CAPTIVE OF DESIRE

"What do you hope to accomplish by keeping me prisoner here?"

Gareth's anger dissipated as quickly as it had come in the face of the uncertainty in Angelica's great silver eyes. Crouching beside her, he raised his hand to her cheek. "Is that what you believe my intentions are, Angelica . . . to keep you a prisoner? No, darlin', nothing could be farther from the truth. I had only intended to talk to you before I left for the mine. But somehow, when I saw you, talkin' wasn't enough."

His hand slipped to the back of her head, cupping it to draw her closer. Angelica could feel his warm breath against her lips, and a paralyzing magic began to permeate her veins. A small voice sounded its protest in the back of her mind, but it was fading . . . fading in the onslaught of the wild sensations assaulting her.

Gareth's mouth was on hers, dissolving her shield of anger, leaving her helpless. She could think of nothing but the sensation of Gareth's warm, eager lips against her own, the familiar taste of his mouth, his strong hands cradling her gently as he lowered her slowly, gently to the blanket stretched out beneath her . . .

Defiant Mistress

Elaine Barbieri

ZEBRA BOOKS
KENSINGTON PUBLISHING CORP.

ZEBRA BOOKS

are published by

Kensington Publishing Corp.
475 Park Avenue South
New York, NY 10016

First printing: June 1986

Printed in the United States of America

Chapter I

1835

Momentarily stunned by the unexpected thrust that slammed her against the bedroom wall, Angelica gave a short, breathless gasp.

"No . . . let me go!"

Rough hands were on her breasts. A wet mouth was crushing hers, stealing her breath, and she struggled fiercely against the heavy male body pinning her with its weight.

"I said let me go!"

"No, damn you! You will not escape me again! I have waited too long . . . too long to take you."

The sneer on the darkly handsome face above hers was accented by the contrast of white teeth against a well-trimmed black mustache as Esteban Arricalde grated harshly, "*Galopina* . . . kitchen maid with the airs of royalty! You bear the proof of your sinful conception in your great silver eyes . . . the same eyes that shout your wantonness to the world! *Puta!* You give your favors to others, and refuse them to me. But you will refuse me no longer. . . ."

Esteban's grip tightened, holding Angelica helpless as he jerked her arms painfully behind her. Forcing her closer against him even as she strove to free herself from his stifling embrace, he ground his mouth into hers. Filled with rage, Angelica endured the enforced intimacy of his caresses as he held her wrists fast behind her.

His chest heaving from the assault of his emotions, Esteban lifted his mouth from hers at last, pulling only far enough away to direct a searing glance into her eyes.

"Now be quiet, little fool. If my mother becomes suspicious, you will be out of this house for good."

"I will not be quiet! I will tell la señora the truth! I will tell her that you follow me around the house, waiting to trap me in lonely hallways and empty rooms! I will tell her that you attempt to force yourself on me . . . that you try . . ."

But Esteban Arricalde's low laugh interrupted her heated retort.

"You are a fool if you think that my mother will believe you. And even if she did, she would not admit to it. After all, why would a man of my stature, heir to my father's fortune and one of the most sought-after bachelors in Mexico, force himself on a servant who should be flattered by his attentions?"

Angelica's bruised lips curled in contempt. "It is yourself you flatter with your words, not I with your attentions! I want no part of you! I only wish to do my work in peace."

" . . . and to earn your seven dollars a month . . ." His observant eyes noting the flush his words had driven to her face, Esteban continued insidiously, "Your family needs that money, is that not true, Angelica? Your little brother is so sick. . . . dying. Padre Manuel is able to do little more for him." Realizing from the shudder that shook her slender body that he had truly struck on the key to her submission, he pressed relentlessly, "And if you are not nice to me, Angelica, you will not be able to earn the money you need, will you?"

"*Puerco!* Let me go!"

Momentary satisfaction at the flush that suffused Esteban Arricalde's face was erased by pain as Esteban twisted Angelica's wrists with new vengeance.

"I told you to be quiet! If my mother hears you, I will be

unable to keep her from dismissing you! You well know that my mother only hired you because of the annoying insistence of the priest. If you are dismissed, you will never work again in the house of a decent family. And I want you here, Angelica, near me, because I intend to have you many times . . ."

"You do not frighten me with your threats!"

"Oh, do I not? Well, maybe that is why I want you even more . . ." Easily subduing her renewed struggle by increased pressure on her delicate wrists, Esteban purred insidiously, "I will have you . . . and I will have you now, Angelica . . ."

The innate confidence in his voice sent a tremor of fear down Angelica's spine. Strengthened by desperation, Angelica unexpectedly jerked herself free and dashed toward the door. She had just pulled it open when she was snatched backward once again, her body slamming forcefully against the wall of Esteban's chest. In a quick, efficient movement, Esteban turned her to face him. His hands were digging into her back as he sought to subdue her, his mouth closing over hers, when an unexpected voice from behind froze their struggles into an almost comic tableau.

"So this is where you are, Esteban."

Tearing his mouth from hers with startling abruptness, Esteban snapped his head up toward the tall man standing casually in the open doorway. The light streaming from the opposite doorway held the man's face in dark relief, not allowing Angelica recognition as she struggled to turn toward him. But Esteban did not suffer the same disadvantage. His response to the softly posed question was quick and emphatic.

"Get out of here, Gareth! This is none of your affair!"

In the moment before the man responded, Angelica attempted to speak, only to feel the pressure on her arms tighten so painfully as to steal her breath.

Slowly shifting his weight, the stranger drawled quietly, "I suppose you're right, Esteban. It makes no difference to me what you're doin', but I thought you might be interested in knowin' that Dona Teresa is lookin' for you. She seemed upset when you disappeared so suddenly from the breakfast table. I have the feelin' she'll be up here herself in a few minutes, and I don't think she'd like findin' you here."

His mouth tightening with anger, Esteban stared unblinkingly into the shadowed face before turning back to Angelica's flushed countenance.

Gritting her teeth against the pain of Esteban's unrelenting grip, Angelica watched the play of emotions across his face as his eyes moved hotly over her lips. His gaze lingered meaningfully before he released her abruptly.

"Next time, my proud *galopina* . . ."

Stepping away from her, Esteban walked toward the man who stood still shadowed by the light at his back. His voice was harsh, his words clipped.

"Yes, I suppose I should return below and set my mother's mind at rest." Making sure to usher the stranger out ahead of him, he added without a backward glance, "My business here can wait for another time . . ."

Still trembling from her narrow escape, Angelica walked quickly down the hallway toward the last of the six bedrooms in the spacious Arricalde hacienda. She would be happy when she would be able to return to the safety of the active kitchen. The upstairs portion of the house was too isolated . . . presented too many opportunities for Esteban Arricalde to press his unwanted advances. Maria, the usual maid, was old and did her work without fear of Esteban's unwanted attentions. But Maria was ill . . . would probably remain unable to perform her duties in the household for at least a week. Until Maria was once again on her feet, the chores of the upstairs maid remained hers.

A new shudder shaking her delicate frame, Angelica took a deep, steadying breath. She had recognized the look in Esteban Arricalde's eyes the first time she had walked into the house a few weeks before. His amorous escapades were no secret, and she had seen that expression too many times not to be aware of the problems it could present.

Moving purposely into the last guest room, Angelica was

8

brought to an abrupt halt by the flash of her own reflection in the dressing-table mirror. The violence of her struggle had worked a long, raven-black strand of hair loose from the single plait trailing down her back. Fine hairs had already begun to curl at her hairline, revealing the natural wave she had been so unsuccessful in controlling. Heated color still flushed her smooth, gold-tinted cheeks.

She frowned at her reflection. She had been marked by the gracefully sculptured planes of the face reflected back at her, by the delicate features which contrasted so sharply with her parents' broad faces and pleasantly blunt features. Her nose was straight and slender. The fine line of her lips, now pressed into a tense line, hid the perfection of straight white teeth. Even her skin, where it was not exposed to the sun on a daily basis, was a lighter color than her parents'. But most of all, it was her great silver gray eyes, lavishly fringed by an incredible length of black lashes, that drew the most comment.

But physical differences between her parents and herself no longer tormented her. She had long ago taught herself to rise above the shouted taunts of children and whispered comments in the marketplace. Her occasional response was a calculated arrogance which only increased the talk about her.

When her mother's dutiful explanation as to her origins had finally come, she had accepted it without comment.

"Papa is more truly your father than the man whose seed conceived you. I do not know who that man was, Angelica. I could not see his face when he forced himself on me. I know only that he was not from this place. But one cannot question the will of God, Angelica. You are a good daughter, and if you are not the child of your papa's body, you are still the child of his heart."

Her mother's words were still clear in her mind. But thankful as she was for the love they conveyed, her rebellious spirit refused to accept unjust accusations as the will of God. Despite Padre Manuel's strict admonitions, she continued to answer each knowing sneer with a toss of her head and a haughty smile.

"*Galopina* with the airs of royalty . . . Like mother, like daughter . . . *puta*. The sin is in her blood . . ."

Esteban Arricalde's words returned to her mind, echoing the taunts she had heard countless times before. Her mother's helplessness and shame had allowed her to tell no one but her husband and Padre Manuel of the physical attack she had suffered. Angelica's birth, a pale-skinned, light-eyed child, had appeared to others physical proof of Margarita's adultery. The arrival of Carlos, her small, dark-haired, dark-eyed brother, nine years later had done nothing to reestablish her mother's fallen status, and the unwarranted silent persecution had continued.

Padre Manuel's response to the occasional tears of her childhood had been a quiet reproof.

"You complain of the skin and hair God gave you because of its texture and shade when others would be thankful for the health their vibrance reflects. You complain about the color of your eyes, when there are others whose eyes do not see. Instead of looking on these things as a curse, Angelica, you should see them as the blessings they truly are . . ."

It was only after Carlos's birth and the difficult, sickly years her dear brother had endured that Padre Manuel's words had taken on a true meaning for her.

Snapping herself back to the present, Angelica reassessed her appearance. No, she could not return downstairs in this state. She could not afford to raise suspicion. Raising her hands to her head, she quickly freed her hair from its simple braid and attempted to rake it into order with her fingers. It was to no avail, and hesitating only momentarily, she reached for the brush on the dresser.

Her mind wandering as she applied a few quick strokes to the thick raven locks, she realized she owed her narrow escape this morning to the unidentified man who had so expertly maneuvered Esteban Arricalde back downstairs. The man was undoubtedly a Texan. His accent had been unmistakable. He had probably arrived late last night with the party el Señor Arricalde had been expecting.

A stinging, unexpected twinge in her shoulder blade

suddenly interrupted Angelica's train of thought, causing her to gasp with pain. Her shoulder had been numbed from Esteban Arricalde's rough treatment and feeling was just returning. Moving it tentatively, she realized her *camisa* adhered wetly to her back.

Sweeping the shimmering length of her hair to one side over her shoulder, she turned to view her back in the mirror. Startled to see that a bloodstain had indeed penetrated the fabric of her *camisa*, she slipped the fabric from her shoulder. But the wound was difficult to see, and frustrated in her attempt, Angelica slipped her arm out of her *camisa* and allowed it to fall almost to her waist in the rear.

The angry marks of Esteban Arricalde's rough treatment were still dark against her skin, and low on her back was a gouge where the blood was only beginning to clot. Experiencing a new flash of anger, Angelica looked toward the washstand. She would wash away the blood before the stain became large enough to cause comment. Slipping her other arm from her *camisa*, she clutched it over her breasts and was about to turn toward the washstand when a sound of movement came from the doorway.

Her eyes jerking in its direction made contact with a dark, unfamiliar gaze. Frozen into immobility by the unexpected appearance of the tall stranger, Angelica stood unmoving as he stepped into the room and closed the door behind him with slow deliberation. Unsmiling, he advanced until he stood towering over her. His eyes swept her unbound hair, the creamy line of her bared shoulders, coming to rest for short moments on the small hands that clutched her *camisa* over her breasts.

Flicking his gaze back to her startled, silver eyes, he mumbled tightly, "I wondered what could've gotten Esteban to the point of agitation where he was willin' to risk his mother's censure. So, Esteban was tellin' the truth . . . You *are* a *puta* . . ."

"I am not a *puta*, señor!"

Angelica's angry response, delivered in unhesitant, perfect English, caused a small flicker to move across the

11

Texan's expression.

"Full of surprises, aren't you?" Reaching out, he closed his hand on the thick twist of hair at the base of her neck, holding her captive as he perused her face.

"Where did you get your beautiful face, *puta*? And those great light eyes . . .? You must have been a surprise to your papa when you were born. But then again, from what Esteban tells me, maybe it wasn't too much of a surprise at that . . ."

Wincing as she made an unsuccessful attempt to break free of his grip, Angelica replied haughtily, "My mother is a good woman. I am proud to be of her blood!"

"So proud that you're followin' in her footsteps?" The Texan's expression stiffened. "It's a hard road you're takin'. Esteban says your mother does the laundry for this household, even though she's not allowed entrance here. Do you think you'll fare any differently?"

Her anger mounting at the Texan's easy condemnation, Angelica spat heatedly, "I care little what you think or say!" Drawing herself up proudly, Angelica made an attempt at control. "Now, if you will take your hand off me, I will continue with my work."

Holding the Texan's gaze unflinchingly, Angelica was extremely aware of the weight of his hand on her hair, the light fanning of his breath against her cheek. His squinting perusal sent a chill down her spine as she waited for his response. His gaze moved to her mouth in a look so intense that she could almost feel its touch and her heartbeat quickened to thunder in her ears. An almost imperceptible smile flicked across his lips as the Texan's eyes fastened on the visible throbbing of the pulse in her throat.

"No, you don't want me to release you, little *puta*. You want me to stay here with you, don't you?" His voice suddenly lowering to a soothing caress, he drew her closer, his hand slipping around her back to stroke her bared flesh. His scent was fresh in her nostrils as he drew her closer.

"And just a few minutes ago you were in Esteban's arms . . ."

"No, I was attempting to escape him. He . . ."

12

"Just like you're tryin' to escape me, little *puta*?"

His lips were trailing across the skin of her cheek, moving in an unaltering path toward her lips. Mesmerized by their tantalizing gentleness, Angelica was unable to move, unable to protest as his mouth moved to cover hers. Unlike Esteban's savage kiss, the Texan's kiss was gently caressing. He was pulling her closer . . . closer still. His grip on her hair loosened as his fingers moved to tangle in the midnight-black silk. His other hand slid lightly over the skin of her back to cup her breast.

Gasping at the intimacy of his touch, Angelica was suddenly struggling to break the Texan's hold. No, she would not be passed from one man's arms to another, as if she was . . .

Startled black eyes snapped to hers as the Texan drew back, still refusing to release her. He muttered a low oath.

"Is this the same game you played with Esteban, little *puta*? Is that why he was almost wild with wantin' you when I interrupted?"

"I play no game . . ."

"Are you tryin' to deny you were waitin' for me when I came in here?" The Texan's eyes narrowed. "Are you sorry you haven't bargained for a price? Or was this little scene deliberate . . . a sample to drive the price a little higher? How much do you want, *puta*? Tell me. Maybe I'll think it reasonable enough to . . ."

"Release me, damn you!"

Angelica's imperious demand resulted in the automatic tightening of the Texan's hold as he jerked her flush against the full length of his body. His arousal apparent in their intimate posture, the Texan whispered stiffly, "You've done your work well, little witch. Name your price. And if it's too high, it'll serve me right for bein' taken in by your well practiced game."

Anger was apparent in the hard lines of the face above hers, but Angelica was immune to its warning.

"I ask nothing of you except that you release me." Echoing his own earlier words, she continued tightly, "la señora will be wondering what is keeping me upstairs so

13

long . . ."

"And you don't want her knowin' the true reason for your delay. No, that would spoil your game, wouldn't it?"

Unwilling to give his question the credibility of a response, Angelica demanded through clenched teeth, "Let me go!"

Releasing her unexpectedly, the Texan watched openly as she struggled to raise her *camisa*. A hot color flooding her face, Angelica turned away from his unrelenting stare and slipped the blouse back on her shoulders. Turning back toward him once again, Angelica steeled herself against his accusing glance before moving toward the door.

"I wouldn't leave like that if I were you." Motioning to her unbound hair streaming past her shoulders in disordered profusion, the Texan grated tightly, "Lookin' like you do, only a fool would believe you were in here cleanin' the room."

Angelica paused, her eyes flicking momentarily back to her reflection. Color was high in her cheeks; her eyes were bright with agitation. The shimmering veil of her hair swayed sensuously against her shoulders, adding the final touch of open sensuality to a picture she dared not name. Reaching up in a jerking movement, she gathered the wayward strands, and without a word began to plait her hair. Within a few moments her hair was again confined in its braid and Angelica turned toward the door. But before she could reach for the knob, the Texan was at her side, his hands on her arms, holding her fast.

"Not yet, little *puta*. I need another sample of your wares if I'm to consider a price . . .'"

Smarting at his words, Angelica hissed, "I have neither a sample nor a price to give you."

"Oh, yes you have . . ."

Before she could respond, his mouth was warm against hers. His lips were relentless in their quest of her arousal, his imprisoning arms both gentle and demanding as his hands moved warmly over her flesh. Releasing her unexpectedly, the Texan stepped back. His breathing was ragged.

14

"Leave now, little *puta*, or you won't leave at all."

Taking the opportunity he provided without response, Angelica paused only to shoot him a contemptful glance before stepping past him and opening the door. Within moments, she was running down the hallway toward the rear staircase.

"Angelica! What has taken you so long? Maria is twice your age and she finishes her work in less time than you!"

Carmela's sharp admonition greeting her as she stepped into the kitchen, Angelica hastened toward the table where a mountain of fresh vegetables awaited her knife. But her silence did not forestall further comment from the angry cook. "Just because you must take over Maria's job for a few days, it does not mean you will be allowed to neglect your own. La Señora Arricalde has many guests. Three more arrived last night and she will be expecting all the meals to be on time."

Her hands already busy slicing and cutting, Angelica nodded. She had no desire to explain the reason for her delay, and she was only too aware of the prejudice against her in these quarters. But Carmela had accepted her generously. She could not afford to lose the large, warm-hearted cook's support or respect.

"*Lo siento*, Carmela. I will be much quicker tomorrow."

Turning back to the dough in front of her without comment, Carmela resumed a vigorous kneading. Angelica took the time to survey the other members of the kitchen staff out of the corner of her eye.

Juanita, a young woman matching Angelica's seventeen years, eyed her contemptuously. But Juanita was nasty and vain and did not wish to share her status as youngest woman in the kitchen with Angelica. Angelica suppressed a sneer. Juanita's personality was similar to that of her ugly, unpleasant mother. Angelica was well acquainted with their disapproving glances, and she pulled her slender frame to its full though meager height and forced a smile to her lips. She would not give Juanita the satisfaction of believing she was uncomfortable in any way.

15

Hernando, the porter, eyed her with his lustful, rheumy eyes. His wife, Josepina, the vicious stick of a woman that she was, watched them both with growing animosity. Angelica did not need to look to know that Isabella, the other *galopina* and a quiet, religious woman, was observing all without expression, preferring to remain uninvolved in the tensions of the kitchen.

Angelica continued with her work. They were waiting, all of them, for just the opportunity Esteban Arricalde and the unknown Texan had almost presented them with today, so they could say they were right about her. Damn them . . . damn them all!

Juanita's coy, high voice interrupted Angelica's thoughts.

"Carmela, who is the Anglo who arrived last night with Señor y Señora Aleman?" Juanita's eyes sparked with interest, twisting the knot of irritation tighter in Angelica's stomach. "He is handsome, is he not? He smiled at me when I served him this morning. I think he likes me . . ."

"You are a fool, Juanita!" Stopping only a moment to shoot the flushed young girl a deprecating glance, Carmela continued kneading. "It is not very wise to look at one of la Señora's guests with the gleam I see in your eye." Turning back toward the annoyed young woman, Carmela gave her another warning glance. "You flatter yourself with thoughts of the gringo's attentions. Even if he did show an interest, you may be certain that interest would be only temporary, and not of the type that would be sanctified by the church."

"Oh, then I suppose I must leave the gringo to Angelica. She is far more accustomed than I to meeting needs of that . . ."

"Juanita!" Carmela's tone reflected the anger that sparked in her tired black eyes. "I will not stand for such talk while I am in charge of this kitchen." Turning to face Angelica, who had taken a quick step in Juanita's direction, she continued in a lower tone, "Angelica, you will please ignore Juanita's loose tongue."

"Loose tongue . . . *si* . . ." Taking a deep breath, Angelica dismissed Juanita's comment with a wave of her hand

16

and a forced smile. "*No importa*, Carmela."

Angelica turned back to her work, her trembling hands the only betrayal of her flaring anger. She would not allow Juanita to bait her.

With careful deliberation Angelica attempted to lose herself in her work, but the effort was a failure. The memory of the Texan's kiss was still fresh against her lips; her skin still tingled from his touch. She felt a moment of true panic as the persistent memory flushed her with a startling warmth. If so much was not at stake, she would walk out the kitchen door right now and never return.

No, she would not allow the pressure of unwarranted gossip that had plagued her all her life to determine the course of her future. The Texan would be here for only a short while and when he was gone, she would never see him again. Don Esteban's lust was a truer threat to her employment. It was he she need fear, not the tall Texan who had so shaken her.

Attacking her work with new resolve, Angelica raised her chin. She would allow no one and nothing to interfere with her employment here in the Arricalde household. It was Carlos's only chance . . .

Gareth walked to the window of the gracious *sala*, his mind wandering from the conversation progressing behind him. He took another sip of pulque, unconsciously realizing his tolerance for the native drink was beginning to grow. He supposed one could become addicted to many things around the Arricalde hacienda.

A memory of great silver eyes returned to his mind, and he felt a responsive stirring in his groin. Angelica . . . the beautiful little *puta* was called Angelica . . . Gareth took a deep breath. His emotions had been under tenuous control since his encounter with her this morning. But he was well aware that he was not in a position to indulge feelings of the sort she raised inside him. He was at the Arricalde hacienda on a business matter, at the request of his father. His deep, inner conviction that a break between Texas and Mexico was imminent lent his mission to the Arricalde

17

mines of San Jose Regla a new urgency.

Gareth frowned in automatic reaction to the direction his thoughts were taking. His father's and his own dedication to Texas and his homestead was uncompromising. Unfortunately, Texas had not meant as much to Emma Walton Dawson. Their move to the homestead more than ten years before had, in fact, succeeded in driving the final wedge between his father and his mother. The breach had never healed and had terminated only upon his mother's death shortly thereafter.

His frown deepening, Gareth adjusted his mental statement. No, he could not blame Texas for first coming between Jonathan and Emma Dawson. He had always known there was a lack of love between his parents. Perhaps the coldness between them accounted for the emotion he himself found lacking in his own makeup. But it had only been after his mother's death that he had discovered his father had found another source for the love denied him. It had been then that Jonathan Dawson had informed his son he was bringing his mistress of many years from New Orleans to live at the homestead . . . that they would be married as soon as Padre Muldoon could be summoned to perform the ceremony.

It was at that time he had also learned that he had a sister, Jeanette DuBois, the seven-year-old daughter of his father's mistress. But he had been fated never to meet his sister or his father's reputedly beautiful mistress. A Karankawas attack had destroyed the entire train which had been to deliver Celeste DuBois and her daughter into Jonathan Dawson's anxious arms. Their bodies had never been found.

The memory of Jonathan Dawson's grief was still vivid in Gareth's mind. It had surpassed totally in scope the pale emotion Jonathan Dawson had displayed at the death of his legal wife, making Gareth realize for the first time the sham his father and mother had lived.

As far as Gareth was concerned, the lesson was well taught. In his dealings with women, Gareth had developed a fondness for a few without ever being touched to the heart. He suspected he never would, and that suited him fine. Never one to deny the needs of the body, he was only too happy to confine his association with the fairer sex to that limited area of his life.

It was his realization that his father still suffered the loss of his lovely mistress and child that had forced Gareth into Mexico to seek an answer to fulfilling his father's dream for their homestead. Jonathan Dawson had suffered enough disappointment in his life. Gareth would not allow him to suffer another.

An enthusiastic rise in the conversation between the two men in the corner of the room drew Gareth from his mental meanderings. The taller of the two, Señor Enrique Arricalde, nodded his well-tended gray head as he continued speaking in an earnest tone. His fine gray mustache twitched with amusement at his companion's comment, and his aristocratic face relaxed into a smile. Gareth knew the sincerity of that smile. Long years of association had proved Don Enrique to be a true gentleman and a friend with a strong sense of loyalty that had so far transcended the strife between Mexico and her Texan state.

Gareth leisurely returned his gaze to the landscape outside the *sala* window. He could well understand Don Enrique's desire to remain at Real del Monte for a good portion of the year, although he had many other houses which were even more luxurious than this particular hacienda. The view was breathtaking—magnificent oak and pine forests resplendent in their primeval beauty, and the village of Real, itself a jewel, set in the side of the mountain. Below him were the sloping roofs of the town houses and the large church which dominated the square, and in the distance he could see the little Indian huts of the miners perched amongst the cliffs.

But Gareth was well aware that this particular hacienda did not hold the same fascination for the younger Arricalde. Gareth shook off his instinctive feeling of distaste at the thought of Esteban. He had known Esteban for many years also, having come to meet him while they were still boys. Always spoiled and self-centered, Esteban had be-

19

come fascinated by the capital scene and the many entertainments it offered. It was well known that he had become so entranced by the pleasures of life that he had neglected to fulfill his duties to his family estate.

Gareth gave a low snort. Now, seeming to have finally realized his duty to his inheritance, Esteban was apparently about to give his patient father another problem with his pursuit of a beautiful *galopina* from his own kitchen.

Aware of his body's annoying reaction to the mere thought of the beautiful little *puta*, Gareth frowned. The girl was a fool if she allowed herself to become involved with Esteban Arricalde. He was notoriously ruthless in his amorous pursuits and completely untrustworthy. Somehow, the thought of the girl's potential future at Esteban's hands disturbed him.

A sudden flicker of movement at the corner of his eye drew Gareth's attention as the same figure who had been dominating his thoughts of a moment before moved into view. Despite himself, he was unable to take his eyes from Angelica's slender form as she moved toward the small herb garden in the sunnier part of the yard. Her stature was delicate, her movements naturally graceful as she leaned over to pluck the matured leaves she sought. Having filled her basket with a suitable variety, she stood at last, her perfect profile in relief against the glorious scenery surrounding her as she stared toward the town below them.

She was beautiful. Gareth's eyes moved over the unmarked loveliness of her face, his eyes touching on her slightly parted lips. He remembered their softness, the incredible sweetness of their taste. His gaze swept the gentle slope of her neck and shoulders and he recalled their warmth, the silky texture of her skin beneath his palms. He felt an almost irrepressible urge to stride out of the confining room to her side so he might take her into his arms and know again the beauty he had sampled so briefly. He wanted to know her better, much better . . .

"Do not allow yourself to become too entranced, my friend. That little beauty is mine. I marked her for myself the first day I returned to Real del Monte, and I do not

20

intend to share her with anyone."

Turning at the sound of a voice in his ear, Gareth regarded Esteban coldly, without the smallest pretense of a smile.

"Are you attemptin' to read minds now, Esteban?"

"I do not need to possess that skill in order to know what you are thinking, Gareth. It seemed strange to me this morning that you had so generously come upstairs to warn me of my mother's interest in my whereabouts. But I now find it easy to see that you came upstairs because of an interest of another sort." A flicker of anger moved across Esteban's handsome, patrician face. "Were it not for the truth of the fact that my mother was indeed concerned about my whereabouts, I would indeed be angry for your interference. But, as things stand, I will acknowledge that you did me a favor. I do not intend to have the beautiful little *puta* driven from this household yet. Her employment here gives me a decided advantage in my game . . ."

"And if Angelica does not care to play your game?"

"So you took the time to inquire as to the *puta's* name . . ." His agitation not allowing him to await Gareth's reply, Esteban hissed, "I do not make empty threats, Gareth. Stay away from her. She is mine!"

As if sensing the growing violence of their exchange, Angelica turned toward the window unexpectedly. She paused, frozen in the gazes that snapped toward her. Her eyes, touching on Esteban's fierce expression, flicked to and held Gareth's gaze. His stomach tightening, Gareth took a spontaneous step forward just as Angelica turned and quickly fled out of sight.

"*Bastardo!*"

Esteban's low epithet turned Gareth angrily toward Esteban's flushed face. The unexpected sound of movement in the hallway and the entrance of Dona Teresa and three other guests forestalled the heated response that sprang to Gareth's lips. Forcing a stiff smile, Gareth remained silent as Dona Teresa's voice rang with pleasure.

"Esteban! See who has come to visit with us! Señor y Señora Valentin y Señorita Valentin! You remember Maria

Luz, do you not, *querido*?"

Esteban turned toward his mother with a fixed smile and advanced toward the group in the doorway. The attention of the others in the room had turned toward them also as a flurry of greetings and introductions began. Waiting his turn, Gareth made a mental calculation. The arrival of the Valentins had swelled the ranks of guests for dinner to nine. Señor y Señora Aleman, two old friends of Don Enrique with whom he had arrived, Señores Flores, Alcazar and Erricavera, business associates interested in the progress of the latest shaft, the Valentins, and himself.

Striding forward in response to Dona Teresa's urging, Gareth extended his hand toward the newest additions to the guest list. The kitchen would be busy tonight . . .

The sun had already set as Angelica gave the kitchen a last cursory glance. Yes, all the pans had been carefully cleaned and restored to their place. The dishes were done, and for the first time that day, work in the kitchen had all but come to a stop. Carmela and she were the last of the staff remaining in the kitchen and she was exhausted. Between her kitchen duties, Angelica had been sent upstairs to ready rooms for the Valentins. There had been a great rush in the kitchen to expand the menu to include three more guests and she had immediately been pressed into service upon her return. Now, hours after dinner, came the first break in the flurry of activity that had begun in the kitchen at dawn.

Satisfied that her work was complete, Angelica turned toward Carmela who rested in a chair before the fireplace.

"I'm going home now, Carmela. I'll see you tomorrow morning."

Turning toward Angelica with a weary nod, Carmela drew herself to her feet.

"*Espera*, Angelica."

Walking laboriously toward the cupboard, Carmela drew it open and removed a large piece of cheese. Taking a knife, she cut off a sizable piece and wrapped it in a cloth. Removing a bowl from the same cupboard, she tipped it to measure honey into a small crock. She sealed it carefully and, turning, held them out toward Angelica.

"Take these home with you, Angelica. This cheese and honey will do Carlos much good. Make sure he eats them tonight so that he may feel their beneficial effects in the morning."

Her eyes widening, Angelica shook her head. "Carmela, this is the creamed cheese delivered just this morning. And the honey . . . It will surely be missed . . ."

"Come, come, Angelica. I am in charge of this kitchen, and I say you will take them home to your brother. I would not give it to Juanita for her greedy family, or to Isabella, because she is not in need. But I know Dona Teresa would not begrudge your ailing brother a little nourishment that will not even be missed in the plenty of her table."

Touched by Carmela's generosity, Angelica nodded her head and took the parcels held out to her.

"*Si*, Carmela. *Gracias.*"

Turning quickly, Angelica moved through the doorway and into the yard. She was well aware that there were very few who truly cared how Carlos fared. Mama and Papa spent the greater portion of their day making sure that Carlos took the sun, rested well, ate all his food, and did not overdo. Papa, in his position of responsibility for the church property, worked very hard, but made little in actual money to show for his many hours in the hot sun. Instead, he was allowed to keep a portion of the food he raised on the church land, as well as a portion of the produce of the church animals, either for his family's consumption or to sell. But there was never much left over to bring to the market.

Mama put in many hours washing the clothes of the Arricalde hacienda, but the pay was meager. It was true what the Texan, Señor Gareth Dawson, had said. Mama was not even allowed in the Arricalde kitchen. At this point in her mother's life, the ugly rumors of Angelica's conception were believed as fact. She supposed the same would be true of the rumors circulated about her in a few years, and the doors of the few houses still open to her would be closed. Angelica shrugged. She had trained herself to care little about those things over which she had no control.

Angelica tightened her hold on the parcels in her hand as the moon moved behind a cloud, plunging the path into darkness. It would have been far better had she borrowed a lantern so that she would not have to negotiate the steep path in the dark.

Angelica stumbled, managing to right herself in time to avoid falling. Her heart beating loudly in her breast, she took a deep breath. The path to the road was uneven and despite its familiarity, she was hesitant about continuing on in the darkness. She clutched her parcels tighter. She would wait a few moments longer. Perhaps the clouds would part again and allow her enough light to continue on in safety.

Taking a few steps toward a tree to her right, Angelica paused and leaned back against the ancient trunk. The night air was cool and refreshing after a long day in the kitchen. She would take advantage of these few moments allotted to her by the caprices of the moon and . . .

"Well, well, what have we here . . .?"

Startled by the unexpected voice to her rear, Angelica jumped, her head snapping around toward a familiar drawl.

"What's the matter? Not the man you expected?"

The shadowed face was becoming clearer as the moon peeked through a fleeting cloud, and Angelica eyed Gareth Dawson's unsmiling countenance.

"I expected no one in this portion of the grounds at this time of night, Señor Dawson." Her eyes shooting back toward the hacienda and the figures still clearly outlined against the *sala* windows, she continued quietly, "La señora usually keeps her guests very well entertained, with little need to wander the grounds aimlessly."

"But perhaps I'm not wanderin' as aimlessly as you might think . . ."

Uncertain exactly what conclusion to make from his remark, Angelica shook her head, only to feel his warm hand take her shoulder unexpectedly.

"Angelica, there's no need pretendin' . . ."

"Pretending?"

"You do your work well . . . maybe too well. I don't really think you realize the state you've gotten poor Esteban into. Poor fella was preoccupied all evenin'. Dona Teresa was becoming quite annoyed with his inattention to Señorita Valentin. He kept lookin' out the window . . . I figured if I watched right along with him, I'd see somethin' real interestin'. That's how I saw you walkin' across the yard. Poor Esteban was intercepted by his mother's summons as he started out after you, but one man's misfortune is another man's gain, you know . . . Of course, I expected I might not be able to catch up with you since you had such a head start." A peculiar light flickering across his dark eyes, he gave a low laugh. "I was wrong of course, 'cause here you were waitin' . . ."

A surge of anger flushed Angelica's face with color at the injustice of the Texan's remarks.

"I was waiting for no one! It was too dark to make my way . . ."

"Funny, I have no trouble seein' you . . ."

Belatedly, Angelica glanced up toward the sky. Of course, he was right. The moon had come out from behind the cloud cover as they had talked and was shining brightly down upon them. Gareth Dawson's features were clearly defined in its silver rays, and Angelica frowned. Somehow those hard features had become burned into her mind. His image had returned to haunt her with annoying frequency during the long, wearying day. She remembered only too vividly the black accusing eyes under dark, arched brows and their squinting appraisal, the harsh line of his uneven profile, the sharp planes of his face, and the deep cleft in his strong, unyielding chin. She had never seen him smile, but she had felt the mesmerizing effect of his well-shaped mouth as it had covered hers. She remembered its touch against her skin . . .

The Texan's thick, dark hair glinted silver in the moonlight, and he shifted his tall, leanly muscled frame. His expression revealed a subdued anger.

Angelica stiffened and attempted to shake off his grip. It

was not he who should be angry! She did not like his inference that she was here waiting for Esteban Arricalde to find her. She did not like it at all, and she would not stand for any more of the Texan's insults!

Ineffective in freeing herself on the first attempt, Angelica attempted again to pull herself from Gareth Dawson's restraining hand, only to have his other hand clamp down firmly on her arm as he jerked her toward him.

"That's all right, little angel. Esteban's not comin', but I can be just as accommodatin' and just as . . ."

His words jerking to a halt as Angelica's heavily laden arms struck against his chest, he mumbled irritably, "What in hell . . ."

His eyes darting to the packages she clutched, Gareth Dawson frowned.

"What's that you're guardin' so carefully, Angelica?"

"It is none of your concern!"

Angelica again attempted to jerk herself free of the arms that still held her breathlessly close. She was intensely aware of the fanning of the Texan's breath against her cheek, the pleasantly familiar scent of his skin as he made an attempt to take the packages from her grasp.

Abruptly she was struggling, her flaring anger unwilling to allow him to search her packages as if she was a thief. But she was no match for his superior strength as the Texan ruthlessly attempted to take the packages out of her hands. Suddenly fearful that he would make her drop them on the ground, Angelica relinquished them with a grudging explanation.

"It is cheese . . . and some honey. I didn't take them from the kitchen. Carmela gave them to me."

"Cheese and honey . . . ?"

"Yes, for my brother. Carlos is ill and Carmela said la señora would not mind if she gave me some for him."

Angelica could see disbelief register on the Texan's face, and she continued heatedly, "I only paused here because the moon moved behind a cloud . . . it was too dark to continue. I waited for no one. I have only one desire, and that is to go home . . . now."

26

The Texan's expression had turned stoic and Angelica felt a fleeting moment's panic. She did not wish to be dragged back to the house to confront Dona Teresa. Despite her innocence, the embarrassment would be too great for Dona Teresa and herself, and she was truly unsure if such an act would result in her dismissal.

Uncertain if the loud pounding of her heart was the result of her fear or the growing awareness of the hard, male body so close to hers, Angelica kept her eyes on the Texan's unrevealing expression. She was intensely aware of the dark eyes that held her gaze, mesmerizing her into stillness. She felt their touch on her skin, the line of her cheek, the soft curve of her mouth.

Returning his gaze to the packages at last, Gareth carefully unwrapped them. The eyes he raised to hers were still unrevealing.

"All right, Angelica, so this much was the truth. Now let's go home and see that poor, sick brother of yours."

Taking the parcels he pushed back into her hands, Angelica had only a moment to cover them roughly before the Texan took her firmly by the arm. His expression was stiff, his voice unyielding as he pulled her into step beside him.

"I'm sure your house can't be far from here."

Suddenly furious with herself for allowing the arrogant gringo to intimidate her, Angelica attempted to free her arm.

"I have no desire to be accompanied home, Señor Dawson."

His grip unyielding as he ushered her forward, the Texan gritted between his teeth, "It should be obvious to you by now that it makes very little difference what you desire, Angelica."

"Oh, yes, it does . . ." Jerking herself to a stop, Angelica refused to move a step farther. "You have no hold over me." Anger pushing her past discretion, Angelica took a deep breath, unaware of the beauty of her animated face as she continued heatedly, "And I do not intend to take you to my home so that you may satisfy yourself as to the truth or

27

falsehood that I speak. It is none of your concern and I . . ."

His grip on her arm tightening painfully, the Texan jerked her abruptly close. Startling Angelica with the menace of his tone, the Texan lowered his head toward hers to mutter between his teeth, "You'll either take me to your home or you'll march right in there to Dona Teresa to show her the little goodies you've stolen from her kitchen."

"I did not steal . . ."

Abruptly aware of the futility of her denial, Angelica snapped her mouth closed. Taking a few seconds to rein her anger under control, she replied quietly, "It will be as you say. But not because I am a thief. I wish to spare Dona Teresa as well as Carmela the embarrassment of such a confrontation. . . ."

"Not to mention yourself . . ."

Her slender lips twitched as Angelica fought to control her response. Had she any choice, she would not allow this *bastardo* the satisfaction he sought. She did not wish to see his dispassionate eyes resting on Carlos's small, wasted face. But the choice was not hers. She glanced quickly back to his unrelenting gaze.

"If you will remove your hand from my arm, Señor Dawson, I will do as you ask."

His eyes narrowing momentarily, the Texan slowly released her arm. Turning as his hand dropped to his side, Angelica started stiffly down the brightly lit path. Her eyes snapped up to the brilliant full moon, and her mouth tightened. Had this same light been available only a short time before, she would have been saved this confrontation. Seething at the relentless step that sounded behind her, Angelica continued on.

His eyes on the proud set of the narrow shoulders in front of him, Gareth kept pace with Angelica's rapid step. In the silver light of the full moon, the graceful sway of her slender body was all too visible and he made a determined effort to rein his rioting emotions under control.

Damn it all, what was he doing on this ragged path with

28

this little Mexican *puta*? And what possible difference could it make to him if she had indeed stolen that pitiful piece of cheese and crock of honey from the Arricaldes' vast kitchen stores? He shook his head at his own confused thoughts.

He had been startled at the violence of his own reaction a few minutes earlier when he had seen the little witch's slender figure moving through the grounds and Esteban's immediate move in attempted pursuit. The strength of the unfamiliar emotion that had shot through him had given him no time for thought. It had merely spurred him into action. When Esteban had been stopped by an observant Dona Teresa, Gareth had simply assumed his place in pursuit.

A resurgence of that unnamed emotion had struck him again as he had spotted the slender figure he sought waiting at the base of that old tree. The perfect meeting place for lovers. From there it would have been easy to fall back into the cool foliage and onto a bed of fresh, damp leaves. Angelica would have had to learn the hard way that Esteban was not a man of honor and could not be trusted to keep his word.

If he had any doubts before in the face of the little *puta's* convincing proclamations of innocence, the sight of her waiting for Esteban under the tree had dismissed them once and for all. Startled at the bitterness the thought induced, Gareth stifled a self-derisive laugh. Those great guileless eyes had almost convinced him. Damn, she was named well. She truly had the look of an angel. It had been all he could do to tear his eyes from her face.

And what in hell was he doing following her now to her home? He didn't give a damn about the things she had stolen from the kitchen, or whether she truly had a sick brother to whom she was taking them. The truth was, he wanted to make sure the little *puta* went straight home, and didn't linger on the grounds, waiting for Esteban to come looking for her again. His eyes moved over the thick black braid trailing down her back, shimmering in the moonlight the soft line of her shoulders as she trudged from the path onto the road at last. The sheer perfection of her beauty as she turned to shoot him a look of pure hatred shook him more than he cared to admit.

Stepping down onto the road beside her, he reached out to grip her arm. The touch of her skin under his palm sent little tremors of desire rippling through him as she turned toward him with a frown.

"Slow down. I'm in no hurry."

The look of contempt on her flawless countenance more expressive than words, Angelica turned away without a response and started walking toward the village.

Stifling a contrary urge to jerk that slender body back toward him and into his arms, Gareth took a deep breath and started after her.

Angelica's step slowed as the small house that had been her home for as long as her memory prevailed came into view. A part of church property, it was made of stone and consisted of three simple rooms. Mama cooked over the fireplace that dominated the main room which served as kitchen, *sala*, and general meeting room for their family. Her mother and father slept in one of the other small rooms, and Carlos and she slept in the other as they had since he was a sickly infant. She had grown accustomed to the sound of his ragged breathing in the night and the bouts of coughing which so debilitated him. She could not count the times she had slipped from her bed to his side to comfort him. His small body had always been frail . . . was frail still. How she wished to see the thinness change to the full bloom of health that was so characteristic of boys his age. But he was not improving. He had, in fact, appeared to grow weaker in the past year.

But if Carlos had been deprived of the blessing of good health, he had been showered with other advantages not held by the average child his age. The family's proximity to the church had allowed Padre Manuel to become a frequent visitor to their small home. He had been quick to see the unusual sensitivity Carlos possessed and, under Padre Manuel's care, Carlos's mind had blossomed.

It was because of Padre Manuel's close involvement with the family that both Angelica and Carlos could read, write, and also speak English, accomplishments of which few others in the village could boast. But where Padre Manuel had often despaired of Angelica's accepting the burdensome twist of fate that had marked her and her mother unfairly, Carlos had accepted his debility fully as the will of God. He was confident that there was another future planned for him in a scheme of things which he did not yet understand.

In the quiet of the night only a few weeks ago, as he had sought to control his labored breathing, Carlos had confided to his sister that he hoped one day to become a priest . . . to follow in Padre Manuel's footsteps. Angelica had smiled and whispered soft encouragements, knowing full well that Padre Manuel had soberly told Mama and Papa only a short time before that he believed Carlos was growing weaker . . . that he would not see his ninth year . . . that his only hope lay in seeing a doctor in Mexico City who had achieved a measure of success in treating illnesses of the type Carlos suffered. But without the funds necessary to finance the trip and the extended stay treatment might involve, it was a hopeless dream.

Carlos was such a loving child, his poor health not detracting from the appreciation for life which shone in his sharp black eyes. His straight black hair gleamed in the sun, and despite his paleness, he was a handsome boy. How many times had she stared at him in sleep, wishing that she also had shared the darkly appealing features which so marked Carlos as her mother's son?

Shooting a quick glance behind her, Angelica frowned. She was well aware that Mama and Papa would be waiting for her, and that Carlos was anxiously anticipating her return. It was his usual custom to tell her with boyish enthusiasm all he had accomplished during the day, and she knew he delighted in her honest praise. It was a time of day she treasured . . . which cleansed her of the whispers and sneers that followed her. She deeply resented the Texan's intrusion into her family and the simple pleasure

31

they had grown to expect from each other.

How would she explain the Texan's presence? She shot another look behind her, and her frown deepened. The Texan's expression was hard, resolute, but they were almost upon her house and she needed to face him.

Her step slowing to a halt, she turned. Her voice was low and hesitant as she raised her eyes to the Texan's enigmatic gaze.

Indicating the small stone structure visible through the trees, Angelica began hesitantly, "That is the place where my family and I live. My parents will not be expecting me to bring someone home with me, especially someone who is a guest at Señor Arricalde's hacienda. They will be surprised and anxious. I do not wish to upset them or my brother needlessly."

A flicker of an unknown emotion flashed in the Texan's eyes, and Angelica waited for a response. But there was little change in the hard lines of his face or in the set of his jaw.

"You should have thought about that before you stole the cheese and honey . . ."

"I did not steal them!"

"So you say."

"And you choose not to believe me."

Her anger growing, Angelica looked up into the Texan's face. His eyes were moving slowly over her countenance and a new tenseness overtook her emotions. She despised this man, his arrogance and his presumption, but the heat of his gaze seemed to penetrate her very soul as he raised his hand to her shoulder. The callused palm of his hand was moving to the curve of her neck, slipping under her hair with a disturbingly gentle touch. He was urging her closer to him, his head descending toward hers. His voice was low and ragged, his breath warm against her lips.

"That's right, I don't believe you, but you could convince me you're tellin' the truth, Angelica. You could convince me of anythin' if you tried . . ."

The Texan's lips were on hers, and Angelica could no longer think. His firm, persuasive mouth, the same mouth which had infuriated her only moments before with unfair accusations, was slowly destroying her will to resist him. His long, strong fingers moved in her hair, against the flesh of her shoulders, urging her closer as his mouth pressed more deeply into hers. Her lips were separating under the onslaught of his kiss, and she gasped as his tongue slipped between them to caress the warm hollows of her mouth. He was kissing her with increasing hunger, his hands clutching her closer, when her burdened arms met solidly against his chest.

Jerking back, his breathing ragged, the Texan darted an impatient glance toward the impediment between them. In a moment he had taken the parcels from her arms and placed them on the ground and within seconds she was again in his arms, pressed tightly against the hard length of his body. He was drawing her back into the deep cover of the trees, his mouth covering hers passionately. A groan echoed low in his throat.

Hardly realizing that her arms had crept around his neck, Angelica felt the cool, heavy texture of his hair under her palms, gasped as his mouth moved from hers to trail heatedly across her cheek to the lobe of her ear where he whispered hoarsely, "I haven't been able to stop thinking about you all day. Angelica . . . with the face of an angel . . ."

A kaleidoscope of swirling colors enveloped Angelica in its midst. She was aware of the trembling of the Texan's strong body, the heavy pounding of his heart against her breast as his mouth moved hungrily to hers once again. She was drowning in the sweet taste of his mouth as she heard him rasp harshly, "Angelica . . ."

But a distant, childish voice penetrated the evening stillness, shattering the brilliantly hued world in which she was floundering.

"¿Mama, viene Angelica? Es muy tarde . . ."

Stiffening as Carlos's familiar voice carried clearly on the silent night air, Angelica snapped her gaze toward her home. She caught a glimpse of her brother's small, thin figure standing in the doorway before her mother ushered him back inside. Abruptly, she was only too aware of the intimate posture of the strong, male body that all but enveloped her.

True realization of her actions striking her for the first time, Angelica made an attempt to extricate herself from the Texan's grasp, only to have him whisper gratingly against her cheek, "Angelica, what's wrong?"

"I . . . I want you to let me go . . ."

"Let you go?" Pulling himself back far enough so that he might look down into her face, the Texan shot an incredulous look into her eyes. "Are you jokin'? Because if you are, it's a damned poor . . ."

"I'm not joking. Please, let me go, Señor Dawson . . ."

"Señor Dawson . . ." Reacting sharply to her formality, the Texan demanded tightly, "I think you can address me by my given name. It's Gareth . . ."

"No, it will serve no purpose. We are not friends or even acquaintances. To you I am nothing more than . . ."

"My name is Gareth. Say it . . ."

Instinctively judging it unwise to challenge him on such a small point while her position was so vulnerable, Angelica repeated stiffly, "Gareth . . ."

His expression intense, the Texan stared silently into her eyes for a few moments before continuing in a lower, controlled tone.

"That's right. And you were right in what you said before. I'm not your friend, or even an acquaintance. But I want to be your lover, little *puta*. I want to make love to you more than I ever wanted anythin' in my life."

Hating herself for her responsive reaction to the need in his voice, Angelica responded tightly, "I am not a *puta*. And I will not allow you to speak to me of things such as this. Let me go."

"You want me to love you . . ." A thread of passion still heavy in his voice, the Texan lowered his head to trail his lips across hers. "You want me to . . ."

"No!"

But his mouth was on hers again, his arm a band of steel around her waist as his other hand cupped her head to hold it still under the heady plunder of his mouth. She was falling back under his spell, her mouth opening to accept the searching caress of his tongue. She was almost lost to the wonder he evoked when a soft, familiar laugh echoed from a distance to snap her back to her senses.

Angelica pushed hard at the broad, male chest so close to hers, staggering back as her unexpected thrust freed her.

"Go away! Leave me alone! I want no part of you and your threats!"

"Threats?" Momentarily puzzled, Gareth gave a small laugh. He had forgotten the small parcels and the lame excuse he had used to keep her with him. He tossed a deprecating glance toward the area where they still lay. "You mean your theft from your employers? Were you afraid I might discover that the poor, sick brother for whom you stole is nonexistent? But you found the perfect way to deter me from my purpose, didn't you, Angelica. You knew once I had you in my arms I'd forget everythin'. And your plan worked so well . . . so well that you were almost caught up in it yourself!"

"You lie! I planned nothing!"

Gareth took another step toward her.

"Stay away from me. I do not want you to touch me!"

"Are you afraid, little *puta*? But you needn't be afraid. I'll be generous. I'll pay you whatever price is necessary to purge you from my mind once and for all."

Her face flaming, Angelica gasped tightly, "I want nothing from you . . . nothing but to be left alone!"

Darting unexpectedly past him, Angelica ran toward the sanctuary of her home. She was within a few yards of its entrance when she stopped running and assumed a normal pace in an attempt to control her ragged breathing. Refusing to turn around, she listened intently for the sound of a heavy step behind her, but there was none. Almost weak with relief, she was about to walk through the doorway when she realized she had left her parcels on the ground where the Texan had tossed them.

Angelica raised her chin with new determination. She would return for them later, when the Texan had gone.

35

Carlos would taste the sweet cheese and honey tonight. And he would be well. She would allow no one and nothing to get in the way.

From the cover of trees, Gareth watched as Angelica's slender figure walked through the doorway of her home. He was shaking, whether from fury or from frustrated desire, he was unsure. Suddenly aware of his total loss of control, he slumped back against the tree under which he stood and shook his head helplessly. The little *puta* with the face of an angel had reduced him to quaking ineffectiveness.

He closed his eyes, and a mental image of Angelica's face returned to haunt him. He had seen desire reflected in those great silver orbs and in the manner in which her heavy lids had fluttered closed as he had tasted her sweet mouth. He had heard her gasping sigh, felt her hands clutch him close. It had not been an act . . . it could not have been. He had sensed the passion rising inside her, gloried in its ascent, reveled in its growing control of her senses.

Suddenly disgusted with himself, Gareth pulled himself to attention and took a deep breath. What in hell was wrong with him, anyway? He was behaving like a fool. He was allowing simple lust to rule his actions and his mind. What difference did it make if the little Mexican whore baited him? There was no doubt she was clever, and there was also no doubt she hoped to drive up her price by raising the level of his hunger for her. He gave a small, bitter laugh. Well, if that had been her purpose, she had certainly succeeded.

He shook his head in disbelief at his almost total lapse of control. He needed keep in mind that his visit to Real del Monte was not a social call. He was here on important business to which he would be dedicating the major portion of his day tomorrow. He need go back to the hacienda and put the beautiful little *puta* out of his mind until a more propitious time.

Refusing to give the small house in the distance another look, Gareth squared his broad shoulders and turned away. He had taken two steps when his foot hit against something

36

on the path, and he glanced down. Angelica's parcels . . . the cheese and honey she had stolen. He frowned and glanced back toward her home despite himself.

Was there really a little sick boy in there to whom she wished to bring the food? A picture of Angelica's clear eyes came before his mind and he felt a strange stirring inside him that all but wiped away his determination of a few moments before. Damn her! Damn her lying eyes and her giving mouth . . . Steeling himself against the strong resurgence of physical yearning her image had evoked, Gareth stepped purposefully over the parcels and continued back toward the Arricalde hacienda, without a break in stride.

Chapter II

"Quickly, Angelica. Hernando is waiting with the wagon."

Hastening to Carmela's command, Angelica carried the heavy pot out through the kitchen door toward the waiting wagon and placed it carefully in the rear. Ignoring Hernando's lascivious glance toward her gaping *camisa* as she leaned forward, she surveyed the food to be transported to the mines: Mole, nopal, frijoles, bananas, fritas, an impressive array of fresh fruit. There was still a morning chill in the air and Dona Teresa had left nothing to chance in her desire to be sure that her guests would receive a warm, hearty meal upon arrival at San Jose Regla.

A small frown moved over Angelica's face. Upon arriving at the Arricalde hacienda in early morning, she had been delighted to hear that la señora had planned on making a small party of her guests visit to the mines that day. Her experience with the Texan the night before had shaken her badly, and she had no desire to exchange words with either Don Esteban or him this morning.

She turned away from the wagon and walked back toward the kitchen in an attempt to evade her own thoughts. Despite her most stringent efforts to shake Gareth Dawson from her mind, his disturbingly masculine scent lingered in her nostrils. Aggravating her even more was the fact that his low, heady whisper still echoed in her ears, and the memory of his touch was still fresh against her

38

skin. She seemed unable to avoid the plaguing memories, and the word that la señora was planning to remove her guests from the hacienda for the entire day had been a welcome relief. It had been only a few moments before that she had been told Hernando, Josepina, Carmela, and she would accompany the entourage to prepare and serve the food. Juanita had been livid with jealousy, and had Angelica not realized that Carmela's selection of her over Juanita indicated a confidence in her dependability, she would have cheerfully remained behind.

La señora had planned a long but entertaining day. The road to the mines was wide and well paved, a product of the English involvement in the mines. It accommodated a carriage very easily, and it was because of this that Dona Teresa had decided to take her female guests along.

They were due to leave shortly, and Angelica released a short sigh. She had hoped to avoid Gareth Dawson and the ever-constant eye of Esteban Arricalde. In any case, it did not appear that Esteban Arricalde would be a problem for the duration of the Valentins' visit. It was obvious la señora considered Dolores Valentin an excellent candidate for marital arrangements for Estaban, and she was doing all in her power to promote things between them. The situation, however temporary, suited her just fine.

The cavalcade to the mines would be small, but mixed. The Arricalde carriage would carry the women, Señor Arricalde, and Señor Valentin. The remainder of the men would be mounted. The kitchen wagon would travel behind, carrying the servants and the food with which the guests would refresh themselves upon arrival. Angelica was well aware that the home of the director of the mines was near the mines, but it was obvious la señora did not wish to impose her guests upon his hospitality.

"Angelica . . . quickly. La señora and her guests are ready."

Carmela's quick instructions were given with a backhanded wave that shooed Angelica in the direction of the waiting wagon. Darting one last glance toward the kitchen, Angelica caught Juanita's dark, jealous glance. Juanita would do all in her power to make her suffer for this small show of partiality on the part of Carmela, but she would be damned if she would allow that nasty little witch to add yet another pall to her day. With calculated deliberation she returned Juanita's frown with a brilliant smile.

Snatching up her rebozo, Angelica walked quickly toward the wagon. Hernando was already helping Josepina up onto the seat beside him. And Angelica flicked a quick glance toward Carmela, who also stood ready to be seated. There would be no room for her in front. Doubtless, she would have to travel in the back of the wagon where the food was being carried. But she cared little. She far preferred to be alone in the back for the duration of the ride rather than squeezed between the considerable bulk of those in front. The wagon was wide and uncovered, and would allow her to take the sun as they rode. In truth, she felt she would be more comfortable than they.

Without further hesitation, Angelica scrambled aboard and adjusted her position between the baskets of food. Despite herself, her spirits were beginning to lift. Yes, perhaps it was going to be a good day after all.

Glancing up as the wagon jerked forward, Angelica suppressed a smile. From the rear view, the three more-than-ample rear portions of those riding up front appeared to be squeezed unmercifully into the narrow seat. Oh, yes, she was indeed fortunate after all to be riding in the back.

The swaying, heavily loaded wagon laboriously rounded the front of the hacienda, and Angelica sneaked a quick look toward the carriage and mounted group that awaited them. Seated casually inside the elaborately lacquered black and gold Arricalde carriage with the careless acceptance of the rich, Don Enrique, Dona Teresa, Señora Aleman, Señor and Señora Valentin, and Señorita Valentin chatted brightly.

Angelica was afforded a better view of the fine features of Señorita Valentin's pretty face and the effectiveness of her smile as the young woman turned to speak. Señorita Valentin appeared to be a truly pleasant person . . . too good for the man on whom she had obviously set her sights.

The sudden movement of her carriage allowed her a clearer view of the mounted men who waited to the side of the drive. Esteban Arricalde's effort to bring his magnificent black stallion under control allowed her a few moments for covert observation. There was no doubt Esteban was born to wear the standard dress of the Mexican nobleman presently in fashion. His black, flat-brimmed hat framed the aristocratic planes of his face to great advantage, emphasizing the dark color of his hair, the narrow brows over his dark eyes, and his finely chiseled profile. The serape he wore slung across his proud shoulders was of a luxurious fabric for which she did not have a name, but the depth of the color and detail of workmanship bespoke a talented hand and added immeasurably to his manly appeal. The same could be said of the dark, tight pants which flared out dramatically in an inverted pleat at his knee. The effect was to emphasize Esteban's slim muscular physique and blatantly male form in a most grand and becoming way.

Angelica gave a low snort. It was unfortunate, the handsome man that he was, that he was totally lacking in the integrity obviously ingrained in his parents. Her sympathy was profound for the noble Señor y Señora Arricalde knowing that they had only this poor, ignoble progeny to show for the proud blood of their family.

Her gaze lingering on the youngest Arricalde as he finally reined his anxious stallion under control, Angelica was startled as Esteban raised his eyes unexpectedly. His irritated gaze caught and locked with hers, the heat in their dark depths abruptly changing to the heat of an entirely different nature as a small smile flicked across his lips.

Immediately averting her glance, Angelica caught the knowing glance of another rider who had just urged his horse into the assembled group. Gareth Dawson's mocking gaze more than she could stand, Angelica turned her head toward the other side of the road, relieved, as the Arricalde carriage started forward and the cavalcade moved into motion.

Raindrops from the brief shower the night before glittered on the leaves and flowers along the road. The trees were green and refreshed, the rocks sparkling with silver as the Arricalde carriage moved leisurely forward on the smooth road. From her position in the wagon a reasonable distance behind the Arricalde carriage, Angelica had a perfect view of the passing scenery in all its magnificence. Having lived in these surroundings all her life, Angelica was still not immune to the beauty of mountains covered with carpets of brilliant flowers, the sight of clear rivulets flinging themselves from rock to rock in careless abandon, the skillful climb of goats scaling the perpendicular rocks to look down upon them from their lofty vantage points.

The abrupt slowing of the cavalcade interrupted Angelica's thoughts, turning her eyes from the passing scenery. They were drawing into the area of the mines, and despite herself, Angelica's anticipation began to grow. It was not often outsiders visited the mines. The area at San Jose Regla was almost totally confined to the Indian laborers of the mines and the British engineers and their families who were responsible for its maintenance.

Her eyes darting to the side of the road, Angelica saw a turn onto which the Arricalde carriage began to move. Straining her eyes, she saw a hacienda in the distance, and she nodded in confirmation of her first guess. Yes, it was the hacienda of the director of the mines. They must be very close to their destination.

Forcing her eyes to remain on the sprawling residence they approached, Angelica was intensely conscious of the lone rider who began to drop behind the other mounted men in their cavalcade. There was no doubt as to his identity. A man of Gareth Dawson's physical proportions could not be missed in this country of modest height and stature. The Texan's expanse of shoulder and trimly muscular proportions would have set him apart, even if his manner of dress had not already accomplished that small fact. But his riding clothes were typically Anglo-Texan, free of the ornate detail and styling that distinguished the Spanish influence, his hat characteristically broad-brimmed and deep in the crown. But in truth, she was

42

uncertain how well a man of Gareth Dawson's physical stature would suit the dandified styles to which Mexico had become accustomed.

She remembered well the width of the tightly muscled chest which had cushioned her body . . . the breadth of the shoulders around which she had curved her clinging arms. She remembered the flat, hard stomach pressed against hers . . . the warmth of strong thighs against her own trembling legs, supporting her. And she remembered the firm rise of his passion against her softness.

A chill that bore no relation to the temperature of the day passed over her slender frame, and Angelica closed her eyes in an attempt to still the trembling that had beset her. Gaining control after the passage of a few seconds, she lifted her lids, only to find the same dark eyes she had fought to elude focused mockingly on her face.

"What's the matter, Angelica?"

Choosing not to respond, Angelica glanced away, only to catch Carmela's assessing gaze.

Noting Angelica's concern with Carmela's steady appraisal, Gareth turned to address the old cook with a smile.

"I've been talkin' with Señores Flores and Alcazar. They're lookin' forward to the food they smelled cooking in the kitchen this morning. They commented that Señor Arricalde is fortunate to have such an excellent cook on his hacienda."

Accepting Gareth's compliment with a small incline of her head, Carmela smiled broadly.

"Gracias, señora. You may tell Señores Flores and Alcazar that they will not be disappointed with the food la señora has instructed me to bring with us today."

"Yes, I have no doubt you have brought a feast."

Turning toward the back of the wagon in the pretense of assessing the baskets and pots surrounding Angelica, Gareth instead focused his eyes on her parted lips. His gaze unmoving, he added quietly, "I have been looking forward to indulging myself all morning."

Not bothering to wait for a reply, Gareth tipped his hat and spurred his horse forward. Within moments he was

43

again riding alongside the others.

Doing her best to avoid Josepina's pointed gaze, Angelica swallowed her anger and turned her attention back to the passing landscape.

Catching Esteban's heated glance as he returned to the other mounted riders, Gareth held his glance coolly. Relieved when Señorita Valentin's polite inquiry interrupted their silent exchange, Gareth watched as Esteban turned toward the young woman with a stiff smile. Gareth frowned. He did not really want to become at odds with Esteban. He did not wish to offend the family which had been so generous to him and on whom he depended for access to the mines.

Whatever had possessed him to drop back toward the little *puta* so obviously? It had been a damned fool thing to do. His short departure from the group doubtless had been noted by others aside from Esteban. Had it been a perverted desire to see the beautiful little witch squirm? Well, if it had, it had only managed to backfire in his face. One glance at her had been effective in starting the heat building inside him again. The memory of the taste of her lips, the sweet fragrance of her skin, the incredible comfort of her body pressed against his aching loins assailed him. He had to purge the little *puta* from his mind. And he knew only one way. . . .

Angelica stood in a small, partially wooded area just above the mines, the spot selected by Dona Teresa for their afternoon meal. She looked down on the mining operation spread out before her eyes, aware that Dona Teresa had selected this spot with that exact purpose in mind. Grateful for the fact that the guests were presently visiting the hacienda of the director where they would no doubt be served tea, Angelica allowed her eyes to move over the unfamiliar scene.

A sadness overwhelming her, she watched Indian miners standing in line to descend into the thousand-foot shaft by way of a narrow opening in the ground. She had heard that the dark caves in which they labored endlessly were damp and airless, lit merely by the light of the candles the miners wore on their caps.

The sight of the miners' silent descent brought into sharp focus the hardships they endured, and it was times like this when Angelica was certain the blood of her unknown father had indeed made her an outsider in her own village. The silent acceptance of their fates with which her people survived was completely foreign to her, and in her heart she was certain it always would be.

But no matter her silent rage, she was well aware she was helpless against the situation that existed at the mines. Here she could only observe in pained ineffectiveness. But at home, in the household where her father, mother, and brother lived, she had long ago determined that she would not remain helpless. She would get the money needed to send Carlos to the doctor in Mexico City, and she would see him happy and well again! She would also see to it that he would have an opportunity to realize his dream. She knew this more surely than she had ever known anything in her life, for she had also determined that she would allow nothing to stop her. Nothing . . .

Gareth listened with difficulty to the detailed explanation delivered with a heavy Scottish burr. He had been startled at first by his own inability to decipher Brock Macfadden's colorful manner of speech, but his ear finally had become attuned to the man's accent, and he was now able to follow his words with reasonable accuracy. It was fortunate, because there was no doubt in his mind that the burly Scottish engineer was exactly the man he needed to see.

Gareth eyed Macfadden's grizzled countenance. Redheaded and red-bearded, with ample flecks of silver in both areas, his face was marked with freckles on the forehead and bridge of his rather hawklike nose. Lines stretched out broadly from the corners of his pale blue eyes, meeting and joining with those just peeping from beneath his heavily bearded face. Gareth experienced a short flash of incredulity. What could be more incongruous in this sun-

45

touched, leisurely land of dark-skinned, dark-haired people than this great, redheaded Scot and the machinery he had brought?

The morning had been spent in a tour of the mine, visiting the apparatus for sawing, the turning-lathe, and foundry. Along with the other Arricalde guests, he had been shown through the buildings for the separation and washing of the ore, the stores, workshops, and offices. He had met the British engineers, and been impressed with the work Horatio Clark, the English director, had accomplished.

But of it all, he had been most impressed by the work of the steam engine, which was Brock Macfadden's area of responsibility, and the work it had accomplished in draining the mines. He had felt an instant affinity with the hard-working engineer and they had immediately fallen into a first-name basis in addressing each other. The other guests had long since filtered back to the area where the luncheon meal was being prepared, but he had remained to press the enthusiastic engineer for further explanations.

"Ye must realize the difficulty we found when we approached this project, Gareth. Aye, flooding in the mines had always been a problem. The Count de Regla had used the only solution available to him when he owned all these tracts of land. It had called for the excavation of a slantin' tunnel nearly two miles in length, most through solid rock, so the mine cou' be emptied into a watercourse at a lower level. The project took years and advanced vera slowly. When the water finally drained oot, the mine proved vera successful and reaped millions in profits. But time and the gradual deepenin' of the shafts made such a manner of keepin' the shaft free of water a twenty-four-hour job and too expensive to be supported."

Gareth's appreciation for the enormity of the project was reflected on his face, and Macfadden continued with a nod of his head. "Aye, profits declined and work was all but abandoned. But a special act of Congress allowed foreign investors to become joint proprietors in these mines, and it was then that we brought the steam engine in here. I dinna need to tell ye the difference implementation of this vehicle has made, Gareth."

"No, it's obvious that the mine is again a great success."

Nodding proudly, Macfadden smiled. His pale blue eyes sparkled with pride. "Aye, we've been successful, and a good thin', too. The great lot of us came a long way."

A new light entering his dark eyes, Gareth nodded. "I've come a long way to meet you too, Brock. Don Enrique has informed you of the project I want to discuss with you?"

"Vaguely, Gareth, vaguely."

Taking a deep breath, Gareth paused. Much depended on his ability now to stir the interest of this engineer. He was in need of a relatively quick response so he might return to Texas as soon as possible.

Turning to the leather-enclosed map he had carried into the office in his saddlebag, Gareth unwrapped it and stated carefully, "I'd like to leave this map with you, Brock. It's a map of our land, my father's and mine." Running his finger over a clearly marked area, he continued. "This part of the land is dry, almost worthless. My father and I would like to turn it into useful land, land that would support a decent crop and good grass for our cattle."

His sharp eyes carefully scanning the markings, the Scot leaned closer. His eyes following the line of the river, he nodded his head. "It appears that yer water supply is convenient, but is it adequate? Is it consistent enough to support a system of this type? Wou' the interruption of the flow of the water constitute other problems for ye and yer neighbors that wou' make this plan unfeasible? Do ye think ye cou' . . ."

Gareth grinned at the questions being fired at him by the sharp Scot and raised his hands in a gesture of surrender. "Wait a minute. Those are the questions we were hopin' you could answer for us, Brock."

A responsive smile stretching across his sunburned face, Brock shook his head. "Aye. Yer nae asking much, are ye? And I'm supposed to answer all this from the basis of this map yer showin' me?"

"This map . . ." Turning, Gareth retrieved another

47

batch of papers from his saddlebag, ". . . and these . . . and these . . . all statistics, accurate to the best of our knowledge, presentin' the situation as it stands."

"Whew!" Taking a step back, Brock shook his head. "This is a grand project ye've presented me, laddie-boy! I hope ye dinna expect an answer on the spot."

"No, I'm intendin' to stay with Señor Arricalde for a short time longer. I had hoped, after you'd had a chance to study the project, we'd be able to discuss its feasibility in detail, as well as the possibility of employin' you to . . ."

"Aye, aye, I understand what yer sayin', but let's nae get ahead of ourselves." Nodding his head, Brock Macfadden continued firmly. "The project is interestin', but I'm nae quite sure I'd be free to take it on right . . ."

His eyes suddenly focusing on a spot outside the office window, Macfadden allowed his words to draw to a halt as his expression moved into a frown. Turning, Gareth caught a glimpse of a slender, redheaded young man walking up the path toward the spot where the Arricalde guests had gathered for their outdoor meal. The young man's objective was obviously not the makeshift table around which the guests were milling. Instead, he was moving directly toward the cooking area and a familiar, slender figure who worked near the fire.

Gareth watched as Angelica turned toward the young man. Her lips moved into a smile as he spoke. A knot constricted in Gareth's stomach as the young man reached out to touch her arm.

"Blast the lad!"

Brock Macfadden's low ejaculation snapped Gareth's head back in his direction.

"With a whole flock of available British lassies in our group to choose from, the fool lad has to find his interest in her!"

Gareth's frown darkened, and he suppressed his own reaction to Macfadden's words as the grizzly Scot continued in a low growl. "The lad has nae a speck of Macfadden common sense when it comes to women. He's done nawt but talk of that lass since he first set eyes on her."

Glancing back to Gareth as if suddenly remembering his presence, the Scot shook his head and mumbled by way of explanation, "The lad is my brother . . . aye . . . the youngest in the family . . . a bairn of my mother's old age. More like my own lad than a brother. He came here just a few months ago. A fine engineer . . . capable man, but blasted slow when it comes to the lassies."

Addressing Gareth, he inquired bluntly, "Ye've seen the lass . . . heard of her, nae doot. The old priest in the village talked Señora Arricalde into hirin' her at the hacienda. Nae a woman in the village wou' have her in the house. Comes from bad stock. Nae a one knows who her father is, but one thin' for sure, it nae be the man she calls Father. When Peter came back from the Arricalde hacienda for the first time, he cou' do nawt but talk about her. Nae a one of us cou' tell him anything. He tries to see her every chance he gets, but the lass is nae vera responsive. Aye, I have to give her credit fer that. She doesna want to get involved wi' the men from the company. Smart lass. From what I hear she's busy enough now that the young Arricalde is back home."

A slow flush was suffusing Gareth's face, and he clamped his teeth tightly shut against the words that rushed to his lips. How could he protest the truth, the truth Angelica herself had demonstrated only too clearly?

Brock Macfadden continued with a short nod. "Aye, 'tis plain to see that ye've seen her. A bonnie lass . . . near has the lad bewitched."

Refusing to comment on Macfadden's remarks, Gareth shook his head in an attempt to change the subject. "About the project . . . what do you say, Brock?"

Glancing down toward the maps and papers that had held his interest so avidly only a few short minutes before, Macfadden frowned. Appearing to consider Gareth's question for a few moments, he finally nodded.

"Aye, I'll take it on . . . at least to let ye know if the plan appears feasible or nae. I may have some questions . . ."

"I intend comin' back here after you've had a chance to familiarize yourself with the drawin's."

"That will be fine."

Extending his hand, Brock Macfadden accepted Gareth's handshake absentmindedly as his eyes shot again toward the window. The Scot's jaw worked noticeably under his beard and Gareth felt a similar tightening in his own stomach. Damn the little witch! Was there no part of his life she would leave untouched?

Striding out the doorway in a rapid step, Gareth headed directly for the cleared area where the Arricalde guests mingled, his mind far from the festive air of the group.

Angelica smiled into the young Scot's face. She liked Peter Macfadden, his gentle manner and his soft, trilling burr. The sound of his voice amused her, and not realizing her great eyes sparkled with the warmth he inspired, she replied quietly, "Yes, it is pleasant to see you too, Señor Macfadden."

"Nae Señor Macfadden, Angelica. Peter is my name, and I wou' be pleased to hear ye call call me by it."

Looking down into her face from his considerable height, Peter Macfadden swallowed tightly. He had never seen a more beautiful woman than Angelica Rodrigo. It mattered little to him that his brother, and the greater portion of the British community at Real del Monte, had much to say about her origins. There was only innocence in the exquisite eyes she raised to his as he waited expectantly for her response.

"No, I think not. I think la señora would not approve. I do not wish to do anything that might jeopardize . . ."

"Calling me by my given name cou' do that?" Shaking his head, the young Scot gave a small laugh. "Nay . . ."

A low snort from behind turned Angelica's eye toward Josepina's tight expression. Much more would be made of this unexpected meeting than it warranted if she did not bring it to a quick end.

Raising hesitant eyes toward Peter Macfadden again, she gave a small shrug. "I am sorry, but it is almost time to serve the meal to la señora's guests. If you will excuse me . . ."

The young Scot reached out spontaneously, his callused

hand taking her arm. Raising her eyes again to the pale blue ones which regarded her intently, she frowned.

"Nay, nae yet, Angelica, please. I . . . I wou' like permission to come to call on ye . . . to spend some time with ye."

Angelica's frown tightened. She did not wish to become involved personally with anyone, much less this handsome young foreigner who would cause considerable gossip by the very act of his attentions to her. She had no illusions about the way she was regarded by the majority of the British community, and she did not wish to give them cause for further gossip. She could take no chances on losing her position. Too much hinged on her continued employment at the Arricalde hacienda.

But the blue eyes regarding her were sincere, she was sure. And she liked Peter Macfadden. She liked the way his brightly colored hair lay raggedly against his neck. She found his youthful face and rough features appealing. The light color of his skin was particularly fascinating, and she never failed to be amazed by the way his heavy golden brows and eyelashes sparkled in the sun. She had never seen the marks of the sun so heavily distributed across anyone's face . . . in little brown spots that concentrated on the bridge of his nose and under his eyes. And she liked the soft, manly timbre of his voice that so belied his apparent youth.

Oh, she knew he was much older than he appeared. His position of responsibility at the mines had determined that in her mind, but he was so slender and tall, as if his body had not quite caught up with his sudden leap in height. He had been politely attentive to her since the first time he had come to Señor Arricalde's hacienda, and she had done her best to discourage his interest. But so far she had been unsuccessful.

He was still smiling hopefully down into her eyes, and Angelica was suddenly overwhelmed with warmth. There was no accusation in his eyes . . . no consideration of gossip that followed her. If only she could . . .

"Peter Macfadden, I presume?"

A deep, familiar drawl abruptly interrupted Angelica's thoughts, snapping her toward the Texan as he approached them in a steady stride.

"Aye, that's my name. And what do they call ye?"

Extending his hand, Gareth offered with a small smile, "Gareth Dawson. I'm visitin' the mines with Señor Arricalde's group of friends. I've just been in conversation with your brother and have left him a map and a set of drawin's on which he wanted to get your opinion. He's told me of your ability, and I'm much interested in what you have to say on the project."

"I'm flattered by yer interest, Mr. Dawson, and I wou' be happy to look over yer drawings with my brother." Turning back toward Angelica with a small smile, he continued in a softer voice, "But at present I'm talkin' with this lass and I . . ."

"Angelica . . ."

Turning at the sound of Carmela's voice, Angelica caught her impatient glance.

"*Angelica, por favor, la comida está preparado ahora. La señora espera.*"

"*Si*, Carmela . . ."

Firmly ignoring Gareth Dawson, Angelica turned back to Peter Macfadden with an apologetic smile. In truth, she was glad the interruption had forced the conversation to a close. The appearance of Gareth Dawson and his dark, accusing glance had spoiled the enjoyment she had been deriving from Peter Macfadden's company.

"If you will excuse me, Señor Macfadden."

Apparently reluctant to relinquish his hold on her arm, Peter Macfadden frowned. Her formal manner of address had not gone unnoted and he shook his head. A small, persuasive smile finally appearing on his lips, he said softly, "My name is Peter, Angelica. It wou' give me great pleasure to hear ye say it."

Peter Macfadden's statement recalled to mind the Texan's harsh demand the night before as he had held her in his arms, and Angelica flushed. Unwilling to suffer his mocking gaze, Angelica kept her eyes trained on Peter's face. The intensity of her stare inadvertently brought a new light into the young Scot's pale eyes as his hand slipped spontaneously up to her shoulder.

"Angelica . . . *ahora* . . ."

Carmela's summons snapped Angelica's eyes once again in her direction. Her flush darkening, Angelica turned a quick, apologetic smile toward Peter Macfadden as she offered, "*Lo siento.*"

Within seconds she had turned away and was hastening toward the fire, leaving the two men standing silently in her wake.

Gareth gritted his teeth against his frustration. The short intimate exchange between Peter Macfadden and Angelica had resulted in the further tightening of the tense knot in his stomach and he fumed inwardly. That prolonged gaze into the young Scot's eyes . . . The little witch actually saw fit to play with the young fellow's emotions in his presence. Damn her!

If he were to be honest he would have to admit she had achieved her obvious purpose with him, too. He was jealous, so jealous of the warmth in the little *puta*'s eyes when she looked at Peter Macfadden that he had had all he could do not to jerk the Scot's hand from her arm and set him straight once and for all. Oh, she was smart, all right.

Not realizing his eyes followed Angelica's slight, swaying form, Gareth watched as she hastened to fill platters with the various tempting treats Carmela had managed to prepare under the less than ideal conditions under which she worked. But the delicious aromas wafting from the steaming trays did little to stimulate his appetite. Hell, his stomach was so filled with lust that he had room for little more. He had no appetite . . . not for food, anyway. The aroma he longed to smell was the lush scent of Angelica's body; the taste he longed for was the sweetness of her flesh; and if he wished to have his appetite sated, it was a appetite which had no relationship at all to physical hunger.

Abruptly realizing that his body was beginning to react predictably to the stimulus of his thoughts, Gareth frowned and turned toward Peter Macfadden. But Macfadden was also engaged in following Angelica with his eyes as she moved around the campfire, and his own agitation increased.

Barely stifling the comment that rose to his lips, he was about to turn away when Macfadden remarked in a low tone, "A bonnie lassie, she is. I've nae seen another to compare. I dinna know how to explain it, but she's nae like the other women here. She's nae like any woman I've ever met . . ."

Biting back his automatic retort, Gareth hesitated, aware that Macfadden's gaze had not stirred from Angelica's form. When he spoke, his tone was heavy with subtle meaning.

"You're right. The people around here would be the first to tell you that she's different from most of them . . ."

Peter Macfadden's head jerked back in his direction, his expression reflecting his sudden irritation. "Aye, I nae be deaf, Mr. Dawson. And I nae be as young as I appear. And were I both, I have nae a doot my brother wou' have overcome it all with his warnin's. I dinna need to hear more . . . and from a man here only long enough to know nawt but gossip."

Doing his best to overcome the flash of anger the young man's response stimulated, Gareth shrugged his shoulders.

"I didn't come to San Jose de Regla to discuss Dona Teresa's kitchen maid. I'm far more interested in the work your company's doin' here, and your reaction to the plans I've left with your brother."

"That will be fine with me, Mr. Dawson. If my brother has accepted the project, ye may be certain I'll give him my opinion if 'tis asked for."

The young man's face was still creased in a frown, and experiencing regret for his hasty words and the tension they had sparked between them, Gareth extended his hand.

"I would appreciate that." Satisfied when Peter Macfadden hesitated only a moment before accepting it, Gareth continued. "And if you'll excuse me, I'll have to be gettin' back to Dona Teresa's party. I can see they're about ready to start."

Within minutes, Gareth was walking back to the area where the Arricalde guests were beginning to seat themselves around hastily erected tables. Unconsciously squaring his shoulders, Gareth gave a small, self-derisive snort. Well, it was obvious young Macfadden was not a man to hesitate in speaking his mind. He had to admire the young fellow for his outspokenness, if not for his judgment. As for himself, he was going to have to get his feelings in hand if he expected to function with any degree of effectiveness, and it had better be soon. He had little time to waste.

Angelica shot a quick look toward the blue sky overhead. Her eye on the position of the sun, she judged it to be well past mid-afternoon and she breathed a sigh of relief. The long, work-filled day was almost over. The early morning chill had long since evaporated under the assault of the brilliant afternoon sun, and the day had turned considerably warmer. But, protected by the lofty umbrella of trees, the grove was a pleasant respite from the unexpected heat.

Angelica turned an unconscious glance toward the Arricalde party which milled about the grove in quiet conversation. The heat of the day and the abundance of food served had resulted in a general air of malaise within the group. Without exception, Dona Teresa's guests seemed in no hurry to bring their pleasant outing to an end, and were obviously content to linger as long as possible before starting back.

Despite the fact that her work for the day had been all but completed, Angelica was anxious to go home. Don Esteban's covert glances were making her considerably uncomfortable, and the knowing smirk on the Texan's face on the few occasions when he had caught her eye had only succeeded in adding the weight of anger to her discomfort. She was intensely relieved that the party had retired into informal groups at the completion of the meal, for it meant that Señorita Valentin had once again managed to engage Estaban in conversation with a few of the other guests. Considering Esteban's present preoccupation with Señorita Valentin, she would not need to suffer a continuance of his poorly concealed interest.

Gareth Dawson was involved in speaking with Dona Enrique and Don Teresa. In the casual atmosphere of the grove, he stood out more than ever from the other Arricalde guests. Having shed his jacket in deference to the heat of the afternoon, he was clad merely in a white lawn shirt, unfastened at the throat, and dark, well-tailored trousers which revealed the long, muscular length of his legs in disturbing detail. She turned her head. She remembered only too well the breadth of his broad chest under her palms, the strength of those arms, and the power in those thighs as he had held her close. She remembered also the eager response of his body as he had clutched her tight against him, and she flushed again at the memory of her own pitiful resistance to the confusing feelings he had stirred inside her.

She glanced toward him once again. His tall, muscular frame was relaxed as he leaned indolently against a great oak, his hand resting on his belt. His expression was pleasant. He turned to address a comment to Dona Teresa, a bright smile flashing across his face as he dipped his head politely at her response. Angelica's heart skipped a beat. The transformation was startling. Gone was the dark, formidable man she had come to think of as Gareth Dawson. In his place was a handsome, charming individual who she could suddenly see as comfortable in the most polished drawing rooms of Mexico City as he was in the Texas homestead which was his home.

Her heart jumped a beat and she frowned in annoyance. His smiles were reserved for Dona Teresa and those he deemed worthy, there was no doubt. He has long since made up his mind about her, and she had long since determined that she would protest his unjust assessment of her no longer. Let him think what he liked! What did it matter the conclusion he had drawn from her brief encounter with Peter Macfadden? The reminder of the silent accusation in his eyes when he had seen her speaking with the pleasant Scot renewed her anger. It mattered little to her that the surly Texan eyed her with contempt. His presence in her life was temporary, and he would be easily forgotten when he left the Arricalde household. She had other, far more alarming situations to deal with, and she was determined she would waste no further time in consideration of the irritating Texan.

Turning back momentarily toward the fire, Angelica noted that Carmela and Josepina were seated a respectable distance from the main group, obviously enjoying their leisure after the long day's work. Hernando was stretched out under a nearby tree, his back propped against its trunk, his eyes closed. Relieved that she was on her own for the first time that day, Angelica turned and wandered onto the path to the stream from which they had taken their water. The glittering ripples of crystal water had beckoned to her from the first moment she had set eyes upon them, and she was determined to make good use of their shallow depth.

Emerging from the heavy foliage surrounding the trail a few moments later, Angelica slowed her step. The thick vegetation around the narrow path came to an end abruptly at that point, as if cleared by a human hand to allow appreciation of the sight that met her eyes. A few feet in front of her the low ground cover stopped at the roots of a huge oak. There a brief bank, verdant with moss, sloped down to a stream gurgling audibly over rocks visibly streaked with silver. The scene was lovely and restful, exactly the refuge she had been seeking.

Walking quickly to the edge of the bank, Angelica sat down and removed her sandals. Inching herself closer, she perched on the edge and dangled her toes into the icy ripples. She gasped. The water was chilling against her warm feet, but it was a refreshing chill which stimulated a small, unconscious giggle. Slowly submerging her feet completely in the freezing sensation, she leaned back, supporting herself with her arms as she raised her face to the sun.

The warm brilliance was bright red against her closed lids as the sun bathed her skin with soothing heat. She could feel herself relaxing, the cares and annoyances of the day slipping away under its tranquilizing rays, and she released a soft sigh. But a dull ache in her forearm brought her back from her serene haven, and she glanced down. She frowned at the sight of the nasty bruise which marked the outer side of her arm almost from wrist to elbow. A visible reminder of the force with which she had struck the wall under Esteban Arricalde's unrestrained attack in the upstairs bedroom the day before, the mark had continued to darken during the night. The soreness with which she had awakened had increased as the day had worn on, resisting her attempts to ignore it.

Taking a moment more to appraise the bruise critically, Angelica reached into the pocket of her skirt and withdrew a cloth. Leaning over, she reached down and moistened it in the cold water of the stream. Cautiously she applied the cold compress against the bruised skin.

"So here's where you're hidin' . . ."

The sound of a low drawl snapped Angelica's head toward the tall figure who emerged from the trail and began walking toward her. The harsh planes of Gareth Dawson's face were unsmiling, putting his words more in the nature of an accusation than a statement.

Her hand dropping back to her side, Angelica responded tightly, "I am not hiding . . . merely taking the opportunity for some time to be by myself."

An unreadable flicker moved across the Texan's expression. "Am I to take it that you aren't lookin' for company?"

"Yes."

But her blunt response had no effect on the Texan's steady advance. He came to stand towering over her, his potent presence effective in escalating the beat of her heart as he slowly lowered himself to sit beside her. His dark eyes caught and held hers in long moments of silence before he began to speak.

"I've come to apologize to you, Angelica. I jumped to an unfair conclusion last night. I just learned in speakin' with Dona Teresa that you do indeed have a ailin' brother. She told me that he is doin' very poorly . . . that the priest in the town in convinced that he won't . . ."

58

Cutting him short of the words she did not wish to hear, Angelica interrupted in a rush, "I do not need to have you tell me what Padre Manuel said. Padre Manuel is certain Carlos will improve with proper care and treatment."

His dark brows knitting into a frown, Gareth surveyed Angelica's sudden flush without comment. He raised his hand to the heated surface of her cheek, his frown darkening as she shook off his touch.

"In any case, I owe you an apology for accusin' you of lyin'."

"That is so generous of you, Señor Dawson."

Appearing determined to ignore her sarcasm, Gareth prompted quietly, " 'Gareth . . .' "

"No, I think not. I do not think it would be wise for me to use your given name. It would give the illusion of an intimacy which I do not intend to allow to develop."

Illiciting just the reaction she had hoped, Angelica felt a flash of satisfaction as Gareth's mouth tightened in irritation.

"No, you seem to save your soft words and glances for a particular young Scot." His voice beginning to reflect a growing annoyance, Gareth continued roughly. "And what do you expect Peter Macfadden can offer you that I can't better?"

"Peter Macfadden offers me friendship . . . consideration . . . he treats me with respect. You do not know the meaning of those words."

Gareth's eyes glittered with a new emotion. "I know what those words mean, and I've employed them on rare occasions. But I would not waste either those words or those emotions on you, Angelica. Instead, I would give you other words, far more suitable to the way I feel when I look at you—desire, passion, and ecstasy, Angelica. I promise you the same ecstacy that I have no doubt you could give to me."

Flushing at his outspoken declaration, Angelica managed a scathing look despite the heavy pounding of her heart. Sincerely wishing to destroy the confidence radiating in his intense gaze, she responded, "You are so sure that is what I wish? You are a poor judge of people, Señor Dawson." A harsh laugh escaped her lips as her eyes raked his face. "You and Esteban Arricalde have much in common . . ."

"Don't compare me with Esteban Arricale . . . or with any man." It was apparent that the Texan's anger was quickly escalating, and Angelica felt a deep satisfaction conflicting with a growing nudge of fear which she chose to ignore.

"I will compare those men I wish to compare. Did you not realize that would be the case when you approached me, Señor Dawson? Did not the reputation which drew you to me give you that indication?" Not waiting for his response, she shook her head with a small, deprecating laugh. "No? If not, then you are more a fool than I thought!"

"I am no fool . . . and I do know what you want, Angelica. You're smart enough to realize that Esteban Arricalde is not a man of his word, and that Peter Macfadden is. But I can offer you more than Macfadden can, in every sense of the word, Angelica." Raising his hand to her cheek, Gareth stroked the smooth skin, his gaze intent upon her lips as his broad chest rose and fell with agitated breaths. "I'm past the point of bargainin'. Name your price, and I'll pay it."

Humiliation and another emotion she did not wish to name sent a wave of color to her cheeks as Angelica jerked away from his touch. "But I do not want you, Señor Dawson!"

Allowing herself just a moment's gratification at the further constriction of Gareth Dawson's facial muscles, Angelica made a quick move to draw herself to her feet. But the Texan's hand snaked out, grasping her roughly, eliciting a gasp of pain as it closed over her bruised arm.

Making certain to hold her fast with his other hand, Gareth examined her arm, his brow knotting in a frown.

"Did Esteban do this?"

Attempting to draw herself free of his hold, Angelica responded tightly, "Let me go. It is nothing. I have had far worse."

His eyes moving slowly to hers, Gareth mumbled, "Yes, I suppose you have."

The heat in his gaze growing, Gareth slowly raised her arm to his lips. With supreme gentleness he pressed his mouth against the battered flesh, covering the aching surface with light, fleeting kisses.

Startled by his unexpected actions, Angelica attempted to snatch her arm away. Her breath was coming in quick, short gasps. A strange light-headedness assailed her, leaving her frighteningly giddy as she shook her head in an attempt to regain full control of her senses.

"Let go! Leave me alone!" Scrambling to free her arm, to draw herself to her feet, Angelica was suddenly conscious of the fact that her trembling legs would not cooperate with her effort.

"No, Angelica . . ." Gareth's eyes glittered with an almost feral gleam. "You don't really want me to leave you alone. And I know I don't want to let you go." He was easing her backward, using his overwhelming strength to subdue her feeble resistance.

The mossy softness of the bank was beneath her back, the weight of Gareth's body holding her helpless with its sensual heat. His grasp moving to her wrists, he raised her arms over her head, fitting his muscular chest intimately against her breasts.

"The taste of you is still in my mouth, Angelica. It's sharp, intoxicatin'. Let me share it with you, darlin'. Let me show you the way you make me feel. Let me give to you . . ."

His lips were moving against hers, his tongue slipping between them to fondle the moist hollows of her mouth. His one hand moved to tangle in her hair, holding her fast under his kiss as the other slid down her side in a stroking caress that brought her bemused senses sharply to life. His mouth was driving deeper, deeper into her own, overwhelming her inept struggle to be free. Despite the strong dictates of her mind, Angelica found her body becoming silent under his, accepting, welcoming, and she raged inwardly at his gradual, seemingly inevitable victory. Her arms were winding around his neck, and she heard his low groan as her lips separated fully to accept the new fervor of his intimate assault.

She heard a soft, throaty utterance. Startled to realize that it was her own, Angelica made an attempt to marshal the last fragments of her quickly waning resistance. But Gareth's heady assault was too much for her newly awakened senses. She was drowning, drowning in a sea of unearthly sensation and soaring emotion, too weak to save herself from wave after wave of the searing tumult that accosted her under Gareth's unrelenting ministrations.

"*Bastardo!*"

The low, venomous expletive reached both their ears at the same time, snapping Gareth and Angelica's heads toward the figure approaching in a rapid step from the edge of the clearing.

His eyes on Esteban's enraged face, Gareth drew himself cautiously to his feet. Scrambling up beside him, Angelica took a few steps backward, only to come up against the trunk of the tall oak which blocked further retreat. Esteban was standing directly in front of Gareth, his handsome face distorted with fury.

"This woman is mine . . . *mine!*" His voice lowering to an ominous hiss, he continued hotly. "Hear me now, for I will not say it again! You are here in Real de Monte at the sufferance of the Arricalde family. In return for our hospitality you will conduct yourself in a manner that is not offensive to us. You will remain a respectful distance from the women of our house, whether they work in our kitchen or . . ."

"Your parents are my hosts, Esteban." His flat, unemotional statement belied by the anger flashing ominously in his eyes, Gareth interrupted Esteban's heated tirade. "And they have given me no such instructions as to my conduct. But if you truly wish to consider your parents' wishes, I think it would be safe to say they would much prefer *you* keep your distance from Angelica, rather than me."

"Then you will consider the effect of your conduct on

me, Gareth Dawson! And I say you will not touch Angelica again. She is my woman . . ."

"I am not your woman!" Finally regaining her tongue, Angelica pushed herself away from the support of the tree, her back stiff with the anger at the humiliating scene being enacted. "I am neither your woman *nor* Gareth Dawson's woman, and I never will be! You both dream wild fantasies that will never become reality. Dolores Valentin awaits you, Don Esteban. Go back to her, for she will welcome you far more warmly than I."

Esteban's incensed gaze raked Angelica's quaking form. His eyes traveled slowly over the flushed perfection of her face, a twisted smile moving across his lips as he muttered in threatening promise, "You may be sure I will remember the words you speak today, little *puta*. And you may be sure I will remind you of them when the time comes for you to refute them, to beg me to take you . . ."

"Never! That day will never come!"

Angelica fought to purge herself of the tremors of fear that shook her as Esteban's sinister smile grew. Somewhere in the back of her mind she was aware that she was making a powerful enemy whom she had no means to fight. Pulling up her slender frame proudly, she struggled to overcome the specter of resolved retribution she saw forming in Esteban's mind.

"We shall see, little *puta*."

His head jerking back toward Gareth Dawson, Esteban looked up into the Texan's coldly emotionless face. He gave a small, mirthless laugh.

"How much did this gringo pay you to accept his meager attentions? The sum must have been great indeed to convince you to allow him to sate his passionless lust on your body. See, Angelica . . . see how cold you have left him? His body was on yours and even then his emotions remained clearly untouched. Perhaps that is because he does not have the capacity for passion! Perhaps it is because he is cold and unfeeling . . . unable to truly love a woman the way she should be loved . . ."

"You've said enough, Esteban . . . more than enough."

Gareth's tone was ominous, vibrating in the silence of the clearing as he continued with tenuous control, "And I think you had best leave now and go back to your guests. Your mother will be wondering where you are . . ."

Shooting him a look of open contempt, Esteban grated insidiously, "You hide behind the skirts of a woman, Gareth Dawson! I care not if my mother comes seeking me. It matters not what she thinks or says. I will do as I wish in any case, as I have always done."

"Not this time. Not if your plans include Angelica . . ."

The two men were squaring off, facing each other with growing animosity. Gareth's hands were balling into fists, and shooting a quick look toward Esteban, Angelica noticed the fingers on his right hand twitching warningly. Angelica felt a new tremor of fear. She was well aware of the fact that Esteban reputedly carried a knife in his boot, with which he was supposedly very adept. She took a quick step forward only to jerk to a stop in mid-stride at the sound of thrashing on the narrow trail.

Within moments Carmela's considerable bulk flashed into view, her broad figure drawing to an abrupt halt as she viewed the ominous tableau. Her observant eyes moving from the unyielding expressions of the two men to Angelica's flushed countenance, she finally ventured in a quiet voice, "Angelica, we prepare to leave. The sky has suddenly become overcast. It will soon storm and Dona Teresa does not wish to be caught on these roads in the midst of its fury."

Noting that no one moved in the silence which followed her statement, Carmela turned toward Esteban and continued quietly. "Don Esteban, Dona Teresa has asked several of the others to seek you out in order to inform you of our leaving. She directed them to the mine buildings in the belief that you had gone down to check on business affairs."

"But instead I came into the glade and found an affair of another kind progressing . . ."

Carmela's eyes snapped to Angelica's flushed face as a sound of spontaneous denial escaped her lips. A stiff smile curving his mouth, Esteban shook his head. "But do not

64

worry, little *puta*. Neither I nor Carmela will reveal to my mother what has happened here today, will we, Carmela?" Allowing his eyes to move from Angelica just long enough to note Carmela's brief nod of acquiescence, he continued tightly. "We will put this incident behind us and forget it ever happened."

His eyes communicating a message of a far different sort as they held Angelica's for a few moments longer, Esteban stepped back. Shooting Gareth one last contemptful glance, he looked up at the sky before gesturing stiffly in Angelica's direction.

"You must return to your duties quickly before any more clouds have had the opportunity to gather. We do not wish a perfect day such as the one we have spent here to end disagreeably." His expression beginning to harden as Angelica remained unmoving, Esteban hissed, "*Ahora . . . pronto!*"

Ignoring her resentment at the imperiousness of his command, Angelica fell in behind Carmela without the briefest glance for Gareth Dawson. She did not want to look at the gringo whose pursuit had nearly brought a personal disaster upon her . . . and she did not want to face the fact that despite her most stringent efforts, she had been utterly helpless against him.

Gareth eyed the rapidly moving clouds, his mind registering their dark, leaden weight with a frown. A sky which had been brilliantly blue only minutes before was now a heavy, threatening black. The wind was rising, and heeding its warning, the concerned Arricalde guests moved quickly to gather their belongings and make their way toward the waiting carriage. His eyes narrowing, Gareth watched with growing distaste the manner in which Esteban deferred to the needs of Dolores Valentin, eliciting a flush on the young woman's delicate features as he assisted her up the narrow steps into the protection of the carriage.

He noted that Esteban's horse had been tied to the rear of the sturdy conveyance, indicating that he intended to ride inside for the duration of the two-hour return trip to the Arricalde hacienda. It appeared to matter little to him that the seating arrangements would be more than cramped, when he was faced with the specter of a drenching from a cold, mountain storm. He would doubtless take advantage of the opportunity to pacify his parents with his attentions to the impressionable Señorita Valentin while his thoughts centered lasciviously on Angelica Rodrigo. Señores Flores, Alcazar, and Erricavera had decided to remain the night at the home of Horatio Clark and had informed Don Enrique earlier that they would return the following day.

Since he had politely refused an offer to ride in the crowded carriage, it seemed it would be only he who would be exposed to elements appearing ready to release a raging tempest at any moment—he and those who would be traveling in the uncovered cook wagon. His brow knitting in concern, Gareth turned toward the cooking fire and the figures scurrying back and forth to the wagon in an attempt to reload before the storm broke. The majority of the cooking gear had been stored in the back. All that remained was to douse the fire and gather up the remaining utensils, and Gareth released a relieved breath.

A short, nervous whinny drew his attention from Angelica's delicate form as she climbed into the rear of the wagon. Gareth turned to pat his chestnut gelding's long, slender neck. Major was always a bit testy before a storm, but the sturdy five-year-old had served him long and well and Gareth knew him to be a stout-hearted dependable animal.

"It's all right, boy. We'll be gettin' out of here in a few minutes and on our way home. But it looks like you're in for a good drenchin' before we get there."

Mounting in a quick, fluid movement reflecting countless hours spent in the saddle, Gareth reached behind him and untied the small roll attached there. Shaking out a shapeless, oversized garment, he slipped it over his shoulders and allowed it to settle around him without fastening the front. A rough cloak made of oiled canvas, it had kept him comfortably dry through many a Texas rainstorm, and he was more than sure it would suffice again. Pulling his

66

broad-brimmed hat down low on his forehead, Gareth urged his horse forward as the Arricalde carriage began a jerking start.

Leaning into the growing force of the wind as thunder rumbled ominously and lightning streaked the dark sky, Gareth shot a quick glance upward. The rushing clouds above him had begun to release the first drops of rain. Noting that the rotund, mustachioed driver of the Arricalde carriage had picked up the pace, Gareth shot a glance over his shoulder to see that Hernando was whipping his horses into a companion pace as the women sitting beside him sought to cover them all with a large tarpaulin.

Allowing his horse to drop back alongside the wagon as the small caravan turned onto the road, Gareth shot a quick glance into the rear. Angelica was sitting in back, the rebozo covering her head and shoulders her only protection against the rain beginning to fall in earnest. Within a few moments she would be drenched to the skin. His reaction spontaneous, Gareth leaned over, and reaching out in a quick movement, curled a strong arm around Angelica's waist and lifted her from the wagon. Appearing to recover from the shock of his actions just as he began to settle her on the saddle in front of him, Angelica began to struggle.

"Hold still or you'll fall!"

"Let me go!" Turning an angry glare into his eyes she demanded heatedly, "Put me back in the wagon! You have done enough damage this day! I will not . . ."

"Unappreciative little witch . . ."

The rain was increasing, the wind whipping the cold, penetrating drops into a steady, pelting abuse as Angelica continued to struggle against him. A bright crack of lightning and the deafening roll of thunder which followed temporarily drowned out his words as Gareth finally succeeded in jerking Angelica astride in front of him. Clamping his arm securely around her narrow waist, his lips tight against her ear, Gareth spoke through gritted teeth.

"Sit still and behave yourself, damn you! It would serve you right if I dumped you back on that wagon and left you to shiver for the next two hours in the storm. At this minute

I'd like nothing better. Maybe a good, cold dousing would cool you off and make you realize . . ." Shaking his head, he continued in a lower voice. "At any rate, you're where you're going to stay until we get back to the hacienda, so if you know what's good for you, you'll sit still and try to stay dry!"

Angelica's struggles came to an abrupt halt, although she remained stiff and unyielding in his arms. Satisfied at that small concession, Gareth pulled the folds of his rough cloak around her to enclose her in its protection. His stiff fingers brushed against the softness of her breasts as he fastened the front to seal her against his warmth. Stifling his intense reaction to the unintended intimacy of the touch, Gareth pulled her breathlessly tight against him. He fitted her back to his body, adjusting her position until her head rested at the side of his neck, shielded by the broad brim of his hat. Secure at last, he wasted no time in spurring his horse forward to regain his position a safe distance behind the carriage.

A jagged flash of lightning cracked loudly overhead, lighting the angry sky and signaling the boom of another deafening roll of thunder. Pulling tightly on the reins of his skittish horse, Gareth tucked his head down against the gusting wind as the frigid rain mercilessly pelted his face. He curved his arm more tightly around Angelica in an effort to spare her some of the force of the storm, but he knew the attempt was useless. They had been on the road for almost an hour. The force of the storm had escalated as darkness began to fall, slowing to a crawl the pace with which the small party had begun its return journey. Water engulfed the roads, swirling around the horses' hooves, as the low roar of the gushing flood in the gullies to either side of the road warned the danger of a single misstep.

The journey was exhausting and far from over. Gareth was extremely aware of the sagging weight of Angelica's fragile frame as she leaned full against him for support. Fatigue and exposure to the raging elements had taken their toll. Angelica was shivering with cold despite Gareth's most stringent efforts to keep her warm. It was obvious that her strength was all but depleted. Adjusting his hold, Gareth pulled her tighter into his arms, unconsciously lowering his cheek as he did to rub it gently against her hair. A warm, sweet scent arose from the damp strands, lighting a familiar spark inside him, and he was suddenly acutely aware of the depth of his unwilling involvement with the unpredictable woman in his arms. He could not remember ever having reacted so strongly to a woman before. What was it about her that brought to life this conflicting raft of feelings inside him?

Angelica stirred again, turning to rest her cheek against his neck as she sought to move closer to his warmth. He suspected exposure to the raging storm had depleted her to the point where she was in a state of semi-consciousness, for he knew nothing would have allowed her to burrow closer to him, were she fully aware of her actions. Her breath was warm against his skin and he gasped as her mouth brushed his throat. The quick reaction of his body was only too predictable, and Gareth experienced a flash of contempt for his own susceptibility.

His heart was pounding, and despite the freezing numbness slowly overwhelming his limbs, he could feel the rise of desire. His mouth ached to taste hers. He had never wanted a woman so badly, been so completely lost to his emotions. In the short time of their rocky acquaintance, Angelica had succeeded in stirring him more than any woman he had ever known. But startling him even more was the fact that ever present with his desire was the equally compelling hunger to keep her to himself, away from the lustful gazes which followed her, doubtless encouraged by herself. And, strangely, although realizing full well the disadvantage he was at in the Arricalde household because of his fascination with her, he was still powerless to combat it.

A new crack of lightning lit the sky overhead, the almost simultaneous roll of thunder indicating a strike nearby. The shattering sound shook Angelica's body with a start, unleashing a new wave of shuddering which he suspected was not entirely related to the penetrating cold. Responding to her silent need, Gareth clutched her closer still. The heavy canvas cape covering them both was almost soaked through and lay like a heavy shroud against his broad shoulders. Angelica had yet to suffer its chilling weight, but it was only a matter of time before it would cease to provide them even elementary protection. If his calculations were correct they were still more than an hour's journey from the Arricalde hacienda. It was too far . . .

Angelica shivered again. His concern forcing a quick decision, Gareth allowed his horse to fall well behind both the Arricalde carriage and wagon. The slow stiffening of Angelica's frame indicated that the last burst of thunder had brought her back to full consciousness. Shifting subtly in the saddle, he saw her eyes were closed against the biting storm, her lips pressed tightly together in an attempt to still her chattering teeth. His eyes searched the darkness to the side of the road, flickering with relief as he saw the turnoff he sought. Taking care to choose safe footing, he guided his horse to the left, following the curve onto the side road. Angelica did not react to their change in direction and he released a tense breath.

A new crack of lightning and the ear-splitting roll of thunder that ensued jerked Angelica upright in his arms, snapping her eyes wide. Suddenly alert, she moved her head from one side of the road to the other as she attempted to ascertain their position.

"Where . . . what happened to the carriage?" She was attempting to turn to see behind them, but Gareth's soft response drew her eyes up to his instead.

"We turned off the road a little ways back . . ."

"Turned off the road . . .?"

A new, more furious gust of wind blew pelting rain into Angelica's face, temporarily stealing her breath as it forced her back against the support of Gareth's chest. Her lips stiff with cold, Angelica faltered. "But . . . but why? We will be home in a little while . . ."

"Not soon enough."

His eyes moving back to the road, Gareth spotted the dwelling Senor Flores had called to his attention that

70

morning. Obviously abandoned, it had served Senor Flores and Don Enrique well on a previous trip to the mines when they had been caught in the same situation. Overgrown and run-down, it would at least be dry and secure against the deluge that battered them.

Reining up before it a few minutes later, Gareth slipped from the saddle, reaching up the moment his feet hit the ground to snatch Angelica into his arms. Holding her tight against him, he ran the few steps to the protection of the overhanging roof and bumped the sagging door open with his shoulder. A rank odor of mildew greeted his nostrils as he stepped into the darkness, along with the sound of tiny, scampering feet.

Aware of Angelica's spontaneous stiffening, Gareth slid her gently to her feet. Returning swiftly to his horse, he drew the gelding forward into the protection of the overhang and snapped off the saddlebags. Turning, he walked quickly through the doorway and into the darkness of the interior. Within minutes he had succeeded in finding a candle and striking a light. He glanced around in quick appraisal. The single room of the small stone structure was almost bare, but thankfully dry. A table and one chair were the only furnishings, with the exception of a narrow cot in the corner of the room, on which a blanket lay in careless disarray. A small fireplace was built into one wall, and he made a quick line toward it. Gratified to see that a supply of wood was stacked nearby, Gareth flung his hat from his head and moved efficiently, with the air of long practice. Within a few minutes a welcome blaze was burning and he turned back to the doorway.

Angelica was standing, outlined against the flashing light of the storm behind her, her body quaking visibly. The extreme pallor of her lovely face snapped him to his feet. Within a few moments he had scooped her up into his arms and carried her to the fireplace.

Standing her gently on her feet, he looked down into her vacant expression. Hesitating only a moment, he reached down into his saddlebag and withdrew a bottle. He uncorked the top and put it to Angelica's quivering lips.

71

"Drink . . . come on, Angelica."

The stinging scent of the liquor was obviously distasteful and Angelica turned her face away. "No, I don't . . . don't want . . ."

Gareth's patience was almost spent. Even chilled to the bone and nearly unconscious, she fought him.

"Angelica, open your mouth and drink. It'll warm you up."

Her great silver eyes moving to his, Angelica shook her head in silent resignation. Raising a cold, trembling hand to cover his, she allowed him to guide the bottle up to her lips. She took a swallow and began to sputter. Gritting his teeth, Gareth waited only until she had caught her breath before pressing the bottle to her lips again and then a third time, forcing her to drink long and deep. She was gasping for breath when he finally lowered it to place it on the table. Well, that ought to do it.

Hesitating only briefly, Gareth lifted the wet rebozo from her shoulders. He frowned. Her *camisa* was soaked through, her skirt in much the same condition. Taking the few steps to the bunk in the corner, he retrieved the blanket and giving it a quick shake, returned to her side.

"You have to get out of your wet clothes, Angelica."

Angelica's half-lidded gray eyes moved slowly up to his with little comprehension. Her body was shuddering so violently that he feared she would collapse, and unable to bear her torment another moment, Gareth raised his hands to the tie on her blouse. She gave no reaction as he undid the cord and began to slip her blouse from her shoulders. She began to sway, and he looked up to see her eyelids fluttering weakly.

"No . . . not yet, Angelica. Hold on a little longer."

The wet cotton clung tenaciously to Angelica's chilled skin, wrapping itself around her possessively as he struggled to pull one arm free of its confines, and then the other. Voicing only a short, slurred protest, Angelica submitted to his ministrations, standing weakly as he finally succeeded in pulling the resisting garment up and off over her head. Stripping away her soaked chemise, Gareth bit back his

72

reaction as Angelica's small, firm breasts were revealed to his view. With trembling hands he reached for the blanket and wrapped it around her shoulders before moving to the closure of her skirt. Within a few moments the soaked merino had dropped to the floor. A new trembling besetting his hands, Gareth undid the tie of her undergarment, his mind registering the unnatural coldness of Angelica's flesh as he allowed it to fall. His eyes followed its descent past the gentle curve of her hip to reveal a dark nest of curls between slender thighs before slipping down her long, graceful legs. Swallowing tightly, Gareth carefully lifted one small foot and then the other free of the saturated garment before securing the blanket tightly around her.

Reaching over, he jerked the lone chair in front of the fireplace, and turning her gently, eased Angelica down into it. But it was plain to see his efforts had been ineffective against the chills which continued to shake her. Hesitating only long enough to remove his own wet jacket and shirt, he crouched beside her. Pulling Angelica close, he supported her against his shoulder, sliding his hands beneath the blanket as he began to massage her back in broad, warming strokes. Satisfied after a few minutes that she was beginning to respond to his ministrations, he moved his attentions to her arms, rubbing their slender length from shoulder to wrist, taking the time to briskly chafe her hands in an attempt to restore circulation into her icy fingers. Content that he had accomplished his purpose there, he took a deep breath and slid his hands to her chest, his hands moving between and around the firm, warm mounds, massaging her in broad, sweeping circles, gritting his teeth against the sweet torture of his platonic touch.

Unable to bear more, he slid his hands past her narrow rib cage to her hips, massaging steadily, allowing his hands to find their way past her taut, flat stomach and the warm delta below to the smooth skin of her thighs. Fighting to empty his mind of thought, he massaged the silken flesh vigorously down to her ankles. Pausing, as Angelica's foot rested in his palm, Gareth unconsciously shook his head. Even her feet were beautiful—small, delicately shaped,

73

with slender, straight toes. Lowering his head, he kissed first one and then the other, realizing belatedly that they were frigidly cold. Experiencing a moment's guilt for his straying sense of purpose, he rubbed them stringently until they glowed with a warm, pink color.

Taking the time to tuck the end of the blanket around them, Gareth rose to his feet, his eyes moving to the battered cot in the corner of the room. In the space of a few minutes he had shaken it free of debris and dragged it in front of the fire. Returning his eyes to Angelica's face, he saw that she was slumped against the back of the chair, her lashes dark, lush fans against smooth cheeks only beginning to regain color.

Suddenly realizing he was perspiring profusely, he shook his head and muttered a low oath. Only moments before he had been as chilled as the beauteous little witch in front of him, but it was obvious that his stimulating massage had been more effective in raising his own body temperature than hers. Damn, had he no control over himself at all?

Afraid to pause a moment longer to examine his wandering thoughts, Gareth gently slid Angelica up and into his arms, pausing for a long moment to savor the sensation as she relaxed automatically against his shoulder. Her eyes flickered open, a small frown moving between her brows as she obviously strained to focus on his face.

"What . . . has . . . has the rain stopped? Are we going to leave now? I must get back. Dona . . . Dona Teresa will wonder . . . I don't want . . ."

Amused by her slurred, rambling speech and the strong scent of liquor on her breath, Gareth could not resist a smile. He shook his head broadly. "No, it hasn't stopped raining, and no, we aren't going to leave yet. You're going to lie down for a while and rest until your clothes dry. Then we'll leave."

But this time there was no fear of an argument from the fragile termagant in his arms. Her head was already lying limply against his chest, her breathing slow and even. Lowering her gently, Gareth lay her down on the narrow bunk, pausing only long enough to watch her curl into a small, warm ball before turning back to the table and the bottle he had left there. Lifting it to his lips, he took a long, deep drag and swallowed roughly. The fiery liquid burned all the way down, hitting his stomach with scorching impact. God, that felt good . . . the only thing strong enough to take his mind off another part of his anatomy which burned hotly with a fire of its own.

Taking a moment to glance back to Angelica's face, he gave his head a short, disbelieving shake and raised the bottle to his lips again. The second and third swallows were even more effective than the first. He was almost feeling in control again.

But he had forgotten something. Reaching out, he quickly gathered Angelica's wet garments from the floor and shaking them out, carefully spread them on the back and seat of the chair. Pushing them as close to the fire as he dared, he did the same with his own soaked clothing. Suddenly realizing he was still wearing his drenched trousers, he gave a small shrug. Oh well, he wasn't cold anymore. No, even asleep, Angelica had taken care of that.

Taking a few steps closer to the cot, he stood looking down at the sweet perfection of Angelica's face. God, he had never seen anyone her match! A familiar stirring began inside him, and frowning against its annoying rise, Gareth leaned over and snatched the bottle from the table. Another long drag satisfied him momentarily. Abruptly disgusted, Gareth moved to situate himself between the fireplace and the cot and lowered himself to the floor. He rested his head against the corner, only inches from Angelica's serene, sleeping face. She was breathing evenly. Her slender, perfectly shaped lips were parted, showing just a trace of straight white teeth. He longed to feel the warmth of those lips . . . to taste the sweetness of that mouth again. He wanted to . . .

Oh, damn it to hell! Lifting the bottle, he took another deep swallow. It was going to be a long, cold night.

Angelica awoke slowly. She was warm . . . so very warm. She strained her eyes to see in the dim light. Where was she? Her memory was blurred. There had been a storm on the return from the mines. The Texan had taken her onto his horse. She had been wet and cold . . . so very cold.

She attempted to move, but her efforts appeared to be restricted by a blanket which had twisted around her and by a heavy weight which kept her pressed against the bed. Managing to move her hand free, she realized she was indeed rolled in a blanket, and she was naked! A soft mumbling in her ear snapped Angelica's head to the side. Gareth Dawson's face was lying beside hers! He was propped on his side next to her on the narrow bunk, his arm clamped around her. He was still sleeping. Angelica's eyes flashed around the unfamiliar room and shot to the closed door. The bright light of morning filtered beneath and Angelica knew a new panic. Mama and Papa would be frantic with worry and Dona Teresa . . .

The haze of memory began to stir and Angelica remembered the Texan had told her to drink . . . had held the bottle to her lips again and again until she had almost choked from the burning liquid. She strained her mind but was successful in remembering little after that.

Her eyes darting to the chair beside the bunk, Angelica saw her clothes stretched out in front of a dead fire, with Gareth Dawson's shirt and jacket hanging close by. She did not remember how they got there. Her last memory was of a slowly encroaching warmth that started on her back and worked its way deliciously down to her toes. She searched her mind frantically for more, only to find the picture of a disturbing pair of dark eyes coming between her and complete recollection.

Turning back to Gareth Dawson, Angelica allowed her eyes to move slowly over his sleeping face. His expression was relaxed. The absence of his frown and the unrelenting glare of his dark eyes softened his hard features to the point where his face took on an almost boyish vulnerability. Her eyes moved over his prominent cheekbones, along the square line of his jaw. The lines slanting from mid-cheek toward the sensuous curve of his mouth were softened, imparting a new facet of appeal in his slightly parted lips.

She remembered the warmth of their touch, the supreme gentleness of which they were capable, the way in which they were effective in transporting her beyond her anger, to a plane of heightened feelings which began to stir again in recollection.

Angry with her wandering thoughts, Angelica forced her eyes from the Texan's face and flicked her gaze across the chest curved so intimately toward her on the narrow bed. Evidence of hard physical labor was obvious in the broad expanse and the firm, well-developed muscles which moved under a network of fine dark hair with each deep breath. There was no other explanation for the total absence of excess flesh on his broad frame and the power of the strong arms she remembered supporting her for the length of the horrendous return from the mines.

Suddenly realizing a light fluttering had begun deep inside, Angelica closed her eyes tightly. Damn him—that arrogant Texan! Fighting to erase him from her mind completely, Angelica gave her head a small shake. She had to return quickly . . . get back to the Arricalde hacienda before anyone realized where and with whom she had spent the night. She could not afford the gossip which was certain to ensue. Her position was too tenuous. She must get up and dress immediately.

Attempting to evade the heavy arm which still lay across her chest without stirring the man at her side, Angelica clutched the folds of the blanket around her. She needed to reach her clothes and get dressed. Then she would awaken the Texan and tell him to take her to her home.

Taking a quick breath, Angelica began to inch herself to the edge of the bunk. Moving was difficult, and she had only managed to move a fraction when she felt a restrictive tug on the blanket. Glancing back, she saw its edge lay under Gareth's body and she frowned in annoyance. Carefully turning back toward the Texan until she also lay on her side facing him, she attempted to tug the blanket free. She pulled carefully, her brow knotting into a frown of concentration as the blanket began to work loose. She tugged a little harder, relieved to see the cloth slipping. Just

77

a few inches more and she would be able to slide off the bed easily without disturbing him. She could then be completely dressed and fully composed before he awoke. She needed that advantage.

She gave another short, careful tug and the blanket worked completely free, only to have a broad hand clamp down unexpectedly on the rough fabric, holding it fast as the other tightened around her back.

"Where do you think you're goin'?"

Jumping with a start, Angelica snapped her eyes up to meet a familiar, wide-awake gaze. His lips curving with only the suggestion of a smile, Gareth drew her closer, sliding his palm up her spine in a way that awoke dim, warm memories Angelica preferred to subdue.

"I don't think I want you to leave yet, darlin'. It feels too good wakin' up and findin' you here in my arms. I think I . . ."

Feeling an edge of panic as the Texan's low, intimate tone began to work a magic on her senses, Angelica interrupted sharply. "I do not truly care what you think, Señor Dawson. I only care what others will think and the position you have forced on me. You seem to have little concern with the conclusion your hosts will reach when they discover you and I did not return last night, but I do not wish to have Dona Teresa thinking that I . . ."

"Don't you think it's a bit late to concern yourself about your reputation, Angelica? I'd say if you did, you should have started before I came to Real del Monte. Maybe then you would have stood a chance of someone believin' you're as innocent as you like to appear."

Stung by his words, but unwilling to give him the satisfaction of knowing how deeply they had cut, Angelica replied with a haughty smile, "I've already told you how very little I care about anything you say or think. You waste your breath, and you also waste my time." A flicker of satisfaction warming her as the Texan's features tightened in reaction to her words, Angelica continued. "So if you will allow me to get up . . ."

Removing his arm from her back while still retaining his

grip on the blanket, Gareth raised his brow in exaggerated innocence. "I'm not stoppin' you from gettin' up . . ."

Gritting her teeth, Angelica looked to his hand and the blanket he clutched, her gaze raising pointedly to his.

"Modest, little one?" His smile taut, Gareth maintained his grip as he raked her blanket-clad body with an insulting glance. "Wouldn't you say it's a little late for that affectation?"

Barely controlling the flush of pure hatred rising inside her, Angelica looked assessingly into the dark eyes level with hers before abruptly averting her gaze. The Texan would persist in thinking only that which he preferred to believe of her. Well, if he chose to believe the worst, she would give him something to truly remember. Raising her lowered lids with slow deliberation until she looked directly into his eyes, conscious of the effect of her sultry gaze as the Texan stiffened visibly, Angelica gave a low laugh.

"Perhaps I am just clever . . . wishing to keep you ignorant of me to 'drive up my price.' Have you not accused me of such a ploy in the past?"

Gareth's hand moved unexpectedly to cup her head, holding her lips a hairbreadth from his, as he responded in a leisurely drawl, "Then I'd say you're wastin' your time, darlin'. I've already seen all you have to offer."

A slow flush transfusing her face, Angelica took a few seconds to recover from the Texan's blatant jibe. She attempted to jerk her head from his grasp.

"So, you finally obtained the 'sample' you spoke of so insistently. Now I fully comprehend the reason for your high-handed manner . . ."

"High-handed manner . . ." His true anger revealed only in the narrowing of his eyes, Gareth responded in a deadly tone. "I suppose you could call me high-handed for deliverin' you out of that storm. Maybe I should thank you for that complement, ma'am. I do think I'm not the man to hesitate when I know somethin' needs to be done." His voice hardening, Gareth continued, emphasizing his words as he looked directly into her seething gaze, "but I don't thank you for thinkin' I took you when you were in no condition to know what I was about. I've never had the need to rape a woman, especially not a *puta* whose favors are for hire. And I don't expect you to be the first, whether conscious or unconscious. You flatter yourself in thinkin' you could push me to that point of desperation, darlin'. I may want you, but I'd tip my hat and say *adios* sooner than stoop to that measure."

Silently uncertain if he was indeed capable of walking away from the beautiful little temptress who drew him even as she harangued him so mercilessly, Gareth watched the effect of his words on her face. Great gray eyes flashed in anger, before abruptly registering a new determination.

"Since you assure me my appeal is so limited, Señor Dawson, I suppose there is no longer need for any modesty at all."

Obeying a driving need to wipe the smug expression from the Texan's face, Angelica took a silent breath and boldly pushed the blanket aside. Moving sinuously, she managed to untangle herself from its folds. Standing with a bravado so false that she was uncertain her trembling legs would support her, she looked down with slow deliberation into Gareth Dawson's widening eyes. Her gaze slowly traveled his face, dropping to measure the breadth of his broad shoulders, the expanse of his chest. It followed the dark line of hair that trailed ever downward to disappear into the swelling bulge below his belt.

"Yes, Señor Dawson, I can see you are a man who has strict control over his body. That fact grows more obvious by the minute."

Satisfied at the slow flush which began to transfuse his face, Angelica gave a low laugh and turned to reach for her shift with trembling hands. Willing them still, she turned her back and donned her undergarments, unaware that the sight of her smooth, well-rounded buttocks bent so temptingly had completed the task she had gone about so deliberately to accomplish.

She was fully dressed when she turned back again. Her color high, Angelica flicked an unsmiling glance over Gareth Dawson's totally clad person, very aware of his silence as his eyes raked her viciously.

"I would like to return now, Señor Dawson. I do not ask you to take me home . . . only to a reasonable distance from it. I will walk the remainder of the way."

"No, I think not, Angelica. I will see you directly to your door. After having gone to so much trouble last night, I would like to make sure you arrive there safely. And surely, there is no need to disguise the fact that you spent the night with me, little *puta*. Your parents must be accustomed by now to your unusual hours . . ."

Snapping her teeth closed in strict refusal to respond to his comment, Angelica snatched up her rebozo and walked directly toward the doorway. Standing rigidly stiff, she jerked open the door and approached the nervous gelding. She still had not deigned to turn back when strong hands abruptly swung her up into the saddle. Taking only the time to fasten his saddlebags, Gareth swung up behind her and slid his arm around her waist, his hand resting warmly beneath her breasts as he spurred his horse immediately forward.

In the brilliant contrast to the weather that had accompanied their journey home the previous day, the sky was a brilliant blue. Its magnificence was matched only by the reflection of the sun's warming rays on a landscape washed clean by the previous night's storm, and the last crystal drops glittering with rainbow hues on the lush landscape. Carefully watching the ascent of the sun in the early morning sky, Angelica could barely restrain her impatience as the Texan held his horse at a maddeningly slow pace.

Intensely aware of the broad hand that rested at her waist, fingers splayed in a manner that supported her breasts as they bobbed lightly on the uneven road, Angelica took a deep breath. Head high, she refused to look down to confirm the fact that the taut crests were pressed revealingly against the coarse cotton of her blouse in blatant proclamation of their arousal. But she knew a sweet, somewhat unsettling triumph in the fact that her close, almost intimate seat in the saddle had not left Gareth unaffected. The warmth of his arousal was warm against her, and she squirmed as he adjusted her position to fit more securely against the heat of his body.

They had traveled a considerable distance when Gareth shifted his reins to the hand he held at her waist. Within a few minutes she felt him picking at her plaited hair. Determined not to allow him to provoke her, Angelica remained silent until the first few strands flew up to whip her face in the brisk breeze.

Unable to withhold comment any longer, Angelica turned to frown into Gareth's unsmiling face. "What are you doing?" Raising her hand, she attempted to brush away his touch.

"Stop . . ."

But even as she spoke, Gareth continued to loosen the braid, the task becoming easier as he neared the top and the weight of her heavy tresses helped to push them free of restriction. Appearing satisfied at last as her gleaming ebony locks streamed free in the breeze, Gareth waited only until the brisk gusts ceased, allowing her hair to again rest against her shoulders before tangling his hand in the silky strands.

"You're hurting me. I told you to stop."

Interrupting her in a tone that brooked no interference, Gareth responded flatly, "As you said to me before, 'what you want makes no difference whatsoever to me.' The braid was becomin' undone anyway, and you wouldn't want anyone knowin' you had other things on your mind this mornin' aside from fixin' your hair."

"*I* had other things on my mind . . . ?" Angelica stopped herself before she began to sputter angrily. She took a deep breath, aware that the position of the hand Gareth still rested against her rib cage allowed him to feel the angry acceleration of her heart even as she began with false calm, "It was not *I* who had other things on my mind this morning, Señor Dawson."

Gareth's hand slipped up from her waist unexpectedly, crossing her chest to grasp and hold her chin fast as he lowered his head to whisper against her lips, "Your thoughts weren't far from mine and you know it, Angelica, my fiery little *puta*. I sleep quite lightly, darlin'. It didn't take much for me to read what you were thinkin' when you looked at me while you thought I was asleep."

"You were awake?" Realizing Gareth had the advantage of seeing the flush that rose to her face as well as feeling its heat against his hand, Angelica attempted to shake her chin free of his hold.

"Oh, no, darlin', not yet . . . not this time."

In a swift, unexpected movement Gareth covered her protesting mouth with his. The unexpectedness of his kiss caught her with parted lips, allowing him the opportunity of passing the barrier of her teeth with ease. Deepening his kiss swiftly, Gareth drew fully of the sweetness of her mouth, his other hand rising to cup her cheek, holding her firm under his dizzying sensual attack. Drawing away at last, Gareth circled her lips with light, fleeting kisses, mumbling almost inaudibly as he did, "I wanted to do this from the first moment I awakened, Angelica, and you wanted it, too, you know you did."

His hand was moving against her breast, stealing her breath as he paused to tease an enlarged crest. "You want me as much as I want you, but I'm not goin' to beg you, darlin'. I don't know what you're expectin' from me, but I tell you now that I'll be fair and generous with you . . . and I'll make you feel good, darlin'. I can feel your heart beatin' now. It's racin' . . . just like mine. We'll be good together . . . real good . . ."

Mesmerized by his low, throbbing tone, Angelica allowed the heady plunder of her mouth once again, her lips separating to permit him full access as his tongue dipped and played in the warm hollows, stirring an aching need inside her which was new to her limited experience. The line of his warm kisses moved across her cheek to the fragile shell of her ear where he teased her with quick, nibbling bites before drawing the small lobe into his mouth to suck it hungrily. A raft of chills traveled her spine, one after another, permitting her little peace, as did Gareth's impassioned, seeking kisses. His mouth had traveled down the curve of her throat, settling at the base to draw the delicate skin roughly into his mouth.

Starting at the stinging pain of his impassioned abuse, Angelica attempted to pull away, only to have Gareth hold her fast as he whispered softly, "Did I hurt you, darlin'? I don't want to hurt you. I just want to love you."

His lips pressed lightly against hers, he whispered in a low, coaxing tone, "And I want to love you now, darlin' . . . now."

Raising his gaze to search the foliage around them, Gareth spied a narrow trail which led to a green, fragrant hollow a distance from the road. Motioning toward it, he urged, "Come with me now. It'll be cool and sweet in there, and if you feel chilled, I'll keep you warm, darlin'. I promise you that . . ."

She was attempting to avoid his eyes and Gareth gave her chin a small shake. "Look at me. I said look at me, Angelica . . ." Unable to resist the note of hunger in his voice, Angelica obeyed his whispered command, her mind registering his short intake of breath as the molten silver of her burning gaze met his.

"Tell me you want me to make love to you, darlin'. Tell me you want it that way between us and you won't be sorry you did. I'll make it beautiful for you . . . more beautiful than you've ever known."

Angelica's mind registered Gareth's words, but she was temporarily past the point of response. Gareth had drawn his horse to a halt. His voice was a low, earnest whisper.

"Angelica . . . darlin' . . . we're almost back to the hacienda. I don't want to take you back . . . not now. If you're worried you won't return to the Arricalde hacienda on time, you needn't. It's early. Say yes, darlin'. You know I'll meet any price you want . . . no matter what it is. God, I couldn't hold back on you now . . . not anymore."

The influx of reality was slow, Gareth's words sinking with numbing effect through the haze of her rioting emotions gradually.

"Price . . . ?"

"Any price, Angelica . . . any price you want . . . but I have to know . . . to hear you say you want me to make love to you, to . . ."

"Culebra!"

The low, angry expletive sound clearly in the early morning silence, snapping Angelica and Gareth's eyes toward Esteban Arricalde's mounted figure as he appeared suddenly on the road a short distance away. His face a livid mask of fury, Esteban commanded in a low hiss, "Take your hands off her!"

Spurring his horse forward abruptly, startling Gareth's mount with his unexpected charge, Esteban reined up sharply at their side.

"Remove your hands from her, damn you!"

Shaking with rage, Esteban looked briefly into Angelica's face, his eyes promising vengeance as he continued to address Gareth in a deeply ominous voice, "Was not last night enough for you? Are all Anglo-Texans as gluttonous as you? Perhaps that is why el Presidente Santa Anna will soon have to teach you all a hard lesson. And when that day comes, you may depend upon it that I will be with him, marching at his side to show you who is master here!"

Gareth's arm had slipped to Angelica's waist. Holding her unyieldingly, his posture stiffening more with each additional word of Esteban's vehement tirade, he waited until Esteban paused before responding with deceiving calmness.

"I'll answer one question at a time, Esteban, just so there'll be no mistakin' my answers. No, I won't take my hands off Angelica. Last night was not enough . . . not for me and not for her, and if you hadn't shown up right now, she'd be lyin' with me right now in that green glade over there . . ."

Gasping, Angelica turned toward Gareth, her face flaming.

"I would not! I would not lie with you, or with Don Esteban, no matter how highly you both estimate your appeal." Her eyes moving between the two men, even as she felt Gareth's arm tighten warningly, she continued in a shaking voice. "Put me down . . . immediately. I need neither of you nor your favors! Nor do I intend to bestow my favors on you!" When Gareth did not respond, made no movement to comply with her request, she demanded hotly, "Put me down, now!"

"You heard la señorita, put her down! You will then be free to face me instead of hiding behind a woman's skirts as is your custom!"

A new fear beginning to permeate her mind, Angelica turned her next remark to Esteban.

"And what do you expect to gain by 'facing' the Texan? Whatever, it will not be *I*! I want neither of you, do you understand? And you . . ." Turning to Gareth with a vengeance, she hissed, "You will tell him the truth . . . that I did not . . . that we did not . . ."

His eyes holding hers, Gareth returned quietly, "Would you have me tell him a lie, Angelica . . . that you didn't lie with me last night . . . that you didn't wake up in my arms this mornin'?"

"No . . . but you know that we did not . . . that . . ."

Turning to look back into Esteban's deepening flush, she swallowed tightly. Anger suddenly coming to her rescue, she had just turned back to Gareth with undisguised antagonism when Esteban interrupted to address Gareth insidiously.

"I care little what this one did with you last night. It is nothing she has not done with others many time before. But I give you my word, what she has done with you, she will not do again. It is in my power to make her pay dearly, and I tell you now, I will not hesitate to use that power. She is a *puta*, but she will be *my puta*, mine alone, to use as I wish for as long as I wish! I tell you this now in solemn warning, Gareth Dawson. You will pay in a way you never expected for your use of this woman if you continue. You will pay more dearly than she is worth! And she will pay even more!"

Dismissing Esteban's threats with a small, unconcerned smile effective in deepening Esteban's heated flush, Gareth gave a short laugh.

"Your threats don't frighten me, Esteban. And for all your talk of payment, I'll tell you somethin' else. Angelica asked no payment of me . . ."

Gareth turned toward Angelica as if in confirmation of his statement. Instinct warning that the warmth in his gaze was calculated to disguise his own anger while inciting Esteban to greater fury, Angelica did not respond. Her silence elicited a low laugh from Gareth as he rubbed his chin lightly against the surface of her hair.

Esteban's cheek jerked in a spasmatic tick and Angelica could sense Gareth's satisfaction as he laughed again. Spurring his horse forward unexpectedly, Gareth took Esteban by surprise, almost succeeding in knocking the furious aristocrat's stallion off balance. Disturbed by the sudden upset, the great horse reared, almost unseating his rider.

Gareth glanced back casually as Esteban fought to keep his seat. A smile flicking across his lips, he called over his shoulder as he turned onto the road to the village, "*Adios*, Esteban. I'll see you at breakfast."

"Stop. Stop here."

Forcing herself to turn toward Gareth as he urged his horse onto the path toward her house, Angelica faced him for the first time since their encounter with Esteban a short time before. They had ridden the few miles in silence. Unwilling to trust her voice, Angelica had chosen not to speak.

The encounter with Esteban had truly shaken her. She had not realized how violent the pampered young Arricalde could become. The memory of his livid face and his vehement threats were still vivid in her mind. She knew only too well how truly vulnerable her position was. It would be so easy for him to have her banished from the Arricalde household, if, indeed, the escapade Gareth Dawson had so conveniently arranged during the storm the previous night had not already managed that fact. But as things stood, if she were to be honest, she really owed Esteban a debt of gratitude. Had he not appeared on the road when he had . . . had Gareth continued his passionate assault, she was truly uncertain if she . . .

But that moment was over, and it would not happen

again! Panic assailing her as her home became visible through the foliage, Angelica turned to face Gareth's unrevealing expression.

"Señor Dawson . . ."

"My name is Gareth, Angelica." His dark eyes probing her expression, he looked down soberly into her face. "Under the circumstances, formality is a bit ridiculous, don't you think?" When she was about to deny his statement he shook his head. His hand coming up to cup her cheek as he reined his horse with a subtle movement, Gareth lowered his head unexpectedly to press a light kiss against her mouth.

"I'm sorry for the scene, Angelica . . ."

"And are you sorry for the untruth you allowed Esteban Arricalde to believe . . . that you and I . . . that we . . ."

"Made love? No, I'm not sorry for that, because you would be in my arms right now in that green glade if that arrogant bastard hadn't shown up when he did . . ."

"You are so sure of that . . . ?"

"Oh, yes, I'm sure of that, Angelica." His dark eyes seeming to darken to a soft velvet, Gareth continued in a whisper. "There's no way you would have gotten away from me again."

"You have told me repeatedly that you do not force women . . ."

"I wouldn't have had to force you, darlin' . . ."

A flush covering her face at the suspected truth of his remark, Angelica attempted to turn her head, but Gareth would not allow it. Forced to hold his gaze, she continued stiffly. "I want you to put me down now. I wish to return to my home."

"I'll take you to your door."

"No. I don't wish to have my mother see . . ."

"Is your mother so unworldly? Rumor would say the reverse is true . . ."

Fury rearing to life inside her, Angelica raised her hand to strike at the cruel injustice of the Texan's words, but Gareth was too quick. Angry frustration renewing her efforts to be free of his despised touch, Angelica pushed

88

and shoved at his chest, tearing at the arm that still held her captive, but Gareth easily overcame her struggles.

Angelica's breath was coming in short, uneven gasps. She strove for control, her voice quaking with fury.

"Do not dare to speak of my mother in that way again! She has suffered much for me . . ." Her voice taking on a new fervor, she repeated, "You will take back those words! You will take them back now or . . ."

His eyes dropping to her trembling lips, Gareth shook his head. "You needn't say any more, Angelica. I apologize."

His unexpected concession halted Angelica's angry tirade. Her struggles ceased just as abruptly. Releasing her wrists, Gareth waited until her breathing had returned to normal before raising her chin until their glances met.

"And now that I've made a concession, don't you think you can make one, too? I'd like you to call me Gareth."

"No, I will not."

"Yes, you will . . ."

Not bothering to reply, Angelica continued in a controlled voice, "I wish to dismount here. I must go home to inform my mother that I am all right. And then I must go to the hacienda . . ."

"I'll take you to your door, Angelica."

"No."

"I must."

Realizing the futility of further argument, Angelica snapped her head forward in silence.

Her shoulders stiff with tension as they reined up before the small stone structure a few minutes later, Angelica moved her gaze to the doorway. Without a glance at Gareth as he dismounted and turned to lift her from the saddle, Angelica looked toward the flurry of movement inside the house. Within seconds a small, frail boy rushed into the yard to throw his arms around her waist.

Angelica's arms closed around Carlos's narrow shoulders, a loving warmth expanding inside her as he buried his face against her midriff. Straining to regain his breath, Carlos lifted glowing black eyes to her face. Her heart wrenching at his pallor, Angelica returned his smile.

"*Gracias a Dios!* I knew you were all right, Angelica. I told Mama that you had been caught in the storm and did not wish to get wet . . . that you would be home in the morning. I was right, wasn't I, Angelica? I was right . . ."

Leaning down to place a kiss on his pale cheek, conscious of its unnatural heat, Angelica said lightly, "Yes, you were right, Carlos. For a young boy, you are too often right. Padre Manuel was right, too. He said your mind runs ahead of your body."

"Oh, Angelica . . . that is because my body is so slow."

Laughing, the boy drew himself away and slipped his hand into hers, his eyes finally rising to the man who stood beside her. But the sound of another step at the door of the house turned Angelica in its direction as Margarita Rodrigo stepped into the yard. Her brow knotting at the concern obvious on her mother's care-worn face, Angelica offered quietly, "*Lo siento, Mama.*"

Refusing to explain the reason for her absence while Gareth listened so intently, Angelica looked silently into her mother's eyes. Feeling the full weight of Margarita Rodrigo's intense perusal, Angelica remained unmoving until her mother nodded her understanding of Angelica's unspoken plea. Her gratitude overwhelming, Angelica swallowed tightly.

Taking her mother's callused hand, Angelica turned proudly back to Gareth's unreadable expression.

"Mama, this man is Gareth Dawson. He is a guest of Señor Arricalde and kindly consented to bring me home. Señor Dawson, my mother, Margarita Rodrigo."

"I am pleased to meet you, ma'am."

"*Mucho gusto*, Señor Dawson."

Her sober expression unchanging, Angelica rested her hand on Carlos's thin shoulder.

"Señor Dawson, my brother, Carlos."

"Pleased to meet you, too, Carlos."

"*Buenos dias, señor.*"

"And now if you will excuse me, Señor Dawson." Her eyes conveying a far different message than her polite words, Angelica continued quietly, "Thank you for your help."

"My pleasure, Angelica."

Turning, Angelica took her mother's arm and urged her toward the house as Carlos followed behind. She was acutely aware that Gareth Dawson did not turn to remount until long seconds after they had walked through the doorway and disappeared from sight.

Standing expectantly in the doorway of the Arricalde library, Angelica attempted to ignore the heavy pounding of her heart as she faced Dona Teresa's unsmiling countenance. Her gaze darting to the side of the room, Angelica started visibly as she spotted Esteban standing stiffly at the window, his back toward her. Realizing the scene portended poorly for her future in the household, Angelica took a deep, shaky breath.

"You wished to speak to me, señora?"

"*Sí.* Come in and close the door, Angelica."

Taking a moment to follow Dona Teresa's request, Angelica turned back and advanced a few steps into the room, suddenly realizing Esteban's hooded gaze regarded her intently.

"I will not waste time with words, Angelica." Dona Teresa's small black eyes glittered with suppressed anger. "Your behavior on the return from the mines yesterday afternoon is an embarrassment to this family. Señor Dawson did not return to the hacienda last night, and my guests and I are all too aware that he was last seen on the road with you seated in front of him on his horse. According to Juanita, he returned early this morning, and I can only conclude from this that you returned at the same time. Do you have anything to say for yourself?"

Angelica exerted a stringent effort to control the slow trembling that had begun to beset her limbs. She could not lose her position here. She could not. Taking another deep breath, she began quietly, "I . . . I am guilty of no wrongdoing, señora. Señor Dawson saw that I had no protection from the storm in the back of the wagon and attempted to share his protection with me. Unfortunately,

91

the storm was too severe to escape and Señor Dawson chose to find shelter against it rather than suffer its rigors any longer. I . . . I did nothing wrong, señora. When morning came, Señor Dawson brought me back home and I came directly here."

"Where did you spend the night?" Dona Teresa's question was direct, her lips pressing back into a straight, uncompromising line as she awaited Angelica's response.

"In an abandoned cabin not far from the road."

"You were alone with Señor Dawson?"

"Yes, but I . . . we did not . . ."

Refusing to allow her to continue, Dona Teresa clasped her small hands in front of her, her small features tight with dismay. Her voice pained, she continued in a low, careful voice. "You are aware that I brought you into this household at the request of Padre Manuel, Angelica. I had hoped you would attempt to live up to his faith in you, and for that reason alone allowed him to convince me to give you the opportunity to redeem yourself."

Inward flinching at Dona Teresa's use of the word "redeem," Angelica forced her expression to remain unchanged as Dona Teresa continued resolutely. "I had thought things were working out very nicely, but Señor Dawson's arrival seems to have wrought a change in you . . ."

"Señora, I did nothing!"

"Do not interrupt, Angelica." Her agitation obviously growing, Dona Teresa took a few moments to compose herself before continuing. "We no longer desire your employment at this hacienda, Angelica. You may return home now and you may rest assured I will inform Padre Manuel of the full reason for your dismissal."

Shocked into silence by the occurrence of the exact event she had so feared, Angelica was unable to respond. Her thoughts raced, pictures of Carlos's thin, white face taking precedence over the myriad images assaulting her mind. She had all but forgotten Esteban's presence until his smooth voice penetrated the tense silence.

"*Madre*, I heartily agree that Angelica is guilty of poor

judgment, but I do not think such a drastic step is truly necessary."

"What are you saying, Esteban? You saw only too clearly the glances exchanged between our guests last evening at Gareth's conspicuous absence! It was a humiliating experience for your father and me! Even you were not left unaffected, if I am to judge by the short temper you showed with Dolores Valentin."

His reaction to his mother's revealing statement reflected only in the momentary flicker of his eyes, Esteban shook his head with a coaxing smile. "*Madre*, all that you say is very true, but I took the initiative to speak to Gareth this morning, and he assures me that he intended only to spare Angelica the rigors of the storm as she claims, and that utmost propriety was observed at all times."

Dona Teresa's face began to show the first sign of uncertainty as her eyes moved over her handsome son's almost benevolent expression in open consideration of his statement. Playing shamefully on the love and trust shining in her eyes, Esteban leaned over to kiss the rounded curve of her cheek.

"*Si, Mama*, it is true. I have Gareth's word that the whole affair was merely a matter of unfortunate circumstance and that both he and Angelica are innocent, despite appearances to the contrary. I do think we should extend our guest the courtesy of accepting his word as truth, don't you? I should not like to see the son of Padre's old friend take insult."

Her brow knitting in concern, Dona Teresa shook her head. "No, I should not like that, either, *querido*." Her glance flicking momentarily to the spot where Angelica still stood unmoving, Dona Teresa hesitated a moment more.

Taking full advantage of the opportunity, Esteban turned to Angelica, his smile almost saintly as he walked toward her. Coming to stand directly in front of her, Esteban raised his hands and placed them on Angelica's shoulders. Out of his mother's range of vision, Esteban's expression rapidly changed. Rage again burned in his gaze, and Angelica could not suppress a shudder from the spontaneous chill it evoked. Appearing gratified by that small show of anxiety, Esteban addressed her with hypocritical concern rampant in his deep voice.

"My mother has no desire to treat you unfairly, Angelica. We are very concerned in being just, but I do believe she, as well as I, would like to hear some assurances from your own lips should she decide to allow you to remain a part of our household. If you are allowed to continue your employment here, we wish to be reassured that you will take special care to correct any misconception our guests may have formed."

Esteban turned back toward his mother, his handsome face again bathed in concern. "*Con permiso, Madre?*"

"*Si*, please continue, Esteban."

Turning back to Angelica once again, Esteban stared pointedly into her eyes as he spoke his next words. "We shall instruct that you have no further contact with our guests at all. You will perform your tasks in the kitchen as required and will devote yourself to comforts of the family alone." Hesitating as Angelica held his gaze silently, Esteban gave her shoulders a small shake. "How do you respond to that, Angelica?"

"Of . . . of course, señor."

"And I am sure you will do all in your power to prove your desire to please in light of our generosity. But then, Dona Teresa is notoriously easy to please, and so am I. You have but to do what is requested of you . . . to fulfill your duties in ministering to our comforts. You are well versed in the duties that will be required of you. You will perform them eagerly, without hesitation and with much enthusiasm to show your gratitude, will you not, Angelica?"

Esteban's hands were now biting into the tender flesh of her shoulders. Innocent on the surface, the true meaning of Esteban's words were reflected in the stiffness of his face and the pain intentionally inflicted by his deceivingly benign hold on her shoulders. Fighting to suppress reaction to all he implied as well as the pain he inflicted with obvious pleasure, Angelica swallowed tightly.

A small smile flicked across Esteban's face as he viewed her discomfort. "Come, come, Angelica, speak up. We wish to hear your pledge of agreement so that we may set our minds at rest that the issue is settled at last."

Unable to control the wince of pain as the pressure of Esteban's hands increased brutally, Angelica nodded.

"Aloud, Angelica . . . my mother wishes to hear what you have to say . . . and so do I . . ."

Abruptly releasing her, Esteban stepped to the side to allow his mother an unrestricted view of Angelica's pained expression. Obtaining the result he desired, he was conscious of his mother's instinctive murmur of regret. Soft . . . his mother was soft. She allowed herself to be manipulated with her weakness. She was already regretting her harshness with Angelica in the light of the pain in her eyes.

But he did not suffer such a limiting debility. The slight discomfort he had inflicted on Angelica's flesh was nothing. She would suffer and suffer dearly for the humiliation she had caused him with Gareth Dawson. For despite the embarrassment she had forced upon him, he was still desperate to have her, and in full realization of the fact that many others had known her before, he was still wild to make that beautiful body his, to feel himself deep inside her. Oh, yes, he would use her, and use her well and she would suffer tenfold for each hour of torment he had suffered at her hands. Revenge would be sweet, almost worth the torment she even now inflicted upon him as she filled his thoughts as no other woman had ever done.

Angelica swallowed hard as a prelude to speech. One glance at Dona Teresa showed she need only declare her good intentions to have an end to these anxious moments. But in speaking, Angelica realized Esteban expected she would be pledging more . . . much more. Angelica shot a quick look into Esteban's face, wincing inwardly at the glow of triumph in his eyes.

Looking back toward Dona Teresa, she took a deep breath before offering quietly, "Dona Teresa, I . . . I regret any discomfort I may have caused you. I will do my best to serve you and your family as well as I am able."

Contempt rose inside him as his mother's eyes filled inexplicably at Angelica's words. Retaining his smile with sheer power of will, Esteban listened as Dona Teresa replied quietly, *"Está bueno.* You may return to your work, Angelica, and we will speak no more about the matter."

"Gracias, Dona Teresa."

Ever the loving mother, Dona Teresa continued quietly. "But first, do you not think you should express your thanks to Don Esteban, Angelica? Without his intervention the outcome of this interview would have been quite different indeed."

Turning a tender smile on her son, Dona Teresa missed the revealing flash of emotion in the silver eyes darting to Esteban's pious expression. The words as bitter as gall in her mouth, Angelica offered quietly, *"Gracias,* Don Esteban."

"That is all, Angelica?" Disappointed at the brevity of Angelica's expression of gratitude and unaware that she played into her son's manipulating hands, Dona Teresa urged softly, "You do not wish to say more to the patron who spoke so well in your defense?"

"Madre, por favor!" Affecting an embarrassed smile, Esteban shook his head. "Angelica has already declared her good intentions."

Realizing Dona Teresa was not yet satisfied, Angelica steeled herself against the humiliation of the words she was about to speak.

"I am deeply grateful for your interference in my behalf, Don Esteban. I . . . will attempt to serve you loyally and well."

Chapter III

His irritation building, Gareth listened to the conversation progressing in the Arricalde *sala*. They had retired to the comfort of the large, graceful room at the conclusion of dinner, but there had been little hope of a pleasant evening after the disturbing political information which had arrived that afternoon.

Opinions at first carefully withheld in deference to Gareth's Anglo-Texan presence had finally surfaced. Felipe Aleman had just finished making a particularly strong statement in favor of his undeclared idol, el Presidente Ântonio Lopez de Santa Anna, and Gareth had remained silent and seething. He was still striving to remember that he was a guest in this house . . . that the accomplishment of his mission at the mines was only a few days away. He had made an error in judgment with Angelica Rodrigo the night before which had stirred resentments he had not anticipated. He did not wish to compound his error by inciting a riot in his host's *sala*. But Felipe had not yet finished speaking.

"*Si*, el presidente is a superior strategist. All other upstart provinces will share fates similar to that of Zacatecas with Santa Anna at the head of our troops. He is invincible."

Unable to bear Felipe Aleman's complacency another moment, Gareth interjected in a low, tightly controlled voice, "When are you goin' to open your eyes to what Santa

Anna is doin'?"

Aware of the fact that Felipe Aleman's narrow face had flushed a bright red at his softly spoken comment, Gareth stepped forward into the group, his eyes carefully touching on each man present. Martin Flores, Pablo Alcazar, and Ricardo Erricavera had returned from the mines that afternoon. They stood side by side as had become their manner since arriving at the hacienda, and eyed him as if with one, disapproving eye. Fernando Valentin stood closest to Enrique Arricalde, his distinguished countenance bearing the same note of censure as his host. Felipe Aleman stood in their midst, their undeclared spokesman. A few steps away, observing silently with a calculating eye was Esteban Arricalde, his animosity betrayed only by the occasional flash of heat in his dark eyes as he glanced in Gareth's direction.

"You are all blind to his machinations, aren't you!" Gareth shook his head, incredulous. "Your wonderful Santa Anna is movin' toward open dictatorship! He has installed a puppet congress and pushed through law after law undeclin' the federal structure established by the Constitution. He was a liberal when he first came into the office, was he not? He then allowed Vice President Farias to institute the changes demanded, allowin' himself to step in later and declare those changes ineffective and his vice president incompetent. It is beyond me how you do not see the pattern that emerges here! He then took aim at Zacatecas, a strongly Federalist state. He ordered the local militia disbanded; and when the state government resisted, led troops to sack the capital. You are celebratin' the downfall of Governor Garcia and his men, men who merely fought the loss of their liberty! Today Santa Anna took their liberty. Tomorrow he will take *yours*!"

"Do you think us all fools, Señor Dawson?" Felipe Aleman responded through stiff lips, his features filled with contempt. "You care little about the fate of Zacatecas, its governor or its people! You are angry because as an Anglo-Texan you feel threatened. You fear only for yourself and your land, and you see it now in more jeopardy than before.

98

But in truth you and your fellow Anglo-Texans merely suffer for your impudence in thinking to set yourselves above the government of our great country!"

"Señor Aleman, you are a fool."

An outraged silence followed Gareth's quiet response.

Don Erique's conciliatory tone was the first to enter the void as he ventured carefully, "Gareth, you are angry and concerned, and we well understand your feelings. You doubtless would wish to be away from here immediately, to return to your home while you feel it suffers threat. Yet you feel impelled to complete the mission that brought you here, and most probably feel trapped by circumstances. But I ask, my friend, that you do not allow your political passions to override either your manners or your good sense. Both you and Felipe are guests in my house. Since I value both your friendships greatly and hope the feeling is reciprocated, I would ask that you both put aside your political convictions for the duration of your stay here, and conduct yourselves accordingly."

Turning toward Felipe Aleman, Don Enrique waited only until the slender gentleman had jerked his head in a brief nod before returning his gaze to Gareth.

Gareth nodded. Taking a deep breath, he looked unsmilingly into Don Enrique's sober face. "Of course, I agree. And I wish to extend my apologies, not for my political convictions but for imposin' them upon you at this time. You are entirely correct. This is neither the time nor the place for a conversation of this kind. *Lo siento*, Don Enrique . . . *señores*."

Relieved to see Don Enrique's face move into a smile, Gareth shot a quick glance toward Felipe Aleman. His small, slight stature was stiff with barely concealed disdain. His head jerked in short stiff movements as he turned to converse quietly with Martin Flores, putting him in mind of a haughty rooster. Barely suppressing the urge to snap his skinny neck, Gareth turned away with slow deliberation.

Walking with measured steps toward the sparkling prisms of the crystal brandy decanter which rested on the sideboard, Gareth picked up the bottle with the grip of a desperate man. This day which had started out in the most stimulating way possible, with the warm scent of Angelica Rodrigo in his nostrils and the rounded swells of her firm breasts under his hand, had deteriorated beyond recall.

Don Enrique was correct . . . much more correct than he realized. He did feel trapped in this place. His emotions had been under attack from the first moment of his arrival when he had first set eyes on Angelica Rodrigo struggling in Esteban Arricalde's arms. This news of Santa Anna's latest moves and the blind stupidity of supposedly intelligent Mexicans who applauded it, had only increased the tension which had been building inside him. They were fools, all of them! They were blinded by Santa Anna's charisma, and refused to see him as the highly ambitious, intelligent but completely unscrupulous man that he was. Yes, he *was* anxious to be out of this place which was proving a true test to his waning self-control. He was needed at home where events were progressing with frightening speed toward an inevitable conclusion.

But if he were to be honest, Gareth had to admit that the disturbing news received tonight was not the sole source of his tension. Annoyed when his hand shook as he tilted the decanter, Gareth poured the amber liquid quickly. Lifting the delicate glass, he took a deep swallow. Damn, he had needed that! It had been a hell of a day! Squaring his broad shoulders, Gareth unconsciously ran a hand through his heavy dark hair and attempted to ignore the low buzz of conversation progressing in the corner of the room.

Gareth fixed his gaze on a distant tree barely visible in the waning light, his mind seeing instead Angelica's face as it had appeared when he had reached up to lift her down from his horse early that morning. Her tension had been apparent in the rigid line of her body and set of her jaw. She had turned toward the door to her home and he had been witness to the incredible flush of tenderness that had suffused her face as the young boy, Carlos, had run out to throw his arms around her waist.

100

His stomach twisting into a familiar knot, he shook his head in disbelief. He had worked that picture over in his mind's eye countless times since early morning. His assessment of Angelica had altered dramatically in that instant, as she had revealed another facet of her already complex character. Beautiful, desirable, calculating, fully conscious of the potency of her appeal, she was also intelligent and proud. Her spirit was indominable, its presence illuminating her great silver eyes, a brilliant challenge which had allowed him little peace.

But the boy's presence had introduced another side of Angelica's personality, and he had ached with the startling, overwhelming desire to experience the warmth of her tenderness. Suddenly disgusted with the line his mind was taking, Gareth shook his head. He had learned long ago that there was only one thing he needed from women. He did not need tenderness from that grasping little *puta*. He need keep in mind that she obviously delighted in playing one man against the other, that she dangled Esteban Arricalde on the string—a dangerous game to play with the spoiled aristocrat—and flaunted a convincing innocence in the eyes of Peter Macfadden until the unworldly young man was almost beside himself with wanting her.

In all honesty he had to admit Angelica Rodrigo had been successful with him also. He had come to the point where he was admittedly willing to pay any price she named in order to purge himself of his desire for her. But his willingness was obviously not enough. She had not had her fill of games.

Memory returned to his mind the casual manner in which Angelica had uncovered her naked body and slid out of bed in the soft gray light of dawn, dressing boldly as he had watched. She had even made certain to turn her back to him, allowing him a view of her firm, well-shaped buttocks as she had reached over to pick up her clothing. The heat of that moment returned with full impact and Gareth flushed hotly. Downing the last drops of liquid in his glass, he shot a quick look toward the sparkling decanter. In a few moments he had returned to the window, his glass refilled.

But in the time since he had returned to the Arricalde hacienda this morning, one obstacle after another had been placed in the way of his seeing Angelica and speaking with her again. The triumph in Esteban Arricalde's eyes when Esteban had faced him across the dinner table had added an even more unsettling note to the situation, and Gareth had become more determined than ever to settle things between the maddening Angelica Rodrigo and himself.

He shook his head, disbelieving his own preoccupation with the beautiful little *puta*. He had never had a problem getting a woman to warm his bed. Yet he could not even get Angelica to name her price . . . a price he knew had been paid many times before. Perhaps that was the true reason for the knot which squeezed tighter in his stomach with each thought of her. Tilting his head back, Gareth drained his glass again, his eyes watering as the scorching liquid slipped down his throat.

"Good brandy was made to be sipped, Gareth. It seems that your frustration is such this evening that you allow all convention to escape you."

Turning toward the sound of Esteban's low, confident purr, Gareth raised a speculative brow. "Not *all* convention, Esteban. I managed to defer to my host's wishes just a few moments ago when my fondest desire was to choke the superior smirk from Felipe Aleman's arrogant face."

"So you defer to the wishes of your host . . . Well, that will not be as difficult for you now as it has been in the past . . ."

A brief silence between them was followed by Gareth's cautious, "And by that, Esteban, you mean . . .?"

"I mean that as far as the *puta* is concerned, you will be spared having to make a choice in the matter. She has decided to devote herself to the full service of her employers."

Gareth was beginning to bristle. "And by her employers you mean . . .?"

"I mean myself, Gareth, of course." Staring pointedly into his eyes, Esteban continued smoothly, "Angelica came

102

to her full senses this morning. We had a long talk when she returned to the hacienda, after which she thanked me for my generosity in giving her another opportunity to serve me. It was a very touching encounter."

"I don't believe you."

"That is unfortunate. But you may hear the words directly from the *puta*'s lips, if you wish. She will be meeting me tonight on the path which leads from the kitchen to the road. *Si*, there is much privacy there and many spots not dissimilar to that wooded glade you spoke of this morning. I'm sure Angelica will be able to convince you. She was very convincing to me this morning when she sought to demonstrate . . ."

"Bastard!"

Esteban laughed low in his throat. "Gareth, you surprise me with your lack of control."

"I don't believe a word you say!"

"Then perhaps you will believe Angelica."

Turning at the buzz of conversation in the doorway, Esteban smiled. Without another word, Esteban advanced toward the doorway and the women who had suddenly appeared there, his eye on Dolores Valentin's expectant face.

Breathing a deep sigh of relief, Angelica stored the last of the dishes and shot a quick look toward Carmela's unsmiling face. She felt a disturbing sadness at the old woman's obvious disappointment in her, and at her loss of the only ally in the Arricalde kitchen. But it was obvious Carmela had succumbed to the gossip that had abounded after her disappearance with Gareth Dawson the night before. Carmela had spoken little to her. Instead, she had adhered strictly to Dona Teresa's instructions, making certain that Angelica had not been out of her sight the entire day. Maria's chores as upstairs maid had been given to Juanita until the older maid had recovered, and judging from the smirk on the conceited little witch's face, Juanita intended to make good use of her opportunity.

The strange gnawing at the pit of her stomach increased

as Angelica wondered if Gareth Dawson would find Juanita more accommodating than she. Somehow the thought gave her little peace. Adding to her unrest were the memories she had been unsuccessful in eluding the entire day: the touch of the Texan's mouth against hers, the exquisitely gentle touch of his lips, and the emotions they had evoked as they had slid down her neck to find more tantalizing play in the hollows at the base of her throat. She remembered his tightly muscled chest moving under her palms, the strength in the hard body pressed so close to hers, the . . .

No! She must also force herself to remember that the same deep voice that had throbbed with need, declaring it openly, had asked for her price. The warmth in Gareth Dawson's eyes had not been for her but for a lust which Juanita would probably not hesitate to sate.

Mentally chastising herself for the turn her mind had taken, Angelica took a last glance around the room. Yes, all had been settled for the night. Carmela was in her usual position seated in a chair beside the fireplace, silent and unsmiling. Taking a deep breath, Angelica approached her.

"Is there anything else you would have me do before I return home this evening, Carmela?"

The weary dark eyes which moved upward to meet hers were filled with sadness, and succumbing to impulse, Angelica dropped to her knees beside the woman's chair. "Carmela, I ask you to listen to what I have to say. I have not spoken to anyone here about what happened last night, for it matters little to me what they think. They have made up their minds about me in any case. But you have been kind to me, Carmela." Her eyes holding Carmela's in open appeal, she continued softly, "I would have you know that nothing that is said of me is true. I am innocent of wrongdoing and innocent of the intention. I hope you will believe me."

The broad hand which moved to cover and pat hers consolingly was unhesitant. "You need not distress yourself on my account, Angelica. I have been searching my heart as I sat here. We are all victims of our fates, are we not? You are a beautiful young woman who was born in sin, but your eyes shine with a heart that is pure. I do not believe life will leave you untouched, but it is not up to me to judge you. I see only goodness in you. That goodness has not changed, no matter the events that occurred yesterday."

"Thank you, Carmela." Swallowing tightly, Angelica began to draw herself to her feet, only to be stopped as Carmela's hand tightened unexpectedly, drawing her eyes back to Carmela's face.

"You must not view the restrictions that I have helped to enforce in this kitchen as a punishment, Angelica. Better you should view them as your salvation."

"My salvation?"

"*Si*, Angelica. In the time you are under my watchful eyes, you are safe from other eyes which desire much more of you than your duties in this room."

Her face flushing, Angelica's eyes dropped from Carmela's knowing gaze.

"You need not feel embarrassment for the lust of others, Angelica. And you need feel no shame for those things which fate presses upon you. A heart remains pure, no matter the demands on the body, when freedom of choice is taken away."

"Carmela . . ."

"No . . . you need say nothing, Angelica." Her lined face creasing into myriad wrinkles to form a smile, Carmela said softly, "I, too, was once young and desirable. Like you, I had little choice . . ."

Angelica's eyes widened in surprise at the woman's words, even as Carmela continued, "But I chose not to bear the child which would proclaim to the world my lost innocence. Though I have since married and lost a husband, I have never conceived another child. At the time of your arrival in Real del Monte with your parents and the obvious gossip that ensued, I pitied your mother for the shame of having borne you. Now I envy her."

"Carmela . . . *lo siento*."

"No, Angelica, it is I who is sorry . . . sorry that I cannot spare you the unhappiness you will suffer as a result of your beauty. But know you have a friend, Angelica, and forgive me the silence of this day while I mourn my own sad memories."

Unwilling to allow release to the tears that choked her throat, Angelica rose quickly to her feet. Patting Carmela's callused hand lightly, she whispered, "*Gracias*, Carmela."

Within moments, Angelica was walking through the doorway and onto the path which led home, grateful for the shield of semidarkness. She took a deep breath as she turned onto the path that led downward toward the road. Carmela's softly whispered confidences had touched her deeply. Carmela's statement had also reinforced her gratitude for her mother's silent strength, the strength that had carried her mother through her own birth and the hard years which had . . .

A strong arm reached unexpectedly from the darkness to jerk Angelica against a hard, male body. Its familiar, cloying scent caused her to struggle spontaneously.

"No, Angelica, no." Pinning her arms behind her, Esteban forced her flush against him with the strength of his captive embrace. "You need not struggle. It is only I . . . the same man who saved you from being expelled from this household . . . the man to whom you owe a deep debt of gratitude."

His words, clearly conveying the covert meaning he intended, registered hard in Angelica's brain. Her struggles ceased as she raised her face slowly to his. She swallowed against the nausea which threatened to overwhelm her as Esteban's hands held her fast.

"That's right, Angelica. We have a strong bond between us now, do we not? You owe me your future in this household, and your brother's future as well. It is a tenuous future which depends heavily upon the manner in which you express your gratitude. And I, in turn, am bound to you with the desire you foster within me. We will serve our bond well, will we not Angelica?"

Unable to speak the words of agreement, Angelica nodded with a short jerk of her head. But Esteban was not content with her meager response. His hands tightening on her wrists until she almost cried out with pain, he whispered softly against her cheek, "You must do better than that, Angelica. It is the very least I will demand of you in the time to come. Let me hear your voice. Tell me you will serve me well. I wish to hear confirmation of that fact from your own lips."

Esteban's words were delivered in a smooth voice which belied the heavy pounding of his heart against her breast. His one hand had moved to knead her breast painfully; his body was beginning to tremble as he awaited her response. His mouth was pressed against her cheek, his sweet, minty breath increasing the nausea which threatened to overwhelm her.

"Yes . . ." Her first word emerging as a low gasp, Angelica struggled for the breath to continue. "I will serve you well . . ."

"Why will you serve me well, Angelica. Tell me so I may be sure you understand . . ."

"Be—because my future lies in your hands . . ."

"That is good, Angelica, very good." Slowly releasing her wrists, his eyes holding hers, wary of the first sign of betrayal, Esteban enclosed her in a breathtaking embrace. "And now you will kiss me, Angelica. You will show me how much you wish to please me, how much you want me to make love to you. Come, Angelica . . . come . . ."

Obeying his softly whispered command, Angelica raised her arms and slid them around Esteban's neck. Nausea assailed her, growing ever stronger as she lifted her mouth to Esteban's triumphant smile. Attempting to restrain her revulsion as her lips touched his, she was unprepared for the violence with which Esteban's mouth descended, the cruel pressure with which he ground his mouth into hers, the pain of his grasping hands as they searched her body in a voracious quest for intimacy. She was gasping under the onslaught of his lust as a silent scream echoed again and again in her mind. She was shuddering with horror engulfing her.

Her restraint was slipping away, the arms wound so carefully around Esteban's neck balling into fists when a voice grated harshly, "Well, seems like I might be interruptin' somethin' again."

Reacting instantaneously to Gareth's voice, Esteban drew his mouth from Angelica's. Still maintaining his hold, he whispered insidiously, "Gareth . . . oh, yes, you were invited here tonight, weren't you? But at the time I extended the invitation, I did not realize you would be interrupting such a loving exchange between Angelica and myself."

His hand stroking Angelica's breast, Esteban lowered his head to her ear to trace its outline with his tongue. His eyes were on Gareth's still face. "She is delicious, is she not, Gareth? You have tasted her before and know only too well her sweetness. That is unfortunate, it it not? For you will remember only too well the pleasure Angelica will bring me. You will have the memory of her sweet taste in your mouth. You will remember the silk of her flesh under your hands, the fullness of her breasts against your lips . . ."

"Bastard!"

Esteban's low laugh echoed in the stillness. With great deliberation he moved his hand from Angelica's breast, sliding it sensually upward to brush her *camisa* from her shoulder. Lowering his head unexpectedly, he clamped his mouth over the smooth white skin.

Gasping as Esteban bit cruelly into her flesh, Angelica pushed spontaneously at his chest, only to feel his hands clamp like steel bands on her arms, holding her captive. Gareth had taken a spontaneous step forward when Esteban raised his head to issue a low warning.

"No! Stay where you are. Angelica does not want me to stop loving her, do you, my little *puta*? A little pain only heightens the senses, does it not? And I shall raise all your senses . . . make them acute, so that when I take you, you will cry out my name and beg me for more."

But Gareth was not waiting for Angelica's response. He was moving toward them, his expression resolute, when Esteban leaned over to snatch something from his boot. The glint of steel flashed in the dim grove, stopping Gareth's quick advance as Esteban hissed, "No, Gareth. I would not wish to be guilty of shedding blood this night, but I tell you now, I will not hesitate. Both of you have earned the cut of my blade, and it matters little to me whether it is the *puta*'s warm blood or your own which it tastes."

Gareth's eyes moved to Angelica's white face. Esteban's low laugh sounded again as Gareth took a short step backward.

"Angelica . . . your name is inconsistent with the emotions you stimulate, little *puta* . . ." His eyes moving over her face as he jerked her closer still, Esteban continued in a low voice, "But it describes her beauty well, does it not, Gareth? She is as beautiful as an angel . . . with her smooth skin and perfect face. An angel of hell . . ."

Angelica was shuddering visibly. Appearing to enjoy her reaction, Esteban moved his knife, carefully catching the dim light on its polished surface as he smiled. "See . . . see how the *puta*'s body cries for mine, Gareth? But it will not be long before I will sate her. Patience, my little one. First you must tell Gareth of your pledge to me."

Angelica's eyes moved to Esteban's, and he urged again, "Yes, tell him so that he may realize that you will no longer allow him use of your body. Tell him, my little *puta*, how you pledge to serve me well . . ."

A cruel twist on her arm elicited a low moan from Angelica and a spontaneous step forward from Gareth, which was halted by a quick, threatening movement of Esteban's knife.

"Tell him, Angelica . . ."

Attempting to swallow the knot of fear which held her silent, Angelica looked into Esteban's wild eyes. Despising herself for the quiver in her voice, she began haltingly, "I . . . I have given Don Esteban my pledge to . . . to . . ."

"*Si*, Angelica, tell Gareth how you will serve me . . ."

"To serve him well and loyally . . ."

Esteban frowned, increasing the pressure on her arm. His voice was a low hiss. "You must be more explicit, Angelica. Gareth would like to know just what you . . ."

Halting in mid-sentence, Esteban snapped his head up unexpectedly as he paused to listen for a sound in the darkness. Within seconds the light of a lantern moved on the entrance to the path as Dona Teresa's voice called quietly, "Esteban, are you out there, *querido*?"

Dona Teresa turned as a second figure joined her. The sound of her voice carried clearly in the silent glade.

"Enrique, Esteban has merely gone for a walk, I am sure. You must not trouble yourself. He has been very tense . . ."

"Too tense, Teresa. It has been a difficult day. But I do not wish to see you upset. Come inside. I shall send Hernando out to find him."

"Enrique . . ."

"Come, Teresa. Our guests will begin to wonder where we are."

The two figures turned away and began walking back toward the hacienda. Esteban's eyes shot back to Gareth's still face, his lips curling in an angry grimace as Don Enrique's voice sounded in the silence.

"Hernando, *vene aqui*."

Anger evident on his handsome face, Esteban addressed Gareth without preamble.

"We are soon to have company, Gareth, so it is obvious we must conclude our conversation another time. If you will return to the hacienda now, I will wait until you are indoors before doing the same. Angelica is on her way home now and that is where she will remain. If you value her good interests, you will make certain you do not bother her with your attentions again." When Gareth still did not move, Esteban hissed ominously, "*Andale! Pronto!*"

Hesitating long enough to give Angelica's pale face an assessing glance, Gareth turned and walked back toward the house as directed. Following Gareth's tall figure with his eyes, Esteban hesitated as Gareth stopped to engage Hernando in conversation.

Turning to look down into Angelica's still face, Esteban whispered with a sneer, "See how the Texan seeks to delay Hernando in order to shield you from being discovered here in the glade with me. Is it his concern for you, my little *puta*, or is it his concern that you will be sent from the

110

hacienda and away from his sight that makes him act in this manner?"

His eyes flashing with a new heat, Esteban leaned over to slip his knife back into his boot. His free hand slipping around her waist, he pulled Angelica tight against his body as his other hand moved to grip the plait which hung down her back. Twisting the braid around his hand, Esteban forced Angelica's head back as he lowered his mouth to cover hers in a vicious, bruising kiss. When he drew his mouth from hers at last, his body was trembling.

"*Puta!* You reduce me to a shuddering youth with my desire for you and the taste of your sweet body. I will not savor my possession of you this night, but anticipation will make conquest all the sweeter. And that day will come soon, my little soiled flower, the day when I will draw from your nectar, and feed upon it until my appetite is sated. Dream of me, little *puta* . . . dream of me and I will not disappoint you. . ."

Releasing her so suddenly that Angelica almost lost her balance, Esteban gave a short laugh. "Now go . . . go before I drag you into the bush and take you while Hernando watches. Were it not that I wish to enjoy you for many nights to come, I would do just that, so great is my desire." When still she did not move, he hissed, "Go!"

The wildness in Esteban's eyes sending a bolt of horror through her veins, Angelica turned instantaneously and began running down the path. The sound of Esteban's low laughter pursued her.

Her chest heaving with deep, gulping breaths, Angelica paused as the small, stone house which was her home came into view. Pressing her hand to the pain which tore at her side, she leaned over in an attempt to alleviate the strain. Remaining unmoving until her breathing had almost returned to normal, Angelica raised a trembling hand to her brow. Her mind was running in wild circles, the image of Esteban Arricalde's savage gaze in endless pursuit.

A deep revulsion again overwhelmed her, sending a new wave of nausea swelling inside her. No, no matter the outcome of her actions, she could not allow this man to touch her again. She would find a way to avoid him . . . hold him off, until she could find an alternative to the degrading act of physical satiation of his lust.

Perhaps if she talked to Padre Manuel . . . No, Don Esteban had been correct. Dona Teresa would never allow herself to believe her son guilty of acts of physical cruelty. Another shudder moved over Angelica's frame. And he had promised her more, had he not? Promised to heighten her senses . . .

The memory of Gareth Dawson's face intruded abruptly into the vision of Esteban Arricalde's savage expression. The knife had been all that had held him back. She had read fear in his dark eyes, but in truth, she did not believe the fear was for himself. She remembered the way Gareth's eyes had shot to her face, the small muscle which had ticked in his cheek as his broad hands had clenched and unclenched revealingly at his sides. She remembered the agitated heaving of his chest. In that moment she had wished desperately to be held safe against him, free of Estaban Arricalde's painful grip.

Pulling herself upright, Angelica took a deep breath. No, she was thinking like a fool! It was only this morning when her mind had railed at a similar lust in Gareth Dawson's eyes. Her face burned in the memory of the words he had uttered in her ear . . . words of desire . . . promise of ecstasy. There was little difference between Gareth Dawson and Esteban Arricalde when it came to that which they wanted of her.

Suddenly weary, Angelica stepped onto the path and started toward her home. She needed its sanctuary this night. She needed it sorely.

Angelica was walking slowly, using the time to affix a mask upon her face. It would not do to allow Mama and Papa to see that she was upset. They would be helpless to aid her, and in the end, the matter was truly up to her to settle.

She was drawing close to her home when Angelica sensed something was wrong. Her eyes flashed to the doorway.

Angelica could hear her mother's low placating tones. She could hear Carlos's sobbing response. Carlos was not a complaining child. He seldom cried. Something was very wrong.

Suddenly running, Angelica entered the doorway just as Margarita Rodrigo bathed away the blood streaming from Carlos's swollen nose. But it was to no avail; a stubborn flow reappeared persistently as soon as it had been cleansed away. Hearing her step, Carlos turned full toward her, his gaze dropping to his lap, but not before she saw the swelling above his eye and the scratches which marked his pale cheek and chin.

Moving quickly to his side, Angelica dropped to her knees and took Carlos's small, trembling hands in hers.

"Carlos, *querido*, what has happened?"

Refusing to meet her eyes, Carlos shook his head. "Nothing, Angelica. It is nothing."

"Nothing! Who did this to you?" Turning to her mother, Angelica pleaded for her response, only to receive a small negative shake of her head not meant for Carlos's eyes.

"It is nothing, just as Carlos said, Angelica. Carlos will be all right in a few minutes, and then he will go to bed. He is very tired, is that not so, Carlos?"

"*Si, Mama.*"

Her eyes on her brother's downcast expression, extremely aware of the fact that he still did not attempt to meet her eyes, Angelica whispered, "You do not wish to have me read to you from one of Padre Manuel's books? I have not read to you in several days."

"No, I am tired. *Por favor*, Mama, I will go to bed now. *Buenas noches.*"

Pulling himself wearily to his feet, his small hand still clutching the wet cloth to his nose, Carlos walked toward his room in a weary step. Waiting only until he had closed the door behind him, Angelica turned to her mother's pained expression.

"Mama, what is wrong? Where is Papa? Why is Carlos . . . ?"

"Your father is working late in the church tonight with

Padre Manuel."

"What has happened?"

"There was much talk about you in the village this evening . . ."

Suddenly motionless, Angelica felt a chill of apprehension move down her spine. "What kind of talk?"

Some of the other boys repeated the stories they had heard their mothers tell . . . about you and Señor Dawson. Carlos defended you, said you were caught in the storm, and they laughed at him. He told them not to speak of you in that way, and when they laughed again, he fought with them."

Angelica closed her eyes momentarily, but the vision of her brother's frail form fighting the stronger boys of the village was more than she could bear.

"I must talk to him . . ."

"He is upset, Angelica."

"I must talk to him . . ."

Walking resolutely toward the small room they shared, Angelica opened the door, and closing it behind her, walked to kneel beside her brother's bed. Straining to adjust her eyes to the darkness of the room, she reached out to take Carlos's small hands in hers. Belatedly realizing he was crying, Angelica reached out to smooth the paths of his tears from his cheeks, a deep sadness adding a hoarse quality to her voice as she spoke.

"Carlos, I am sorry you were hurt. You must learn to ignore gossip. Such talk comes from people with idle minds."

"It was Jose Morales who said bad things, Angelica. He said he heard his mother tell his aunt that you were to be dismissed from the hacienda because of your conduct with the Texan who brought you here yesterday. He said you have proved that Dona Teresa should not have allowed you to work in her house by becoming involved with one of her guests. He said no other decent family would hire you now. He said . . ."

Aware of the fact that Carlos's breathing was again becoming agitated, Angelica lay her hand gently across his lips in an attempt to halt his rush of words, but it was to no avail. Brushing her hand away, Carlos continued heatedly. "But I told Jose that his mother was a fool . . . that all the women are jealous of you because you are so beautiful. I told him that his mother and sister were ugly and wanted to make everyone look as ugly as they and . . ."

"Carlos, you didn't . . ."

"Yes, I did, Angelica, because it is true. You are so beautiful . . . as beautiful as the angel Mama named you for. You are too beautiful for their ugly eyes . . ."

"Carlos . . ."

"And I will not let them say things about you . . ."

"You will not be able to stop them, Carlos. You cannot fight everyone."

"Then I will tell Señor Dawson, and *he* will fight them! He is big and strong . . ."

The lump in her throat growing, Angelica shook her head. "Shhhh, Carlos. We cannot look to Señor Dawson for help. He will soon be leaving Real del Monte. The rumors will stop then and all will be well. You must learn to ignore loose tongues, *querido*, like I do."

The silence which prevailed after her whispered statement was of short duration, broken by Carlos's softly whispered question.

"It is not true, is it, Angelica? You were not dismissed from the hacienda . . ."

"No, it is not true, Carlos. La señora was concerned and spoke to me this morning, but all the difficulty was cleared up and there is no longer any problem. You must not worry, *querido*."

"Then I will tell them tomorrow . . . *all* of them! I will tell them how wrong they were! I will tell them that you still work at the hacienda, and that la señora . . ."

"No, Carlos, you will tell them nothing. They will see for themselves in a little while, and they will then know the foolishness of their words."

"But, Angelica . . ."

"They will see their error then, Carlos . . ."

There was a short silence while Carlos assessed the

firmness in her voice. His response was a reluctant "*Si*, Angelica."

Lowering her head, Angelica pressed a light kiss against her brother's forehead, the raised heat there stirring a small frown, "You are feeling all right, Carlos?"

"*Si*, I am just tired. I will be better tomorrow."

"Sleep well, *querido*."

Drawing herself slowly to her feet, Angelica walked to the doorway of the room and let herself out, making sure to close the door firmly behind her.

A low gasping drew Angelica slowly from her sleep. Momentarily disoriented, she sought to define the sound, sudden realization snapping her to an upright position in her bed. Her eyes jerked to the smaller bed in the corner of her small room, her heart beginning to pound with fear as her eyes focused on Carlos's writhing form. Throwing off her covers, Angelica jumped to her feet, moving immediately toward him.

"Carlos, what is wrong? *Querido* . . ."

Carlos's pale face, barely visible in the meager light filtering through the window, turned toward hers. Startling Angelica with the wildness in his eyes, he rasped and fought for breath.

"I . . . I cannot breathe . . . Angelica . . ."

Panic beginning to build inside her, Angelica raised her hand to Carlos's brow, her senses jolting at the furious heat burning there. She moved her hand to his frail, heaving chest, her tension mounting at the furious pounding of Carlos's heart against his thin-ribbed body.

"*Querido*, you must try to be calm. You must not be frightened. This will soon pass, and you will be better once again."

"Angelica . . . *por favor*. Do not . . . leave me . . ."

The sudden tightening of her throat creating a momentary obstruction to response, Angelica fought her growing fear as Carlos's wild eyes moved over her face. She dared not allow Carlos to see her fear, to know the panic which was beginning to overwhelm rational thought. She dared

116

not allow herself to remember Padre Manuel's dire warnings of the possible result of another attack. She dared not . . .

"Carlos, *mi corazón*, you must not be afraid." Startled at the level quality of her own tone, Angelica continued with a low, calm insistence that belied her inner quaking. "I must leave you for a few moments. I must wake Mama and Papa so they may stay with you while I go to fetch Padre Manuel."

"No . . . no. I want you to stay!"

Carlos's small hands were clutching at hers, the small fingers talons of fear, strong with panic as he rasped for breath. Prying them loose from her arm, Angelica clutched Carlos's hands firmly between her own. Realizing that the heaving convulsions of his chest were becoming even more violent, she lowered her face to his cheek. She could not wait much longer. She must get Padre Manuel . . . now!

"Carlos, *por favor*, you must be brave for a few moments. Will you do that for me, *querido*? Will you remain quiet and calm so that I may leave you without fear? If you will do that for me, I will return in a few moments with Mama and Papa. Will you put aside your fear for me, Carlos?"

The desperation in her tone appearing to filter through his terror, Carlos raised his eyes to hers. Her heart breaking at the smile he strove to bring to his lips even as a harsh rattling joined the sound of his ragged, shattering breaths, Angelica heard his low response.

"*Sí.* Go. I . . . I will not be afraid . . ."

Taking only a second more, Angelica drew herself swiftly to her feet. Within moments she had awakened her parents and returned with them to Carlos's side. Confirmation of the fear she had herself experienced was written on their dark faces and Angelica's shuddering grew. The heaving convulsions of Carlos's small body were escalating, shaking him with each breath, the sound of his anguished rasps echoing in the silent room as she watched helplessly. With horror she saw blood rise to color Carlos's white, even teeth, swelling to trickle out of the corner of his mouth and

117

run down his cheek.

Panic overwhelming her, Angelica jumped to her feet. Stopping only to snatch at a rebozo to cover her nightshift, she ran from the room. Picking up the lantern in the kitchen, she jerked open the door and started in the direction of the church. Unconscious of the stones which cut into her bare feet Angelica ran, her breath coming in deep, sobbing rasps as she flew over the uneven path. She was running with all the speed her shaking body could muster when strong arms unexpectedly reached out of the darkness, jerking her to a halt against a hard, unyielding wall of male strength.

Her eyes darting upward, focused on Gareth Dawson's frown as she demanded harshly, "Let me go! I must go . . ."

"Where are you goin', Angelica? What's so important . . ."

"Carlos . . . he is sick. I must get Padre Manuel. Let me go, damn you!"

Not realizing tears streamed down her cheeks, Angelica struggled against Gareth Dawson's restrictive embrace. Holding tight to the lantern in her hand, she punched and clawed frantically at his unyielding chest with the other.

"Angelica, stop. Stop!"

Angelica reacted unconsciously to the command in the Texan's low tone, her struggles coming to an abrupt halt as she fought to suppress the sobs which choked her throat. Taking her lantern with one hand, Gareth took Angelica's arm firmly with his other.

"It isn't safe for you alone on this path at night. I'll go with you to get your priest. Come on."

Allowing her to lead the way, Gareth steadied Angelica's shaking frame as she started rapidly in the direction of the church once again. Knowing an overwhelming need to protect the vulnerable young woman whose body quaked so wildly under his touch, Gareth adhered to Angelica's frantic pace as they followed the endless path to the rear of the church. Without pause, Angelica raced to a small building behind the impressive structure and pounded on

118

the door.

Stepping back as Angélica raised her hand to pound again, Gareth waited in silence, his eyes moving over her slender, trembling form. The lantern he held etched her perfect profile against the darkness. She was clad only in a light nightshift through which the outline of her long, slender legs was all too apparent. She clutched a rebozo over her shoulders, mercifully obscuring the outline of firm, high breasts and a narrow waist he remembered only too vividly. The black, unbound silk of her hair hung past her stiff shoulders, swaying with her anxious movements. He raised his eyes to her face again. The shining paths of tears were still apparent on her cheeks, but she was crying no longer. Her eyes were wide, frantic with fear as she raised her hand to knock again. But the door opened unexpectedly, swinging wide to the short, squinting man dressed in dark Franciscan robes.

"Padre . . . quickly. It is Carlos. He is very sick, much worse than the last time."

The priest nodded, his gaze moving from Angélica's panic-stricken expression to Gareth's silent presence. Without comment he turned and moved back into the house, only to emerge a few seconds later with a small leather bag in his hand. Jerking the door closed behind him, he stepped down into the yard and moved unhesitantly toward the path. Turning to Gareth, Angélica reached out and took the lantern from his hand.

"*Padre, un momento, por favor.* The path is dark."

Stepping in front of him, Angélica held the lantern high to illuminate the darkness as the silent procession started back.

Aware only of Padre Manuel's step behind her, Angélica moved quickly on the path, refusing to allow herself to think. They would soon be home and Padre Manuel would remove his medicines from his small bag and attend to Carlos. Carlos's breathing would then slowly come under control, and he would slip into an exhausted sleep. It would take several days for him to overcome the aftereffects of such a severe attack, but he would slowly recuperate.

119

Past experience told her that Carlos would be a little weaker than before as a result of the siege, but that weakness would be temporary. Within the year she and her parents would have saved the amount needed in order to go to Mexico City and consult the doctor Padre Manuel recommended. They would stay there as long as was necessary to accomplish his cure, and Carlos would return to Real del Monte healthy and completely recovered.

Yes, that was the way it would be. She would allow no negative thoughts to enter her mind, for she had determined long ago that Carlos would be cured. A merciful and loving God would not allow Carlos to slip away from life before having fulfilled the promise of his future. His was too beautiful a light to be snuffed out before having an opportunity to fully illuminate the lives of those around him.

Emerging from the wooded trail, Angelica walked quickly across the yard toward the house, conscious of the fact that Padre Manuel followed closely at her heels. She entered the house, her certainties of a few moments before vanishing as the sound of Carlos's ragged breathing echoed ominously in the silence. The attack continued unabated. It had been a long time. How much longer could his valiant heart continue to beat under the weight of such stress?

Restraining a sob, Angelica stepped back to allow Padre Manuel entrance to the small bedroom, her eyes touching on Carlos's small, gray face. Blood stained the pillow beside his head, and Margarita Rodrigo raised her hand to wipe the slender path of blood from his cheek. Hemorrhage . . . Padre Manuel had said the danger of excessive, unrestrained bleeding caused by the rupture of vessels in Carlos's chest was the greatest threat to his life. This was the first time he had bled . . . Her eyes moved to Carlos's lips, and Angelica allowed herself a moment of hope. The bleeding appeared to be constant, but mild. There appeared to be none of the gushing flow of which Padre Manuel had warned. Surely this slender trickle of blood meant little . . . did not constitute a threat to Carlos's life.

Angelica's eyes searched Carlos's face for a sign of

welcome, but there was none. Instead, he appeared to be hardly conscious, his prolonged struggle for breath seeming to have sent him into a temporary limbo which did not allow him recognition. Fear expanded inside her as Angelica glanced first to her mother's and then her father's grief-stricken face for assurance that did not come.

Padre Manuel was bent over Carlos's bed. His hands were moving among the bottles in his bag, his expression dark. He turned to Margarita Rodrigo's frightened face.

"The attack is severe. Carlos was content and happy when I visited here earlier in the day. What happened to upset him? Surely something must have occurred to bring about an attack of this severity."

Margarita Rodrigo remained silent, but Angelica did not need to hear the words that echoed so blaringly across her mind. It was her fault. She was to blame for this attack, and she feared it was Carlos's very love for her that would ultimately drive him to his . . .

Refusing to think any further, Angelica raised her head and walked toward the kitchen door. For the first time since arriving at Padre Manuel's house, she remembered Gareth Dawson. She looked into the yard, but he was nowhere to be seen. He had been waiting for her in the darkness, but he had found little satisfaction of the type he sought this night. Did nothing discourage his intentions? Not Juanita, not Esteban, not . . .

Turning away from the door, Angelica walked to the fireplace and stared into the leaping flames. Carlos's harsh, rasping breath echoed within the small room and she could not escape the sound.

The velvet black of night was yielding to the soft gray of dawn. Her hands covering her face, Angelica rested her elbows on the kitchen table, her mind on the stillness that now prevailed. A soft mumble of voices sounded from the small bedroom in the rear and she raised her head. Padre Manuel was the first to emerge from the small room, followed by her mother and father. Her mother's face was without color. Moving her to her feet, Angelica raced to take her arm.

"I am all right, Angelica. I am merely tired, as are Padre Manuel and your father." Her eyes shot to the fireplace where a pot boiled, emitting the fragrant aroma of coffee, and she managed a smile.

Ushering her mother to a chair, Angelica motioned Padre Manuel and her father to their seats and hastened to place cups in front of them filled with the hot, fragrant brew. Realizing her throat was too tight to allow passage of the beverage, Angelica sat at the table, her eyes on Padre Manuel's sober face.

"Padre, Carlos . . . he will be all right . . .?"

His eyes lifting to Angelica's white face, Padre Manuel raised his shoulders in a small shrug. "*Quien sabe*, Angelica?"

A stillness came over the room at his cryptic response. Realizing the eyes of all three were on his face, Padre Manuel allowed his gaze to remain on the beautiful, colorless countenance that faced him with growing horror.

"But . . . but you said Carlos would be well. You said the doctor in Mexico City could cure him . . ."

"Angelica, time is running out for Carlos. He is growing weaker. His body cannot withstand the rigors of another attack such as this."

"But . . . but we will soon have the money to take him to Mexico City. My employment at the hacienda . . ." Swallowing tightly, Angelica looked to her father's pinched face for support. "We will have the money for the doctor within the year . . ."

"My child, I fear that will be too late . . ."

"Too late . . .?

Her body rigid with shock, Angelica held Padre Manuel's gaze without moving until his warm, gentle hand moved to pat hers. His brown eyes bright with compassion, he offered softly, "*Quien sabe*, Angelica? It is in the hands of God."

"No!" Suddenly springing to her feet, uncaring of Padre Manuel's concerned frown, she shook her head adamantly. "No, Carlos will not die! I will not let him die! I will not!"

Pushing her chair roughly from the table, Angelica was unaware of the grating sound of the quick movement, or the creak that broke the silence as it fell back against the floor. Knowing only a need to escape, she snatched at her rebozo, and flinging it around her shoulders, ran out of the house into the growing light of dawn. Within moments she had disappeared into the foliage of the trail.

The small house was in complete silence when Angelica returned. Dawn had fully broken through the darkness, bringing the first blush of a brilliant new day upon the verdant landscape. Birds chattered noisily amongst the branches under which she walked, but Angelica was unmindful of all sight and sound as she stepped silently into the kitchen. Her father sat in a chair before the fireplace, his gray head resting against its high back, his slight body slumped uncomfortably. Her mother was doubtless resting on her bed after the long night.

Walking softly to the door to her room, Angelica opened it and stepped inside. Tears welled in the eyes she rested on Carlos's white, sleeping face. He was too young, too innocent, and too loving to die. She would fight his death with every weapon she possessed. And she had many, did she not?

Restraining the urge to press a kiss against her brother's smooth cheek, Angelica moved silently instead to her bed and took up her clothes. She slipped her feet into her sandals, and snatching up a cloth and a few other articles from the shelf beside her bed, slipped from the room. Within minutes she was moving across the yard.

She had come to a decision in the time since she had fled Padre Manuel's shattering statement. And she had formed a plan in her mind. Carlos could not wait a year for her to earn the money to save him, so she would have to get the money more quickly. She need prepare herself before she took the first step.

Turning onto a path used by her alone, Angelica walked silently, her mind registering the familiar gurgle of the stream which moved rapidly beside the trail. Her step remained steady as she followed its winding route, only slowing as she neared the spot she sought. Pausing, she came upon the familiar beauty of a small pool where the clear water welled before escaping in a narrow stream down the mountainside. She dropped the articles she carried carelessly to the grassy bank.

Unmindful of the morning chill, she allowed her night-shift to slip to her feet. Naked, she walked into the cool water, grateful for the startling sharpness as it moved over her feet to her calves, and slowly up the long line of her legs before engulfing her body. Her gradual descent into the crystal stillness was soothing to a mind tortured by the frightening series of events of the day before. She stood waist deep in the verdant silence for a brief moment, her eyes skimming the serene beauty of the pool, before continuing onward until the water met her shoulders.

Aware that the shallow depth would allow her no further respite Angelica slowly lowered herself beneath the surface. Relaxing beneath the clear water, Angelica opened her eyes and looked around the silent world she had temporarily invaded. The sun easily penetrated the transparent depths, illuminating the scene with a soft, golden light. Green plants waved their welcome on the sandy floor, their small blossoms pulsing in vain display. Renacuajos played hide-and-seek between rocks sparkling with silver. She reached out to touch the small, darting creatures, only to have them elude her with a flick of their minute tails.

She languished in the cooling freshness, allowing herself to float beneath the surface as the long black spirals of her hair rose around her in graceful undulating swirls. It was beautiful and silent here. There was an absence of care, a beauty which she wished to hold within her. Her chest was beginning to ache with a desire for breath, her head grew light, but she would not allow herself to surface. She needed to remain, to cleanse herself of horrors that had become too real, of decisions she had not wished to make. She opened her mouth to accept the cleansing liquid . . .

Gareth walked silently on the same path he had followed

only a few hours before. He had not remained long after having followed Angelica and the priest back to her house a few hours earlier. He had been an outsider to the drama progressing inside the small stone structure and had not wished to intrude.

He had not been certain exactly what had brought him to stand staring at Angelica's home in the darkness in the first place. Certainly, his inability to drive Angelica's face from his mind and the sleeplessness which had resulted had been part of the reason. But why should this particular woman affect him so strongly, this little *puta* who would slip forever from his life when he left Real del Monte within a few days' time?

And why did the memory of Esteban Arricalde's hand moving against her body, his mouth crushing hers, all but tear him apart? There had been no doubt Esteban had sought to give Angelica pain with his touch. He was also certain he had seen fear in Angelica's eyes. The realization that Esteban would have used his knife on Angelica as easily as he would have used it on him had been all that had held Gareth back.

He had needed to talk to Angelica alone, to make certain she had truly chosen Esteban as a lover. If that was true, he had convinced himself that he would not interfere . . . would walk away and forget the desire she stirred inside him. And he would . . . he would . . .

It had been a few hours since he had left Angelica and the frantic scene at her house, but only a few minutes before he had found himself again arising and walking to the washstand beside his bed to splash cold water on his face in an attempt to clear his mind. He had looked up into the mirror and run a tentative hand over his cheeks. He had stared at his image.

He wondered still. What did Angelica see when she looked at him? Did she see a man who had no room in his heart for a woman, who did not trust the whole breed enough to allow them any more of him than the traitorous part which continued to draw him to them? He had never cared what women thought about him before. There had not been a one whose reaction he had valued enough to care. What was the hold this fiery little beauty had gained over him?

He was well aware that his actions were not solely prompted by desire. A strange anxiety burned inside him, a need that would allow him little peace until he returned to her home this morning, to make certain all had gone well with her brother. He needed to talk to her . . .

He was nearing her home and he paused, his eyes moving around the deserted area in time to see a flicker of movement to the other side of the yard. The brief flash of white had looked like the nightshift Angelica had worn, and that fleeting glimpse of black silk her unbound hair. Taking only a moment to survey the silent household, Gareth made a quick decision and turned in the direction of that flash of movement.

Experiencing momentary satisfaction, Gareth discovered a well-used trail. The path was narrow, the clearance poor, forcing him to lean over to avoid the low-hanging branches. His shoulders brushed the foliage on either side. The person or persons who used it were obviously quite small if they had managed to wear such a slender path. The sound of a stream gurgling over rocks accompanied his steps. He followed the winding trail, his pace slowing as the path gradually widened. He drew himself to a halt, his eyes moving to the edge of a pond behind which a great, glorious sun was beginning its ascent.

Angelica stood poised, outlined against its golden glow, her graceful, naked figure magnificent in its supreme purity of line as she began to walk into the water. Mesmerized by the ultimate grace and beauty she personified, Gareth watched as the gilded ripples slowly engulfed narrow, dainty ankles, slender calves, moved above well-shaped knees to cover the creamy skin of her thighs. The dark triangle of Angelica's womanhood was gradually hidden from his sight, and he mourned its loss as the ever-encroaching water moved to her narrow waist.

Abruptly halting the steadiness of her advance, Angelica paused, her eyes moving over the surface of the pool. An ache completely unrelated to physical desire expanded inside him. His gaze consumed the sheer perfection revealed to his eyes alone, and a deep, silent gratitude welled inside him. He longed to go to her, to run his hands over the smooth line of her shoulders and arms, to cup the small, rounded breasts in his hands, to taste the sweetness of their flesh. He ached to lift her chin until her great, glorious eyes looked up into his, to cover her lips with his, to whisper her name against their softness . . .

But she was walking deeper, the shimmering glow of the water consuming the black silk of her hair until it reached her shoulders. She was in the center of the pool. Unexpectedly she disappeared below the surface of the water. The suddenness of the deprivation caused a spontaneous protest to escape his lips. He waited anxiously for her reappearance, his heartbeat beginning a slow escalation as she failed to appear.

He walked quickly to the edge of the pool, but she still had not come to the surface. He was beginning to panic as his eyes skimmed the smooth surface, his heart thudding against his ribs. He waded into the water, moving quickly to the spot where he had last seen Angelica. He was searching the crystal depths when he spied her graceful form floating motionlessly below the surface. Her dark hair splayed out in graceful wings, her arms and legs undulating on the smooth current, she had become part of the silent, primeval tableau.

Moving spontaneously, Gareth pulled Angelica's motionless body from the chilling water. Knowing a flash of true fear, he scooped her up into his arms, intensely aware that her eyes were closed. She was unmoving. He was wading quickly back to the bank when Angelica began to sputter and cough in his arms.

She was still gasping for breath when he reached the bank and lay her down on the velvet moss. He reached for the clothes she had dropped on the ground. His hand closed on a large cloth, and he snatched at it to blot the water from her face and eyes before shaking it out to cover the full length of her shivering body.

His hands moving swiftly and surely, he rubbed her chilled flesh through the cloth in an attempt to stimulate her circulation in the same manner of treatment he had used once before. His heart was pounding wildly. Angelica's lips were chattering, but he suspected less from cold than from the shock of her narrow escape.

Unwilling to face his thoughts, Gareth ministered to her quaking frame, smoothing and stimulating her cold flesh in an effort to avoid the chill he feared Angelica would suffer in the aftermath of her terrifying experience. He was still working feverishly when he realized that Angelica's shuddering had come to a halt. Slowly raising his eyes, he saw Angelica's eyes trained on his face. Her regard was startlingly sober, considering.

Leaning closer, he smoothed a strand of hair from her cheek. Without conscious thought, he dipped his head to follow the gentle gesture with a quick brush of his lips. His voice was hoarse with the myriad emotions brought to life within him in those few moments in the pool.

"Angelica, I thought . . . I saw you go under the water and when you didn't come up . . . I couldn't find you at first. Then when I did see you . . . God, I thought . . ."

Unable to finish his statement, Gareth abruptly slid his arms under and around her, scooping her tight against him as he closed his eyes against the thoughts he could not speak. His heart pounding against her breast, he clutched her breathlessly close.

Angelica's voice was soft in his ear.

"I . . . I was all right, you know. I was safe under the water. I would have been fine . . ."

Drawing away, not comprehending her words, Gareth frowned. Her expression was so calm.

"What do you mean, Angelica? You weren't breathin' . . . Even when I pulled you up, you had trouble gettin' your breath . . ."

"I was all right. You shouldn't have worried. I'm sorry I frightened you."

Not quite certain what to make of her comments, Gareth shook his head, his eyes moving over her face. He was close, so very close to her. At this distance she was even more flawlessly beautiful. Her hair was clinging wetly to her scalp, accenting the perfect oval shape of her face. Her narrow brows were darkened with moisture, her lashes curled tightly, supporting the last remaining drops of water. Gently, he smoothed the reluctant drops from their lush haven, conscious of the tingle that moved up his arm as her lashes brushed his palm. He lowered his head and kissed one transparent lid, and then the other. He trailed his lips to the gently beating pulse in her temple and moved to trace the curve of her cheek and chin. He pressed light, fleeting kisses on its firm tilt, sliding his mouth up to the invisible spot where an errant dimple winked in and out as she spoke.

Her lips were smooth and still. He hungered for them, wanted them more than he could remember ever wanting anything in his life. He swallowed tightly. A few minutes ago she had been close to drowning, despite her protestations to the contrary. He could not take advantage of her weakness to press himself on her . . .

Just a taste . . . just a taste of her mouth would sate him. Cupping her face gently in his hands, Gareth ran his tongue lightly across the pink surface of her lower lip, following its contour lovingly. Her lips moved under his, separating to allow a peep of white teeth beneath. His heart pounding, he traced their perfection, knowing a driving hunger as her lips separated further. Spurred by a sharp, spontaneous need, he deepened his kiss, moving to taste the moist, inner hollows of her mouth, finding and caressing the sweet warmth of her tongue. His senses reacted violently as Angelica moved sensuously under his touch.

Just a taste. But a taste was not enough . . . His eyes moving to catch and hold hers, Gareth saw her glance was clear, unclouded by the passion which was slowly setting him afire. Her voice was a soft whisper.

"Do you still want me, Señor Dawson?"

Gareth shook his head in protest of her formality.

"My name is Gareth, Angelica. Gareth. I want to hear you say it . . ."

129

Hesitating only a moment, Angelica whispered more softly still, "Do you still want me, Gareth?"

Her soft pronunciation of his name reacting erotically on his senses, Gareth gave a small nod. "Oh, yes, I still want you, Angelica."

"Did you mean what you said . . . that you would pay any price I ask?"

Her question was unexpected. Stunned, Gareth was momentarily unable to respond. Somehow he had allowed himself to forget . . .

Fool . . . he was a fool! He had played his part well since the first moment of his contact with her, and the moment of blind intoxication which had just passed had been his crowning glory. A small, self-deprecating smile flicked across his lips. But there was no denying he wanted her still. More the fool, he.

"Yes, I meant what I said." Surprise was beginning to fade and anger was quickly filling the gap. "Name your price."

"Then I would have a gold piece, Gareth . . . a five-dollar gold piece."

Gareth remained silent, his mind revolting at the bargain he was being asked to strike. He had not wanted it to be this way between Angelica and him. He was not above paying for a woman. He had paid before and enjoyed the freedom the honest exchange had afforded him. But he had not thought, despite the heated words that hung between them, that it would come to this. He did not want to buy Angelica's response to him. He wanted . . .

Refusing to think any further, he responded gruffly, "A five-dollar gold piece. High payment for a woman who earns seven dollars a month."

Her face stiffening at his response, Angelica made a sudden attempt to move from his touch, but Gareth was too quick. His one hand moved to grip her shoulder as the other tangled in her hair, holding her face turned up to his. His mouth thinning into an angry line, he grated harshly, "I told you I would pay your price."

Angelica's expression changed subtly at the anger reflected in his dark eyes.

"Then we need talk no more." Her gaze steady, Angelica slowly slid her arms around his neck.

Unable to explain the small ache that began inside him even as his body reacted instantaneously to Angelica's show of compliance, Gareth slowly slid his hand from her hair to trail his fingers across her flawless cheek. But his anger was such that he was unable to resist another cruel taunt.

"You don't demand payment in advance, *puta*? It seems to me to be a dangerous practice . . ."

Uncertainty flashed momentarily in her silver eyes.

"I think you are a man of honor, Gareth."

"Unlike Esteban?" Gareth's angry response was spontaneous. "And what will you do when Esteban finds out you sold yourself to me?"

A telltale heat rose to Angelica's cheeks. She stiffened in anger at its betrayal of her emotions.

"What do you care, Gareth Dawson? You buy me now, this moment, and then you will be finished with me. My future is my own."

Her words inciting a new, silent fury, Gareth nodded stiffly, "Yes, I suppose you're right, *puta*. I'm wastin' words."

Drawing himself to his feet, Gareth kept his cold gaze unmoving from her face as he slowly unbuttoned his wet shirt.

He was angry with her. Angelica was uncertain why. Perhaps he resented the needs of his body, or perhaps he balked at the price she had demanded of him. The spark of anger inside her grew to a healthy flame, effectively negating Angelica's anxiety of a moment before. He had told her he would pay any price she asked, and she would not accept less than the price she had asked . . . not from him. She had determined in the few hours after Padre Manuel's visit that she would get the money needed for Carlos in any way that was open to her. Her body was her own. It was all she had of value to sell, and surely Carlos's life was worth such a small sacrifice.

And if Gareth Dawson was to be the first, he would pay

the price. Strangely, she had not considered anyone else when she had decided what she need do, despite Gareth Dawson's obvious contempt for her. She had refused to consider her reasoning, perhaps because she feared there was little reasoning involved. Instead there was the memory of his supremely gentle touch, low, whispered endearments, and the promise of more . . . so much more . . . read in his eyes . . . pledged by his unspeaking, tantalizing lips. She would not think now of what would come when this was over . . . when his desire for her had been sated. There were others who wanted her, but . . . Forcing away the sense of dread that all but overwhelmed her, Angelica refused to continue those thoughts. She would take one day at a time. . . .

Her calm demeanor belied by the quaking which had begun inside her, Angelica watched as Gareth Dawson slowly peeled the wet shirt from his body. She followed the line of his shoulders as they were revealed to her gaze, the broad chest heaving with deep, agitated breaths, and her trembling increased. Her gaze observed the muscular power of his arms. She remembered well their strength.

In a facile movement, Gareth slipped off his boots. His hands moved to the fastening on his trousers. She swallowed again. He was slipping them from his flat, male hips and down the long length of his legs. He leaned over to retrieve the sodden heap at his feet and twisted to toss the clothes over a low-hanging branch. He turned his back toward her, the naked length of him broad and intimidating. Angelica's eyes followed the ever-dwindling line of black hair down his chest, past his flat waist. She suppressed the gasp that rose to her throat as Gareth's full arousal was revealed to her for the first time.

Her teeth tightly clenched against their chattering, Angelica kept her gaze steady as Gareth dropped to the ground beside her and turned his full, naked length toward her. His hand moved to the cloth that covered her and another shudder shook her frame. Unable to bear the shattering contact of his eyes a moment longer, she dropped them closed, only to hear Gareth's low, whispered command.

"Open your eyes, Angelica."

Pride coming to her defense, Angelica followed his instruction, her breath catching at the sudden heat in Gareth Dawson's gaze. His hand moved to push aside the light coverlet that shielded her body from his eyes, and her heart began a wild palpitation. His gaze moved slowly to encompass her nakedness and returned to peruse her face intently. His eyes locked with hers, holding her motionless as he lowered his head to brush her lips with his.

"I want you to look at me, Angelica . . . to memorize my face as I take you. I want there to be no confusion who is making love to you. And I will make love to you, my beautiful little *puta*. This will be no fast affair. I've waited too long for this moment."

Gareth's palm was stroking her cheek, sending little tremors of anticipation down her spine, and Angelica fought to control the wild racing of her heart. He trailed his fingertips along her cheekbone, his expression momentarily bemused.

"Your skin is like velvet. . . ."

He lowered his head to follow with his mouth the course his fingertips had trailed only moments before. The touch of his lips was gentle, light . . . butterfly's wings brushing against her skin. He moved his mouth to her ear and traced the delicate outline with his tongue. A tension grew inside her and her shuddering deepened. She clenched her eyes briefly closed against the memory of Esteban's similar caress. Gareth pulled her closer, his hand tightening unexpectedly in her hair until she winced with pain.

He had hurt her. Gareth frowned, startled at his own unexpected reaction to the picture which had suddenly invaded his mind. Esteban . . . his mouth pressed against Angelica's ear in a sensual caress, his eyes hot and gloating. But Angelica had not submitted to Esteban's demands willingly, he was sure of that. Instead, she had offered herself to him. She was compliant and unmoving in his arms. He could see the throbbing of the pulse in her throat, echoing the rapid beat of his own heart. Regret filled him at the pain he had unintentionally inflicted.

"*Lo siento*, Angelica. I didn't mean to hurt you."

He looked to her eyes only to be startled at the brightness of restrained tears. He had frightened her. No, he didn't want it to be that way. He moved to brush her lids with his kiss, a tremor shaking him at the stroke of her lashes against his lips. He kissed them again. Her eyes were beautiful. They were great, glaring reflections of her quick mind. He had seen anger, frustration, exhaustion, discomfort, resentment, tenderness, pride, and occasional fear reflected there, but he had never seen joy. He yearned to put joy in their shimmering depths.

Stiff with a sudden, inexplicable fear, Angelica blinked away the sting of tears. Gareth was trailing his mouth to her lips. He fitted his mouth slowly over hers, his touch gentle and coaxing, but she was unable to respond. Her emotions were frozen. She could no longer control her trembling, and Gareth frowned. His mouth moved to hers once again, brushing her lips lightly, circling them with fleeting kisses, his gentleness gradually chipping away at the fear which threatened to consume her. His hand moved down her side to stroke her. His touch was warm, compassionate, sensuously acute. He nipped tenderly at the softness of her mouth.

A slow warmth was beginning to permeate Angelica's senses. The knowing stroke of Gareth's hands was soothing, gradually freeing her from the unanticipated talons of fear which had held her helpless. His touch was lifting her on light, delicate wings, as his hands moved to her breasts, cupping them gently, massaging their fullness. His mouth was worshipping the skin of her cheek, the bridge of her nose, trailing to the corner of her mouth to linger tantalizingly. With a small, subtle movement, Angelica sought to capture the healing touch of his lips, only to have them escape her with each attempt.

A small core of warmth was beginning to expand inside her as Angelica strained to catch Gareth's caressing mouth, to know its sweet solace. A strange, frustrated need mounted as it continued to elude her. The core of warmth grew to a burning ache, an ache she longed to assuage with the renewing gentleness of Gareth's mouth.

A soft, frustrated moan escaped her, and Angelica lifted her arms around Gareth's neck. Her hands slid into the dark thickness of his hair, clasping his head tightly to draw his mouth down full upon hers. A sweet elation soared to life inside her at the moment of their touch.

Gareth's lips moved deeply, hungrily against hers and Angelica moved to accommodate his seeking kiss. With loving care he stroked the moist hollows of her mouth, fondling, tasting, drawing deeply from its confines. She was floating, drifting in a hazy world of careening colors and heady sensation when he drew his mouth unexpectedly from hers. A low protest escaped her lips, and Gareth smiled, extending her anticipation as he gradually lowered his mouth again to hers. He traced her lightly parted lips with his tongue, restraining her gently as she sought to deepen the contact.

A slow hunger building inside her, Angelica sought to sweeten the caress, her tongue moving tentatively against the fullness of the mouth that so tantalized her. The responsive shudder that shook Gareth's strong frame flushed her with a startling elation. Moving her hands in the sensuous weight of his hair, she boldly stroked his firm lips with her tongue. His low gasp sent a new shudder over her frame, and she entered his mouth freely in a seeking thrust. Gareth accepted her exploring quest, stroking the warmth of her tongue with a light, sucking pressure she had no wish to evade.

Appearing unable to bear her sensual torment a moment longer, Gareth closed his mouth tightly over hers, his kiss sinking deeply, hungrily into hers, seeking, drawing, ravaging her with unconcealed hunger.

Angelica was gasping from his tender onslaught when Gareth tore his lips away, his mouth moving in a steadily descending path down the white column of her throat. Worshipping the delicate flesh, he pressed hot, consuming kisses against the deep hollows at the base of her neck, the curve of her shoulders. His eyes stopped at the small, rounded bruise that marred the white surface of her skin, the mark of Esteban's savage attack. Covering the mark with his mouth, he bathed it with tender, cleansing kisses.

But he was not satisfied long with such limited game. Raising his head, Gareth dropped his gaze to Angelica's white, rounded breasts. The waiting buds were pink . . . virginal. . . .

Her gaze following the slow descent of his head as it moved to her breasts, Angelica gasped as his lips closed over the waiting crest, drawing it deeply into his mouth, fondling the tender bud with his tongue even as he drew deeply on her sweet flesh.

Her senses reacting violently to this new assault, Angelica strove to catch her breath, the wild pounding of her heart compounding the impossible task as Gareth moved his attentions from one aching breast to the other.

Angelica's low gasps seeming to feed the tumult that drove him, Gareth circled the delicate mounds with deep, drawing kisses and sharp, loving bites, succumbing to a driving need to again take the blushing crowns inside his mouth.

Her emotions aflame, her heart pounding wildly against her ribs, Angelica felt the deep tension in her groin begin to expand, overwhelming her to take control of her scattered thoughts. She was drifting out of herself, entering a sphere of sensation completely foreign to her experience, and a wild panic began to assail her. Suddenly she was pushing at Gareth's chest. Her voice was a breathless plea.

"No, please, I can stand no more."

Her eyes focusing on Gareth's passion-filled face, Angelica saw a small, tender smile move across his lips as he whispered in return, "But there is more, darlin' . . . so much more . . ."

Easily subduing her struggles, Gareth clipped her wrists together with one broad hand and drew them carefully over her head. He kissed the moist palms lingeringly, trailing his lips down the slender length of her arms in a wandering, aimlessly loving trail to the waiting breasts which had eluded him only moments before. He settled over the taut

136

crests in tender homage, his body throbbing as Angelica twisted and turned in an agony of ecstasy under his loving attack.

Beside herself in the whirl of unearthly sensation Gareth had induced so well, Angelica was not aware of the first moment that Gareth's sensuous touch began to stray. She felt only the wild surge of emotion as his hand slid across the flatness of her stomach to tangle in the damp curls beneath. Covering her mouth with his, Gareth circled the gleaming mound with his touch.

Slowly drawing back, Gareth watched with a sense of wonder the play of emotions on Angelica's beautiful face, the flutter of heavy lids as he stroked the warm delta; her gasping breaths as he circled it with his touch; the sensuous parting of her lips as he entered the moist slit; her low moan as he found the bud of her desire and stroked it to full, aching life.

She was trembling, shuddering, and he paused. His lips moved to cover hers deeply, fully, lovingly drawing from her mouth even as his hand sought to draw from her body the ultimate proof of the passion he effected within her.

But he was only too conscious of his own tenuous control. Tearing his mouth from hers, he brought her cautiously to the pinnacle of her need, holding her there as he whispered hoarsely against her lips, "This is what I promised you, darlin'. . . this and more . . . so much more. But you must give to me now, darlin' . . . now . . ."

The throbbing sound of Gareth's voice penetrated the ecstatic mist that surrounded her. The storm of beauty he had brought to life within her rose to a roaring crescendo, lifting her higher, higher, tossing her wild and free, as her body shuddered in wild, quaking release of the glorious, searing tribute he had so lovingly sought.

His eyes intent, Gareth watched the exquisite play of ecstasy on Angelica's beautiful face until her body was once again still. He swallowed tightly. An aching tenderness mingled with his passion. She was so small and delicate, but she had given warmly and freely to him and he needed, oh so desperately, to return her loving gift.

Her fluttering lids were closed and still as Gareth moved to cover Angelica fully with his length. He cupped her face with trembling hands, holding her mouth against his as he whispered, "Look at me, Angelica. Open your eyes and look at me. I want you to see my face when I become part of you, darlin'. I want you to welcome me, to draw me in . . ."

Angelica's eyes opened slowly. There was an indefinable flicker in their clear depths as the throbbing point of his need moved intimately against her. He paused briefly at the warm, moist haven he sought, his mind registering a growing stiffness in her body which he could not comprehend. But he was past the point of contained consideration. It was too late to do else but fill her, quickly, deeply as he had so eagerly sought.

In one swift thrust he was inside her, and Angelica gasped, closing her eyes at the suddenness of the pain his entry had evoked. There was a brief pause and she raised her lids to Gareth's startled gaze. But his hesitation was brief, his dark eyes glazing over with passion as he began a slow, rhythmic movement within her.

A new tension was building inside her, a new throbbing heat that sought to exceed the soaring emotions of only a moment before. Raised by the fervor of Gareth's loving onslaught, Angelica met and welcomed his rhythmic assaults, riding high in a plane of heightened consciousness, traveling in a world of kaleidoscoping colors that stole her breath. She was paused at the brink of a yawning precipice, her heart pounding in unknown expectation. Clinging to Gareth's strength as he moved in a final, searing thrust, deep and full within her, she plunged with him, falling, spiraling, lost in the whirling vortex of searing emotions that left her shaken, exhausted, unmoving in the circle of his arms.

Gareth lifted his head from the fragrant pillow of Angelica's hair; his gaze slid to her still face. Her eyes were closed, her lashes dark fans against her flushed cheeks. He frowned. Slipping from her body, he consumed her with a gaze that lingered on her parted lips, the warm, rose-tipped swells of her breasts, and came to rest on the dark valley between her thighs.

Evidence of her lost maidenhead stained her white skin and a tremor of shock shook him. Incredulous, Gareth glanced sharply to Angelica's face. His voice was brusque in low command.

"Angelica, look at me."

The heavy lids lifted slowly. He looked deep into the clear, almost transparent depths of her eyes.

"Why didn't you tell me? If I had known . . ."

The soft vulnerability of a few moments before slowly disappeared in the face of Gareth's accusing gaze. Angelica shook her head, a slow realization dawning upon her. He had paid for a *puta*, for expertise she did not possess, and instead he had gotten an inexperienced maiden. Gareth was obviously not pleased with the trick fate had played upon him. But she was as much a victim of its caprice as he and she was determined not to allow him his righteous anger.

In sharp contrast to her passion of a few minutes before, Angelica spoke in a voice void of feeling.

"It was of little consequence."

"Little consequence! But I . . ."

Her eyes cold gray ice, Angelica interrupted evenly. "I do not believe I disappointed you. As for the other matter, if it had not been you this day, it would have been someone else."

Gareth stiffened at the impact of Angelica's emotionless statement. His hands moved to grasp her arms in a cruel grip, holding her fast as she attempted to roll from him.

"Why did you choose me?"

Angelica hesitated. Anger had hardened the planes of Gareth's face, returning the ruthless expression she had first associated with his unyielding character. Unwilling to admit to the last ripples of warm emotion which still echoed inside her, she replied coldly, "Because you are a wealthy Texan. I knew you would have the gold piece I sought, and I believed you would keep your word."

His only reaction to her words a quick, almost indiscernible blink of his eyes, Gareth stared silently into her dispassionate face. Declining response, Gareth released her. Turning away, he drew himself silently to his feet. He stood looking down at her for a few long seconds before offering her his hand.

Angelica reached up to accept his aid. Pulling her to her feet, Gareth startled her by cupping the back of her neck with his hand in a swift movement and drawing her mouth to his. His kiss moved warmly against her lips and Angelica fought the heady reaction of his touch. But she was not far enough from the intimate experience of a few moments before to control the spontaneous parting of her lips. The result was a sweet plunder of her mouth that lit a new familiar flame inside her.

Unexpectedly jerking his mouth from hers, Gareth ignored her soft gasp as he whispered hoarsely against her lips, "It was worth the gold piece, Angelica. It was worth every penny."

Turning just as unexpectedly, Gareth slid his arm around her waist and urged her silently into the pool. He stopped abruptly when the water had reached to cover her breasts. Uncertain what to make of his behavior, Angelica raised her eyes to Gareth's emotionless face.

Gareth shook his head. "No, Angelica. No deeper."

Turning her toward him, Gareth pressed a light kiss on her lips. His eyes flickered with an emotion she could not identify as he whispered, "Yes, the services performed were more than worth the price."

His arm firm around her waist, Gareth moved his other hand to her thighs. He stroked the tender flesh gently beneath the water, rubbing it clean of the stain which had marked her. Becoming absorbed in his intimate ministrations, he broadened the circle of his stroking caress, his heart beginning an accelerated beat as he felt Angelica's tension slipping away under his soothing touch. His eyes moved over the sensuous droop of her lids, the slow acceleration of her breathing. His own breathing becoming labored, he moved his hand to the dark mound of her pleasure and caressed it gently. Angelica's protest was instinctive as his hand moved into the moist slit, but he silenced her with a slowly deepening kiss.

A victim of Gareth's continuing sensual assault, subservient to the need he brought to life within her, Angelica floated in a strange netherworld of his creation. She was floundering, drowning more effectively in the overwhelming feelings he awoke within her than she had been in the clear water only a short time before. She was lost to his searing touch, floating in a realm introduced so brilliantly to her untutored body. She was limp in arms that moved to support her, clasping her close. She was unaware of the extent of Gareth's involvement until the firm rise of his passion moved roughly against her.

Tearing his mouth from hers, Gareth looked down into her bemused expression.

"I can't get enough of you, darlin' . . ."

Sliding his hands down to cup her firm buttocks, Gareth moved lightly against her before he crouched in a quick, facile movement, to thrust deep and sure inside her. Pausing to savor the moment of complete possession, Gareth looked down into Angelica's eyes. The hard gray ice was now a warm silver velvet, beckoning to him, drawing him closer. Lost in their wonder, he held Angelica's eyes intently with his own as his slow, rhythmic assault began.

Mesmerized by the intensity of Gareth's gaze and the gradual wealth of emotions stirring to life inside her, Angelica moved instinctively to accommodate Gareth's gentle thrusts. Without her realization, her arms slid around his shoulders to support herself, relying on his strength as he moved with ever-increasing impetus. She was gasping, clinging, her eyes closed against the emotions assailing her when Gareth paused. His hoarse command snapped her eyes open to look into his passion-filled face.

"Angelica, look at me. Say my name, darlin'."

"Gareth . . ." Angelica's eyes held his. Her voice was a breathless whisper. "Gareth, what do you . . .?"

"Tell me you want me, Angelica."

"Gareth . . . please . . ."

"Tell me!"

Her heart was pounding, and Angelica gasped. She

could stand little more. "I want you, Gareth."

"Say it again."

"I want you, Gareth . . ."

Gareth's response was a deep, searing thrust, the groan that echoed low in his throat carrying Angelica with him in a brief, wild burst of rapture that left them clinging tightly together in the aftermath of the sweet abandon they had shared.

His passion spent, Gareth was abruptly aware of the sudden droop of Angelica's fragile frame. Scooping her up into his arms in a swift movement, Gareth turned to walk toward the bank. Laying her gently on the cloth she had abandoned only a short time before, he covered her gently. He left her briefly, only to return a few moments later to lie on his side beside her. He stared down into her face, his eyes following the fluttering movements of her lashes as he absentmindedly brushed a few silken strands of hair from her cheek. Sliding his hand beneath the light coverlet, he took her hand, pressed two coins into her palm, and wrapped her fingers around them.

Startled, at the contact of the cold metal against her skin, Angelica snapped her gaze to Gareth's. His eyes were twin midnight pools, their darkness unfathomable. Finally breaking his silence, Gareth whispered hoarsely, "Two gold coins, Angelica. Payment in full for services rendered."

A new coldness starting in the pit of her stomach, Angelica held Gareth's gaze. Her fingers tightened around the hard, cold coins until they ached.

Chapter IV

With visible impatience, Esteban made his way down the staircase of the Arricalde hacienda to the first floor. Impeccably dressed as was his custom, he adjusted his well-tailored waist-length jacket and the cuffs of his fine, lawn shirt. He smoothed his hand against his freshly combed hair and absentmindedly brushed the surface of his thin mustache.

It was early. The Arricalde guests had not yet arisen and he was relieved. He had long since tired of entertaining the tedious Dolores Valentin. She was a pleasant enough young woman who would doubtless make the perfect wife, content to remain at home and bear a man's children while her husband attended to the more rewarding and entertaining aspects of life. For that reason alone he had pacified his anxious mother by paying the accommodating Señorita Valentin courtly attention. He was well aware of the fact that he would not be able to escape the state of holy matrimony much longer.

He was already well past the age when he was expected to supply his parents with grandchildren and heirs. He suspected it was mainly that reason and the fact that his parents were suspicious of his long absences at the capital which had caused them to call him home. Were it up to him, he would have remained in the exciting atmosphere of the capital indefinitely, but his parents had seen fit to tighten the purse strings, putting severe stress on the style to which he had become accustomed to entertaining himself.

But if he was to be truthful, his return to the Real del Monte had provided more stimulation than he had expected. Angelica Rodrigo had only come to work at the hacienda a short month before his return. He remembered still his first sight of her. He had walked into the kitchen in search of the provocative little twit, Juanita. She was an ambitious young woman whom he remembered as anxious to please him and he had been of a mood to take advantage of that desire.

Angelica's back had been turned to him as she had worked at the table. He remembered being struck by the delicate line of her body, her graceful proportions, and the almost aristocratic carriage of her shoulders. A single plait had hung neatly down her back, contrary to the usual custom of allowing hair to fall wildly around the shoulders often uncombed. In a country where a servant's rebozo often hid more than her hair, he had been fascinated by the clean shimmer of the raven braid as a beam of sunlight had filtered through the window to rest on her bent head.

He remembered waiting with considerable anticipation as the old cook, Carmela, had addressed her, causing her to turn in his direction. And he also remembered only too vividly the casual manner in which she had turned, realizing he was there for the first time and slowly raised that magnificent face toward his. The full impact of his first contact with the true radiance of her startling silver eyes was with him still. Even now he remembered little of what happened after that, the manner in which he had attempted to engage her in conversation, and her properly subservient tone as her eyes had dismissed him so effectively.

Even the strict disadvantage of servant's status had not thwarted her success in escaping his attentions. And each time she had eluded him, he had wanted her more. In truth, he had wanted her desperately from the first moment she had responded to his questions in the soft, smooth tone that was hers alone. It had not taken him long to seek out her family history. Hernando, old lecher that he was, had been only too happy to supply the story of her sinful conception and of Angelica's proclivity to follow in her mother's less-than-admirable footsteps.

But if he had dreamed of the moment when he would touch her smooth flesh, feel it under him as he possessed her completely, and when he would see a tender plea in the great, shining discs of her eyes, he had only been allowed to dream. His anger returned at the memory of the Texan's interference with his plans for the beautiful little *puta*. Even last night on the darkness of the trail he had been fully aware that it had only been his blade which had kept the Texan from coming for him. And he had also been aware that Gareth Dawson's fear had not been for himself, but for the fact that his knife also threatened Angelica's smooth, white skin.

His mind far from the hallway into which he had turned, Esteban walked swiftly toward the door at the end. Hernando had delivered the message that his father wished to see him in the library. He felt another flash of annoyance. His memories of that room were not his most pleasant. It was the place where his father had most often called him to complain of his behavior, his spendthrift ways, the stories which had reached his ears of the wild life he led in the capital. He anticipated more of the same this morning, and he was in no mood to listen. Whatever his father said, he would do exactly as suited himself. His status as only heir of the family fortune and lands left him secure in the knowledge that no matter his conduct, all would be his.

He slowed his step as he approached the door of the stuffy room. He had never been able to understand the reason his father spent so much time there. He had always been oblivious to its questionable charm. Admittedly large, with well-polished floors covered only by occasional rugs, his father's sanctuary was dominated by a large, imposing

145

desk in its center. Well-used leather furniture lined the far wall. He cared little for the impressive array of books which filled a bookcase that stretched from ceiling to floor on the opposite wall. He had never felt the need to make use of their knowledge, preferring instead to learn through avid participation and to direct his efforts to those things which gave him the most pleasure. Women . . . horses . . . cock fighting . . . exciting war games . . . and games in which a far more intimate strategy was involved. Those were the things which sent the blood coursing hotly through his veins.

The room's one saving grace were the French doors which led out to the rear patio, affording a view of the landscape behind the house. Esteban was also aware that the view would afford him the opportunity of maintaining covert surveillance of the approach to the kitchen. He was impatient with his father's interference in the schedule he had set for himself that day. He had arisen early and had intended to be waiting when Angelica Rodrigo made her way toward the house. If he was not careful he would miss her arrival, and he was only too conscious of the difficulty he would encounter in attempting to set up a rendezvous with her later in that event.

And he needed to see her. He had spent a long uncomfortable evening after allowing Angelica to escape him the previous night, and he had slept poorly when he had finally bid the Arricalde guests a good night and retired to his room. He did not intend to allow his frustrated appetite for the haughty little *puta* to hinder his sleep any longer. He was pleased, so very pleased with his manipulation of the beauteous little bitch. He had preferred that she come to him willingly, but he had begun to look forward to the persuasion he would employ in order to bring her to heel.

She had no way to escape him now. She needed her position at the hacienda for her anemic, ill brother. He had seen the boy once, and the sight had sickened him. He had no patience for sickness or deformity, and as far as he was concerned, the sooner the boy was out of his misery, the better. But the boy was serving his purpose. He supposed he should be grateful. Perhaps he would send the boy a gift. His generosity would doubtless impress Angelica . . . perhaps even cause her to show her gratitude to him in a very tangible way . . .

Suddenly realizing the direction of his thoughts was having a very obvious result on his body, Esteban attempted to adjust his skin-hugging trousers to afford himself more comfort. Damn! He would make the little bitch pay for every moment of his discomfort . . . and pay well. He would take her with great pleasure and use her until his passions were so sated that the sight of her revolted him. A picture of Angelica's flawless countenance returned again to haunt him, and Esteban shook his head. Yes, he would do that, but even in the privacy of his own mind he could not make himself believe that he would quickly reach a point of complete satiation. No, he suspected that day would be long in coming.

Slowing his step as he approached the library door, Esteban glanced down to his smooth-fitting pants. He snorted his satisfaction. The evidence of his thoughts could no longer be read on his body. He was grateful for that, at least. But he would be more content tonight, when Angelica's smooth flesh lay pressed against his. Yes, she would begin payment for the chase she had run him, and she would pay well. And how he would enjoy that payment . . .

Making an attempt to conceal the impatience which pricked him, Esteban raised his hand and rapped sharply on the library door. Don Enrique's response was immediate. Obeying his bidding, Esteban reached for the handle, and opening the door, walked slowly into the room. His father was standing near the window, his erect slender form outlined against the brilliant sunshine streaming in behind him. Put to a disadvantage by the fact that his father's face was shadowed by the sun, making his expression unreadable, Esteban hesitated.

"Come in, my son. I am grateful that you have responded promptly to my summons." Walking toward his desk with measured steps, Enrique Arricalde reached for a missive which lay upon it. He held it out toward Esteban, his face reflecting an austere expression as he turned into the light.

His brow moving into a small frown as he accepted the letter, Esteban looked down to see a familiar seal. An official document . . .

Appearing to read his mind, Don Enrique nodded. "Yes, an official document. I admit to some apprehension when a courier arrived earlier this morning and relayed its importance. I called you immediately, Esteban."

Hardly hearing his father's words, Esteban stared at the envelope, his frown tightening. Not now . . . not now. His hand tightened unconsciously on the unwelcomed missive.

So intense was his anger at the ironic twist of fate he expected the document represented, that Esteban moved with a start as Don Enrique questioned quietly, "Aren't you going to open it, Esteban?"

Raising his head to his father's gaze, Esteban nodded, his hand moving to loosen the seal. Slowly he withdrew the letter and unfolded it, reading without obvious reaction.

"Well, Esteban? What does it say?"

Raising his eyes to his father's increasingly anxious face, Esteban gave a small shrug. "It is an appointment, *Padre*."

"An appointment?"

"Yes, an official appointment . . . to el presidente's service."

"El presidente's service?"

Beginning to become annoyed by his father's parroting of his words, Esteban nodded stiffly. "Yes. You asked me many times what occupied my time in the capital. Well, this is what occupied my time." Shaking the letter lightly, he continued in an arrogant voice. "I was fortunate to be able to spend considerable time in el presidente's company while in Mexico City. He is a brilliant man. His personality is such that he draws men to him. He has many great plans for Mexico. I was privy to many of those plans, and it was my great desire to aid him in accomplishing them."

His father was obviously stunned at his words. Experiencing great satisfaction at the flush of pride that colored Don Enrique's aristocratic face, Esteban struggled against the laugh which rose to his lips. His father was proud of his nobility, his interest in the affairs of his country. It was a joke! He had in his hand an appointment he had diligently sought for the sole purpose of having an excuse to remain in the capital. He had avoided returning to Real del Monte when he had received his father's many summonses. Life had always been boring in this small mining village, and the affairs of his father's mine even more tedious. He would have used any excuse to avoid them both.

On the other hand, life in the capital was never dull, especially in el presidente's company. El Presidente Santa Anna enjoyed the best of life. La Señora Santa Anna remained at Manga del Clavo, their country estate, as was her duty, leaving her charismatic husband the freedom he deserved. Antonio used it well, and Esteban had enjoyed the good life in his wake. Delicious food, marvelous drink, beautiful women flocking to him as he stood basking in the light of the acclaimed hero of the country, short days, and long, eventful nights . . . What more could a man ask?"

But the appointment as Antonio's aid had not come. Sorely disappointed, he had been forced to return to Real del Monte, condemned to a monotonous existence and a futile search for a reason to start his day. And then, on his first day home, he had seen Angelica Rodrigo.

A slow fury began to descend upon him. Why now? Why did this appointment have to come now? He was so close . . . so very close to possessing her. He wanted time, time to explore Angelica's body, indulge himself in its beauty. He wanted to hear her sighs of ecstasy. He wanted to hear her beg for him to take her. Why did this appointment have to come when he no longer had inclination or desire to follow its request? There had to be a way to avoid this call . . . there had to be . . .

His father walked slowly toward him even as Esteban's mind raced in silent rage. He extended his hand, smiling as Esteban accepted it with a stiff smile.

"Congratulations, my son. It seems . . . it seems I owe you an apology."

"An apology?"

"Yes, for thinking you spent your days and nights in the capital in frivolous pursuits. It gives me great pride to see that El Presidente thinks enough of you to appoint you to his staff."

Esteban smiled. "Your apology is accepted, *Padre*. How could you know of my interests when I sought to keep them from you? I did not wish to see you suffer a disappointment should this appointment not materialize." Suddenly realizing he need break to his father the news that he had no intention of leaving at this time, Esteban continued. "But since I am home, *Padre*, I see the need for me to reman here, to take some of the burden from your shoulders. I shall dispatch a letter immediately to Antonio and explain . . ."

"No, Esteban, you must not do that."

"*Padre . . .*" His brow knitting into a frown, Esteban observed his father's determination. The fool! He was nobly releasing his son for service to his country when his son wished only to service the beautiful *puta* in his own kitchen . . .

"When does el presidente want you to leave?"

Esteban's eyes darted back to the letter and he read it slowly to the end. "El presidente has returned victorious from Zacatecas. The country hails him its savior, but he is concerned with the audacity of the Anglo-Texans who flaunt the country's laws. He is contemplating a punitive sweep . . ."

"*Madre de Dios!*"

"This information I give you is confidential, *Padre . . .*"

"*Si*, I am aware of that, my son. You must go immediately to the capital. You must do your best to dissuade el presidente from such an action. I am well acquainted with the temperament of the Anglo-Texans. They are proud people . . ."

"As are we!"

"Esteban, they seek only to protect their liberty."

"Then let them obey the laws and the laws will protect them!"

"Esteban, you must understand, that is part of the

problem. They do not have adequate access to the courts. Gareth has explained this problem well to me. They are disturbed because they are bound by the law, but not privileged to its protection. The courts are too far away from them. They live in an untamed section of our country where they must bend the law for their own protection. They suffer unduly from its restrictions, have no protection in the courts from those who break it, and their messengers have all but been ignored in the capital."

"*Padre*, you listen too much to the traitorous words of Gareth Dawson." His hatred reflected in his eyes, Esteban hissed, "Were I in the position, I would have him taken into custody to share the fate of his compatriot, Stephen Austin!"

"Esteban, *por favor!*"

"*Por favor!* You defend the traitorous gringo! He seeks only his own gain! Were it up to him, Texas would no longer be a part of Mexico but a country of its own where he would aid in making the laws!'"

"Esteban, you are wrong. Gareth is a serious young man, interested in his family's land, that is true. He has dedicated the greater portion of his life to it, has worked by his father's side from dawn to dusk. He saw his mother's life sacrificed to its hardships and all possibilities for his father's happiness destroyed not long afterward by the Indians who feed upon it. There was no protection from the law through all those trials. They had no one but themselves and their strong will."

His anger mounting, Esteban raised his hand in a dismissing gesture.

"I do not wish to discuss Gareth Dawson any longer, *Padre*. It is obvious we shall never agree. He will be gone in a few days at any rate and he will no longer be of concern to us."

"But you will be in a position to influence el presidente on the Anglo-Texan cause."

"No, I will not."

"You will not?"

"No, because I do not intend to leave Real del Monte."

Don Enrique's eyes were beginning to show the first hint of suspicion.

"Is there some reason why you do not wish to leave . . . other than desiring to relieve me of the workload here?"

"No . . . of course not! Is that not reason enough for a responsible son to remain by his father's side?"

"No, it is not, Esteban . . . not when you are called to the service of your government."

Fighting to conceal his disgust with his father's sickening nobility, Esteban took a long, tight breath.

"When does el presidente ask you to report to him?"

Trapped by his own words, Esteban flicked another glance down to the letter in his hand.

"Immediately. He wishes to have me present when he conducts a series of affairs intended to consolidate support for his move against the undisciplined, upstart Anglo-Texans."

Don Enrique nodded his grey head. "Have Hernando bring up your cases. Senor y Senora Valentin are leaving before noon. I am certain Dolores will be delighted to have your company on the trip."

"No doubt."

Don Enrique frowned at his caustic comment. "Dolores Valentin is a very lovely young woman . . ."

". . . who would doubtless make me a very fine wife . . . if I were in the market for a wife, *Padre*."

"And you are not?"

"At present my only concern is to pack my bags and make ready to return to the capital. And at present that will have to be enough for you."

"Dolores Valentin will be returning to the capital with her parents . . ."

"*Si*, I am aware of that, *Padre*."

Unable to resist a smile at his son's rapidly deteriorating disposition, Don Enrique reached out to clap his hand on Esteban's broad shoulder.

"So, if it is not time for you to take the step which would please your mother and me, I will console myself that you go off in service of your country." Walking with him as his son began to move toward the door, Don Enrique turned as he drew it open. His eyes on his son's handsome face, relief apparent in his eyes, he said simply, "You make me very proud, Esteban. I go to tell your mother of your imminent departure while you instruct the servants as to your packing."

"*Si, Padre.*"

Within a few moments, Esteban was striding back down the hallway, wondering how the situation had so quickly slipped out of his hands. Entering into the large central hallway, Esteban called imperiously, "Hernando . . . Hernando!"

Waiting only until Hernando's face had appeared around the corner, he instructed, "You will bring my cases up to my room and pack all my clothing. I will be leaving Real del Monte in Señor Valentin's carriage."

Exhibiting marked surprise, Hernando nodded his head, his unkempt hair flapping ludicrously. "*Si,* Don Esteban."

"And be quick about it!"

Walking quickly toward the front entrance, Esteban jerked open the door and strode out of the house and into the yard. His destination was the wooded area to the side of the house and a circuitous route around the back of the house to the path which led to the kitchen. If he was lucky he would be able to catch Angelica before she was into the kitchen and out of his reach.

Frustrated beyond belief, Esteban clenched his hands at his sides as he lengthened his stride. Damn el presidente for his untimely interference! Damn his father for his rigidity! Damn Gareth Dawson for the bastard that he was, and damn Angelica and her beautiful silver eyes! Damn them all!

Angelica stepped down from the narrow wooded path which led from the forest pool to her yard. She walked silently, refusing to look back. She approached the rope strung between two trees used for the drying of the family laundry and lay the damp cloth she carried across it. Certain she could feel Gareth Dawson's keen eyes following her, she covered the distance between herself and the doorway to her home in a quick step. She had left him only a few moments before. He had insisted on accompanying her as far as her house, and it had only been due to her insistence that he had remained hidden instead of accompanying her to the door. No, she did not want her mother to see him. She was not up to answering her questions. Her emotions were too ragged, shame too vivid a specter for her to face her feelings now.

She walked into the house and hesitated momentarily, waiting for her eyes to adjust from the brilliance of the morning sunshine to the restricted light of the kitchen. Her eyes scanned the sparsely furnished room.

Papa was no longer sleeping in the chair before the fireplace, and Mama was working at the table. She looked up as Angelica entered, her eyes reflecting her fatigue.

"*Hola*, Angelica. I see you have bathed." Her eyes dropping at her mother's comment, Angelica walked toward her bedroom door as Margarita Rodrigo continued. "Your father has gone to work and Carlos is resting peacefully. *Querida* . . ."

Within a moment, Angelica felt her mother's light touch on her arm. Turning toward her, Angelica was faced with her mother's small, encouraging smile.

"Do not despair, Angelica. Padre Manuel . . . he is not always right. I am sure God will watch over Carlos . . . allow him to improve . . . get well . . ."

"We can afford to sit and wait no longer, Mama!" Her despair boiling to the surface in the face of her mother's acceptance of what she considered to be the working of fate, Angelica shook her head.

"Does it not say in Padre Manuel's book that, 'We are responsible for our own way in life'?"

"But that is only in matters of conscience, Angelica."

Her mother's innocent comment striking a tender nerve, Angelica shook her head with heated emphasis. "No, Padre Manuel's book tells us that He will help those of us who attempt to help ourselves."

The suspicious brightness in Margarita Rodrigo's eyes

grew considerably heavier as she raised her shoulders in a weary shrug.

"*Quien sabe*, Angelica? I cannot read . . ."

Suddenly regretful of her curt words, Angelica slid her arms around her mother's rounded shoulders and hugged her hard. Releasing her a moment later, she said quietly, "*Lo siento, Mama*. I am . . . upset."

"Yes, it has been an eventful morning, has it not?"

Angelica's eyes searched her mother's face for a meaning to her words other than the more obvious, and relieved to see only love and trust in her eyes, Angelica responded hoarsely, "Yes, it has." Anxious to change the subject, she continued. "I must go to the hacienda in a few minutes, but first I must look in on Carlos."

Turning away from her mother, Angelica walked the few steps to her room. Quietly opening the door, she slipped inside. Her eyes moved immediately to the small bed in the corner on which Carlos's thin body lay. He was breathing evenly in a restful sleep, and she approached him silently.

She came to stand beside the bed and looked down into Carlos's sleeping face. His eye was bruised from the fight of the day before and his cheek scratched, but what worried her more than the ugly bruises was his warm color. Leaning over, she placed her hand lightly against his forehead. Yes, he had a fever.

Angelica glanced to the table to see that Padre Manuel had left some of the medicine used to combat the sudden rises in temperature which were becoming more and more frequent. Yes, the medicine would help Carlos . . . temporarily.

Reaching down into the pocket of her skirt, Angelica closed her hand on the two coins in her pocket. She drew them out slowly and allowed them to rest in the palm of her hand. Two gold coins . . . two. Carlos's first step toward Mexico City. Now she would have to determine how she could arrange for his second.

Moving quickly to the flowering potted plant which rested on the windowsill, Angelica pushed the gold coins down into the moist dirt and covered them over carefully.

155

Soon the pot would be filled with gold and Carlos would be on his way to the doctor who would cure him. She would see to it that it was so . . .

Gareth entered the hacienda quietly, his eyes scanning the empty foyer. Sounds of activity came from the kitchen. As he had expected, the preparation of breakfast had most of the household engrossed, and this portion of the hacienda was all but empty. Moving quickly up the staircase, he walked toward his room. Within moments he was inside and closing the door behind him. He breathed a deep sigh of relief. He had had no desire to be seen in clothing that was still suspiciously damp. Questions would have been certain to arise, and he was of no mood to counter them. He had too many questions of his own hounding him.

His hands moving absentmindedly to his chest, Gareth unbuttoned his shirt and stripped it from his body. He unfastened his pants, and pulling them off, tossed them onto a nearby chair. They would be dry within a few hours. If only his problems could be as easily solved.

Walking to the wardrobe in his characteristically fluid step, he drew open the door and pulled out his change of clothing. He turned, his eye catching on his reflection in the dressing table-mirror. He hadn't realized he was frowning. It was hardly the expression he usually wore after an extremely rewarding session with a whore. His stomach jerked into a tight knot, and Gareth frowned more darkly. Furious with his own mental confusion, he walked to the bed and threw the clothes down.

Damn! Even now, after paying the beautiful little *puta* handsomely for her favors, he could not face the fact that she was a whore. Strong, unnamed feelings raged unchecked inside him, warring with common sense to counter with the fact that Angelica had been a virgin until this morning. He had seen the physical evidence of that fact. And surely a common *puta* could not arouse in him feelings of the scope he had experienced when making love to her. And he had made love to her. More than a meeting of bodies and the execution of a physical act he had performed

156

many times before, their coming together had stimulated a whole raft of feelings within him of which he had not believed himself capable.

He remembered well the deepening flush of passion on Angelica's beautiful face as he had worshipped her sweet flesh; the flash of panic in her eyes when culmination was near and the tenderness that had swelled to life inside him; the revealing trembling in her voice as she had whispered, "No, please, I can stand no more . . ."

But there had been more, so much more. The knot in his stomach tightened painfully and a strange yearning swelled inside him. It had been all he could do to let her go. He had wanted to give her joy, and instead, she had awakened a supreme joy inside him that had been almost shattering. He could not remember ever having been touched so intimately or so deeply before. Angelica had brought to life a mind and heart carefully schooled against such emotions . . .

That was it . . . the reason for his strange sense of disquiet . . . this feeling akin to desperation! She had made him vulnerable where he had never known vulnerability before, and he didn't like it. He didn't like the fact that he had taken her so completely, but was as yet unsated. There was a fury burning inside him in the knowledge that despite the emotion he knew she had experienced at his hands, she had accepted the gold he had offered without hesitation or embarrassment. He had felt shattered that while a full range of tender emotions still ran rampant inside him, she had been able to dismiss him so easily.

More than that, a slow rage had begun to build inside him until he was now all but overcome by the thought of someone else holding Angelica the way he had held her; someone else touching her, using her sweet body, the sweet body he did not wish to share . . .

A new, more reasonable voice entered his mind. He had gotten what he had wanted, hadn't he? He had offered Angelica payment for her services and she had accepted, for whatever reason she preferred to use. She had been true to her bargain . . . given all she had to offer with her limited experience. She had held nothing back. There was a

157

certainty deep inside him that her passion had not been feigned. God, no . . . He remembered still her soft, breathless voice saying his name, her spontaneous quaking as passion assumed control.

Now fully dressed, Gareth looked down to the smooth line of his trousers. The evidence of a resurgence of his need was pressed tight against its surface, and he gave a low snort. How very wrong he had been. He had been so certain that taking Angelica would purge him of her, while in truth, it had only succeeded in establishing his desire more firmly inside him.

He was now even more certain than before that he would not suffer Esteban Arricalde's lecherous hands on Angelica. He would establish his priority over Angelica with Esteban today, so there would be no further incident.

He would establish his priority over Angelica with her also. He doubted that would be difficult. She had been quite honest about what she wanted from him. A few more gold pieces and a week to exorcise this passion she aroused in him should be sufficient to free him of this debilitating emotion to which he had fallen prey.

Stepping back, fully dressed once again, Gareth surveyed himself in the dressing table-mirror. Reaching out, he took up the brush and gave his heavy brown hair a few quick strokes. His narrowed gaze made a quick pass over his fresh white shirt, left open at the neck, and dark trousers which now lay smoothly against his body, before coming to rest on his boots. They were still damp, but not obviously so. Reaching for the brocaded vest which lay on the bed, he slipped it on in deference to the air of formality which prevailed in the Arricalde household. He had no desire to wear a jacket. He was far too accustomed to the casual attire of the working Texan to have patience with its restrictions. This would have to do. He could spare no more time before he talked to Esteban. He had important matters to settle . . .

Steadfastly ignoring the quaking which had begun inside her the moment the Arricalde hacienda became visible

158

through the heavy foliage, Angelica raised her chin defiantly. She had taken an irreversible step that morning. Strange, she had hidden the two gold coins in the flowerpot in her room, but she could still feel the imprint of the hard, metallic shapes against her palm, almost as if they had branded the skin there.

But this day had been fraught with experiences which had branded her more surely than those small coins. Carlos . . . so close to death . . . the only thing that stood between him and its grim specter the sum needed to make the journey for treatment. Gareth Dawson . . . He had delivered her from the silent, unfeeling world into which she had sunk in the depths of that forested pool. Once she had been in his arms in that secluded glade, it had not been difficult to respond to his embrace, to allow his intimate touch. Her skin was still warm from the memory; the clean scent of his body was still fresh in her nostrils. She remembered the weight of his hair as it slid between her fingers, the startling beauty he brought to life inside her with his flesh pressed intimately against hers. His hoarsely whispered words had echoed again and again in her mind.

"I can't get enough of you, darlin' . . ."

Angelica shook her head in a futile attempt to shake his voice from her mind. It would have been so easy to dismiss Gareth Dawson if he was truly what he had appeared to be at first—hard, unsympathetic, and uncompromising. But Gareth Dawson was an enigma whom she was beginning to believe she would never truly understand. For all the strength and power of his tall, lean body, he was supremely gentle in his touch, and despite his often grim, angry words, she found herself responding to an unknown emotion, a tenderness which she sensed just below his surface appearance.

Whatever the case, she need now forget him entirely. He had had his satisfaction from her body and he had paid her price. Swallowing hard against the lump which formed in her throat, Angelica raised her chin a notch higher. She need decide where she would go from here, and then she would . . .

Her mind intent on her thoughts, Angelica did not see the man who awaited her on the trail until it was too late to avoid him.

"You are late this morning, little bitch."

Anger flushing her face a dark red at Esteban's greeting, Angelica attempted to elude him, only to have his arms snake out to take her captive. Infuriated by her attempt to avoid his touch, Esteban tightened his grip cruelly.

His mouth only inches from hers, he hissed with a note of pain in his own voice, "Bitch . . . *puta* . . . if you seek to drive me mad with wanting you, you are near to succeeding. And now . . . now that I am so close to taking you, I must leave . . ."

"Leave . . . ?"

"Yes, leave." Esteban maintained a strained, momentary silence as he allowed his eyes to move hotly over her face. "Face of an angel . . . soul of a *puta* . . ."

"I am not a . . ."

"Bitch, you are all I say and more!"

Shaking his head with an incredulous expression, Esteban suddenly dipped his head to cover her mouth in a hot, seeking kiss. Forcing his mouth painfully against hers, Esteban jerked her closer still, welding her body to his with the heat of his obvious arousal. His hands moved greedily over her body. He curved a broad palm against her buttocks, forcing her tight to his throbbing manhood as he twisted her gleaming plait in his hand, forcing her prolonged contact with his punishing mouth.

Her lips separating under the pain of his kiss, Angelica felt a swell of revulsion as Esteban's tongue raked the inner confines of her mouth, plunging deeply again and again, almost gagging her with his voracious thrusts. She was struggling in his arms, seeking to escape him when his hand wrapped tighter around her braid, eliciting a sharp gasp of pain.

Drawing his mouth from hers, his heart pounding against her breast, Esteban drew her head back even further, to run his lips down the side of her neck. His mouth closed on the white skin with deliberation, his teeth

160

sinking into the tender flesh until she cried out in pain. Her spontaneous outcry the signal he awaited, Esteban covered her mouth again hotly with his.

Suddenly coming to life in his arms, Angelica began to struggle wildly, her pounding heart echoing loudly in her ears, drowning out all sound except that of her own ragged breath. With an unexpected thrust, Esteban pushed her hard against the tree to her rear, reacting instantly as her head struck the hard surface, momentarily stunning her into immobility.

Grasping her wrists with one hand, he jerked her arms behind her, forcing her face up to his as he grated heatedly against her lips, "With every step, with every move you make, you only succeed in making me want you more. You are such a tempestuous little she-cat, are you not, my beautiful little *puta*? I have dreamed of the time when I would feel your softness under me, your body writhing in the throes of the passion I will raise inside you. Had I the time I would take you here, now . . ."

"I do not want . . ."

"It makes no difference what you want, *puta*! You must remember that above all! And remember this!" Tightening his grip until pain forced tears from the corners of her great silver eyes, Esteban laughed low in his throat. "I satisfy my father now by going to the capital, but I do not forget what lies unfinished between us. I will be back, and when I do, you will pay well for all the discomforts you have caused me. You will serve me, and serve me well, and I will take great pleasure in that service . . . Oh, yes, my beautiful *puta*, very great pleasure."

Releasing her with a sudden thrust, Esteban watched as Angelica sought to regain her breath, his eyes slipping to her heaving breasts before jerking back up to her white face.

"Now go!"

Taking a step toward her when she did not move, he grated, "Wipe the tears from your eyes and go to the kitchen where you belong. Go!"

Snapping into sudden movement even as her hands rose

161

to wipe the tears from her cheeks, Angelica began running toward the hacienda. Jerking to a stop as she was about to emerge into the yard, Angelica paused to regain her breath. Once again in control, she raised her chin and started forward, aware of the heat of the unseen gaze which burned into her back.

"What do you think, Carmela? Do you think Dona Teresa will convince Don Esteban to accept Señorita Valentin?"

Juanita's insistent whisper echoed again in the kitchen on a theme she had not been content to let lie for the duration of the morning. Taking advantage of the fact that only Carmela, Angelica, and she were presently working in the kitchen, Juanita had continued in endless speculation as to the reason for Don Esteban's leaving. Her disappointment was obvious, and disgusted with her stupidity, Angelica listened without comment.

When it was apparent Carmela did not intend to respond, Juanita continued unperturbed. "I cannot believe that Señorita Valentin could have been successful in winning Don Esteban's heart. After all, he is a man of the world, accustomed to the beautiful women of the capital, and Señorita Valentin is so pale and . . ."

"Juanita, I am not interested in your opinion of Señorita Valentin, and neither is anyone else in this kitchen. I have told you several times that I neither know nor care what caused Don Esteban's abrupt decision to return to the capital. I only know that he will be leaving soon in the Valentin carriage."

"More than likely he is leaving on a ploy conceived by Dona Teresa. She dotes on Señorita Valentin. She no doubt believes Señorita Valentin will breed well . . ."

"Juanita!"

"Well, it is true, is it not? Don Esteban would marry her for no other reason." Lifting her hand to brush back a few unruly strands of hair which had fallen forward as she worked the dough slated for the noon meal, Juanita shot a boastful glance toward Carmela's shocked face. "Don

162

Esteban prefers a woman with spirit. He told me so himself. He said that is what drew him to me . . ."

"Are you truly fool enough to believe Don Esteban is infatuated with you? First you set your sights on Señor Dawson, and when that proves fruitless, you set them even higher!" Carmela's voice was filled with derision, effectively wiping the smile from Juanita's face as she continued in a low voice. "You fool yourself with your vain daydreams."

"They are not daydreams! Don Esteban told me himself that he found me very appealing. Were it not for Señorita Valentin's presence, I know he would have sought me out when he returned from the capital."

"Fool, if he had sought you out it would not have been to flatter your vanity."

Her voice rising with irritation, Juanita shot angrily, "Oh, you are just jealous because you are an ugly old woman . . ."

"And you are a very stupid, vain *young* woman!"

"Carmela . . . Juanita . . . *qué pasa*?"

Dona Teresa's interruption was unexpected, snapping the heads of all present toward her unexpected appearance in the doorway of the kitchen. Her pleasant face was unusually disturbed.

"*Hay nada, señora. Lo siento*. Juanita and I were having a small disagreement, but it is over now, is it not true, Juanita?"

Carmela's question, directed into Juanita's nervous expression, was more in the form of a command, and elicited exactly the response she had sought as Juanita responded with a small jerk of her head.

"*Si*, Carmela. *Lo siento, señora*."

"Then let us have no more of this. Don Esteban is soon to leave on a summons from el presidente himself." Her lined face flushing with obvious pride, Dona Teresa continued. "And I do not intend to have his last memory of this house colored by shrewish bickering from the kitchen! Now, is the picnic lunch ready for the Valentin carriage?"

"Almost, señora." Nodding toward the huge basket over

163

which she still worked, Carmela added, "I have taken the chicken fresh from the fire so it will still be warm when it is eaten, and have only to put in fresh fruit and . . ."

"*Si, si.*" Not allowing Carmela the opportunity to finish her statement, Dona Teresa interrupted absentmindedly, "You must make haste, Carmela. The carriage is ready and everyone is gathered and waiting to leave. Bring it out as soon as you are finished."

"*Si, señora.*"

Waiting only until la señora had turned on her heel and left the room, Carmela directed another sharp glance into Juanita's flushed face.

Her tone was hushed. "Now do you still think you have captured the eye of Don Esteban? *Tonto!* He would use you once and throw you away when he was done! The ladies of the capital will entertain him far more lavishly than you could ever dream!"

Her eyes intent on Juanita's sullen face, Carmela was not aware of the impact of her words in another quarter. Her head lowered, her fingers working nimbly slicing the vegetables for the soup that simmered over the fire, Angelica closed her eyes against the pain of Carmela's statement. Giving silent thanks to a Divine Providence which had seen fit to deliver her from Don Esteban's lascivious intentions, Angelica remained silent.

Carefully wrapping the last of the fruit and tucking it in the basket, Carmela covered the basket with a clean cloth. A satisfied smile curved her lips.

"Now, it is finished. Dona Teresa will be proud of the meal her guests are to share on the trip back to Mexico City."

Turning from the hopeful gleam in Juanita's eye with disdain, Carmela glanced purposely toward Angelica.

"Angelica, you will take this basket to la señora. Quickly. Everyone is waiting to leave."

Ignoring the flash of discomfort she experienced at Carmela's command, Angelica walked quickly to the table and picked up the basket. Shooting Juanita a quick glance, she saw the anger that colored her sullen face and gave a small mental shrug. She would have preferred Juanita take the basket to the carriage. She had not seen Don Esteban since their encounter that morning, and she was not anxious to be present at his farewell. But Juanita's comments were too fresh in Carmela's mind to put her to the task of delivering the basket, and no one else was available.

Walking quickly through the rear exit of the kitchen, Angelica rounded the hacienda, her eyes moving over the scene of imminent departure that met her eyes. The Valentin carriage, a large, black, luxurious conveyance, stood ready for departure with Esteban's stallion tied to the rear. Angelica recognized Esteban's luggage amongst the Valentin cases, and noted that he had ordered all his cases packed. He obviously intended a long stay. A team of four anxious horses was carefully controlled by Pedro, the Valentin coachman, and a quick glance into the carriage revealed that Señora and Señorita Valentin were already seated inside. Her eyes moved to the two men still conversing with Don Enrique and Dona Teresa. Grateful that Esteban had his back toward her as she approached, Angelica made her way toward the carriage, hoping to deposit the basket inside without being noticed. But Dona Teresa's soft, unanticipated comment precluded that possibility.

"Angelica, bring the basket over here, please. Don Esteban will take it. I am sure it is too heavy for the ladies to lift into the carriage."

Aware of the fact that Dona Teresa's comment had turned the eyes of all present toward her, Angelica gave a small obedient nod and walked toward Esteban. Raising her eyes to his, she held the basket out to him with a silence he obviously did not intend to allow.

"Ah, yes, Angelica. So you bring us our lunch for the journey. I hope your offerings are ample. I have a ravenous appetite."

His eyes imparting a significance to his words meant for her alone, Esteban eyed her flush with obvious satisfaction.

Closing his hand over hers as he reached out to take the basket, Esteban smiled at her discomfort, prolonging the contact as Dona Teresa responded, "Carmela assures me she has made a special effort to give you a pleasant repast. Is that not right, Angelica?"

"*Si, señora.*"

Releasing her hand at last, Esteban allowed the basket to swing to his side, his free hand closing on Angelica's shoulder as he said with hypocritical affection, "And I am sure you did your part in preparing this feast for us, did you not, Angelica?"

Uncomfortable in the attention he purposely drew to her, Angelica shook her head, anger sparking in the eyes she turned up to his hypocritical smile.

"I did little, señor."

Esteban's hand was tightening on her shoulder, causing her covert pain. Smiling as Angelica's lips thinned into a straight line while she sought to control her reaction to the strong fingers which bit into her flesh, Esteban nodded. "Modesty becomes you, Angelica."

Dona Teresa's smile benevolent, she nodded. "*Si*, Angelica has shown a true desire to please, Esteban. We are all very satisfied with her contribution to the household of late."

"Yes, and I am sure Angelica has much more to contribute, do you not, Angelica?"

His grip tightening to the point where she was almost gasping with pain, Angelica struggled to maintain an impassive facade.

"Will you not respond to Don Esteban, Angelica?" Dona Teresa's voice held a note of censure at her hesitation.

Starting at an unexpected voice from behind, Angelica snapped her head toward Gareth as he interrupted opportunely.

"Esteban, I'm afraid I lost track of the time and almost missed sayin' good-bye." Extending his hand, he forced Esteban to relinquish his grip on Angelica's shoulder. Conscious of Esteban's rapidly deteriorating smile, he continued in a casual tone which did not quite match the angry gleam in his eye. "It's unfortunate we didn't have the opportunity to finish our discussion the other night. I understand you're bein' called to the capital by President Santa Anna, but you can rest assured I'll devote much time and effort to the matter we discussed while you're gone. Yes, I expect to devote every spare moment I find to its resolution."

Esteban's eyes darted revealingly to Angelica, a flash of pure hatred sparking in their depths as he turned back to Gareth with a cautious tone. "Then I must continue to advise caution, Gareth. Your intentions will afford you much danger. I should not like to see you injured or worse . . ."

"I think there is little fear of that, Esteban . . ."

"Esteban, Gareth . . ." Don Enrique's voice interrupted the tense vocal exchange, "This is neither the time nor the place for a political conversation. Here, at this hacienda, we are friends, not adversaries. I beg you to keep that in mind."

"Of course, Don Enrique." Making an attempt to shake off the coldness which had begun to permeate his senses, Gareth turned immediately in the elder Don's direction. "My apologies."

"No apologies necessary, Gareth." Waiting briefly for a response from his son, Don Enrique frowned his annoyance at Esteban's silence. Extending his hand toward his son, he drew him closer in a few words of quiet farewell.

Gareth's eyes followed the soft exchange for a few seconds before moving to Angelica's pinched face. His eyes snapped to her shoulder, noting the marks of Estaban's hand on the white flesh. Fury suffusing him, he reached out to take Angelica's arm as she began to turn back toward the house. His eyes holding her startled glance, he stayed her proposed flight, moving to stand securely behind her as Esteban turned back in their direction.

Paling even further at the leap of fury in Esteban's eyes as they raked Gareth's possessive stance, Angelica watched as Esteban turned toward the carriage in a quick jerking step. Within moments he was seated stiffly inside.

Unable to move without creating a scene, Angelica stood fast on the spot, her anger flaring anew at Gareth's open, proprietorial display. She remained so until the last of the farewells had been spoken and the Valentin carriage began to move down the road. Carefully disengaging her arm from Gareth's grip, aware of the fact that Gareth and she were the focus of the Arricaldes' attention, she then moved quietly back toward the kitchen, a silent sense of foreboding dogging her every step of the way.

". . . and I feel it is my duty to warn you that my son's summons to the capital does not bode well for the immediate future of the Anglo-Texan cause."

His sober, aristocratic face marked with concern, Don Enrique faced Gareth across the ancient, scarred desk in his library. Motioning Gareth to follow behind him as soon as the Valentin carriage had turned the corner of the road, Don Enrique had drawn him toward the privacy of that room. He had begun without hesitation the moment the door had closed behind them.

His eyes narrowing assessingly, Gareth responded with caution. "What are you tryin' to tell me, Don Enrique? Is Santa Anna contemplatin' a military move against . . ."

"Gareth, please do not question me. I am not at liberty to tell you more, and in fact, I know of no decisive plans in that regard. I only know that my son has told me of Santa Anna's concern. There is no doubt you are aware of my son's feelings with regard to the political actions of the Anglo-Texans. I am afraid the relationship between you has suffered as a result. I can only tell you, my friend, that I would advise that you conclude your business in Real del Monte as quickly as possible and return home."

His brow knitting into a tight frown, Gareth stared silently at Don Enrique a few moments longer. There was no doubting the man's sincerity. It was exhibited clearly in the sober dark eyes that beseeched his understanding, as well as in the noble lift of his chin, which signified he would refuse him any more information than he felt he could ethically convey. Making the silent observance that if Santa Anna possessed the merest portion of Don Enrique's integrity, the upcoming revolution in Texas would be nonexistent, Gareth nodded his head.

"*Muchas gracias*, Don Enrique. You may rest assured I will consider your warnin' well, and make every effort to wind up my business as soon as possible."

"Gareth, my friend . . ." His expression suddenly contrite, Don Enrique shook his head. "I only wish that my mission in taking you in here could have been to ask you to remain longer, instead of advising you to leave . . ."

"Don Enrique, you demonstrate your friendship for my father and me more truly with your advice this mornin' than you could have in any other way. I appreciate both your concern and your honesty."

"*Hay nada*, Gareth. I wish it was in my power to do more."

Accepting the hand Don Enrique extended, Gareth moved silently toward the doorway, and within a few minutes he was moving rapidly up the staircase to his room.

Angelica paused with her hand on the knob of the morning-room door. Having received a summons from Dona Teresa a few moments before, she had made her way from the kitchen with increasing trepidation. Damn that Gareth Dawson! He was aware of her shaky situation in this household. Had he purposely striven to put her in the position she now faced? What possible purpose could there have been for forcing her to remain beside him until the Valentin carriage had driven out of sight? Dona Teresa had already been annoyed by her failure to answer her beloved son's question, and Gareth's interest in her had been the final blow. She did not dare to think of the result of this next interview.

Striving to control her trembling, Angelica raised her hand and knocked on the door. Dona Teresa's response was immediate. Obeying the softly spoken command to enter, Angelica opened the door and walked in, closing it behind her. Her eyes touching on Dona Teresa's unsmiling countenance, Angelica took a deep breath in expectation of the words which were forthcoming.

"Yes, Angelica, you do well to look apprehensive." Her

169

thin brows tightening in an uncharacteristic frown, Dona Teresa continued quietly. "I see I need not tell you that I am extremely disturbed by this morning's occurrence."

"Dona Teresa, there was no one else in the kitchen to bring the basket to the carriage . . ."

"Had you only brought the basket to the carriage as you were instructed, there would have been no problem, Angelica."

"But . . ."

"Please allow me to continue." Dona Teresa took a short breath, her small nose twitching in annoyance. "It appears you value very little the fact that my son interceded for you, out of his good heart, with the hope that you would prove yourself worthy of an opportunity to redeem yourself. Your lack of appreciation was evident in your sullen silence to my son's spoken concern."

"Had I the opportunity to respond, I would have assured Don Esteban of my loyalty . . ."

"Yes, of course. But your loyalty is not in question here. It is your moral conduct and the reflection it bears on this household which is under dispute."

"Dona Teresa, I . . ."

"You will please hold your silence until I have finished speaking, Angelica."

"*Si, señora.*"

"I am not blind, Angelica, and I am not so old that I did not recognize the manner in which Senor Dawson put his hand on you. I do not appreciate untruths, and both you and he assured me that you were completely innocent of wrongdoing on the evening you returned from the mines."

"That was the truth, señora."

Her eyes widening at Angelica's interjection, Dona Teresa made a small, strangled sound in her throat. "You still maintain your innocence on that night . . . that Señor Dawson did not . . ."

Thankful that Dona Teresa had phrased her question in a manner that enabled her to answer affirmatively, Angelica nodded. "*Si, señora.* It was the truth." Taking the risk of her next words, Angelica added, "Don Esteban believed me . . ."

"*Si*, and how did you thank him? Neither was I blind this morning to the fact that my son was angry almost to the point of losing control with Señor Dawson's obvious familiarity with you. There could be no other explanation for his reaction than the fact that he, too, felt you had betrayed his confidence in you."

Her gaze holding the older woman's eyes intently, Angelica barely contained her amazement. Dona Teresa was indeed blind when it came to her son. But more accurately, she chose to be blind to those aspects of her son's character of which she could not approve.

Responding in the only manner open to her, Angelica replied in a subdued tone, "I truly regret your disappointment, Dona Teresa, and I . . ."

The sudden opening of the door interrupted Angelica's statement, and turned her toward Don Enrique's abrupt entrance.

Immediately realizing he had stumbled upon a sober exchange, Don Enrique hesitated. "*Qué pasa*, Teresa?"

"I was speaking to Angelica of a very important matter . . . her less than becoming conduct this morning."

"Her conduct?"

"Yes, with Señor Dawson."

Don Enrique frowned. "Your problem is about to be solved, Teresa. Gareth Dawson will soon be leaving Real del Monte."

Shock that was almost pain brought Angelica rigidly erect. Gareth was leaving soon? Angelica raised her chin and blinked away the wet heat that had begun to gather beneath her eyelids. Gareth's whispered endearments echoed in her ears, and Angelica raised her chin a notch higher. She had known . . . had expected just the eventuality which had come to pass. His lust sated, Gareth was moving on to more important matters than his temporary passion for her. She had known . . . so why this supreme sense of loss?

Her expression darker than before, Dona Teresa inquired solemnly, "Why is Gareth leaving?"

"The situation in Texas grows more threatening by the day, *querida*. He can afford to waste no more time here. He will probably go to the mines tomorrow to speak with Brock Macfadden. If Senor Macfadden has completed the work Gareth requested, I have no doubt Gareth will leave immediately."

Taking a few moments to digest her husband's words, Dona Teresa nodded her head. Finally turning back to Angelica's direction, she stated adamantly, "Gareth's leaving does not negate the fact that Angelica has not kept her word. Esteban was good enough to intercede for her and she betrayed his trust . . ."

"Teresa, you excite yourself unnecessarily."

"Unnecessarily! Did you not see Esteban's expression this morning as he walked to the carriage? He was livid!"

"*Si*," Appearing suddenly weary, Don Enrique shifted his gaze to Angelica, his eyes moving over her pale face in unspoken understanding. "I saw his face, *querida*. He was upset, but perhaps not for the reason you believe."

"You must be more specific, Enrique. I do not quite understand your statement." Dona Teresa's uncharacteristic challenge of Don Enrique's statement was delivered with a stiff set to her softly rounded shoulders.

His expression briefly flashing a clear perception of his son's character, Don Enrique smiled into Angelica's stiff face. Turning back to his wife's defensive posture, he offered quietly, "I believe Gareth and Esteban had a falling-out. Esteban is not one to easily forgive. You know that, *querida*."

Grudgingly accepting her husband's declaration of that small flaw in Esteban's makeup, Dona Teresa nodded her head. "*Si*, that is true. It would account for Esteban's anger, but that does not change the manner in which . . ."

"Teresa, this discussion is to little avail. Gareth will soon be gone, and the source of your anxieties for Angelica go with him. I suggest you ignore this morning's irritation and chalk it up to our unhappiness at Esteban's departure. Should you find yourself similarly disquieted by Angelica's actions in the future, you may take action at that time."

Hesitating only briefly, Don Enrique walked the few steps to his wife's side and raised his hand to rest it lightly on her shoulder. "Would that not be a better arrangement than to act now while we are upset over Esteban's unexpected departure?"

Dona Teresa's small brown eyes suddenly filling with tears, she nodded. Holding rigidly to her control, she turned back toward Angelica.

"Angelica, perhaps Don Enrique is right. In any case, I should not like to feel my judgment has been affected by my temporary sense of loss. Once again one of the men in our household has come to your defense. I hope you will show your gratitude by proving yourself worthy."

"I will try, Dona Teresa."

"The security of your position will depend on your efforts. That will be all, Angelica."

Turning away at Dona Teresa's dismissal, Angelica walked unsteadily toward the door and pulled it open. Within a moment she was walking back down the hallway toward the kitchen, her knees quaking. Once more she had received a reprieve. Don Enrique's appraisal of his son was undoubtedly more realistic than his wife's, and his innate honesty had not allowed her to be dismissed as a result of his son's frustrated lust. But instead of relief, Angelica was staggered by an overwhelming sense of loss, the cause for which she adamantly refused to name.

Hastening her pace as she sought to escape her own thoughts, Angelica returned to the kitchen. Her eyes averted from the openly inquisitive stares which met her appearance in the doorway, Angelica walked to the table and resumed her work.

His hands moving through his saddlebags in a short, cursory check, Gareth mentally checked off his necessities in the event of an overnight stay at the mines. He shot another look around his room, his eyes coming to rest on the clothes that lay on the chair, still damp from this morning's interlude at the forest pool. His heart reacting predictably to the flash of memory, Gareth jerked his gaze back to his saddlebags. He need only get overnight supplies from the kitchen . . . some cheese and bread in the event he was delayed. It was not necessary to revert to the stringy beef jerky that had been the staple in his diet on the long trip from his homestead. No, he would be depending on that unappealing fare soon enough.

Don Enrique's words had forced him to a quick decision. He had decided he would leave for the mines immediately after lunch. He would then arrive there in early afternoon. In the event Brock Macfadden had completed his assessment of his father's plans for their Texas land, he would have plenty of time to discuss the work before nightfall. If not, he would stay overnight until the estimate had been completed.

It was obvious that he could not afford to extend his visit. He was absolutely certain Don Enrique would not have called him to that unexpected conference were he not certain something was in the wind. And he had no desire to be caught in this country when he was needed at home.

Yes, all was ready for his imminent departure for the mines. If he were to be honest, it would perhaps be wiser to leave right now, which would allow him even more time for discussion of the plans, but somehow . . .

A flash of self-disgust moving across his mind, Gareth slapped his saddlebags back down on the bed and ran an impatient hand through his hair. Damn! The true reason for his hesitation was obvious enough. He just preferred to avoid facing it. He didn't want to leave right now . . . not before he had had an opportunity to talk to Angelica. She had been angry with him this morning. It had been in her eyes when he had claimed her so openly in front of Esteban's assessing gaze. And he had no doubt that if Esteban had been free to follow his inclinations at that moment, he would easily have used that little knife he carried in his boot.

The memory of the mark of Esteban's hand, red against Angelica's flesh, sent a new wave of fury surging through him. Yes, and if he had been free to follow his own inclinations at that time, Gareth knew he would have beat the arrogant Esteban Arricalde to within an inch of his life. His own actions had been unwise, admittedly so, but he had been compelled to establish his priority over Angelica so that Esteban would no longer even dream of . . .

But what was he thinking? He would be gone from this place within two days' time at the most, and Angelica would stay. When Esteban Arricalde returned, she would be here, waiting for him to take up where he had left off. He would be hundreds of miles away while Esteban indulged himself in Angelica's sweet flesh. What was it Angelica had said?

"It was of little consequence. If it had not been you, it would have been someone else . . ."

But he didn't want it to be someone else, damn it! He didn't want anyone else getting close enough to see the startling gold and green specs flare to life in Angelica's great eyes. He didn't want her to whisper anyone else's name in the throes of ecstasy. He didn't want anyone to touch her.

No, he didn't want to leave yet. He needed time to exorcise his passion for the little *puta*. At this point it mattered little that she had sold herself to him for the price of a gold coin. He gave a small laugh. At least she had the good sense to set her price high. Or perhaps that price had been only for him—the "rich Texan." He laughed again. No description could be more inaccurate. Were Angelica more worldly, she would have realized that all Texans were land rich and working-capital poor. Perhaps it was best he was leaving after all. He had few gold pieces left to spare.

But no matter his reasoning as he mind warred with a driving need inside him, he knew he was hesitating to leave in the hope of having an opportunity to see and speak to Angelica before he left for the mines. But he had made a silent determination that he would not allow his passion for a beautiful *puta* to make him forget his reason for coming to this damned spot. He would not.

Stopping to brush a tear from her cheek, Angelica threw the last crumbs from her basket into the fenced enclosure.

175

She watched the scrambling chickens absentmindedly. The large coops which supplied the Arricalde household with a daily supply of fresh eggs and poultry were a cautious distance from the hacienda. Realizing Carmela had purposely sent her out of the kitchen on a chore that normally fell to Hernando so she might have a few moments to herself, Angelica walked to the shelter of a large tree and leaned thoughtfully against its trunk.

Carmela had generously granted her permission to return home for a brief period while lunch was being served so she might check on Carlos's state of health. But the short visit had allowed her little relief from the worry that had nagged her the morning long. Padre Manuel had visited Carlos again just before noon, but he had been less than encouraging in his comments. Time was drawing very short for Carlos. Padre Manuel was convinced Carlos would not be able to survive another attack in his present condition.

Two gold coins . . . Two gold coins and an ache deep inside were all she had to show for her grand plan to save him. She dared not think of the glow in the Texan's dark eyes when he had made love to her, his impassioned whispers. She dared not consider for a moment her desire to have the soft consolation of Gareth's strength hold her safe from reality. She had made the mistake of coming to depend on that strength for a few short hours, only to have Don Enrique's statement snap her back to the reality.

Gareth Dawson was leaving. She could not afford to indulge the memory of the warmth which permeated her veins when his eyes touched hers, or the memory of the singing emotions he had awakened inside her. Somehow it had seemed so right, when she had lain in Gareth's arms and abandoned herself to his lovemaking. There had been no thought in her mind of the promised gold coin, only the sweet promise of his touch. But the soft glow she had witnessed in his eyes was temporary, forgotten the moment his lust was spent. He would soon be gone, and her anxieties for Carlos were no less than before.

She was confused. Unfamiliar emotions were assaulting her from so many directions at once that she was truly uncertain what she felt. The only emotion she recognized without doubt was fear . . . fear for Carlos. She knew only that she dared not lose her position at the hacienda. It was her only security in the turmoil which assailed her.

The sound of a soft, nearby whinny brought Angelica back sharply from her thoughts the moment before a horse and rider came into view over the rise of ground. There was no doubting the broad width of shoulders silhouetted against the afternoon sun, or the distinctively casual manner of sitting a horse that was thoroughly Texan.

Gareth Dawson . . . A startling panic touched her mind. She could not abandon herself to his touch again. She dared not. To allow Gareth to penetrate her defenses any further would be a mistake. For all his tenderness when he had held her in his arms, he had been completely honest as to the intent of his dealings with her. The outline of the gold coins still burned the palm of her hand. She was only too keenly aware that she had now truly earned the name of *puta* which she had borne for so long, no matter the reasons for the step she had taken.

Determined to avoid him, Angelica made an attempt to move past Gareth even as he drew his horse to a stop beside her and dismounted in a facile movement. But the Texan's strong hands reached out to grasp her arms and turn her in his direction. He stood towering over her, holding her fast. A frown creased his brow as she raised an unsmiling face to his.

"What's wrong, Angelica?"

"Nothing is wrong. I am expected back in the kitchen. I have no time . . ."

His eyes narrowing, Gareth interrupted stiffly. "You had 'time' for me this mornin' by the pool." Pausing, he added on a hoarser note, "Or do you only 'have time' when there's promise of a gold coin involved?"

A new flush suffusing her cheeks, Angelica raised her chin defiantly. "Our business of this morning is over and done."

An almost imperceptible light flickered in his dark eyes before Gareth's expression hardened visibly. The small smile that curved his lips was devoid of warmth.

"You're a hard-hearted little bitch, aren't you, Angelica . . . despite your inexperience. You're well suited to your chosen profession." Reaching into his pocket, he pulled out a gold coin and held it up in front of her. The sun glinted on its bright surface as he looked deep into the gray ice of her eyes.

"Is this the key to makin' you greet me with a smile, *puta*? But I think it would be wise for me to bargain price now that you're no longer a virgin. Yes, I would say that I hold the upper hand, especially since my competition has left for Mexico City."

Hating him for his words, and refusing to allow him his victory, Angelica raised her brows with a well-controlled, mocking smile.

"And what makes you think there is no one else who would be willing to pay my price for the privileges you enjoyed this morning, Gareth Dawson?"

His reaction to her statement revealed only by the almost undetectable blink of slitted eyes, Gareth studied Angelica's face for a few moments in silence before responding.

"And if I'm unwillin' to share you with other . . . patrons?"

"Gareth Dawson, you do not seem to understand." Angelica held his gaze unflinchingly, her frigid tone calculated to leave no further room for discussion. "You have no choice in the matter."

A muscle in Gareth's cheek ticked warningly.

"Oh, but I do have a choice, Angelica. Didn't I prove that to you this mornin' . . . with Esteban?"

"You proved nothing but that your rivalry with Don Esteban is stronger than your good sense!"

Making an attempt to brush past him, Angelica was suddenly jerked back to Gareth's openly angry face.

"No, not yet, Angelica. I haven't finished . . ."

"But I have, Señor Dawson. I am no longer available for your hire."

A burning rage beginning to seethe within him, Gareth drawled with deceptive calm.

178

"So you tire easily of your patrons. That's unfortunate. Whose hire *are* you available for, since you've so obviously tired of me?"

"I have not yet decided, Señor Dawson. But I do not expect I will waste much time in deliberation."

"Oh, of course, the anxious young Scot . . . Peter Macfadden . . ." His rising anger becoming apparent, Gareth continued tightly. "Your proposition will be a shock to him, little *puta*. He thinks of you as an angel."

Gareth's verbal barbs were hitting their mark too closely for Angelica to continue their painful conversation. Taking a deep breath, she prepared a parting shot.

"If Peter Macfadden pays the price, Señor Dawson, I will be whatever he wants me to be."

The flash of fury that colored Gareth Dawson's face was unexpected, as was the suddenness of his action as he curved his arm unexpectedly around Angelica's waist and swung her up onto his saddle. Within seconds, he had mounted behind her and spurred his horse into movement.

Her momentary shock suddenly dissipating, Angelica began to struggle, only to feel Gareth's arms snap around her in an iron grip as he spurred his horse to a faster pace. Helpless against the unexpectedness of her situation, Angelica could do no more than attempt to keep her seat as they galloped over the rise and out onto the road.

The first drops of rain were unexpected. They had been on the road for over an hour as rapidly darkening clouds had gathered overhead. A swift reversal in the direction of the breeze blew damp mountain air into Angelica's face in a signal that portended poorly for the weather to come, but her anger held her oblivious to its threat. She was conscious only of the warm wall of Gareth's body supporting her back, and the strong arm still clamped around her waist. Firmly resisting her traitorous desire to lean back full into his warmth, Angelica took a firm hold on her control and broke the uneasy silence that reigned between them.

"This madness has gone far enough. I demand that you take me back, Señor Dawson."

A low response rumbled from the strong chest supporting her. "You're in no position to demand anythin', *puta*."

"I must return to the hacienda. I will be dismissed if I am missed!"

Gareth's response was unrelenting. "You should have thought of that before."

"Before? Before what? This madness of yours had nothing to do with anything I said or did!"

"Oh, but that's where you're wrong . . ."

Hunching his shoulders against the rain which was beginning to come down in a steady pattern, Gareth turned his mount unexpectedly off the road. Her eyes searching their new direction, Angelica recognized the trail and the small stone hut becoming visible between the trees. She turned in an attempt to assess the Texan's expression.

"Where . . . where are you taking me?"

His eyes unfathomable in the shadow of the wide brim of his hat, Gareth Dawson drawled with a hint of steel, "Haven't you guessed, darlin'? I'm deliverin' you to your new patron."

"But . . . but this isn't the road to the mine."

"We're goin' to make a brief stop to get out of the rain. You want to greet your new patron lookin' your best, don't you."

"I want. . . ."

But the remainder of Angelica's statement was lost as the rain began to pelt them in earnest and Gareth spurred his horse to a faster pace.

Moving more from instinct than conscious thought, Gareth gave silent thanks to the unknown hands which had stocked the small hut so carefully with firewood, and threw more wood on the fire. His eyes flicked to Angelica's stiff, unmoving figure where she sat on the blanket he had spread on the floor, looking into the bright flames. She had not spoken a word since he had lifted her from his horse and gruffly directed her inside. The cabin had been cold and damp. He had been very aware of her shivering and had hastened to light a fire. The room was now considerably warmer, but occasional shudders still shook her slender frame.

His eyes moved over her delicate profile etched against the flickering flames, and a raft of warm feelings stirred inside him, despite himself. Beautiful . . . she was so beautiful. He doubted she realized how truly lovely she was. Certainly no attempt was made to capitalize on the gleaming black silk of her hair. Instead, she seemed content to keep it tightly braided and out of her way. He longed to set its beauty free, to spread his hands in its shimmering warmth.

Her perfect features needed no artifice to enhance her appeal. There was no improvement to be made on the narrow winged brows and the thick brush of lashes that contrasted so remarkably with the clear silver depth of her eyes. She employed no coy fluttering of those delicate lids or enticing smiles from those pink, well-shaped lips. Instead, the question she had posed to him beside the pool had been direct . . . delivered without shame.

"Do you still want me, Señor Dawson?"

He had paid her price, and tasted her sweet body. He had been the first to claim her. His moment of realization of that truth was burned vividly into his mind.

The silent hour since they had entered the cabin had only caused his frustration to mount. She had dismissed him so easily, while he had been able to think of little else but the sense of wonder she had inspired within him beside the forest pool. The knot in his stomach tightening, Gareth turned his face from Angelica's sweet perfection and drew himself to his feet. He reached for his canteen and poured some water into the small pot on the table and hung it over the fire to boil.

He turned away from the fire in time to see the spontaneous shiver that again shook Angelica's frame. He was not sure what he had expected to accomplish by forcing her to come with him. The only thing of which he was certain was that he had been unable to tolerate her cool dismissal. He could understand his own actions no more than he could understand the sudden change which had come over Angelica after she had left the pool. He had searched his mind again and again for a clue to her behavior, but there was none.

And if he were to be completely truthful, he would have to admit that part of his anger was directed at himself and his own preoccupation with the beautiful little *puta* who had so coldly turned her back on him. He supposed there was a measure of ironic justice in the situation. This time it was he who was being dismissed without a second thought. Strange, he had not thought himself vulnerable to the type of pain which now tore at his insides. Indeed, he had not thought he could care enough.

His eyes moving over the gentle slope of her shoulders, Gareth remembered vividly the sensation of Angelica's smooth skin beneath his palms . . . the taste of those warm hollows at the base of her throat . . . the spontaneous shudder which had convulsed her body when his mouth had closed over the pink, virginal crests of her breasts. He remembered the texture of those delicate buds against his tongue. He remembered the scent of her skin as he had bathed them with deep, drawing kisses.

He remembered the ecstatic sensation of enveloping Angelica's sweet beauty with his eager warmth, the welcoming wetness that had greeted his surging penetration of her body. But most of all he remembered the overwhelming tenderness that had pervaded him as he had held her in his arms. The feeling had been new to his experience, evoking the vulnerability which plagued him. He swallowed tightly, closing his eyes against the bittersweet pain of his thoughts.

Abruptly determined to distract his mind from things which would allow him no peace, Gareth walked to the table and reached for his saddlebags. Removing a small container, he returned to the fire and shook a measure of tea leaves into the steaming pot.

Angelica barely reacted to his movement, startling him all the more as she said unexpectedly, "How long do you expect to keep me here, Señor Dawson?"

She had not even bothered to turn in his direction.

"So, we're back to formality again." His tension was

growing, but Gareth resisted its rigors. "Do you have an aversion to my given name, darlin'?"

"I simply wish to know when you will allow me to return home."

Anger returned in a heated flash, and Gareth grated under his breath, "When I'm good and ready."

Angelica's eyes snapped unexpectedly to him. "What do you hope to accomplish by keeping me prisoner here?"

Gareth's anger dissipated as quickly as it had come in the face of the uncertainty in Angelica's great silver eyes. Crouching beside her, he raised his hand to her cheek. "Is that what you believe my intentions are, Angelica . . . to keep you prisoner? No, darlin', nothin' could be farther from the truth. I had only intended to talk to you before I left for the mine. But somehow when I saw you, talkin' wasn't enough."

Taking a deep breath as he held Angelica's unblinking gaze with his own, Gareth dropped to his knees beside her. He cupped her face with his palms. His voice was husky with the myriad emotions assaulting him.

"Angelica, darlin', I'll only be here for another two days at most. I'd like to spend part of that time lovin' you." Gareth gave a small, self-derisive laugh and shook his head. His voice was a hoarse whisper. "As a matter of fact, darlin', makin' love to you has become more important to me than I ever expected it could."

But Angelica was shaking her head. Her low protest was almost inaudible. "No, no more. You will soon be leaving and I . . ."

"Yes, darlin', I'll be leavin' soon. We have so little time left and I have so much to give to you, Angelica. I want to make love to you, darlin'. . . ."

His hand slipped to the back of her head, cupping it to draw her closer. Angelica could feel his warm breath against her lips and a paralyzing magic began to permeate her veins. A small voice sounded its protest in the back of her mind, but it was fading . . . fading in the onslaught of the wild sensations assaulting her.

His mouth was on hers, dissolving her shield of anger,

leaving her helpless. Conscious thought was fading. She could think of nothing but the sensation of Gareth's warm, eager lips against her own, the familiar taste of his mouth his strong hands cradling her gently as he lowered her slowly, gently to the blanket stretched out beneath her.

He was bathing her face in gently seeking kisses, his hands moving in a sensuous touch that undermined her will to resist him. She was not conscious of the moment when the fabric of her *camisa* slipped to her waist, when his searing assault moved to the warm swells of her breasts. She was not aware that her hands had slipped to cup his head, clutching him close against her as he ravaged her tender flesh. He was drawing from her deeply, all but devouring her when his insatiable hunger could be restrained no longer.

His hands were working at the closure to her skirt. His lean fingers were slipping the unwelcome hindrance from her hips, pulling it down and off her legs, baring her flesh in one sweep of his hand as he tossed her skirt behind him. His mouth followed the line of the forgotten garment, ever downward to the dark nest of her womanhood. He was nuzzling the tight ringlets, pressing a spray of gentle kisses against their fragrant warmth. His kiss was sinking lower, seeking the moist crevice of her desire. His lips were moving warmly against the aching slit. The first penetration of Gareth's tongue sent a searing jolt through Angelica's veins which stole her breath.

She made a scrambling move to escape, only to have Gareth's hands clamp onto hers as he stretched himself against the length of her legs. Imprisoned by his weight, she directed a look filled with panic into his impassioned face, only to be mesmerized by the tumult raging in his eyes and his husky, throbbing murmur.

"Let me love you, Angelica. I need to love you completely, to savor the taste of you. Nothin' else will sate me. We're both prisoners, here, darlin'. I'm as much your prisoner as you are mine. We're in a prison of our own makin', and only lovin' can free us. Give to me, darlin', and let me give to you, and I'll set us both free. . . . "

184

His eyes holding hers for only a few moments more, Gareth slowly lowered his head to the warm mound which drew him so insistently. His hands slipped from hers to cup her firm buttocks as he raised her slowly to accommodate his loving quest. Her mind soaring, Angelica abandoned herself to his intimate kiss, reveled in its glory. He was drawing from her. He was loving her deeply, fully caressing the velvet petals of her passion with his tongue, consuming the sweet dew that rested there. He was relentless in his loving ravishment, insatiable.

A deep shuddering began to shake Angelica's slender frame. Gareth's kisses deepened, his caresses expanded, feeding the flame that threatened to consume her. A shattering ecstasy lifted her higher, higher. The harrowing wave of emotion crested, breaking suddenly in a crashing, quaking climax that tossed her spent and breathless into the searing wonder of total reward.

Drinking deeply of the sweet homage of her body, Gareth waited until the last convulsive shudder had passed her slender frame. Drawing himself to his knees, he moved quickly, efficiently stripping away his clothes. He crouched atop her. Gradually, savoring the joy of anticipation, he lowered his flesh to hers.

A tender smile worked across his lips as Angelica's heavy lids slowly lifted. Passion had stirred the green and gold flecks to life in the silver eyes lifted to his and Gareth was humbled by their brilliant glory. Lowering his mouth to hers, Gareth whispered softly against her lips, "I've drunk from the well of your passion, darlin'. I've taken all you have to offer me, but I need more, darlin'. I need to seal my claim, make you mine completely. Welcome me . . . take me in. Bring me home, darlin'. Set me free . . ."

His mouth claiming hers, Gareth raised himself to move within her even as Angelica's thighs parted in silent, willing acceptance. His first, searing plunge shook her, separating her lips in a low groan which was smothered by the wealth of his kiss. The second thrust penetrated more deeply, the third sent her again into the realm of vivid, soaring wonder she had relinquished only moments before. The deep rhythm of Gareth's thrusts became part of her, echoing in her brain, blending with the rapid beat of her heart. She was one with Gareth, suddenly careening high on a shaft of shimmering light, abruptly thrust in the burst of its brilliant explosion and abandoned to drift slowly, gently back to earth in the cushion of Gareth's loving arms.

Her heart was still pounding, her breathing ragged when she became aware of the echo of Gareth's heart racing against her own. He was holding her close, his body welded to her by the moist veil of their mutual passion. Gareth's sweet breath fanned her cheek as he lifted his head to look down into her eyes. His low whisper was torn between wonder and despair.

"I thought to set us free, darlin'. But I failed. Instead I've only succeeded in binding us closer still. There is no escape for us, darlin', none at all. . . ."

The light of afternoon was rapidly slipping into night. Lifting his head, Gareth looked down into the beauty of Angelica's sleeping face. He smiled, his mind wondering how he could have spent his passion so completely and still feel so filled with desire. But this desire was a new experience. It was a need, felt deep inside, to hold and cherish her, keep her close. His body had been sated, but his spirit had not. He wondered if . . .

A sudden clap of thunder broke the silence of the room, jarring Angelica awake with a frightened start. Angelica frowned as her eyes focused on his face. But the small lines between her brows disappeared under the caressing warmth of his kiss. Her eyes dropped closed under the familiar stroking of his warm mouth, and her lips parted.

His mouth curved in a smile, brushing hers lightly as he whispered against its warm surface, "Get up, darlin', our shower is waitin'."

Angelica's eyelids fluttered and slowly lifted. Her expression confused, she shook her head. But she had no time to respond. Gareth was drawing her relentlessly to her feet. His intentions finally becoming obvious, Angelica shook her head with growing protest.

"Gareth, you don't mean . . . not the rain! It's too cold!"

Stopping to press a light kiss against her lips, Gareth whispered, "And if I promise you won't be cold for long . . . ?"

Another clap of thunder sounded overhead and Angelica shook her head with growing adamance.

"No . . . no. I won't. It's too. . . "

But her protest was to no avail as Gareth scooped her up into his arms and started toward the door. Struggling to escape him, Angelica was rewarded by his tightening grip as he continued walking unaffected. Reaching out, he swung the door open, and within moments she was gasping as the icy drops splashed against her heated skin. Her words of protest died in her frantic attempt to catch her breath. She had never been so cold, so completely lost to the elements.

She was struggling no longer as the steady drumming of the pelting drops against her flesh became more refreshing than cold. She closed her eyes and raised her face to the ceaseless deluge, hardly hearing the crack of thunder that sounded again close by.

Gareth was slowly lowering her to a standing position. Her eyes still closed, she felt the texture of rough forest grass beneath her feet. Opening her eyes, she gave a low laugh, only to have it die in her throat as her eyes met and held Gareth's sober gaze. The rain had plastered his hair blackly to his scalp and was running down his face as he cleared his forehead with an impatient hand. Reaching out, he began working at her braid, not stopping until he had undone the plait and the black silk of her hair was lying against her wet skin in long, swirling spirals.

A smile flicking across his lips for the first time, he gently smoothed a few errant strands back from her cheek. His touch was caressing.

"You look like a wood nymph, a creature of the storm, darlin', ready to weave your spell." The smile slowly dropping from his lips, Gareth appealed softly, "Work your magic on me, little witch. It'll be easy, darlin'. I have no

187

will to resist you."

Taking her hands from her sides, Gareth wound her arms around his neck, his eyes dropping momentarily closed as Angelica's sweet flesh closed against his.

Mesmerized by the dark-eyed gaze that met and held hers, Angelica felt again the stroke of Gareth's naked length pressed against her. Responding to a compulsion neither questioned nor understood, she raised herself on tiptoe, reaching up to taste the rain-washed lips which had loved her so well. She brushed them once . . . twice . . . They were cold. She sought to warm them with her own and she covered them fully, her lips parting at the response she sensed coming to life.

Gareth's lips were cold no longer. They were moving warmly, hungrily against hers, his strong arms closing around her as thunder boomed and lightning crashed, creasing the dark sky above them in a shaft of ragged brilliance. Tearing his mouth from hers, his eyes darting to the sky overhead, Gareth gave a low laugh and scooped her back into his arms. In a few long steps he was once again within the protection of the cabin and setting her on her feet.

The cold cabin floor was startling, effective in bringing her back from her bemused state to the reality of her sodden condition. Suddenly she was shivering, her teeth chattering so violently that she could scarcely speak. Taking her by the arm, Gareth drew her close to the fire. Urging her to sit on the blanket he had spread on the floor, he reached over for the other blanket which lay close by and wrapped it around her head and shoulders.

Noting that her quaking did not abate, Gareth hesitated only a moment more. Cupping her head with his hand, he pressed her back against the floor, his body moving to cover hers even as he unwound the blanket and sealed it closed around them both in a warm coccoon of mutual warmth.

Gareth's naked length was stretched full against her, his body cool, damp, erotically stimulating against her sensitized skin. The curling hairs on his chest teased her enlarged nipples as he moved in a slow, sensuous rhythm to caress her flesh with his. His breath was warm against her ear as he whispered softly, "I promised you I wouldn't let you get cold, darlin'. I always keep my promises."

His whispered words were slipping into mumbled, unintelligible endearments. The shaft of his passion was swelled against her and Angelica ached to feel its stroking caress. She opened her softness to him, a low gasp escaping her lips as he slid into the sweet sanctuary she offered so willingly. All conscious thought leaving her mind, Angelica could think only of the sensuous rhythm which was consuming her mind, the brushing caress of hard muscle against smooth flesh. There was no time or space, only the two of them in intimate joining. A deafening clap of thunder accompanied the peak of their climax. The almost simultaneous lightning which lit the flickering darkness wedded their blazing passion, drew it to a close, only to have it sputter and die, to fade back into the darkness from whence it had come.

The cabin was silent, the only sound the pounding of relentless rain and the rasp of short, gasping breaths. Gareth mumbled inaudibly into the damp silk of Angelica's hair. He clutched her close, still unwilling to release her, and in her bemusement, Angelica was suddenly aware that Gareth had been true to his promise. Yes, she was cold no longer.

Chapter V

Esteban bit back the curse which rose to his lips as the Valentin carriage sank into yet another jarring rut on the flooded wash of road. He forced his gaze out the window. The driving rain which had persisted through the long night had washed the last cloud from the sky, leaving it a brilliant, unbroken expanse of blue. The sun was warm, unusually so for early spring, but Esteban felt none of its clement rewards. Instead, his mind was far from the green of the rolling landscape which moved past his window.

His situation in the Valentin coach was intolerable. For the duration of the ride he had been subjected to Concepción Valentin's broad hints as to his intentions toward her witless daughter, and that daughter's boring, pointless conversation. His patience was stretched to the breaking point.

How long had he been in this black torture chamber which threatened to jar his bones from his body? Had it been merely a single day? He had worn out his polite conversation during the first hour of the journey the day before, the memory of Gareth Dawson's possessive hand on the beautiful *puta's* shoulder effectively driving both the desire and the ability to converse from his mind.

He had recognized the light in Gareth Dawson's eye. He had no doubt the bastard had claimed the little bitch again, right under his very nose. His eyes shooting to Dolores Valentin's pinched face, Esteban felt the rise of revulsion.

What man in his rights would prefer this pale wretch to the haunting beauty of the beautiful little *puta* who obsessed him? Surely not he.

It had been her fault . . . hers! His eyes flashed again to Dolores Valentin, his animosity so strong that it threatened to consume him. What was he doing in this carriage, returning to Mexico City? How had he allowed his father to persuade him to leave so quickly, before he had had time to collect his thoughts? He did not need to go to the capital in such haste. The appointment that he had received had already waited months. He had been anxious for it at one time, but that time was past. He had new priorities now . . . priorities which would allow him no rest.

How many days was it to the capital? He dared not even think. The journey stretched before him in his mind, endless and unrewarding. Were he traveling with the beautiful *puta*, his situation would be quite the reverse. Were it Angelica Rodrigo in this carriage rather than Dolores Valentin, he would be able to think of any number of ways in which to pass his time in a more entertaining manner.

A sudden thought coming to his mind, Esteban drew himself from his slouched position in the carriage. Yes, of course. He would not be driven into blind obedience of his father's wishes like a spineless fool. If he was unhappy with his circumstances now, he would change them! He was only a day and a half away from the hacienda. On horseback he would be home in even less time. It would be an easy matter to collect Angelica Rodrigo and take her back with him to the capital. It mattered little to him what his mother or father would think of his behavior. They had no recourse but to accept him, whatever he did.

And the *puta*? He would make it worth her while to accompany him. Then, when she was dependent upon him, he would see she paid for all the torment she had made him suffer.

He had made his decision. He knew what he would do.

Raising his hand suddenly, unexpectedly, Esteban thumped heavily on the inside roof of the carriage, calling out loudly as he did, "Pedro . . . stop the carriage! Stop it immediately!"

His unexpected command drew startled exclamations from all within the vehicle and Esteban smiled with true pleasure for the first time since he had entered.

"*Esteban, qué pasa?* What is wrong?" His grizzled countenance wrinkled with alarm, Fernando Valentin eyed him apprehensively as the carriage drew to a shuddering halt. Reaching out, Esteban took Dona Concepción's hand.

"*Por favor*, Dona Concepción, I have decided that I must return to Real del Monte. Business there, left unsettled, will give my mind no peace. If I am to function properly in the capital, I will have to bring this matter to a satisfactory conclusion."

Turning to Dolores Valentin, Esteban took her hand and drew it to his lips. Smiling at the flush that rose in the girl's insipid face, he purred gallantly, "Ah, senorita, it is my greatest sorrow that I must deprive myself of your divine presence in order to fulfill my obligation. But duty must come before the great pleasure I would derive from remaining in your company. *Lo siento*. Please forgive me for interrupting your journey."

Turning to Señor Valentin, Esteban extended his hand, his handshake firm with hypocritical concern. "I beg your understanding and your pardon, Don Fernando, for the poor spirits I have inflicted upon all of you."

"Esteban, I am ever a man to put duty before my own personal preferences." Don Fernando's face reflecting understanding, he considered solemnly, "For that reason I well comprehend your feelings, and admire you for your devotion to your obligations. God's speed on your return journey. We will look forward to seeing you when you have returned to the capital."

Accepting Don Fernando's bidding with a subdued smile, Esteban turned to exit the carriage. Signaling the release of one of his cases from the top of the carriage, he waited only until Pedro had dispatched it to the ground before untying his horse from the rear. Securing his case to the saddle, he mounted quickly and raised his hand in a parting salute to the monstrous conveyance and the three faces which peered out at him in sad farewell.

Waiting only until the carriage was once again in motion, Esteban turned his stallion back in the direction from whence he had come, his handsome face marked with determination.

Angelica came awake slowly. She was too comfortable to move. Enclosed in a cozy cushion of warmth, she turned her head to avoid the light shining brightly against her closed lids, only to feel warm lips brush against her own as a husky whisper sounded in her ear.

"Good mornin', darlin'. A real fine, good mornin' . . ."

Her eyes suddenly snapping open, Angelica was momentarily startled by the face so close to hers. Propped on one elbow as he looked down at her, Gareth raised his hand to her cheek. Sliding his fingers into the hair at her temples to hold her fast, he dipped his head to press another kiss against her lips.

Angelica was suddenly conscious of the fact that Gareth's naked length was stretched out against hers under the light blanket. Total recall of the night before brought a flush to her face, and she attempted to avoid the dark eyes looking into hers. No, that wanton creature who had met kiss for kiss, languished under Gareth's intimate touch, and who had actually sought to return a portion of the loving which he had imparted, could not have been her! No . . . she had not wanted any part of another intimate encounter with Gareth Dawson. Why then had she reacted so illogically to his passionate plea to allow him to love her?

His dark eyes sought her glance, but Angelica continued to avoid them. She had always steadfastly denied the name put so easily to her by circumstance . . . *puta*. But last night, even more indelibly than the morning's first encounter, she had marked herself worthy of its stigma.

Gripping her chin firmly, his fingers gentle despite their refusal to allow her to turn away, Gareth forced Angelica's eyes up to his as he scrutinized her face. His dark hair lay smoothly against his neck, gleaming in the beam of sunlight which reflected on its ruffled surface, but his expression was slowly stiffening, moving into familiar hard lines. His eyes were narrowing in squinting appraisal, his brows drawing into a straight line to impart an almost sinister appearance as the former softness began to leave the curve of his lips. The blanket had fallen away from his chest to reveal the broad curve of his shoulder and the strongly muscled chest covered with a light mat of black hair. She remembered so well the erotic sensations evoked as the finely curling mass had tantalized her naked breasts. Her flush deepened and she attempted to avoid his gaze once again.

But Gareth was having none of it.

"What are you thinkin', Angelica? You don't really want to run away from me . . ."

"I . . . I want to be away from here . . . as . . . as quickly as possible."

With a quick movement, Angelica attempted to roll away from his grip, but Gareth could not be caught unawares.

"Why are you suddenly so anxious to leave, Angelica? After your first protests you seemed quite happy to be with me last night."

"I had no choice but to remain. You carried me here forcibly . . . against my will. Had I a true choice right now, I would be at home in my own bed."

"You did have a choice last night, Angelica." A spark of warmth returning to his gaze, Gareth ran his eyes over her mouth, sending little tremors up her spine as he continued quietly, "You had a choice when it came to my lovin' you. I told you I've never been guilty of rape, and last night was no exception. You gave yourself to me willin'ly, darlin'. That's somethin' you can't deny, no matter how hard you try."

Angelica's flush darkened. What was wrong with her? She was acting like a child. Gareth Dawson had just stated he would not force her to do anything against her will. All she need do was insist she wanted to leave.

Taking a deep, shaking breath, Angelica nodded.

"Perhaps. But you will not find me of a similar mood

194

this morning. I would like to get up."

The brief flicker in the dark eyes so close to hers was almost indiscernible, and while Angelica still paused to consider its fleeting appearance, Gareth suddenly uncovered himself and lifted himself to his feet. Reaching down, he took her two hands and drew her up beside him.

"You're right. It's time to be moving."

Turning to reach for his clothes, Gareth did not see Angelica's startled expression the moment before she reached for her own clothes.

She was stepping into her skirt as Gareth turned back toward her, fully dressed. Her eyes averted, she did not see the manner in which his gaze roved her slender form, the frustration obvious only too briefly as he restrained his desire to reach out to touch the gleaming strands of hair which swung down past her shoulders in riotous disarray. Unbound the night long, they had moved into thick, heavy waves. He remembered too well their sweet scent as he had buried his face in their fragrance. He wanted to hold Angelica close again, to bury himself in her completely, so that there would be no mistaking his claim, but Angelica obviously had other things on her mind. Whatever her game, he had decided he would play it her way.

Angelica was turning back toward him when a low rumbling sound broke the silence between them. Gareth was unable to restrain the smile that picked up the corners of his lips.

"Sounds like you're hungry."

Annoyed at her stomach's traitorous appeal, Angelica raised her chin, refusing to return his smile.

"I have been hungry before. You need not concern yourself."

The tightness returned to Gareth's expression. "Well, there's no need for either of us to go hungry this mornin'."

Glancing to the fire which still smoldered, Gareth turned and took a few steps to the door. Opening it to the bright light of morning, he retrieved the small pot he had placed outside before retiring. Leaning over, he gave it a small shake. Satisfied that he had collected enough water for tea,

195

he turned, closing the door behind him. Within a few minutes the pot was hanging over a small but blazing fire.

"I would prefer to leave now. I do not wish to wait for tea." Refusing to admit the true reason for her desire for a quick exit was distrust of her own rioting emotions, Angelica held Gareth's glance stiffly.

The small muscle ticking in his cheek revealed Gareth's growing agitation. His tone was flat, allowing no room for discussion.

"Unfortunately, I'm not ready to leave, Angelica. Although my stomach isn't as vocal as yours, I'm just as hungry, and I don't expect to spend the mornin' in discomfort just to accommodate you."

Turning, Gareth reached for his saddlebags and withdrew a small wrapped package. He shot her a quick look over his shoulder.

"You'd might just as well make yourself comfortable. I don't intend budgin' until I've eaten."

Suddenly furious, Angelica plopped herself down on the blanket and stared into the fire. She was angry and growing more hungry by the minute. Her eyes moving to the wedge of cheese he had unwrapped, Angelica realized it was the fresh cheese which had been delivered to the hacienda only the day before. Actually salivating as her eyes took in Carmela's golden-crusted bread as well, Angelica swallowed and forced herself to turn away.

Disdaining the use of the filthy table, Gareth lay the cloth in which the food had been wrapped on the blanket in front of her. Sitting beside her, he withdrew a pocketknife from his trousers. Unable to keep her eyes from returning to Gareth, Angelica felt her stomach tighten as he moved with maddening slowness to slice the cheese and bread.

Angelica was not a stranger to hunger, but, in truth, this morning she was famished. Refusing to admit to the possible reason for her unusual appetite, Angelica waited in silence, managing to avert her face just before Gareth glanced up.

Ignoring her apparent disinterest, Gareth moved to the fire and shook some tea leaves into the pot.

"Well, the tea should be ready in a minute."

Furious at his maddeningly slow pace when she was both famished and anxious to depart, Angelica startled herself by the haughty shake of her head and her own perverse reply.

"I don't want anything to eat."

Hesitating only a moment in response, Gareth gave a small shrug. "If that's the way you want it, I'm not goin' to force you."

Reaching out with great deliberation, Gareth picked up a slice of cheese. He consumed it slowly, savoring its taste with obvious appreciation before reaching for a piece of bread. Not stopping until it had been consumed completely, Gareth reached over to retrieve the pot from the fire and poured a cup of tea. He was on his second slice of cheese when Angelica's traitorous stomach growled loudly once again. This time Angelica was certain she saw a fleeting smirk on Gareth's face before he stuffed an especially large piece of cheese into his mouth and chewed vigorously.

Her stomach was providing a loud accompaniment to each of Gareth's smacking chews when Angelica could stand it no longer. She was about to draw herself to her feet when Gareth's hand snaked out to grasp her arm. Making an attempt to shake off his grip, Angelica raised angry eyes to Gareth's openly amused face.

"Admit it, darlin'. Your spirit is willin' to go hungry for the sake of principle, but your body isn't." Hesitating only a minute more as Angelica shot him an even haughtier glance, Gareth picked up a piece of cheese and offered it to her with a broadening smile.

"Come on, Angelica. You know you're hungry."

"No, thank you. I do not choose to eat this morning. And I would appreciate it if you would release my arm so I might go outside to wait while you are finished."

"If you think I'm goin' to let you anywhere near my horse without me, darlin', you're sadly mistaken." His eyes beginning to show a touch of annoyance, Gareth shook the tantalizing wedge in front of her face. "So you might as well eat somethin'."

"I told you, I don't want anything to eat!"

"Stubborn little . . ."

Slipping his arm unexpectedly around her shoulders, Gareth pulled Angelica firmly against his chest as he waved the cheese under her nose.

"Smells good, doesn't it, darlin'? And you know damned well you're hungry, so why don't you break down and eat? It's goin' to be a long mornin' until we . . ."

"I told you, I don't want to eat!"

Making an attempt to squirm out of his grip, Angelica was fighting in earnest when Gareth abruptly released her. His eyes reflecting his frustration he gave his head a short shake.

"Angelica, why do we always end up at odds when we both want the same thing? You're hungry, darlin', and I want you to eat. There's more than enough for both of us."

Raising the cheese again to her lips, he said softly, "Take a bite, come on, darlin'. I can hear your stomach tellin' me how much you want this."

Gareth was brushing the cheese lightly against her lips and Angelica fought her waning resistance. No, she could not let him win out again over her resolve. She could not . . .

His brow furrowing into a frown, Gareth's frustration grew. How had the whole damned thing come about? He had managed to put her on the defensive again, when all he wanted was to have her happy, well fed, in his arms.

Lowering his head on an impulse inspired by his conflicting emotions, Gareth pressed a light kiss against Angelica's mouth. Startled at his unexpected tactic, Angelica lifted her eyes to the sober lines of his face.

"Angelica, come on, darlin' . . ."

Gareth raised the cheese again to her lips and unable to bear his open expression of concern any longer, Angelica took a small bite. She chewed slowly, expecting any moment to see victory dawn in the depths of Gareth's dark eyes, but his gaze remained unfathomable. Instead, when she had swallowed, he kissed her lightly once more. He fed her another bite, waiting only until she had finished to cover her lips again with his. He was pressing her back against the blanket, waiting only until she rested in the curve of his arm to continue feeding her, alternating food with kisses. When she had consumed the last of the cheese, Gareth reached for the cup of tea and, supporting her head, brought it to her lips.

Angelica sipped the hot brew carefully, watching as Gareth drew the cup from her mouth. Taking a brief swallow, he returned it to her lips. Placing the empty cup on the floor at last, his smile was gentle.

"That wasn't so bad, was it, darlin'? We don't always have to be at odds . . . not when we both want the same thing."

Angelica's hand was against Gareth's chest. His heart was pounding heavily against her palm, echoing the beat of her own heart. A panic began to overwhelm her as he caressed her cheek.

"You eat like a child, darlin', enjoyin' every bite." A smile flicked across his lips. "You have crumbs on your cheek."

Angelica raised her hand to brush them away, but Gareth shook his head. "No, Angelica . . ."

Slowly lowering his head, Gareth trailed his mouth against her cheek to flick the light, almost invisible crumbs from its surface with his kiss. His tongue followed the trail of powdery flakes to her throat, lifting them gently from her skin. Lost to his intimate service, Gareth trailed his mouth downward, his tongue darting out to snatch errant crumbs from the rise of her breasts.

Gareth was breathing heavily, his eyes moving up to hold hers with a glow that lit a fire deep inside her. His hand moved to curve over her flat stomach.

"Has your hunger been sated, darlin'? Tell me . . ." His mouth worshipped hers again and he urged, "Tell me, darlin' . . ."

Angelica nodded, her breathing so erratic that she could not find her voice.

Noting her assent, Gareth grated, "Then let me sate

mine, Angelica. My hunger is for you. Your taste is sweeter in my mouth than anythin' I've ever known. I need to sate that hunger, darlin'. I must . . ."

He was kissing her deeply, fully, drawing of her taste. His mouth was savoring her sweet skin, his tongue fondling its texture. Her blouse slipped away and he devoured the soft swells beneath, sought to consume the blushing crests. He was beside himself with wanting her.

Within moments he was deep inside her, his appetite voracious, his need compelling. Too far gone in his desire to sustain his passion, he plunged deeply a final time, consuming even as he was consumed, until his need was spent.

Angelica's innate fragrance was in his nostrils and he breathed deeply of her scent. Why was it he could not get enough . . . that even when his physical hunger was appeased, he knew a desire to keep her close, still a part of him?

Lifting his head, Gareth looked down into Angelica's passion-flushed face, and a sweet, singing emotion rose inside him to which he could not put a name. The hunger . . . it was with him still.

Gareth was intensely aware of Angelica's silence. Strangely, their moments of ecstasy had seemed to erect a barrier between them far stronger than the one he had overcome in bringing her into his arms only moments before. They had dressed in silence. Gareth had put out the fire and packed his saddlebags, noting that Angelica stood near the door, awaiting him.

He approached the door slowly, his eyes on her averted face. Unwilling to allow the uneasiness between them to continue, Gareth slid his arm around her shoulders and lowered his head toward her lips. She turned instinctively, avoiding his kiss, and Gareth's frustration grew. Each encounter with Angelica seemed to leave her colder toward him than before, while each time he took her in his arms his desire for her grew. It was an endless, maddening circle that was driving him wild.

Pausing to strap on his saddlebags, Gareth hesitated only

a moment before swinging Angelica up onto his horse. Within a second he had mounted behind her and had spurred his gelding forward.

It was a lovely morning, the foliage fresh-washed and sparkling from the deluge of the night before, the sun sparkling on the remaining drops that spotted the verdant wall around them. Cool and fragrant, alive with the sounds of life, the forest was renewed, and Gareth breathed deeply.

But Angelica sat stiffly in front of him in the saddle. Suddenly impatient, Gareth closed his arms tighter around her, pulling her back until, despite her restraint, she leaned full against him. He pressed a light kiss on the surface of her hair, moving to rest his chin against her temple. Consoling himself with the warm pulse beating there, he reasoned that no matter her reservations, he was close enough to her that he could feel her life pulsing through her veins. He knew no man had been closer to her before. He consoled himself with that thought, refusing to think further than two days hence when he . . .

But she was stiffening again in his arms. They had turned off the trail onto the road to the mine and Angelica demanded sharply, "Where are you going?"

Gareth's reply reflected his annoyance at her tone. "You know where we're goin'. I told you I had to go to the mine to talk to . . ."

"To the mine!" Jerking around, directing an incredulous look into his face, Angelica shook her head. "But I cannot! I have been away all night. Mama, Papa, will be frantic and Carlos . . . you know he is ill. I cannot worry him."

"I told you, you should have thought about that yesterday . . ."

"You pretend . . ." Her voice quaking with anger, Angelica rasped, "You pretend concern for me, but you think only of yourself! You know Dona Teresa is suspicious. She will send someone to my home to look for me when I do not come to work, and when she finds out we are both missing, she will know. I will be dismissed!"

"You'll find another position."

"No one else will hire me!"

Gareth's reply was unrelenting. "We're goin' to the mine."

Taking a deep breath, Angelica swallowed her pride. Turning, she directed the full force of her gaze into Gareth's eyes.

"*Por favor* . . . please, Gareth, I ask you to take me home. It is not only my future which depends on my position, but . . ."

"You're wastin' your breath, Angelica. I expect to conduct my business and return to the hacienda today. If I took you back now, I'd waste too much time."

"Then go to the mines if you must!" Her voice exploding in anger, Angelica continued hotly, "But put me down, now! I will walk back home!"

"No."

"We are only an hour away. I can walk there easily. Then I can . . ."

"I told you, no!" Not allowing Angelica to continue and not stopping to question his motives, Gareth continued flatly, "You're comin' with me. I don't intend to let you walk back on this road by yourself."

"No, you would rather that I lose my position because of your whim!"

"If you're worryin' about your time, darlin' . . ." Reaching into his pocket, Gareth extracted the coins he sought. Taking her hand, he pressed them into her palm with a meaningful expression. "It was always my intention to pay you well for your time. And I won't haggle price, darlin'. I've told you before, you're worth every penny."

Whitening at his words, Angelica jerked her face suddenly forward in silence. Her anger was apparent in the rigidity of her frame, but Gareth ignored her attempt to pull out of his embrace. Dismissing her protest, he pulled her closer still, not satisfied until she was deep in the circle of his embrace. His only concern was to keep her close to him. He wasn't ready to let her go.

"What do ye think, mon?"

His bushy brown brows furrowed over his nose, Brock

Macfadden awaited Gareth's response. He had studied the maps and diagrams the Texan had left with him while he had sat before the fire the night before. Mary had been annoyed when he had failed to respond to her soft chatter, but the project the Texan had left had fascinated him from the first. Judging from the papers he had been provided, the Texas land the Dawsons had settled was as different from the terrain of Real del Monte as could possibly be imagined.

He was intrigued by the wild country, fascinated by the idea of men and women coming into a raw, virgin land and carving a home from the wilderness with the strength of their bare hands. He and Mary had taken a great step in accepting the position he now held. It had involved leaving the home of his father and his father before him. But with them had traveled a whole colony of Scots and English. Homes had been waiting, along with the problems of the mine they were to address. There had never been a thought that the land might not provide them food for their families, or the elements might eliminate the roofs over their heads. There was no threat of hostile Indian raids.

The very vastness of the country mapped out before him had been startling. Gareth's homestead itself . . . unbelievable! Four thousand six hundred acres. The size of an entire hamlet on which hundreds of people lived in the old country . . .

Brock's eyes moving assessingly over the Texan's face as Gareth studied the partial report he had prepared. Only strong, relentless men succeeded in the type of environment spelled out on the maps before him, and Gareth Dawson was doubtless one of those. It was written on the sun-darkened planes of his face, the tiny creases fanning out from the corners of his eyes despite his youth. It was also reflected in the power represented by his well-muscled expanse of shoulder, and the smooth, soundless manner in which he walked despite his size. It was a face accustomed to the elements, and a body developed by hard, physical work and honed to respond with lightning reflexes. He had no doubt those reflexes and the keen scrutiny of his watchful eyes had saved the Texan's life on more than one occasion.

Brock admired him and the unknown man who had the foresight to dream a dream for potentially valuable land otherwise thought worthless. He respected Gareth for his devotion to the land, his tenacity in forging a growing empire out of the wilderness. There was no doubt all these elements of his character would be put to a sore test before long. Even in the mountains of Real del Monte, word of the trouble brewing between the central government and the distant state of Texas had come. Santa Anna . . . the country was wild about the man, calling him a hero, a savior. He had seen and heard of men like Santa Anna before. He was not impressed.

Gareth looked up from the papers in his hand, his eyes meeting and holding Macfadden's glance.

"This is exactly what we wanted, as far as it goes."

"I dinna know if I can give ye a true assessment without knowin' more than these papers provide. The maps are good, but the scope of the project is vast, mon. I've nae seen one its like."

"I wouldn't expect you to set us on a course of action without seein' the land, Brock. I have a suspicion this bit of work will have to wait, in any case. I have the feelin' my father will be involved with other matters when I return."

"Aye, I've heard the rumors of trouble brewin'."

"Then you realize all I'm lookin' for is a general assessment and a brief outline of the work involved if you think the project feasible. We wouldn't expect a final recommendation until you've had a chance to see the land for yourself."

"Aye, I would like that. But for yer present needs, I need more time and more information, Gareth."

Turning over the pages he still held in his hand, Gareth shot Macfadden a short glance.

"I'm pressed to return to my homestead. Do you think you could finish a preliminary evaluation tonight, Brock? From what I've read, you think the plan has merit. You've only to outline a specific plan . . . mark the points where we would start . . . give us a general idea of how big a job we're undertakin'."

His brow furrowing in thoughtful deliberation, Brock moved the papers on the desk before him. "I suppose. If ye stay to answer any questions which may arise, I can start work on it, and if necessary, work through the night." Raising his eyes to Gareth's, he nodded his head in agreement. "Aye, I'll get the job done for ye. And ye'll have the benefit of another good engineer's opinion, too. Peter has been studyin' the project with me. Mary will be happy to fix a place for ye to rest yer head shou' ye tire. We've nae had guests in our house for a long time."

"I'll be happy to stay and work with you, Brock, but . . ."

Hearing the note of hesitation in his voice, Brock snapped up his graying head, his eyes catching a flicker of concern.

"Be there a problem, mon?"

"I'm not travelin' alone, and considerin' your comments on our last meetin', I'm not certain my friend would be welcome in your house."

"Yer friend?"

His eyes following Gareth's gaze to a point outside the window where Angelica had just walked into view, Brock frowned, his face jerking back toward him with a low exclamation.

"Ye brought the lass with ye?"

"Yes, I did."

"Are ye crazy, mon, gettin' involved with that one? She'll bring ye nothin' but trouble."

"I expect that's my concern, Brock. In any case, you haven't answered my question."

His grizzled face moving into a tight scowl, Brock shook his head.

"Ye ask a hard thing. My brother lives with Mary and me and ye know the lad is daft about the lass. He'll nae like seein' the two of ye together."

Gareth frowned. "The decision is yours, Brock."

"Aye . . . aye." Scratching his red beard thoughtfully,

Brock directed another glance toward the window, his frown darkening as Peter Macfadden walked into his line of vision. Not stopping to see that similar frown drew Gareth's face into tight lines, he mumbled under his breath, "It dinna take the lad long to make his way to her side. He'll nae like it, but I canna call myself a Christian and be content to leave ye both in the cold."

"We'll be able to manage. I don't want to make trouble for you with your wife."

Brock turned his eyes back to Gareth, his expression composed. "Mary will welcome ye both." His eyes showing only temporary hesitation, Brock added in his characteristically outspoken manner, "We'll not be providin' ye with sleepin' arrangements, just a warm meal and a comfortable chair to pass the time until I can finish the report. If that satisfies ye, mon, we can begin work this afternoon."

His eyes moving back to the two figures standing outside in the late morning sun, Gareth nodded. "That will be fine. Brock. The sooner I'm able to leave, the better."

"Good day, Angelica."

"Good day, Señor Macfadden."

His sober face creasing into a small grimace, Peter Macfadden attempted a smile. But his heart was not in it.

"I saw ye ride up a short time ago. I was unable to get away from my work sooner or I wou' have come right out to greet ye."

"That's all right. I've managed to amuse myself while Señor Dawson conducts his business with your brother."

"Aye, they're no doot discussin' the project the Texan left with Brock. It be a vast undertakin'. Brock and I have been studyin' it nightly."

"We will be leaving as soon as Señor Dawson has collected the plans."

"Then I expect ye'll be here for some time, Angelica. My brother has only begun to compose his report."

Angelica's eyes snapped up to his in alarm. "You are saying he has another hour's work . . . maybe two?"

"Nay, I'd say nae less than five or six hours, maybe

more."

"But . . . but I cannot stay!" Panic beginning to become obvious on her pale face, Angelica shook her head. "I've been gone too long already."

Peter Macfadden's face showed the first flicker of disapproval. "Then perhaps it wasna wise to come with Gareth Dawson in the first place."

Sorely tempted to tell the young Scot how she actually came to accompany the Texan to the mine, Angelica looked up into his steady blue eyes. No, she could not. In the end, she was not guiltless and she would not allow this pleasant young man to become involved in a situation which would only result in trouble for him.

"Yes, perhaps it was not."

Suddenly reaching out to touch her hand, Peter Macfadden shook his head. His mouth curved in an apologetic smile that touched her with its sincerity.

"I dinna mean to speak so harshly, Angelica." Giving a quick glance around the area, Peter frowned. He was intensely aware that the few workers milling around the compound were casting interested glances in their direction. He resented the intrusion. He gripped her hand more tightly.

"I dinna think this be a good place to wait or to talk, Angelica. If I apologize for my poor behavior this mornin', wou' ye consider walking wi' me for a little while? The trail to the higher ground where Dona Teresa entertained her guests is close by."

Making an attempt to dislodge her hand from his, Angelica shook her head. "No, I think I would rather stay here."

"Are ye thinkin' Gareth Dawson wou' object to yer walkin' with me?"

Angelica's chin came up with an annoyed jerk. "It is not Gareth Dawson's concern whom I speak to or walk with, señor."

"Then ye will walk with me . . . ?"

Realizing she had trapped herself into accepting Peter's proposal or giving him a blunt refusal, Angelica felt a flush

207

of frustration. She did not wish to encourage this nice young man. His eyes were too open, his smile too sincere. But his expression was too hopeful for her to make it fall into disappointment with a negative response.

"All right, for a little way. I do not wish to be far should Señor Dawson decide to return to the hacienda."

Doing her best to ignore the immediate leap of pleasure reflected in his face, Angelica turned at Peter's urging and started toward the trail.

Moving ahead of her as they climbed the steeper portion just before the ground leveled off again, Peter turned to Angelica to extend a hand. Gratefully accepting his assistance on the last step up, Angelica found herself suddenly looking into sober blue eyes that regarded her with obvious concern. But Peter Macfadden did not wait to voice the thoughts that obviously plagued him as they began a slow step.

"Angelica, surely ye realize the impression yer arrival gave to the folk here. Tongues will be waggin' for days to come."

Startled at his outspokenness, Angelica was momentarily at a loss for a response. Finally giving a small shrug, she returned softly, "I think we both know that tongues were already wagging about me, señor."

Peter stopped short in his tracks, the frown that passed over his youthful face stimulating a warm appeal.

"I wish to speak to ye frankly this day, Angelica. I will find it more in keepin' with me words if ye'll call me by my given name. I ask it as a favor of ye, please. My name is Peter."

"All right, while we are in this place . . . Peter."

Hesitating, Peter burred softly, "The name on yer lips has a beautiful sound, Angelica." His gaze moving briefly over her face, Peter turned and began walking again. His eyes moved unseeingly to the trail in front of them as he obviously sought the right words with which to begin. Finally turning back toward her as they walked, he began carefully.

"The last time ye were here I asked permission to come

to call on ye. Ye didna have time to respond, and now I'm thinkin' Gareth Dawson's interruption of our conversation was not the coincidence I thought it to be. It didna give me pleasure to see ye ridin' into the yard with him." Peter's face flushed with the growing heat of his words, but he continued resolutely. "I dinna like the thought of the mon's arms around ye. It is my feelin' the mon has no regard for women, other than for the physical comforts they cou' bring him."

Taking only a few steps more as they reached the grove of trees, conscious of the fact that they were now shielded from prying eyes, Peter drew Angelica to a stop. He turned to face her. His eyes intense, he shook his head.

"In truth, Angelica, I dinna like the thought of any mon's arms around ye. No mon but me . . ."

"Peter . . . I . . . I think you have gotten the wrong idea. I . . ."

"No, Angelica. I nae think I have. There be a change in ye since the last time I looked into yer eyes. Ye avoid my glance when before ye didna hesitate to face it squarely. And I didna miss the way the Texan lifted ye to the ground . . . the way he touched ye . . ."

"Peter. . . ."

"Nay, I ask that ye hear me out. I have waited too long to speak frankly to ye. I blame myself for listenin' to others and not followin' the urgin's of my heart. So I ask ye now, and I ask ye to answer me truthfully. Do ye care for the mon?"

The bright morning sun glinted on the young Scot's long golden lashes and brows as Angelica returned his earnest gaze. She allowed her eyes to move over his pleasant features, coming at last to rest on the tight line of his mouth. His was a mouth more accustomed to laughter than the strain she had put there, and she wished most sincerely she could restore its former softness. She wished . . ."

"Tell me, lass." His voice a soft rasp, Peter interrupted her thoughts to grip her shoulder tightly, his gold brows furrowing into a tense frown. "Tell me quick and spare me the pain of nawt knowin'. Do ye truly care for the mon?"

"I . . . I don't really feel I want to answer that question . . ."

His eyes dropping closed for the briefest second, the young Scot shook his head. "That means ye do . . . ye do care for the mon. . . ."

"No, it does not!" Immediately regretting her impulsive response as the light of hope returned to Peter's pale eyes, Angelica continued quickly. "It only means that I don't wish to encourage such talk from you. You are aware of my position here and you know gossip follows me. I do not wish to involve you . . ."

"Ye didna hesitate to involve Gareth Dawson . . ."

"I don't have the affection for Gareth that I have for you."

Peter's face stiffened as a sudden flush colored his fair skin. "If affection for me will keep ye in Gareth Dawson's arms and out of mine, I dinna want yer affection! What is it ye feel for the Texan? I would rather ye feel that for me!"

Making an attempt to turn away from the rapidly deteriorating situation, Angelica was stopped by Peter's soft remorseful goan and his staying hand.

"Nay, dinna leave, Angelica." Contrition reflected in his voice, he continued quietly. "It's just that I dinna ken. Ye feel affection for me, but that affection keeps ye from me."

Angelica made an attempt to brush away his hand and Peter's earnest face crumpled into despair.

"I'm beginnin' to believe my brother is right, that I dinna know much about women. There's so much in my heart that I feel for ye, and it's comin' out all wrong. So I'll say it as best I can and I hope ye'll ken." Pausing, Peter looked soberly into her eyes. "I dinna care that ye went with the Texan first. I dinna care if all that 'tis said about ye is truth. The Texan will leave Real del Monte soon. When he does, I wou' like a chance to prove to ye that I'm more the man than me looks appear. My next birthday I'll be twenty-six years old. I'm not so young as I look, and I'll not disappoint ye. I'll love ye well, for as long as ye let me, and I'll nae let a word be spoken against ye in my presence."

210

Distressed by Peter's unexpected outburst, Angelica shook her head.

"I don't want to hear any more, please."

Immediately contrite, Peter was still unwilling to release her from his grip. "Just one word more. I ask ye to consider what I say. When the Texan leaves . . . if ye need somebody, I ask ye to let that somebody be me. I'll treat ye well, and I'll love ye well. For as sure as I'm standin' here today, I love ye already, Angelica. Yer deep in my heart and yer there to stay."

His eyes intent on her face, Peter whispered as he drew her closer, "I wou' like to kiss ye, Angelica. The longin's been with me since the day I first saw ye . . ."

"Peter . . ."

"Just once . . ."

Peter's strong arms closed around her with a swiftness that was unexpected. His mouth covered hers as he pulled her firmly against his lean height. His kiss moved warmly against her lips. It was pleasant, comforting, and Angelica accepted it passively, only resisting as he sought to deepen the contact.

Allowing her to draw away with obvious regret, Peter raised his hand to brush a strand of hair from her face. His voice shaken, he whispered softly, "Ye'll remember what I say this day, Angelica?"

Looking up into his eyes, Angelica nodded. "Yes, I will remember."

Turning away, Angelica felt Peter's hand cup her elbow as he walked beside her back toward the mines. They had only taken a few steps out of the wooded area when Gareth came up the rise of the trail. Standing stiffly erect as he touched level ground, Gareth waited as they approached him. Reaching out the moment they were alongside, he carefully disengaged Peter's hand from Angelica's arm. His expression solemn, unreadable, he turned her firmly toward the trail and escorted her down, leaving Peter to take up the rear.

Ignoring his stallion's fatigue, Esteban spurred him to a

faster pace on the rough mountain road. He had left the Gonzalez hacienda at dawn. Were he in a better humor he would have laughed at the old gentleman's surprise when he had shown up to spend the second night in succession at his hacienda, this time on his way back to Real del Monte. In truth, he was irritated to be forced to spend yet another night on the trail. Were it possible, he would have ridden straight through to Real del Monte so his mind might be at rest from the thoughts that plagued him.

But he had returned to the trail that morning well prepared for the ride ahead of him. He had allowed his horse only minimal rest. His decision made, he had only one thought on his mind. He would return and take Angelica back with him. She had no choice but to do as he proposed. If she resisted, he would see to it that his mother dismissed her. Deprived of her only means of lending support to her ailing brother, she would gladly accept the opportunity to come to the capital. She would come with him in any case. He would see to that.

How he would enjoy her. He had spent most of the previous night in contemplation of the pleasures she would bring him. He would take her directly to his quarters in the city. Perhaps he would not announce his arrival to el presidente for a few days. He would need time to exorcise the heat the little bitch had fostered in his loins and the madness she had inspired in his mind.

He would then arrange for her new wardrobe. He would engage the services of the most popular couturiere in the city. The little *puta* would be a sensation at the capital. El presidente himself would envy his possession of her. A sudden stab of jealousy drained the smile from Esteban's face. But no, not even for el presidente would he give up his prize. And she was a prize, a toy he would enjoy for countless hours.

The sudden vision of Gareth Dawson's face returned to disturb Esteban's pleasant thoughts. Damn the Texan . . . It was not bad enough that Dawson had gotten to the *puta* first, but his own stupidity had allowed the Texan even more time to sate his lust on her slender body. He had little doubt that Gareth would protest her removal from his affections, but it would make little difference. Angelica would be his, no matter what he had to do to get her.

Glancing up, Esteban judged the position of the sun in the bright, cloudless sky. It was late afternoon. He would soon be home. He was perspiring and uncomfortable. He was unused to the rigors of extended travel on horseback. More accustomed to the easy life of the capital and the less tiresome travel by coach, he found that muscles, grown lazy from disuse, were beginning to complain vigorously. He growled his annoyance. Another thing for which to repay the beautiful little whore. But she would be worth it . . . all the inconveniences he had suffered, all the irritations she had caused. He knew without doubt that her body would provide him more satisfaction than any other woman he had ever known. He doubted that she possessed the expertise of some of the more sophisticated whores of the capital, but when he was through with her, she would be more knowledgeable of how to please a man than all of them. He would see to that.

A smile slipped across his lips as Esteban turned onto the well-paved road to Real del Monte. He consoled himself with the realization that he would be indulging himself in fantasy for only a short time more. Then he would be indulging himself in the pleasures of a warm bath, a comfortable bed, and the little *puta*'s soft, accommodating body.

A familiar tightening stirred in his loin. Damn the witch! The time would not come fast enough!

Gareth ran a weary hand through his hair and blinked his eyes. Lifting his hand, he shot a quick look toward the clock on the mantel. Eleven-thirty. Brock McFadden and he had been working at the dining-room table of the modest house Macfadden had been provided since the conclusion of dinner. The house consisted of five small rooms, a kitchen, dining room, living room, and two bedrooms, leaving little choice as to where they could conveniently spread the maps and drawings on which Brock worked. As

213

a result they had all but taken over the living room and dining room, with charts and papers spread on every available surface in well-organized confusion.

It had been a long day and Gareth was beginning to feel the effects of its rigors. But the burly Scot was showing little signs of tiring. Gareth shook his head with a trace of incredulity, a smile turning up the corners of his mouth. He and Brock Macfadden had been working for over six hours on the set of drawings which they were now bringing to a finish, and the man's concentration had not diminished in the slightest. The Scot was a wonder, possessed of a keen mind, a tireless spirit, and an enthusiasm for his work which was unmatched in his experience. Damn, the man was wasted in this environment. They needed men like him in Texas . . .

But there was little chance of inducing Macfadden to try his luck on that frontier while the present threat remained. A sound of movement in the kitchen turned Gareth toward the buxom figure of Mary Macfadden as she bustled into the room. A handsome woman in her mid-thirties, she was obviously devoted to her husband, fond of her brother-in-law, and well adjusted to her adopted community. If he did not miss his guess, she would not look favorably on a suggestion that they change their present circumstances in favor of an uncertain future in the more uncertain state of Texas. He also had no doubt that her opinion weighed heavily in Brock Macfadden's mind. He had already seen her unspoken opinion, if not thoroughly accepted, then carefully weighed and digested by her husband.

Contrary to his expectations, Mary Macfadden had taken an immediate liking to Angelica. It had been obvious in her gentle manner in the face of Angelica's discomfort and the pains she took to make Angelica feel accepted. His eyes moved back to Mary and he saw an almost maternal smile flick across her austere expression as her eyes fixed on Angelica's sleeping face. There was no understanding women. But he was not alone in his surprise. Obviously Brock had been just as startled by his wife's acceptance of the controversial young woman.

Gareth's gaze lingered on Angelica. His anger of the afternoon, when he had seen her walking with Peter Macfadden, had all but dissipated. Instead, tenderness combined with a familiar yearning as his eyes touched on her. She had finally fallen asleep and was curled up on the couch at the other end of the living room, her cheek resting against the high back. He had wondered just how long she would be able to remain awake. She had done her best, but the hours had drawn too long and the fire in front of her too comfortably cozy.

His expression slowly tightening, Gareth found the memory of the long, angry afternoon he had spent with Angelica eating into his temporary mellowness. Angelica had resented his "high-handed" attitude when he had firmly removed her from Peter Macfadden's guiding hand earlier in the day. Anger nagged again at the memory of the young Scot's possessive touch. Damn her, she was fortunate that he had done no more than remove that hand from her arm!

A small grimace slipped over his lips. She had taken the first opportunity to walk off with young Macfadden, and he had a suspicion that he would have reacted far more strongly if he had come upon them in that grove of trees in which they had hidden from sight. A wave of an emotion he could classify as nothing else but jealousy tightened a familiar knot in his stomach.

He had realized then that he dared not turn his back on Angelica, that the young Scot would do her bidding without hesitation. He had begun to realize that the fellow could very easily be prevailed upon to arrange for a horse so that she might return to the hacienda. Or worse, he might even decide to accompany her back. In any case, he had no intention of letting her out of his sight. His time in Real del Monte was limited, and no matter the manner in which he spent the time remaining, he had already determined she would spend it with him. He did not question the reason for his decision. It mattered little.

Angelica had protested heavily his declaration that they were to spend the evening in the Macfadden household. Well aware of the attitude of the foreign community toward

215

her, she had been unwilling to expose herself to the censure of Brock's wife. He was certain that Mary's acceptance of her and the actual affection with which the woman had begun to treat Angelica had come as much as a shock to Angelica as it had to him. But, if he were to be truthful, he would have to admit that an honest, open woman like Mary Macfadden would find it difficult to resent the courtesy with which Angelica treated her despite her discomfort.

He had strained his ears to hear their conversation while the dishes were being washed and dried and the kitchen put to right. He was certain he had heard Angelica mention her brother's name. The love ringing in her tone had tightened the knot of jealousy in his stomach even further and he had been momentarily disgusted by his own uncontrolled feelings. But the tone had not been wasted on Mary . . . had obviously gone straight to her heart. For he was certain he had seen her austere expression softened by restrained tears when she had bustled briefly into the dining room shortly thereafter.

If there had been any discomfort during the evening, it had been the times when Peter Macfadden had been unsuccessful in drawing his eyes from Angelica, despite his brother's dark looks. The fellow was obviously deeply under Angelica's spell, and he made little effort to hide his feelings. Out of deference to his position as guest in the household, Gareth had restrained his anger, choosing instead to demonstrate his possession of Angelica with small proprietorial gestures, the effect of which registered clearly on the young Scot's expressive face.

The fellow was wildly jealous . . . and if he were to be honest, he would have to admit that he, himself, was not in a much less desperate state. It had been too long, too many hours had passed since he had held Angelica in his arms . . . tasted her mouth. He needed to renew his possession of her, to know the security of his mastery over her body, even if that was the most she would give him.

"Gareth."

His eyes snapping back to Brock's face, Gareth noted the pale blue eyes had followed the direction of his stare only to return to his with annoyance.

"If ye be able to keep yer mind on business, mon, I need to know the flow of the river at this point, here." Pointing to a spot on the map, he commented, his brow furrowing more tightly, "It seems to me ye chose poorly in choosin' to bring the lass with ye. She's a distraction to ye and to my fool of a brother. Ye'd be gettin' much more work out of him this night if his mind wasna fixed on the lass's pretty face."

"I apologize for my lack of attention, Brock, but I have no control over your brother's actions. It seems to me you should hold him to account for them, not me."

"Ye may depend on it that I'll do just that!"

The vehemence of Brock's response left no doubt in his mind that the young Scot was in for some stern talk. Feeling the first speck of commiseration for the young fellow's predicament, Gareth frowned and devoted his attention to the map. Brock was right. His mind was wandering too far from the business at hand. He would make certain it would not happen again.

Peter lay stretched out on his bed fully dressed, his arms cushioning his head. He had been staring at the ceiling for the past hour in the forlorn hope that sleep would come to relieve his mental anguish. But it had not. His mind would allow him no rest.

He had been a fool to allow considerations at the mine to take precedence over his intentions toward Angelica. But his period of orientation to the mines was just coming to a close. It had been difficult to find the four hours necessary to make the journey to see Angelica and return. He now realized, too late, that it would have been worth the hardship if there had been any chance of preventing today's occurrence. Gareth Dawson had not hesitated, and unless he was mistaken, Angelica . . .

Dropping his eyes briefly closed against the pain of that unfinished thought, Peter released a soft sigh. Had it been anyone else but Angelica, he would have turned away at the thought of her intimacy with the Texan. He had steadfastly resisted the talk of her promiscuity. He resisted it still. The clear gray eyes raised to his had not been the eyes of a loose woman. For whatever reason, if she had allowed Dawson to love her, she was not happy with her actions. It was in her eyes, the manner in which she avoided Dawson's gaze, the strange animosity that seemed to prevail between them for all the Texan's show of intimacy.

He had heard Angelica speaking to Mary of her brother and her concern for his health . . . her desire to return so that she might relieve herself of that anxiety. She obviously was anxious to be away from here. Why had she come with Dawson? Had he misrepresented the situation to her? Had he trapped her into accompanying him, hoping to flaunt their intimacy? What did he have to gain by such measures?

Peter had left the dining room and his attempts to concentrate on the drawings his brother and he had discussed in detail. He had been unable to keep his eyes from Angelica where she had sat silently before the fire. Aware that he had begun to prove a distraction to his brother's concentration, he had come in to bed. But sleep had eluded him. It eluded him still.

Suddenly disgusted with his wakefulness, Peter drew himself to his feet and slipped on his shoes. He walked slowly to the door of his room and pulled it open to squint into the semidarkness of the kitchen. Avoiding the entrance to the dining room, he walked toward the living room, his eyes intent on the couch and the small, motionless figure in the corner. The fire had begun to burn low, and Angelica was curled up into a small ball in an attempt to keep warm. A wave of tenderness overwhelming him, he turned and walked swiftly back to his room. Taking the blanket from his own bed, he walked directly into the living room. His eyes intent on Angelica, he approached the couch, hesitating only a moment to indulge himself in her beauty before crouching to tuck the blanket carefully around her.

She was beautiful, as beautiful in sleep when her perfect features were composed and serene, as she was with her expressive eyes completing the thoughts she would not speak. It was so easy to lose himself in those eyes. He had never known anyone like Angelica. Her hair was so black, vibrantly alive, with the flicker of the flames dancing in its sheen. He had never seen her wearing it loose the way she did now. She had been beautiful before, with her hair worn in a single plait down her back, but with that glorious mane surrounding the perfect oval of her face, she was magnificent.

Before he had first seen Angelica, he had carried in his mind a mental picture of his idea of the ideal woman. She would be a sharp, quick-minded Scot, unhesitant in speaking her mind. She would be tall and slender, ample in the bosom as was Mary, but far more slender than she elsewhere. She would be fair, with sand-colored hair and blue eyes. Her soft burr would lull his children to sleep, and she would bring a touch of the homeland with them wherever they wandered.

He gave a soft laugh, his hand moving tentatively to Angelica's smooth cheek. Velvet skin . . . darker than the woman of his dreams. Black hair . . . blacker than any hair he had ever seen before, with waves and curls that reflected an almost silver sheen in the light. Great, almost transparent eyes, reflecting an inner torment he longed to assuage. And she was small, standing not as high as his shoulder, of a delicate body structure that appeared almost fragile to his hungry eyes. Small breasts, ultimately more appealing because they were a part of her . . . lips that withheld comment, restrained reaction . . . sought to find the exact word before responding to his urgent pleas. Contradictions of his image of the perfect woman, yet she was more perfect than any woman he had ever known . . . perfect for him.

Gareth Dawson had loved her first . . . he and possibly others. But he would love her last. He had already made up his mind to that.

She was stirring. He felt a flash of remorse. He hadn't meant to awaken her. Her awakening would mean he was no longer free to indulge himself in her beauty, to touch her. Her eyes were opening, and he smiled.

"Did I awaken ye, Angelica? I'm sorry. I cou' nae sleep thinkin' of ye out here on the couch. Ye appeared cold. I brought ye a blanket."

Moving to his knees beside the couch, he smiled as he tucked the blanket around her, extending the moments while he had an excuse to be near her, to touch her.

"*Gracias*, Peter."

His eyes snapping to hers at the use of his given name, Peter gave a small laugh. Strange how the sound of his name on her tongue gave him such pleasure. But he had experienced more pleasure still at just the touch of her lips. He had tasted them only briefly before. He was well aware of the fact that he had enjoyed the contact more than she. He had been plagued by the thought that she had merely endured his kiss. But she had been upset, anxious to get home. She was anxious still. He was certain that when the time came for them, he would be able to make her happy.

He realized his youthful appearance was a drawback. He had grown to despise it when he held himself in comparison with Gareth Dawson's virile, mature image. But he had had considerable experience with women. During the term of his engineering education in Glasgow, he had earned an education of another sort. His boyish appearance had not hindered him then. It had, in fact, stirred even the most hardened of whores to take more time with him. He was thankful for that education now.

Swallowing hard, Peter made a great effort to see that Angelica was thoroughly covered, his hands moving to tuck the blanket more firmly around her. The hand that moved against her back slipped up to catch her hair. He smiled again.

"I dinna think ye cou' be more lovely than the first time I saw ye, but with yer hair unbound, ye take away my breath." His hand moved to her cheek to brush away a wayward strand, but it remained there to caress its smoothness.

"Angelica. . . ." His voice a husky whisper, Peter held the great silver eyes turned up to his. "Ye . . . ye will nae forget what I said this afternoon. When ye are done with the Texan, ye will nae turn to another. Ye will give me the chance to prove to ye how I feel. . . ."

The great silver orbs turned up to his were beginning to register distress and Peter stopped short. He was pressing her again, making her uncomfortable, adding to the anxiety which had been present in her eyes since her arrival at the mines.

He lowered his face closer to hers, anger with his own stupidity showing in his pale eyes as he brushed her cheek with his lips. "Nay, ye needna answer me. I beg yer pardon and ask ye to forgive my stupidity."

Angelica frowned and made an attempt to rise to a sitting position, but his hands moved out to hold her fast. "Nay, I will leave so ye may get yer rest. It will do nawt but distress us both shou' I say more. Good nicht. I am goin', Angelica . . . but ye remain with me."

The hush of his words soft between them, Peter dropped his mouth to hers for a brief kiss.

Leaning back in the stiff dining-room chair as Brock worked tirelessly over yet another chart, Gareth raised his hand to rub the aching tenseness from his shoulder. It was that same spot, the shoulder he had broken when he had been thrown from a mustang in his youth. It plagued him whenever he was overly tense.

He was not accustomed to this type of restrained activity. He had discovered himself, grown to adulthood in the saddle. He had learned that in the end, he must learn to depend on himself and his determination to persevere. He had found out long ago that love was transient, emotions fickle. Only the land remained true, endlessly prevailing. As long as he remained close to it, he, also, would prevail. Whatever other needs he experienced were merely temporary, purely functions of the body. He had learned to relegate those needs to their proper place . . . until now.

He frowned. He did not enjoy his present subservience to his body. He did not like the fact that even as he sought a quick resolution to his mission here, his mind rejected his concentration. His eyes sought to return to the small figure on the couch behind him. The more tired he became, the more he wanted to see her . . . be with her. It had been all he could do for the last hour to keep his eyes on the charts Brock drew so diligently. Hell, it was a fine thing . . . the Scot working into the early morning hours while he mooned over his frustration at being kept from the side of his little whore! But somehow he wasn't . . .

The sound of a soft whisper behind him broke into Gareth's thoughts. He turned around slowly, his eyes moving to the couch. He drew himself gradually erect in the chair, his body tensing, his hands balling into fists. It was a joke . . . it had to be . . . Peter Macfadden on his knees, beside the couch . . . Angelica looking up at him as he stroked her hair. The whisper he had heard, it had been Macfadden's voice. He was speaking softly to her. He was kissing her . . .

Hardly realizing he had crossed the room in a few fluid steps, Gareth grabbed the young Scot's collar and jerked him to his feet. Enraged, he hurled him staggering backward, his chest heaving with fury as Peter struck the wall hard with his back.

Gareth's eyes were fixed on the startled Scot's face, his voice ominously soft.

"You'll keep your hand off her, do you hear? I didn't think I would have to make things any clearer to you than they are, but I'm goin' to tell you straight out. Angelica isn't here for your pleasure. She's here with me. While she is, you'll stay away from her or you'll answer to me!"

Gareth was still shaking with rage when Brock Macfadden stepped between the two men. His eyes moving to this brother's stiff expression, Brock managed to check the young Scot's sudden lunge forward.

Restraining him physically, Brock growled, "Are ye crazy, mon? Do ye nae realize what yer doin'? This lass is travelin' with this mon of her own free will. Ye have nae a right in the world to the liberties ye were takin'! Remember yer place, mon! And it is nae at this lass's side! She has chosen her mon, and it is nae you."

His fair skin flushing at his brother's words, Peter Macfadden took a step backward, his eyes moving to Angelica's white face as she drew herself to her feet.

Ignoring Gareth's presence completely, he whispered stiffly, "I beg yer pardon again, Angelica. My behavior has been less than admirable this day. I ask ye nae to think less of me for it."

Aware that he had no recourse, Peter turned swiftly on his heel and left the room.

Turning back to Gareth, his eyes moving only briefly to Angelica, Brock shook his head wearily.

"I dinna know what to say, Gareth. The lad is daft over the lass." Unaware that his words had brought the color flushing back into Angelica's face, he continued. "But he'll nae try that again . . . nae this nicht. I give ye me word on that. In any case, I'll be done here in a few minutes. Ye can then take yer rest here in the livin' room and start out in the mornin'. It will be Mary's pleasure to send ye on yer way with a good breakfast."

Aware that Gareth's chest still heaved heavily in anger, he added quietly, "Will that satisfy ye, mon?"

Nodding stiffly, Gareth held Brock's sober gaze until the exhausted Scot had turned away and was again working at the table. His jaw still tense with restrained anger, he turned for the first time to face Angelica. Her eyes held his levelly, her gaze steady despite her trembling.

Barely holding himself in check, Gareth allowed her to absorb the full weight of the fury that filled him. He wanted her to realize that she had been wildly successful if she had sought to torment him. But he also wanted her to know that no matter her intentions, his tolerance was limited.

Infuriating him even more was his realization that even now, in the face of her actions with the young Scot, his strongest compulsion was to snatch Angelica into his arms, to hold her close. It was only with the strictest constraint that he managed to remind himself that this emotion he felt was temporary . . . that this need which raged through him would fade.

Her eyes widening with surprise, Juanita watched the figure which emerged through the trail to the side of the

223

hacienda. Don Esteban! He had returned! She turned to quickly scan the yard behind her. No, no one else was near. All were busy with midmorning chores. Even she would not have seen his covert arrival had she not been set out to air the bed linens at this particular moment.

Dropping the heavy coverlet into the nearest basket, Juanita ran her hand over the surface of her hair and smoothed her *camisa* against her full breasts. Surely providence was smiling on her today. Whatever the reason Don Esteban had returned, he obviously did not wish to be discovered immediately and his stealth afforded her the perfect opportunity to approach him. Now that Angelica was not present to distract him with her pretensions, she would prove that she could capture and hold the interest of the handsome young aristocrat. He had shown his interest in her many times prior to the *puta*'s arrival. They had merely been lacking in opportunity to expand their relationship. The occasion she had waited for was now at hand.

Not stopping to question the reason Don Estaban tied his horse to a tree at a distant point in the yard and why he began moving toward the seldom used side entrance to the hacienda, Juanita went quickly in his direction. She chose to ignore the frown that tightened Don Esteban's handsome features as she approached him in a swift step. Her full lips curved in a confident smile, her eyes raised provocatively toward his, she reached out boldly to take his arm.

"Don Esteban, we were not expecting you back so quickly. I hope nothing is wrong."

His expression reflecting his annoyance at her familiarity, Don Esteban flicked his eyes over Juanita's animated face. He restrained his contempt at her forwardness. He was at a loss to understand how he had ever thought to find even temporary amusement with this woman. For all her boldness, she had little to recommend her besides the considerable bosom she went to great pains to flaunt in his face. In truth, she all but nauseated him with her coarse Indian features and damp skin. He must, indeed, have been desperate to make his first overtures to her. But she was malleable to his bidding. He could use her today, if not in the way she obviously hoped.

Turning on the full force of his practiced appeal, Esteban smiled, fully aware of the effect of his even white teeth against his well-shaped lips.

"I left unfinished business here at the hacienda, business that would allow me no rest. I do not wish to have my family know of my arrival until I've had an opportunity to accomplish my purpose in returning. You may be of help to me today, Juanita."

"*Sí*, Don Esteban. You know how much I wish to please you."

"Very well." Resisting the desire to brush the blunt-fingered hand from his arm, Esteban nodded. "You must then go to the kitchen and wait for the opportunity to tell Angelica quickly, without being overheard, that I wait for her here. I do not wish to have anyone know she leaves to meet me and . . ."

Her smile dropping from her face, Juanita interrupted sharply. "You need say no more, Don Esteban. Your instructions come too late. Angelica is gone."

"Gone?" A flicker of annoyance compromising his smile, he prompted stiffly, "Where has she gone? Is she home, perhaps, with her brother and . . ."

Juanita's laugh was shrill, bringing a flush of color to Esteban's face with its hint of ridicule. "You give Angelica credit for far more noble qualities than she possesses. She is not here because she has gone off with the Texan!"

His eyes suddenly cold, Esteban shook his head. Reaching out unexpectedly, he snatched Juanita's shoulders with a cruel grip as he gave her a hard shake.

"Tell me the truth, bitch! Where is she? I will listen to no more of your jealous tales! If she is not in the kitchen, where has she been sent?"

Her face paling under the assault of Esteban's sudden rage, Juanita began to tremble. All hint of arrogance gone from her voice, she responded fearfully. "I have told you the truth, Don Esteban. The Texan went on an errand to the mine and she was seen riding away with him on his horse. They have been gone two days and nights and have not yet returned."

Refusing to accept the words he did not wish to hear, Esteban shook Juanita again. Seething, he hissed, "I tell you, do not repeat those lies once more. I know she is here. You seek to advance your own cause but it is hopeless. I have no more desire for you than I have for the poorest street beggar in the capital. Tell me, bitch! Tell me quickly or I will make certain that you never speak another lie!"

Fear assuming control, Juanita shook her head wildly. "It is true! It is true, Don Esteban. Dona Teresa was furious. She sent Hernando to Angelica's home to inquire where Angelica was, but her mother and father were at a loss to explain her absence. But they know now where she is. Everyone knows, and no one is surprised. Señor Dawson made no attempt to hide his interest in her and he . . ."

"Bitch!" Releasing her with a shove, Esteban sent Juanita staggering backward. His face filled with contempt he directed imperiously, "Get back to the kitchen where you belong! And if you are wise, you will not encourage the talk about Angelica Rodrigo. She will soon be in a position far above you, and you may suffer the effects of your words against her. Now go!"

His eyes on Juanita's scrambling figure as she ran back toward the hacienda, Esteban waited only until she had disappeared inside before turning to untie his horse's reins. Walking slowly, he led his horse around the front of the house, his mind traveling a far faster rate than his feet.

There was no reason to hide his arrival from the household now. He would calmly announce that the would be detained at the hacienda another few days before he again left for Mexico City. He would take a bath and change his clothes, and he would then sit down for a leisurely meal. He would determine the true story about Angelica, and he would find her. No matter the events that had transpired since he left Real del Monte, he did not intend to change his plans. Angelica would return to the capital with him . . . one way or the other . . ."

Gareth packed the carefully folded drawings into his

saddlebag. Looking up with a relieved expression, he glanced across the dining-room table where he had spent the greater portion of the night and saw the same relief reflected on Brock Macfadden's weary face. Extending his hand toward the great hulking Scot, he smiled.

"I am much indebted to you, Brock. You have made this visit more profitable than I had imagined it could be. My father will be extremely pleased with the detail you have managed on the basis of the limited information you were afforded, and I thank you as much on his behalf as I do on mine. We'll be expectin' you at our Circle D as soon as you have the opportunity to travel. When my father sees the work you've done, he'll be anxious to see your opinion confirmed by an on-site evaluation. Barrin' any unforeseen problems, I know he'll want to start on the project as soon as possible."

His expression sincere, Brock took his hand firmly. "I confess to a great curiosity ye have stirred in me, Gareth. I will nae let ye doon. Ye'll see me there before the summer is oot."

Taking his saddlebag into his hand, Gareth glanced around the small room. The object of his search was standing in the kitchen talking quietly to Mary and Gareth hesitated as his eyes touched on Angelica's slight form. After Peter had been dispatched for the night, he had known considerable relief. Work on the plans had continued for another hour longer, finally coming to a halt in the wee hours.

Bidding him a gruff good night, Brock provided him with a blanket and walked silently to his room to make the best of the night that remained without a backward look to see where Gareth had placed the blanket. Without hesitation, Gareth had approached the couch where Angelica sat curled into the corner in sleep, her head resting against its high back. He had suffered another jealous twinge when his eyes had touched on the blanket he had seen Macfadden tuck so carefully around her. He had forcefully ejected the memory of Peter Macfadden's hands moving in the tender service and had consoled himself by sitting down beside

227

Angelica's slumped figure and pulling her into his arms.

Angelica's sleepy protests had been spontaneous, directed at being disturbed rather than the fact that he had taken her into his arms. But she had quickly adjusted to the comforting heat of his body, and had curled against his side to rest her head against his neck. He remembered still his reaction, the warmth the contact had stirred inside him, the way he had held her as tight as he had dared for long seconds until he could again bear to loosen his hold.

He had held her in his arms most of the night, dozing until the first light of dawn had begun to cast its silver shadows through the window across from them. He had stirred only when Mary had moved silently into the kitchen to begin preparing breakfast. Her mind had been easy to read as she had glanced toward them and then at the doorway to Peter's room.

In deference to her unspoken request, Gareth had carefully lowered Angelica back to the couch and walked into the kitchen to greet his hostess. He had been standing at her side when Peter had emerged from his room. With only the gruffest of greetings for him, the young Scot's eyes had moved immediately toward the couch and Angelica's stirring figure. With obvious disregard for Gareth, he had walked directly to the couch and crouched beside her to whisper smilingly into her face.

Gareth's step in their direction had been halted by a gentle, restraining hand on his arm and Mary's soft plea.

"Gareth, I beg ye to be generous. Ye be lucky enough to have the lass Peter has set his heart on. It's not been easy for him seein' ye together. And I'll tell ye true, unlike me own mon, I wou' have nae a single objection if Peter had brought the lass into this house as his chosen one. She be a bonnie lass, as unlike the rest of us as can be, to be sure, but I cou' nae help takin' to her. But ye'll soon be leaving the mine, and ye'll have her back to yerself again. All Peter'll have will be his regrets. Be generous, mon. He strives for just a few minutes more with her."

He had nodded and turned to go outside, certain if he had remained all his good intentions would have been for naught, so strong was his desire to stride forward and jerk Peter Macfadden from Angelica's side.

Angelica had been silent at breakfast. She had, in fact, spoken less to him than any member of the household since she had arisen. She was anxious to get home. She was concerned about her position at the Arricalde hacienda, her brother, her parents. . . . Gareth had given little thought to those considerations which nagged her. His own mind had been too filled with his own problems, the greatest of which at the present time appeared to be Angelica herself.

Walking toward the two women in a rapid step, aware that Brock followed slowly behind, he stopped at Mary's side and smiled a rare smile into her upturned face.

"Mary, Brock Macfadden is a fortunate man. It has been my pleasure to meet you and to spend time in your home. I thank you, ma'am, for all you've done, and I hope I'll be seein' you again soon."

"Yer a fine man, Gareth Dawson. I enjoyed havin' ye in my home . . . ye and Angelica. I'm sorry that ye must be gettin' back to yer home in Texas, but. . . ." turning to Angelica, Mary continued with a warm smile, "perhaps we can look forward to seein' more of Angelica. I wou' . . ."

Interrupted gruffly by her husband, Mary turned to Brock's frown.

"We shou' nae be keepin' them from the road, Mary. We've had a long nicht so that Gareth cou' get an early start back to the Arricalde hacienda, and it wou' nae do to delay them now."

Her frown as dark as her husband's, Mary responded unhesitantly, "Peter's nae yet said his good-byes. . . ."

"If the lad has nae the sense to remain nearby, he canna expect . . ."

But this time it was Mary's turn to interrupt. Glancing toward the window with obvious relief, she nodded. "We need nae discuss it any longer. Peter be outside waitin' by Gareth's horse." Turning to Gareth, she said with a glance of silent appeal, "It appears he had Joseph saddle yer horse for ye."

A stiff nod the only response he could manage, Gareth

slid a possessive arm around Angelica's shoulders and ushered her forward. His teeth clamping tightly closed as she stiffened under his touch, he pulled her closer to his side as they emerged into the yard. Forced to forsake his hold as he approached his gorse, he swung his saddlebags onto the saddle and turned to face Peter Macfadden. He extended his hand, his expression sober.

"I'd like to put aside our frictions, Peter, and say good-by as friendly business associates. I appreciate the work you did with Brock on the project and your suggestions on the drawin's."

"The project was a fine challenge and I enjoyed the work. As for our personal differences, they all come to naught now that ye be leavin'. I wish ye a speedy journey back to yer home."

"Yes, I'm sure you do."

The hint of steel in the young Scot's grip did not go unnoticed by Gareth as he shook his hand soberly and turned to scoop Angelica up and onto his horse. Mounting quickly behind her, he took a few moments to settle her comfortably in front of him, aware of the fact that Peter Macfadden's teeth clenched tightly as he bit back comment. Lowering his head until his lips grazed her cheek he addressed Angelica directly.

"Did you have time to say your good-byes, Angelica?"

Turning just enough so that the angry glint in her eye did not go unobserved, she responded quietly, "I think you forget. You are the one who is leaving to return to Texas, not I. I shall doubtless continue to see these people as I have in the past. Ours is only a temporary farewell."

"And mine more permanent in nature. Yes, I suppose you're right."

Looking back to the three faces who watched them with mixed emotions, Gareth gave a final wave and turning, spurred his horse in the direction of the main road. His own arm slipping around her waist, he pulled Angelica closer. He could not get out of this place fast enough.

"It's hard to believe . . ."

Gareth's first words since the inception of their return journey almost an hour before appeared to startle Angelica. Maintaining her silence, she turned to direct a short glance toward his face.

Not waiting for her response, Gareth replied with a shrug, "We've been on this road for almost an hour and there isn't a sign of rain."

His eyes moving to the brilliant blue of the sky overhead, Gareth shook his head. He was almost disappointed. The rain and this road had provided him with some very memorable hours. The thought of them warmed his blood. Time was passing too quickly. They would soon be at the hacienda, and he would be making arrangements to return to Texas. He had been looking forward to the day when he would return home, but. . . ."

Turning his horse to the side of the road, Gareth directed him toward a narrow path that led into the deeper brush. Angelica's reaction was immediate.

"Where are you going?"

Resenting her tone, he responded quietly, "I can hear a stream and I figure it's time for my horse to get a drink. I also figured you might want to get down and stretch your legs a bit."

Appearing relieved, Angelica gave a small nod. He had lifted Angelica down and was watering his horse when Angelica appeared back at his side. She stood silently beside him, her eyes on the glittering ripples of the small stream. Her words had been few since their departure from the mine, and he wanted her to talk to him. The only time they seemed to talk was when they were making love or arguing. There seemed to be little neutral ground between them and Gareth was suddenly conscious of that deficiency.

Reaching out, Gareth picked up a few gleaming strands of her hair and raised them to his face. He inhaled them deeply. His eyes met the silver ones raised to his.

"Your hair smells good, darlin', just like you."

Angelica raised her hand to brush the strands from his palm. Reaching back, she scooped her hair over her one shoulder and separated it into three equal portions in a prelude to braiding.

"No." Taking both her hands in his, Gareth forced her to release her hair. "I don't want you to braid it yet."

A familiar light flashed in Angelica's eyes. "It matters little what you want, señor."

"Oh, so we're back to 'señor' again. What do I have to do to make you call me Gareth, Angelica? Do I have to make love to you again? Is that what you want?"

Angelica attempted to step back, her eyes clearly flashing her answer. Her spontaneous reaction resulted in the inevitable tension which sharpened Gareth's tone.

"Are you savin' yourself, darlin'? What did Peter Macfadden say to you last night? Did he tell you that he'd wait patiently until I left Real del Monte for you to come to him?" The flush that colored Angelica's face was more revealing than a response, and Gareth's anger began to escalate. "Damn the bastard! He didn't waste much time, did he?"

"What does it matter? You will soon be gone and your interest here will come to an end. You will find another '*puta*' with which to amuse yourself. You have had many, have you not?"

Her coolness deceiving, Angelica returned Gareth's intense stare. She recognized the light that was beginning to burn in his eyes. Shamefully, it lit a similar spark deep inside her. But unlike Gareth Dawson, she did not wish to indulge her weakness. She had had her feeble resistance to Gareth Dawson's unexpected flashes of tenderness demonstrated only too clearly in the past few days. She had no desire to experience again the tumultuous emotions which had left her so vulnerable to his touch. No, far better if he considered her cold, unresponsive to the current of emotion moving between them.

"Yes, I've had a few." Gareth looked down at the small hands he still held in his. Long fingers, slender, delicate hands, which looked as if he could crush them with the smallest of efforts if he chose. But he did not choose to crush them. Instead he lifted one small hand to his lips and then the other. He hesitated. "But none of them ever raised the feelin's inside me that you do, Angelica."

Lowering his head, Gareth kissed her hands again. Uncurling her tightening fists, he flattened her palms against his chest. She made an immediate attempt to withdraw them, but he held her wrists fast.

"No, Angelica. Don't pull away. It occurred to me that I take every opportunity I can to touch you, and you shrink from the contact. Angelica, look at me."

When Angelica did not respond but held her head firmly averted, Gareth questioned softly, "Are you afraid to look at me, Angelica? Is that it? You feel the same thing I do, don't you. You want to touch me as much as I want to feel your touch." Slowly unbuttoning his shirt with one hand as he held Angelica's wrists easily captive, he pressed her palms against his bared chest. Managing to suppress a gasp as her hands touched his skin, he ordered softly, "Angelica, look at me, darlin'."

Angelica's eyes slowly rose to his. He would have been prepared for anger, passion, or even coldness in the silver eyes that held his gaze, but the pain in their sober depths was unexpected. Her lips were parting. She was slowly succumbing to his seduction, and she suffered at the realization of her waning resistance. He shared her pain, knowing a similar distress of his own, and a wave of tenderness all but overwhelmed him.

Releasing her wrists, he slid his arms around her and pulled her close against him. Pressing his cheek against her hair, he whispered softly, "I know, darlin'. I know how you feel because I feel the same way."

Her heart was pounding against his chest as Angelica's muffled voice came from the circle of his arms.

"Gareth . . . I must go home. My parents . . . they will be beside themselves with worry, and I must see Carlos. Gareth, a gold coin will not make the difference now, when I must be home . . ."

His arms stiffening at her mention of a gold coin, Gareth moved far enough away so that he might look down into her face. The silent plea there put a swift end to his anger. He held her gaze in silent contemplation. It would not be difficult to take her now, despite her words. She was trembling, the first stirrings of desire moving through her veins, dawning in her troubled eyes. But he could not ignore her plea, no matter the strength of his desire.

Lowering his head to brush her lips lightly with his, Gareth smiled.

"All right, darlin'."

Lowering his hands to her waist, Gareth gripped her securely and swung her up onto his horse. Within a few moments he was mounted behind her and they were making their way back to the main road. His hand holding her firmly against him as they continued back toward the hacienda at a steady pace, Gareth kept his silence. He had no words for the emotion that burned inside him . . . no words at all.

Chapter VI

Angelica was beginning to tremble and Gareth frowned. It was just past mid-morning and they were riding into sight of her home. His hand resting at the curve of her rib cage, he could feel her heart pounding against his palm. She had spoken little since their return to the main road earlier that morning but he had felt the tension slowly stiffening her frame as they had neared the turnoff to her home. He had not anticipated such a reaction.

Angelica's house came into full view and he scanned the empty yard. The stillness was foreboding. His chestnut gelding had broken from the trail into the clearing and they were approaching the door when Angelica's mother emerged, relief filling her eyes. Glancing behind her, Gareth saw a man he could only guess to be Angelica's father come to stand behind her. It was easy to see the reason why Margarita Rodrigo had been found out so easily when she had presented a newborn Angelica to this man. Short with a bulky frame, his dark skin and blunt features spoke only too clearly the Indian blood in his veins. There was none of the refinement of feature present in Angelica's face nor the instinctive carriage with which she walked. But his dark eyes raked Gareth with the suppressed fury of a man who sought to protect his child from the abuses of the world. It was unfortunate, but the man's anger was too late.

Gareth held his stare levelly, challenging the man's anger. He would not accept blame for the outcome of the emotions Angelica had raised within him. She was too beautiful, too desirable, and too willing . . . for a price. In truth, Rodrigo should consider it fortunate that it was Gareth who had taken her. It had merely been a matter of time, and Angelica had made it only too clear that if it had not been him, it would have been someone else. Inwardly flinching at the thought of Esteban Arricalde's well-tended hands abusing Angelica with his sadistic lust, or Peter Macfadden's anxious mouth moving against hers, Gareth pulled himself stiffly erect. He felt no guilt. He had remained true to his bargain with Angelica. He had loved her gently and well, the emotion and tenderness he had experienced were new and startling to his own jaded sensibilities. And she had several gold coins to her credit as a result of their encounter.

But the gravity of Rodrigo's expression was having a far different effect on Angelica. She was beginning to shudder so violently in his arms that Gareth had almost determined to turn his horse around and leave when Angelica turned to shoot him a silent plea. Succumbing to her unspoken persuasion, Gareth dismounted and reached up to lift her down to his side.

Angelica turned to her father's silence, and Gareth suddenly realized that her anxiety was not for herself or fear of her father's anger. Instead, it was directed toward the circumstance of his unusual presence at that hour of the morning and its portended meaning.

"Papa, why are you home this time of day? Is . . . is something wrong? Where is Carlos?"

His dark eyes flicking heatedly to Gareth's stiff countenance, Juan Rodrigo responded softly, "Your brother is in his room. He is yet too ill to leave his bed. If you have any concern at all for him, you will present yourself and relieve him of the anxiety he has suffered at your disappearance."

"Papa . . . Mama . . . *lo siento*. I . . ."

"I do not wish to hear more. Go into the house, Angelica."

Instantly obeying her father's low command, Angelica walked stiffly into the house without a glance for Gareth as he resolutely stood his ground.

"And you, señor . . ." Addressing him coldly, Juan Rodrigo raised his dark eyes to Gareth. "You will leave here,

236

and you will not come back. Angelica will have nothing to do with you after this day."

Not waiting for a response, Juan Rodrigo directed his wife back to the house with a steady hand and turned to follower her. He was a man of few words, and his speaking was done.

Filled with apprehension, Angelica walked rapidly to her room. Pausing at the door, she took a deep breath and attempted to draw her emotions under control. It had been two days since Carlos's attack. It was unusual for him to be bedridden so long after an episode, even one of such obvious severity. Refusing to consciously acknowledge this ominous sign of his worsening condition, Angelica clenched her hand around the gold coins in her pocket and dropped her eyes briefly closed. These few coins were not enough . . . not enough. She needed more.

Attempting a smile, Angelica entered the room, her breath catching on a sob at the joy on Carlos's pale face as she moved rapidly toward him.

"Angelica!" Throwing his frail arms around her neck as she knelt beside the bed, Carlos hugged her tightly. She could feel the moistness of his tears as he whispered in her ear, "I am so happy you are home. Papa was so angry, and Mama was so worried. I heard them talking. They said that you were seen leaving with the Texan . . . that everyone said you were with him."

Drawing back, Carlos looked solemnly up into her face. "I told them if you went with him, then he must be a nice man who would take care of you and they shouldn't worry." His voice dropping lower a notch, Carlos avoided her eyes. "But you must not go off without telling us again, Angelica. I . . . I was frightened. I was afraid you would not come back."

Unable to respond for long seconds, Angelica returned the strength of Carlos's embrace. He was thinner than he had been only two days before. Beginning to feel the press of panic, Angelica sought a normal tone as she drew away at last and smiled. She raised her hand to smooth the shining paths of tears from Carlos's cheeks.

"*Lo siento*, Carlos. I am happy to be back with you, too. It was thoughtless of me to go without telling you I was leaving. But if you will promise not to tell anyone, I will tell you a secret."

His eyes widening with youthful curiosity, Carlos nodded. "A secret, Angelica?"

"Yes, do you promise?"

"*Si.*"

"All right. Look what I have."

Withdrawing her hand from her pocket, Angelica held the gold coins out to him in her palm. Doing her best to retain her smile, she continued softly. "I was able to earn these. Soon we will have enough for you to go to the capital to see the doctor who will make you well! You will be happy then, won't you?"

Engrossed in the wonder of the gold coins, Carlos touched them lightly with his fingertips. Raising his eyes to hers at last, he nodded. "Yes, I will be very glad. I do not like staying here in this bed all day. But in truth, I am too tired to get up and go outside. Padre Manuel says I will feel better in a few days. He has been coming to see me several times each day."

A low mumbling in the room outside their door caught Carlos's attention. "Padre Manuel . . . he is here now, Angelica."

Quickly snatching back her hand, Angelica dropped the coins into her pocket and held a finger up to her lips.

"Remember. It is our secret."

"*Si*, Angelica."

His quick smile reflecting his pleasure in the shared confidence, Carlos held Angelica's hands tightly as padre Manual walked into the room.

"*Buenas dias*, Angelica."

Padre Manuel's old eyes bore a light of censure as he approached the bed. Acknowledging her soft reply with a brusque nod, he walked to Carlos's bedside. He noted the reluctance with which Carlos relinquished Angelica's hand so that he might assume her place at his side, and he commented lightly, "So, you are happy to see your sister again, Carlos. Yes, we are all glad that Angelica has returned. Your father will make certain that she does not leave so unexpectedly again."

"Angelica is happy to be back home, too. And she is sorry everyone was worried, aren't you, Angelica? And . . ." Hesitating, a light coming into his dark eyes, Carlos continued slowly, "And she is a good sister. You are not angry with her any longer, are you?"

His face reflecting his concern, Carlos looked into Padre Manuel's observant eyes. Anxiety was beginning to produce little beads of perspiration on Carlos's brow and upper lip, and anxious to dispel his tension, Padre Manuel nodded his head.

Avoiding a direct answer, Padre Manuel responded quietly, "We are all relieved that Angelica is back with us. Your papa has told me that the Texan delivered her safely to the door, and she looks to have fared well during her two days away from us."

"Yes, Angelica is fine, and now that she is home I will soon be well."

"*Sí*, Carlos."

Touching the boy's forehead with an assessing hand, Padre Manuel turned to Margarita's worried expression.

"You have been giving Carlos the medicine as I have instructed?"

"*Sí, Padre.*"

"Then we can do no more."

Turning back to Carlos, Padre Manuel took his hand. "Your mama tells me you were breathless again last night . . . that you did not sleep well."

Noting Angelica's quick look of concern, Carlos shook his head. "I was not too sick. I will be well soon. Angelica. . . ." Looking to Angelica, Carlos smiled. "Angelica says I will be well soon."

"Well!" Unable to resist a smile at the boy's expressed confidence, Padre Manual nodded emphatically. "If Angelica says you will be well, then you will be! But for now you must rest. Angelica and I, and your mama and papa

239

will leave so that you may sleep undisturbed."

His eyes darting to Angelica, Carlos inquired softly, "You . . . you will be here when I wake up?"

Speaking past the knot that choked her throat, Angelica managed a soft response.

"I must go to the hacienda. Dona Teresa is no doubt wondering what has kept me away so long. But I will return tonight, Carlos, and I will read to you."

"And I will sleep a long time this afternoon so I will not be tired tonight when you return."

Waiting only until Angelica had leaned down to press a light kiss against his cheek, Carlos closed his arms around her neck and whispered into her ear.

"I won't tell anyone our secret, Angelica."

Smiling a silent response as his arms dropped from her neck, Angelica waited only until his weary eyes had closed before following Padre Manuel out of the room.

His eyes moving to hers the moment the door had closed behind her, Padre Manuel shook his head.

"I need not tell you my opinion of your conduct of the past two days, Angelica."

Her head coming up stiffly, Angelica nodded. "No, you need not, Padre." Her eyes moving to encompass the three figures who regarded her so solemnly, she continued quietly. "I regret you were caused concern on my account. In truth, I did not want . . ." Hesitating as her father's expression darkened, she continued quickly. "But it is over and done. It will not happen again."

Long experience had taught Padre Manuel the futility of attempting to talk to Angelica when she was in her present state of mind. Determining to put aside their discussion until a more appropriate time, he responded in a tone of temporary dismissal, "We will speak again, Angelica."

Turning back toward Margarita Rodrigo, Padre Manuel's expression turned grave. His voice dropped a notch softer in a manner which sent a flicker of apprehension down Angelica's spine.

"You say Carlos had another attack last night?"

Angelica's eyes flicked to her mother as she whispered

her response.

"*Si, Padre.* It was not so severe, but I fear Carlos is much weaker this morning."

"There is no doubt that he is."

Confirming Margarita's concern with a weary wag of his head, Padre Manuel took a deep breath before continuing with obvious regret. "I am sorry. I can do no more for Carlos. I fear you must accept each day with grace and enjoy him as much as you can. I do not believe he will be able to withstand the rigors of his illness much longer."

Angelica's low gasp drew all glances in her direction. Her face drained of color, she managed stiffly, "But . . . but you said the doctor in the capital . . ."

"Angelica, with each day that passes Carlos's prospects for recovery are more dim. If his health continues to deteriorate at its present rate, he would stand little chance of surviving the journey to the capital, much less of responding favorably to treatment."

"But if he were to leave soon . . ."

"It would have to be very soon, Angelica."

Swallowing tightly at the portent of Padre Manuel's remarks, Angelica turned blindly toward the door. She did not hear her mother's soft words of consolation as she walked blindly into the yard and started toward the path to the hacienda.

Gareth pulled his horse up before the Arricalde hacienda and dropped his reins into Hernando's hands. He did not miss the old man's sneer, nor his look of open assessment. His annoyance doubled. The old lecher was doubtless trying to determine if he looked sated. The leering bastard had probably spent the last two days thinking and wondering.

As far as he was concerned, he himself had spent more than enough time thinking about Angelica. Damned if she hadn't been almost the sole thought on his mind for the entire duration of the trip back from the mine. It had been impossible to concentrate on anything else with his arm around her slender waist, her breasts bobbing against his hand. He could still smell the warm scent of her body, feel the black silk of her hair brushing his chin. And the mere thought of those rheumy eyes lusting after Angelica raised his rage anew.

That brief encounter with her father had left him vastly dissatisfied, but in truth, he supposed he should be grateful that the man did no more than give him warning. He was very conscious of the fact that Angelica had not told her father that she had accompanied him under duress. He had not yet made up his mind as to her thinking on that account. Perhaps she feared for her father should he attempt to go up against him . . . or perhaps she considered she had been well paid for her time.

The thought left him little peace. Who would be the next person to offer her a gold coin . . . or any coin at all? Would her reaction to her next man be as spontaneously loving? Would she give her new patron the supreme ecstasy he had experienced in loving her? His thoughts efficiently tying his stomach into tight knots, Gareth walked through the front door and started up the steps toward his room.

It was time for other considerations now. His work completed at the mine, he was free to return to his homestead and the trouble brewing in Texas. He would not like to be caught on the ground in between should a conflict begin. No, he had worked too long and hard not to be there to defend his land should Santa Anna be planning a covert strategy against them.

He did not trust the arrogance of the man. There was no doubt Santa Anna considered loyal Texans upstarts. A man of his type demanded blind obedience to his avowed dedications, which usually fluctuated with the pressures of the moment. There could be no clearer statement as to his character than the type of men with whom he chose to surround himself. Esteban Arricalde . . . vain, self-centered, with an exaggerated idea of his own worth . . . a man little interested in the affairs of his country other than the personal stimulation and comfort it could afford him. He truly pitied Don Enrique and Dona Teresa their exceedingly handsome but worthless son.

Esteban *was* handsome. Perhaps that was the reason for his success with women . . . Angelica's attraction to him. Esteban would not be good for any woman . . . much less Angelica. The knot in Gareth's stomach tightened. If he were to be honest, he would have to admit his mind would allow him to accept the thought of no other man but himself with Angelica, but that same honesty forced him to remember that a gold coin was the key to her favors.

Damn, what did he care? His mind was wandering again . . . losing track of the fact that Angelica, for all her youth and beauty, was a *puta* by her own choice. Yes, she was now young, relatively inexperienced, but the short time she had spent in his arms had shown that she learned fast . . . breathtakingly fast. If he were to return here within a year he would probably not recognize her for the woman she would have become. Gareth swallowed hard at the pain the thought evoked.

Striding quickly to his room, Gareth walked in and closed the door firmly behind him . . . just as firmly as he had determined to close his mind to thoughts of the *puta* who had managed to monopolize his thoughts. He walked quickly to the dresser and gathered his few belongings. Picking up the small case in which he had carried the few things he had brought with him, he proceeded to stuff them carelessly inside. Don Enrique had already volunteered supplies for his return journey to Texas. He need only arrange to have them packed and make his farewells. He intended to travel as light as possible. He had the feeling he needed to be out of this territory quickly, as much for his own peace of mind as for the possible threat involved.

Angry that clear, silver eyes were again invading his thoughts, Gareth roughly swept the drawer clean and dumped the contents into his case. He did not hear the movement at the doorway until a familiar voice jerked his head upward.

"Ah, Gareth, you appear to be in a very irritated state of mind. Was not your idyll with the beautiful little *puta* as rewarding as you had intended?"

Stunned at Esteban's appearance in his doorway, Gareth

slowly straightened, maintaining his silence as Esteban's laugh echoed in the small room.

"That is truly unfortunate, because you will not have another opportunity with her."

Walking slowly into the room, Esteban paused. His face twisted into a deprecating sneer.

"You are wondering why I have returned to Real del Monte. The answer is simple, Gareth. I have returned to take Angelica back with me. It occurred to me while on the road that the little slut would shine in the capital. She is a true beauty for all her lack of breeding. I have no doubt she will be able to carry off a pretense to a far more suitable background with a minimal amount of instruction. And I intend to devote much time to instructing her." His sneer widening into a vicious smile, Esteban walked to within a few feet of Gareth, suppressed jealousy burning in the depths of his dark eyes.

"So you have had her first and you took care to take her away with you so you might put your mark more deeply on her . . ." Esteban's voice trailed away, his rage thinly veiled with his smile. "I admit to anger when I returned to find that you had taken the girl with you to the mine. But from outward appearances I can only assume you did not come away from the experience as you expected. I suppose I cannot fault you for your decision to take your opportunity after I had left for the capital, despite my warnings to stay away from her. I admit to a mistake in leaving so precipitously, but I have returned to correct my error. Angelica and I will leave for the capital tomorrow."

"You're so sure of that?"

"Oh, yes, Gareth. I am as sure that Angelica will be returning with me to Mexico City as I am than I will take great pleasure in ridding my country of one more unwise Texan should you attempt to go near the *puta* again."

Gareth's lips moved into a smile which did not reach the frigid depths of his eyes. "Am I to take that as a threat, Esteban?"

"You may take it any way you wish. From appearances, my statement comes a bit after the fact as you seem to be preparing to leave. It is unfortunate that you will not have the opportunity to bid Angelica and me farewell when we depart tomorrow. We will not have the blessings of either set of parents, but I have never allowed those considerations to stop me in the past. I do not intend to allow them to influence me on this occasion, either."

"You've spoken to Angelica about your plans?"

"Gareth, you well know she has not yet returned to the hacienda. I confide my plans to you before I offer them to Angelica. A poor business, is it not? But I care little. My objective was to caution you so you might not inadvertently interfere with my plans."

"You expect Angelica will jump at the opportunity to go with you?"

"She will have little choice. But you need not worry on her account, Gareth. I will go to great lengths to give her pleasure. And then I will teach her the way to give it to me in return . . . "

"Bastard!"

All pretense of civility disappearing from Esteban's facade with the explosion of Gareth's single expletive, Esteban hissed, "You call me a name far more suited to yourself! But names mean little. The sweet Angelica is a *puta*, but no less desirable for the name she carries. And I will taste her, Gareth . . . many times. You may count on my words. You may think about them as you travel on your lonely return to your backward state, and I will enjoy the thought. For I know from experience that contemplation of no other woman will be successful in exorcising the *puta* from your mind. She is like a poison in the blood, is she not? You see, I know what she is. And I also know that she will be mine! And I tell you now, more clearly so that my words will not be misconstrued. Do not go near her again or you will pay with your life, Gareth Dawson!"

Pausing only long enough to allow a few moments for the impact of his words to register fully, Esteban turned on his heel and strode from the room, leaving Gareth silent in his venomous wake.

Angelica stepped off the trail. Her chest was heaving from the strain of her rapid flight through the woods as she approached the rear door of the hacienda. Numb from Padre Manuel's words, she had all but run the entire distance, but she had been unable to escape their ringing sound. Carlos was going to die . . . Carlos was going to die . . . All her fierce determination to manipulate his destiny had been but a whisper in the wind, the gold coins for which she had traded her honor shallow tokens of her loss.

No . . . no, he could not die. He could not!

Perhaps Padre Manuel was wrong! Perhaps Carlos would improve, at least grow strong enough to last the few months necessary for her to get the rest of the money needed for his care. The gold pieces were a good start. She needed just a little more time.

She was entering the kitchen, suddenly aware that all eyes turned in her direction as she walked toward Carmela.

"So, she has the nerve to return . . . to expect Dona Teresa to take her back!"

Juanita's shrill exclamation ringing in her ears, Angelica turned toward Carmela, her eyes lifeless gray pools.

"Carmela, I have returned to assume my work. Do you have any order to the contrary for me?"

Carmela's face reflecting her distress, she gave a small nod.

"*Si.* Dona Teresa has given me instructions to send you directly to her should you return. But in truth, she did not expect you to do so. None of us did.

Angelica nodded. "But I am here."

"Dona Teresa is in the library with Don Enrique."

Turning on her heel, Angelica ignored the stares which followed her, her eyes directed forward as she entered the hallway and walked toward the library door. She knocked once, aware of the stunned silence that met her appearance in the doorway as she obeyed the admonition to enter and walked in.

Dona Teresa's silence was short, her words rasping as she instructed in a shaking voice, "Close the door behind you,

Angelica."

Her small features twitching with anger, Dona Teresa shot a short look to her husband's frown before turning back to face Angelica squarely.

"I admit to surprise that you returned to this household, Angelica. You are far more brazen than both Don Enrique and I gave you credit for. You were clearly warned in this very room, in the presence of Don Enrique, what the result of another transgression would be. You know that it was only Don Enrique's intercession which prevented your dismissal at that time. Not only did you choose to ignore Don Enrique's words on your behalf, but you also chose to betray the confidence my son placed in you!"

Shaking her head, Dona Teresa fell back a step. "It is unfortunate that a pressing matter caused Don Esteban to return this morning to witness your disgrace . . . after his beautiful appeal in your behalf. I can no more forgive you for failing my son than I can forgive you for breaking the word you spoke to me in this very room! Señor Dawson is my guest! You have shamed me by consorting with him openly with full knowledge of my distaste for such proceedings! I do not blame Gareth. He is but a man and subservient to the demands of his body. It was from you I demanded and expected obedience! Since you cannot seem to obey my wishes, Angelica, I have no recourse but to dismiss you from service in this household."

Glancing toward her husband as the words had left her mouth, Dona Teresa nodded her satisfaction as he maintained his silence. Turning back to Angelica, she added, "As you can see, you have lost your last defender here. Even Padre Manuel will not bring me to task for my decision. Whereas it is up the Lord to forgive, Padre Manuel can ask no more of me than the chances I have already given you to redeem yourself. Angelica, you may leave. You are no longer a part of this household."

The peculiar numbness with which Angelica had entered the hacienda was spreading to encompass her mind. Almost unable to function under its influence, Angelica nodded a stiff assent and turned toward the door. She had closed it

247

behind her and started walking back down the hallway when a familiar voice turned her in its direction at the same moment a strong hand reached out to grip her arm. Within moments she had been pulled into the morning room. Turning as the door closed behind her, she faced Esteban's angry hiss.

"So you have survived an encounter with my mother's wrath and emerged unscathed. Bravo, Angelica. Let us now see how well you will escape mine! Bitch!"

Raising his hand, Esteban slapped her full across the face, the force of his blow snapping her head roughly to the side. Hesitating only long enough to allow her eyes to return to his face, he slapped her again, holding her firmly upright as she staggered backward under his blows. Her eyes smarting under the force of his attack, Angelica took a deep breath in an effort to keep at bay the darkness that sought to envelop her.

"No! You will not escape into unconsciousness! You will look into my face and hear what I have to say, for I give you choice to do little else!"

Suddenly pulling her close, Esteban ripped her head back cruelly to avail himself of her mouth. His mouth ground into hers, his hand tightening in her hair as he crushed her against him. He was punishing her with his kiss, purposely inflicting pain with an act meant to give pleasure and he reveled in his power. Jerking his mouth from hers at last, he said savagely, "You are through bending others to your will with the lure of your sweet body! You are finished in this household, and you will find no employment elsewhere. But I will save you from yourself, Angelica. You see, I have a plan."

Taking her chin with hard, biting fingers, he held her fast under his bruising grip. "You will be flattered to know that I returned from my journey for the sole purpose of bringing you back to the capital with me! Do you realize the extent of the trouble I experienced just to return for you, Angelica? It involved lying to the saintly Valentins, imposing on the hospitality of my father's friends, and putting my body to the rigors of a long return trip on horseback. All that for you, little *puta*, and when I returned you had run off for a two-day idyll with the Texan."

He was squeezing her chin, causing her intentional pain, but Angelica could not bring herself to struggle against him. It was worthless, all of it, all of it . . .

"Did you hear what I said? You will come back to the capital with me tomorrow morning. My mother will be scandalized, but I expect your parents will put up no stronger objections than they obviously did to your departure with the Texan. You will, after all, be leaving in better company . . . improving your station. You will stay with me in my apartments in Mexico City . . . will function as my mistress. You will serve me well. You will give me an opportunity to evaluate your talents, and I will teach you those things that especially please me. We will have a fine exchange, little *puta*. A very fine exchange."

Appearing suddenly conscious of the fact that Angelica neither responded nor attempted to fight him, Esteban gave her a hard shake, anger lighting his eyes. "Have you been listening, *puta*? Did you hear what I said?" When she still did not respond, he gave her a vicious shake. "Answer me, *puta*, or I promise you, you will never speak another word!"

"Y—yes, I heard you." Angelica managed a halting response despite the fact that her tongue had gone as numb as her emotions.

"And what is your answer? Come, I wish to hear you speak the words."

Swallowing once again, Angelica rasped, "How much will you pay me?"

His handsome face going stiff with shock, Esteban stared into the silver ice of Angelica's eyes. The sudden burst of laughter that escaped his lips echoed in the empty room.

"Pay you? Pay you? You wish to bargain with me for price?"

Uncaring of the result of her words, Angelica took a breath and pressed unyieldingly. "I care not what you do to me, Don Esteban. My future is sealed from this point on, but my brother's is not. If you will give me the sum necessary for him to travel to Mexico City to the doctor who can help him, I will go with you willingly."

"You will go with me in any case, *puta*. I will see that you have no choice. Your family is vulnerable, is it not . . . especially your poor, sick brother . . ."

"But if you will pay me, Don Esteban, I will serve you well." Steeling herself against the nausea which began to envelop her, she continued steadily, "I will be a willing pupil to your teachings. I will extend every effort to see that I far surpass your wildest dream of my accomplishments, and then I will pleasure you even more."

Aware of the betrayal of his body and its revealing swell, Esteban hissed raggedly, "Bitch . . . bitch . . . You seduce me with your words as effectively as you seduce me with your beautiful face and warm body." Hesitating only a moment as his eyes moved lasciviously over her face, Esteban gave a small, jerking nod. "All right, I will pay you. I will put a sum into your hands tomorrow morning before we leave this place. I will watch you give it to your bitch of a mother, and then I will take you with me. And you will pay for that piece of bargaining, Angelica. You will give me my money's worth many times over. Is that understood, *puta*?"

Experiencing the beginning of hope, Angelica did her best to ignore the hands that roughly massaged her breasts, the mouth that moved to bite into her neck. Her response was soft.

"Yes, I understand."

The glare of triumph in Esteban's eyes almost more than she could stand, Angelica was preparing to accept another of his savage kisses when Dona Teresa's step was heard in the hall.

"Esteban . . . Esteban . . ."

Muttering harsh epithets under his breath, Esteban pushed Angelica away from his grasp. Looking quickly to the door to the patio, he ordered gruffly, "Go . . . get out of here, now! I will come for you tomorrow morning at dawn. I warn you now to be waiting for me, Angelica . . ."

"Yes, I will be waiting, Don Esteban."

Turning quickly, swallowing against the bile that rose to her throat, Angelica took a few quick steps to the patio door. Jerking it open, she ran onto the patio and into the yard. Within minutes she was running down the trail toward her home. She did not look back.

Glancing up toward the cloudless blue sky, Gareth frowned. It was shortly past noon and he was anxious to depart. Dressed in traveling clothes, his gunbelt slung low around his hips, he had descended the front staircase of the Arricalde hacienda only a few minutes before to find Don Enrique and Dona Teresa waiting to say their farewells. Securing his case firmly to his saddle, he turned back toward them once again where they stood on the front steps of the hacienda. He closed the distance between them in a few long strides and extended his hand toward Don Enrique.

"*Muchas gracias* for your hospitality, Don Enrique . . . Dona Teresa. You've been very generous both in opening your home to me and in allowing your engineers to work with me."

"It was our pleasure, Gareth."

Echoing her husband's response with a stiff smile, Dona Teresa held herself rigidly erect as Gareth took her plump hand briefly in his.

"I only hope I haven't caused you discomfort in any way, Dona Teresa. It would be poor payment indeed for your splendid hospitality."

Her small eyes more eloquent than her words, Dona Teresa nodded briefly. "You are our guest, Gareth. As our guest you are under no restrictions here. It is only our employees who follow instructions in order that they may maintain their position. You will always be welcome here."

Dona Teresa's words imparted a message far clearer than her statement, and Gareth frowned. Had not Angelica accepted the damned gold pieces he had given her, he would have felt compelled to defend her. But a hard core of an unknown emotion refused to allow him to assume responsibility. It has been a business matter, pure and simple. Angelica had offered herself to him and had accepted payment each time they had made love. She had made it clear that although he had been the first, he would not be the last.

That last thought stiffening his resolve, Gareth turned again toward Don Enrique.

"I would like to thank you again for your advice, Don Enrique. I will keep it in mind, and I appreciate your efforts in my behalf."

"You are not leaving without saying good-bye, are you, Gareth?"

Esteban's unexpected interruption snapped the attention of all three toward him as he appeared unexpectedly from the front doorway and approached them with a brilliant smile.

"I thought we had accomplished that earlier, Esteban."

"Perhaps. But since I am to leave again tomorrow, it will probably be the last time we will have an opportunity to speak for some time to come. There were some things we left unfinished in our last conversation, were there not?"

"Were there?" His eyes narrowing in suspicion of Esteban's obvious good humor, Gareth bobbed his head. "If so, we had best get them settled." Turning back to the Arricaldes' puzzled regard, Gareth gave them a genuine smile. "*Adios* and *muchas gracias* from both my father and me. We can never thank you enough for your friendship."

The Arricaldes' warm farewell still sounding in his ears, Gareth took his horse's reins and turned to walk companionably beside Esteban as he started down the drive.

"Gareth, the truth is, I have some details to impart to you that will doubtless set your mind at ease."

His expression wary, Gareth maintained his silence, extremely conscious of Esteban's confident strut as he matched Gareth's steady stride. Waiting only until they were out of the Arricaldes' range of hearing, Gareth dropped all guise of friendship.

"All right, Esteban. Out with it. I haven't any time to waste if I expect to make any time at all before nightfall."

"Such impatience. And all you have to look forward to tonight is an empty bedroll. While I . . . oh, yes, Gareth, I have much to look forward to in the nights to come."

"What are you tryin' to tell me, Esteban? You're right. I'm gettin' damned impatient."

"Oh, that is unfortunate. My intentions were to allow you to leave with a settled mind. I would not want you to leave wondering what will happen to the little *puta*."

Gareth's expression tightened.

"Oh, yes, she reported to work this morning, shortly after we talked. It was a decidedly stupid thing to do. She must have realized my mother would never have her in the house again."

Gareth stiffened. "Is that what you wanted to tell me?"

"No, that is only the beginning, my friend."

"You're no friend of mine."

Esteban's laugh sent the blood rushing to Gareth's face.

"Ah, but since I will have Angelica, I confess the loss of your friendship will plague me little, Gareth." Realizing he had gained Gareth's acute attention, Esteban continued with relish. "Yes, I will have a very willing companion in Mexico City, Gareth. Angelica came very gladly into my arms. She made no protest whatever . . . delighted in my loving attentions. The taste of her is unique, is it not? It still warms my mouth and stirs my blood. Oh, yes, I will enjoy myself intensely on my long journey to the capital."

"You're a damned liar, Esteban."

"But she wants another man, Gareth. She was not terribly happy to be dismissed from service in the hacienda. That little brother of hers, you know. He is so sick, *pobre niño*. But I admit to being startled when she asked me how much I would pay her . . ."

Cursing the spontaneous jerk of his head that gave Esteban just the answer he had sought, Gareth clamped his teeth tightly shut against his stupidity.

"Oh, so! You paid the *puta* for her time, too! She is a greedy little slut, is she not? But tell me, how much did you pay her, Gareth? I need not ask if she was worth the price, because I can see on your face that she was worth any price you paid."

"Shut up, Esteban."

"Does the truth disturb you, Gareth? It is a statement of fact, a business arrangement of money exchanged for services rendered. And she has promised me that she will render them well, Gareth . . . that she will learn all I have to teach her and then she will pleasure me more . . ."

"Lyin' bastard . . ."

Triumph shining brightly in his eyes, Esteban laughed again. "You wish to believe I lie, but I do not, Gareth. So you had two days which you paid for handsomely. But you did not leave your mark on her, did you? That is always a blow . . . so damaging to one's ego. You were no more to her than another man to service. And tomorrow I will put a sum into the little slut's hands and she will come with me willingly . . . very willingly. You see, but I will differ from you in one respect, for then I will make *her* pay, Gareth, and pay and pay and pay . . ."

"Do whatever you want with her, I don't give a damn!"

Unable to listen to more, Gareth turned and mounted his horse. Without another look he spurred his gelding forward, turning his back on Real del Monte and all who lived there.

The peculiar numbness had not yet left her. Her eyes moving blinding to the foliage that surrounded her, Angelica adjusted her position on the large boulder to the side of the trail. She had not been able to make herself return home. She was all but certain her father had returned with Padre Manuel to the church. There were few excuses for Papa to spend a leisurely day, and he would doubtless be working all the harder in an attempt to work out his despair at Padre Manuel's words.

She must return home soon. She must talk to Carlos . . . read to him as she had promised. And then she must tell him that she would be leaving in the morning. She would explain that it would not be for long, that he, too, would be coming to Mexico City as soon as arrangements could be accomplished. In her heart she suspected that Don Esteban would frown on any attempt by her to communicate with her family once they arrived. She had no doubt she would suffer the weight of his hand many times if she attempted to cross him. But she feared him little. Somehow, it seemed that the pain she bore inside made physical pain all but ineffective.

Angelica's eyes moved to the sky overhead. The sun was past the midpoint. It was at least an hour past noon. She had no doubt the Texan had already started back. He was anxious to return to his home. His fears for his homestead had assumed the spot of major importance in his mind. She had been forgotten, relegated to the same place in his mind as all the other women he had bought and used well. But he had been honest from the first in declaring his sole interest in her. He had desired her and had paid the price she asked. She had no right to expect more.

But if Carlos died, there would be nothing at all.

A flush suddenly rising to Angelica's face, she felt shame for the first time. Now, when Carlos needed her most, she was allowing the deadening weight of reality to overcome her. She was so close . . . so very close. Tomorrow she would get the sum needed from Don Esteban. She would place it in her mother's hands and she and Papa would only need to wait until Carlos was fit to travel before starting out for Mexico City. Padre Manuel would help. A dedicated man of the cloth, he was also practical enough to realize that money, however obtained, was Carlos's only chance. Carlos would be well. And when Don Esteban tired of her, she would be free. All would be well.

Suddenly revisited with the memory of Esteban's savage kiss, Angelica felt a flash of revulsion. There would be no tenderness, no soft words whispered in her ear in the throes of passion. She knew instinctively Esteban would be a cruel taskmaster who would hold her stringently to her rash promises. But she had been left with no other choice.

A vision of Peter Macfadden's earnest face returned to her mind and her throat tightened with emotion. No, she could not involve him in so cold a bargain . . . demand a price from him which he could not afford to pay. And she could not bring herself to come between him and his family. She had no doubt involvement with her would bring a separation of ways between Brock and Peter Macfadden. She, of all people, knew the true value of family. She could not add the weight of that burden to those she already carried.

Pulling herself to her feet abruptly, Angelica took a deep breath. She had devoted enough time to pathos. She had much to accomplish this day . . . unpleasant tasks that would only become more unpleasant as they were left to wait.

She had taken several steps back in the direction of her home when the sound of hoofbeats on the trail behind her turned her in their direction. Startled at the sight of the familiar chestnut gelding as it came into view, Angelica lifted her eyes to the face of its rider. His stiff expression formidable, Gareth held her gaze without warmth until he drew his horse to a halt. Dismounting, Gareth dropped his horse's reins over a low bush and came to stand close beside her. His eyes were cold black onyx, his voice harsh.

"It's true, isn't it? You've sold yourself to that bastard Esteban Arricalde."

Spontaneous anger, inflamed by the contempt in his voice, forced Angelica's chin to a proud tilt as she met and held his gaze.

"I see no need to answer your question, Gareth Dawson. Our association has come to a close. You are on your way back to your home, are you not? What I do here in Real de Monte . . .

"But you won't be in Real del Monte. You'll be in Mexico City. Have you ever been there, little *puta*? Mexico City is large . . . complex. People have been very conveniently lost there, with few to remember or care that they ever existed. You're makin' a mistake going there with Esteban. He can't be trusted."

"If I am making a mistake, then it will be I who will pay, not you! What are you doing here now? I had expected that you would be on the trail back to Texas."

Refusing to admit that he had indeed been on the road

but had been unable to go on, Gareth reached out to grip Angelica by the shoulders. Her spontaneous wince drew his eyes to the flesh his hands had touched. Ugly bruises were already darkening there. Raising his eyes slowly to hers, he noted Angelica sought to avert her gaze, inadvertently turning her face to reveal another bruise beginning to darken the soft skin of her cheek. He raised his fingers tentatively to her face and traced the outline of the mark.

"Is this how Esteban convinced you to go with him, Angelica?"

Angelica jerked her face from his touch, stung by the pity in his low voice.

"It was not necessary for Don Esteban to convince me. I was most agreeable to going to the capital with him. Don Esteban had much to offer me."

"Much to offer you?" Anger filling the eyes which only moments before had been soft with compassion, Gareth gave a harsh laugh. "Are gold coins that important to you? What purpose do you have in mind for this fortune you are attemptin' to amass? Do you dream great dreams for yourself? If you do, Esteban Arricalde won't help you to achieve them."

"I will achieve my purpose before I leave Real del Monte. I will have the money that I . . ."

"Money?" His hands moving again to grip her arms, Gareth grated in barely controlled anger, "What will money buy you that is worth the chance you take with Esteban Arricalde?"

"It will buy my brother's life!"

Stunned by Angelica's response, Gareth shook his head. "What has Esteban promised you?"

"I need no promises from Don Esteban other than the money I will receive tomorrow. That money will allow him to see the doctor in the capital who will cure him."

"What doctor?"

"Padre Manuel knows of him. Money is the only thing that keeps Carlos from becoming well. Now he is dying. My virtue is a small thing when weighed against his life."

"So you did it for your brother . . ."

257

Pride coming to her defense, Angelica raised her chin a notch higher. "Carlos's illness forced me to take a step I would doubtless have taken in any case. There is little for me here in Real del Monte. Minds have been closed against me since the day of my birth. My future lay in only one direction, and I am not so sure it is not better than the fate of many of the women of the village. A life of poverty and endless children at the side of a man who forces me to walk in his shadow was never a life I aspired to."

"Is that the way it is in your family?"

"No!" Responding spontaneously before the thought registered that he had no right to such a question, Angelica shook her head vehemently. "My father is a good man. There is no question of the love he bears my mother, and for his love he has suffered ridicule since the day of my birth. When my brother is well, I will use my new 'profession' to gain him freedom from the yoke he has been made to bear because of me."

"He has borne the burden of your mother's actions, not yours."

Her eyes turning to silver ice, Angelica hesitated before responding, making an obvious attempt to rein her emotions under control.

"Like the others, you choose to believe my mother had guilt in my conception. That is because you are a fool!"

At the conclusion of her rasped statement, Angelica stared belligerently into Gareth's eyes, challenging his response. But the picture of her beauty, all the more magnificent for the fire which burned in her great eyes and the flush that colored her perfect features had a far different effect than that which she sought. Despite himself, Gareth felt the draw of the warm flesh beneath his palms, the lure of the mouth which spat her contempt. Somewhere in the back of his mind he accepted the accusation. Yes, he was a fool for wanting her still . . . for being unable to leave knowing Esteban Arricalde would soon be holding her in his arms.

"Do you care for him . . . for Esteban?"

Startled at the unexpected question, Angelica hesitated.

258

But it was too late to hide the revealing flicker of denial in her eyes.

"You know what he is, don't you?" Gareth was incredulous. "And you'll still go with him . . ."

"He gives me what I need. It is Don Esteban's intention that I will remain with him in the capital. That is well. In that way I will be able to get additional funds should they be needed for Carlos."

"And when he is through with you?"

Faced unexpectedly with the question she had sought to avoid, Angelica felt a small tremor shake her frame. She took a deep breath. "That is too far in the future for me to consider now. I . . . I must take one step at a time . . ."

Hesitating only momentarily, Gareth questioned softly, "What if I would give you all Esteban Arricalde offers you, and the answer to my last question as well?"

Angelica hesitated, at a loss for words.

"Wh—what are you proposing?"

"I've decided that I'd like some company on the journey back to Texas. If you come with me, I'll give you the amount you need for your brother's treatment. A year, Angelica. The sum will buy me the same rights it buys Esteban, but for only a year. After that you may return to Real del Monte or go any place you wish."

Angelica's heart began a steady pounding in her chest. Her gaze flicked over the dark, unrevealing eyes, the strong planes of his face, and across the firm lips now drawn into an unsmiling line. She remembered the sweet persuasion of that mouth, the wonder it had evoked inside her. She swallowed tightly.

"There would be no objection to my presence at your homestead?"

"We have a large workin' ranch in Texas, Angelica. There are several women workin' in the kitchen, but there's always room for one more. You'll receive the same pay as they do for your work there."

A flash of a burning, unrecognizable emotion jolted through her.

"Do these women perform 'personal' services for you

also?"

A short, spontaneous laugh escaped Gareth's lips.

"No, Angelica. I don't run a brothel. You're more likely to end up in one if you accompany Esteban to the capital than if you come with me." Raising his hand to her cheek, Gareth continued softly, "No . . . I have no other women in the house that I have any desire to love."

But the unexpected warmth in his tone was fleeting, replaced moments later by a hint of steel. "And while you're in my household, Angelica, your 'services' will be reserved for me only. There'll be no exchange of coins between you and anyone you might fancy."

Refusing to reveal the pain his statement had evoked, Angelica allowed her heavily lashed lids to hood her eyes as she appeared to consider his offer. When she was again in control, she raised her eyes slowly to his.

"A year, and I may return?"

"I will provide you with transportation to whatever place you wish. You may also arrange for letters to be delivered to Padre Manuel through the lines of communication our committee has set up to the area of Real del Monte."

"I . . . I will be able to find out how Carlos is progressing . . . send money if it is needed?"

Allowing himself to feel the first spark of hope since he had made his unexpected proposal, Gareth nodded. He exerted stringent control over the desire to take Angelica into his arms . . . to persuade her to accept his offer in a way that would give them both pleasure. But he would not allow himself to use tactics similar to the obvious physical coercion Esteban Arricalde had used. Instead, Gareth nodded again, holding his breath, his eyes intent on Angelica's face.

Perversely refusing to speak her instinctive assent, Angelica hesitated. "But what will I tell Don Esteban?"

"Nothin'. Damn it . . . nothin'."

His hand slipping up to cup her chin, Gareth held it firmly as he searched her eyes for the words she refused to speak. A flood of elation sweeping his mind at the unspoken consent there, he lowered his mouth at last to hers.

Lingering there only briefly despite his inclination to the contrary, Gareth lifted his head and swallowed against the familiar need building inside him.

Her pink lips still moist from his kiss, Angelica swallowed visibly. "When will we leave?"

"Now."

"But . . . but I cannot!" Panic moved across Angelica's face and she shook her head. "I cannot leave without explaining . . ."

But Gareth would not allow her to continue. "Then go to your house now and speak to your family." Turning toward his horse, Gareth unfastened his saddlebag and reached inside. Within a moment he had withdrawn a pouch. Removing a portion of the coins inside, he turned back to Angelica and put them into her hands. Carefully assessing her expression as her eyes touched on the sum, Gareth waited only until Angelica had raised her face again to him before continuing.

"It's enough?"

Angelica nodded and slipped the money into her pocket.

"I'll have to stop in the village before we leave, but I'll be back for you within the hour. I want to be well away from here by dark, Angelica. Will you be ready?"

"*Si*. I will be waiting."

Gareth's eyes moved briefly over the determination in her beautiful face. Sliding his hand around to cup her neck, Gareth drew her toward him as he lowered his mouth briefly to hers once more.

"An hour."

Releasing her with more regret than he dared admit, Gareth followed Angelica's figure until it had disappeared down the trail. He turned and mounted his horse. Within moments he was riding toward the village.

Angelica walked to the door of the darkened room, her eyes moving to the small figure on the bed. Reacting instantly to her appearance in the doorway, Carlos raised his head.

"You are home early, Angelica."

"I am home early because I am no longer employed at the hacienda." At his instinctive look of alarm, Angelica approached the bed quickly. "No, do not despair, *querido*." Her hand moving to Carlos's warm brow, Angelica suppressed a frown. "Do you remember the secret I told you?"

"*Si*, I remember, Angelica. I have told no one."

"Well, you will be leaving for the capital sooner than we all thought." Smiling at the immediate widening of Carlos's expressive eyes, Angelica nodded. "*Si*. All has turned out well. You were correct to have faith in the Texan. He has furnished the funds for your treatment in exchange for my employment at his hacienda."

"But his hacienda is in Texas . . . far away from here . . ."

"That is right, *querido*. We will have to be separated for a while, but it will not be for long. I would not be able to accompany you while you go for treatment to the capital in any case."

"How long will you be gone, Angelica?"

"A year."

"A year! But I will be all grown up in a year!"

Unable to restrain a laugh, Angelica leaned forward and pressed a light kiss against Carlos's thin cheek. "No, you will not be grown up in a year, but you will have grown well. And when you return to Real del Monte, I will return shortly afterwards. We will all be together again. It will be very wonderful, Carlos. You will be able to play with the rest of the boys . . ."

Carlos appeared to consider her words.

"I am not so sure I wish to play with some of them. Some of them are not very nice."

"Then you will play with those of them whom you like. And you will grow big and fat and I will laugh at you."

"Oh, Angelica!" Laughter sparked in eyes filled with doubt only moments before, and Carlos shook his head. "I will not get fat, only well rounded like Jorge Morales. But I will be tall and strong, like Miguel Santos, and I will run very fast . . . much faster than Pedro Alvarez." Leaning closer, Carlos reduced his voice to a confidential whisper. "I do not like Pedro Alvarez, Angelica. He is a bully and a

262

braggart. But when I am well I will be able to run very fast and I will be very happy to beat him in a race."

"And when I come back you will race for me and I will laugh at Pedro when you win."

The smile slipping from his face at the reminder of her imminent departure, Carlos raised questioning eyes to Angelica once again.

"Will you be happy in Texas, Angelica?"

Seriously considering the question for the first time, Angelica offered simply, "I will not be happy until I am back again with you and Mama and Papa." Feeling instant regret at her statement in the face of Carlos's immediate frown, Angelica added with a forced smile, "But . . " Realizing she had again caught Carlos's attention, she continued. "I do know one thing. Don Esteban offered to take me to the capital when he leaves, to serve in his apartments." Leaning forward in the same manner as Carlos had only moments before, Angelica whispered confidentially, "I do not like Don Esteban very much, Carlos. Like Pedro, he is a bully. I much prefer the Texan to Don Esteban. The Texan is a fair man."

"Then I am glad you are going with the Texan." His momentary smile fading, Carlos took her hand, his eyes moving to her slender fingers as he said softly, "When are you leaving?"

"Within the hour."

"An hour? But Papa will not be home! He will be angry if you leave without telling him."

"And you must explain to Papa all that I have explained to you, Carlos. You must tell him that I will return when I have finished my employment. The Texan has promised to arrange for transportation back to Real del Monte and I know he will keep his word."

His dark head bobbing soberly to her instructions, Carlos watched as Angelica drew herself to her feet and walked to the window to remove the flowerpot resting there. Intent on her actions, he followed her return to the bed as she placed the pot on the table beside him. His narrow brows moving into a frown, he watched as she dug into the dirt and pulled out three gold coins. Cleaning them off against her skirt, she placed them in his hands.

"These are for you, Carlos."

Carlos nodded. "I will give them to Mama."

"No, they are for you." Smiling at his surprise, Angelica continued softly. "Mama has more than enough money to take care of expenses at the capital. The markets in the city are vast, Carlos. When you are feeling well again you will enjoy walking there. You will be so big and strong that you will not fit in these small clothes anymore. You will need new ones, and when that time comes you must buy them and other things you will need when you come back to Real del Monte."

"*Si*, and I will buy something for you! It will be a surprise when you return." At Angelica's immediate look of disapproval, he continued with soft assurance. "You need not worry, Angelica. I will choose very carefully. I will pick something that will match your beautiful eyes, and you will be proud to wear it."

"Oh, Carlos . . ."

Angelica allowed her gaze to move over Carlos's loving face, hoping to store his image in her mind for the long months ahead. Experiencing a swell of love so strong that she was almost overcome, Angelica reached out to encircle Carlos in a fierce hug.

His small arms no less emphatic in their silent statement, Carlos whispered against her ear, "I will miss you, Angelica."

Gently extricating herself from his clutching embrace, Angelica pulled back to look carefully into Carlos's brimming eyes.

Swallowing against the lump in her own throat, she said softly, "I will not be gone so long, *querido*. It is important that I go with the Texan to fulfill my obligation, and it is important that you go to the capital so that you will be well. It is a small sacrifice, Carlos, and one well worth the pleasure of seeing Pedro Alvarez's face when you run past him to finish the race. We will both enjoy that, will we not?"

"*Si*, Angelica."

Heavy tears still hung in his great black eyes, and unable to stand their mute appeal any longer, Angelica raised her hand to the shelf over Carlos's bed and picked up the book resting there.

"All right. I promised I would read to you tonight. We are almost through Padre Manuel's book."

"Who will read to me when you are gone, Angelica?"

Her eyes moving to Carlos's sad face, Angelica hesitated. "You will be going to the capital very soon. Perhaps you will buy a book there that you will be able to read by yourself. Then you must save it and read it to me when I return. In the meantime, we will ask Padre Manuel to allow us to borrow this book again so that we may finish reading it when I come back." Her smile encouraging, Angelica nodded. "You will have much to tell me of the capital when next we see each other, and I will tell you all about the primitive state of Texas."

"*Sí*, Angelica."

Attempting to ignore his less than enthusiastic tone, Angelica opened the book and began to read.

Trailing a small sorrel filly attached to his lead, Gareth made his way cautiously back up the trail he had traveled only a short time before. He had spent a busy hour in the village. It had not been easy securing another mount. It had only been by the greatest stroke of luck that he had been able to find the undersized animal he had bought. He suspected it was only due to the presence of Europeans in Real del Monte that the animal was available at all. It seemed an enterprising merchant had thought to make himself a handsome profit when one of the Scots from the mine was looking for a mount for his wife. But he had failed to take into account the natural frugality inherent in that breed of European. As a result, he had been stuck with the animal. His enthusiasm upon hearing Gareth's inquiry as to a mount had been restrained as result of his inborn bargaining sense, but it had not been difficult to secure a good price.

He had also negotiated for extra supplies which he had

loaded equally between the two horses. He intended to waste little time in hunting en route. It was his desire to arrive at his ranch as quickly as possible, and if that meant long days in the saddle, and léss than appetizing meals at night, that was the way it was going to be. But somehow he expected he would hear little complaint from Angelica.

Gareth gave a small grunt. They needed to make it back to the homestead quickly. His funds were all but nonexistent. When he had made his plans to come to Real del Monte, he had not taken into account the expense of a beautiful little *puta* whom he could not leave behind.

Oh, he had tried. Upon leaving Esteban earlier in the day he had made directly for the main road out of the village. But he had not gone more than a mile when Esteban's words began to gain greater proportion in his mind. Vivid mental pictures of Angelica in Esteban's arms had given him no rest. It had done no good to tell himself that she was going with Esteban of her own consent . . . that she had agreed to accept payment to allow Esteban to love her . . . that she deserved whatever she got as a result of her bargain. And it had done no good to tell himself he was driven by anything but his own unrelenting desire for the greedy little *puta*.

In the end, he had decided that until he could exorcise the insatiable hunger she had created inside him, he would pay her price and keep her exclusively his. Emotions of the scope that presently ruled him were doomed to a short life. He had no doubt that by the time he reached Texas he would begin to question his sanity in bringing her with him. She would doubtless grate on his nerves as much as she stimulated his lust now. A year . . He would be free of this compelling need for her by then. He would have to be.

He was drawing nearer Angelica's home. Its outline was becoming visible through the trees. Disgusted with the racing of his heart, Gareth searched the yard for a sign of Angelica, but there was none. He frowned, a slow agitation beginning inside him. She could not change her mind now, damn her! She had struck a bargain. It made no difference to him if her parents, the priest, or the rest of the world

266

disapproved, she would come back with him!

He had determined that even before she had given her voluntary approval. He had determined that he would take her with him to Texas and use whatever force was necessary. His feelings had not changed in that regard. She would come with him with or without her consent. He would not spend his nights dreaming of her in Esteban Arricalde's arms, thinking of his hands on her flesh, his mouth tasting hers. She was his now, bought and paid for! And, damn it, he was going to go inside and take her!

Urging his horse down off the trail and into the yard, Gareth approached the front door of the house. His eyes scanned the surrounding area cautiously. He could afford to take no chances.

Gareth dismounted and secured his mounts. He approached the door in a smooth, silent step. The door was open, but there was no one in the small kitchen. He walked noiselessly inside, his eyes flicking to a doorway off the main room and the low buzz of voices coming from it. Unwilling to yet announce his presence, he approached it with caution, his step slowing at the sound of Angelica's voice.

". . . must go now, *querido*. I can stay no longer, but I will come back to you as I promised. You must remember everything I told you, and remember to keep the secrets we share. We will not be apart long. And you must also remember . . ." A low huskiness entering her voice, Angelica hesitated before continuing. "I . . . I will always love you best, *querido* . . . and I will think of you all the while I am gone."

The love in Angelica's voice had set his heart to a jealous pounding. The silence that followed her statement spurring him into action more quickly than the sound of a shot, Gareth moved rapidly to the doorway of the room. His hands balled into tight fists, he started into the dimly lit room, only to draw to a jerking halt at the sight that met his eyes.

Angelica was sitting on the edge of the narrow bed in the corner of the room, her arms wrapped securely around the thin body of a child. It was obvious the child was crying and

Angelica attempted to comfort him. They were unaware of his presence until Margarita Rodrigo spoke from the darkness in the corner of the room.

"Angelica, Señor Dawson has arrived."

Her head snapping up, Angelica frowned. The boy's arms moved to wrap around her neck and she turned back to him, her expression immediately softening.

"I may stay no longer, Carlos. You see, Señor Dawson has come for me. It is necessary that he be away from here before nightfall and I must not delay his departure."

His eyes moving to Carlos's thin face, Gareth felt a shock move through him. How long had it been since the last time he had seen the boy . . . two days . . . three? But his physical deterioration was so marked that it was almost unbelievable that so short a time had elapsed. His eyes darted to Angelica's face, and he felt her pain.

But Carlos's strangely adult eyes drew him back as he began to speak.

"Angelica is ready, Señor Dawson. She only came in here to say good-bye to me because I am not yet well enough to walk to the door with her. But I will be leaving for the capital soon and I will be well. Then Angelica will come back home again. She has promised me. Angelica does not break her promises. She is a good sister."

Taking a deep breath, Carlos slowly allowed his arms to drop from around Angelica's neck. He took a deep sniff and attempted a smile as Angelica drew herself to her feet. Taking a few steps toward the bed, Gareth leaned forward and extended his hand in Carlos's direction. The hand which slid into his was pathetically small, but the strength of the grip which attempted to respond to his brought a small smile to his lips.

"*Adiós*, Carlos."

Carlos's dark eyes studied Gareth's face openly before a smile picked up the corners of his mouth.

"I am glad that Angelica is going with you, Señor Dawson. I do not like Don Esteban. He is not a kind man."

Withdrawing his hand, Gareth was about to respond when Angelica leaned over to press a light kiss against

268

Carlos's face.

"*Adiós*, Carlos."

Turning back to the woman who stood silently in the corner, Angelica walked forward and placed her arms around her for a short embrace. "You will stay with Carlos until I leave?"

"*Si.*"

Turning quickly, Angelica walked toward the doorway, pausing as she stepped over the threshold to glance back over her shoulder. Sliding his arm around her waist, Gareth bid her mother a quick farewell and urged her on into the kitchen. Realizing the necessity for a quick break, he waited only until she had snatched up her rebozo and a small bundle from the table before urging her on toward the front door. Intensely aware of her trembling, he led her to the side of the sorrel, and placing his hands firmly around her waist, swept her into the saddle. Taking the small parcel from her hands, he secured it to the saddle behind her without a word and turned to mount his horse. In a fluid movement he was in the saddle and moving across the yard, aware that the sorrel followed docilely behind.

They had stepped onto the trail when Gareth looked back to Angelica for the first time. Her face emotionless, she returned his glance without comment. Gareth was stunned by the impact of her gaze. It was as if she had turned to stone.

They had been traveling at a steady pace for over an hour. His eyes moving to Angelica, Gareth made a sudden decision. He turned to survey the road ahead of them. Finding a break in the wall of foliage, he guided his horse in its direction, pausing only to shoot Angelica a short glance as he moved onto the narrow trail. Satisfied when they had finally drawn into a small clearing beside a stream, Gareth dismounted and turned toward Angelica. Reaching up, he lifted her easily from her horse. Setting her on her feet beside him, he slid his arms around her and drew her close against him. Her body was rigid in his embrace, and he drew her closer, pressing light kisses against the surface of her hair. Sliding his hand up beneath the gleaming mass, he cupped her neck with his palm as he

269

whispered softly, "Angelica, look at me, darlin'."

Angelica raised her face obediently and Gareth felt a stab of pain at the silent despair in her eyes.

Unable to find the words he sought, Gareth raised his hand to touch her cheek. "Let me console you, darlin', for just a little while . . "

Gareth's eyes were intent on her face as he lowered his mouth to hers. His kiss was gentle, a soft caress as it brushed her lips and moved to dust her fluttering lids with light kisses. He sensed the heat of her tears as he trailed the line of her cheekbone, seeking to find her mouth once again. He was kissing her warmly, his arms straining her close, lending her his strength. His mouth was moving deeply into hers, his heart beginning a rapid beat as her lips separated to his urging. His one hand moving in the black silk of her hair, his other stroked her back, urging her to lean fully into him, use his strength, give to him . . .

A familiar hunger was growing inside him and Gareth groaned low in his throat. No, he had not meant things to go this far. He had just wanted to hold her, console her, break the frozen barrier she had set up between them. But his effort was backfiring. He didn't want to . .

The sound of movement behind them alerted Gareth to a presence the second before a familiar voice sounded in the stillness of the clearing.

"I suppose I must be thankful for your opportune passion, Gareth. It has allowed me the chance to catch up with you at last. I admit to considerable doubt that I would reach you before nightfall. But then, you always do the unexpected, don't you, Gareth?"

Snapping around, Gareth maintained his hold on Angelica, realizing that she had begun a sudden trembling at the sound of Esteban's voice. Allowing her to step away from him as Esteban dismounted and walked toward them, Gareth turned fully in Esteban's direction.

His heightened color betraying the full extent of his anger, Esteban purred softly, "I hope you have enjoyed your farewell kiss, Gareth. I suppose it is only fitting that your parting should be warm. Its memory will have to keep

270

you company for the remainder of your journey back to Texas."

"I think you're mistaken, Esteban. You see, Angelica has decided that I've offered her the better proposition. She's goin' back to Texas with me."

Directing his next words to Angelica, Esteban turned the full heat of his silent fury into her eyes. "You must tell Gareth that he is the one who is mistaken, *puta*. Your bargain was with me. I do not take kindly to such reversals in commitment. I have already warned you of the dangers of erratic behavior." Pausing for effect, Esteban continued on in a soft voice. "But I have decided to forgive you if you will explain to Gareth that you regret your foolishness. But you must tell him now . . . immediately. I admit to a rapidly dwindling patience in this affair."

Angelica's face was whitening, and unable to stand her fear a moment longer, Gareth stepped directly in front of her, blocking her from Esteban's view.

"I think you've had your answer, Esteban. But just one more thing before you leave. I stopped to talk to Padre Manuel before I left the village today. He is aware of the situation between Angelica and me, aware of our destination and just how long it will take us to get there. He also has the information regardin' the location of my homestead . . . and how to get in touch with it. His is aware of your interest in Angelica. I know he will be very interested to find out how well you handle your disappointment. He has informed me he will make certain to watch your reactions carefully, so that he may inform Don Enrique should there be a problem . . . or should the Rodrigos experience any unexpected difficulties."

Pausing only long enough to allow his words to be absorbed by Esteban, Gareth said abruptly, "Now why don't you go home? Angelica and I have a lot of miles to travel yet before nightfall and I . . ."

"Stand back from the *puta*, Gareth." All pretense of civility disappearing in the wake of Gareth's statement, Esteban demanded hotly, "I warn you to stand back now. I do not intend to leave this place without her. She is mine!

271

Our bargain was struck according to her own terms, and I intend to hold her to it!"

"That's unfortunate, Esteban, because there's only one way that you're going to get Angelica to come back with you, and I don't think you're prepared to go to that extreme."

Shaking his head, his face filled with contempt, Esteban responded softly, "Once again you underestimate me, Gareth. You are a fool, because that 'extreme' does not bother me at all."

Leaning forward unexpectedly, Esteban slid his hand down to his boot. His hand coming up again in a rapid movement that showed only the glint of steel, he lunged forward in a deadly thrust. Managing to avoid the full weight of Esteban's attack, Gareth felt the knife penetrate his side. A low gasp escaping his throat, he drew his gun in a quick, spontaneous movement, jerking it up to Esteban's face even as Esteban prepared to strike again.

"No you don't, damn you!"

A hot warmth was beginning to seep down his side, and Gareth cursed his own stupidity. He should have realized the depth of Esteban's rage. Should have been prepared . . .

"Drop that knife, Esteban! Drop it, or you're dead!" Waiting only until the bloodstained knife had fallen to the ground, Gareth hissed, "Now, get out of here, Esteban. Get out of here now! And don't come back, do you hear? If it wasn't for the debt I owe your parents, you wouldn't be alive to see this gun wavin' in your face. No matter what you think or say, Angelica is comin' back to Texas with me. I'd let you hear it from her own lips, but I know that wouldn't make much difference to you. There's only one thing that'll make a difference. So I'll tell you straight out. Next time I won't hesitate to shoot, Esteban. This is the first and only chance you're goin' to get from me. Now turn around and get goin'!"

"You are making a greater mistake than you think, Gareth. It is only by chance that you are still alive. Had you not turned, my knife would have found your heart."

Aware of Angelica's gasp behind him, Gareth gave a low laugh. "Esteban, you missed the only chance you're goin' to get. Get out of here! I'll give you just three more seconds to get back on that horse."

Hesitating, his eyes moving to judge the weight of Gareth's warning, Esteban turned slowly and remounted his horse. He was about to speak when Gareth jerked Esteban's rifle from his saddle and threw it to the ground behind him.

"Now, Esteban. My patience is wearin' thin . . ."

His handsome face livid, Esteban shot a quick look to Angelica as she moved to Gareth's side. But she was not looking at him. She was staring at the rapidly widening circle of red on Gareth's shirt. Gareth swayed, and Angelica slid her arm around his waist in a steadying movement.

Sliding his free arm around her shoulder, Gareth grated, "Move! Now!"

Turning his horse, Esteban galloped quickly down the trail he had entered so silently just a few moments before.

When he had disappeared from sight, Gareth turned to Angelica, his expression disturbed.

"I have a feelin' we haven't seen the last of him." Furious with himself, Gareth realized he was beginning to become light-headed. Slipping his gun back into his holster, he attempted to stem the flow of blood from his side. Moving quickly back to her horse, Angelica reached up to her small bundle. Untying it quickly, she pulled out her other chemise and ripped it into several strips. Wadding up a small portion, she started toward the stream to moisten it when a sudden thundering of hoofbeats sounded behind them.

His head jerking up in the direction of the sound, Gareth heard Esteban's wild yell over the crash of his horse's sudden burst through the foliage. Drawing his gun in a flash just as Esteban was upon him, the glint of steel descending, Gareth fired.

The thud of Esteban's body as it hit the ground echoed in the sudden silence. Moving quickly to his side, Gareth bent over Esteban's still body and felt for the pulse in his neck. It was throbbing.

His eyes moved to Esteban's shoulder. His shot had caught him there, ending the downward plunge of yet another knife that was supposed to put an end to Gareth's life. Disappointed his aim had been so poor, Gareth turned back to Angelica.

"He's still alive. Hold his horse. I'm goin' to get him back up on it."

"Gareth, you can't. You . . ."

"I damned well can! Now hold that horse!"

Bending down, ignoring his own pain, Gareth hoisted Esteban's limp body across the saddle. Taking a deep breath, he walked slowly back to his horse. Within a few moments he had returned with a rope and had tied Esteban firmly in place.

He turned back to Angelica. Beads of perspiration were visible on his brow and upper lip.

"Mount up."

Hesitating only a moment, Angelica moved to follow Gareth's brief command. Mounting with difficulty, Gareth reached over for the reins to Esteban's horse. He spurred his gelding back toward the main road, trailing Esteban's horse behind. Waiting only until Angelica was beside him on the road, Gareth turned Esteban's horse back toward Real del Monte and gave it a hard slap on the rump. Withdrawing his gun, he fired a shot into the air, sending the frightened animal into a faster pace as it turned the curve of the road and disappeared from sight.

Grimacing against the hot pain in his side, Gareth turned back to Angelica.

"With any luck, the damned horse will get lost, and that'll be the end of Esteban Arricalde. But it's more than likely he'll head right back to the hacienda and Esteban will soon be in tender loving arms. Hell, there's no justice."

Angelica's eyes moved to the spot Gareth clutched at his side. Blood was streaming through his fingers and Gareth was getting more pale by the moment. But his determination was unrelenting.

"Don't worry about me. It's just a scratch. A little pressure will stop the bleedin' and I'll be fine. Where's that cloth you were tearin' when Esteban interrupted?"

Silently handing him the cloth she still held in her hand, Angelica watched as Gareth wadded it and stuck it beneath his shirt. Clamping his hand tightly on the spot, he looked up. His lips were tight with pain. "That'll do until tonight. Come on, we have ground to cover before nightfall."

Spurring his horse forward, Gareth was only too aware of the lapse of time before Angelica moved to follow his lead. Waiting only until she drew up alongside him, he urged his horse to a faster pace.

His disposition deteriorating with each mile they traveled, Gareth grimaced at the waning light of day. The pain in his side was worse. The bleeding had all but stopped, but heat was building inside the wound. He needed to stop and cleanse it thoroughly, but he was yet uncertain that they were not being followed.

Damn, he had been a fool to send Esteban back. But in truth, he had not been able to pay the generous Arricaldes back by allowing their only son to die, no matter the circumstances which had brought about the situation. But if anyone deserved what he had gotten, it had been Esteban. Twisted bastard that he was, it had been obvious Esteban could not wait to get his hands on Angelica and make her pay for reneging on their bargain.

In truth, the whole situation was the beautiful little *puta*'s fault. There would have been no conflict between Esteban and himself if it had not been for her. And his mission to the mines could have been handled without the complication caused by Peter Macfadden's infatuation with her. Right now he could have been much farther along in his journey back to Texas, and most certainly he would not have been burdened with a knife wound that was making him absolutely miserable. Damn her!

Shooting a heated look to the woman who rode silently at his side, Gareth frowned again. She was so damned beautiful. Silhouetted against the waning light, her profile was more perfect than a cameo with the light of the pink sunset reflecting on the silken sheen of her hair. The line of her slender neck and shoulders was straight and perfect, despite the fatigue he knew she must be feeling. For he was feeling it too. They had to stop

275

soon before it was too late to find a good place to camp for the night. But he had no doubt there were any number of streams in this area where they might make themselves comfortable. He had only to keep alert and . . .

His keen hearing catching the sound of trickling water, Gareth turned his horse sharply to the right and searched the darkening roadside for the sign of a trail. His eyes catching on just the spot he sought, Gareth directed his horse off the main road, not bothering to watch if Angelica followed behind. He knew she would. She had been silent and cooperative since Esteban's horse had disappeared around the curve of the road. The shock of Esteban's appearance and the events which had transpired afterward had had a sobering effect on her. He was glad. He was not of a mood to do much talking. All he wanted right now was some food in his stomach and a place to rest his head.

Pulling his horse to a halt as he reached a spot obviously used before for a night camp, Gareth dismounted. Turning to Angelica's horse, he reached up and swung her down, wincing severely at the resulting pain. Somehow the concern on Angelica's face only increased his annoyance.

She spoke for the first time in a low, anxious tone. "Your wound needs to be attended to. I can . . . "

"Angelica, let's get somethin' straight right off." His expression knotting into a frown, Gareth interrupted unhesitantly, directing the full force of his annoyance into her silver eyes. "I can tend to my own wound. I've had worse. I don't need you fussin' over me. That's not the kind of service I bought from you."

Angelica stiffened. All trace of concern vanishing from her expression, she turned back to her horse. She was removing a few personal articles from her bundle when she heard the breaking of twigs behind her. Turning, she saw that Gareth was gathering firewood and placing it near the charred remains of a previous fire. Catching and holding his gaze, Angelica questioned coolly, "Do you have any objections to my helping with the food? I suppose since I'm to eat too, you won't consider me interfering if I attempt to get some water boiling for tea."

The ache in his side was worsening. Striking a fire quickly,

Gareth blew on the flames, waiting only until the light tinder had caught to turn back to Angelica. "To tell you the truth, Angelica, right now I don't give a damn what you do. I'm goin' to the stream to wash this cut. Where's that cloth you ripped up earlier?"

Turning to retrieve the last of her shredded chemise, Angelica placed it silently in his hand. Nodding, Gareth walked to his horse and searched out a bar of soap in his saddlebag. Gritting his teeth at the throbbing pain, he walked warily to the side of the stream and dropped to his knees. He raised his hands to unbutton his shirt. Damn, if everything wasn't an effort. He must've lost more blood than he thought. Hell, this was just the kind of complication he needed.

Carefully pulling off his shirt, Gareth dropped it to the ground, his eyes moving to the bloodied rag which covered his wound. He pulled it carefully from his skin. He was well aware that he ran the risk of starting the bleeding again, but the wound had gone long enough without being cleansed.

Dropping the makeshift bandage to the ground beside him, Gareth surveyed the jagged cut. Damn, Esteban had done a good job. The bastard had been absolutely right in his appraisal. If he hadn't turned in time, the knife would've gone right through his heart. As it was, the knife had entered his side just below his ribs. The cut was ragged and deep, the skin on either side of the penetration beginning to redden and swell. He was going to have a problem if he wasn't careful. And he didn't need any more problems. He had enough on his hands with that little black-haired beauty who would allow his mind no rest.

Leaning over, Gareth moistened the cloth Angelica had given him in the stream and rubbed it into the soap until he had worked up a lather. Carefully working the soap into the wound, he winced against the pain, grimacing against the fresh flow of blood. Well, there was nothing else he could do. Satisfied that he had done the best he could, he carefully rinsed the cloth and wiped the soap from the wound. Leaning over, he picked up the remaining dry piece of cloth. His eyes touched on the narrow row of frayed white lace that trimmed the edge, and he frowned. Angelica had torn one of her undergarments for his

277

use. He was quite certain she had few to spare. Judging from the circumstances in which she had lived with her family, there was little money for her to waste on clothing. Well, he owed her for this one she had ruined for him. He wouldn't forget it.

Picking up the cloth, he folded it and covered the surface of his wound. Drawing himself to his feet, he walked to his horse and withdrew a fresh shirt. Shrugging it on with considerable difficulty, he tucked it carefully into his pants, allowing it to hold the bandage secure. Turning, he walked back to the stream and carefully washed out the bloodied cloths and shirt. The small effort all but depleting his strength, he returned to the campfire at last and stretched the wet articles out on the nearest branch.

He turned to see Angelica pick up the pot and walk to the stream. Within minutes she returned and set it on a flat stone which rested in the middle of the fire. Well, he guessed that was as good a way as any to heat the water for tea. He noted that she had taken out the bread and cheese Carmela had packed from the hacienda kitchen. Warm memories stirred in his mind and he shot a quick glance to Angelica's face. He noted that her face was carefully averted and a fresh annoyance rose inside him. Damn, why had he gotten involved with the *puta* in the first place? She was nothing but trouble, had caused him a problem from the first . . .

As if sensing his perusal, Angelica turned to meet his gaze. Her great silver eyes moved slowly over his face, touching on the tight line of his brows, the anger in his eyes, the hard set of his jaw, and dropped at last to the harsh, unrelenting line of his mouth. Her glance lingered there for the briefest moment, her face drawing into a frown. He could almost feel the touch of her great eyes. They burned into his soul. His mouth was suddenly dry and he felt a familiar stirring inside him.

Suddenly furious with his own susceptibility, Gareth turned to walk toward the horses. Unwilling to look back, he unsaddled them and settled them for the night before removing his blankets and walking back toward the fire. Angelica was dropping the tea into the steaming pot. She had already sliced the bread and cheese and laid it out on a cloth. She did not speak but began to eat without turning as he came to sit beside

278

her on a nearby log.

Unable to draw his eyes from her, he watched as she alternated bites of cheese and bread. Taking a few steps to the fire, she took the steaming pot and poured the tea into her cup, hesitating momentarily before filling his cup as well. Turning, she held it out to him. Accepting it, Gareth placed it on the ground at his feet.

Angelica's voice was unexpected, drawing his eyes to hers as she said softly, "I do not understand, Gareth. If you despise me so, why did you not let Esteban take me? It would have been far easier, and you would not have been wounded . . ."

An unreasonable anger flushed him with heat. "Is that what you would've preferred?"

Angelica's hesitation was momentary. Her color faded at his obvious anger. "No, it is not. I . . . I just do not understand."

Unable to understand his own unreasonable agitation, Gareth responded tightly, "The answer is simple, darlin'. I wasn't goin' to let that bastard have you. You're mine, Angelica. For the next year, nobody's goin' to put his hands on you . . . nobody but me. Is that clear enough?"

Holding his glance only a moment longer, Angelica turned away and raised her cup to her lips. Finally realizing she did not intend to respond, Gareth turned to devote his attention to the food which had lain untouched before him. He was suddenly exhausted.

Gareth threw a few more pieces of wood on the fire and glanced back toward the stream. Angelica had been gone a long time. He had no intention of lying down before she returned. He was so exhausted that he was certain he would fall off to sleep the moment his head hit the blanket and somehow he could not make himself rest until she . . .

There was a small movement from the shadows near the stream as Angelica suddenly came into the light and approached the fire. She had obviously bathed. The hair around her face was curling in little tendrils and she had loosened her plait so that her hair streamed in curling profusion around her shoulders. She was so beautiful that she took his breath away.

Her step drawing to a gradual halt as she saw the two blankets which he had placed side by side, Angelica frowned.

Hesitating only a moment, she walked to the edge of the farthest one and slowly lowered herself onto it. Turning her back to him she drew the loose edge around her shoulders.

Gareth drew himself laboriously to his feet, wincing as the pain in his side throbbed to life. He took the few steps to his blanket and lay down beside Angelica. Reaching out unhesitantly, he ignored the pain in his side and turned her toward him. Still silent, Angelica raised her gaze to his as he drew her closer. Realizing the pain in his side would allow him to do little more, he lowered his head and covered her parted lips fully with his. He drank deeply of their drugging nectar. Drawing away at last, he settled her as close to him as his aching wound would allow, and adjusted the blanket over them both.

Angelica was silent in his arms. He was drifting off to sleep when her soft question sounded in the resounding quiet of the grove.

"Was it your pride, Gareth? Was that why you chose to fight with Esteban rather than give me up to him? Pride seems the only plausible reason for both Esteban's pursuit and your defiance of him. Both of you have had many women. What possible difference could it make to either of you whom you use to sate your bodies. Surely it is worth neither of your lives . . ."

With a quick, assessing glance, Gareth realized that Angelica's question was sincere. She truly did not understand. She had no comprehension of the hunger he felt for her, the need that burned hotter inside him than the fire in his wound. She had no realization that he would indeed have killed to keep her from Esteban's hands or the hands of any other man who sought to take her from him. Pride? No, it wasn't pride. If he had any pride he would've continued on down the road after Esteban had told him of his plans, and not given in to the jealousy which had allowed him no peace.

It was obvious from her question that he had not been successful in stirring a reciprocal emotion in her. His uneasiness increased. She had committed herself to him for a year, but she had made a commitment to Esteban and seen fit to break it when he had made a better offer. Would she do the same to him if a better opportunity came along? His instinctive reaction was immediate. Over his dead body . . .

She was still waiting for his response, her exquisite face turned up to his. He pulled her closer, tucking her head under his chin, ignoring the pain in his side as long as he dared.

His response was gruff. "Does it really matter? You're with me now, and that's where you're goin' to stay. That's all you have to know. That's all you need to know."

And she felt so good in his arms . . . so damned good. That was all that mattered . . .

Chapter VII

"Welcome, Senor Macfadden! It it our pleasure to see you at the Arricalde hacienda."

Genuine pleasure reflected on his face, Don Enrique extended his hand to the lanky Scot as Peter Macfadden strode across the foyer. Accepting his hand, Peter shook it firmly. He followed the smiling aristocrat down the hallway toward the library as Don Enrique continued hospitably.

"We will soon be taking our afternoon meal. You are most cordially invited to join us. It is not often we have the opportunity to repay the courtesy extended by the members of your group to our guests. I most especially owe you and your brother a debt of gratitude for your quick work in helping my old friend Gareth Dawson with his project." Turning, he added with concern, "I hope you have not come expecting to find Gareth here. He has already left for Texas . . ."

"Aye, I was aware of his plans. I dinna expect to find him here." Peter fought a niggle of annoyance. He had not come to discuss Gareth Dawson or his project. He had, in fact, sought to push thoughts of the Texan and the jealousy that inadvertently followed from his mind. Following Don Enrique into the library, he waited until the door had been closed behind them before continuing. "I came here today to bring ye the monthly production reports from San Jose Regla and to take care of some personal business of my own."

"That is good. From the little Gareth told me of the work your brother and you did on the project, I understood you both felt Jonathan Dawson's plan very workable . . ."

"Aye, Brock did the preliminary work, but he dinna

choose to commit himself fully without an on-site evaluation."

Peter noted the manner in which Don Enrique assessed his expression, and he made a greater effort to control his impatience. Don Enrique's surprise at seeing him the bearer of the monthly reports from the mine had been evident. The task of delivering the reports and the detailed explanation which usually accompanied them was more commonly reserved for one of the senior engineers. But he had needed an excuse to come to the village. It had either been that or an unprecedented day's leave from his work in order to accomplish that task.

He needed to see Angelica. A full two days had passed since she had left the mine with Gareth Dawson. He had had no doubt Dawson had left immediately for Texas. He was well aware of the Texan's anxiety to be home in this time of escalating danger to his homestead, and it had been only with the greatest expenditure of willpower that he had forced himself to stay away an additional day so that Angelica might have an opportunity to review her feelings without the pressure of his presence.

But he had been able to stand no more. He had come to the point where he had to make certain of Angelica's feelings toward him. He remembered only too well her silence when he had spoken to her in the living room of his brother's house. He remembered the taste of her lips . . . soft, so very warm under his. He wanted to taste them again, to know that she would reserve the sweet intimacy of their touch for him alone.

But he need dispense with mine business first, so he might free himself for the remainder of the day.

With a careful smile, Peter placed the envelope he carried into Don Enrique's hands.

"Brock and I worked on the production reports until late last night in an effort to get them up to date. Brock tells me that ye were concerned last month that production had fallen off in one of the shafts. As ye can see—" Taking the particular report he discussed into his hand, Peter pointed out the favorable rise in production figures, "the problem has been overcome and the shaft is once again producin' up to expectations."

His sharp eyes moving to the figures Peter pointed out, Don Enrique nodded. Raising his gaze to Peter once again, Don Enrique smiled.

"Please be seated, Peter. It will only take me a short time to read these reports and unless there is an unforeseen problem, my questions should be minimal. In the meantime . . ."

Interrupted by a short knock on the door, Don Enrique lifted his head, his face creasing into a frown.

"*Entra.*"

The door swung open immediately upon his response. Dona Teresa bustled into the room, an expression of extreme agitation replacing her characteristic calm.

"*Con permiso*, Enrique, but . . . but I am in need of your assistance. Esteban . . . he is upset. He insists he is well enough to be able to sit his horse. He says he wishes to go after the men who shot him. I have already told him that we have sent men out to cover the roads, that the bandits that shot and robbed him evidently have left the area. But he will not listen. He . . ."

"*Madre de Dios . . .*" Muttering under his breath, Don Enrique turned toward Peter, annoyed.

"My son was the victim of a robbery two days ago. He returned home wounded and suffering great loss of blood. He is extremely weak, but his debility has not lessened his desire for revenge. However, he does not seem to understand the true extent of his injury. If you will excuse me momentarily, Peter, I must go upstairs and attempt to speak to him."

"Of course, senor."

His eyes following the two anxious figures as they moved toward the library door, Peter was about to assume a seat when raised voices on the staircase caught his attention. A deep flush darkening his features, Don Enrique moved quickly to the doorway, his mouth tightening in anger the moment before he stepped into the hallway.

"*Esteban, qué pasa?*"

"I am going out!" Turning to Hernando's protesting figure as the servant descended the steps cautiously beside him, Esteban said haughtily, "Fool, leave me alone. I do not need your assistance. I need no one's help!"

His eyes on Don Esteban's descending figure as he moved slowly down the staircase, Peter noted his uneasy step. Springing automatically to his feet, Peter followed Don Enrique to the library doorway. His reaction spontaneous as Don Esteban's stiff figure began to sway more openly, he rushed past Don Enrique and started up the staircase in time to catch Don Esteban's arm as he stumbled weakly.

But there was no gratitude in the dark eyes raised to his. Instead, Esteban hissed menacingly, "Take your hands off me, fool! I do not need your help! You are in my way!"

"Esteban!"

Don Enrique's shocked voice echoed from the foot of the staircase, snapping Peter's eyes in his direction as he ascended to take his son's arm.

"You are the fool here, not this man! You have him to thank for saving you from a serious fall."

Relinquishing Esteban's arm to his father's firm grip, Peter turned and walked back to the foot of the staircase. He had no desire to become caught up in a domestic argument, but his curiosity had been aroused. He had not been aware of bandit activity in this area.

Refusing to be swayed from his course, Esteban continued down the staircase, his father's arm supporting him despite his protests. Watching carefully as Esteban allowed himself to be led into the *sala* and lowered himself shakily to a chair, Peter maintained his silence. His appearance in the household had been poorly timed. From the look on Don Enrique's face, it was only his presence which kept the older gentleman from delivering a scathing reprimand to his arrogant son. But uncertain which was the more prudent course of action, to return to the library or follow the rest of the household into the *sala*, he lingered hesitantly in the foyer as Don Enrique turned in his direction.

"Peter, *por favor, entra.*" Turning to the servant who

hovered anxiously at the foot of the staircase, Don Enrique ordered quietly, "Hernando, serve the brandy, please. I believe we will all benefit from its strengthening powers."

"I do not need brandy! I need nothing but to regain my breath before I leave. Hernando, saddle my horse!"

"You are going nowhere, Esteban!" His patience finally breaking, Don Enrique faced his son in true anger. "You will remain exactly where you are until you are sufficiently recovered to return to your bed upstairs!"

"I have told you where I am going! I do not intend to allow the men who wounded me to escape. I will see their blood shed and I . . ."

"Silence!" His patrician countenance flushed with rage, Don Enrique continued slowly, obviously in tenuous control. "You will do only one thing right now, Esteban. You will stand on your feet and follow me into the library where we may discuss this matter sensibly. Your quest for vengance has waited for two days. The delay of another few minutes will not allow the bandits to put much more distance between them and you than they have already accomplished."

"I do not intend to . . ."

"You have little choice, Esteban!" Turning to the servant who vacillated uncertainly in the doorway, Don Enrique snapped, "Hernando, you will serve Don Esteban and myself brandy in the library and you will instruct Juanita to bring tea to la senora and our guest in the *sala*."

Turning back to Peter, Don Enrique offered politely, "*Con permiso*, Peter. I apologize for this unexpected interruption, but I will not be long."

Waiting only until his son had pulled himself laboriously to his feet, Don Enrique turned sharply on his heel and strode toward the library. His eyes moving to Dona Teresa's face as the library door closed behind them, Peter experienced a flash of compassion. The woman was obviously at the point of tears, her round, pleasant face pinched with the effort she expended to restrain them.

His gaze direct, Peter offered softly, "Ye be concerned for yer son's welfare, Dona Teresa. I will nae find it difficult to entertain myself in here if ye choose to go to the library to be with yer husband while he discusses the matter with yer son."

Her response trembling on her lips, Dona Teresa nodded. "You are very understanding, Señor Macfadden. Hesitating a moment, she continued. "Juanita will be here within moments with tea. You must not hesitate to consider this house your own. Neither Don Enrique nor myself will forget your quickness in coming to our son's aid when he wavered on the staircase." Hesitating only a moment more, she added with a flush, "And we hope that you will accept our apology for Esteban's angry words. My son . . . his pride has been injured by the unexpected attack he suffered and he takes his frustration out on those around him."

"Ye need nae explain, Dona Teresa."

"*Muchas gracias*, Senior Macfadden."

Drawing herself carefully to her feet, Dona Teresa shot him another grateful look before bustling through the doorway and turning in the direction of the library. It was only after her rounded figure had slipped out of his sight that Peter released a tense breath. It appeared he was to be delayed in this section of the hacienda longer than he thought. His frustration was mounting. He was so close . . . only a few feet away from the kitchen where Angelica doubtless labored unaware of his presence.

Unable to stand the pressure of his own thoughts, Peter rose and walked to the window, his mind moving to the scene he had just witnessed. Esteban Arricalde . . . He had heard much of the spoiled Arricalde heir. He had also heard rumors of the rake's involvement with Angelica. His hands automatically balling into fists at the thought, Peter shook his head. No, he would not allow himself to fall victim to idle talk now. He would talk to Angelica and he would win her over. She was honest . . . he had seen the honesty in her eyes. Once she gave her word to him, she would be his and his alone. That was what he wanted and dreamed of . . . the goal he sought. He would take her to—

A sound of movement at the entrance to the *sala* turned Peter toward the doorway as a maid entered carrying a tray.

His eyes flicked over the young woman, only to be startled at the sultry glance she returned as she offered softly, "Do you wish me to pour your tea, senor?"

About to refuse, Peter suddenly had a better thought. Affixing a smile on his lips, he approached the low table on which the tray was set and nodded.

"Aye, I wou' appreciate that, lass. Tea wou' be vera welcome right now."

Obviously flattered by his friendly tone, the girl assessed him openly for a few long seconds before she leaned over to pour the tea. Her full bosom displayed freely for his benefit while performing the service, she finally raised the cup and offered it to him with a raised brow.

"Senor, I hope you enjoy. It is my wish to please. If there is anything else I may do . . ."

Accepting the cup, Peter restrained a frown. He had already had more than enough of the lass's free and easy looks. He suddenly found it difficult to fathom how Angelica had come to obtain her accepted reputation when this one was working beside her in the kitchen.

Accepting the cup, Peter responded carefully, "What be yer name, lass?"

Her manner warming noticeably, the maid answered in a hushed voice. "My name is Juanita, senor."

"Juanita . . . Aye, Juanita, there be somethin' ye can do for me. There be a lass in the kitchen I wou' like to speak to. If ye wou' tell her that I am here today, and will be lookin' to see her later, I wou' be much obliged to ye."

Her smile freezing, Juanita replied haltingly, "A lass? There is no other young woman in the kitchen. All the others are old . . ."

Startled at her response, Peter shook his head. "Surely ye be mistaken. The lass's name is Angelica . . . Angelica Rodrigo. She works . . ."

"Angelica Rodrigo does not work in the hacienda any longer, senor." Her manner suddenly abrupt, almost angry, Juanita turned away and was about to leave the room when Peter reached out to stay her.

"Wait, Juanita . . . She was workin' here only two days

288

ago . . ."

Attempting to shrug off his hand, Juanita turned in obvious anger.

"She left Real del Monte two days ago with the Texan . . . Gareth Dawson." At his startled look, Juanita replied with a shrug, "It was to be expected, senor. She was known for her easy ways. Dona Teresa dismissed her from service here because of the scandal she caused with the Texan. Everyone is glad to be rid of her, most especially I."

The unexpected turn of events almost too much for him to comprehend, Peter shook his head. No, Angelica would not have left with Gareth Dawson . . . she would not. She had told him she would consider his suit . . . would think seriously of . . .

"No, ye must be wrong! Where does she live? I'll go to see her there."

"You can go to her home in the village, but you will not find her there! If you do not believe me, ask Dona Teresa. She will tell you."

When Peter made no response, Juanita continued coldly, all trace of her former warmth gone, "*Por favor, señor.* Release me."

"Aye . . . aye . . ."

Dropping his hand from her arm, Peter waited until Juanita had left the room before replacing his cup on the tray. Stunned at the news the maid had imparted, he turned stiffly and walked to the window. He closed his eyes against the bright, glaring sun and the pain that had entered his heart. It could not be true. It could not be true that Angelica was gone . . . that he was too late . . .

Esteban walked to stand stiffly in front of the library window, staring out into the yard beyond. Taking a deep, furious breath, Don Enrique closed the door to the library behind him. His son's turned back was yet another silent insult to his authority and he had taken enough from this son whom he loved more than his life. Yes, perhaps that was the problem . . .

"Esteban, you will turn and face me. I do not appreciate

the sight of your back when I am attempting to converse with you."

Esteban turned in a jerking movement, his pale face all the more startling in his anger. "But you do not attempt to converse with me at all, *Padre*. Instead, you expect to dictate to me, and to have me listen and obey. Well, you are doomed to disappointment! I have no intention of following your commands like a well-trained servant!"

"I have no desire to discuss your imagined grievances, Esteban. I have brought you in here to discuss your present actions. You are behaving like a spoiled child and causing your mother unnecessary grief. You are not yet well enough to ride despite your claims to the contrary. If it had not been for Senor Macfadden, you would doubtless have fallen on the staircase only a few moments ago because of your excessive pride."

"Again you imagine situations that uphold your stiff opinions. I am indeed well, and I will go after the men who attacked me."

His eyes darting to the doorway behind him as Dona Teresa slipped into the room, Don Enrique hesitated only momentarily, his brow drawing into a frown. He had hoped for a few words alone with his son, but it appeared he was no longer going to be able to protect his wife from the knowledge of his son's excesses. Taking a deep breath, he turned back to Esteban's stiff expression.

"Esteban, do not flatter yourself that you fool me with your pretensions."

Momentarily taken aback with his father's reply, Esteban hesitated, allowing his father the opportunity he sought to continue.

"I have known from the beginning that your story of being attacked by bandits was false."

"False!" Dona Teresa's echo was a rasping whisper as her startled gaze moved between father and son.

"*Si, Madre*, that is what Padre said! False! He accuses me of lying . . ."

"Do not compound your deception with further lies, Esteban!" Don Enrique's lined face was livid with anger.

"My shock was as great as your mother's when you arrived at the hacienda tied to your horse and wounded. And my anger knew no bounds. As soon as you were able to speak and told us of being attacked, I sent men to search the roads for a sign of the band you say attacked you. There was none, and no sign of such a band has been reported since."

"And for that reason you call me a liar!"

"No, not for that reason, Esteban. For the simple reason that I know you to be dishonest, as much as I have sought to escape the fact in the past. I also know you to be vicious and scheming, accustomed to having your own way and willing to do anything in order to satisfy your every whim."

"To whom have you been listening? Padre Manuel . . . or Gareth Dawson perhaps? You have long been infatuated with the Texan's great 'devotion to the land.' Well, I have no such devotion, and I do not intend to develop one."

"There are other traits I would have you develop in your character if the choice were mine, Esteban. Not the least of them would be integrity, but I have begun to despair of ever seeing you exhibit even the slightest shadow of that virtue. But I tell you now, I will no longer countenance the despicable traits you have demonstrated since you have returned to the hacienda . . ."

Swaying weakly, his strength slowly deserting him, Esteban reached for the desk chair to support himself. His shoulder was throbbing wildly, the pain forcing beads of perspiration to his brow.

"I don't know what you're talking about!"

"You did not meet up with bandits! You rode after Gareth Dawson! Your mother was fooled by your pretensions of concern for Angelica Rodrigo, but I was not. I am not so old that I did not recognize the lust in your gaze when you looked at her. Nor did I fail to see the fear in her eyes when she looked at you. For that reason I was almost relieved when Gareth was taken with her, and even more relieved when I realized he had decided to take her back with him to Texas."

Shock at his father's words combining with his waning

strength forced Esteban into a few wavering steps toward the chair in the corner. Lowering himself slowly, Esteban brushed aside his mother's concerned rush to his side.

"So you were pleases that your Texan ran off with a woman from your kitchen. *Padre*, you continue to surprise me . . ."

Ignoring Esteban's remark, Don Enrique shook his head. "I should have realized . . . been prepared. The great mystery of your return to Real del Monte after leaving with the Valentins . . . You had returned for the woman, hadn't you? And when you were not expecting it, she left with Gareth. Your pride was injured. It could not sustain the blow . . "

Not bothering to deny his father's accusations, Esteban shook his head, incredulity apparent on his face.

"Inconceivable, is it not, that the bitch should prefer the rough Texan to me? But there is no accounting for the taste of an uneducated woman. And I am determined to educate her, *Padre*. She has escaped me only temporarily. I intend to go after her. And when I find them this time, I will not fail! My knife will find Gareth Dawson's heart . . . not be deflected into a less vital area by a caprice of fate. He will not be allowed a chance to raise his gun against me again. My blade has but tasted him . . . it knows the need for complete satiation."

Dona Teresa's gasp flicked Esteban's gaze in her direction. He gave a small laugh.

"Did you not believe your son capable of such passion, *Madre*? I assure you, I am. But you need not worry. The bitch is well known for her dalliances. I will merely be taking advantage of a service she offers. I will take her back to the capital with me, but there will be no shame in that. A beautiful woman is easily absorbed into society. I need only establish a plausible reason for her to be my guest. It will be readily accepted, and far from being the object of gossip, I will be envied, you may be sure."

"Esteban . . . Padre Manuel installed Angelica in my household under my protection . . . to guard against just such a circumstance . . ." Aghast, Dona Teresa allowed her voice to trail off in the face of her son's open sneer.

"If that was Padre Manuel's intention, he showed outrageously bad judgment, did he not?"

"No, Esteban, Padre Manuel is not guilty of showing bad judgment. Far better you should look to yourself for that." Outrage reflected on his face, Don Enrique looked to his wife's shocked expression. His voice softened.

"Teresa, why do you not go to attend to our guest. You are not needed here. Esteban and I will be able to speak more frankly if . . ."

"No, I think you should stay, *Madre*. You are shielded from the facts of life, and in such a way do not live in the real world that exists outside the walls of your hacienda. Far better that you see your son for the total man that he is, not the weak fop he is expected to be. . . ."

"Esteban, that is enough!" His eyes flaring wide in rage, Don Enrique took a warning step forward. "I will not allow you to torment your mother. It is not she who avoids the 'real world.' Rather it is you who seeks to avoid it . . . to indulge your weaknesses . . . to pretend to all that your excesses are strengths instead of the deep flaws in your character which they truly are! But the time for such indulgences are past . . ."

"*Padre*, you waste your breath on sermons . . ."

"Yes, I have found that to be true . . . that is why I intend to preach to you no longer."

"That will be a decided relief." Drawing himself weakly to his feet, Esteban turned toward the door, only to be stopped by Don Enrique's low command.

"Sit down, Esteban."

Esteban's quick look in his father's direction was accompanied by a short laugh.

"You do realize that your are at a decided advantage, *Padre*. I find I have indeed overestimated my strength. In this particular case I shall have to concede your point. I am too weak to travel today. But there will be tomorrow . . . or the next day. I do not intend to allow the Texan his victory over me. I will . . "

"You will do nothing!" His voice low, Don Enrique

directed a look of steel into his son's startled gaze. "You will rest here until your wound has healed. Your mother is a dedicated nurse, are you not, Teresa?"

"*Si . . . si . . .*" Her expression bewildered, Dona Teresa nodded vaguely.

". . . And when you have recuperated completely, you will go to the capital as originally planned and report to el presidente. You need not worry that he will be angry at your delay. I have already sent a messenger to tell him that you met with a mishap on the road . . . that you will be delayed for a short period of time. I conveyed your regrets . . ."

"That was very wise of you, *Padre.*" His eyes beginning to gleam, Esteban nodded. "It will allow me the time to find Angelica and bring her . . ."

"You will do nothing of the kind, Esteban."

His handsome face freezing, Esteban faced his father squarely.

"And how do you expect to stop me, *Padre?*"

Don Enrique gave a small laugh. "My device is simple. Money, Esteban . . . money . . ."

"Money?"

"Yes. You do realize you are completely dependent on me for that necessary vehicle?"

His handsome face beginning to twitch, Esteban snapped, "I live on my inheritance, those funds that come to me as a part of my grandfather's estate!"

"You live on the funds I supply to you! Your grandfather's estate came to me! I am the sole beneficiary of his will! You are and always have been dependent on my good will . . . and you have managed to completely destroy it, Esteban. My good will toward you is now nil."

Shooting a quick look to his mother for confirmation, Esteban saw the drop of her head. A new rage suffused him. Taking a deep breath he squared his shoulders with considerable pain and managed haltingly, "And what are the conditions under which your good will will be restored?"

"Your return to the capital, of course, and responsible

conduct that will be worthy of the name Arricalde. I will also expect you to abandon any thought of retribution for the wound inflicted by Gareth Dawson. It appears you managed to inflict a similar wound on him. It is my hope that it did no serious damage . . ."

"It was my hope that my blade would pierce his heart, but I was not to have that wish granted! No, your precious Texan is well . . . was well enough to inflict this wound on me and obviously strong enough to tie me to my horse and send it galloping back here! Yes, I believe we can assume Gareth Dawson is strong and well . . ."

"And he will remain that way, Esteban . . . with no interference from you!"

"And the Rodrigo bitch?"

"She left with him of her own free will. I can only assume you offered her a choice, but she decided in favor of Gareth . . ."

"More the fool she. She will live to regret that decision."

"If she does, it will not be as a result of an action you have instituted."

"So, I am not to seek her out, either."

"That is correct."

"And if I choose to follow my own course of action?"

"Then you will lose all support of the Arricalde name and finances. I can no longer countenance the use of our honored name in a manner that brings shame to our family. Esteban, this is my final warning. You are my son, but I will no longer acknowledge that fact if you choose to bring humiliation and shame to this household by your actions. Do you understand all I say to you now?"

His eyes cold, Esteban nodded. "I understand completely. You have chosen the son of your friend, Jonathan Dawson, over your own."

Ignoring his mother's softly gasped plea, Esteban shook off her touch, but Don Enrique was unrelenting.

"If you choose to interpret my words in such a way, it is your choice. But I will have your answer here and now, Esteban. What will it be?"

Estaban's laugh was shrill. "Do you leave me an alternative, *Padre*? Of course I will follow your directions. I will return to the capital as soon as I am well, and I will work in the service of my country. I will serve el presidente honorably and make the Arricalde name revered."

"I ask only that you serve to the best of your ability."

"But of course, *Padre*."

"You know I have your best interests at heart, my son."

"And my best interests do not include the Rodrigo *puta* . . ."

"Only if she chooses to come to you."

"And how would she do that . . . from the state of Texas?"

"Then I suppose you shall have to strike her from your mind."

His eyes holding his father's unfaltering gaze, Esteban abruptly gave a short nod.

"Of course, *Padre*. But for now I will return to my bed. And I will make certain not to overestimate my strength again."

"That is wise, my son."

Turning to his mother as Dona Teresa slid a supporting arm around his narrow waist, Esteban suppressed his instinctive desire to push her from his side. He needed no one . . . no one. But a second sense caused him to reconsider. Yes, he did need help now. He was caught in a web from which he was presently too weak to break free. But he would be stronger soon, and he would go to the capital as his father insisted. He would insinuate himself into a position of power beside el presidente, and then he would see. Then he would see . . .

Forcing a smile to his lips, noting his mother's immediate brightening, he nodded.

"*Gracias*, Mama. *Muchas gracias* . . ."

Esteban walked up the staircase, his mother at his side, fully aware of his father's strict appraisal. He lifted his head and continued steadily forward, silently seething. This was all Angelica's fault . . . his violent break with Gareth Dawson, his injury, his father's reprimand, and the strict circumstances under which he would be forced to live as a result. Infuriating him even more was the fact that despite all that had happened, the little bitch was with him still. Silver eyes haunted him, and desire burned full and strong inside him. Yes, this was the final humiliation for which the *puta* was responsible, and she would pay. No matter how long it took him, she would pay . . .

Angelica slipped her rebozo from her head and allowed it to fall to the saddle behind her. The heat of the day was becoming too strong to bear its weight despite her need for protection against the afternoon sun. It was indeed fortunate that despite the fact that they were well into their third day of the journey from Real del Monte, they had not left the coolness of the mountains. They were still blessed with a verdant wall of green that bordered the road and an undulating cover of leafy boughs that shaded the road on either side. In all too short a time they would be out of the mountains and into the lowlands where there was no respite from the merciless sun and the burning landscape.

An unexpected movement on the horse beside Angelica turned her eyes in Gareth's direction. The knot of anxiety in her stomach tightened at the stiff, swaying posture of his tall frame. They had been traveling for three days, and it was obvious that with each passing hour it became more difficult for Gareth to maintain his seat in the saddle. The gradual worsening of his condition had become apparent with the passage of time, and now, pale and uncomfortable, he tensed his facial muscles as he fought his pain.

Angelica swallowed against her fear. The wall of silence that had sprung up between them after Esteban's unexpected appearance had grown to a living, palpable force. Gone was the warmth that had colored Gareth's gaze and tone when they had instituted their bargain and begun their journey. In its place had come a watchfulness, a distrust that stung her deeply. She was only too aware of his covert perusal of her, his reluctance to let her out of his sight.

He had steadfastly refused to allow her to tend his wound, although his own attentions were decidedly ineffective in giving him relief. She had no doubt his pain was increasing, that infection was complicating an already vicious wound. She had seen Gareth's growing tendency to favor his unwounded side, the perspiration that broke out anew on his forehead with each new physical exertion. His agony was now such that he found it difficult to mount and dismount his horse, but he allowed himself little respite.

Her fears were beginning to escalate. Despite the fact that he had not made love to her since the inception of their journey, Gareth had steadfastly spread their blankets side by side each night. She had slept in the curve of his body, his arm wrapped possessively around her waist. She had grown accustomed to his warmth, the scent of his body, the reassurance of his presence. But this morning Gareth's skin had been unnaturally warm to the touch. The flush with which he had awakened had darkened as morning had turned to afternoon and a deep-seated fear was beginning to shake her.

Unable to keep her silence any longer, Angelica turned in Gareth's direction with a frown.

"Gareth, you are in pain. Should we not stop for a while?"

Gareth jerked his eyes in her direction, appearing to have difficulty in focusing his gaze.

"I'm fine."

"You are not fine! You are hardly able to sit your horse! Why must you be so stubborn? Why will you not allow me to help you?"

His eyes suddenly bright with suspicion, Gareth snapped tightly, "I don't need your 'help', Angelica. It occurs to me that if I suddenly succumb to my wound, you'll be free to return to Real del Monte. I've done you a great service, haven't I. I've eliminated the one person who threatened your situation there. Esteban Arricalde is no longer a problem. Your brother has the funds necessary to go for treatment, and if you arrive home in time, you may yet accompany him to the capital with your family. It would be quite an adventure for you, wouldn't it, Angelica? Much more excitin' than accompanying me to a homestead where you have nothing to look forward to but long days filled with work, and long nights sufferin' my attentions. It's just too bad that Esteban's knife wasn't just a little more accurate. You could've had it all then. But as things stand, you're goin' to have to keep your bargain."

Angelica was startled at his unexpected verbal attack. "You are wrong in your assumptions, Gareth. I have no intentions of . . ."

"Well, darlin', it doesn't make much difference what your 'intentions' are, does it?" The harshness of his voice making a mockery of the endearment with which he addressed her, Gareth continued in a slurred voice. "Because I'm goin' to make sure you follow the terms of our agreement to the letter."

"Are you so sure I seek a way to escape our agreement, Gareth?"

Apparently unwilling to talk any longer, Gareth responded flatly, "I'm not sure of anythin' right now, Angelica . . . most especially you. But for the record, you can forget any plans you've made for the next year which don't include me. You're bought and paid for, darlin', and I don't intend givin' you up."

Flushing at his words, Angelica snapped her face forward once again. It was useless. He would not listen. To his mind she was one thing, and one thing only . . . a *puta* who could only be trusted to keep her word while she was in his sight. The fact that he continued to desire her only succeeded in deepening his anger and his distrust. She was helpless against his suspicions.

The sun was beginning to set and Gareth spurred his horse to a faster pace. He remembered this area. He had camped close by on his way to the Real del Monte. Yes, they would soon be upon a large wooded glade where a stream widened to form a pool. The ground around it was flat and covered with a comfortable moss. It would make a soft bed for the night, a comfortable place to lie with Angelica in his arms.

Gareth gave a low snort, his eyes darting to the smaller horse beside him. Angelica sat a horse gracefully. He had long ago come to the conclusion that there was nothing Angelica could do that would not appear pleasing to his eye. He had come to that conclusion at the same time that he had made the admission to himself that he was totally enraptured by the beautiful little *puta*. It had been a source of bitter frustration to him since the beginning of their journey that he had been unable to do else but hold her when she had lain in his arms. His inclination had been to do far more, but the nagging pain in his side would allow him no peace, frustrating every effort he had made to overcome its limitations.

He had been unwilling to admit the full scope of his injury, but he was aware that his wound had become infected. Esteban's knife had cut deep, and he had a need for better treatment than he had been able to afford himself under his present conditions. But he had neither the time nor the patience to seek a doctor in this backward country. He would wait until he reached Texas. There he would find a good Texan doctor who would put him to right quickly. In the meantime, he had determined that he would just have to suffer his present discomfort.

His eyes still scanning the area, Gareth spotted the turnoff he sought. Obeying a sudden impulse, he spurred his horse to a faster pace. The rushing of the wind against his face was pleasant, relieving the heat that flushed his skin. Ignoring the growing ringing in his ears and the pain in his side, Gareth felt a sense of exhilaration sweep his mind. Yes, this was what he needed . . . to ride wild and free, to forget the pressures which drove him. It had been too long since he had felt this kind of freedom. Anxieties for his homestead; the fight for justice from the central government; worries for the threats against his land from the elements, Indians—all had combined to cut short his youth . . . to force him into maturity long before his time.

He had almost forgotten what it was like to experience true joy. He had been preoccupied of late with duty. But Angelica had penetrated the shield he had erected around himself all too easily, and he had been unable to let her go.

His eyes flashed behind him. Angelica was trailing him,

her smaller animal unable to keep up with his own's escalated pace. She was frowning, and he felt remorse. He had no desire to frighten her. He only wanted to love her. He wanted very badly to love her.

He was reining up his horse, slowing to a trot that allowed Angelica to catch up with him. Her bewilderment as she drew up alongside him stimulated a sudden burst of irrational laughter. Impulse assumed control and he spurred his horse forward once again. A sense of euphoria all but overwhelmed him as he urged his horse to breakneck speed. His side was almost numb . . . free of pain. The ringing in his ears was growing louder, but the floating sensation that appeared to take control of his mind freed him from pain . . . from care. With a quick command he turned his gelding off the road and onto the trail to the grove.

Within a few minutes he was breaking into the glade. He reined his horse to a slower pace. Yes, there it was, the pool. It looked cool and inviting. He was anxious to relieve the heat that burned his skin. Yes . . . he would feel better after a swim. Angelica and he would swim together. He frowned. He would have to watch her closely. She had almost failed to surface from the water once before. He had almost lost her. God, he would not have been able to bear that.

He pulled his horse up beside the pool and dismounted, turning to see that Angelica came up the trail behind him. A fierce, burning pain shot through his side and he gasped. The world was reeling around him and he took a moment to steady himself against a tree. Angelica was looking at him strangely and he laughed.

"We're goin' for a swim, *puta*."

His voice sounded strange to his own ears and he laughed again. Angelica had reined her horse up beside his and was attempting to slide to the ground. Within a few steps he was at her side and swung her to her feet. The pain was minimal. She was so light . . . like a feather in his arms. Succumbing to a wave of desire, he pulled her close and covered her mouth with his. She tasted so good . . . so very

301

good.

But he was hot. The heat was consuming him. He could wait no longer to cool the fire that threatened to devour him. Taking Angelica's hand, Gareth pulled her toward the beckoning surface of the water.

"Gareth, no. You aren't well. Please lie down before you fall."

Gareth spared only a moment to look down into the great silver orbs turned up to his. Concern . . . did she really care what happened to him? He smiled. She needn't worry. He'd be all right.

Angelica was speaking again, but he couldn't make out the words she spoke. He shook his head against the buzzing in his ears that drowned out her voice. It was growing louder, louder still. The glade was darkening rapidly around him. He had never seen night fall so quickly. His head was beginning to spin, the sights and sounds of the area blurring into a rapidly widening spiral which stole his breath. He was falling . . . falling, the humming in his ears turning to a roar that eliminated all sound . . . all sound but the faint echo of Angelica's voice . . .

"Gareth . . . Gareth!"

Fear closing her throat, Angelica held tight to Gareth's slumping form, managing to cushion his fall, sinking to the ground with him as he lapsed into unconsciousness. Unwinding herself from the weight of his body, Angelica drew herself to her feet. Her heart pounding, she stared, momentarily unable to react as Gareth lay sprawled out on the ground in front of her.

He was burning up with fever! The few short moments during which Gareth had held her in his arms had brought a resounding shock of realization. His illogical attitude of the past few days, his wild behavior of a few moments before, all had been signs she should have recognized.

Taking only a moment more to pull herself under control, Angelica took a few steps to her horse and removed the saddlebags. Within a moment she had the laundered bandages and a small pot in her hand and was hastening to the side of the pool. Quickly filling the pot with cool water, Angelica rushed back to Gareth's side. She dampened a cloth, and ran it across Gareth's forehead and cheeks. Worried when there was no immediate reaction, Angelica heated the cloth and repeated the process several times, her breathing only beginning to return to normal as Gareth's eyes fluttered and began to open.

But his gaze was dazed, disoriented, renewing Angelica's fear as she whispered, "Gareth, how do you feel?"

There was no immediate response and Angelica had begun to despair when Gareth frowned in response.

"Angelica. . . .?" Lifting his hand to take hers, Gareth looked at the cloth in her hand and shook his head. "No, it's too hot. This isn't doing any good. I'm goin' swimmin'. Come on . . ."

He was attempting to lift himself to his feet, and Angelica swallowed hard against his useless effort. He was burning up. Yes, perhaps that would be the quickest way to reduce his fever. She was well aware of the danger when fever raged out of control. She did not wish to see its ravages overcome Gareth. No. The water was cold, it would lower his temperature rapidly, and when he came out she would tend to his wound. He was no longer in a condition to protest.

Restraining him carefully, Angelica smiled into Gareth's wandering gaze.

"Yes, I'm coming, Gareth. But first you must take off your boots . . . your clothes. You cannot allow them to get wet. They will take too long to dry . . ."

Looking to his feet, Gareth frowned. He reached for his boots, a dazed expression slipping across his face as he was unable to accomplish the task of removing them.

Moving quickly, Angelica jerked off one boot and then the other. Seeing that he was all but helpless, Angelica moved to kneel beside him as Gareth slumped weakly back against the ground. Her hands moving to the buttons on his shirt, she whispered encouragingly, "Gareth, you want to go into the water, don't you? Let me help you to take off your clothes. First your shirt . . . that is right."

Her trembling fingers worked quickly at the buttons until the surface of his heaving chest was revealed to her gaze. Urging him to a sitting position, Angelica attempted to pull his shirt free of his trousers, her eyes touching on the bloodied bandage stuck fast to his side. The area surrounding it was red and swollen, and she darted a quick look to Gareth's face.

His response was a slurred, "It's a mite tender . . ."

His hands moving to his shirt, Gareth assisted her in pulling it free, a spasm of pain crossing his features as he moved to slip his arms out of the confining garment.

Taking a deep breath, Angelica moved her hands to Gareth's gunbelt. Within seconds she had snapped it free and was working at the closure to his pants. Sensing his perusal, she jerked her eyes upward. His eyes intense despite the brightness of fever, Gareth stayed her hand. Reaching out, he cupped the back of her head with his palm and drew her close, his mouth moving over hers with a passion that matched the heat consuming him. But she resisted his kiss, pulling away against his soft protest.

"No, Gareth. We're going into the pool . . ."

Abandoning any further attempt to undress him, Angelica assisted Gareth to his feet. Swaying, Gareth accepted Angelica's supportive arm, his gaze slipping to her tense face.

"You can't go swimmin' with all your clothes on."

Nodding, Angelica allowed Gareth to support himself against a tree as she kicked off her sandals and stripped off her blouse and skirt, leaving on the bare wisp of her chemise.

Gareth's small ironic laugh brought her to sudden realization of an arousal that was suddenly clear, despite the slur of his tone.

"I've been dreamin' of this for two nights now, and when it finally comes to pass, I'm too damned weak to take advantage of it."

Ignoring his remark, Angelica slid her arm around Gareth's waist and guided him toward the water. Suppressing a gasp as the cold ripples met her feet, she continued steadily forward, not stopping until the water covered her breasts. Supporting Gareth steadily with her arm, Angelica looked up, only to be startled by the intensity of his gaze.

"I won't let you go, Angelica . . ."

"I . . . I do not expect to leave you, Gareth. Our bargain . . . remember? A year . . . our agreement calls for a year. You have been true to your word, and I will be true to mine."

But the brightness of the fever burning in Gareth's eyes was reflected in his tone.

"I want you with me, Angelica. . . "

"And I will stay with you, Gareth. But first you must get well. You have a fever. Your wound, it is doubtless infected. I have brought some medicine with me . . . some of the herbs Padre Manuel prescribes for Carlos. Mama insisted, because she had heard the fever was rampant in Texas. I will make a fire and make you an herb tea. It will help you, Gareth."

"I don't want an herb tea . . ."

Angelica bit back the response that rose to her lips. Frustration soared anew, bringing a frown to her brow.

Gareth curled his arm more tightly around her shoulder, searching her face with his concerned gaze.

"Are you angry with me, darlin'? I don't want you to be angry . . ."

His unexpected gentleness brought a rush of tears to her eyes as Angelica struggeled against the myriad emotions assaulting her.

"No . . . I . . . I am not angry. I merely want to help you . . ."

A sudden spasm of pain crossed Gareth's face, the abrupt assault staggering him. Panicking at his sudden weakness, Angelica struggled for calm.

"Gareth, I think we should go back to the bank now. I find I am tiring . . "

"All right." Gasping, Gareth leaned more heavily into her supporting grasp.

"Gareth . . . you must help me get you back to the bank."

Nodding, Gareth drew himself erect with obvious difficulty. Still supported by her arm, he turned and waded staggeringly back toward the bank.

Releasing an anxious breath as they emerged from the water, Angelica carefully assisted Gareth toward a tree a few feet away and helped him to lower himself to the ground. Moving quickly to her horse, she removed the blanket and covered him. She was intensely aware of the shuddering that had suddenly beset his broad frame. Returning to Gareth's saddlebags, Angelica searched until she came up with the bottle she sought at last. Back at his side within seconds, she undid the cork and held the bottle up to his lips.

"Gareth, drink . . . please."

"What is it?"

"It is the bottle from your own saddlebag. You're shivering. This will warm you."

His broad hand moved to cover hers as Angelica guided the bottle to Gareth's lips. He drank deeply. Angelica attempted to withdraw the bottle only to have Gareth's hand tighten as he drank deeply once again.

Allowing her to withdraw the bottle at last, Gareth murmured stiffly, "I have to sleep for a while . . . for just a little while. When I've rested, we'll start out again."

Gareth's fevered confusion shaking her more than she dared admit, Angelica managed a smile.

"Yes, Gareth. Rest. I'll take care of everything."

But he had already slipped from consciousness and Angelica released a shaky breath. Her hand moved immediately to Gareth's forehead. Unless she was mistaken, he was cooler. The cold water had done its job. She had no doubt his wet pants would be effective in keeping down his body temperature for a short time. As long as she did not allow him to get a chill, they would not create a problem.

Taking a moment to adjust the blanket around him, Angelica raised her hand to Gareth's cheek once more and allowed her eyes to move over his sleeping face. He was not resting. He had merely succumbed to exhaustion and fever. He grimaced. He was not free of pain even in unconsciousness. His wound could not go untended any longer. Drawing herself to her feet, Angelica shot a quick glance around the area. Within minutes she had gathered a supply of wood and had started a fire. She had no time to lose.

The water was boiling rapidly over the fire when Angelica felt the weight of someone's gaze. Turning, she saw Gareth had drawn himself to a sitting position, his back propped against the tree. So intent had she been on her purpose that she had not heard him move. Angelica felt a flicker of despair. She had hoped she would be able to treat his wound before he awakened. But it was not to be . . .

Taking the time to shake the herbs into the pot, Angelica then removed the other small pan from the fire and carried it back in Gareth's direction. Kneeling at his side, she placed the hot water beside him and removed the remainder of the bandages from the saddlebag. Noting that Gareth's eyes followed her every movement, Angelica lowered the blanket to reveal the area of his wound. The bandage was still stuck fast to his side, and Angelica grimaced.

Raising her eyes to his, she said softly, "I must change this bandage, Gareth. I am afraid it will hurt . . ."

Gareth's gaze was still lacking clarity, and he shook his head in spontaneous protest.

"No, I'll take care of it."

"You are too sick to take care of it now, Gareth." Her hand moving to the bandage, Angelica prepared to remove it, strengthening herself against the pain she needed to inflict when she pulled it free. But Gareth's hand clamped down on hers.

"I said no." His face darkening, Gareth refused to relinquish his hold.

Angelica looked pleadingly into the dark-eyed gaze holding hers. Not realizing her despair was clearly reflected in her expression, Angelica whispered, "Why, Gareth? Why do you refuse to trust me? You are ill. The infection from your wound is spreading. It must be treated immediately or you will be unable to go on."

"Are you tellin' me you want to help me, *puta*? Why? Wouldn't it suit you just fine to be free of our agreement?

307

You could return to Real del Monte. You wouldn't need to spend the next year in payment of your obligation . . . sufferin' my touch . . ."

"Gareth, I told you I had no such intention . . ."

Ignoring her protests, Gareth pushed her hand away from his wound. "No, I'll take care of myself."

Her eyes moving slowly over the hard set of Gareth's jaw, Angelica felt desperation assume control. Fever had twisted his thinking. She needed to convince him of her intent . . . to prove to him that she wanted only to help him. She took a deep breath. She knew only one way.

Gareth's grip on her hand was painfully tight as Angelica moved closer, closing his grasp between their bodies. She lifted her mouth to fit it lightly against his. Her other hand slid into the heavy hair at the back of his neck, drawing his mouth against hers, urging his participation as she kissed him gently. He resisted the inducement of her kiss and Angelica leaned fully into him, drawing his taste into her mouth, her heart beginning a slow pounding as a spontaneous warmth began to pervade her senses.

A small gesture, begun as persuasion, gradually assumed control, causing her to seek a deeper intimacy in the familiar pleasure of Gareth's mouth, the comfort of his arms. Her arm wrapping around his neck, Angelica kissed his lips again, the deep cleft in his chin, the rough surface of his cheek, holding him fast as she returned to brush her mouth back and forth across his until his arm snapped up to crush her close, deepening the contact. His kiss seared her, stole her breath. Her heart was throbbing, echoing the pounding of Gareth's as she drew herself away from him at last. Aware that one of Gareth's arms still strained her close while his other hand caressed her breast boldly, she drew back from his kiss, and directed the full weight of her heated gaze into his eyes.

"You see, Gareth, I do not suffer your touch. Feel . . . feel how my heart is pounding . . ." Her hand closing over the broad hand that caressed her breast, Angelica held it tight against her, the warmth inside her growing as Gareth's eyes held hers.

"I have no desire to escape our bargain, Gareth. It was made in good faith. You have been generous. My brother will soon be on the way to good health because of you. If I have any wish at all, it is to repay you for what you have given me. I know only one way, Gareth. And in that way I give to you willingly."

Angelica's voice deepened to a husky whisper as she continued earnestly. "You have bought and paid for me, Gareth. Your words are true, but I do not begrudge you your possession. You have bargained for a year, and I give it to you gladly. I hold nothing back from you as you have held nothing back from me. We have much to give each other, Gareth, for the time that we will be together. But you must trust me, Gareth . . . you must."

Drawing back slowly, the flush of her ardent statement coloring her flawless cheeks, Angelica watched the play of emotions in Gareth's fevered gaze. He was silent as he obviously sought to weigh her words. Finally drawing her close again, Gareth kissed her fully, deeply. His chest was heaving from the strain on his waning strength as he pulled away at last.

"I have no defense against you, Angelica. The true fever in my blood is you. It consumes me, darlin'." Lowering his mouth to brush hers again, he shook his head. His voice dropped with exhaustion. "Do what you like, Angelica. You're worth any risk I take . . . anythin' at all . . ."

Swallowing as Gareth slowly released her, Angelica sat back on her heels. Her hands trembling, she placed the clean cloth in the hot water. She took a deep breath before reaching for the soiled dressing which still covered Gareth's wound. Pulling it back quickly from the skin, she gasped as the full extent of the infection was revealed to her for the first time. Her eyes jerked up to Gareth's in disbelief.

"You . . . you allowed this to happen just because you doubted me? You took the risk of its consequences rather than . . ."

Gareth's low, self-derisive laugh interrupted Angelica's incredulous whisper.

"I've played the fool before, Angelica. I expect I will

again. I'm not sure of much right now, but there's one thin' I've been sure of since the first moment I saw you. And that is, that you're worth every chance I take darlin'."

Holding his gaze only as long as she dared, Angelica dropped her eyes to Gareth's wound. She could afford to think no more.

"All right, mon, out with it! What happened? Did the lass turn ye doon? Was she nae interested in what ye went to offer her?"

His eyes snapping across the table to his brother's impatient face, Peter hesitated. His eyes darted to Mary where she sat in silence at the end of the table. Her discomfort was evident. He had no intention of increasing the strain evident among the three of them since his arrival back at the mine. Slowly drawing himself to his feet, Peter was about to leave the dining room when Brock's angry voice snapped him back in his direction.

"I asked ye a question, mon! I dinna expect ye to leave without the courtesy of an answer."

"And if the question ye ask is none of yer business . . . ?"

Brock's face flushing a bright red, the older Scot drew himself slowly to his feet. His voice soft, he said slowly, "Ye be a part of me, lad. Whatever ye do concerns me. I dinna like to see ye unhappy. Rather than that, I would have had ye bring the lass back with ye." Directing a quick look toward his wife's concerned expression, Brock shook his shaggy head.

"Mary has spent the day talkin' in my ear, and what she says makes sense to me at last. It does nae matter what I see in the lass. It is what ye see in her that counts. I dinna think ye would be fool enough to ask the lass to be yer wife." At a short sound from Mary, Brock shook his head, and began again. "But whatever ye decide is a matter of yer own choice. I dinna expect to try to force my own opinions on ye again."

Pausing to assess the reaction of his words on Peter's unyielding expression, Brock continued into the silence that remained between them. "But by all that's holy, mon, we've waited the day to know the outcome of yer visit. Ye cannot expect us to wait . . ."

Silencing his brother's words with a raise of his hand, Peter shook his head. A bright color flooded his fair skin. His voice was gruff.

"Yer words come a bit late, Brock. Ye could have saved yerself the entire declaration if ye'd but waited until I was able to speak with more control of my words. But since ye canna wait, I'll tell ye straight out. I dinna speak to the lass."

"Ye dinna speak to her?" Incredulous, Brock shook his head. "Did ye change yer mind? Did ye . . ."

"Change my mind?" Peter gave a low, self-derisive laugh. "Damned fool that I be, I did nae believe the truth when it was spoken to me at the hacienda. I had to to to the lass's house . . . to see for myself that she was gone . . ."

"Gone?"

His words choking in his throat, Peter nodded, the heat that rushed to his eyes carrying with it a huskiness to his tone that was all too revealing.

"Aye, that's what I said. The lass was gone. I was too late. Yer friend, Gareth Dawson, was not the same fool as I. He dinna let the grass grow under his feet. He took her back with him to Texas . . ."

"Took her back . . ." Mary's spontaneous response turned Peter's stiff face in her direction as she pressed softly. "Did he marry the lass?"

Peter shook his head. "No, he dinna marry her, and it seems she dinna care that he nae did. I was the fool who wou' have offered her marriage if I'd but thought she'd have me."

"Peter . . ."

Hearing the despair in Mary's soft tone, Peter laughed again. "So I've learned my lesson the hard way." Turning back to Brock, he continued harshly. "Ye were right about the lass from the beginnin'. She dinna care for me. If I am to be honest, I must say she dinna say she did. It was my own wishful thinkin' that got up my hopes, and I'm more the fool for that. She has the man she wants, and it is nae me. 'Twas a long ride back from the hacienda, and I did some hard thinkin'. I came to a conclusion I will nae forsake. I'm done with the lass. I'm puttin' her out of my mind." Hesitating a moment before turning from the table, Peter shot a quick look between his brother and Mary's shocked faces.

"And I ask ye not to mention her name again. It is my wish to forget the lass ever existed."

Turning away, Peter heard Brock's low acquiescence.

"Aye, lad . . . aye."

The words echoed in Peter's mind as he walked out the door into the yard, as he sought to ignore the ache inside him that would not cease.

"Angelica!"

Reacting immediately to Gareth's summons, Angelica raced to his side, but the feverish light in his eyes allowed no recognition. Squinting toward her, he shook his head. "Damn it, she's gone. I knew she would leave. I knew . . ."

"Gareth . . . Gareth look at me. I'm here, beside you." Taking his hand, Angelica raised it to her face, moving it slowly against her cheek. "See, Gareth, I'm here . . ."

Recognition dawning gradually in his eyes, Gareth nodded. "It's dark, Angelica. Why aren't you sleepin'? We have to get up early in the mornin'. There's no time to waste."

"No, Gareth. You need to rest . . . allow time for your wound to heal."

"No . . . no . . ."

Gareth was straining to get up and Angelica began to panic. She had been working continuously over his wound for the past few hours. He had lapsed in and out of consciousness, seeming hardly aware of her ministrations. He had drunk freely of the herb tea she had offered to him, but it had seemed to do little good. The effect of his brief time in the pool lessening as the night wore on, Gareth's fever was again raging.

Persisting in the only treatment she knew, Angelica

continued to coax Gareth to drink, emptying the pot of herb tea only to brew some more. But the majority of her time had been spent working over the surface of his wound. Continuous hot applications had resulted in a lessening of the inflammation surrounding the area, but the bleeding had started again.

Straining her mind, Angelica sought to remember Padre Manuel's instructions on the occasions he had treated Carlos, but her confused mind could come up with nothing more than she was already doing. How desperately she wished for the comfort of Padre Manuel's presence, his instinctive knowledge of healing. But she had no one to depend on but herself. Gareth was helpless, a hindrance to his own treatment in his flaring bouts of delirium.

He was still straining to get up and not knowing what else to do, Angelica took his face between his palms, forcing his eyes to hers.

"Gareth, it is night. You should be sleeping. If you don't rest, you can't get well." Realizing she had captured his attention, if only temporarily, Angelica continued quickly. "You're tired, Gareth. I'm tired, too. It's time for us both to sleep. Lie down . . . that's it . . ." Pressing him back against the ground, Angelica moved to lie down beside him. She pulled the blanket up over them both as she curled against his side, adjusting it so that it covered Gareth's bare chest.

He had turned toward her, his eyes on her face, and she forced a smile as he reached up to touch the curling wisps at her hairline. His eyes searched hers restlessly, his mind in obvious torment.

"The bastard Esteban would have hurt you, Angelica. His kind of lovin' is like that. I'll never hurt you . . ." A gasp of pain suddenly escaped Gareth's lips, temporarily cutting off his rambling words. She could feel the tensing of his strong chest muscles beneath her palm, and a new wave of helplessness swept her mind. But he resumed speaking in a breathless tone as soon as the spasm passed. His hand moved to stroke the surface of her hair.

"You're goin' to like belongin' to me, darlin'. I'm goin'

to take good care of you, and I'm goin' to love you well."
His attention suddenly moving to speak to a person visible
only in his mind's eye, Gareth shook his head vehemently.
". . . don't give a damn what you say! You had your
woman and you didn't give her up, no matter what Ma
said! She hated you for it. She got back at you, huh . . ."

Suddenly Gareth was laughing. His eyes appearing to
focus on her face again, he said, "Big Jon Dawson . . . his
only son the image of his wife. He never lived that down,
me dark-haired and dark-eyed like my ma, and him blond
and light-eyed." Taking Angelica's hand, Gareth moved it
to his scratchy cheek. "This face is all Carson, like my ma's
side. Homely bastards, the whole lot and Ma was proud of
it."

"But you are not homely." Running her hand over the
warm skin of his cheek, Angelica frowned. She remembered her first reaction to the harshness in his gaze, the
uncompromising stiffness of the sharp planes of his face.
But she also remembered his smile, the full lips stretching
wide across white, even teeth, transforming that harshness.
Gareth did not smile often . . . not truly, but the effect,
when it came, generated a warmth inside her she had
experienced with no other. She longed to see that smile
again, to feel its glow.

But Gareth was frowning, his eyes wandering her face.
"You look like your daddy, don't you, darlin'. That sure
enough has to be because there's no trace of your mama in
your face. That fella's walkin' around this earth not knowin' a part of him's lyin' in my arms. He'll never know you,
darlin' . . . have you to brag on . . ."

Gareth's wandering words touched on an old wound.
Had she her fondest wish, she would carry her mother's
soft, blunt features with pride . . . would not be possessed
of features so fine that they made her an outcast in her own
village . . . eyes so light that her every glance caused people
to stare . . . a personality so unlike her dear parents' quiet,
accepting natures that it set her apart from them more
surely than the physical marks of her unknown sire. She
despised carrying the visible characteristics of a man she

had never seen, a man who had forced her conception upon her mother and left her beaten and unconscious. She felt nothing but hatred for this unknown man whose sole legacy to her was a face and body which stimulated lust and a disrespect for all she valued.

Suddenly humiliated, Angelica responded harshly, "Would you not say it is a case of 'like father, like daughter,' Gareth? A father who rapes, and a daughter who sells herself?"

Gareth held her gaze soberly. "Since I'm the only one you sold yourself to, darlin', I'm not complainin'. I'd say I owe the fella a debt of gratitude for givin' me you. I'm not about to damn him, whether he forced your mama or not."

His statement finished, Gareth moved his hand to Angelica's face, tracing the high rise of her cheekbone, down the straight line of her perfect profile, the surface of her hair and slid down to grasp the heavy plait. His eyes were beginning to drop closed, but he fought his weakness. His voice was low, confused.

"Loosen your hair, darlin'. I want to see you lyin' beside me with your hair unbound. Your hair's beautiful, Angelica . . . you're beautiful."

A harsh laugh escaped Angelica's lips.

"I care little for beauty, Gareth. It is the heredity of a sire I do not know . . . whom I will never know. It is that heredity you lust for . . ."

"No, darlin' . . . it's not only that. I love the way you feel in my arms, the way you taste, the way you look at me. And when I make love to you, darlin', I . . ."

But Gareth was losing his trend of thought, his chest beginning to heave with strain. His hand tightened on her hair.

"Loosen you hair, darlin'."

Gareth's fingers were working feebly at her braid, when Angelica relented at last. She need remember that he was delirious. He was confused, rambling. She was allowing him to tax himself unnecessarily, and experiencing considerable guilt at her foolish reaction to words he would not remember when his fever was spent, she raised her hands to her hair. She pulled the plait over her shoulder and quickly undid it, giving her head a quick shake to loosen the lustrous waves.

Looking back to Gareth, Angelica turned on her side, her arm slipping back around his chest in a gesture that both caressed and restrained him. Her mind subconsciously reacted to the burning heat that met her touch.

"Now will you sleep, Gareth?" Her voice dropped to a coaxing whisper. "I am tired and I cannot sleep until you are resting."

Gareth nodded. He covered the small hand that rested against his chest with his own. His words were low, almost inaudible.

"I'll be well tomorrow, Angelica, and then we'll go on."

"Gareth . . ."

"Go to sleep, darlin'."

At her hesitation, Gareth strained to keep his eyes open, and Angelica frowned. She would have to close her eyes for a little while to satisfy him. She was tired . . . more tired than she realized. Yes, she would rest for just a little while . . .

Angelica snapped abruptly awake. The bright light of morning was startling. Her heart pounding, she lifted her head, her eyes shooting to Gareth's face. Careful not to disturb him, she raised her hand lightly to his forehead. It was not free of fever, but it was cooler. She released a ragged breath.

Gareth was sleeping restfully. Her glance slipped to his hand. A lock of her hair was wound between his fingers. She frowned in memory of the words he had spoken in delirium. So his father had kept a woman. It was not unusual. She had known many men whose custom it was to keep a steady stream of mistresses while their legal wives functioned only as nursemaids to their children. She felt an instinctive contempt for such a situation and for the men who practiced such an arrangement.

But it appeared Gareth embraced that philosophy . . . found it strangely amusing, although he had appeared to find a bitter satisfaction in the fact that his mother had managed to have the last laugh. Whatever the case, it was obvious that Gareth was extremely loyal to his father, going to the extreme of coming to Real del Monte to pursue a dream his father had for their land. It was all so confusing, as was Gareth's attitude toward her, fluctuating between supreme tenderness and suspicion of her intentions.

Angelica shook her head and drew herself to her feet. Whatever the case, she was committed to him for a year. Her own integrity would not allow her to consider any other course of action. There was consolation in that decision. Gareth's words echoed in her mind.

"I'll never hurt you, Angelica."

No, she would never need to fear physical abuse from Gareth. He was too strong . . . too proud to resort to such a manner of handling a woman. Unlike Esteban Arricalde, his strength was exhibited in gentleness. His words were not mere vocal exercises as were Esteban's expressions of concern. It would not be a difficult year for her to bear. She was already becoming accustomed to his touch, her body responding more spontaneously than she would prefer. She need keep in mind that their arrangement was temporary, that despite Gareth's gentleness, he still used the name "*puta*" interchangeably with her own. She need also keep in mind that she had earned that designation fully. But it was only for a year . . . a year . . .

Taking a deep breath, Angelica turned toward the remains of the fire. She need heat water again and prepare more of the herb tea. She only hoped Gareth would not balk at the bitter-tasting drink now that his fever appeared to be going down. She need also check his wound. If it was not markedly better, she was uncertain what she would do. Perhaps it would then be best to leave him here and ride to the nearest town for a doctor. But if his fever should escalate again, if he should attempt to come after her . . .

Putting an abrupt halt to the worries assaulting her mind, Angelica began scouting the area for firewood. One step at a time . . . She could not afford to borrow trouble.

Her eyes moving around the area, Angelica frowned. She

had all but cleared it of firewood in her efforts last night. It was obvious from the remains of other fires, that this was a well-used camping area for travelers, making it all the more difficult to find the wood she needed. But it was a necessity that she find fuel. She could not afford to allow whatever good had been accomplished to lapse because of her inability to continue treatment.

Raising her hand anxiously to her head, Angelica brushed back her hair. The memory of Gareth's request brought a sudden flush to her face. She would keep her hair unbound temporarily. It was little enough to do to ensure his cooperation, but in truth she could not understand Gareth's fascination with the disorderly, curling strands. She had long despised the fine texture of her hair and its penchant for curling annoyingly. She would by far have preferred her mother's straight, heavy hair. Its coarse texture lent more easily to braiding and seldom became unruly.

Angelica suppressed her annoyance. She had found only a few pieces of wood, far too little to start a fire. It would be necessary to go to the other side of the trail, beside the flat, grassy area where she had tied up the horses so they might graze. She looked back to Gareth. He was still sleeping. Making a sudden decision, she hurried across the trail and ran into the wooded glade beyond. She needed to return quickly, before Gareth awoke and wondered where she had gone. She did not want to stir a recurrence of suspicion which plagued him. She could not depend on his rationality now.

She had been gathering wood for some time when she looked back to see that Gareth's sleeping form was no longer visible between the trees. She looked to the pile she had accumulated. She would start to carry some back now and come back for the rest later. She could afford to stay away from Gareth no longer.

But what was that? Freezing in her step, Angelica listened again. Voices and the sound of horse's hooves . . . Someone was on the trail. They were riding toward the pool. She could see the flash of movement between the heavy foliage. A shiver of fear coursing through her, Angelica dropped the log she held in her hand. The sound carried in the silent glade, halting the figures who moved on horseback just a few feet away.

"Clay, do you hear somethin'?"

"I think so . . ."

Angelica took another step. She did not recognize the voices, but her first thought was to get to Gareth. She did not want to have them come upon him when he was helpless. She took another step when suddenly with a crash of movement the two horses broke through the foliage, sending her back several steps to get out of their way. Her heart pounding, Angelica stared up at the two strangers. She felt a tremor of fear. It was apparent they had been on the road a long time and had traveled rapidly, with little time for the necessities. Their traveling clothes were badly stained and in need of washing. They showed several days' growth of beard on faces that were less than clean. But more threatening still were the guns they wore low in their hips and the ammunition slug in readiness across their saddles.

She was still studying them silently as the first man dismounted and took a step in her direction. Pushing back him broad-brimmed hat, he leered as he advanced slowly toward her.

"Well, I'll be damned if we haven't got us a little chili pepper here to spice up our day, Jimbo."

"Clay, damn it, we don't have time for that now! We ain't even sure if them fellas are still chasin' us!"

"That's the point, ain't it? What would you feel like if you found out later that them boys gave up tryin' to catch us and we let this little senorita get away without showin' her the proper attention. You wouldn't be able to live with yourself then, would you?"

"Clay . . ."

"Come on, Jimbo, get off that horse. You're only wastin' time, and she has to get on with her work, don't you, you pretty little thing . . ."

"*Señor, por favor*, I must get back . . ."

"So you speak English, do you? Now, ain't that nice. I always like my women to know what I'm whisperin' in their ears when I have them under me. And I like to know what they're screamin' at me, 'cause I don't like nobody callin' me names. It makes me mad . . ."

The first fellow was advancing steadily toward her, his eyes carefully scrutinizing her movement as she backed away cautiously. He was getting closer. The rancid stench of his perspiration reached her nostrils and she shuddered with revulsion as his leering smile widened to reveal yellowed and rotten teeth. A movement at the corner of her vision caught her attention. The second fellow had dismounted and began circling to his friend's right. They were cutting off any hope of escape back in Gareth's direction, and Angelica began to panic. She could see the oily sheen on the first man's face, the excitement shining in his rheumy eyes.

"What are you doin' out here, little beauty? You got a house around here somewhere's? Hey, Jimbo, maybe there's another one like her in her house. Then you could get a girl of your own and we won't have to share. I kinda think I'd like to have this one to myself for a while. She looks real sweet and tender."

"Clay, damn it, let's get this over with. We ain't got time to . . ."

Distracted by the second man's statement, Angelica did not anticipate the first man's unexpected rush forward until it was too late. Rough hands clamped down on her arms and she struggled fiercely as he shouted over his shoulder, "Come on, Jimbo, I did the work for you as usual. I got her, don't I honey? Yeah, and since I got her I'm goin' to be first to . . ."

But Angelica was not listening. She was fighting desperately to be free when a sudden voice from behind them jerked her eyes to Gareth's swaying form as he moved into sight between the trees.

"You're not goin' to first to do anythin'!"

"Gareth!"

Still bared to the waist, the bandage on his ribs showing

signs of fresh bleeding, Gareth leaned heavily against the tree, his side arm in his hand. Angelica made another attempt to break free of the grip that held her, but the stranger had no intention of releasing her.

"Well, looks like there's two of 'em after all. But this fella here ain't got much left, do you, fella? As a matter of fact, it looks like he's goin' to fall down in a heap in a few minutes and save us the trouble of knockin' him down."

"I wouldn't count on it, friend." His voice low, Gareth ordered again, "Turn her loose, now! You're right, you know. I'm not goin' to last too long on my feet and I know it. So I'm tellin' you again. Let the lady go, or I'm goin' to stop you right now, the only way I know how before I pass out. Your buddy here goes first, because he's a clear shot, and then you . . ."

"Turn the bitch loose, Clay!" Beginning to panic at the menace in Gareth's tone, the second fellow demanded again, "Turn her loose! Either way, if this fella shoots, it's goin' to bring that damned bunch down on us again . . ."

Sensing the first man's hesitation, Angelica suddenly jerked herself free. Running to Gareth's side, she stood beside him, her chest heaving with fear as Gareth said quietly, "Are you all right, Angelica?"

"Yes, Gareth."

His eyes moving between the two who still watched him expectantly, Gareth motioned with his gun. "Drop your gunbelts and mount up."

"I ain't droppin' my gun. Hell, I ain't . . ."

"It's your choice. Either drop them quick, or I pull the trigger. I'm not stupid enough to let you fellows out of here armed so you can come back and finish what you started. You got three seconds to get those guns on the ground!"

Angelica watched expectantly as the strangers' hands moved reluctantly to their belts. She breathed a silent sigh of relief as their guns hit the ground.

"Now mount up and get out of here."

Turning, the two men walked back toward their horses. They had mounted and were wheeling their horses around when Gareth fired two shots into the air.

The effect was instantaneous, setting the two men into motion as they spurred their horses back onto the trail and in the direction from which they had come. Lowering his gun slowly as the racing hoofbeats faded into the distance, Gareth turned toward Angelica. His face was ashen.

"That set those bastards to runnin'. Those gunshots will bring anybody they got chasin' them up fast, and you can bet they won't be back again lookin' for us."

Nodding, Angelica slid her arm around Gareth's waist. Supporting him with her arm, she attempted to urge him to turn back toward their camp. But Gareth was not about to move.

"Angelica . . ."

Angelica's eyes snapped up to Gareth's pale face, aware of the tension there.

"Don't ever leave camp without tellin' me again. Another few minutes and . . ."

"*Si*, I know Gareth. I will be careful from now on. But now we must get you back."

"I made it here by myself and I can make it back the same way. Give me those gunbelts. It won't do to let them lay here to give somebody ideas if they stumble over them. Take the firewood. I don't want you leavin' me for any reason for a little while . . . until we're sure those fellas are long gone."

Her hesitation earned her a dark look from Gareth, and deciding it would cause him more stress if she disputed the limits of his waning strength, Angelica retrieved the gunbelts. Frowning as Gareth draped them over his shoulder, Angelica picked as much wood as she could carry and walked at his side back toward the pool. Her mind on Gareth's unsteady step, Angelica dropped the wood on the remains of last night's fire and hastened to aid him as he attempted to lower himself to the blanket. Supporting Gareth as he slid to the blanket beneath him, Angelica took the guns and put them in a pile beside him. Realizing his supreme effort had weakened him to the point of exhaustion, Angelica quickly covered him, and moved to wipe the sweat from his brow.

Angelica's voice was shaken as she whispered into his pale face. "*Muchas gracias*, Gareth. If you had not come . . ."

"Angelica, there was only one thing that would keep me from gettin' between you and those two, and I'm not dead yet, darlin'. I told you, you belong to me now. And what I have I keep . . ."

But his strength was slowly slipping away, and realizing his debility, Gareth whispered, "I'm goin' to rest now. If you hear anythin', wake me up right away. It doesn't take me long to get my eye set when I have a gun in my hand."

Realizing his words were not just idle talk, Angelica nodded. A sudden warmth heavy under her lids, she averted her eyes, only to feel Gareth's hand turn her chin back toward his face.

"Now kiss me, darlin'. I want the taste of you fresh in my mouth when I close my eyes."

Following his directions without hesitation, Angelica lowered her mouth to Gareth's, only to be startled by his strength as his arm closed around her. His words were soft against her ear as he drew her down against him.

"You don't have to be afraid, darlin'. The only arms that are goin' to hold you are goin' to be mine."

Angelica closed her eyes. Yes, she would be all right while Gareth's arms were around her. Suddenly, of that she was very sure.

Chapter VIII

She was swathed in sheet of blue velvet, reveling in its exquisite texture as it moved against her skin. She had longed to experience the caress of the glowing fabric. It was an unspoken hunger buried deep in the back of her mind, an overwhelming desire born of a muted dream. The sensation did not disappoint her. She gasped her delight as its smooth luminescence moved against her breast in a subtle stroke that left her breathless. She pulled the voluminous fold closer in an effort to indulge herself further. It caressed the flesh of her stomach, gently traveled her hips . . . It fondled her buttocks, smoothed her thighs, found the heart of her desire. She was gasping, wishing never to leave its sensuous warmth as it touched the skin of her cheek again. It brushed her lips. It was gentle, loving. It abandoned her mouth and she cried out against its loss.

She reached up to clutch it closer, only to find it cool and damp under her fingers. She stirred and its dazzling warmth covered her mouth again. Its taste was familiar, stirring. She separated her lips as she sought its texture more fully. It was good . . . so good . . .

She sighed her contentment, only to hear a low whisper in return. The sound lifted her from the velvet haven in which she languished. She did not want to leave the unadulterated bliss, to have it slip from her grasp. But a stronger force called her, taking a step beyond the sensuous mist induced by the lustrous, billowing length.

The blue velvet was slipping away, falling from her grasp. She emitted a gasp of regret only to be consoled by a warmth of another kind, building deep inside as a voice murmured again in her ear, "Angelica . . . darlin' . . ."

Light kisses punctuated the whispered caress . . . soft velvet against her skin. The brilliant netherworld which had held her in its grasp was slipping away. The blue velvet was fading . . . gone at last, replaced by the fathomless black velvet of Gareth's eyes as he lowered his mouth to hers again.

Realization was slow in coming as the touch of velvet moved from her lips to brush her fluttering lids. Her words were a hushed whisper.

"Gareth . . . it's you . . ."

Gareth's head came up slowly at the bewilderment in her tone. She could feel the spontaneous tensing of his body. The black velvet was turning to brittle onyx.

"Yes, it's Gareth."

Angelica shook her head in instinctive denial of the obvious conclusion which had sprung to his mind.

"I thought it was . . ." She hesitated, suddenly embarrassed by the irrationality of her familiar dream. But the glow in his eyes was turning chill and unwilling to allow it to slip away she continued haltingly. "I thought . . . I thought it was the velvet . . ."

Gareth frowned his lack of comprehension.

"The blue velvet of my dream. The velvet is beautiful . . . warm. It holds me gently, Gareth. When I was a child, it came to me in my sleep when I was frightened or unhappy. It held me safe in its folds. It loves me, Gareth . . ."

Angelica's words dwindled to a halt with the realization of her intimate revelation. She averted her face. She had never confessed her dream, her secret source of consolation to anyone before. He had caught her at a vulnerable moment. She had been a fool to tell him. He would laugh at the childish escape her mind employed. She would not be able to bear ridicule . . . not his, not in this . . .

But Gareth's touch was gentle. He turned her back to meet his gaze. There was understanding there, a tenderness in his tone which was reflected in the endless depths of his eyes.

"Darlin', look at me. No, don't turn away." A sensitive

smile curved Gareth's lips, softening his features. "You won't be needin' your blue velvet anymore . . . not when you're with me. No dream will hold you safer than I will, darlin', nor more gently . . ."

Gareth employed no more words. His mouth completed his whispered promise with its worship of the delicate lids which fluttered under his mouth. His hands were moving against her flesh, flesh startlingly bared of the chemise in which she had slept. The blue velvet was caressing her again in his touch and Angelica closed her eyes against the glow it restored inside her. But there was as deeper color to the aura Gareth created, a fathomless depth that held her breathless as his mouth consumed hers with his sweet passion. She surrendered to the pulsating warmth it induced, her lips separating to allow him the freedom he sought. She had no desire to resist him. She had no will to escape the glory he renewed within her.

His knowing hands smoothed her shoulders, following their curve lovingly. Her breasts warmed under his caress. The budding crests burgeoned to life in aching expectation. He fondled the sweet, womanly swells, his mouth following the sensitized trail he had created only moments before.

A low gasp escaped her throat as Gareth's mouth adored her with the warm, moist touch of his lips. The need inside her was building with each drawing kiss, each taunting bite. Her searing torment was so strong that she sought to free herself from its sweet ravages, only to become the beloved prisoner of Gareth's tender passion as he clamped his hand strongly around her wrists and drew them to the ground over her head.

Tasting, drawing deeply, he ravaged her with his loving attack, raising her response to audible gasps which echoed in the stillness of the silent glade. He was taking her slowly, carefully to a plane of heightened desire, the billowing, radiant swells far surpassing the warm velvet of her dreams. She was floating buoyant on waves of glittering rapture which swept all conscious thought from her mind, holding her helpless on their undulating heights.

Gareth's tender assault became more exacting in the

gradual descent of his searing hunger. Uncertain at which moment he had freed her wrists, Angelica felt the warm caress of his touch against her hips, cupping her buttocks. She felt his mouth pressing its sweet ministrations against the flat surface of her stomach, the dark curls between her thighs.

He was separating her legs with gentle persuasion, nudging them apart with nuzzling kisses that set her afire. He was worshiping the bud of her desire, coaxing it to bloom, fondling the moist petals intimately to taste their sweet nectar. He was drawing deeply, his tongue stroking a wild hunger to life within her. Her need was voracious, consuming, and she clutched him close even as she opened herself to him, accepting his homage with a matching hunger of her own. A new shuddering beset her and she cried out in awe of the kaleidoscoping colors of ecstasy rapidly springing to life inside her. He was bringing her to the breathless precipice, holding her at the brink, pausing before the breathless descent.

The pause lengthened torturously as Gareth's lovemaking was withdrawn. Angelica's eyes fluttered open in sweet anguish to see Gareth had risen to his knees above her.

His gaze intent on her face, Gareth slipped his pants from his hips and discarded them quickly, moving again to straddle her restless form. Indulging himself in the torment visible on Angelica's face, Gareth felt the escalation of the already mind-consuming passion that ruled him. He ran his eyes over her flushed face, her parted lips, lowering his gaze to caress the soft swells of her breasts still rosy from his heated kisses. He followed the curve of her slender form, his eyes descending to the moist mound for which he hungered still. He hesitated, prolonging the anticipation he saw mounting in her eyes. He smiled at her desperation . . . her need. He needed that visible proof of his power over her . . . needed to know that he could stir the same need inside her that all but consumed him.

She was swallowing tightly, her lips moving in wordless entreaty as she raised her arms to him.

"Gareth . . ."

He lowered himself slowly, the hard shaft of his passion moving against her moistness. Her lips separated in a low gasp, her heavy lids dropped closed, and he gasped at the supreme beauty of her passion. He entered her, plunging deeply, his own joy soaring as her arms clamped tight around him, drawing him in. She was meeting his thrusts, her slender body rising to accept his joining, encouraging him. The glory was growing in magnificence, the splendor escalating. He was trembling at the brink, holding Angelica with him as he paused to contemplate its wonder. Unable to restrain himself a moment longer, Gareth plunged into the breach, carrying Angelica to soar high in the breathless plane, clutching her close, wishing fervently never, never to be free.

Still holding her close, loathing to separate from her, Gareth raised his head at last. Her eyes were closed, her cheeks flushed with spent passion, her lips slightly separated as her breathing sought to return to normal. He needed to taste those sweet lips again. He joined his mouth to hers, and Gareth felt anew the rise of the incredible emotion Angelica inspired within him.

The dawning of realization was startling in its abrupt clarity. He would never get his fill of her . . . his Angelica. This was no ordinary passion. Lowering his head, Gareth tasted her mouth again, barely restraining the words which rose to his lips as he drew away at last. No, he could not tell Angelica he loved her. The realization was too new, the words too strange to his tongue. He could not ignore the nagging voice in the back of his mind that forced unpleasant truths into his mind. Angelica was beautiful, giving. He had no doubt it was entirely due to her care that he had survived the infection of his wound. She was more desirable than any woman he had ever know. But she had not come to him in love. *Puta* . . . The word haunted him. He had bought her for a year.

Gareth forced away all trace of wishful thinking stimulated by her uninhibited response to his lovemaking. He need be honest with himself. Angelica had committed herself to him for a year, and at the end of that time she intended to leave him. She had not hesitated to make that clear even while pledging her fidelity. She had told him she would hold nothing back in giving her body. She was but being true to her word. He was her first man. The sweet consolation in that knowledge was great indeed. He need now make sure that he would be her last.

His mind moved to her words on awakening. Blue velvet . . . As strong and resilient as Angelica had proved herself to be, her mind still sought consolation from reality. Blue velvet . . . a place to hide . . . a place to feel safe. Gareth swallowed against the tenderness which rose within him. She would need her velvet no longer. He would be her consolation . . . her blue velvet. He would protect her from unpleasantness, her fears. And he would win her love before he declared his own.

A familiar flush of jealousy soared to life inside him. No one would come between Angelica and him. Angelica was the warmth . . . the beauty which had been missing from his life. Too many years had passed without warmth in a home embittered because of love's demise. That bitterness had been reenforced by fate's caprice in the death of his father's beloved mistress and child . . . killed before they could restore love to that home.

For the first time Gareth had full understanding for his father's passion, his inability to give up his mistress and child, even in death. The thought of surrendering Angelica to their bargain in a year's time had haunted his fevered dreams of just a few days before. It haunted him still.

His eyes still on Angelica's face, Gareth stroked her cheek, watching as her eyelids began to flutter and slowly rise. Molten silver, her gaze seared his. He bit back the words he longed to say. It was not yet time. He had tutored her body well, but he had yet to touch her heart.

Slipping his arms under her, Gareth enclosed Angelica in the circle of his arms. He had a year to make her love him. A year would be long enough. It would have to be.

Gareth's light touch on her cheek drew Angelica back, brought the world slowly into focus around her. She was suddenly conscious of the green leafy boughs which swayed above their heads in the cool, morning breeze, and the shaft of sunlight glinting on Gareth's dark hair. Gareth was still lying atop her, the full length of his nakedness stretched out against her own. She reveled in his apparent strength as he released her from the circle of his arms at last and rolled to the blanket beside her.

Angelica turned her face toward his perusal. She steeled herself against the fluttering within her that his warm glance provoked.

This was the first time in a week that she had not been the first to awaken in the forest glade, but she could relax her vigilance at last. The return of health was apparent in Gareth's face. There was no trace of fever in his gaze. There had been none for the past three days. She had been gratified at the gradual healing of his wound and the return of his strength. She had been aware of the growing warmth in his eyes that had accompanied his returning health. It had preceded their loving exchange of a few moments before. It shone brightly on her now, all but consuming her.

Her eyes moved to the bandage at the base of his ribs and she touched the spot gently. "No more pain, Gareth?"

Gareth lifted her palm to his lips, moving her hand to cup it against his cheek. "No more pain. You've cured me, darlin'." Lowering his head, Gareth kissed her lips lightly. "You've taken care of me for a week, and now it's time for me to take care of you."

Drawing himself to his feet, Gareth reached down to pull Angelica up beside him. His sudden smile sent unexpected joy coursing through her.

"Come on. The water is callin' us. We'd better take advantage of it while we're here. We'll be startin' out again tomorrow and leavin' this place behind us."

Startled at her sudden sense of regret, Angelica averted her gaze and started toward the pool. But Gareth's arm circled her waist to stay her, his eyes intent on hers.

"What's the matter, darlin'? You don't look very happy to get away from here."

Raising her eyes to his, Angelica nodded and attempted a

smile. "Is this such a bad place after all, Gareth? With the exception of those two men . . ." Hesitating, her brows knitting temporarily into a frown at the memory of the two men Gareth had driven away at gunpoint, Angelica continued determinedly, ". . . we have been safe here. And those men are . . ."

". . . are either in jail someplace or in a bar, lamentin' the loss of their guns." Continuing quietly, sensing her discomfort, Gareth shook his head. "No, this isn't such a bad place, but Texas is better, darlin'. You're goin' to like it there." Silently determining to make certain his words proved true, Gareth urged her into the water beside him as he continued talking. "Texas women are handsome and proud, darlin', but I don't know a one who holds a candle to you. I'm goin' to have to beat the boys away from you with a stick." Suddenly realizing the truth of his statement, Gareth shook his head, his arm curling more tightly around her to draw her close. "And they'd better not get any ideas, 'cause I'm not sharin'."

Raising her eyes fully to his, Angelica responded soberly, "You need not worry, Gareth. There is no man in Texas who will take precedence over you in my eyes."

Unable to respond without revealing himself, Gareth reached out and drew her close. His arms closed around her and he held her slender, naked length breathlessly tight. He had known all along, hadn't he, that he'd never be able to let her go?

Ignoring the pain in his shoulder, Esteban pulled himself up to strict attention and forced a smile. Resplendent in a perfectly tailored dark uniform lavish in gold braid and epaulets, he advanced slowly into the crowded palace ballroom. He was aware of his striking appearance. He had made a generous assessment of himself before leaving his apartment, and he was more than satisfied that he would probably be the most handsome man in the room.

But even his superior physical appearance would not overshadow el Presidente Antonio Lopez de Santa Anna. Were Antonio not a handsome man in his own right, he would still steal attention at any affair with the lure of his outstanding charisma. It was an invaluable tool he used with great skill. Esteban gave a small laugh. Even he had been temporarily taken in by the passionate political zeal displayed in Santa Anna's large, moody eyes, his beautifully modulated voice. He had been all but hypnotized by the dreams el presidente espoused for his country. But Esteban was not a fool. It had not taken him long to see Santa Anna for what he was.

If he were to be totally honest, he would have to admit many groups had good cause for complaint against Santa Anna, among them the Texans. Antonio had changed his political position countless times to suit his purpose, moving at last from federalist toward his present goal of a centralist form of government. His position with regard to Texas had been difficult to ascertain, had fluctuated in accordance with whom he was speaking at the time. In speaking with representatives of Texas, Antonio had often declared his support, but he had then gone to the opposite extreme of imprisoning the Anglo-Texan duly elected representative, Stephen Austin, for almost two years without benefit of trial. It was Esteban's secret suspicion that el presidente had not a sincere thought in his mind in regard to that rebel state. He was also beginning to believe el presidente hoped to be put into a position where he could use his military might against Texas, just as he had in Zacatecas, to demonstrate his power to those who might choose to defy him.

And as far as Esteban was concerned, that would be well and good on all counts. The majority of Mexico's people were ignorant. He agreed wholeheartedly with Antonio that it would be an impossible task to attempt to educate them. The aristocrats, those with fine Spanish blood in their veins, were the only people of intelligence in this backward land. It was up to them to lead the rabble. Mexico needed a strong leader who would take its mongrel people by the hand and direct their destiny. If that strong leader was Antonio Lopez de Santa Anna . . . and if el presidente chose to make a life of luxury and power for himself as he did that, he was only receiving his due. Esteban had no objections . . . as long as he maintained a share in that wealth and power.

Esteban was satisfied that he had taken a good step in that direction. He had arrived in Mexico City only a week before. He had remained at Real del Monte only as long as necessary, fleeing his mother's smothering care as soon as he was well enough to travel. His obvious injury and the fact that he had hastened to the capital in spite of it had impressed el presidente favorably, and he had been immediately installed in a position of confidence. He had only just begun his duties. Much of them were tailored to his talents. He was mainly to circulate as el presidente's representative at social affairs such as this boring ball. He was to test the political climate in his charming manner, gather information, and submit it to Antonio.

He had been informed that his opinion was highly respected and that his thoughts would be given much consideration. Esteban had suppressed a laugh at Antonio's comment. He supposed that was so because Antonio and he were so very much alike that Antonio could feel that Esteban's ears were virtually an extension of his own.

Esteban moved between the laughing groups in a steady, unwavering pace that declared a set destination. Nothing could be farther from the truth, but he was not about to be caught in yet another boring conversation with an earnest matron who hoped to advance her daughter's cause.

Strangely, he had been startled at his own reaction to his return to the brilliant capital scene. He had resented his father's summons to Real del Monte when it had come a few months before. It had interfered with his enjoyment of the perpetual festivities in the magnificent city. He had also resented his deliverance from the free and easy ladies of the capital. His dalliances had become a daily event, his conquests many. He had enjoyed the challenge, the diversity.

But he had obviously returned a different man. His wound, now almost healed except for painful twinges that occasionally beset him, had little to do with his preoccupation. Before returning to Real del Monte, the sound of gay music throbbing on the sultry night air, the reflection of candlelight in magnificent crystal chandeliers, the spark of witty conversation, the sight of women magnificently attired and bejeweled, and the thought of gardens with conveniently dark corners and beds of comfortable grass—all had been sufficient to lend purpose to his day. Those thoughts now left him cold.

Making his way through the milling crowd, Esteban chose to ignore the music of the gay waltz and the couples sweeping around the floor to its lilting rhythm. The sound of the high-pitched, feminine laughter which somehow managed to penetrate the overwhelming din annoyed him. He struggled to overcome his contempt for the flirtatious glances sent in his direction from behind fluttering fans. Ugly, ignorant bitches, all of them!

His smile becoming decidedly strained, Esteban spotted a familiar face in the far corner of the room and walked in the gray-haired gentleman's direction. He could not fathom how he had been so enraptured with this same scene only a few short months before.

He hesitated to admit that the true cause for his disenchantment might be the fact that he had not returned to the capital in the manner he had planned. No, had he had his choice, he would be crossing this room now with Angelica Rodrigo on his arm. She would be dressed in a magnificent gown of black lace, the dark beauty of which would be challenged only be the deep ebony silk of her hair. Her faultless face and shoulders would be displayed in a daring décolletage that allowed a tempting glimpse of her small, firm breasts. Full sleeves of delicate black lace would allow only the outline of the slender grace of her arms. The bodice would nip in at her waist, tempting his hands to circle its minuscule dimensions, and the full skirt would sweep out in endless tiers to her dainty feet. She would wear diamonds at her throat which would outshine those of any woman in the room, and which would be paled only by the brilliant glow of her great, luminous eyes. On the small, perfectly shaped ears which he would explore lovingly with his kisses, she would be wearing matching earbobs which he himself would have had the pleasure of fastening in place.

Yes, he had had great plans for the little *puta* and he chafed at the despoiling of those dreams. He would have been the envy of every man in the room, for surely there was not a woman present who could compare with the beautiful Angelica. He had spent many long house since Gareth Dawson's success in stealing the *puta* from him in contemplation of what could have been. Even now, while she probably lay in the Texan's arms on the hard ground, en route to a meager homestead where she would most likely be put to work as a common kitchen maid, he could not drive thoughts of her from his mind.

He had never known a woman with such fire. *Puta* that she was, possessed by many men, lying now with a man she preferred over him, he found thoughts of her still strong enough to drive desire for any other woman from his mind. He had lost her, but only temporarily. She would be his. Yes, she would be his . . .

The face he sought in the crowd momentarily passed from his view and Esteban felt another flicker of annoyance. He needed to find a purpose for his presence at this boring affair, for his own satisfaction. He could not possibly abide another evening of stilted conversation and heavy-footed maidens whose only attributes were the fact that they were willing.

His eyes snapping onto Colonel Botin's distinctive features once again, Esteban felt a flicker of relief. He could depend on this gentlemen for the relief of intelligent conversation. And he had much to learn . . .

Affixing a smile on his face, Esteban extended his hand enthusiastically in the older gentleman's direction.

"Arnoldo! *Cómo está?*"

Suspicion was rampant in the dark eyes of Arnold Botin. In his fifties, gray haired and slightly overweight, he did not have the appearance of military man of great ability. But his disarming appearance hid a keen intelligence and the heart of a patriot. Knowing these things Esteban expended his most charming manner, fully aware that Colonel Botin eyed him with great skepticism. Esteban shook his hand warmly. As never before he appreciated this man's keen powers of observation, for Esteban knew in Colonel Botin he would find the truth of the rumors presently circulating in capital circles.

"Esteban . . ." Botin's voice was cautious. "It has been some time since I have seen you in the capital. I had heard that you had returned to the family mines on a matter of business."

"*Si*, that is correct, but a summons from el presidente brought me back to the capital."

"A summons from el presidente, eh? That sounds quite important." His eyes moving over Esteban's magnificent uniform, he continued with badly concealed amusement. "And what rank has Antonio bestowed on you? Oh, yes . . ." His eyes studying Esteban's uniform more closely he continued with a raised brow. "You are very impressive, Colonel Arricalde."

Esteban's smile stiffened. "Only from you would I accept such an implied criticism, Arnoldo. A man with a record of service to his country as great as yours is certainly allowed his private joke at a political appointment. In any case, it matters little. As you can guess, this uniform is for appearances only. Antonio feels it is important for me to present an official appearance if I am to represent him."

"And are you representing him, Esteban?"

"*Si*, in many ways. But tonight I am merely representing myself. My personal interest of late has moved in the direction of the Anglo-Texan state, and since that is your province of concern, I should like to ask you personally how the situation stands there."

"And does your good friend, Antonio, not keep you informed?"

"Arnoldo, it is my duty to serve el presidente—not have have him serve me. I would not bother him with my petty concerns. I have come, instead, to you for information. If you feel you are not of a mind to answer my questions . . ."

But Arnoldo Botin was not to be easily led. Taking his

time, he considered Esteban's discomfiture. Yes, it was obvious the man was sincere in his interest, although he could not fathom why the self-serving young man would have an interest in the unrest in the distant state of Texas. But no one could say Arnoldo Botin was a fool. A small favor now for Arricalde, and perhaps a large favor later for Botin. His mind quickly made up, Arnoldo took Esteban's arm and guided him toward the terrace doors.

"If we are to talk, Esteban, perhaps it would be best outside, away from this annoying din." His lined face reflecting amusement, he offered with an unexpected smirk, "I suppose this will be the first time you have taken a walk into the gardens of the palace with a person of my age and state of overweight . . . much less a male at that! If I am to believe the rumors that circulate about you, Esteban, several ladies of the capital were bereft when you were called back to your home."

Esteban's face twitched with annoyance. "Yes . . . well, my return home has put me in a more serious mind of late. At present my interests lie in a different direction."

"Ah, you have met a young woman who has stolen your heart?"

Esteban's annoyance increased. "I had not realized you were a romantic, Arnoldo. Is it possible that you truly believe such nonsense about losing one's heart . . . one woman for life?"

"You forget, Esteban. Señora Botin has carried my name for more than twenty-five years, and, yes, I do believe it will continue to remain one woman for life for me . . . But then Angelica has always been homely enough to appreciate the love of another homely individual like myself . . ."

"Angelica . . ?"

"Si, that is my dear wife's name . . ."

Grateful for the semi-darkness in which they walked, Esteban cleared his throat nervously. "Oh, I had not realized . . ."

"A lovely name, is it not? And my dear wife does it true justice, not for her beauty of face, but for the beauty of her

337

heart . . ." Suddenly appearing embarrassed by his own sentimentality, Arnoldo frowned. "But enough of that. You did not approach me to hear me speak sentimentally of my dear old woman. What is it you wish to know, Esteban?"

"Lorenzo de Zavala. Antonio will not allow his name to be spoken in his presence. His fury is intense. Word has it that he has fled the governorship of the state of Mexico and is seeking asylum in Texas."

"*Si*, I am afraid that is true. That firebrand is thought to be presently making his way to that trouble spot. He will find many to listen to his incitements there. It is further rumored that he intends to meet with Sam Houston, to lend his insight to the situation which exists in the capital. I have no doubt Zavala will influence their cause greatly. He and Viesca have been very vociferous in their denunciations . . . their incitements. Viesca was reported speaking only the other day . . ."

His expression darkening, Colonel Botin quoted, " 'Citizens of Texas, arouse yourselves or sleep forever! Your dearest interests, your liberty, your property—nay, your very existence—depend upon the fickle will of your direst enemies. Your destruction is resolved upon and nothing but that firmness and energy peculiar to true republicans can save you!' Bah! I have little patience with that kind of talk!"

This submission to anger brief, Colonel Botin drew himself firmly under control, his eyes moving directly to Esteban's intense gaze.

"But it is my thought that Antonio will not sit idly by for that. Knowing his temper, I would not put it past him to send a force to apprehend both Zavala and Viesca."

"Perhaps." Esteban was aware that Botin was fishing and he was too wise for that probing type of remark. He had made the contact to obtain information, not to give it. Realizing the old gentlemen had no more to offer in that regard, he changed the subject adroitly.

"And the trouble at Anahuac?"

"Ah, yes, another mishandled situation. You are aware of the background of the discord there?"

"*Sí*, to an extent. It is a problem of smuggling, is it not?"

"As you say, to an extent, Esteban. You are aware of Anahuac's geographical position and the fact that it is a port conducive to the smuggler's art."

"*Sí.*"

"Captain Tenorio and a small garrison were stationed there for some time to guard the port against just such occurrences and to afford protection to the collectors of customs. He was often annoyed and harassed by the merchants' opposition to payment of high duties upon imports. Well, it seems many riotous demonstrations occurred and Captain Tenorio was forced to arrest two merchants for agitating against taxes. That proved to be an unfortunate mistake, for it provided enough fuel for a healthy showing of Texans on court day in San Felipe."

Colonel Botin took a short breath before continuing in an annoyed tone. "As fate would have it, while the Texans gathered in San Felipe, an army courier arrived. He was seized by the Texans as he rode up the street and the three messages he carried intercepted."

"And those messages were . . ."

"The first was from General Cos, addressed to the alcade of San Felipe, stating that the civil government in Coahuila y Texas had been suspended; Cos was to be in complete charge. The fact that General Cos is el presidente's brother-in-law only added fuel to the fire. Another from General Cos was addressed to the Captain Tenorio, stating that troops were on the way to bolster his garrison in Anahuac. The third, and most upsetting to the Texans, was from another general close to el presidente. It stated that as soon as el presidente felt the time was right, he would personally lead the troops on a punitive sweep across Texas."

"The courier's capture was an incredible stroke of poor luck."

"Which will have far-reaching circumstances, I fear." Arnoldo Botin shook has gray head wearily. "I have no doubt that when word of the dispatches circulates, Texan sentiment will swing solidly behind the war party. It is my personal conviction that Captain Tenorio's position is badly

339

threatened, especially now that the Texans are aware of the force which is on the way."

Esteban took a deep breath. Pausing in his step, he turned to face Colonel Botin squarely. "It is obvious that you are extremely well informed, Arnoldo. What would be your advice on a manner in which to save the situation at Anahuac?"

Colonel Botin frowned. He could not quite figure out this new Esteban Arricalde. A second sense told him there was more to his interest than concern for his country's welfare. No, the passage of a few months' time could not have changed this handsome, spoiled young man that much. It was more probably that his interest evolved from a personal matter which he was driven to right. But Arnoldo Botin also realized that this was a golden opportunity to have his comments taken directly to el presidente. He was not willing to pass up that chance for the sake of a few details which he had not yet had time to figure out.

"My advice . . .?" Looking directly into Esteban's intense expression, Arnoldo offered slowly, "My advice would not be welcome in some quarters, but I will give you my opinion as you request. My opinion is this: General Martin Perfecto do Cos is a fool! He does not respect the intelligence of the Texans, and in that way underestimates them time and time again. To send him into this highly tense situation is a ghastly mistake. If there is to be any negotiating, it would be far better to allow Colonel Ugartechea to take over in that regard. He is not regarded unfavorably by the Texans, and his integrity is generally well respected."

"You were correct when you made your original statement, Arnoldo. Your opinion would not be well received in many circles. But I respect it, nevertheless." Urging Colonel Botin back toward the ballroom, Esteban continued softly. "You may rest assured I will keep your confidence, and you may also rest assured that you have earned yourself a favor in return if I am ever in a position to return one to you."

They had reached the lights of the ballroom once again and Esteban extended his hand in his companion's direction.

"*Muchas gracias*, Arnoldo. I have taken up enough of your time tonight. I will allow you to return to your wife . . . your Angelica. El presidente is fortunate to have a man of your caliber in his service."

Lifting his eyes as Señora Botin started in their direction, Esteban made a silent observation. Arnoldo had been entirely truthful. La señora was decidedly homely, with few physical attributes in her favor. He suppressed a low snort. Colonel Botin had obviously never needed to defend his Angelica against the desire of others. But such would never be the case for the man who possessed Angelica Rodrigo. However, he was more than certain possessing her would be worth whatever trials he need suffer, and possess her he would. Arnold Botin had just placed him another step closer to that goal. For that he was decidedly grateful.

Excusing himself, Esteban started toward the doorway. El presidente had just entered. His timing was perfect . . . perfect for his purpose.

"General Cos will handle the situation at Anahuac, Esteban, and I do not wish to hear another word about it! I am sick to death of the upstart Texans and their cries for liberty! They were not so arrogant when they petitioned our government for permission to settle on our lands. They are fools, all of them! Only fools would send Stephen Austin into our hands. And only a fool like Stephen Austin would address a letter back to Texas advising anarchy, and then allow word of that advice to fall into our hands."

Esteban faced an agitated Santa Anna across the desk in the private portion of the palace where they had retired to talk. Esteban frowned. El presidente had not received his comments well. Antonio Santa Anna's proud stature and broad shoulders were rigid, his handsome, aristocratic face stiff with displeasure. Esteban had not expected such a violent reaction to his statement, but he was not yet willing to give up hope for his plan.

"Antonio, the problem here is not a new one. The Texans are determined, proud individuals. Where they are decid-

341

edly lacking in breeding, education, and the social graces, they are not lacking in courage. We cannot afford to underestimate the importance of that quality in their makeup."

"And you overestimate them, Esteban! Do you not understand, we hold their leader? Stephen Austin now languishes in our custody. He will return to Texas only when I say he will return, yet I have managed to convince him that I work steadily in an effort to free him . . . that it is the courts which hold him, not I! The Texans are very fond of Señor Austin. They will do nothing which might threaten him in any way."

"Antonio, I beg to differ with you. The Texans have suffered great agitation at Anahuac. Action will be instituted. I propose that you send me to this point of action, allow me to assess it for you personally. You may expect a prompt report and a quick evaluation of the . . ."

"*Silencio*, Esteban!" His face flaming a deep red, Antonio Santa Anna had heard enough. "I have no intention of sending you anywhere! You are of more use to me here, in the capital. I will hear no more of this foolish talk! You have been engaged to listen and to advise me of what you have heard. You have not been engaged to direct me in guiding this country! You must guard against allowing your new uniform to overpower your good sense, and you must remember just who is *presidente* here!' "

"Antonio, not for a minute did I forget . . ."

His agitation lessening at Esteban's apologetic tone, Antonio Santa Anna took a moment to rein his anger under control. He nodded his head. "That is fortunate, Esteban, because I would not like to lose you. You are a good man who can be extremely useful to me."

"That is my most fervent desire, Señor Presidente."

A full smile returning to his face, Antonio Santa Anna walked around the desk and slapped Esteban companionably on the shoulder.

"That is good. Now, let us return to the ball. La Señora de Santa Anna is regrettably in residence at Manga de Clavo, as is her usual custom. I find myself desirous of female company this evening. My eyes and heart are set on a particular beauty, and I anticipate a long, eventful evening. We must make the best of our time and our opportunities, must we not, Esteban?"

Turning toward the doorway at Santa Anna's urging, Esteban nodded. He had never agreed with Santa Anna more.

"*Sí*, that has always been my thought, Antonio."

"Well, then we are in agreement on this point, my friend."

Guiding him into the hallway, Santa Anna began to speak as they turned in the direction from which the music of yet another waltz originated.

"I appreciate your effort to keep me informed, Esteban. Perhaps next time we will be able to agree on the action to be taken."

Affixing a smile on his lips, Esteban murmured agreeably, "Yes, perhaps we will."

A hasty retreat in the face of Santa Anna's strong opposition, but Esteban had not given up. In fact, the brief setback in his plan made him all the more determined to succeed. He had not been able to persuade el presidente to send him as his ambassador to Texas this time, but he would convince him the next time . . . or the next. Yes, he would travel to Texas in an official capacity, and when he returned, he would not be alone.

Angelica grimaced against the taste of dust in her mouth, its gritty rasp against her skin. The mountains' endless walls of green foliage, the crisp scent and moistness in the air were far behind them. Instead, the glare of the afternoon sun beat down relentlessly on a desolate landscape that stretched as far as the eye could see. The heat rose in little shimmering waves to lend an eerie, tremulous quality to a silent scene broken only by the sound of their horses' hooves and the perpetual buzzing of insects.

Angelica took a deep breath and adjusted the large straw sombrero she had adopted as a protection against the burning rays which abused her skin. She was thankful for

Gareth's thoughtfulness in providing for that protection. Her rebozo had been too heavy a shield in the sultry air of the lowlands.

Accustomed to the more pleasant climate of the mountains, Angelica had been unprepared for the heat. Her discomfort was intense, growing more with each hour and each mile they covered. A strange sort of unrest had seemed to infiltrate her mind. The heavy, moist air was a faint memory which she could not summon to total recall. She remembered only vague shadows of days spent in torturous discomfort, the sun burning her skin, long anxious thirsts, and an endless ride from which there seemed no deliverance.

She had finally abandoned her attempt to revive the memory of her childhood and devoted her energies to the endurance of the endless journey which lay before them. But her efforts were to little avail.

Turning her eyes back to the trail, Angelica urged her horse to a faster pace in order to keep abreast of Gareth. She did not wish to fall behind.

Chapter IX

She was running, straining to catch the whisper of velvet which fled from her grasp. There was no light. The angry darkness fought to overwhelm her and she gasped against its suffocating weight. Where . . . where had it gone? A wild panic sent her running faster, faster, but she could not escape. Her heart was pounding, her breath catching in her throat in frantic sobs. The darkness pressed deeper, deeper, forcing the air from her lungs. She was choking, expiring in the lightless, silent void. There was no more space. The only sound her own tremulous cry, she was beginning to succumb . . .

"Angelica! Angelica, wake up."

The deep voice that penetrated the shadows of her fear was demanding, forcing her from her breathless agony. Struggling to raise herself from the obscurity which held her in its grasp, Angelica reached out, her hands coming into contact with a familiar warmth.

"Gareth. . ."

"Angelica, you were dreamin'. Open your eyes, darlin' . . . that's right. . . ."

Gareth's husky voice comforted her, lending her the strength to take the last step into consciousness. Angelica raised her heavy lids, her eyes focusing on the concerned face shadowed by the darkness of night. Gareth was lying beside her on the hard ground. His arms clutched her close, protecting her against the shades of unreasonable fear which had seen fit to revisit her. Yes, she remembered where she was. She was on her way to Gareth's Texas homestead with him. They had been on the trail over a month. They had finally entered Texas, and that had been when the nightmares had begun.

The nightmares were terrifying, allowing her no consolation from their rigors. They assailed her almost nightly, and she was defenseless against them. Vague memories of similar dreams suffered in her forgotten childhood hovered in the back of her mind . . . visions from long ago, before the velvet had come to console her. But the velvet, soft and blue, had disappeared. She had only the strength of Gareth's arms to save her from the horrendous assaults of fearful dreams which would allow her no peace.

Angelica swallowed hard, forcing her eyes to remain on Gareth's face, to absorb his strength. The light from the small campfire that still burned a few feet away played against its harsh planes, but she found only comfort in his glance . . . a sense of escape from the horror of the dreams that pursued her.

Gareth's broad hand was stroking her cheeks, smoothing the paths of tears from their surface.

"Was it the same dream, darlin'?"

Nodding her head, Angelica attempted to respond, only to find that the words could not pass the remains of terror lodged deeply in her throat. It froze her tongue, made it impossible to speak. The great silver saucers of her eyes widened as she struggled to overcome her frightened state.

"No . . . don't try to talk if you're not ready. It was a stupid question to ask. I know it was the same dream . . . the same, damned dream."

Gareth's arms closed tightly around her, and Angelica gasped at the strength of his embrace. It was almost pain, but she suffered it gratefully. The heat of the lowlands had not abated even in night, the weight of the damp air adding to its distress, but the moist warmth of Gareth's bare flesh against hers was a solace she could not sacrifice to discomfort. Ashamed of the fear that lingered, hating herself for submitting to its nameless shadows, Angelica pressed herself against the familiar wall of Gareth's body. His arms were her only respite, and in her mindless fright, she accepted them fully.

Morning dawned bright and clear, the brilliant, rapidly rising sun having no effect on the damp air which lay oppressively against Gareth's skin. Following the routine of long weeks on the trail, Gareth worked at reloading the horses as Angelica rolled the blankets and secured the last details of their night camp. His eyes returned again and again to Angelica's efficient movements, lingering on the almost imperceptible trembling of her hands and the tense set of her face. Those dreams . . . they had begun shortly after they had entered the state of Texas. Surely that could not have been a coincidence, the fact that each mile which drew her closer to his homestead seemed to increase her nightly desolation.

Gareth turned sharply away from the sight that so distressed him, back to his horse, working to tighten the cinch on his saddle. There was no doubting the absolute terror each episode inflicted upon Angelica. Gareth fought his growing sense of guilt. Was the thought of remaining with him to complete her year of commitment so oppressive that it laid her open to nightly assaults of her mind? Somehow the thought was incongruous with Angelica's reaction to his lovemaking. During their nights on the trail, Angelica had come to him willingly, almost eagerly. He could not believe her passion feigned. There was a spontaneity there, a warmth that sprung to life at his touch. He had almost begun to believe his campaign to stir in her the same wealth of emotion Angelica had brought to life within him was knowing success. But then the nightmares had begun.

Now he was uncertain, confused. Each debilitating occurrence appeared to make her turn to him all the more spontaneously in the darkness of night, while changing her to silent stone in the full light of day. They had completed a silent breakfast only a short time before, in stark contrast to Angelica's former interest in the course of the day on which they were to embark. He had been unable to get her to talk about her dreams. Instead, she seemed determined to avoid the subject of her almost nightly bouts of terror. He had felt no accusation in her avoidance of the subject, just her fierce, unspoken determination which he could not overcome.

The horses saddled and loaded, Gareth turned back to Angelica to see her draw herself to a standing position over the last carefully packed saddlebag. There was no mistaking her exhaustion. Her face was chalk white under its surface color, the shadows under her eyes increasing the appearance of fragility which had marked her of late. He was well aware that she had remained unsleeping in his arms almost until the first light of dawn after the particularly frightful dream she had suffered last night. No, she could not go another day with such limited sleep. He would have to take care of that deficiency.

Taking the few steps to Angelica's side, Gareth took the heavy saddlebag from her hands. Aware that she followed close behind him, he walked to Angelica's horse and threw it over his back. Securing it tightly, he turned back to Angelica's startled gaze as she noted the majority of their equipment had been loaded on the smaller animal's back.

Not bothering to respond to Angelica's unspoken inquiry, Gareth gripped her tightly around the waist and swung her upon his horse. At her vocal protest, he mumbled gruffly and mounted unhesitantly behind her. His voice was low as he adjusted her against him.

"You're goin' to ride with me this mornin', Angelica. You're exhausted. You need sleep. When you feel drowsy you can close your eyes and lean back against me."

A frown wrinkled Angelica's smooth brow.

"You are as exhausted as I, Gareth. I do not wish to be a burden to you during the daylight hours as I have been during the night. I would prefer to ride my own horse."

Gareth's response immediate, he cupped her chin with his hand and turned her face toward him.

"We're goin' to be havin' a long day today, Angelica. If you're worryin' about bein' a burden ridin' with me, then you can remember that it's no hardship on me ridin' with you in my arms. the hardship would be in not bein' able to make Goliad before nightfall. I'm intendin' to stop for supplies and some information on the state of affairs at home. I'm also intendin' to sleep in a real bed tonight, and anythin' that keeps me from realizin' those goals will be the real imposition." Pausing only a moment as Angelica appeared to consider his words, Gareth continued firmly. "So lean back, darlin', and rest." A small smile flicked across his lips. "If you start snorin', I promise to wake you up. I can't abide a noisy woman . . ."

But there was no responsive smile as Angelica studied his expression. Instead, she turned her face resolutely forward in silence. Refusing to allow her silence to bother him, Gareth spurred his horse into motion. His relief was profound as Angelica leaned fully back against him.

They had switched back to separate horses at their last rest stop even though it had been Gareth's inclination to continue riding double as they had most of the day. It had been a heady feeling traveling with Angelica in his arms again. He had almost forgotten the pleasure he derived in Angelica's slender form swaying against his. The heavy, moist air and the uncompromising heat had not been the problem he had anticipated. As the morning had worn on, he had been aware of the gradual relaxing of her slim body against his and he had experienced a startling sense of fulfillment as the tension had left her body completely. Her head had begun to loll back against the support of his shoulder and he had shifted her slightly to brace her more comfortably against his chest. Her head had rested against the curve of his neck and he had delighted in the feathering of her breath against his skin.

Angelica had dozed for a short time in the morning, seeming almost embarrassed as she had awakened. She had pulled herself upright and shot him a small frown. Feeling oddly bereft, he had drawn her back against him again. She had not opposed the contact.

Goliad was only a little way down the road, and Gareth

was relieved. He had been determined to make the town before nightfall. He was glad that he had made the decision to allow Angelica to assume her own mount at their last stop. It would not do for both of them to arrive in the busy little town on one horse. As it was, his arrival with Angelica was bound to stir talk. Despite the fact that settlements were widespread in the territory, and communication poor, his homestead was large and well known. He did not wish to cause such a stir that news of him and his traveling companion would precede his arrival at the ranch.

He was fully aware that their stopover in Goliad might accomplish that fact, but he felt forced to take the chance. He was unable to protect Angelica against the anxiety which stimulated the wild nightmares. He could not help but suspect they were caused by Angelica's unconscious rejection of the commitment she had made. What else could explain her tortured flight in each dream, or the fact that the dreams became more frightening, more effective in inducing a silence between them with each mile they came closer to his home?

Gareth shot a quick glance in Angelica's direction as the town of Goliad came into view and he suppressed a bitter laugh. He had promised her that he would be her "velvet," that he would provide her consolation. Instead, he had provided a source for the nightmares from which she could not escape. That realization did not rest lightly on his mind.

She needed a night back in civilization, a break from the fatiguing journey that still stretched out in front of them. The realization that Texas was not all wilderness, heat, and glaring sun, that it had much more to offer, would relax her. They would get more supplies so their meals on the trail would have a little variety again. The Golden Steer Hotel still provided the best accommodations in town and he was going to make sure Angelica and he took full advantage of them.

Signaling Angelica to follow his lead, Gareth spurred his horse to a faster pace. First things first. He was going to arrange for a room so that Angelica might have a few minutes to freshen up while he took the horses to the livery stable to bed them for the night. It was just past mid-afternoon and the hotel was often filled by the time the night hours approached. He was not going to take that chance. When he lay with Angelica tonight, it was going to be on a soft mattress. When he made love to her, it was going to be in full comfort. Angelica deserved the best he had to offer her.

Reining up in front of the hotel, Gareth dismounted. He reached up and lifted Angelica down from her horse before turning back for his saddlebags. Angelica's belongings were packed carefully along with his. He had seen to that early on in their journey. Taking her arm, Gareth ushered Angelica onto the porch and into the modest lobby.

Forcing himself to ignore the interested glances and knowing smirks his registration induced, Gareth led Angelica up the staircase a few moments later. He had failed to take into account the possible effect of those under-eyed glances and whispered comments on Angelica. He shot her a quick look. Her chin high, she walked stiffly up the steps. The vulnerability he sensed just below her surface calm was carefully masked, and he was determined to do nothing to upset its tenuous balance. Stifling the fierce flood of protective warmth that all but overwhelmed him, Gareth walked silently at her side, touching her arm only when they had arrived at the doorway to their room.

His spirits lifting the moment his eyes touched on the broad bed that dominated the center of the room, Gareth walked in. He closed the door behind them and turned toward Angelica as he threw the saddlebags on the bed. His mouth moved into a pleased smile. Miraculously, the tension began to fade from Angelica's frame and she returned his smile.

"We'll be sleepin' in comfort tonight, darlin'." Lowering his head, he pressed a light kiss against her lips. "You can get cleaned up while I take the horses to get bedded down for the night. I'll do the same when I come back, and then we'll go for supplies and some information. After that, our time's our own, and we'll make the best of it, darlin'."

351

Gareth paused for another brief kiss, relieved to feel the surge of Angelica's response. Yes, she was starting to feel better already, and so was he. It was going to be a good evening. He had a feeling.

An hour later, Gareth and Angelica were striding across the busy main street of Goliad toward the general store. His hand cupping Angelica's elbow, Gareth smiled down into her eyes. There was a flicker of tension in their silver depths, and Gareth felt her discomfort. It had emerged as they had descended the staircase at the hotel and all eyes had turned in their direction. But he could not really blame those trail-weary cowboys for staring.

The long journey in the hot summer sun had only added to Angelica's magnificent beauty. Her skin, now colored a soft golden brown from indirect exposure to the unrelenting rays, gave dramatic contrast with her great luminous eyes and the black, incredibly thick, spiky lashes which surrounded them. The creamy texture of her skin seemed smoother, the planes of her cheeks more exotically pronounced. Her hair, still damp from washing, was unbound and moved in gleaming swirls past her slender shoulders. The worn simplicity of her clothing could not hide her petite dimensions or the instinctive grace with which she walked. She was beautiful . . . the most beautiful woman most of these men had seen in a long time. He would try to explain that to Angelica later tonight, when he held her in his arms, but he doubted she would believe him.

His arm curving around her waist as they entered the store, Gareth ushered Angelica inside. An emporium of considerable dimensions, it served as a meeting place for many of the matrons of the town, several of whom were browsing amongst the bolts of cloth. The immediate buzzing that commenced between them upon Angelica's and his entrance did not go unnoted by Angelica's keen eyes. She instinctively raised her chin and turned deliberately to Gareth.

"We need more tea, Gareth. And we also need . . ."

"Darlin', tell the clerk what we need and he'll put it

together for us." Gareth raised his eyes to the balding gentleman who stood expectantly behind the counter. "Isn't that right, friend?"

Waiting only until the smiling fellow gave a short nod and Angelica had started in his direction, Gareth moved instinctively toward the proclamation pinned to the wall in the far corner. He had not had an opportunity to speak to anyone about the progress of political events in Texas, but he had a feeling his questions would be answered by the long, printed article. It had the look of an official document, and he did not waste any time moving in its direction.

Surprised to find it was a statement printed by the Committee of Safety, relating the events which had led up to the arrest of two merchants in Anahuac, Gareth read with great interest. He had almost reached the bottom of the article when a deep voice sounded in his ear from behind.

"You're wastin' your time, partner. Them's not the most recent details. If you're wantin' to be brought up to date on what's happenin', just you turn around, and I'll be pleased to help you."

Gareth turned slowly. The low laugh that sounded in the throat of the leathery-faced fellow standing directly behind him elicited a similar response.

"Gareth Dawson, you're the last man I expected to see in Goliad! I expected with your pa takin' off for the States a few weeks back, you'd be high-tailin' it back to your homestead!"

"That's just the direction I'm headin' in, Lester, and damn if I don't know I'm gettin' close when I see your ugly face!" Reaching out his hand, Gareth grasped the callused one extended in return and shook it warmly. "Well, well, Lester Small. What are you doin' in this town, and what's all this braggin' about bein' able to catch me up on the latest news?"

"I ain't braggin', Gareth. Hell, it's plain to see by the way you read that old notice that you ain't heard nothin' about the little trick William Barrett Travis pulled on the garrison in Anahuac a little while after that paper was posted."

"I know Bill Travis, all right. He's a brave man and a true patriot. I'm proud to number him among my friends. But you're right. I haven't heard anythin' about his 'little trick'."

"Well, you read how dispatches were intercepted while bein' carried down the main street of San Felipe on court day . . . the day when the merchants that were arrested in Anahuac were goin' to be tried."

"I sure did. I can't say the messages surprised me. Santa Anna is one of the most arrogant men I've ever known. I wouldn't put anythin' past him."

"Well, let me tell you, Gareth, when word of the dispatches circulated, the Texas War Party got more converts than it had in the past year. Public meetin's were held in San Felipe and there was general discussion about expellin' the Anahuac garrison before Cos's troops arrived to reinforce them. Heedin' the call, Travis and twenty-five men took up a trusty cannon and started out from San Felipe. They fired but one shot, Gareth, and the garrison surrendered. Bill Travis disarmed Captain Tenorio and his men and gave them the polite order to 'Be seen in San Felipe as soon as God would let them.'

"The only problem was, when Travis returned to San Felipe the municipality of Liberty and the central committee condemned his action. Hell, they even wrote a letter to the Mexican authorities condemnin' Travis's rashness and apologizing, sayin' that Travis's actions were not by the vote of the majority. Travis was even forced into the position of writin' his own apology. But General Cos wasn't havin' any. Last I heard, he was demandin' that Travis be arrested and turned over to him."

"They're not goin' to do . . ."

"Hell, no, Gareth! They're a bunch of fools in San Felipe, but they ain't stupid, and they ain't turnin' no loyal Texan over to a Mexican firin' squad!"

"Well, that's damned good to hear!"

"That's about all the good news there is, but . . ."

"Lester, you sure like to play out a story. Come on, get on

354

with it!"

"Well, the last I heard, Cos was expected to move his troops into Texas. If he does, it looks like Texans will have to fight or submit."

Gareth frowned. It was coming faster than he thought. Hell, he needed to get back to his homestead. He had no time to lose . . ."

Lester's voice drew to a slow halt as his eyes moved to a point behind Gareth's head. He let out a low whistle and his voice dropped to a conspiratorial whisper.

"Damn, what have we here? That's sure enough the prettiest little thing I've seen in a dog's age! Look at them eyes! Hell, I don't think I'd be able to breathe if that little woman set them eyes on me, even at my age!"

Turning, Gareth followed the direction of Lester's gaze. The supplies they needed lying in a pile on the counter, Angelica had moved to the table covered with bolts of cloth. Her hands were moving curiously over the fabric. At a word from the clerk, she turned and shot the balding gentleman a small smile. Lester Small's gasp tightened the knot in Gareth's stomach.

"Lord Almighty!"

Lester's close-set eyes all but bulged as he shook his head disbelievingly. "I didn't believe them boys at the Green Pond Saloon when they was talkin' about the little señorita that came into town. Hell, I figured they was just too long on the range. There wasn't no woman that looked as good as they said she did. But I was wrong, Gareth. It's a damned lucky fella, whoever he is, that hooked onto that one, Mex or not."

Lester was rambling on, his eyes glued to Angelica's face. Gareth made an attempt to distract him, only to have the smitten Texan shake his head with a frown. "What in hell's wrong with you, Gareth? I came all the way over here from the Green Pond Saloon just to get a glimpse of that little girl. I suspicioned that bunch in there was pullin' my leg, but I wasn't goin' to let them old boys get one up on me." Small shook his head, incredulous. "But, hell, they wasn't lyin' after all."

Rambling to a halt, Lester moved his eyes around the cluttered store. A small grin picked up the corners of his mouth.

"What do you think, Gareth? Looks like the little senorita's man left her alone for a while. Do you think she'd be able to warm up to an old range rider like me? Hell, I got a lot of good years left in me . . ."

"Lester, save your breath and your energy. That little lady's man isn't goin' to let anybody get near her. You can take my word for it."

Gareth was finding it exceedingly difficult to maintain his sense of humor. Lester wasn't exactly the "old range rider" he chose to call himself. In fact, he was no more than ten years older than Gareth himself, and that made him a man in his prime of life. He didn't like the idea that this man, or any man in town, would feel free to approach Angelica. The desire to set this fellow straight, friend or no friend, was becoming too strong to ignore. But Lester was not about to be put off.

His eyes showing a rare sparkle, Lester puffed out his chest and absentmindedly smoothed his handsome graying mustache. "Well, as far as this old boy is concerned, it's work takin' a chance. Any fella that'd be fool enough to leave that little senorita unprotected in a strange town deserves whatever he gets. And if he's that much of a fool, she'll most likely be better off with me than him anyway."

"Lester . . ."

Gareth's warning tone went completely unrecognized and would have resulted in sharper words had not Angelica glanced up in their direction and caught their intense stares. Flushing, Angelica dropped her hands from the bolt of cloth she had been examining. A small frown tightened her brow at the annoyance obvious on Gareth's face, and she glanced toward the supplies waiting on the counter.

Aware of Lester's low, unintelligible comment as Angelica started in their direction, Gareth took a firm hold on his control. Moving directly to his side, Angelica fastened her uncertain gaze on his.

"The supplies are ready, Gareth. I have told the storekeeper to put them aside until you have approved of my selection. There will be no difficulty if you don't feel . . ."

"Whatever you've chosen will be fine, Angelica."

Pulling her into the curve of his arm, Gareth turned silently toward Lester.

"Well, I'll be damned . . ."

His incredulous voice breaking the silence between them, Lester swept his range-weary hat from his head, and ran a callused hand through his thinning hair.

"You always was a damned lucky bastard! Well, ain't you goin' to introduce me to this señorita, Gareth?"

Gareth's hesitation was brief. The look on Lester Small's face showed there was no way he was going to be put off.

"Lester, this lady's Angelica Rodrigo. She's travelin' back home with me. She's goin' to work for the Circle D for the next year." Turning to Angelica, Gareth offered in a softer voice, "Angelica, this here fella's an old range rider by the name of Lester Small. He's been on the trail for a long time, so if his manners are a little rusty, I guess we'll both have to forgive him."

Angelica nodded her acceptance of the introduction, noting the stiffness in Gareth's manner.

"Real pleased to meet you, ma'am. I was just tellin' Gareth that you're the prettiest little thing I've seen in a dog's age, and any man'd consider himself right lucky just to spend some time feastin' his eyes on you."

"That's a real pretty speech, Lester." His annoyance beginning to dissipate in the face of Lester's obvious sincerity, Gareth managed a short smile. "But you're just goin' to have to find yourself a little lady from the Green Pond Saloon to 'feast your eyes on' tonight. Like you said, any fella that didn't keep his eyes on Angelica in a town like this would be a real fool, and I'm not about to allow myself to suffer in comparison to your 'golden tongue,' you old rascal."

"Oh, hell, Gareth, you know I'm all talk. You ain't gonna let my big mouth keep me from enjoyin' this lady's company. What do you say we go to Maude Pierce's boardinghouse for supper. I was about to go there myself, and I'd be right happy to have your company . . ."

"You mean Angelica's company . . ."

The twinkle returning to his small eyes, Lester nodded. "You just might be right there, Gareth. But just to show you my intentions are honorable, I'll buy you both supper." Turning toward Angelica, Lester offered politely, "What do you say, little lady?"

Angelica's reply was a short glance in Gareth's direction, and unable to restrain his smile a moment longer, Gareth nodded. "Well, you wore me down, Lester. If you'll wait until I pay for our supplies, Angelica and I will be happy to have you buy us dinner tonight. As a matter of fact, it'll be our pleasure, won't it, darlin'?"

"Sí . . . yes, it will be our pleasure, Señor Small."

"Call me Lester, darlin'." And at Gareth's sharp look, the older Texan said gruffly, "Hell, loosen up, Gareth! And go pay for those supplies so that we can get on to our dinner. I can feel my appetite growin' as I stand here."

Making sure to urge Angelica alongside him as he walked toward the counter, Gareth shot a small smile into her face. Hell, he was just going to have to get used to it. He had no doubt it was going to be the same wherever Angelica and he showed their faces. This was not going to be easy . . . not easy at all . . .

Laughing heartily, Gareth spontaneously urged Angelica closer to his side as they crossed Goliad's main street. The light of day had long since faded, the hours racing by in Lester Small's entertaining company. Sending a short glance toward Angelica as they stepped up onto the porch of The Golden Steer, he was relieved to see true enjoyment visible in her demeanor as well.

Obviously unwilling to allow them to get away, Lester sent a quick look toward the empty chairs on the porch.

"It's a real pleasant night, ain't it? Too nice to call it a day already. What do you say we sit here for a spell? There's three chairs waitin' for us over there, and if I ask them real nice inside, I bet I can talk somebody into bringin' us somethin' refreshin' to drink."

Gareth shot Lester a wary look. True to his word, Lester

had brought them dinner and caught him up on the latest news. Through him he had found out that Jonathan Dawson had left for Louisiana just the week before, with intentions to travel even farther in response to a summons from a federal official of the U.S. government whom he did not care to identify. It appeared his father's work in relation to Texas liberty was beginning to bear fruit, and Gareth had been pleased. Unconsciously he had been relieved that his father would not be there upon his arrival. It would give Angelica time to settle in at the homestead, to feel more secure when she would finally have to face his father. He knew from experience that Jonathan Dawson's steely-eyed stare could be demoralizing, and with his past history of disappointments in matters of the heart, he was uncertain how his father would react to Angelica's installation in the household.

But he could not afford to indulge Lester any longer. The man had been all but salivating through the whole course of their delicious dinner at Maude Pierce's boardinghouse, and he was certain the tempting chicken and biscuits were not the sole cause. Angelica's cautious regard of his friend had turned to acceptance after she had learned to accept the steady barrage of flowery but heartfelt compliments with which he had continued to shower her. There was no doubt Lester was smitten, and were he not so obvious about his reaction to Angelica's beauty and the reserved affection with which she had begun to treat him, Gareth doubted his reaction would have been so temperate. But it was time to call the evening to a halt. They had had a long day, and he did not want to wait until Angelica and he were both exhausted before retiring. No . . . his plans tonight most definitely did not include going right to sleep the moment his head touched the pillow.

Holding Angelica firmly in the curve of his arm, Gareth smiled into Lester's hopeful face.

"Yes, it is a nice night, Lester. And I have no doubt you'd be able to talk somebody into bringin' us somethin' refreshin' out here. I got to admit, I never realized what a smooth talker you are. But we've had a long day, and we're goin' to be gettin' up early tomorrow mornin' . . ."

"Sensing his refusal, Lester pulled his lean body up tall in strident objection.

"Gareth . . . hell, man, I ain't had such a good time in months. You can't go turnin' me back to The Green Pond now. The evenin's just begun . . ."

"Just begun for you, partner, but endin' for Angelica and me . . ."

The disappointment on the leathery face looking into his was almost comical. Barely suppressing a laugh, Gareth shook his head.

"All right, just one drink." Lester's face had just begun to reflect his relief when Gareth added, "I'll go back to The Green Pond with you, but Angelica's goin' upstairs. You're tired, aren't you, darlin'?"

Not quite certain of Angelica's true reaction to his question, Gareth saw a guarded look pass over her gaze as she responded simply, 'Sí, I am tired.

But Lester's reaction was far more spontaneous.

"You ain't sendin' Angelica upstairs? Hell, Gareth, you ain't half as pretty as she is, and I ain't had my fill of lookin' at her yet! Beggin' your pardon, ma'am." Turning back to Angelica, Lester offered simply, "I got a long trail ahead of me for the next few week, and I was hopin' to fortify myself with a few more pleasant memories."

"Lester, please. . . ." Raising his eyes in a silent plea for patience, Gareth continued quietly. "You're just goin' to have to be satisfied with memories of my company for another few minutes. That's my final offer."

"Well, if you're sure of that . . ."

"I'm sure." Turning toward Angelica, Gareth offered with a small smile, "I'll be back in a few minutes, darlin'. When you go upstairs, lock the door behind you, and just make certain you open it only to me. There're a lot of lonesome cowboys in this town . . ."

"You needn't worry, Gareth."

"Angelica, ma'am. . . ." Lester's low, gravelly voice called their attention to his forlorn expression. "Bein' with you and Gareth this evenin' has been the greatest pleasure

360

I've had in a long time, and knowin' that you'll be at the Circle D is sure to make me stop by on the way back from this little job I have to do." Reaching out, Lester took Angelica's hand. Slender and graceful, it looked decidedly out of place in Lester's broad, callused palm as he closed his hand around it and raised it to his lips in a surprising gesture.

His face flushing as he released it, Lester nodded. "Thank you for the evenin'." Turning to Gareth, he frowned. "Let's get goin' then, Gareth. I get the feelin' you're goin' to have a short night at The Green Pond."

"You're right, Lester. I'll be with you in a minute."

Following Angelica inside, Gareth watched her as she quickly climbed the staircase, his eyes not relinquishing her form until she had slipped through the doorway of their room and closed it behind her. Letting out a short sigh, Gareth walked back onto the porch. His voice was gruff.

"Let's get goin', Lester. I'm gettin' more and more tired every minute."

"Tired, hell! It ain't sleepin' you got on your mind . . ."

Gareth gave Lester a sharp look that resulted in a sheepish glance.

"Don't you recognize envy when you see it, Gareth? If you don't, then get a good look at it and memorize the way it looks, 'cause you're goin' to be seein' a lot more of it wherever you go with that little señorita . . ."

"Is that so?"

"Yeah, that's so. Let's get goin'. I got to go drown my sorrows. You just broke my heart . . ."

Gareth gave a small laugh. "A little Jim Crow will put it back together again, you poor fella. . . ."

Throwing his arm companionably around Lester's shoulders, Gareth laughed again. Hell, he was a lucky bastard, and he wasn't about to stretch his luck by a long stay in The Green Pond. As a matter of fact, the sooner he got there, the sooner he'd be coming back. Spontaneously increasing his pace, Gareth urged Lester along.

A bottle in one hand and two stemmed glasses in the

other, Gareth mounted the steps toward his room at the Golden Steer. He was frowning. He was still uncertain what had made him pay such an outrageous price for this bottle of champagne and two stemmed glasses. Damn that Roxy Miller! You'd think a woman would have a softer heart when it came to romance, but that redheaded barkeep had a heart of stone. He winced at the thought of the dent the purchase had made in his reserve funds.

Well, it would be worth the expense if it ensured Angelica a restful, uninterrupted night's sleep. Hell, he owed her that. Besides saving his life, she had added to it to such a degree that he could not imagine being without her.

He was standing in front of the door to their room. Raising his hand, he knocked lightly. There was no response and he knocked again. A jiggle of apprehension moved along his spine. The door was locked but there was no sound from within. She had to be inside. He knocked again, a light panic beginning to edge his mind. No . . . she could not . . . she would not have taken this first opportunity he had afforded her to sneak away . . . to leave him. He knocked harder, the side of his hand shaking the scarred wood as a slow fury began to build inside him. He had all but decided to apply his shoulder to the unmoving barrier when the door pulled open abruptly and Angelica's sleepy face poked around the corner.

"Gareth, what's wrong?"

Pushing inside and kicking the door closed behind him, Gareth stared down at Angelica's startled face. She was obviously still groggy from sleep and unable to comprehend his agitation. The ridiculousness of the conclusion to which his mind had jumped suddenly struck him, and he released a tight breath.

"Nothin's wrong, Angelica, except you opened the door without even askin' who was there." He gave a quick glance to the brief chemise in which she was attired, realizing she had obviously been in bed. "And I don't have to tell you what might've happened if you'd answered the door like that and it hadn't been me."

"Oh . . ." Belatedly remembering his instructions of a

short time before, Angelica frowned. "I was asleep. You startled me . . ."

Not wishing to pursue the subject, Gareth put the bottle and glasses on the night table beside the bed. Taking the few steps back to Angelica, Gareth curved his arm around her neck and pulled her close. Damn, he had awakened her. If he hadn't had this little celebration planned, he wouldn't have gone to the Green Pond with Lester in the first place. But he had wanted Angelica to have something special to remember, to occupy her mind and keep the dark dreams at bay.

Her slender length against him was working its usual magic, and slipping his arm around her waist, Gareth leaned her back over the curve of his arm to trail his lips along the hollows at the base of her throat. Her skin was sweet and smooth and he resisted the urge to deepen his kiss. Instead, he released her slowly, his eyes moving back to her face. The sleepiness was fading, and in its place a familiar glow began to warm her gaze.

His heart beginning to pound, Gareth scooped Angelica up into his arms, covering the distance to the bed in a few short steps. He sat her there, propping the pillows comfortably behind her before sitting beside her and turning back toward the bottle and glasses.

He had little difficulty in popping the cork. The brief time he had spent in Mexico City a few years before had taught him that skill, but he had had little use for it since. Tonight he was intensely glad he did not need to waste time.

Her eyes intent on his actions as he poured the sparkling liquid into the glasses, Angelica commented quietly, "I have never had champagne."

"It's not very common in Texas, darlin', but in Mexico City it flows with abundance. I developed a real likin' for it when I visited the capital a few years ago. And I wanted tonight to be a special celebration . . ."

"Surely your friend Lester would have enjoyed . . ."

Gareth's short glance forced her statement to an aborted end. Her face flushing, Angelica averted her glance, only to

363

have Gareth tip her chin up to his face.

"Let's forget about Lester, darlin'."

Turning back to pick up the filled glasses, Gareth placed one in Angelica's hand, his eyes intent on hers.

"It won't be long until we reach the Circle D, and I wanted us to drink to the time we'll be spendin' there." His warm gaze holding hers, Gareth proposed huskily, "May you love Texas, darlin', as much as Texas will love you . . ."

Raising his glass to his lips, Gareth watched as Angelica did the same. He supressed amusement as she frowned at the first sip. He drained his glass without thinking and waited for Angelica's comment.

"It . . . it has a rather strange taste. It is a bit bitter, is it not?"

"Bitter? A little, I guess . . ." Leaning forward, Gareth cupped her head with his palm. Covering her moist lips with his, he kissed her lingeringly. Reaching for her glass as he drew away, he drew it up to her mouth. Her lips separated to admit the golden liquid. Waiting only until she had swallowed, he leaned forward to carefully kiss away the remaining moistness from their surface.

"But the taste is sweeter on your lips, darlin' . . . much sweeter." He kissed her again, his mouth moving earnestly against hers. With careful deliberation he alternated kisses with wine until her glass was drained.

Unsure which was more potent, Gareth drew away to fill the glasses once more.

"This is a special night, darlin'. I can feel it deep inside me."

Draining his glass, Gareth watched as Angelica sipped cautiously. A light flush was beginning to color her face. She was not accustomed to alcohol, and he had no desire to numb her senses.

Disposing of her glass, Gareth reached out to run his hands gently along the curve of her shoulders. Dislodging the straps of her chemise, he followed the garment with his gaze as it fell to her waist. His eyes lingered on her breasts and the warmth inside him grew. They were small, round, perfectly shaped. Leaning forward, he touched his mouth to one pink crest and then the other. Without conscious thought he slipped his arm around Angelica's back to arch her into the increasing fervor of his ardent caresses. Her flesh was sweet . . . oh so sweet. He was lost in the wonder of loving her, his hands moving spontaneously to strip away the last scrap of her clothing until she was naked against the whiteness of the sheet. Beautiful . . . so beautiful . . .

Drawing himself to his feet, Gareth divested himself of his own clothes. Within moments he was lying beside her, his heart pounding with the supreme beauty of the meeting of their flesh.

Unwilling to draw his eyes from Angelica's magnificence, clear in the soft light of the room, Gareth shifted her in a gentle movement until her fragile, naked length lay stretched out atop him. Cupping her face with his hands, Gareth kissed her tenderly, his lips coaxing her into ardent participation. Her mouth was fresh with the taste of the wine she had consumed, and Gareth drank deeply of its subtle intoxication.

His thirst for Angelica insatiable, his need overwhelming, he slid his voracious quest down the column of her throat to the gleaming swells beneath. Warm and inviting, they called to him. He was lost in the wonder evoked with their tender intimacy, the low murmurs of passion which escaped Angelica's lips increasing the already ragged beat of his heart.

He was adjusting the warmth of her body atop him, fitting her moist heat intimately against him. In a quick, subtle movement he slipped inside her, gasping his elation at the full glory of their joining.

Her palms were resting against his ribs as Angelica supported herself above him. Hesitating, Gareth allowed himself to consume the full magnificence of the woman so completely a part of him. Black, velvet lashes fluttered against the flushed cheeks as she sought to restrain the emotions assailling her. Her lips were parted, her chest heaving with the strain of the passion that sought to consume her. The molten silver of her eyes cleaved to his, burning him with their heat. He moved subtly within her, and her eyes flicked briefly closed.

But desire, stirred anew, conquered restraint, leaving him helpless against the heat that suffused him. He lifted himself into the moist warmth of her body, searing her with his loving thrust. He lunged again and again, his eyes unmoving from Angelica's face as ecstasy flooded its graceful contours, stealing her breath, taking her higher and higher into a plane of sustained rapture. Gareth fought to curb the approaching climax of the glory they created so ardently. He needed a few moments more to consume the magnificence that was Angelica, to seal it in his mind. His Angelica . . .

But his level of emotion was too intense to sustain. Cupping his hands on the gentle curve of Angelica's hips, he held her fast against him as he thrust deep inside her once, twice, a third time, and he was there. Kaleidoscoping colors, soaring sensation . . . profound, sublime . . . Angelica . . . totally his and his alone . . .

Angelica's slender weight was slumped against him in exhaustion. Curving his arms around her, Gareth clutched her close as he strained to bring his breathing back to normal. He buried his face in her hair, smoothing his cheek against the gleaming silk. God, he loved her . . . he loved her so much it was an ache deep inside him which would not abate. She would learn to love him, too. She would have to, for it was clearer to him now than it had ever been. He would not be able to let her go.

Gareth shifted Angelica beside him. She was silent, unmoving in the curve of his arm. Turning her toward him, he trailed his lips against her cheek, pressing light kisses against the lids that shielded the brilliance of her eyes, the bridge of her perfect nose, her soft, endlessly appealing lips. His voice was a husky whisper.

"Angelica, darlin', open your eyes. Look at me . . ."

The heavy lashes fluttered and lifted slowly.

"The way you feel in my arms, darlin', the beauty we have together, it's sweeter, more heady than wine. And it's ours . . . ours alone."

Gareth waited only a moment, until his statement had registered clearly in Angelica's eyes, and then he was kissing her again.

Almost an hour had passed, and Gareth was intensely aware that Angelica still had not fallen asleep. Doing her best to conceal her wakeful state, she had turned her back in Gareth's embrace, but her ploy had not been successful. Concerned by her wakefulness, Gareth finally turned her to her back, supporting himself on his arm as he questioned quietly, "Is somethin' wrong, Angelica?"

Angelica's eyes opened, but she sought to avoid his gaze.

"What is it, darlin'? Is there somethin' on your mind?"

"It . . . it is just that I was wondering. I have been wondering since that first day . . . when Don Esteban came after us. . . ."

Gareth's brow knotted into a frown. Esteban Arricalde . . . even now he was not free of him. . . . But it was best he hear what Angelica had to say. She had obviously been storing these thoughts from the beginning of their journey, and he need hear them, no matter how distasteful they might be.

Taking a deep breath, Gareth nodded. "What were you wondering, Angelica?"

"I was wondering if . . . if it was true what you said . . . that you had truly stopped to speak to Padre Manuel before we left . . . had truly left the address at which letters might be addressed to me while I am in Texas . . ."

The question she posed a complete surprise, Gareth hesitated momentarily. He remembered well his brief meeting with Padre Manuel. It had not been pleasant, but then he had not expected it to be. He had merely wanted to assure that Angelica would receive news of her family . . . of her brother's progress . . .

"Yes, it's true, darlin'. He wasn't particularly pleased, but he accepted the note I gave him."

Gareth strained to see Angelica's face in the dim light of the room. She was silent for long moments. When she finally spoke, her voice was a tremulous whisper.

"That . . . that means when we get to your homestead, I may have a letter waiting for me, telling me that Carlos has improved enough to enable Mama and Papa to take him to Mexico City . . ."

"I suppose that's possible, darlin', but I wouldn't get my heart set on it. The mail isn't always too dependable and . . ."

But Angelica's hand reached up to his lips, silencing him in mid-sentence. Her voice was hushed, touched with emotion.

"Thank you, Gareth."

Her gratitude affecting him deeply, Gareth was momentarily unable to respond. Instead, he pressed a fleeting kiss against her lips, managing a hoarse whisper at last.

"Go to sleep now. We've got an early risin' tomorrow mornin'."

Moving closer into his embrace, Angelica mumbled in soft agreement. Within minutes she was asleep.

Gareth finished adjusting the cinch on his saddle and turned toward Angelica and smiled. They were standing in the Goliad livery stable yard. It was a fine day, as days went for that time of year in Texas. He had just paid the board for his horses, and other than the fact that his funds were getting a little low, he was in good shape.

He was aware of the fact that he had been grinning like an ape since he had awakened this morning. His strategy had worked out perfectly. Angelica had had a perfect night's sleep, free of the nightmares he had so diligently sought to prevent. They were both well rested and, speaking for himself, feeling on the top of the world. Angelica looked beautiful enough to stop his breath each time he looked at her, and she looked almost . . . happy.

They had stopped for an early breakfast at Maude Pierce's boardinghouse, thankful that the hardworking woman was up at dawn. They were all but set to start out. He had only to . . .

"Well, what do you know? Guess we're both leavin' at the same time this mornin'. Too bad we're goin' in different

368

directions, ain't it?"

His eyes moving to Lester Small's smiling face as he appeared around the corner of the stable, Gareth took a hold on his patience and shook his head.

"I don't know. I think it's kinda lucky for us . . ."

His expression distinctly hurt, Lester straightened his narrow shoulders. "You tryin' to tell me somethin', Gareth?"

"Nothin' you don't know already, friend. I'm right glad to have run into you again, and I'll be lookin' for you to come to the ranch to visit, but I'll be damned if I want you travelin' with Angelica and me. Your sweet talk's just too much competition, and, frankly, I can do without it."

His spirits seeming to have picked up at Gareth's indirect compliment, Lester shrugged his shoulders. "I suppose you're right, Gareth. If I was you, I wouldn't want anybody stickin' his two cents in between this little lady and me."

Turning to Angelica, Lester said unexpectedly, "With you permission, ma'am." Not waiting for her response, he place his hands around her waist and swung her unexpectedly up into her saddle.

Accepting the reins he put into her hands, Angelica managed a startled, "*Gracias*, Lester."

Lester bobbed his head politely.

"You're as light as a feather, Angelica, ma'am. It was my pleasure. And I want to thank you again for one of the most memorable evenin's I've had in a long time." Pausing as his expression turned a bit sheepish, Lester continued. "If the truth be known, I'd have to admit that I came out here especially to see if you looked as good in the full light of mornin' as you did last night. I was truly hopin' to be disappointed so I could consider myself gettin' the better of this rascal here. But, the truth is, ma'am, you're even more beautiful . . ."

Turning back to Gareth, Lester shook his head wearily. "Damn you, man, you have broke my heart."

Unable to suppress a laugh, Gareth turned to mount his horse. Looking down at his forlorn friend, he said lightly, "Well, I guess that's better than you breakin' mine. Good-

369

bye, friend. We'll be waitin' to see you at the Circle D when you're back in the area. Don't disappoint us."

His face picking up considerably at the invitation, Lester shook his head. "Hell, no, I ain't goin' to miss a chance at seein' this little lady again." Turning back to Angelica, Lester doffed his hat, his eyes glued to her smiling face. "I'll be seein' you, Angelica, ma'am."

"I will be looking forward to it, Lester."

His smile challenging the brightness of the morning sun at Angelica's response, Lester stood watching as Gareth spurred his horse into a trot and Angelica followed close behind.

It was only after the town of Goliad had disappeared behind them that Gareth finally turned to Angelica with a smile.

"You have broken that man's heart, Angelica."

Angelica's smile was spontaneous, warming him to the core.

Yes, it has been an entirely satisfactory stopover in Goliad. And now it was time to go home.

Chapter X

A long, solitary wail resounded in the darkness. She was alone and afraid. She had not noticed the slow passage of light, the gradual drifting into a blackness that now overwhelmed her. Breathing, heavy and labored, sounded in her ears. There was pain in each breath, a gasping that echoed in her own chest as she strove to identify the source. The breathing was growing more ragged. It was faltering, the torment in each rasp tearing at her own heart. Expiring . . . the breathing was expiring. Soon there would be no more. Death would come then. Death in darkness . . . death without light . . .

No, she could not allow it to happen! Suddenly struggling, she fought the weight of the oppressive blackness, screamed as the rasping breath became more ragged still. There was a rattle . . . a low choking sound . . . and the breathing faltered again. Then it was done.

The absence of sound was deafening . . . louder than a roar in her ears. She cried out against the blackness which had stolen life, fought as it sought to overpower her as well. No! She would not give in to its pressure, submit to the eternity which waited to overwhelm her. She would not . . .

"Angelica . . . Angelica, wake up, darlin'."

Gareth . . .

Striving to catch her breath, Angelica opened her eyes to the black night. She had been dreaming again. Concern obvious in his expression, Gareth smoothed the paths of tears from her face. Her breathing was so affected that Angelica had trouble responding to his low entreaty. Finally regaining control, Angelica nodded tightly.

"I . . . I am sorry, Gareth."

Sorry. She had said she was sorry again, but it was to little avail. The nightmares had resumed, their frequency escalating until she had but to close her eyes and the sound of labored breathing began again. Aware of her fatigue, Gareth had begun to take her on his horse for several hours each afternoon while on the trail, allowing her to sleep in his arms in the realization that only in the bright light of day was she able to sleep without painful dreams assailing her.

She had become a burden to Gareth, a weight that dragged him down more and more each day. A bargain well struck had turned to a hardship from which he could not escape. No, he did not deserve that . . . not Gareth.

Gareth did not bother to respond to her apology. He had heard it many times before. Instead, he drew her against the curve of his body. His breath was warm against her hair, his voice gentle.

"Close your eyes, Angelica, and try to remember that you're in my arms. I'll protect you, darlin'. You don't have to be afraid."

Angelica nodded, inwardly realizing in her desperation that Gareth's consolation would be negated by the terror which would ultimately gain control. The blue velvet was gone, and the black velvet of Gareth's eyes was only visible in the full light of day. Only then was there safety from this shattering fear which would allow her no rest.

Realizing she could do little more, Angelica moved close into Gareth's embrace. This nameless terror was consuming her. There was no escape.

Angelica's body was tense in his arms, shuddering in the aftermath of the horror which had revisited her. His helplessness more than he could bear, Gareth clutched her close in an attempt to lend her his strength, and he whispered against her hair.

"Angelica, listen to me. We'll be reachin' Circle D land

tomorrow. Just one more day, darlin'. You'll be safe, sleepin' in a bed instead of on the hard ground, and then you'll be free of these dreams. You'll see. When we get there, we'll send a letter off to Padre Manuel, tellin' him that you've arrived with me, that you're all right. We'll remind him to send us word of Carlos as soon as he hears anythin'."

Angelica's trembling was lessening in reaction to the soothing tone of his voice and Gareth felt a spark of hope. He didn't know what Angelica needed to feel safe again, but he was going to try damned hard to give it to her, whatever it was. He resumed talking, realizing that the soft rumbling of his voice was lulling her into a sense of safety and semisleep.

"You're goin' to like it on the Circle D, darlin'. The buildings have grown over the years. Pa and I've added extensions to the main house twice already. The first time it was because my mother wanted a room of her own, and the second time it was because my Pa was expectin' to bring home a new wife and child. But we get good use out of those rooms now, with Pa's and my involvement in the Committee of Safety. There's always somebody stayin' over.

"The hands all come in to eat in the house at dinnertime, you know. Pa always insisted on that, despite my mother's objections. He said that brought the boys a sense of belongin' there. He was right. Most of them have been with us for years. We add a fella now and then as the need arises, but they're pretty much a steady lot.

"You're goin' to like the women in the kitchen." Flinching inwardly at the fact that she would be put to work there, Gareth consoled himself with the thought that he would bring Angelica to her proper place in the household at the first opportunity. But for the present it would not do to pressure her. She needed to feel she had a place, a job which would be respected. She was proud. She would not suffer being merely a kept mistress, and he dared not tell her yet that he wanted much more from her than that. No, the time would come, but first he must overcome her fear.

"We have two women in the kitchen, Angelica—Maria

373

and Sophie. But there's always need for a new pair of hands. You'll be welcome there, you'll see. And I'll make you happy, too, darlin'. You won't want for anythin'. The first thing I'm goin' to do when we get home is to buy you some new clothes. These clothes you're wearin' have seen enough wear. We're goin' to buy you somethin' pretty . . . somethin' soft and delicate to wear underneath, too. Your skin was made for lace, darlin'. It's soft and smooth . . . perfect, made for beautiful things. I'm goin' . . ."

His voice trailing off as he realized Angelica's breathing had become slow and even, Gareth pulled far enough away to peruse her sleeping face in the semilight of the fire. He resumed speaking in a low, intimate tone, words he knew she would not hear.

"And I'm goin' to love you, darlin'. I'm goin' to love you so much that you'll forget everythin' but lovin' me back. And when your year is up, you won't want to leave. You'll never want to leave me, and I'll never let you go. I love you, Angelica . . . God, how I love you . . ."

Holding her tight, his love a consuming flame inside him, Gareth brushed Angelica's lips with his and closed his eyes to sleep. Yes, tomorrow they'd reach his homestead, and everything would be all right. It had to be . . .

"There is no longer any doubt! Zavala has arrived in Texas and has been welcomed by the insurgents there!"

The veins in his forehead bulging with the zeal of his statement, Antonio Santa Anna faced the men gathered in his palace office. The ban on mentioning the name of Zavala in his presence had been lifted with the arrival of that morning's courier, and the furious presidenté had summoned his advisers immediately. All elaborately uniformed and silent, they observed his rage.

"I will not tolerate that traitor's inflammatory presence in that rebel state." Turning to his secretary, Santa Anna waved his hand with a flourish. "Ricardo, you will formulate an order for Zavala's arrest. You will also see that an order is issued for the arrest of the ringleaders of the hostile party, and all who took part in leading the affair at

Anahuac. Most especially, we demand the incarceration of persons Johnson, Williamson, Travis, Williams, and Baker to be held for trial. You will also see that it is understood that we will be sending a sufficient force to effect their capture if our demands are not carried out."

Turning back to the men assembled, Antonio Santa Anna glared his anger. "We are a great country, destined for greater things, and yet we allow a band of ignorant ruffians to thwart us at every turn!"

Santa Anna's dark eyes flashed, moving over the uncomfortable men who stood in their glare. His sharp mind was moving rapidly . . .

One general, two colonels, a trusted adviser—military men, all of them, except for Esteban Arricalde. Santa Anna focused his attention on the young aristocrat's handsome face. Intelligent, cultured . . . yes, but also crafty, self-serving, and wise enough to realize that by serving Santa Anna and his country he also served himself. Yes . . . he trusted a man who had personal goals which drove him, and Esteban was certainly one of those. This was the perfect opportunity to use his talents. The perfect . . .

"Esteban, you have been anxious to leave the capital, have you not? You have hinted on several occasions that you wish to be sent to that rebel state which causes me this anxiety."

"*Si, Señor Presidente.* That has long been my wish. But you have chosen to have me serve you here, and your wish is my command . . ."

"Yes, Esteban, of that I am certain." His voice bearing only the slightest note of sarcasm, Antonio Santa Anna continued thoughtfully, "Some time ago Captain Thomas M. Thompson was engaged into our service as a naval officer. Are you familiar with this gentleman, Esteban?"

Esteban's face clearly reflected his reaction to Santa Anna's question. "I know him only by reputation, Señor Presidente."

"And what is that reputation, may I ask?"

Esteban raised his brow in exaggerated surprise. "You are certain you wish to have me repeat rumors about one of

375

your officers?"

"If they are rumors, you may rest assured I have heard them before. So tell me, what do you know of Captain Thompson?"

"I know he is an Englishman by birth and a man of unprepossessing appearance. I also know him to be somewhat of the buccaneering stamp, a man who seeks his own fortune in your service."

"A quality that does not negate his value to me."

"I have also heard that he is skilled in his craft and respected by his men."

" . . . which makes him invaluable, do you not agree?"

"To an extent, Señor Presidente."

"I intend to send him to Anahuac on the schooner *Correo* to protect the revenues."

"My opinion is that you will be taking a great chance in doing so."

"And to guarantee that he does not exceed that extent you mentioned, I propose to send you on that ship as an adviser . . ."

"To Anahuac?"

"Are you not pleased with the idea, Esteban?"

Esteban hesitated. "What authority will this responsibility carry, Señor Presidente?"

"Captain Thompson will retain full command of his ship, but you will retain the powers of your rank, and a direct line to my ear should a problem beset Captain Thompson which he is not qualified to handle."

"Will my services be confined to the *Correo* and the activities of those connected with that ship?"

"I would prefer you travel freely within that city, Esteban. I value your powers of observation too highly to limit your services."

Esteban strove to conceal his satisfaction. Anahuac. The hot spot of the current conflict in Texas. A place to make his name . . . to strike fear in the hearts of the arrogant Anglos. It was but a small step from Anahuac to his ultimate destination and his ultimate goal. Allowing a reserved smile to move across his lips, Esteban responded with admirable humility.

"I am honored that you express such confidence in me, and I will be honored to serve you in any way that I may, Señor Presidente."

"Excellent, Esteban!" His expressive face reflecting his satisfaction, Santa Anna continued enthusiastically. "Then you will be ready to sail within one week's time. Captain Thompson has already been informed of his assignment. I will send a communication to him immediately so he might prepare for your presence on board."

"*Muchas gracias* for your confidence in me, Señor Presidente."

"You need not thank me, Esteban. You need only prove my opinion of your value in this capacity to be valid."

"I will not disappoint you."

Santa Anna's observant gaze noted the spark that glowed in Esteban's eyes, the flush of triumph that colored his handsome face. He smiled.

"I have no doubt that you will serve me well, Esteban."

His disposition much improved, Santa Anna turned back to the gentlemen who until that point had remained silent observers to the conversation.

"In the meantime, gentlemen, I would like to have your opinions on allowing Martin his way. General Cos, my Commandant General of the Eastern Internal Provinces, still takes his orders from me and has requested permission to take his 1400 regulars to San Antonio. What is your opinion on that move?"

The reaction to Santa Anna's question was immediate and heated. Silently observing the vehement exchange between the military men assembled, Esteban allowed his mind to drift into the opportunities afforded him by Santa Anna's unexpected proposal.

Ah, yes, he was finally on his way. And if he knew anything at all, he knew he would not allow this opportunity to pass him by.

The panorama stretching out as far as Angelica's eye could see was breathtaking. Day was coming to an end. An endless rolling landscape fed into a horizon colored brilliant hues of pink and gold by the setting sun. Lazy brown and white cattle, a greater number than she had ever seen congregated into one herd, dotted the land, grazing leisurely in the light of the waning sun. She had been startled when Gareth had informed her that they all carried the Circle D brand. It had been too overwhelming a premise for her to comprehend, and she had concentrated instead on his declaration that the buildings of the Circle D would soon be coming into view.

Angelica strained her eyes into the distance. The first sight of a small group of buildings turned the beat of her heart to a heavy thunder in her breast. She shot a quick glance toward Gareth. His gaze had taken the same direction, and a smile was growing on his face. He turned toward her.

"There it is, darlin', the Circle D. We'll be there within the hour."

Appearing suddenly conscious of the apprehension she strove to hide, Gareth frowned. He did not offer her assurances. It was obvious that he felt he had been more than conscientious in his consideration of her, and Angelica could not fault him in that regard.

Turning her eyes back to the trail, Angelica took a deep breath and steeled herself against her anxiety. Two months of the year to which she had committed herself had already passed. Her silent fear that they were the easiest of the long months yet to come despite the rigors of the long journey would give her little rest. On the trail it had been just Gareth and herself. She had lain in Gareth's arms each night under the stars. There had been no one to judge their bargain, to put a name to her that she now thoroughly deserved.

The immediate future which stretched out before her was uncertain, and she chafed at her inability to accept it without anxiety. Closing her eyes momentarily against the new world into which she was riding, Angelica summoned her waning strength of will. The long, sleepless nights on the trail, the horror of her unrelenting dreams, had debilitated her beyond her realization. Suddenly ashamed of her weakness, Angelica pulled herself erect in the saddle in an attempt to shake off the fears and insecurities which sapped her strength.

Angelica took a deep breath. She had made this bargain with Gareth freely. There had been no pressure put upon her, no restraints. The situation which had necessitated her decision still remained, and her departure with Gareth had been the first step in the process of a change which she was determined to effect.

Carlos . . . she had long ago decided that she would do what was necessary to see his return to health. He was doubtless under treatment in Mexico City right now. There was even a remote possibility that a letter waited for her at the Circle D . . . possibly carried via boat by one of Padre Manuel's many acquaintances. In any case, she had accomplished the first step in her goal, and the money she would earn as a *galopina* in Gareth's kitchen would finance the remainder of Carlos's treatment for as long as it was needed. To that end she would bear accusing glances and the humiliation they caused. She would bear them proudly.

She need keep an eye to the future . . . a future in which she might return to her family, to a Carlos bright with the flush of health. She would not need to stay very long in this foreign society where Gareth Dawson was her only link with the past. In any case, she would take it one day at a time . . .

"Gareth Dawson! You rascal! So you're finally home!"

Pausing as he came out of the door of the house, a lanky fellow with a gray handlebar mustache turned to call loudly over his shoulder before starting in their direction.

"Get out here, boys! This ranch has a legitimate honcho on board again!"

Walking rapidly toward their horses as Gareth and Angelica reined up in front of the sprawling structure which was the Dawson homestead, the enthusiastic fellow extended his hand in Gareth's direction.

"It sure is good to set eyes on you again, boy! Your pa

379

left this place a few weeks back with less than peace of mind. You know how he feels about a bona fide Dawson bein' in residence here at all times. That old hard case never did learn to trust nobody."

"But he trusted you, didn't he, Brett?"

Dismounting, his eyes showing true warmth, Gareth accepted the hand held out to him and shook it vigorously.

"Well, he didn't have no choice, did he now? But I'm tired of playin' *segundo*. I'm more than happy to turn the whole works over to you again."

Brett's gaze was openly assessing as Gareth turned around and lifted Angelica from the saddle. His smile took on a wary light.

"Well, now, we wasn't expectin' you to bring back no souveniers from your trip . . ."

"Brett Willis . . . Angelica Rodrigo . . ."

The whoop of enthusiastic welcomes as a stream of men emerged from the house interrupted Gareth's introduction, turning him toward the friendly hands stretched out in greeting. Accepting them with equal enthusiasm, he exchanged a few words with each man before turning back to Angelica.

"Boys, I'd like you to meet Angelica Rodrigo. She's goin' to be workin' in our kitchen. Angelica, you already met Brett Willis. This is Michael Holley, Charlie Stiles, Wilson Harper. And this fella here," he motioned to the tall Negro who had joined the welcoming crowd, ". . . is Harvey Snow." Turning, he smiled at the slender Negress and the middle-aged Mexican woman approaching from the house. Giving each woman in turn a warm greeting, he turned back to Angelica.

"This is Sophie, Harvey's wife, and Maria. Maria has the misfortune of bein' married to Charlie, here. Bad stroke of luck for her . . ."

Laughing at Charlie's loud growl of disagreement, Gareth slid his arm around Angelica's waist and urged her toward the house.

"Maria, Angelica and I were hopin' you and Sophie were up to your old tricks this evenin' and cooked enough for an

380

army. We rode right through dinnertime."

"Like an old horse that smelled home, right, Gareth? You wasn't goin' to spend another night on that hard ground . . ."

"Damned right!"

Angelica was aware that Gareth's proprietary hand at her waist had not gone unnoticed. The quick look exchanged between the two women had spoken for itself and Angelica turned her head to conceal her discomfort.

Angelica's eyes flicked carelessly around the house as they entered. She did her best to hide her surprise at the unexpected luxury of lace curtains on sparklingly clean windows, well-kept furniture and rugs in the spacious living room, and a large dining room with of set of gold-trimmed dinnerware carefully displayed in a corner cabinet. This was not her mental picture of a homestead on a wild frontier.

Within minutes they were installed around the long table that dominated the dining room, steaming plates of a rich chicken stew and biscuits in front of them. Feeling considerably out of place in face of the fact that Gareth had installed her at the dining table like a guest instead of the servant she truly was, Angelica found her appetite all but nonexistent. The weight of the hired hands' obvious curiosity managing to destroy her little remaining appetite, Angelica picked lightly at the food.

Gareth turned as a good-natured exchange continued between Michael and Charlie. It had not missed his notice that Wilson Harper, the youngest and newest member of his crew, had been unable to take his eyes off Angelica. Gareth's dark brows moved into a frown as the spark of a familiar emotion tightened his stomach muscles. Willie was young and earnest, probably just a few years Angelica's senior. Sandy-haired, light-eyed, his build was slight, his manner polite and sincere. He had the look of a choir boy, but Gareth knew from experience that deceiving exterior hid a personality that had seen considerable success with the ladies. Determined to assign to its proper place, the interest peaking in his blue eyes, Gareth turned his head

381

toward the seat beside him where Angelica sat silently. Sliding his hand under the heavy plait that hung down her back, he massaged her neck with an open familiarity that spoke for itself. He deliberately ignored the raised brows of his crew.

"What's the matter, darlin'? That Circle D stew is the best around. I can vouch for that. You're not givin' it a decent trial with that pickin' and dabbin'."

Darting a quick look to the two women's faces, Angelica responded in a low voice, "The food is delicious, Gareth." Halting momentarily, realizing that she had used his given name in a situation where she should have displayed more formality, she continued hesitantly. "But I . . . I find I am truly too weary to eat. In truth, I would prefer to go to my sleeping quarters . . ."

Aware of Angelica's discomfort, Gareth nodded and raised his eyes toward the two women who stood casually near the door to the room.

"Sophie, be a good girl and show Angelica where the west bedroom is."

The silence that fell round the table sent little prickles up Angelica's spine as she rose to her feet. Sophie's eyes snapped wide with obvious surprise. Her response was spontaneous.

"But . . . Mr. Jon . . . he ain't gonna like . . ."

Sophie's words dwindled to a halt as Gareth's expression became formidable. The tension in the room was rising, and Angelica was unsure why.

"I said the west bedroom, Sophie . . ."

"Yes, sir . . ."

Bobbing her head, Sophie waited until Angelica made a move in her direction before turning and walking quickly toward the staircase. Her pace rapid, the slim Negress did not stop until she had reached a door a little way down the narrow hallway. Angelica waited in the hall as Sophie moved inside, and within a few minutes a lamp was burning welcomingly.

Angelica let out a short gasp. It was no wonder Sophie's reaction had been so intense. Large and beautifully decorated, the room had obviously been prepared with great care for the lady of the house.

Taking a spontaneous step back, Angelica shook her head. Her face flushing with color, she met Sophie's glance.

"No, I cannot stay in this room, Sophie. Surely there is somewhere else . . . a more appropriate room."

"Mr. Gareth says he wants you in here. His room be right next door . . ."

Pulling herself erect, Angelica held Sophie's eye steadily. "I would prefer a place closer to the kitchen, where I will be working."

Appearing abruptly relieved, Sophie nodded. "If that's what you wants, it be best if you talks to Mr. Gareth. I has my orders . . ."

"Whose room is this, Sophie?"

"This be nobody's room. Mr. Jon got it ready for the lady he was bringin' here to be his wife, but she never see'd it. There ain't been nobody sleepin' in this room in all the years since."

And it was doubtless true that "Mr. Jon" would not take very kindly to finding her in it when he returned. Truly understanding Sophie's reaction and uncertain what Gareth hoped to accomplish by installing her in there, Angelica was suddenly extremely grateful for the honesty of Sophie's response.

"Thank you, Sophie." Forcing a smile, Angelica stepped back another step. "Please put out the lamp. I think I'll go back downstairs and wait until later to discuss this with Gareth."

Sophie frowned her hesitation.

"If you don't mind, I's gonna leave this lamp lit until Mr. Gareth tells me to put it out."

Understanding Sophie's reluctance, Angelica nodded and turned back toward the staircase, her mind still attempting to sort out Gareth's reasoning in attempting to install her in that particular room. Was their situation not already obvious enough? Did he feel the need to flaunt their relationship? Somehow, she had not expected this of Gareth . . .

Angelica was suddenly amused by her own gullibility. No, she had not expected this of Gareth, but she should have. Somewhere along the trail from Real del Monte to Texas she had lost track of the true Gareth Dawson. Was he not the same man who had all but kidnapped her so that he might indulge his lust during his brief visit to the mines? He had paid her well and had obviously felt that compensated completely for the repercussions which had followed. He was obviously of the same mind here in his own home.

She had not stood up to him before, finding his purposes also suited her own. But this was different. No, she must live and work among these people. She need command some respect if she was to function within this household. Their agreement for the next year was twofold. She was to work in the kitchen and be paid for her services there in the same manner Sophie and Maria were paid. Equal pay demanded equal work. She would not be able to live with any other arrangement.

As for the more intimate services she would provide Gareth, he was obviously reluctant to sacrifice easy accessibility to convention. That was unfortunate. Gareth's tender concern for her during the long nights on the trail had earned him her gratitude. But it was time she assumed her proper place in this less than ideal situation, and on this position, she was determined not to relent. Lifting her chin with determination, Angelica stepped down from the staircase onto the first floor and turned in the direction of the animated conversation progressing in the dining room. She had a feeling this was not going to be easy.

The study was as much Mexican in flavor as it was Anglo. Colorful woven rugs covered the wooden floor and hung decoratively on the corner wall of the room. An old, scarred desk, piled high with ledgers and paperwork and worn leather furniture, obviously brought from another time and place, completed the meager furnishings. The wall behind the desk housed a surprising library of books which appeared to encompass everything from history to popular novels.

It was the old Gareth who faced her within the confines

of the well-used room. His hard features in a stiff, unyielding mask, his dark, arched brows in a tight line, his eyes were assessing slits from which squint lines fanned into his temples. All trace of softness had disappeared from his gaze. She had sensed the tension in his tightly muscled frame as he closed the study door behind him and approached her.

Gareth had risen from the dinner table within minutes of her return downstairs. He had taken her arm and guided her urgently into the study. A quick assessment of her face had brought him to his present state. He knew her well . . . sensed her opposition before she had had an opportunity to voice it. Raising her chin in unspoken defiance, Angelica waited for the question she knew was to come.

"All right, Angelica . . . what is it? I know that expression . . ."

"I would like another room. I cannot sleep in the room to which you assigned me."

"Sophie . . . did she say anythin'? Damn that girl and her gossipin' ways. She . . ."

"I had only to look into that room to see it for what it is . . . the room readied for your father's mistress . . ."

Gareth was suddenly hostile. "And do you put yourself above her, Angelica? You forget . . ."

"No, I do not forget, and I do not put myself above that woman. How could I hope to judge her when I find myself in much the same situation? But in truth, there is a vast difference between us. I will be here for a year only . . . even less than that, considering the time that has already passed. During that period I am also to function as a kitchen maid. I was promised a salary equivalent to that of the other women in your kitchen and I do not wish to lose the opportunity of that sum. With that thought in mind, it would be better that I occupy accommodations more suitable to my position here."

"I don't give a damn about your kitchen duties!"

"But I do!" Pausing to control her rioting emotions, Angelica took a deep breath. Anger faded from her great silver eyes as she said softly. "Gareth, you need not think that I will forget my obligation to you. Such is not my intention. I owe you much for your consideration of me on the journey." Her words bringing a flush to her face, Angelica continued determinedly, "I am well aware of the trouble I caused you."

Gareth's gaze was unrelenting.

"Then you will stay upstairs, in the room which I assigned . . ."

Angelica's flush deepened.

"No, I will not."

"Where do you expect to stay? In the bunkhouse with the boys? Somehow I don't believe that would work out."

"Sophie said there is a room near the kitchen. It is used for storage now, but . . ."

The muscle ticking in Gareth's cheek gave Angelica cause to exercise caution, and her words slowed to a halt.

"You're speaking of the room Sophie used before she and Harvey were married . . ."

"Yes, that will be fine."

"It's small and airless, little more than a closet."

"It will be adequate to suit my needs. I have little in the way of personal articles."

"But it will not be adequate to suit mine!"

Taking an abrupt step forward, Gareth took Angelica by the shoulders and gave her a small shake.

"I have no desire to make love to you under those circumstance. I did not bring you here, all the way to Texas, to hide you away as if I am ashamed to have anyone know . . ."

"Gareth, I am sorry, but I will not sleep in that room upstairs . . ."

"One of the other rooms, then . . ."

"No, I am not a guest. I am a servant in this house . . . and a *puta*. You have not used that name for me in a long time, Gareth, but it was very frequently on your lips before we arrived here. I have no doubt that name will be used for me again before I leave this place in view of the circumstances under which I have accompanied you here. I do not wish . . ."

"Angelica, this conversation is pointless. You will take the room I have assigned you. I will have it no other way . . ."

"No . . . no, I will not."

Truly uncertain of the force driving her adamance, Angelica felt Gareth's hands tighten on her rigid shoulders. A flicker of an undefinable emotion crossed his face before he released her.

Gareth's voice was cool.

"The room Sophie refers to has not been used in two years except for storage. The bed was removed and taken to the small house in the back where Sophie and Harvey live. I do not intend to assign anyone the added chore of cleaning that room or moving a bed into it when there are suitable bedrooms upstairs which you may use."

Angelica's hesitation was only momentary.

"Then I will sleep in the barn."

Fury flared in Gareth's eyes. His face stiff with anger, his hands balling into frustrated fists at his sides, he stared into her flushed face. Turning abruptly on his heel he walked stiffly toward the door. Jerking it open, he grated harshly over his shoulder, "Do as you damn well please!" Within moments he was gone.

Biting her lips to still their trembling, Angelica stood woodenly, uncertain if he intended to return. When she finally realized he had truly left the matter in her hands, she took a deep, shuddering breath and followed the line of his rapid departure into the hallway. Closing the door behind her, she shot a quick look around her. It was curious that a house so full of sound only a few minutes before could now be so silent and empty. Walking in the direction of the kitchen, Angelica was aware of the quaking in her limbs. She need find Sophie so she might be guided to the barn. It would serve temporarily, and tomorrow she herself would begin cleaning out the storage room. She did not need a bed. She had slept on the floor before. It would not force an unfamiliar hardship upon her.

The picture of the beautiful room upstairs returned to her mind, and Angelica shuddered. No, somehow she could not make herself use it, even for a night. It had been readied for another woman, one who had never lived to see it. She would not take her place in that beautiful bed. The barn would be better, and it would only be a short time until she was installed where she belonged.

Gareth stamped up the staircase and turned down the hallway toward his room. His eyes flicking to the doorway beside his, he glanced inside. A single lamp glowed in the darkness, lending its softness to the meticulously kept room which had never known the love for which it was intended. He had thought to rectify that unintentional neglect by installing Angelica there. But it was as if Angelica sensed his intentions and was giving him full notice that she would fulfill her bargain and nothing more.

But he wanted more . . . much more, and he would not have her relegated to the small room behind the kitchen. He had had a twofold purpose in mind in sending Angelica to this particular room. He had wanted her firmly settled in the house when his father returned home. Surely, Angelica's installation in the room of the woman his father had truly loved would carry Gareth's message clearly.

But Angelica was difficult, hard and proud. She now accepted the name of *puta* as due her, but bore it with a perverse kind of pride that made her determined to function as a working part of the household despite it. He suspected in that way she intended to use her legitimate position as an invisible wedge between them.

Damn, he had been a fool to suggest her employment in this household. He should have demanded that she function solely for him. But he had been desperate to make the position appealing to her and he had thought that the promise of an additional sum received on a regular basis might turn the tide in his favor. He had not wanted to lose her to Esteban Arricalde, and he had been uncertain if she had truly harbored tender feelings for the spoiled bastard. As it was, Angelica appeared to have as little true feeling for Esteban as she did for him.

If there was one thing with which he could console

himself, it was the fact that Angelica reacted like fire to straw when he made love to her. The thought of the spontaneity of her response unleashed a familiar wave of desire which Gareth fought to control. She had learned to depend on him on the journey to Texas. He intended to enlarge that dependence until she was as lost without him as he would indeed be without her.

Gareth took a moment to light the lamp on his night table. Throwing his saddlebag on the chair, he flopped down on his bed, hardly registering its comfort as his mind slipped back to Angelica.

Let her sleep in the barn tonight if she chose, damn her! It would serve her right if she did not sleep a wink. After a few such nights, she would soon come around. And then he would make up for the time they had lost through her stubbornness.

Why was she afraid? Darkness had never been her enemy . . . not before the journey to Texas. Closing her eyes, Angelica breathed deeply of the sweet-scented hay on which she lay, the aroma of horses and stored grain. She heard the restless rustling of the great animals that bumped against their stalls, and the more subtle sound of scampering feet and darting movement which indicated an activity of an entirely different kind in the large barn.

No, she would not think of the small creatures which moved in darkness. They were not her enemies. Her enemy was the blackness which sought to suppress breath and life, but she was unable to get any clearer definition of that force in her mind.

She closed her eyes and sought the blue velvet. It had long ago abandoned her, but now she was twice bereft. She had become accustomed to sleeping in the circle of Gareth's protective embrace. She had begun to become dependent on the security of his presence, knowing he would be there should the horror of her nightmares again assail her. That had been a mistake. It had not taken her long upon arriving at this homestead where she was so obviously an outsider and a temporary addition to the household to realize that she had been lax in allowing that to happen. No, she had learned long before that she need depend only on herself. Passion was a fleeting emotion, a fierce but temporary flame. She need be prepared for the time when it would begin to flicker and eventually became extinguished.

Angelica again sought the comfort and texture of blue velvet, its sweet scent, its gentle warmth. It eluded her, and she twisted on her bed of hay in an attempt to reclaim its gentle reassurance. It flickered tantalizingly just beyond her grasp, and she attempted to pursue it. But it was a fleeting illusion just out of her line of vision.

Frustrated tears slipped out of the corners of her eyes, and Angelica wiped them away with disgust. So this is what had become of her firm determination. It had melted into salty drops of ineffectiveness.

No, she would not submit to the humiliation of fear and despair. Taking a deep breath, Angelica steeled herself. She would think of kinder times . . . Mama and Papa's gentle faces and Carlos's laughter. They would see her through. They always had in the past. They were her lifelines. She needed no one but them. She would think only of the time when she would return to the warmth of their unfailing love. It would not be long . . .

Gareth twisted on the wide bed, his discomfort growing more intense by the moment. What perverse sense had allowed him to become so accustomed to sleeping with the hard ground beneath him that he now found it difficult to get comfortable in his own bed? His eyes darting to the clock on the desk in the corner of his room, Gareth shook his head. Surely the shadows of the moonlight were distorting his vision. It could not be merely one o'clock. The night must be close to being over.

Gareth strained his eyes again. One o'clock . . . he had not been mistaken. He had retired only a few hours ago after watching Angelica from his window as she had made her way to the barn. Lantern held high to guide her steps, she had not hesitated upon entering and had quickly disappeared from his sight. His frustration had known no bounds. He had not intended that Angelica's and his first night spent in his own home would find them estranged from each other. No, on the contrary, he had anticipated an intimate celebration. Instead, his arms were empty and his joy upon arrival had fallen flat.

Damn, he had behaved stupidly. How had he allowed control of the situation to escape him? Angelica had declared to him that she was no more than his employee, had she not? All right, so be it. If that was to be the relationship she wanted to establish, than he would turn it to suit him. He'd remind her that he had paid for her services, and they did not include her sleeping in the barn while he lay in his lonely bed. She would follow his orders like every other employee on the ranch. Yes, and he'd be damned if he would allow another moment to pass before he straightened things out.

Having settled his determination, Gareth drew himself to a sitting position and reached for his pants. Frowning at the realization that his hands were trembling, Gareth took a deep, steadying breath. God, he was sick with wanting her. The desire to hold Angelica in his arms was all but consuming him, and no matter the rationalization his mind devised to protect him, the hard truth was that he needed her. He no longer felt complete without her.

Sobered by that realization, Gareth made his way down the staircase and out the back door of the house. He had not bothered with his shirt, and the warm, moist night air was heavy against his bared chest. Taking a moment to pick up a lantern at the rear door, Gareth lit it quickly and walked directly toward the barn. He had been a fool to allow Angelica to make her own decision as to where she would sleep. He should have realized that her stubbornness would not allow her to back down once she had voiced her refusal to sleep in one of the upstairs bedrooms. Well, he would take the matter out of her hands now.

His hand on the barn-door latch, Gareth drew it open and held the lantern high in an effort to dispel the darkness inside. The responsive whinny of his gelding met his ear, but he hardly registered the sound as his eyes searched the darkness. Where was she? He supposed the only place that would afford comfort in the huge, airless building was the hayloft. Raising his lantern a little higher, Gareth walked directly toward the ladder in the rear of the building.

Within minutes he had climbed the ladder and was peering into the darkness of the loft. A slight shadow moved on the pile of hay closest to the window and he started immediately toward it. Yes, it was Angelica. Small and vulnerable, she lay asleep on the fragrant hay. But her sleep was anguished. Obviously in the throes of another nightmare, her breathing was labored, her beautiful face distorted with fear. She was whimpering softly, the words she mumbled inaudible as she fought an invisible threat. Tears were slipping down her cheeks and she choked on the sobs filling her throat.

Knowing an anguish of his own, Gareth hung his lantern on a peg and crouched beside her. His throat tightened, all trace of the anger he had nourished for the past several hours fading in the face of her helpless despair. He could not stand to see her cry. The sight of her tears was all the more effective because of her impotence against the invisible force which stimulated them.

Moving to lie beside her, Gareth gently drew Angelica into his arms, cushioning her against his body. Her response was instinctive as she clutched him close, her body seeking the protection of his strength.

"Angelica . . . darlin' . . ."

His hand moving to stroke her hair, Gareth attempted to get his words past the lump which had formed in his throat.

"Angelica, come on, darlin', wake up. You're dreamin' again." Guilt seared him. Nightmares that robbed her of a restful sleep . . . they were his fault. Of that he no longer had any doubt. Her mind protested her situation, fought the control he had over a year of her destiny despite her conscious determination to live up to her bargain. He had placed her in this torment, and even facing that hard truth, he could not make himself free her. For to free her would be to give her up, and he would rather give up his life . . .

"Angelica . . ."

Her body was beginning to stiffen in his arms, and he realized she was awakening. Yes, that reaction was instinctive, too . . . her desire to escape him. But he could not let her go. Instead, Gareth drew back just enough to allow her to see his face as he tilted her chin up toward him. The smooth skin of her cheeks was pale and streaked with tears, her eyes still clouded with the dark horror which had visited her in sleep.

"Darlin', listen to me. I can't let you stay in this place. You have to come back to the house . . ."

"No . . . no, Gareth. I can't stay in that room . . ."

The desperation that flickered in her eyes as she spoke startled Gareth with its intensity. It was akin to fear, stimulating a spontaneous response of his own.

"You don't have to stay in that room, darlin', not if you don't want to. But come back to the house with me. We've both wasted the better part of this night in stubbornness. We can make decisions in the mornin', but you're goin' to spend the hours remainin' tonight with me. That's the only thing that makes sense now, and the only thing that will allow either of us any sleep."

Angelica's eyes were fixed on his, her expression unrevealing. She was so damned beautiful, her face so pure that he was all but overcome. Lowering his head, Gareth touched her lips lightly with his, his desire for more succumbing to better judgment.

"Come on, darlin' . . ."

The great silver eyes turned up to his reflected Angelica's consideration of his urging. Her hesitation was brief before she responded by allowing herself to be drawn slowly to her feet beside him. Not allowing a moment for reconsideration, Gareth reached for the lantern and within minutes they were moving down the ladder.

They stepped down on the ground and Gareth curved his arm around Angelica's slender shoulders. Adjusting her body against his side, he drew her along with him.

Depositing the lantern at the rear door of the house, he continued to draw her with him toward the staircase to the upstairs rooms. Within minutes they were moving through the doorway of his room, and waiting only until the door was closed behind the, Gareth turned toward her.

With a gentle touch he removed Angelica's clothes, leaving her clad only in her chemise. Pausing in his efficient ministrations, he slipped off his pants and threw them to the chair. He turned, and in a fluid movement scooped Angelica into his arms. Taking the few steps to the bed, Gareth placed her on the broad surface and lay beside her. His hands moving to her plait, he efficiently freed her hair. Only after the black silk was a gleaming swirl against the whiteness of the pillow did Gareth relax. A low sound of satisfaction escaped his throat as he drew Angelica into the circle of his arms.

"You know this is where you belong, don't you, darlin'. And this is where you're goin' to stay."

But Angelica was stiffening again in his arms. "Gareth, I cannot share your room openly. Please do not ask that of me. I have neither the desire nor the intention of depriving you of your rights to me. Whenever you want me, I will be yours . . ." Angelica raised tremulous lips to his. Her kiss was brief and sweet. ". . . but . . . but to flaunt our relationship openly in your home . . ." Angelica shook her head.

Frustration tightening his grasp, Gareth drew her close. "We'll talk about it in the mornin', darlin'. Go to sleep now. It'll be light before too long and day starts early around here."

Angelica was silent and compliant in his arms as Gareth drew his words to a halt. He would have to be satisfied with that for now. Yes, they'd talk everything out tomorrow. Tomorrow was soon enough.

Angelica had been intensely aware of Sophie's assessing gaze. The young Negress had come into the kitchen in the morning and had been obviously startled to see Angelica had already begun to heat the water for coffee and had started mixing the biscuits. Maria had arrived only a few moments later, her surprise just as marked when she had found Angelica working alongside Sophie. Maria had im-

394

mediately joined in and the three women had prepared the breakfast meal in remarkably short order.

Angelica sensed their approval and was relieved. Somehow the acceptance of these two women was important to her. Their manner had been stiff upon her arrival the day before. They had been wary of her, uncertain of her position in the household. Gareth had gone to great pains to set his unspoken claim upon her, and from the manner of their reactions, Angelica could only surmise that they were uncertain as to what to expect. But she did not want any special treatment. She did not intend to take advantage of her intimate position with Gareth, even though it appeared he would prefer that she did. No, she would not be such a fool. When Gareth's interest began to wane, she wanted her position to be secure, at least as far as her work was concerned, so that she might finish up her year in dignity before leaving.

She was also intensely aware that Gareth's father might have an objection to her if preferential treatment was extended. And she had no desire to be the cause of a rift between Gareth and his father. No, she had too strong a sense of family for that. As long as she was functioning as a working member of the household, she was certain the elder Mr. Dawson would not object to her stay at the Circle D.

"Sophie, I hear the men coming into the house. You must start putting the food on the table. Mr. Gareth will most certainly want to start the men out early today."

Aware that Maria hesitated to give her similar instructions, uncertain as she was of the status Angelica was to assume in the household, Angelica pulled the last tray of biscuits from the oven. Yes, they were perfect, their surface a warm, golden brown. Placing the hot tray down on the top of the stove, Angelica transferred the biscuits onto a platter. It was obvious that Maria was the unofficial head of the kitchen, and deferring to that position, Angelica stated quietly, "I'll start taking in the food, Maria."

Platter in hand, Angelica walked toward the door to the dining room. Refusing to allow her trepidation to show, she entered the room in a brisk step, her mind registering the low rumble of male voices in conversation around the table. A brief silence fell over the table as she advanced into the room, but Angelica refused to allow it to affect her as she moved between Charlie Stiles and Willie Harper to place the platter on the table. The silence was suddenly broken by a chorus of appreciative comments.

"Damn, those biscuits look good!"

"Hell, they ain't Sophie's biscuits! She ain't never turned out nothin' as pretty as them!"

Ignoring Michael and Charlie's comments, Willie Harper turned a small smile in her direction. His pale eyes and low voice revealed an appreciation of an entirely different sort.

"Good mornin', Angelica. You sure are a pleasant sight to start the mornin'."

"Yes, she is, isn't she, Willie."

Gareth's voice carried a note of censure which did not go unnoticed by the men. Restraining comment, Angelica returned to the kitchen to help with the remaining trays. She was filling the coffee cups around the table to a chorus of low thank-you's and sober glances when she, finally reached Gareth's side. She was pouring his coffee when she felt Gareth's hand slip around her waist to stay her departure.

"I'm goin' to be ridin' out with the boys right after breakfast, but I'll be returnin' a little before noon. Tell Maria to make a list of anythin' she needs from town, and tell Harvey to have the wagon ready for when I get back. You and I will be goin' into town this afternoon."

Extremely conscious of the weight of Gareth's arm and the familiarity it clearly demonstrated, Angelica responded quietly, "but I have already told Maria I will be helping her with . . ."

"Maria will have to do without you this afternoon, Angelica. There's some things I want to do in town."

"But . . ."

Angelica's continued protest had begun to draw Gareth's face into stiff lines when Michael Holley's voice interrupted the growing tenseness of their exchange.

"I sure wish somebody'd offer me the afternoon off! Gareth, if Angelica don't want to go with you, I sure as hell will . . ."

The strain passing out of the moment, Gareth turned with a smiling reply.

"Who do you think you're foolin', Mike? You have every afternoon off. You never needed an invitation to stretch yourself out under a big green tree and let the rest of the world slip by."

"Why, Gareth!" Feigning an injured expression, Mike turned his weathered face toward the men for support. "Tell him, boys! I'm a hard-workin' fella! I'd no more think of sleepin' on the job than I'd think of . . ."

"Collectin' your pay on payday? Hell, I know that well enough!"

The chorus of laughter that rounded the table dispelled the atmosphere of stiffness. Realizing it was the perfect moment to make her escape, Angelica attempted to move away only to have Gareth's arm tighten even more securely.

"You can tell Maria we'll be back in time for supper."

Angelica held Gareth's gaze for long seconds. He was deliberately refusing to allow the men to look upon her as just another servant in the household. Had it been Willie's complimentary remark that had pushed him into this action? Realizing she would not be free of his hold until she responded, Angelica nodded. His eyes holding hers for a second longer, Gareth dropped his hand from her waist.

Taking her opportunity, Angelica escaped to the kitchen. Making certain to stay there while the morning meal progressed in the dining room, Angelica allowed Sophie to refill the platters, ignoring the young Negress's pointed looks. No, she could not face the men again . . . not so soon. Gareth was in a strange mood, and she did not wish to test it.

The loud scraping of chairs against the wooden floor announced the end of the meal in the dining room and Angelica released a sigh. She would wait only until the table had been cleared and the cleaning up accomplished before starting to work on the storage room. She would not spend another night in Gareth's room, and it was obvious Gareth would not allow her to stay in the barn. It had been difficult enough waking before the others so that she might not be seen coming from his room this morning. As it was, she had arisen while Gareth was still asleep and managed to slip away without awakening him. But she did not wish to make early morning stealth a regular part of her life. No, she needed a room of her own.

The sound of voices had moved through the front door of the house and into the yard. The men had left. Judging it safe to enter the dining room, Angelica walked rapidly in its direction. She had only taken two steps into the room when an arm slipped around her waist and pulled her up against a familiar muscled length.

"Gareth!"

Drawing her with him into the privacy of the hallway beyond, Gareth pulled Angelica flush against him. His mouth was hungrily insistent, not satisfied until her lips had parted with a low sigh to allow him the freedom he sought. When he drew away at last, Gareth still held her close. His voice was a low whisper against her ear.

"I didn't like wakin' up to find you gone, darlin'. You're goin' to have to get over this shyness. Everybody here knows you're more than just an employee, and that we're more than friends. And for those that don't quite accept it yet, I'm aimin' to make myself very clear."

Angelica frowned. Gareth could be referring to no one other than Willie Harper. But he would allow her no response as he continued softly. "And you just make sure you're ready when I come back for you later on. There're some things we have to do."

His dark eyes promising her more than his words conveyed, Gareth released her reluctantly. He was about to speak again when his eyes moved back to the dining room. Sliding his arm around her waist, Gareth urged her back into the room with him as Harvey entered.

"Good mornin', Mr. Gareth, Miss Angelica. Sophie said you was ready for me now."

"Good mornin', Harvey." Nodding in response, Gareth directed his next words to Angelica. "Harvey is goin' to set up the storage room for you, Angelica. That's what you wanted, isn't it?"

Her face flushing at his unexpected consideration, Angelica had only managed a short nod when her reply was cut short by Mike's shout from the doorway.

"Hey, Gareth, are you comin' or not? The men are mounted and ready to leave. Brett said to tell you if he was still head honcho here, you'd sure be catchin' it for holdin' us back."

Annoyance flicked across Gareth's face. His reply carried a pointed message which did not go unnoted.

"So I guess it's a damned good thing I'm the boss, not Brett, isn't it?"

Watching until Mike made his silent retreat, Gareth turned back to Angelica. His formerly pleasant mood had obviously disappeared.

"Make sure you're ready when I come back."

"I will be ready, Gareth."

His eyes flicking over her face, Gareth nodded before turning toward the door. Angelica's eyes followed his tall, well-muscled frame as he disappeared into the yard. Yes, it was obvious that Gareth had chosen to make himself very clear.

The storage room was very small indeed. Angelica surveyed its limited confines. Formerly relegated to the storage of spare foodstuffs which had overflowed the pantry, spiderwebs, and all manner of junk, it was now spotlessly clean. Appearing to take his work extremely seriously, Harvey had stripped it bare before commencing to scrub the floor and walls vigorously. Due to his unrelenting efforts, the single window in the room had been forced open and cleaned. The late morning sun, just achieving its zenith, shone through unrestricted. The trapped heat was beginning to build, and Angelica frowned at the sample of the temperature which it would achieve in the full heat of the day. She shuddered at the thought.

But as small and airless as it was, Angelica was intensely relieved to have this space of her own. At present Harvey was working at assembling the bed he had transported into the room, piece by piece. As it had begun to take shape, she had been amazed at its proportions. Quietly advising that a smaller bed would suit far better than the full-sized one, Angelica had been informed that Gareth had been very specific as to which bed he wanted in the room. Her face flushing at the freedman's knowing glance, Angelica had silently returned to her kitchen chores.

But curiosity had drawn her back as Sophie had arrived with the linens and commenced to dress the bed. When she had attempted to assume the chore, Angelica had been advised that Gareth had left strict orders which linens were to be used and Sophie was going to make sure everything was done the way she had been instructed. Within a few minutes a small washstand had been squeezed into the corner and a dresser into the only remaining wall space still available in the room. She had been about to comment that she needed no more than the hook behind the door to store her limited wardrobe, but fearing another recitation of Gareth's orders, Angelica had declined her comments. All but groaning as Maria arrived with the necessary hardware to hang curtains on the windows, Angelica turned away.

Had Gareth done this purposely to humiliate her? The sound of a familiar step jerked her head up just as Gareth walked into the kitchen. Without hesitation he walked to her side, sliding his arm around her waist as he drew her with him toward the stuffy room. His frown adequately bespeaking his thoughts, he turned back to Angelica.

"So now that you see what it'll be like, do you still insist on sleepin' in this room, Angelica?"

All three faces within turned in her direction, and intensely aware of their regard, Angelica nodded. "It will be fine."

His mouth tightening, Gareth did not bother to respond. Instead, he turned toward Maria.

"The boys will be back in about an hour for their noon meal. Angelica and I will be goin' into town for a little while."

Town. In the rush of the morning's activities, she had almost forgotten. Angelica nervously raised her hand to her tightly plaited hair, seeking out errant strands. Were they going to check to see if any mail had arrived for her . . . or perhaps send a letter? But she had no money yet. Perhaps she could ask Gareth to pay for the postage with the promise to repay him from her salary at the end of the month. The thought of home brought a rush of tears to her eyes. Irritated by her submission to the untimely rush of sentiment, Angelica turned away.

Startled by the glaze of tears which suddenly brightened already brilliant silver eyes, Gareth frowned and raised his hand to her cheek.

"Is somethin' wrong, Angelica?"

"No, I just wondered . . ."

"Wondered what?"

"If it would be possible to send a letter to Padre Manuel . . ."

Gareth clamped his teeth tightly shut as his eyes moved assessingly over Angelica's face. He should have realized that flush of emotion was not for him. Home. She was thinking of her family and wanting to return home. But damn it, the Circle D was her home now, and despite the fact that she was presently unaware of it, she was never going back to Real del Monte. He would make certain of that.

Taking her arm, Gareth ushered Angelica toward the kitchen door.

"Yes, we can send a letter if you want . . . and check to see if any have been received for you." His anger softening at the obvious relief his words evoked, Gareth continued to guide her into the yard toward the waiting wagon. "Will that make you happy, darlin'?"

"Yes, I would be very pleased."

Swinging her up onto the seat, Gareth proceeded to climb onto the wagon beside her. Taking the reins in his hand, he slapped them lightly on the gray's back to start the great horse into motion and turned in her direction. His voice was low with promise.

"That's all I want, darlin' . . . to make you happy . . ."

Gareth accepted the letters the clerk held out to him. Appearing to immediately recognize the scrawling hand on one, he spent a few seconds in silent perusal of the other before starting to open the first. Angelica's eyes darted to him again in mute appeal. Frowning as he ripped open the envelope, Gareth looked back toward the clerk who appeared to be waiting expectantly for his next words.

"You're certain, Teddy . . . no letter has come for Angelica Rodrigo in care of me or the Circle D?"

"I'm sorry, Gareth."

Unconsciously allowing her eyes to linger moments longer on the clerk's florid face, Angelica was unaware of the discomfiture her intense stare caused the balding young fellow. Turning away, unaware that Teddy Wright's light brown eyes followed her, Angelica spoke as Gareth quickly scanned the contents of the letter he had received.

"I suppose it was foolish to expect word so soon. We have only just arrived. It was asking too much to expect Padre Manuel to be able to dispatch a letter that would arrive the same time as we. But I had hoped, in light of our delay at the beginning of the journey . . ."

Her voice trailing away, Angelica swallowed hard against her disappointment. His eyes lifting from the missive in his hand, Gareth folded it and slipped it into his pocket before sliding his arm around her narrow shoulders. Her anticipation had been marked in the tenseness of her beautiful features as they had approached the large general store which also served as the post office for the small Texas town. Her disappointment was keen, and intensely aware of her distress, Gareth tipped up her chin so that she looked into his face. His voice was gentle.

"It's too soon to expect word from the priest, Angelica. But you did say you wanted to send word home that you've arrived here safely."

The spark that lit Angelica's pale eyes sent a little niggle of jealousy moving up his spine. Someday her eyes would sparkle like that for him . . .

"Yes, Gareth. I would like that very much. I will repay you for the postage after my first month of service."

Choosing to ignore her promise of repayment, Gareth turned and took the few steps back toward Teddy Wright. Noting with annoyance that the fellow had not moved a muscle since they had turned away, but had remained staring in their direction, Gareth spoke with added sharpness in an attempt to shake him from his bemusement.

"Teddy!"

"Yes, sir, err . . . Gareth."

"Do you have a piece of stationery and a pen so that Señorita Rodrigo might post a letter?"

"Certainly, Gareth. Come this way, miss."

Obviously enjoying the opportunity to talk directly to Angelica for the first time, Teddy all but pushed Gareth aside in his bid to usher Angelica toward the large desk in the corner.

"We've provided this desk for just such a purpose. So many people in town haven't had the time to learn to write properly, and I've been only too happy to provide that service whenever necessary. Now, miss, if you'll just tell me what you'd like me to write . . ."

"*Gracias*, but that will not be necessary, señor. I am able to write."

Uncertain whether the young man was flushing from surprise, embarrassment, or strictly from the pleasure he obviously derived in being addressed by the object of his intense scrutiny, Gareth snorted his impatience.

"Sit down, Angelica. Teddy . . ." Turning to address the fellow obviously tonguetied with bemusement, Gareth continued tightly. "I don't have all afternoon."

"Oh, certainly, Gareth . . ."

Reaching behind him, Teddy took a piece of paper and put it on the desk as Angelica settled herself in the chair. Pushing the pen and ink within her reach, he also retrieved an envelope from the shelf behind him and placed it to her left.

"Now, if you need anything else, just give me a call. I'll

be only too happy to help."

"We'll be sure to call you if we need anythin', Teddy. But for now the young lady would like a little privacy."

"Oh, surely. Excuse me. I'll be close by if . . ."

"Yes, we know. If she needs you for anything, she'll call."

Waiting only until the flustered clerk had moved out of hearing, Angelica turned to Gareth with a frown. "Gareth, he was merely being kind. I was not annoyed by his offer of help."

"But *I* was!"

The vehemence of his response obviously startled Angelica, and Gareth mentally chastised himself for his flaring jealousy. Lester had been right. He was going to have to learn a greater tolerance for the kind of attention Angelica drew from men . . . at least to a point. He was doing himself and Angelica no good reacting like . . .

Refusing to follow his uncomfortable thoughts any further, Gareth shook his head and mumbled gruffly, "I'll give Bart the order for the supplies while you write your letter. Call me when you're done."

The picture of Angelica's small frown fresh in his mind, Gareth turned and walked away.

His hands moving absentmindedly through the rack of clothing he was examining a few minutes later, Gareth's thoughts ran between the letters he had just received and the small woman bent over the desk a few feet away. His father's letter had been brief, relating that he had been successful in obtaining support for the Texan cause, and that he expected to be starting home within the month. He had promised explanation in more detail when he returned, but it was the other letter which stirred his thoughts even more. Brock Macfadden . . . He had not expected to hear from the Scot so soon. Written not more than a few days after Gareth had left, Macfadden's letter explained that an unexpected break of activity at the mines had cleared enough time for him to make the journey to Texas. If all went according to Brock's plans he would be arriving at the Circle D within a month. His father should be returning home just about that time also. Gareth's frown tightened. If all went well with his plans, he should have Angelica firmly entrenched in his life by then. He did not think . . .

An unexpected touch on his arm interrupting his rambling thoughts, Gareth turned toward Angelica. A neatly addressed letter in her hand, she said quietly, "It is all ready to go, Gareth. I have but to give the clerk money for the postage . . ."

Taking the envelope from her hand, Gareth walked back toward Teddy. He was intensely aware that the fellow's gaze had not left Angelica since they had entered the store, and he strained to keep his patience.

"Teddy, weigh this up, will you? And take the price of the postage out of this." Slapping a five-dollar gold piece down on the counter, he added with more sharpness than was necessary, "We're in a hurry."

"Sure, Gareth."

Clumsy in his haste, the fellow accepted the letter and turned to the scale. Dropping the weights in his first attempt to adjust them, his eyes bobbed up to meet Gareth's sheepishly as he made a second adjustment. Finally counting out Gareth's change, he flashed him a quick grin while turning the bulk of his attention toward Angelica.

"If you need any help in the future with something of this sort, miss, you know who to ask for. My name is Teddy Wright, Miss . . . er . . ." Checking the return address on the letter, Teddy concluded brightly, "Miss Rodrigo."

"*Muchas gracias*, Señor Wright."

"Yes, thanks, Teddy. But if Angelica needs any help, she knows who to come to . . ."

Taking her arm firmly, Gareth ushered Angelica toward the other end of the store. Waiting until they were out of earshot of the embarrassed young man, Angelica turned to frown into Gareth's stern expression.

"Gareth, the man was but doing his job."

Unwilling to discuss the matter any further, Gareth urged Angelica toward the far corner of the store.

"Let's forget about Teddy Wright, Angelica. Come over

here. I have something I want you to see."

Steering her to the small rack of ready-made women's clothing he had been examining, Gareth adjusted her position so that she stood in front of him. Looking over her head, his eyes intent on the garments, he frowned.

"There doesn't seem to be much choice here. Most of these dresses look to be sizes too large for you. There're only two that seem to be anywhere near your size, and they're not at all what I was thinkin' of."

Angelica's eyes flicked to the clothing and back to Gareth's face.

"I am not in need of new clothing, Gareth. What I have is more than adequate for my needs."

Gareth's eyes carefully assessed the stiffness which had beset her lovely features. The adamance that slowly overcame his expression turned him to the Gareth of old as he stated flatly, "I don't agree, Angelica. I told you I expected to get you some new things when we arrived . . ."

"I am already indebted to you for the price of the postage for my letter. It is not my intention to enter into extravagance that will find me just as poor at the end of the month as I was at the beginning. I have better use for my money than to cover my back with garments for which I will have no use . . ."

"But you will have use for them, Angelica. You'll dispense with these rags you're wearin' and wear the new dresses on a daily basis . . ."

"New clothes to work in the kitchen?"

"Yes! I don't intend that your labor will be such that these simple cotton dresses will prove a problem. And I don't expect to be reimbursed for the things I buy for you."

Angelica's face flamed a deep red."

"I will not accept your gifts!"

His own color rising as well, Gareth gripped Angelica's shoulders firmly. Intensely aware of their lack of privacy and the fact that the growing heat of their conversation was already drawing the attention of the clerk and several of the matrons who browsed amongst the bolts of cloth nearby, Gareth lowered his voice to an angry hiss.

"You will accept money for your 'services,' but you will not accept gifts, even if they are more in the way of necessities than luxuries? You are behavin' like a fool, Angelica! Or do you have a more subtle method behind your thinkin'?"

Momentarily confused, Angelica shook her head.

"A 'more subtle method to my thinking'? You talk in riddles, Gareth!"

"Riddles? Perhaps you are hopin' to stir the sympathy of someone in particular . . . someone to whom you've taken a likin'. It would be easy to claim mistreatment by me, wouldn't it? I've taken you from your home and delivered you into a strange environment, and it has to be obvious that I can't keep either my hands or my eyes off you. You've been installed in a mere closet of a room which is little less than an oven. And on a homestead where even our freed Negress is more than adequately dressed, you function in clothing that even our poorest slave would not have been expected to wear. Poor Angelica! Mistreated, worked like a servant during the day and expected to function according to the whims of her employer's desire at night, given only the barest necessities while others in the household . . ."

"Stop, Gareth! You are insane! To whom would I appeal with such a distortion of the truth? There is no one here . . ."

"No one here? Is there someone somewhere else whom you would expect to call upon, someone who . . ."

"Gareth, please." Unable to believe the wild suspicions which had surged to life in Gareth's mind with her simple refusal, Angelica shook her head once again. Gareth's grip on her shoulders had tightened to the point of pain and she whispered softly, "Gareth, you are hurting me."

Gareth's hands immediately dropped from her shoulders, his lips tightening into a straight line which emphasized the firm set of his jaw. She could bear no more of the accusation in his dark eyes, or the anger which had replaced the gentleness he had exhibited only moments before. Sliding her hand onto his arm, she looked up at him in mute appeal. But Gareth's adamance was unrelenting, and unwilling to allow the anger to continue between them, Angelica offered a conciliatory smile.

"I truly do not understand your reasoning, Gareth. I do not believe I have done anything since arriving here to cause you suspicion of my motives. But I am your employee, and if I am an embarrassment to you in my present manner of dress, I suppose I cannot refuse your generosity. But I must insist upon repaying you . . ."

"No!"

"Gareth . . ."

"No, damn it, no!" Frustration again welled inside him. How could he explain his desire to give to her . . . his absolute need to demonstrate his right to take care of her?

The sterling glow of her eyes moved over his face for a few moments longer before Angelica bobbed her head reluctantly.

"All right, Gareth"

Angelica turned to face the rack once again. Gareth's breath fanned the side of her neck, sending little shivers down her spine as she raised her hand to examine the dresses. She drew out the two smallest of the garments, her eyes moving over the blue and white gingham and the simple gray cotton. She would wear whatever he wanted for the duration of her stay at the Circle D. She could do no less since she would be functioning as part of his household. But she would keep her old clothes and when she left she would leave behind whatever he insisted on buying for her now. She would only take home with her that which they had originally bargained for and that which she had earned. But for the present she would go along with Gareth's demands, for it appeared she had little choice.

Turning back to Gareth, Angelica realized he was frankly suspicious of her abrupt about-face. Her eyes dropped back to the dresses with confusion.

"I confess that I do not know which of these garments to choose. Do you have a preference, Gareth?"

"I'm impressed with neither of them, but if you think they'll fit, we'll take them both."

"Both!"

"And while we're here we'll stop at the dressmaker and have her measure your size . . ."

"Gareth, please! This is wasteful! I have no need . . ."

"But *I* have a need, darlin'."

Gareth's voice suddenly dropping to a husky whisper that solicited her understanding, he lowered his head to press a kiss against the smooth curve of her neck that tempted him so outrageously. Realizing his emotions were warming to a dangerous degree, Gareth continued in a low voice. "And my needs are diverse when they come to you, darlin'. So indulge me, and I promise they'll give us both pleasure."

Angelica was still engrossed in the velvet depths of Gareth's eyes when the hiss of whispers reached her ears. Turning, she found herself the object of the disapproving glances of the two browsing matrons, and she flushed.

His arm curving around her, Gareth lifted his head to smile boldly in the women's direction.

"Good afternoon, Mrs. Colby . . . Mrs. Waters. Nice day, isn't it?"

Mumbling their replies, the two women scurried away, prompting a low oath as Gareth urged Angelica toward the counter.

"Damned busybodies. Their tongues are goin' to be waggin' all over town for at least the next week." His jaw working with irritation, Gareth tightened his arm around her waist and pulled her close. "Well, I hope they enjoy themselves 'cause I sure as hell am."

Lowering his head, Gareth pressed another light kiss against her throat and pulled Angelica into step beside him.

Angelica's arm under his, Gareth turned out onto the street. Looking down to Angelica, Gareth noted her somber expression, and he whispered encouragingly.

"Smile, darlin'. You're not goin' to the gallows . . . just for a bite to eat at the Sunset Cafe. Isabel Jeffers is a real nice lady, and a great cook. And I have to admit, my appetite is growin', darlin' . . . it's growin' more every minute."

His eyes lingering on Angelica's lips, Gareth managed to wipe the grimness from their soft contours, and feeling more carefree than he had in months, he walked rapidly toward the building at the end of the street. The first step in his plan was going well. He was leaving no doubt in the minds of everyone in town as to whom Angelica belonged, and whatever other conclusions they drew be damned!

The concentrated heat of late afternoon had turned Angelica's small room into a stifling, airless box. Angelica brushed back the straying wisps which had adhered to her moist temples and adjusted the simple gray cotton dress around her waist.

Gareth and she had returned home only a short time before to find Maria and Sophie deep into preparation of the evening meal. At Gareth's request she had gone reluctantly to her room to change into one of her new dresses. Uncomfortable in its luxury, despite the fact that the material was lighter and less bulky than that to which she was accustomed, she would gladly have changed back to her *camisa* and skirt had it not been for Gareth's direct instructions to the contrary.

Frowning, Angelica moved to the small mirror on the washstand and assessed her appearance. Scoop-necked and short-sleeved, the pale cotton was simple and free of detail, with the exception of the narrow row of white lace which trimmed the neckline and sleeves and ran down the front closing of the dress.

Gareth had been correct in his assessment. The dress was slightly oversized for her small proportions. The generous cut made it more ample in the shoulders and deepened the neckline a bit lower than intended. Adjusting it to the best of her ability, Angelica was thankful for the wide matching sash that allowed her to tighten the waistline more comfortably and thereby give the garment a greater semblance of proper fit. Somehow her long black plait seemed out of place with the new picture she presented, and succumbing to impulse, Angelica twisted it into a secure knot at the back of her neck. The effect was not particularly becoming,

410

but far more in keeping with her new manner of dress.

But her present discomfort was just another element in the long afternoon of discomfort for her. Feeling herself akin to a pet cat on display, Angelica had accompanied Gareth first to the Sunset Cafe where she had been introduced to the friendly Isabel Jeffers. But the same welcome had not been extended to her by the young woman who worked alongside the matronly brunette. To the contrary, Marian Wells had flushed to the roots of her pale flaxen hair when Gareth politely introduced her, and Angelica had experienced a true conflict of emotions. It was obvious that Gareth had spent time in cultivating the young woman's acquaintance in the past and that she still harbored warm feelings for Gareth. In the time they had eaten their afternoon meal, Angelica had silently compared herself to the quiet Miss Wells. The contrast between them could not be more distinct.

Tall and slim, except for a more than ample bosom, Marian Wells was extremely fair of complexion. Her brows and lashes were light brown, almost gold, and her eyes were a bright blue. Although she was not truly a beautiful woman, Marian Wells had a particular combination of fair coloring and clear features which Angelica had heard referred to as wholesome. Angelica was very aware that she would never bear that distinction, and would probably never attain true acceptance in their society as well.

She had been aware of the intense scrutiny of the townsfolk as she had walked at Gareth's side. She had submitted uneasily to the dressmaker's touch as the woman had taken the measurements for the three dresses for which Gareth had contracted. Small sounds of disbelief had accompanied each measurement the tape had registered. Angelica had tried to ignore the comments she had overheard made to Gareth about her "petite proportions," and how different they were from the majority of the women in the area who were of "Anglo-Saxon" heritage.

Gareth's response to the comments had been too muffled to reach her ears as she busied herself with the material in the rear of the store, but she had noted that the talkative

Mrs. Sinclair had guarded her words carefully after that.

Contrary to Angelica's wishes due to the lateness of the hour, Gareth had stopped the wagon in a small grove on the way home from town. They had spent a leisurely hour there while Gareth had made love to her slowly, with great passion. The depth of her own response and her realization that she was less in control of her emotions each time Gareth took her into his arms, had truly shaken her. She risked much in giving herself to Gareth so completely and her fear of the outcome grew stronger each day.

But there was little time for retrospect now. She was well aware that her late return to the kitchen had been frowned upon by Sophie and Maria, and she really could not blame them for their censure. Gareth's preferential treatment was the surest way of causing herself problems with those two hard-working women. Steeling herself against their reaction to what she was certain they would consider the flaunting of her questionable position when she appeared in this new dress, Angelica turned away from the mirror and walked toward the door.

Her hand poised on the knob, she acknowledged her realization that Gareth's approval—the particular warmth that lit his increasingly frequent smile, the glow that only she could light in that somber darkness of his eyes—was worth any censure she might be forced to suffer.

The silence that greeted Angelica as she stepped into the kitchen was all she had expected. Lifting her eyes to Maria's stiff face, Angelica saw her sniff of disapproval. Sophie's eyes reflected more of the same as she inquired with a quick assessment of her attire, "Will you be eatin' in the dinin' room from now on, Miss Angelica?"

"An afternoon out of the kitchen and more suitable working attire does not change my status in this household, Sophie. With the exception of this evening meal, I will still be working alongside you and Maria, and I will be eating with you as well."

The sound of male voices from the next room indicated that the men were waiting for their meal to be served, and having stated her position clearly, Angelica reached for the

412

platters which had already been readied to be served. Taking a deep breath as she approached the dining room, Angelica walked briskly into the room.

" . . . and Pa said everythin' went well with his meetin' within the 'federal official.' " Gareth hesitated as Angelica entered the room, his gaze moving briefly in her direction. Not stopping to gauge its approval, Angelica slid the platter onto the table as Gareth continued slowly. "He said he expects to be back here with the month . . ."

The unexpected announcement brought a round of approval from the men and snapped Angelica's gaze toward Gareth, registering her surprise. Why had he not mentioned that his father had indicated the time of his return. Had he hoped to keep it from her? Did he think his father would . . . ?

But the men were getting restless, anxious for their meal, and Angelica returned to the kitchen to fetch another platter. She caught the last of Gareth's statement as she turned back into the room.

". . . and he says that pressure has been put upon Santa Anna that will undoubtedly result in Stephen Austin's release. Pa is expectin' that they won't be holdin' him much more than a month longer. I'm hopin' he's right and all this bickerin' between the committees can be settled at last. I'm gettin' damned tired of this limbo we've been livin' in . . ."

A low rumble of agreement moved around the table, covering Willie Harper's smiling comment as she leaned past him to slide the last of the platters onto the table.

"I ain't never seen nothin' as pretty as you in that dress, ma'am, and I don't expect I ever will."

Nodding a soft thank-you, Angelica made a fast escape. She had been increasingly aware that the men's attention was drifting from Gareth to wander in her direction. She had not dared to face his gaze in light of his unexpected behavior of that afternoon. She was truly uncertain exactly what would set him off on another tangent, and she had no desire to face another of his outbursts.

Skillfully managing to have Sophie take over the last chore of pouring the coffee for the men, Angelica released a tense breath and began the work of clean-up in the kitchen.

She had been congratulating herself on her success in avoiding another trip into the dining room when Maria turned in her direction.

"Angelica, you will please remove the plates from the table and refill the men's cups. Sophie will bring out the sweet buns I have prepared."

Taking a deep breath, Angelica nodded her head. Silently scolding herself for her discomfort, Angelica turned toward the dining room. This time she walked directly to Gareth's chair and reached down to take his plate. Hesitating momentarily, she allowed herself to meet his eye at last, only to be mesmerized by the unexpected warmth of his smile.

"You look beautiful, Angelica."

"You are beautiful, Angelica . . ."

Gareth's husky whisper was warm against her flesh as his mouth moved to worship its sweetness. His naked length stretched out atop her, Gareth trailed his lips along the lower curve of her breast, his tongue flicking out to caress the erect, roseate bud which awaited him. Indulging himself for long moments, he lifted his head to her half-lidded gaze.

The hours from suppertime until he had been free to hold her again in his arms had been excruciatingly long. Accustomed to the solitude of the long journey to Texas, he chafed at the restrictions imposed by the presence of others. It had been endless torture to wait until Maria and Sophie had retired to their own rooms for the night and he had been free to seek Angelica out. He had not lasted more than a few moments in the heat of Angelica's room, but instead had wordlessly scooped her up into his arms and carried her up the stairs to his. The night breeze was refreshingly cool, blowing across their nakedness through the open window, and Gareth's heart was filled to bursting.

He loved her. He loved her so desperately that his love was a burning ache, crying to be acknowledged. But he dared not speak yet. His eyes, tangling with Angelica's crystal gaze, recognized the warmth his touch evoked inside her and his heart filled to bursting.

He had a month . . . at least a month more before his father would appear to complicate matters, and by that time Angelica would be more securely his. She was growing closer to him each day . . . each hour. The conflict which had once been constant between them had already begun to change. Cautious not to sacrifice her sense of self, Angelica was giving herself to him more and more with each loving contact. The supreme beauty of that gift was all the more satisfying with the realization that Angelica did not share herself easily, that each concession reflected a measure of her trust. He would soon turn that trust into love. It could be no other way . . . not for Angelica and him, for he knew now, with a deep certainty, that she was all he had ever wanted . . . ever needed to make his life complete.

Lowering his mouth to hers, Gareth indulged himself in the beauty that was Angelica, more certain than ever that their love was meant to be . . .

Chapter XI

Esteban Arricalde surveyed the scene being enacted on the dock before his eyes with growing disgust. A line of merchants, their faces grim, were being guarded by armed soldiers as they were herded in single file past a makeshift desk and a smirking soldier with a large ledger. Tariffs and taxes, assessment being made and payment demanded, from men who claimed to be unable to pay the price. The resulting furor was growing greater with each invasion of the liberties these people seemed to value over their lives, and Captain Thompson had not the sense to see the error in his method of handling them.

Captain Thomas M. Thompson was a fool! It had not taken him long to assess the man's worth. The voyage to Anahuac and several in-depth conversations with the haughty Englishman had brought him to that conclusion, and he had been proved right again and again in the time since. Arrogant, with an inborn sense of superiority which seemed characteristic of his nationality, Captain Thompson had sailed into Anahuac with all the boldness of an invader. He had immediately assumed his responsibilities with a heavy hand, allowing no time for orderly compliance. The Texans, ignorant oafs that they were, had been pushed to the wall, and the Texan War Party was gaining new recruits in the bustling port city each day.

Buffoon . . . charlatan! Had Santa Anna hoped to put a man into the situation who would cause an immediate commencement of armed hostilities, he could not have made a better choice. Pulling his slender muscular frame up to its full height, Esteban barely suppressed his sneer. El presidente would have done far better to have put him in control of this situation, with Captain Thompson as his subordinate. Then the job would have been done properly. The mentality of these uneducated misfits who hoped to pass themselves as true Texas patriots had not been difficult to figure out, and he would have been able to handle them easily. Granted, he would have had to modify his original thoughts on the matter . . . force was truly not the answer, but he was confident he would have been able to talk their leaders into easy compliance with Santa Anna's new tariff laws. Had he not been complemented on his superior powers of negotiation? Had not his ability in that respect been compared to el presidente himself. He had never had a problem molding others to his line of thinking with the earnest manner and sincere expression he found so easy to assume.

Instead, he had been helpless in his capacity as observer. His communications going strangely unanswered by Antonio, he had been forced to watch as he did now while Captain Thompson bullied the citizens and traders of the port. Flicking his eyes toward the stern, narrow face of the autocratic Englishman as he looked on the scene unblinkingly, Esteban saw the man had not the sense to realize the depth of his error. Fool that he was, he had actually threatened these people with burning the town if they did not comply with the law!

Even as he watched, a wild altercation broke out between the merchant presently being assessed and the arrogant officers proceeding under Captain Thompson's orders. A public spectacle . . . forcing these men to behave as heroes, molding them into martyrs with stupidity. Were he in command, he would pursue a finer course with these people. He had studied them carefully in the time since he had arrived. They were not truly desirous of revolt. In their hearts they were cowards who were merely being forced into these outrageous acts of revolt by fools acting in the name of el presidente. Did not the dispute between the "War Party" and the "Peace Party" demonstrate that point vividly? The Texan Peace Party had retained command despite all the petitions of incitement distributed. It was el presidente's

417

men themselves who were providing the War Party their greatest aid.

Even enraged as he was with stubborn Texans, el presidente was too intelligent to force a situation in this manner. No, he would have proceeded with his usual sincerity of expression and empty promises, and he would have held the revolutionary movement at bay with the sheer power of his mesmerizing charisma. But el presidente could not be everywhere at once, and this mistake in putting Captain Thompson at the helm of the *Correo* was going to cost him heavily in Anahuac.

Esteban's lip curled in contempt as he pulled his impeccably uniformed figure up proudly. Yes, he should have been in charge of this situation, and he was going to make sure Antonio knew the true error of his decision. He would have been wise enough to use his superior intelligence to outwit this leaderless herd of Texans whose poor mentalities would have had no defense against his persuasive skill and his own particular brand of charisma.

A crowd was gathering by the customs house, their protests growing louder. At Captain Thompson's command, several soldiers rushed froward to restrain the protesters, using the butts of their rifles to force them back in line. Esteban surveyed the growing heat in the expressions of the spectators, his eyes snapping back to Captain Thompson's stern, unyielding face. Arrogance. Blind, ignorant arrogance was stamped there as the Englishman ordered five more of his men into the line suppressing the protestors, guns drawn. There would be bloodshed yet, and the War Party would have even more ammunition with which to agitate!

Unable to stand the sight of such idiocy any longer, Esteban turned and walked abruptly in the direction of town. He signaled his two private guards to accompany him, fully realizing the sight of his uniform was a provocation in its own right among these harassed citizens. Yes, were he handling these fools, he would have them eating out of his hand . . . begging to pay the tariffs demanded as good citizens of a great, benevolent country.

Instead, Captain Thompson was pushing matters to the point of no return.

His mind moving to the conversation Captain Thompson and he had had that morning, Esteban stiffened. Yes, he could delay no longer. Captain Thompson had greater goals in store for himself, and Esteban wanted no part of them. Thompson's plan to go after the American brig *Tremont*, presently engaged in the Texan trade, would be a gross error, a ludicrous step in face of the present state of affairs. Antonio must be warned. In any case, Esteban had no intention of becoming associated in any way with the fiasco which was certain to follow.

A quick glance over his shoulder showed his guards were in place, and Esteban hastened his pace as he flicked an unconscious finger across his meticulously trimmed mustache. No, he would not allow the idiotic Captain Thompson to pull him down with him. Captain Thompson's stupidity was doomed to failure, and Esteban was determined to emerge on the winning side.

He would make his excuses and arrange for transportation back to the capital immediately. He had too much to lose . . . his future, his fortune, and most importantly, his revenge. He had come so close, so very close to achieving his goal right here. He was in Texas, surely not more than a few days' travel from the Dawson ranch, but the time was not right. He was not yet in the position of power he desired. The desire for revenge was a festering wound inside him, but retribution would be all the sweeter for this torment he now suffered. All these aggravations would seem petty when he indulged himself in the complete destruction of the homestead to which Gareth Dawson had devoted most of his life. But his greatest elation would come when, as the spoils of his brilliant campaign, the fiery little *puta* would come to him at last. Oh, yes, revenge would make all his torment worthwhile.

Angelica raised her hand to her forehead and strained her eyes into the golden, sunswept distance. August had come to the Circle D with unceasing heat and the weight of heavy air which was almost a burden to breathe. In the brief periods between waking and sleeping, the nudge of memory had brought to mind similar nights of her childhood in the crisp air of Real del Monte. But somehow she had been hesitant to coax that reluctant veil into rising for total recall. That memory was too closely tied to the dark dreams which haunted her still.

But Gareth had been true to his word. A powerful, nameless flush of emotion all but overcame her as Angelica recalled the night before when his strong arms had been her defense against the labored breathing which had assaulted her in nightmare and the heavy, smothering darkness which sought to steal her own breath from her lungs. His arms had held her . . . his deep voice had called her back to the security of reality . . . and his strength had protected her from the dark, threatening horror which gave her little peace.

Gareth's arms had truly become her blue velvet, the touch of his lips the breath of life which drew her back. Somewhere in the many long nights she had lain in his arms, she had given up her war against becoming dependent on his strength. She needed him now, and he was there. She had learned she must deal with the present in order to face the uncertain future which lay before her.

The endless distance was empty of man and beast and Angelica strained her eyes toward the winding road Gareth had taken earlier. He had gone into town with his men in early morning. The boys had been in a frivolous mood, which had raised Maria's brow. The resulting look she had sent in Charlie's direction had spoken Maria's thoughts clearly to her husband of many years, and Angelica doubted that look would go unheeded.

In the month since Angelica had come to the Circle D, a tolerant peace had come to exist between Angelica and the two women in the kitchen. She had managed to earn their respect and that of the ranch hands despite the obvious intimacy which existed between Gareth and herself. Although Gareth would have it otherwise, she continued to return to her room behind the kitchen so each morning would find her in her own bed, despite the time spent in Gareth's arms the night before. She had found that compromise the only one with which she could live, but Gareth still chafed at her insistence at maintaining separate quarters. His impassioned words, spoken only that morning in the hours before dawn, echoed in her ears, renewing her tension.

"I don't want you to leave, Angelica. I want to wake up with you in my arms. I don't care what anyone thinks. You belong to me . . ."

But his insistence had been to no avail, and her adamance in returning to her room had been the cause of a particularly bitter argument. Gareth's angry accusations had haunted her the day long. She had been bewildered by Gareth's stored jealousies, astounded that he could harbor such thoughts in light of her obvious abandon to his lovemaking. Her words had been angry in return, resulting in a parting that morning in sharp contrast to the love they had made only a short time before.

Gareth had left with the men, without a glance in her direction. His hostility had been such that she was certain Gareth harbored little desire to hold her in his arms. Sophie had confided that this monthly pattern was all but ritual at the Circle D. Payday, and the boys would go to town to renew themselves with an ample indulgence in Jim Crow, the gaming tables, and the willing ladies that worked in the local saloon. According to Sophie, Gareth had never been one to hold back on such occasions, and it appeared this day was to be no different.

But Gareth had made her a promise before their bitter parting to check at the post office to see if a letter had been received for her. She had had no response from her letter to Padre Manuel . . . had heard no news of her family in the time since she had left Real del Monte. In the absence of news her mind had reverted to playing wild tricks and she was badly in need of peace of mind.

The brilliant red-gold sun was setting, and Angelica turned back toward the house with a low sigh. Another day . . . she would have to wait another day to find out if there was a letter for her from home. Refusing to admit that the tension deep inside her might be caused by thoughts other than those, Angelica walked back through the front door of the house and made her way to the kitchen. She would amuse herself by writing another letter to Carlos, one which she would incorporate into her response when an answer was finally received from Padre Manuel.

She attempted to raise her spirits with the thought that she had received her pay at the same time as the ranch hands. The entire amount was secreted in her room, the first of a sum to be saved for the time when she would return to Real del Monte. She had determined she would spend only the amount needed for the posting of her letters. The rest would be saved to provide an alternative for her family if Real del Monte was no longer feasible for them in light of Carlos's illness. This year of insecurity and uncertainty would not be wasted. It would make a new life for the three people she loved most in the world, those who had sacrificed so much for her in their love.

Love . . . it was rare indeed.

Her spirits dropping even further with the setting of the sun, Angelica made her way into the empty kitchen, her heart feeling as empty as the small, silent room.

A stroking touch in the darkness awakened Angelica with a start. Momentarily unable to focus her eyes, she stared at the vague outline which knelt beside her bed in the stifling room. Her low gasp was smothered by the warmth of a kiss laced with the unfamiliar scent of tobacco and alcohol and she struggled to escape. But she was no match for the strength imprisoning her in the shadow's embrace. Tearing her mouth free, she was about to call out in her fear when Gareth demanded in a slurred tone, "Still angry, Angelica?"

"Gareth!"

"Yes, Gareth. Does that disappoint you, Angelica?"

"Gareth, you are talking nonsense."

"Does it? Answer me, damn it!"

"No, it does not disappoint me!"

"That's good, because if you've spoiled me for any pleasure I could get from other women, then I sure as hell am goin' to spoil you for any other man!"

"Gareth!"

Her protest to no avail, Gareth leaned forward and scooped Angelica up into his arms. Ignoring the protest of her flailing arms and kicking feet, he jerked her tight against him, his arms steel bands cutting into the soft flesh of her arms and legs as he turned toward the door to her room.

"Stop it, Angelica." His voice a low threat despite its revealing slur, Gareth whispered warningly, "You know you're tied to me just as surely as I'm tied to you. And we're goin' to make the best of the bargain we've struck."

They were moving through the silent house and up the staircase, the liquor Gareth had obviously consumed having little reaction on his ability to negotiate the familiar path with her in his arms. Angelica abandoned her fight. It was senseless, only adding to Gareth's unreasonable and unyielding anger.

They were moving through the doorway to Gareth's room and within moments Angelica felt the softness of the bed beneath her back. The night was clear, the light of the moon illuminating the room brightly. In its silver glow, Gareth's face was sober and unrelenting as he sat beside her, his gaze intent on her face.

Holding her eyes with his, Gareth began to strip away his shirt as he whispered in the silence of the room, "You're where you belong now . . . you know that, don't you, Angelica?"

"Gareth . . ." Her hand moved up to touch the bared flesh of his chest as Angelica offered softly, "I have never denied you . . ."

"That's right, darlin', you've never denied that you belong lyin' beside me, but you've never acknowledged it, either." Standing up, Gareth tossed his shirt to the nearby chair, his hands moving automatically to his trousers. Within minutes they had followed the same course as his shirt. He was lying beside her, his body curved to hers

423

before he spoke again. His hands slipped her shift from her shoulders to bare her breasts and a sound of satisfaction echoed low in his throat. His hands were moving over the smooth, white flesh as he lifted his gaze to hers.

"I was furious with you when I left here this mornin'. So damned stubborn . . . so determined to have your way. You slept every night in my arms on the journey here . . . became a part of my life. And now you take every opportunity to remind me that I paid to have you lyin' beside me. You insist on playin' the *puta*, leavin' me before dawn each day to return to your own bed."

As he spoke Gareth continued to stroke her intimately, and Angelica fought to suppress the spontaneous response his touch evoked. He was working the same magic again . . . the magic against which she had no defense, and she closed her eyes in despair.

"No, Angelica, don't close your eyes. I want you to look at me."

Waiting only until her gaze once again met his, Gareth lowered his head to trail his lips across hers, teasing her with the fleeting contact.

"I have a lot of old friends at the Oasis saloon, darlin'. They were real happy to see me. I figured all I needed to do was to spend a little time at the bar and I would wander naturally in the direction of the 'friend' who stirred the fondest memories. I worked hard at it, darlin', but you know somethin'? I couldn't even get up enough interest to take Lucy upstairs, much less get about doin' what the rest of the fellas were so busy at. It finally occurred to me I was wastin' my time. The only woman I wanted was here, and I was lettin' stubbornness get in the way. So I finished up my drink and told the boys I'd be seein' them."

Gareth's mouth had slid down the slender column of her throat and was roaming freely against her breasts. He was tugging at the erect nipples, sucking them with growing fervor. His voice was low, almost inaudible against her soft flesh.

"And I decided on the way back, darlin', that I was goin' to make you want me more than you've ever wanted me before, and that you were goin' to stay with me . . . here . . . in this bed until mornin'. And I decided you were goin' to walk down those steps beside me, not carin' who saw us, because that was the way it was meant to be . . ."

His seeking mouth was sliding down the flat surface of her stomach, finding the moist heart of her desire, stroking it to life with the warmth of his tongue.

Angelica was beginning to whimper in protest against his heady assault, but Gareth gave no quarter. With steady deliberation he stroked the petals of her desire, coaxing them to unfold. With gentle persuasion he drew the sweet nectar to the surface, urged her passion to blossom full and sweet within her. Enthralled with the wonder flowering between them, growing in magnificence, Gareth deepened his intimate caress, tasting, fondling, loving her completely, leaving no portion of her body stranger to his tender succor.

Angelica's slender body was heaving with rioting emotions, her ragged breathing echoing his own when Gareth paused at last, searching her face to determine the full extent of her passion. With tenuous control, Gareth drew back allowing her torment to grow, fighting his own aching need as he resisted her entreaties with the sheerist force of will.

Angelica's arms reached up to draw him close, her eyes flicking open to search his face as he sat back on his heels, his knees straddling her slender body. His eyes were hard as onyx, his voice a breathless, determined whisper.

"Tell me you want me, Angelica. I want to hear you say you need me as much as I need you. Tell me there's no one else that will do for you, just like there's no one else who will do for me . . ."

"Gareth . . ."

"Tell, me, Angelica. Tell me, or I swear I'll walk out right now and leave you here to find your way back to that damned room you insist upon. And I'll do the same thing tomorrow night and the next and the next until you . . ."

"Gareth, please . . ."

Unable to stand her urgent plea, Gareth swooped down to kiss the welcoming mound once again, the heat of his stirring kisses eliciting a soft cry from Angelica's lips. He was drawing from her deeply, indulging himself in her sweetness when he felt the first shudder shake her frame. Drawing back immediately, his voice was an urgent plea.

"Tell me, Angelica . . . tell me, damn you. Let me give you all the lovin' I have stored up inside for you. Let me give to you, darlin' . . ."

Angelica could no longer think. Her body was crying for the joy Gareth promised, crying out her need. She raised her hands in supplication only to hear Gareth's voice demand shakily, "Tell me you want me, Angelica . . ."

"Oh, I do want you Gareth. I want you very much . . ."

"Tell me you need me . . ."

"I need you . . ."

"How much?"

"Very much . . . very . . ."

"Tell me there's no one else for you. No one else . . ."

"There's no one else, Gareth. There never has been . . ."

"And there never will be . . ."

"Gareth . . ."

Angelica's eyes moved to his, registering her resistance to his final demand. His voice was a harsh command.

"Say it! I want that, too. I want it more than . . ."

"Gareth, please. I can't say . . ."

But Gareth could hold out no longer. His mouth moving to the core of her womanhood, he seared her with his kiss, drew from the font of her passion until she gave to him in burst of searing rapture, her joy erupting in shaking, convulsing spasms which brought her careening from the summit of passion where she had lingered torturously for so long.

She was still gasping when she felt Gareth slip atop her, felt the shaft of his manhood probing her intimately. Within moments he had filled her, his gasp of satisfaction raising her again on great diaphanous wings, higher, higher with each jolting plunge until their mutual explosion of joy rocked the multicolored world of their glory, setting them free.

Gareth was lying atop her, his breathing still ragged

when he began his loving again. He had not been sated . . . could not get enough of her. He needed to sear into his mind the fervor of her words.

"I want you. I need you. No one else will do . . . no one else but you . . ."

His arms pillowed under his head, Gareth lay on his back in bed. His eyes moved over Angelica's naked outline, silhouetted against the bright light of morning shining through the window of his room as she dressed. A breeze just beginning to edge with heat lifted the ends of her hair from her shoulders, and he envied the silken strands their gentle caress. She was so lovely. The joy of her made him truly complete.

The night had been long and fulfilling. The memory of Angelica's soft whispers, her gasps of passion, the touch of her hands against his skin in exploring caress, lingered with him still. Determined to set the precedent which would define the course of the year that lay before them, Gareth had returned to Angelica's room while she slept and brought back her clothes. She would walk down the staircase beside him this morning, and later in the day, when the least attention would be called to his activity, he would transfer her meager belongings to his room. He would establish her firmly in his life, allow her no separation from him. She was a part of him more certainly than if he had spoken his vows, and it would be only a matter of time until Angelica felt the same. He sensed it . . . felt it deep inside him, and his spirits soared.

The wisp of her lace chemise slipped down over Angelica's flawless skin, and Gareth swallowed hard. He had bought the fine undergarments against Angelica's wishes, but had never had the opportunity to view her in them unrestricted due to the covert nature their loving had assumed since arriving at the Circle D. For the first time since they had arrived he was free to observe her leisurely in the privacy of his room in the full light of day. He was all but overcome with the joy at the sight provided him. She was slipping the simple blue and white gingham dress over her head, allowing it to fall against her slenderness, struggling to fasten the buttons on the back of the garment. He drew himself to his feet. Walking to stand behind her, Gareth smiled as Angelica turned tentatively in his direction.

"I'll do that for you, darlin'."

Waiting only until Angelica had again put her back to him, Gareth gathered the sprawling silk of her hair into his hand and drew it over her shoulder. Leaning down, he kissed the nape of her neck. Her head snapped toward him momentarily, and he rewarded her glance with the light brushing of her lips with his own.

But he was only too aware that this type of amusement was unwise. Emotions still ragged from the night before surged to life at the contact and Gareth fought their burgeoning power. No, Angelica was anxious to get downstairs. It was a matter of pride to her that she functioned as a working part of the household. He had made one important change in her life. He would have to wait, bide his time before making another.

His fingers moved quickly to fasten the buttons, anxious as he was to spare himself the temptation of the smooth white flesh exposed to his touch. Releasing a short sigh as the job was completed, Gareth turned Angelica toward him, his eyes moving over her supreme beauty in silence as she raised her eyes to his face. He touched her cheek lightly and smiled, his fingertip moving to brush the incredible length of lashes surrounding her great silver eyes. Succumbing to the emotion running hot inside him, he allowed himself one more taste of her mouth before he stepped back firmly.

"I know, you want to get downstairs, darlin'. I have a few things to do, too. I don't remember tendin' to Major very well last night when I came home. I had other things on my mind, and I think the old boy deserves better treatment than that. But I sure hope Maria gets breakfast ready fast. I've worked up a considerable appetite . . ."

Turning her face away as a revealing color began to pervade its contours, Angelica glanced toward the dresser.

Her eyes touching on the brush that rested there, she said tentatively, "Gareth, if I might use your brush . . ."

Unreasonably annoyed that she should seek permission for such a simple matter, Gareth frowned and grumbled his assent. With that simple question she had succeeded in putting a measure of distance between them and he resented its intrusion into the intimacy of the moment. He reached for his clothes. He had donned his trousers and boots, and was reaching for his shirt when he became aware of Angelica's perusal. His eyes flicking up, he caught her stare, his heart jumping a beat as she took a step closer to him. Reaching out her hand, she placed her palm against the bare skin of his chest, her fingers moving almost unnoticeably in the dark hairs which peppered the muscled surface. Her translucent silver gaze was pensive.

"Gareth, you are again angry with me. I admit to confusion with your rapidly vacillating moods. I only begin to believe I understand you and you are once again another person. Will I ever truly comprehend your Anglo ways?"

His annoyance softening under the weight of her sincere concern, Gareth covered her hand with his, pulling her palm up to his mouth to press a warm kiss against its heart.

"It isn't a matter of Anglo difference, Angelica. No, that isn't the key . . ." Realizing he could not yet explain that it was his frustrated love for her which caused him torment, he continued huskily. ". . . but you'll find that key soon. It's there darlin', waitin' for you . . ."

Her hair was combed into a smooth bun, and he curved his hand around the back of her head, delighting in the silky texture of her hair under his palm. He risked one last kiss. Quickly pulling on his shirt before his determination failed, Gareth buttoned it quickly and opened the door. He slid his arm around her waist and urged her into the hallway. They were walking down the staircase side by side when the feeling hit him. It was all going to work out well. Angelica would grow to love him . . . want him as deeply as he wanted her. He knew it . . . could feel it in his bones. God, he felt so good!

Angelica brushed a straying wisp of hair from her cheek and placed the last of the biscuits on the baking tin. The kitchen had barely been cleaned up from breakfast, when preparations for the afternoon meal had begun. The men had been unusually quiet at breakfast, and she suspected aching heads and testy stomachs had been the main cause for their silence. She had done her best to ignore the knowing glances which had moved her way as she entered the dining room. Gareth's early departure from town had been duly noted the night before, and his warm perusal as she move around the table had received equal attention as well.

It had taken all her determination to force herself back into that room again. But she supposed she had to force herself to become accustomed to such knowing glances. Gareth would no longer tolerate their separation at night. He had made that abundantly clear, and if she were to be entirely honest she would have to admit she felt a deep satisfaction in again awakening in his arms. In any case, she no longer had any choice. Her determination to keep Gareth's possessiveness at bay was a war she stood no chance of winning. Time . . . time would now determine the course of her future status, and she no longer chose to give that uncertainty the weight of her concern.

If anything, she felt a deep gratitude for Maria and Sophie's reaction to her emergence from the upstairs rooms that morning. There had been no hint of scorn in their glances. Instead, she had read acceptance in their eyes, a sense of inevitability that she herself should have determined weeks before.

"Angelica . . ."

Turning at the sound of Maria's voice, Angelica noted the older woman's gesture in the direction of the freshly washed and dried plates.

"The table must be set for the noon meal."

"But . . . it is early, is it not, Maria?" Glancing to the clock on the mantel over the fireplace, Angelica checked her instinctive assessment of the hour.

"*Si*, but the men will be starting out early this afternoon.

Mr. Gareth has allowed them the morning for lesser duties which would put the least stress on their aching heads. It is an unspoken consideration he provides his men, and one which is greatly appreciated. But he will allow them no respite from work this afternoon, and he will be expecting the table to be ready early so that he might make certain to waste little time in getting them back to their main tasks of the day."

Nodding her head, finally understanding the reason for the men's milling about the yard and stable area, Angelica moved immediately to her task. She had returned to the kitchen for the cups when she heard the first muffled shouts from the yard beyond the entrance to the house. Pausing at the unexpected commotion, she saw recognition dawn first on Maria's and then Sophie's face. Her own realization came a few minutes later, causing a knot of tension to tighten in her stomach as smiles brightened the two women's faces.

Maria's declaration confirmed Angelica's conclusion.

"Mr. Jon . . . he has come home. Quickly, Sophie, put the meat on the platter. Mr. Jon will be hungry. We do not want to keep him waiting."

As if responding to Maria's words, the sound of hearty male voices and laughter filtered into the kitchen. The men were entering the house, and not waiting for an invitation, Maria and Sophie moved toward the dining room. A hearty male voice greeted the two women the moment they stepped into sight, its depth of tone evoking a strange sense of unease. Gareth's father . . . Her heart was beginning to thunder in her chest and perspiration broke out on her brow. Apprehension set her to trembling, and she closed her eyes against the sound of that same deep voice in light-hearted conversation with men who were obviously sincere in their welcome.

Gareth's voice, remarkably similar in tone to his father's, reached her ear. In her state of agitation, she did not comprehend his comment, but the uneasy silence that fell on the meeting increased her trembling. No . . . she did not want it to be this way . . . She could not face him in front of

431

the men. Her trembling increased and an encroaching darkness threatened her. Breathing deeply, she steeled herself against it, fought the echo of labored breathing which sought to overcome her. No . . . she would not allow her nightmare to overcome her in the bright light of day, to threaten reality.

She heard Gareth call her name, and she took another deep breath. Forcing a surface calm in direct contrast to the shattering fear which had suddenly beset her, Angelica took a step toward the living room. Gareth called her name again, and she took another step and then another. She was nearing the doorway when she heard Gareth's deeply affected voice.

"Pa, I have someone I'd like you to meet. Angelica . . ."

Angelica stepped into the doorway of the room, her eyes snapping to the graying blond head which turned in her direction. The buzz of voices went on around her, refusing to register in her mind as Angelica's glance locked with the man's incredulous blue-eyed stare. She continued walking slowly toward him, as if propelled by an unseen force that controlled her shaken mind. She could feel the color draining from her face just as it drained from the lined face of the man who could not draw his eyes from her.

She did not see Gareth's instinctive movement toward her which was stopped by his father's soft cry.

"Gareth . . . God . . . where did you find her?"

Within minutes Jonathan Dawson's arms were around her, the strength of his embrace causing her a sweet pain as he repeated his choked question into Gareth's astonished face.

"Gareth, where . . . where did you find your sister?"

The room was in total silence. Numb, Angelica remained motionless in the tall man's embrace, her eyelids fluttering weakly as he drew back to study her face. Tears were overflowing the brilliant blue eyes so close to hers, running down the shakingly familiar lined cheeks. She shook her head. No . . . no, it could not be true . . .

"You do remember me, don't you, darlin'? You were a big girl when I lost you . . . almost eight years old. You

432

must remember somethin' about me. Say somethin', Jeanette. Tell me you know . . ."

But Gareth was pulling her from his father's arms, his eyes blazing.

"No, Pa, you're wrong. This isn't Jeanette. I never thought you'd think . . ." He hesitated, swallowing roughly as he sought a way to make his father understand.

Angelica was shuddering visibly, swaying in the hands of an unknown force which kept her eyes pinned on Jonathan Dawson's white face. His blond brows knotting in confusion, he turned away from his son. His words were low, muttered under his breath.

"It has to be Jeanette. It's like seein' Celeste come alive again. There was never anyone with eyes like Celeste. Only Jeanette . . . never anyone so beautiful. Tell him, Jeanette. Tell Gareth who you are . . . my daughter . . . his sister. Tell him, darlin'. Tell me. . ."

Jonathan Dawson's voice was reverberating in her mind, releasing visions long suppressed. Angelica opened her mouth and tried to speak, but the effort failed. She could hear Gareth's voice in strident protest, could hear Jonathan Dawson's low entreaty. The world was whirling around her, the same darkness beginning to gain control. She heard the sound of labored breathing and her eyes snapped wide in fear. It was closing in on her and she was a child again, alone and afraid. She saw her father's face, his brilliant blue eyes lighting the rapidly enveloping blackness. She cried out his name, the words tumbling out from between her frozen lips in the moment before the lightless void opened up to swallow her.

"Papa Jon. *Au secours!* Help me! *Je t'aime . . . Je t'aime . . .*"

The numbing darkness was lifting. A refreshing coolness brushed the skin of her forehead, her cheeks, aided her effort to cast the blackness aside, and Angelica sought to open her eyes. But the heavy curtain which covered her mind was unwilling to cooperate and she felt a growing panic. She was lost . . . lost in this limbo . . .

"Angelica . . . darlin', are you all right? Open your eyes . . . talk to me . . ."

Responding to the familiar sound of Gareth's voice, Angelica increased her efforts, finally knowing the first measure of success as a slit of light penetrated the darkness which had held her in its grasp. She was coming slowly back to consciousness. Unable to remember the cause of her sudden departure from reality, she sought a line to safety, finding it in Gareth's gaze as he looked down earnestly into her face.

She was in Gareth's room . . . the same room they had shared the night before. She was lying on his bed and he was pressing a wet cloth against her forehead, her cheeks. As her gaze became more steady, his hand dropped away, only to come back within a few moments to tenderly caress the damp surface. His voice was a low, worried whisper.

"Are you all right, darlin'? I need to hear you talk to me . . . tell me you're all right."

"Gareth . . ."

But another face came into her line of vision as a tall, blond man moved to stand behind Gareth. His appearance stole her breath, and Angelica gasped. She was beginning to tremble and Gareth darted a quick look over his shoulder.

"You're frightening her, Pa. You'd better leave."

"No. I have to talk to her. Jeanette, don't you . . ."

Gareth's tone was suddenly vicious. His hands moved protectively to Angelica's arms. "I told you, she's not Jeanette, damn it!"

"She is! Didn't you hear what she said before she fainted? She called me Papa Jon. Jeanette always called me that. And she spoke in her mother's native tongue. She asked me to help her . . . said she loved me." Turning toward Angelica, Jonathan whispered with obvious difficulty, "Tell him, Jeanette. Tell him, so we can settle this thing once and for all. You remember me, don't you, darlin'."

Aware of the intense scrutiny of both men, Angelica swallowed tightly. Her mind was a maze of rapidly chang-

434

ing shadows, hushed echoes of labored breaths, but a light was growing in the center of the shifting mists . . . a light suspiciously alike in color to the brilliant blue of Jonathan Dawson's eyes. She remembered. She remembered . . .

"Jeanette, come quickly. We will be leaving soon. Have you packed your special box?"

"Oui, Mama."

"Papa will be waiting for us. We are going home at last . . ."

The shadows were shifting, and she cried out. The sun was going down on a plain that rolled endlessly to the sky, but there was no peace in the setting of the sun. Gunshots and savage screams filled air clouded with dust, the thunder of hoofbeats, and moans of the dying. The hooves of Indian ponies pounded the earth, riding past the wagon under which she lay. Gunshots were ringing closer, hitting the ground near her and she hid her face in her mother's blue velvet dress. She crushed its softness against her, no longer fearing to mark its loveliness. Her mother strained her close in a frantic grip. The echo of her mother's racing heart was beating against her ear when they were jerked apart with horrifying abruptness and she was suddenly bereft.

She looked up, the sight of her mother's terrified gray eyes halting her frightened scream. They were taking her away, those long-haired men whose reddened, bared skin shone with sweat and dirt. They were dragging her roughly, their hands twisted in her long, dark hair, and her mother was screaming, calling out to her. One of the men lifted his hand and struck her. Her mother's screams stopped and she tumbled forward, striking the ground with startling impact, and was then still. Her eyes riveted on her mother's unmoving form, she saw the blue velvet of her mother's gown mingling with dust and blood on the scarred ground. A savage hand reached down, rending the dress from her shoulder to waist, and she screamed her protest. No! It was Papa's favorite dress. Mama had worn it because they would be seeing him at the end of that day's journey. They had almost reached their home!

But her mother was stirring! Drawing herself to her knees, she scrambled from beneath the wagon. Within minutes she was at her mother's side, only to be snatched away by a vicious hand. There was the sound of hoofbeats beside her and she was suddenly scooped up into the air and jerked onto horseback in front of another of the foul-smelling, naked men. She was screaming, calling out in her terror, but her mother was helpless to aid her. Her breasts all but bared by the cruel, savage hand, her mother stood swaying unsteadily, blood running from the corner of her mouth as another of the barbarians, his pony on the run, swept her roughly to its back and galloped into the encroaching darkness . . .

"Jeanette . . ."

Gareth's arm snapped out roughly to keep his father from Angelica's side, breaking into the shifting shadows which had overwhelmed her mind. His voice was a vicious snarl.

"Get away from her, Pa. She is not Jeanette, I tell you. She's Angelica Rodrigo. I brought her back from Real del Monte with me. She's not my sister, she's my . . ."

"Gareth!" His lined face draining of the last of its color, Jonathan Dawson halted Gareth's declaration. "I don't know what you think, or how you came to find her, but this girl is Jeanette DuBois. You never met Celeste . . . never saw her. If you did, you'd know she could be no one else."

"No!"

"Gareth, ask her! Ask her who she is. I don't know what she told you before, but she remembers, I know she does."

"It's a mistake . . . a coincidence. Angelica was taught by the padre in the village. She speaks a few languages, and French . . ."

". . . French was her mother's tongue . . ."

"No, damn it, no!"

"Ask her, Gareth."

Angelica's eyes were moving back and forth between the two men. The younger was dark-haired, and -eyed, fury

436

coloring the hard lines of a face which had been filled with tenderness only short hours before as he had held her in his arms in this very room. Angelica felt a flush of pain. The older one was blond, as unlike the younger as could be imagined in physical appearance, the only similarity manifesting itself in the uncompromising lines of his face as he stared into his son's eyes.

But the shadows intervened, blotting out reality, bringing her back to a night of darkness. Fear, stark and all encompassing again controlled her mind. She sitting on the ground in a rough, hide dwelling, her mother's arms holding her tight. She could feel her mother's trembling as the savage drumming continued outside, accompanied by wild shrieks and guttural calls which failed to disturb the primitive rhythm. She heard it again, the cry of pain, deep and penetrating, curdling her blood, echoing in the night, and she buried her face in the battered velvet of her mother's dress. Yes, she could hide there as she always had. Her mother would keep her safe.

Footsteps sounded close by, approaching their shelter. Her mother's arms stiffened, clutching her closer as a ragged flap was jerked upward to reveal the towering height of a naked savage. He swayed unsteadily in the entrance before stepping forward to stagger toward them. He jerked her mother from her clutching embrace and dragged her to the entrance of the shelter. Screaming her protest, her mother scratched and kicked at her captor in an effort to break free, but it was to no avail. Dragging her brutally by the hair the naked man threw her onto the ground outside the door, his hands roughly ripping her mother's dress from her shoulders.

Angelica saw the reflection of the fire which roared behind them dancing on her mother's white flesh . . . saw the horror in her mother's eyes as the savage dropped down atop her, forcing his body onto hers. She heard her mother's screams, was raising herself to her knees to go to her aid as her mother fumbled at the strap slung around the man's naked waist. Her searching hand found the knife sheathed there and swept it free to swing it roughly toward

437

the red, shining back.

There was a slash of red on naked flesh and a sharp outcry. There was a glimpse of black, glinting eyes, filled with fury before a brutal hand jerked the knife free from her mother's grip and raised it high to plunge it deeply into her naked chest.

The echoes of her own, horrified scream reverberated again in Angelica's mind, shaking the channels of memory, returning the terror of the moment when she drew herself to her feet. The savage had abandoned her mother, left her on the ground as he had staggered into the flickering darkness. She scrambled to her mother's side, leaned over to see her face even as she struggled to cover her naked flesh. There was blood . . . blood streaming from a deep gash, trickling from the corner of her mother's pale lips. Her mother's breathing was deep, labored, and she cried out, only to be halted by her mother's gasping whisper.

"Jeanette . . . do not be afraid, *ma chérie*. Do . . . do not be afraid when I leave you. Your papa . . . he will come. *Oui*. He will take you from these people. He loves you, Jeanette. He . . . he will find you . . . take you home."

Her mother's breathing was growing more ragged. It was faltering, the torment in each rasp tearing at her own heart. Expiring . . . her breathing was expiring . . .

But there was one last, strained whisper.

"Tell him, Jeanette. Tell Papa for me, *'Je t'aime . . . Je t'aime' . . .*"

There was a rattle . . . a low choking sound . . . and the breathing faltered again. Then it was done.

The memory was gone, but the horror remained. She was back, lying on the bed in the sunny room. She strained to pull herself to a sitting position despite the protest of the man who sat at her side. She looked past him, seeing only one face.

Her eyes locking with brilliant blue eyes trained on her face, she raised her arms and called out with a shuddering sob, "*Je t'aime . . . je t'aime*, Papa Jon. *Je t'aime . . .*"

Gareth allowed himself to be pushed aside. He pulled

himself to his feet as his father assumed his place at Angelica's side and drew her into his arms. Incredulity flooded his mind with disbelief even as he saw Angelica's tear-streaked face pressed against his father's shoulder, heard her sobbing words and his ragged replies. No, it could not be true? Angelica could not be his own . . .

He could not say the word, even in his mind. Rage suffused him. God, no! It could not be true! Angelica . . . his Angelica . . .

Bile surged to his throat, and Gareth turned from the scene of his torment. He swallowed against its bitterness and took a deep breath. This was wrong . . . all wrong. He need keep his calm and reason this whole thing out. The ragged sobs behind him tore at his heart as he took his first step toward the door, and then his next. He would allow his father this time with Angelica but it would be limited at best. He would find out the truth, and everything would be all right again. And then he would tell his father that he loved Angelica . . . that she was his. Everything would be all right and Angelica would be his again . . .

Chapter XII

Gareth stood adamantly in front of his father's desk, his chest heaving with agitation. His eyes flashed toward Angelica's tense figure as she stood a few feet away and he despised himself for the surge of hunger the sight of her evoked inside him. His jaw ticking in an attempt to control his emotions, he took a deep breath. He had not been allowed to be alone with Angelica for two days. She had spent most of that time in the room beside her father's, talking to no one except him. Each attempt to speak to her had found his father close on his heels, and Gareth could countenance his deprivation no longer. He had demanded to talk to them both, and his father had finally relented.

"All right, what did she tell you?" Gareth's voice grating on the silence of the room, he flashed a look of pure hatred in Angelica's direction. Ignoring her paling visage, he continued harshly, "I don't believe a word of all this. You've managed to convince yourself she's telling you the truth because it's what you want to believe! Angelica is not my lost half-sister, Jeanette DuBois!"

"Gareth, please . . . sit down."

"I don't want to sit down!"

His eyes moving over his father's weary face, Gareth stated harshly, "There's only one thing I want . . ."

"And you can't have it, Gareth . . ." His piercing eyes reflecting his pain, Jonathan Dawson shook his head. "You . . . you have to forget everything that's happened before this. Jeanette didn't know . . . couldn't remember . . ."

"Don't call her Jeanette!" His eyes flashing again in Angelica's direction, he fought his reaction as Angelica lowered herself slowly to the chair behind her. "Her name is Angelica. Angelica Rodri—"

"Gareth . . . she's Jeanette DuBois. There's no other explanation for the memories which are returning to her more clearly each day . . ."

"It's a trick . . . she planned all this. I should have known . . . should have realized that the change in her was too quick . . . too complete. You didn't know her in Real del Monte. She fought me every step of the way. She . . ." Gareth's voice choked to a halt and he swallowed deeply in an attempt to continue.

"Gareth, I don't want to hear . . ."

"But you're going to hear it, damn it! I don't have to tell you how I felt the minute I saw her. Hell, I didn't stand a chance. But she fought me at every turn. She managed to hold off that bastard, Esteban Arricalde, too, and she never gave an inch. I had never seen anythin' like her. But Arricalde got to her . . . was pushing her into going with him to Mexico City. I . . . I couldn't stand the thought of that, so I offered to take her back here with me.

"She jumped at the chance. I was too stupid to realize there was somethin' behind it. Damned fool that I was, I was so damned caught up in her . . ."

"Gareth, I told you, I don't want to hear this!"

Gareth's voice hardened. "You're missin' the point, Pa, so listen to me, and let yourself understand. Angelica is the daughter of the town whore in Real del Monte. Ask her . . . go ahead and ask her. Her life's been hell since she was born because her mother's reputation washed off on her. She hadn't been able to get a decent position until the priest talked Señor Arricalde into taking her into service in the Arricalde hacienda. She needed money. She needs it

441

still. It couldn't have been hard for her to learn about my background when I arrived . . . the Arricaldes know all about us . . . you and Celeste DuBois . . . about the Indian raid and the way Celeste and Jeanette disappeared without a trace on the way to the Circle D. And servants talk."

Gareth looked again toward Angelica. She was sitting motionlessly in the chair, her face expressionless. She was pale, exhausted. The light shadows under her sober silver eyes lent her an almost ethereal beauty. A lovely, deceitful vision . . .

"She told me she came to me the first time because I was 'a rich Texan.' " Gareth gave a low, mirthless laugh. "I had no mind to correct her. I figured in comparison to her, in her meager circumstances, I was rich. But I should have. I knew her mind was quick, that she was intelligent and resourceful, but I underestimated her . . . and I trusted her. We struck a bargain and fool that I was, I truly expected her to live up to it.

"But instead, she obviously had a better plan in mind. She wasn't going to be satisfied with a kitchen maid's salary for the year she was to be here. Oh, no, not when she could be the lady of the house . . . the long lost daughter of the patron. In that way she could have it all, and there would be no strings attached. She would even manage to free herself of me . . ."

"Gareth . . ."

Flashing her a vicious look, Gareth hesitated only briefly at Angelica's soft admonition. He leaned forward, his palms flat on the desk as he stared unblinkingly into his father's eyes.

"Think about it, Pa. She's been talkin' to you for two days, hasn't she? Has she said anythin' that couldn't have been dreamed up with some basic information about us and a little imagination? Has she given you any details that only Jeanette could know? Has she explained to you how she just happens to have a family, a father of sorts, a mother and a brother in Real del Monte?"

Gareth paused, his heart thundering in his chest as he

waited with bated breath for his father's reply.

"No, Gareth. Jeanette can't remember everythin'. She still has blank spots in her memory, but I'm convinced . . ."

"I'm convinced, too, Pa. I'm convinced she's a liar and out to get all she can, and you're a fool if you accept everythin' she says on just her word."

"No, I'm not goin' to do that, son . . ."

Momentarily taken aback, Gareth frowned. He had been so certain his father had been totally taken in. Hope surged to life inside him. Perhaps . . .

"Jeanette is upset about this thing with her family in Real del Monte. She asked me to write a letter to Padre Manuel, to find out the truth. I did it just to set her mind at rest. I had Brett take it in to town to the post office yesterday. She said the priest would know the truth, and she said that . . ."

Turning toward Angelica, Gareth shook his head, his eyes holding her shaken glance as he growled in a low voice, "No, I don't want to hear you tell me what Angelica said. Nobody has to do her talkin' for her. I want to hear her tell me herself. Talk to me, Angelica. Tell me why you asked my father to write to the priest . . ."

Angelica's face was working, her facade cracking under Gareth's steady perusal. When she finally spoke, her voice was a hoarse whisper.

"Gareth, none of what you said is true. I did not plan to deceive you. If I did in truth deceive you, then I deceived myself also. I . . . I need to know for sure what these dreams mean, Gareth, if I'm truly Jeanette DuBois. Because if I am, who is Angelica Rodrigo, and how did she come to be?" Pulling herself to her feet, Angelica took a step forward. She was trembling visibly as her gaze held Gareth's intently. "I need to know, Gareth. I need to know if you are truly my brother . . ."

"I'm not!" Gareth's denial was vehement, spontaneous. Despite himself, he had to fight the desire to take Angelica into his arms, to wipe the haunted look from her eyes. Despite it all—her devious machinations, her deceit—he

443

wanted her still. He could not see a method to her request to have his father write Padre Manuel, but he was certain the old priest was not in on her plan. His confrontation with the man had been too sharp, too filled with reproach to be insincere. No, she probably expected to brazen the matter out, hoping by the time a return letter was received she would have his father so wrapped around her little finger that no one would be able to touch her.

But she wouldn't get away from him. His mind had run the whole gamut of emotions in the two days since she had sprung this surprise on him. He had been incredulous, disbelieving, then suspicious and, in turn, angry. His anger had turned to rage as his father had erected a barrier between Angelica and himself, keeping her away from him. His rage stemmed from the realization that Angelica had probably planned it that way. He had come to realize that she had just been lulling him into a sense of security so that he would be ineffective against her when she put her plan into effect. Her loving compliance . . . her gasping passion . . . an act he had allowed himself to believe because he had so much wanted to believe. He gave a low, self-deprecating laugh. He had been taken in far worse than his father, and he was more the fool, because he wanted Angelica still.

And he would have her again. When the response was received from Padre Manuel, he would not allow his father to dupe himself. He would set the whole situation straight, and then he would take it from there.

Beautiful, deceitful Angelica. And he loved her. And he wanted her. God, how he wanted her . . .

"Gareth . . ."

Angelica's low whisper snapped him from his thoughts as she took another step closer. He could see the heavy heaving of her chest, the brightness of tears that turned her eyes to molten silver. Her trembling had escalated to shuddering, and he ached to hold her. But he steeled himself against her. She was a superb actress. She had taken him in completely. She would not do it again.

"Gareth . . . I'm sorry. I wish . . ."

Almost at the end of his control, Gareth rasped harshly,

"What do you wish, Angelica?"

Paling even further under the weight of his gaze, Angelica turned away, and the ache inside him grew as Jonathan stepped forward to take Angelica comfortingly into his arms. Unable to stand anymore, Gareth turned abruptly and strode out of the room. He slammed the door closed behind him and paused to take a deep breath. The house was empty and silent. It had been that way since his father had returned, and he was beginning to realize it would probably stay that way until this entire charade with Angelica was settled.

How long would he have to wait for a response to the letter. One month . . . two? It was a lifetime . . . a lifetime if he must spend it seeing Angelica and not be allowed to touch her. She wasn't Jeanette DuBois! He would have known . . . would have sensed it if she truly was his father's illegitimate daughter. He would have known. God, she couldn't be his . . . She couldn't . . .

No, he would not entertain even the possibility in his mind! She was Angelica Rodrigo, the beautiful little *puta* who had sold herself to him. And she was the only woman he had ever truly loved. Waiting would be hard, but when proof came of her deceit, he would make up for the time they had lost. He would make up for it in every possible way.

The door slammed behind Gareth, and Angelica leaned against Jonathan Dawson's chest as his embrace tightened. Her mind registered the familiarity of that embrace, memory stirring again as he rubbed her back comfortingly in an unconscious circular movement effective in reducing her anxiety. The veil which still clouded her mind parted slightly, allowing a flicker of memory past its diaphanous folds.

She was curled on a comfortable lap, dozing against a broad chest. She was looking up sleepily to see a reassuring warmth in the brilliant blue eyes that returned her gaze. A wide hand was moving against her back in a relaxing motion, making slow circles that lulled her to the comfort of sleep. She smiled and raised her hand to touch the man's cheek. It was rough, but his skin was cool and she was filled with contentment in his arms. She was snuggling her head back against his chest and the memory ceased.

Looking up, Angelica caught and held that same blue-eyed gaze of her memory, a low sob catching in her throat at the inescapability of realization that ensued.

"It is true, isn't it. I'm Jeanette DuBois. I must be. There is no other explanation."

The grief in her voice was undeniable, bringing a frown to Jonathan Dawson's brow.

"Is that so bad, Jeanette?"

Angelica's low response was almost inaudible.

"I don't know . . ."

"You're referring to Gareth. It's new to him. It's come as a shock that you are his sister. He has deep feelings for you. It will take time, but he . . ."

Angelica could stand no more. Drawing back from his arms, she said stiffly, "I'm tired. Please excuse me. I'm going to my room now, but first I must stop to talk to Maria. I have been neglectful of my duties of late. I want to reassure her . . ."

"You no longer have any 'duties' in this house, Jeanette." His blond brows working into a frown, Jonathan Dawson stiffened. "You're not a servant here."

A peculiar panic moving across her colorless face, Angelica shook her head.

"Please, Papa Jon, do not take that away from me. I need something . . . a way to avoid the pictures that haunt my mind."

Relenting in the face of her despair, Jonathan Dawson offered softly, "You're free to go wherever you want in this house and to do whatever you like. But the word 'duty' doesn't enter into it. The only duty here is mine to you as your father." Jonathan paused, understanding written in the deep lines of his face. "Jeanette, try not to worry. Gareth will be able to accept the new status between you in time."

Unable to respond, Angelica allowed her eyes to absorb

his concern for long moments before silently nodding and turning away. She was walking through the doorway and into the hall when the response formed itself clearly in her mind for the first time.

"Yes, but will I?"

Chapter XIII

Esteban carefully assessed the crowded conditions of the great hall from his position at its rear. Accustomed to clothes tailored to his specific measurements, he was uncomfortable in the simple, ready-made clothes he wore. Texan garments . . . a plain cotton shirt and trousers, a broad-brimmed hat, a vest, each piece free of the elaborate detail and trim which set Mexican garments aside from those of such inferior quality. He kept his face carefully averted from curious gazes. One glance in the mirror had told him that despite his disguise, his partician features marked him of a class far above the people of the common herd who jammed these inadequate facilities—even with the full two days' growth of beard he sported in an attempt to aid his masquerade.

He consoled himself that he had only just arrived in the Texan port city of Brazoria and for that reason would not be easily recognized in his position of covert observer of the newly returned Stephen Austin. Oh, yes, he was a representative of el Presidente Santa Anna in extremely good standing . . . Esteban suppressed his grunt of satisfaction. Despite the fact that his warning to Antonio about Captain Thompson's poor handling of the situation at Anahuac had come too late to avoid the major damage of its effect, he knew Antonio had been impressed with his clear assessment of the situation. The fact that Captain Thompson had been stupid enough to pursue his goal of capturing the *San Felipe* and had failed, only to be forced to surrender and to be taken prisoner to New Orleans by the Americans, had only served to bear out the validity of his assessment.

He had received as his reward the assignment to determine and report back to el presidente the course Stephen Austin would take after his release. Antonio was hopeful that the sober-minded Austin would heed his warnings and advise his people to follow a cautious course of action and remain loyal to the central government of Mexico. Antonio recognized the importance of the word Stephen Austin would spread among his followers . . . knew that these people would be greatly influenced by this man whom they considered the father of the Texas colony.

Had he received this assignment only six months before, Esteban was certain he would have revolted against orders which caused him this discomfort, this danger, but now . . . yes, they suited his plans exactly. With each step he drew closer to his ultimate goal. General Cos was presently heading toward Texas with a large armed force. He was to immediately report his findings to Cos and await Cos's disposition of the information. He would then remain to aid Cos in whatever action he chose to take. Yes, he had no doubt that within the next month, he, Colonel Esteban Arricalde, would be in the exact position he desired in this hostile state. However, all his plans hung in the balance of Austin's comments tonight and for that reason he found himself as anxious for Austin's remarks as the Texans who milled around him.

The great hall was filled to bursting. An air of expectancy hung over the Texans gathered there, the same expectancy which had hung over the town of Brazoria itself since Stephen Austin had arrived back in Texas. Antonio had been ingenious in the way in which he had managed to hold Austin hostage for the good conduct of his colony by shifting the questionable charges against him from one court to another while he had been incarcerated. But his ploy had finally been played out and Antonio had found it wise to release Austin at last.

At present Austin's followers jammed the hall for his welcome, anxious to lend him their support. Tension was rife as Austin drew himself to his feet and prepared to address the waiting crowd.

Startled gasps echoed from the crowded floor, accompanied by worried glances from those familiar with Austin's former appearance. It was only too obvious that the prison experience had adversely affected his health. Austin's face was palid and lined, his demeanor that of a man far older than his forty-two years. Always slender, he appeared to have diminished to a point just short of emaciation. A persistent cough interrupted his attempt to begin his comments, necessitating still more patience from a crowd whose patience with waiting was already long exhausted. But silence reigned, allowing the Texan the opportunity he sought to regain his breath.

Esteban raised his head, aware of the fact that all eyes were now focused on Austin's face. In a voice often interrupted by a hacking cough, Austin began slowly. Esteban's eyes narrowed as Austin related in great detail his conduct in Mexico City and discussed the position of Texas. The Texan's voice growing in strength, he stated he recognized the critical state of affairs and the almost inevitable result. Patiently, he related that he felt it was his duty to convey Santa Anna's friendly messages and his wishes for the prosperity of Texas, and his intention to use his influence to give to its people a special organization suited to their education, habits, and situation. Austin informed them of his advice to Santa Anna not to send troops to Texas . . . that war would be the inevitable result, but he also conveyed his thoughts that Santa Anna would not heed his warning. He stated that he felt the federal constitution would be overthrown and a central government established.

Esteban's attention to Austin's comments, as well as the attention of the others who overflowed the hall, was unwavering, despite the fact that Austin had been talking for almost an hour. His frown of concentration increased as Austin paused, obviously nearing the conclusion of his statement. Total silence prevailed as Austin surveyed the sea of faces waiting expectantly for his next words.

"The crisis is such as to bring it home to the judgment of every man that something must be done, without delay. The question will perhaps be asked, 'What are we to do?' I have already indicated my opinion. Let all personalities or division or excitements or passion or violence be banished from among us. Let there be a general consultation of the people of Texas as speedily as possible . . . to be convened of the best, calmest, most intelligent, and firmest men in the country. And let them decide what representation ought to be made to the general government, and what ought to be done in the future."

Raising his hand, Stephen Austin offered his glass in toast, his voice rising strongly, to be heard clearly around the crowded hall.

"The constitutional rights and security and peace of Texas—they ought to be maintained! Jeopardized as they are now, they demand a general consultation of the people."

Glasses were raised as voices echoed Austin's sentiment, and Esteban turned to make a hasty exit. Within a few minutes he had slipped from the hall and was walking down the street, intent on returning to his room. His annoyance was increasing.

Damn the man! Santa Anna had underestimated him! He was far more clever than both he and el presidente had thought. Austin's remarks were set in exactly the right vein. He had managed to warn the settlers . . . stir their spirit without causing the agitation that would provoke foolhardy acts. And he had also established the need for unity, cooperation between rival factions. That rivalry had allowed neither side any measure of success and had been the greatest asset to el presidente. Judging from the manner in which Austin's remarks were received, that would no longer be the case. el presidente would doubtless find that to his distinct disadvantage.

Esteban could only hope hot-headed agitators would continue their harassment and deter the unity certain to be stimulated by Austin's plea. Cos would be arriving in Texas shortly and needed only a little more time to become firmly entrenched. And once he was in the position he sought, these poorly disciplined, ignorant Texans would not stand a chance against him. The rebellion would be short-lived, and he had no doubt that the Texans would be easily whipped into compliance by Cos's strong hand.

His hand . . . his own unyielding hand would be effective in bringing the Texans to heel once the conflict was over! Esteban felt a flush of elation. He had already voiced his desire to become the administrator of a particular district in Texas when the conflict was over. He had stressed his strong desire to serve el presidente in that capacity and that he was particularly suited to such duties. He had stated firmly that he felt he would do el presidente credit in that field.

He remembered the lifting of Antonio's brow and the small smile which had flicked across his lips. Antonio admired his audacity . . . his ambition. He had proved himself in Antonio's service, and he had no doubt he would get the post he sought.

Esteban approached the hotel and ascended the steps to the front door quickly, his alert gaze making a quick, assessing sweep of the lobby as he made his way to the staircase. He would be leaving Brazoria early . . . at dawn. He would make his way back to his prearranged point of meeting with his personal guard. He had sacrificed their protection in this particular case to avoid suspicion, but when properly uniformed, he would again have them at his heels and be on his way. A copy of his report would soon be in Antonio's hands, and when Cos arrived he would report to Cos personally and take his place at the general's side.

Yes, everything was working perfectly. His revenge would soon be complete. The arrogant, ignorant Texans would be chastised, and he would make certain Gareth Dawson would suffer the full weight of the poisonous emotion inside him, eating so unceasingly at his vitals, refusing him peace. Angelica . . . the beautiful, gray-eyed bitch would then be his. Yes, retribution was almost at hand.

Exhilaration brought a smile to his face as Esteban walked into his room and slammed the door behind him. He had only to wait a little longer . . . just a short time more . . .

Angelica tossed restlessly on the broad bed, her eyes moving to the window through which shone a brilliant half moon. She was grateful for its light, realizing it would be successful in dispelling the darkness outside her room. There would be no difficulty in navigating the road safely tonight, no matter the time or the condition in which Gareth came home.

Angelica's eyes moved to the dresser and the small clock that rested there. It was almost two . . . Her eyes remained on the small, painted face of the dainty clock. It was really quite beautiful. There were many beautiful things in this room she had occupied since the day Jonathan Dawson had come home to the Circle D. Had she been in better condition, she might have resisted him more effectively and insisted on maintaining her old room. But she had been overwhelmed by fragmented memories inundating her mind, bits and pieces of a life which still was not clear to her.

But Jon had moved her directly from the room in which she had awakened . . . Gareth's room . . . to the room beside his. She was grateful he had not offered her that one . . . She still could not face it . . . the room he had prepared for her mother . . . the one she had never seen.

Her heart skipped a beat. Sometimes she was so certain, and other times so unsure of just who she truly was. The nightmares . . . they continued still, but not as frequently. The difference was that each visitation now opened a new facet of memory. Total recall firmly resisted her, and she was beginning to become uncertain if she would ever remember the events of her past with full clarity. Padre Manuel's response to Papa Jon's letter had still not arrived, and her anxiety was such that she was uncertain if she truly wished to see it come.

Angelica turned away from the face of the clock and twisted restlessly in an attempt to make herself more comfortable. The bed was large, the sheets smooth and fresh. A lovely sleeping garment of white cotton trimmed with lace caressed her flesh. Gareth had bought it for her before . . . had insisted that her skin was meant to be touched with lace.

Angelica closed her eyes against the heat which accumulated there and swallowed tightly. Thoughts held at bay during the light of day overwhelmed her even as she struggled to resist them. Gareth's arms around her, holding her close, the warm flesh of his chest pressed against her cheek. She remembered the fanning of his breath against her hair, the scent of his skin in her nostrils. She remembered the stroke of his hand, the taste of his mouth as it moved against hers. Her breath choked on a sob.

No, she could not allow herself to think . . . not until she was certain . . .

Her mind returned to the supper table that evening. Due to Jon's insistence, she occupied a place to his right—had done so since he had returned. Gareth had not been present at the table that evening, and the atmosphere had been tense. Jon's question as to Gareth's whereabouts had been answered by Brett's surly response.

"He went into town. He told me he wasn't sure when he was comin' back." Jon's expression had tightened, and Brett had flicked an accusing glance in her direction before turning back to Jon. "It ain't my place to say, but I figure he's earned as many nights in town as he wants. Hell, he's been drivin' himself for the past month . . . stayin' out ridin' the fences long after the rest of the men have come in for the night . . . some nights not comin' in at all. He ain't let up on himself nohow, and the rest of the boys and me . . ."

"You're right, Brett, it isn't your place to say." His eyes blue ice, Jon clipped his words in a manner which clearly defined his anger. "We're all aware that the situation is difficult at present, and we don't need you to remind us. Gareth is a grown man. The way he conducts himself is his own concern." His voice dropping a notch, Jon continued. "But Jeanette isn't . . ."

"Her name ain't Jeanette. It's Angelica . . ."

Unable to stand the tension a moment longer, Angelica had risen to her feet and quietly excused herself from the table. Jon had come after her and she had taken the opportunity to plead his understanding of the circumstances that had caused Brett's outburst. The men were fully on Gareth's side, believing her a usurper at best. She could not blame them.

In all honesty, she was unsure how much longer she would be able to bear the uncertainty under which she was presently living, and the ache inside her which each thought of Gareth stirred to life. She closed her eyes and Gareth's image returned clearly. She longed to stroke his dark hair from his troubled brow, to smooth the tension from his cheeks. She longed to see warmth return to eyes that had turned to brittle onyx. Their gaze cut her . . . pierced her as sharply as a knife. She could bear it no longer . . . she could not. There was only one thing she could do . . .

Slumping in the saddle, Gareth allowed his eyes to drift closed for a fraction of a moment before forcing them open once again. He focused unsteadily on the moonlit road in front of him. Hell, the trip into town had been a complete waste of time. Approximately six hours earlier, desperation had forced him to the conclusion that a short night at the bar and some time with Lucy or one of the other girls would relieve his tension. But that treatment had been no more effective on his malady this time than it had been the last. He had accomplished little else with that exercise in frustration except to prove to himself even more acutely that Angelica was the only woman he wanted.

Damn, nothing was effective in easing his desire for her. Everything else paled into insignificance beside the dilemma that faced him. The only relief he had had from his tortured thoughts this night had been the short time while he had talked to Jeremy Barnes. Steve Austin was back in Texas. He had been surprised and relieved at the news, and he was well aware that his good friend Bill Travis would be intensely gratified by the changed tenor of Austin's thinking. War . . . it would soon come to that, but strangely, that prospect which had filled his thoughts and directed much of his activities prior to his journey to Real del Monte was suddenly far removed from his plane of thought.

Angelica . . . Angelica . . . She was all he thought about, the only light at the end of the long, black tunnel which stretched out ahead of him. How much longer before it came to an end and Padre Manuel's letter freed him? She had not relented a moment in her campaign to convince his father that she was indeed Jeanette DuBois. Her innocent confusion was so convincing, her vulnerability so excellently feigned. And she employed her "nightmares" well, only now it was his father who awoke her from their throes, not he. A furious jealousy burned him as he jerked his head to the side to squint at the turnoff onto the trail to the Circle D.

He rubbed a weary hand over his face and allowed it to drop back to his side. He was exhausted to the bone, but the thought of Angelica persisted. Her face in front of him, he allowed his eyes to drift closed. If only for a few exhausted moments, he needed peace.

The moonswept buildings of the Circle D came into view, and Gareth spurred his gelding to a faster pace. Major gave him little resistance, obviously as anxious as he to rest for the night. Forcing himself to head for the barn instead of the main house, Gareth dismounted and led his horse to his stall. Barely managing to unsaddle him, Gareth slapped the stall shut behind him and walked wearily across the yard and up the front steps of the house.

He reached for the doorknob, and turning it quickly, hesitated only a moment to take a last glance at the brilliant half moon. How many times had he lain beside Angelica on the long journey to Texas, watching her sleeping face in its silver glow? Would he ever be able to forget the way she looked with its silver light playing against her perfect skin?

Taking a firmer hold on his wandering thoughts, Gareth pulled open the door and squinted into the darkness in an attempt to adjust his eyes to the dim light of the room. It would do him no good to torture himself with such thoughts. What he needed now was sleep. Morning would come fast and he had no intention of . . .

A sudden movement in the darkness jerked Gareth to a stop. Turning abruptly, his eyes focused on a slender figure standing in the shadows near the window and his heart began an escalated beating. Was it truly Angelica or a

456

figment of his frustrated desire seeing fit to haunt him? Unwilling to wait a moment longer for confirmation, Gareth took the few long steps to the window and reached out. The warmth of Angelica's flesh met the palms of his hands and he pulled her unhesitantly into his arms.

"Angelica, I've missed you, darlin' . . ."

"Gareth . . . no, please . . ."

Angelica was stiffening in his arms, seeking to free herself from his embrace, and Gareth felt a moment of panic. His arms tightened, refusing her the freedom she sought.

"No, don't pull away, Angelica. I don't care, darlin'. I was angry as hell at first, but I'm not anymore . . . not now. I don't care how many lies you told Pa and me, we'll forget them all. We'll explain to Pa that you needed security and were just tryin' to get it for yourself in the only way you could. He'll be angry, but he'll understand eventually. You'll have him eatin' out of your hand again, you'll see. But in the meantime . . ."

"No, Gareth, please let me go. I didn't come here tonight for this. I just wanted to talk to you."

Unable to deny the true resistance he was meeting to his touch, Gareth allowed Angelica to draw back just far enough so that he might study her expression. He swallowed tightly at her beauty, steeling himself against the havoc it played on his senses. Her slender brows were drawn into a frown, her face earnest. Her lips were trembling, reflecting the quaking of her slender frame. She bit down sharply on their softness before attempting to speak.

"Gareth, I . . . I only wanted to talk to you . . ."

Gareth's voice was rough. His hands tightened on her shoulders.

"It isn't talking I have in mind, darlin'."

The sudden rigidity of Angelica's frame darkened Gareth's frown.

"You really don't believe me, do you, Gareth? I wasn't sure whether. . ."

"Is that why you're waitin' for me here tonight, Angelica?" Anger flared to life, tightening Gareth's grip on

Angelica's shoulders as he gave her an unconscious shake. "You're just wantin' to see if you've taken me in as completely as you have my father, aren't you . . ." Not waiting for her reply, seeing confirmation in her gaze, Gareth was silent for long seconds before his head dropped back and he gave a low, disbelieving laugh.

"It just goes to show you what a true fool I am about you, Angelica. Hell, I thought . . ." Gareth's laugh this time was more bitter as he forced himself to say the words. "I thought you were wantin' me as much as I've been wantin' you. I thought you were goin' to tell me you wanted to call this whole thing off before the priest's letter gets here . . . that you wanted me to go with you to my father and . . ."

"Gareth, I haven't been lying. This whole thing that's happened isn't a scheme. It's the truth. I don't understand it but . . ."

"No! You're lyin' again!" Jerking her tight against him, Gareth refused to listen. Grasping Angelica's chin, he turned it up to his until his lips were brushing hers with the fury of his words. "What do you feel when you're in my arms, Angelica? Does your body cry out, wantin' me to touch it? Do you ache to feel my arms around you . . . to feel me strokin' your skin? Does your mouth yearn for the touch of mine? Do you want to feel me deep inside you, darlin' . . . makin' love to you . . . fillin' you . . . showin' you just how right it is for me to be there, a part of you . . . ?"

"Gareth, please . . ." Angelica's trembling had turned to a deep shuddering that his strength could not suppress. The crystal depths of her eyes were pleading, her stiff lips fighting to form words appearing to be caught in her throat. "Gareth, I wanted to talk to you tonight, to plead with you to believe me. You were so angry . . . hated me so much. I could see the hate in your eyes when you looked at me, and . . . and I don't want you to hate me."

"What do you want, Angelica? Tell me that! Do you want me to love you . . . like a sister?" Gareth gave a low, explosive laugh. "No chance of that! You're wastin' your time . . ."

Unexpectedly, Gareth jerked her even closer, cupping her rounded buttocks with his hand, forcing her body against the rise of his passion as he grated harshly, "This isn't brotherly love . . . and there's no way you're goin' to convince me that I wouldn't know . . . wouldn't feel it in my bones if you were really Jeanette DuBois. No, Angelica, darlin', you're my little *puta*, Angelica Rodrigo, and the sad truth is that no matter what you've done or are tryin' to do, I haven't stopped wantin' you."

His mouth was closing over hers when Angelica began to fight him wildly, scratching and clawing at him in her frantic attempt to free herself from the touch of his lips. Startled at the open panic she exhibited, Gareth allowed a separation to come between them while suppressing her frantic struggles until she was once again still.

Tears streaming down her cheeks, she raised her eyes to him in open appeal. "Gareth, please believe me. Please. Whatever the outcome of Padre Manuel's response, whatever we eventually learn, I never lied to you. All I can tell you is that those dreams are becoming clearer. I'm remembering more and more, and . . ."

"No! You're not rememberin' anythin'. You're makin' this whole thing up." Beginning to experience a panic of his own, Gareth shook his head. "Don't ask me to believe you, Angelica, because . . ."

"You're goin' to have to believe her, Gareth—"

The unexpected voice which came from the hallway behind them snapped their heads in its direction as Jon Dawson walked toward them. "—because she's tellin' the truth."

There was a moment's silence as Gareth realized the futility of further discussion. Releasing Angelica, he clamped his teeth tightly shut in frustration as his father slid his arm around her and pulled her against his side. Gareth shook his head, and the weariness which had eluded him for a few short minutes returned. He met his father's gaze with true understanding.

"Pa, you're a damned fool. When that letter comes from

the priest, you're goin' to realize just how much a fool, but I'll be the last one to tell you I told you so. Hell, I've got no room to talk . . . no room at all."

Shooting Angelica one last look, Gareth allowed his eyes to move over her tear-streaked cheeks, to linger on her lips. His eyes flicked upward to hold her gaze, the unspoken questions that tortured him bright in his gaze.

Why, Angelica? Why? I told you I would be your blue velvet. Why couldn't you understand . . . ?

Muttering a soft good night, Gareth turned away and headed for the staircase to the second floor. It wouldn't be much longer, and then he would be free to explain himself more clearly to Angelica. He'd tell her that he'd be her blue velvet, and she could wrap herself in him for the rest of her life. In truth, he didn't want it any other way.

"You know what this means, don't you, Pa?"

Raising his eyes from the missive his son had just placed in his hands, Jonathan Dawson met his son's troubled gaze. The message from the Committee of Safety, conveyed by the young man who still stood at their side, could not be more clear.

"There's goin' to be a war."

"Damned right, sir!"

The unexpected comment expressed by Dennis Fairclough, eldest son of their nearest neighbors to the north and runner for the Committee of Safety, darkened father's and son's brows.

"I can't say the thought makes me too happy, most especially now when the situation is right upon us."

Nodding to his father's statement, Gareth added mentally, ". . . especially now . . ." He did not want to leave the homestead now with the situation between Angelica and himself unsettled. If that letter from the priest didn't arrive soon . . . But his father was still speaking and Gareth dragged his mind back to the conversation progressing between him and the excited young man.

" . . . that damned Santa Anna. He knows exactly what he's doin'. Austin warned him what sending troops into

460

Texas would mean." His eyes reverting back to the message, Jon shook his head. Five hundred more troops marching toward San Antonio with General Cos . . . Austin was urging that militia and volunteer companies be organized, concluding by stating that it was his duty to say as chairman of the Safety Committee that conciliatory measures with Cos and the military were hopeless. Jon reread the lst paragraph of the missive, the words burning into his mind.

War is our only recourse. There is no other remedy. We must defend our rights, ourselves, and our country by force of arms.

Unwilling to discuss the matter any more fully without careful consideration, Jon nodded in the young man's direction. "Dennis, I thank you for bringin' this communication to us so fast. You can tell your father for me that all the men from the Circle D will be at the meetin' in town tomorrow."

"All right, sir. I only have one more stop to make and I'll be happy to deliver that message."

The young man was mounting up when Gareth's eyes moved back to the road. Another mounted figure was moving steadily in their direction, his moderate pace steady. Gareth frowned into the afternoon sun in an attempt to identify the rider.

"It's nobody from around here, Gareth. I passed him on the way in. He said he wasn't goin' to push his horse because he'd come a long way. I didn't bother to ask him how far. I didn't have time for conversation."

"We appreciate that, Dennis. You tell your father what I said and when we see him tomorrow . . ."

Jon was still talking, but Gareth's eyes were fastened with unblinking intensity on the slender mounted figure. There was something about the carriage of the fellow's shoulders, his unusual seat in the saddle. Dennis was right. The man was no Texan. No, his manner of sitting a horse was different, almost foreign. It was as if . . .

The horse was drawing closer even as Dennis mounted and spurred his horse onto the road in a pace just short of a gallop. The unknown horseman lifted his hat from his head for the space of a second as he wiped his arm across his forehead. The man's hair glinted a fiery red in the sun, and Gareth's frown deepened. Those shoulders . . . they weren't broad enough to be Brock Macfadden's, but that hair and the way the fellow held his head . . .

The wait was interminable as the rider continued to approach. Gareth's face was set into a stiff mask, his hands balled into tight fists as the rider pulled up at last, dismounted and extended his hand.

"Hello, Gareth. I expect ye dinna think to see me again so soon."

"No, I didn't." Accepting the man's hand without a smile, Gareth turned toward his father. "Jon, I'd like you to meet Peter Macfadden, brother of Brock Macfadden, and one of the engineers who worked on the plans I brought back to you."

The strain between the two men was obvious. Uncertain what to make of the situation, Jon offered as cordially as possible, "You're welcome here, Peter, although I admit we were expectin' your brother."

"My brother's wife was feelin' poorly, and he dinna wish to leave her. And since I was intendin' on comin' this way . . ."

"You were comin' this way on business of your own?"

Peter answered Jon's question with a short glance toward Gareth.

"Aye. Personal business."

Turning to his saddlebags, Peter withdrew a letter. There was no doubt it had traveled long and far with him, and Gareth felt a tremor of premonition slip down his spine as Peter handed it solemnly to Jonathan Dawson.

The tension of the moment caused Jon's fingers to shake as he tore open the envelope and unfolded the sheets inside. His eyes darted to Gareth as he turned the pages to check the signature.

"It's from the priest."

His face slowly draining of color, Gareth moved to his father's side. His eyes settling on the flowery hand, he read silently along with him:

My dear Señor Dawson,

I apologize for the time taken in composing this reply to your letter. I need not tell you that I was totally unprepared for its arrival and the questions it posed. My conversation with your son prior to his leaving with Angelica was less than cordial. I disapproved of Angelica's actions, although I readily understood her desperation in the face of her brother's deteriorating health. Despite your son's statements to the contrary, I suspected he would not be true to his promises to her and she would find herself abandoned among strangers at some point in the near future. I need not tell you that your letter demonstrated his true faith and I offer you both my apologies. Now to respond to your questions.

My delay was due to the need to wait for the return of el Señor y la Señora Rodrigo and their son from the capital. I wish to inform you that I set this story down on paper exactly as was told to me, and with their full permission. It was the lack of this permission which has kept me silent these many years and would have kept me silent still were the situation different. I will answer your questions by starting at the beginning . . .

Margarita and Juan Rodrigo were married many years when their first child was born to them. She was a beautiful child whom they considered a gift from God since they had given up hope of having a child. She gave meaning to the existence of her parents, and was all they had ever hoped for in a child. But the ways of God are shrouded in mystery, not to be understood, but simply to be accepted with faith. When the child was eight years old, she fell sick from the smallpox which visited their village and died shortly thereafter.

Margarita was desolate, her grief so intense that she could no longer stay in the same village that bore so many memories of her dead child. She convinced her husband to take her to the mountains she had visited once when a child and where she had felt happy and close to God. They were on their way there when they came upon an Indian encampment in the mountains. The Indians were not native to that area, had obviously traveled many miles, and traveled quickly. Juan suspected they were part of the marauding band which had been driven out of Texas most recently. It grew dark, and they were unable to put much distance between themselves and the Indian camp, but had to content themselves with cautiously working their way around them. They awoke at dawn determined to get away as quickly as possible.

They had loaded their animal quietly and were preparing to depart when Margarita's gaze was drawn to the camp by the sound of a baby's cry. The child cried on and on, and there was no attempt to halt the sound. Realizing that silence was demanded by Indian mothers of their children, that no child would have been allowed to cry unattended for that length of time, Margarita disobeyed her husband's wishes and moved closer to the camp. She was startled to see that there was no activity in the camp. More surprising still, there were no horses or other animals at the camp. No campfires burned, no one moved between the hasty shelters, and yet the baby cried on, the only sound breaking the eerie silence.

· Impelled by the baby's cry, Margarita moved closer still. The sight that met her eyes was horrifying. Prostrate bodies lay on the ground, some already in a state of decomposition which gave off a horrid stench. There was no sign of life except for the baby's weakening cry. Margarita immediately concluded that this place of death had been abandoned by the healthy who had felt their only hope lay in escape.

Driven by a force stronger than her fear, Margarita

made her way between the temporary shelters, finding at last the spot from which the weak choking cry came. She entered the hide shelter to find a fevered infant lying in her dead mother's arms. No stranger to smallpox, Margarita took the child from her mother's arms and attempted to minister to her with her limited knowledge, but it was too late. The child died in her arms a few moments later, and Margarita was inconsolable.

Juan had just convinced her to leave that place of death when a sound at the doorway drew their startled eyes in its direction. A child stood there staring at them, her great gray eyes glazed. Her dark hair was matted, her simple buckskin garment stained with the filth of her sickness. She did not speak despite Margarita's attempt to communicate with her in Spanish, but even as she persisted in the attempt, the child collapsed in the doorway. One touch revealed that she was burning with the fever that had taken the lives of those around them.

But Margarita was determined not to lose another child to the disease which had already left two children dead in her arms. She and Juan carried the child away, setting up camp as far distant from the stench of death as they could manage with the sick child. They nursed her carefully during the three days that followed, washing the filth from her hair and body and burning her disease-ridden clothes. Many times they feared she would slip away as had their own child before her. But the child was strong, and after the third day she began to improve.

Magarita Rodrigo was elated at the child's improvement, believing then as she does now that she had been sent by God to that place so she might claim this beautiful girl child as her own. With great joy she dressed the child in her own daughter's clothing.

The child was beautiful, so close in age to their own lost daughter, and Margarita and Juan considered themselves blessed by God. But the child did not

465

speak. Her fever appeared to have left her brain burned clear of all thought and memory prior to awakening to Margarita's smiling face. After fruitless hours, Margarita abandoned the attempt to learn the girl's name and christened her instead Angelica, the child sent to them by the angels.

When the child was well enough to travel, Margarita and Juan Rodrigo resumed their journey to Real del Monte. They arrived strangers to the town and not entirely welcome in an area already beset by foreigners. The child was an additional hardship on Juan and Margarita because of her light eyes and skin that was noticeably fairer than that of the two claiming to be her parents. Fearing that she would lose the child, Margarita allowed it to be believed the child was the product of a forced union . . . that the child's true father was unknown. But rumor took fruit on the soil of the mountain, growing to damage the name and the reputation of Margarita Rodrigo beyond repair.

Unable to find work, Juan was about to accept employment in the mines, but Margarita came to me and confessed the full story. Determined not to allow an act of kindness . . . and, indeed, courage . . . to be rewarded so poorly, I employed Juan at my church, and he has served me faithfully ever since.

As for the child, she gradually regained her ability to speak and grew with no memory of her former life. She was a surprising strong and adamant child who would allow no one to speak her mother's name with disrespect in her presence. Margarita conceived another child a few years later, and her happiness was boundless. She felt her life fulfilled, despite the fact that the male child delivered to her was of poor health and appeared destined not to live to maturity. The birth of Angelica's brother, as she knew Carlos to be, brought as much joy to Angelica's life as it did to the lives of Margarita and Juan, and her true devotion to him has never faltered.

Such is the story you have requested of me, Señor Dawson. I can only hope it will help you to find peace. The only assurance I can give you as to Angelica's birth is that she is not the natural child of Juan and Margarita Rodrigo, but instead is a child taken in an Indian raid. For her identification I can offer only the small gold ring which Angelica was wearing when she was found. She had obviously worn it many years for it was all but impossible to remove from her finger even in the child's emaciated state when Margarita found her. Juan thought it best to take it from her while the child was in her delirium, and I have held it all these years in good keeping for just such a time as this.

Upon hearing of Peter Macfadden's intention to come to your homestead, I imposed upon him to deliver this letter. I have also written a letter to Angelica, conveying Margarita's thoughts and feelings, and I am asking that Peter deliver that message to her as well. I wish you happiness, and confess to relief that the truth is out after all these years. Do what you will with it for I believe you are an honorable man.

Yours in Christ,
Padre Manuel Santiago

Gareth's eyes followed his father's frantic search of the envelope, his chest beginning to heave with agitation as his father's trembling fingers closed on a small article rolled in a piece of paper. Clenching his fists against the trembling that had beset his own hands as well, Gareth watched tensely as Jonathan Dawson unwrapped the article quickly. Jon's revealing gasp as the narrow gold ring was uncovered shook him deeply. The tears that filled his father's eyes started a slow desolation building inside him.

Offering the ring to Gareth, his emotions obviously torn, Jon rasped, "I . . . I gave this ring to Jeanette for her sixth birthday. See . . . her initial 'J' is engraved in the top. It was gettin' too small for her, but she didn't want to take it off. Celeste couldn't bear to take it from her because she treasured it so. I often thought that she . . ."

His words dwindling to a halt, Jon allowed his eyes to move slowly over Gareth's pale face.

"Gareth, I'm sorry."

But Gareth did not hear his father's words. His mind refuted the proof exhibited before his own eyes. He shook his head, his adamance growing stronger.

"No . . . there . . . there's a mistake. There were many children taken in Indian raids. Angelica's not your daughter. She's not my . . ."

"Gareth, there's no longer any doubt. This ring . . . Margarita Rodrigo's story . . . the priest's testimony . . ."

Gareth was shaking his head when the sound of movement at the doorway of the house turned all eyes toward Angelica. Obviously startled at Peter Macfadden's appearance, Angelica walked toward them, her expression freezing at the sight of the letter Jon Dawson still held in his hand. Sparing her the agony of suspense a moment longer, Jon offered simply, "It's the letter from Padre Manuel."

Stopping still in her step, Angelica swallowed tightly, her eyes flicking to the small gold circle Jon held in his hand. Lifting his hand, he held it out to her in silence. The light of the afternoon sun glinted on its surface, releasing a multitude of whirling memories to assault her brain in a dizzying flood. Her left hand snapped to her right, massaging the finger which had worn the carved gold band so long ago. She remembered . . . she remembered Papa Jon's face as he put the ring on her finger, and she remembered . . . oh so clearly . . . the look her mother and Papa Jon had exchanged. Oh, God . . . no . . . She was spinning around and around in the ever tightening circle of fragmented pictures and sounds, but she fought to escape, her eyes seeking one face.

Gareth . . . His black eyes were dark, forbidding pools in his white face. They would allow her no peace. Even now she longed for his arms, their comfort, their joy. She longed to hear him tell her that this was a dream, that they would be together again . . . that he would hold her and love her, make her his own. But agony was reflected in those obsidian depths, the agony of acceptance of the reality he had fought so diligently. Never again . . . she would never know the joy of Gareth again . . .

Angelica took another step forward, but the ground was swaying beneath her feet. Gareth . . . She said his name only to hear it reverberate a thousand times in the chambers of her mind. Gareth . . . She reached out. He was not there to take her hand, but his eyes held hers, their desolation echoing in her heart, a heart that was racing, pounding in her ears, drumming out all sound. There was no reality but Gareth, no breath but the life only he had breathed into her, no light but the eternal flame he had lit in her heart. But it could no longer be. With a force that rocked her, realization dawned full and clear. It was done.

Her mind shut out the light that was Gareth, leaving her in darkness. She accepted the rapid assault of obscurity, submitted to its stringent demands and allowed it to conquer her senses. Harsh reality was extinguished with the light. The velvet blackness which had sought to consume her, which had been her enemy, was now her only consolation . . . her only peace.

Chapter XIV

The night was shrouded in fog, the Guadalupe river invisible to the eye. Intensely aware that dawn would soon be breaking, Gareth inched his way with the covert force of Texans toward the Mexican camp. His body flush to the cool ground, his heart beat an erratic tatoo in his breast. His eyes darted from side to side as he strained to assess their advance, almost two hundred Texans, determined that they would no longer suffer the indignities forced upon them by a government which was not their friend.

Colonel Ugartechea's demand that the people of Gonzales surrender their cannon had been the final straw. In his position of garrison commander at San Antonio, Ugartechea had already overstepped his bounds by ordering houses to be searched, confiscating weapons, disbanding "suspicious" groups of loyal Texans. Now the culminating affront, demanding the return of the cannon which had been given to Gonzales years before . . .

Sent by Colonel Ugartechea, Lieutenant Castaneda had been met by a group of armed Texans and a banner which challenged, "Come and take it." The Mexican officer had found it impossible to take a cannon that was so well hidden but the people of Gonzales knew the matter had not ended there. A frantic call had been sent out for volunteers by the Gonzales Safety Committee, and the response was the group which now crawled under cover of the remaining darkness toward the encamped Mexican force. Certain that

Castaneda intended to attack that day, they realized that surprise was their greatest asset against the superior Mexican force.

Gareth shot a quick glance toward the rear. The cannon in question, freshly dug up from the peach orchard where it had been hidden, was being dragged along with them. The fog was an excellent cover. They would soon be within striking range, and the battle would begin.

Suddenly, from within the Mexican camp, Gareth heard a shot and shouts of alarm. Halting uncertainly, he glanced around, only to see that the curtain of fog was lifting. His heart beginning an escalated pounding, Gareth was astounded to see that the lines of opposing forces were almost facing each other, separated by a breach of about three hundred yards!

An arrogant Mexican demand shattered the stillness of the dramatic tableau.

"Surrender your cannon or face the dire result of your actions!"

And the taunting reply:

"Come and take it!"

The rattling of muskets broke the pulsating stillness. Shots! The battle had begun! From a position to his rear, Gareth heard the roar of the cannon, watched as a shower of nails and old horseshoes flew into the midst of the Mexican soldiers. The unexpectedness of the powerful shot was the determining factor. The shaken Mexican commander called for an immediate parley.

The time loomed long for the men waiting in the field, but the whispered word was soon passed that the Mexican commander was stalling, waiting for reinforcements. Raising his head, Gareth watched as the leaders of the opposing forces retired to their respective lines. Within moments the six-pounder sounded again, its deadly barrage obviously finding its target as cries of the wounded Mexicans sounded in the gray dawn. A few scattered shots rang out in reply before Castaneda's men unexpectedly broke ranks and fled to the road back to San Antonio!

Catcalls and exuberant cries rang in the air from within

the Texan ranks, and a smile spread across Gareth's lips. An easy victory, without a single Texan wounded! It had been far easier than anyone had thought to rout the cowardly Mexicans. The revolution had begun!

Rising to his feet, Gareth clasped the hands held out to him in ecstatic celebration. Making his rounds, Gareth joined in the revelry, thankful that for the first time in the weeks since he had left the Circle D, the ache inside him was mercifully numbed.

Unexpectedly a beautiful, pale-eyed vision saw fit to visit him, and Gareth attempted to expel the unwelcome specter from his mind. He forced a smile to his lips. No, he had put that portion of his life aside. Freedom and independence for Texas was now his first priority, and if that same pale-eyed vision saw fit to haunt him in the quiet hours before sleep, to taunt him unmercifully, he would exorcise it from his mind. He had made that determination many weeks before, the afternoon the gold ring had been delivered and he had realized that he no longer had any choice.

Angelica spurred her horse forward, unmindful of the fact that she had left her companion in the dust at her heels. The brilliant horizon, ever changing in shades of pink, red, and subtle gold was calling her, and she had no choice but to heed its summons. The pleasant October air was flying against her face, brushing the curling tendrils from her hairline to flatten them against the shining silk of her restrained coiffure. She was momentarily mindless in the joy of her rushing escape, the freedom temporarily gleaned from her careless pursuit. There was a joy in the vacuum created by whistling of the wind in her ears, the panting of the horse beneath her, and the challenge of fitting her body to the rhythm of the animal's elongated stride as her mare's hooves pounded the ground under her.

The horizon was endless, stretching out in magnificent defiance of her attempt to conquer it. She spurred her horse faster, faster, her heart escalating to a thunder in her breast, the sound echoing to roar in her ears as she leaned over her horse's neck in an attempt to become one with its breathless rhythm.

She was gasping with exhilaration, reveling in her deliverance from her driving thoughts, when she suddenly became conscious of the pounding of hoofbeats to her rear, the gradual gaining of the sound as a horse and rider came up into her line of vision. She was no longer alone, the appearance of the man who now rode beside her intruding into her escape, erasing the glow from her eyes. She glanced to the side, catching his concerned expression, and Angelica felt a moment's remorse. Gradually reining her horse to a more conservative pace, she became aware of the relief reflected on the man's face. Waiting until they were traveling at no more than a canter, she turned toward him with a small smile.

"It was glorious, was it not, Peter? There is no more beautiful time of day here than the hours before sunset, and no more beautiful way to spend it than rushing into the setting sun."

"It is my feelin' that yer horse wou' nae agree with that thought, Angelica."

Unable to suppress a short laugh at his dry comment, Angelica shook her head.

"Perhaps not, but it is a small indulgence . . ."

"It wou' be a more thoughtful indulgence should ye allow yer animal a brief rest after her hard rush."

Her pale eyes touching and holding Peter's sober gaze, Angelica took another look at her mare's heaving sides and nodded.

"Of course, you're right Peter."

Reining her horse to a stop, Angelica was about to dismount when Peter's arms reached up to lift her easily to the ground. She was only too aware of his sudden intake of breath as he slid her down his length, the almost imperceptible flicker in his eyes as he allowed her to step back and take her horse's reins. Doing the same himself, he assumed a step at her side as Angelica began walking her laboring mare.

"I have had it on my mind to talk to ye about a certain matter, Angelica, but I have hesitated to voice my concern."

Her brow slipping into a frown, Angelica lifted her eyes to Peter's sober face.

"What is bothering you, Peter?"

Peter's response was hesitant, his expression pleading her indulgence as he offered softly, "Have ye written to yer mother, Angelica . . . to Margarita Rodrigo? I dinna wish to ask the question, for I knew it to truly be none of my concern. But the woman was present when I took the letters from the priest's hand, and she was greatly agitated. It is my feelin' that it wou' be an act of mercy to respond as quickly as ye can."

Angelica's mind flicked back to the day Peter arrived, and she closed her eyes temporarily against the pain memory evoked. She raised her free hand automatically to her neck, to the chain on which the small gold ring was strung. The ring had been the key to unlocking memories stifled by her frightened mind, and she had awakened from her swoon with the benefit of almost total recall.

Her mother's body lying in the dust . . . her Indian captors' impatience with her tears . . . long, terrified days during which her only solace was the small piece of blue velvet she had managed to salvage from her mother's gown and the echo of her mother's whisper.

"Your father will come to rescue you. Do not be afraid . . ."

Strangely, the only lapse that remained was the time of her travel to Real del Monte and her early life in that place. Memory surged to life again with the picture of her mother Margarita's smile, when she was already fully her child.

With the emergence of her true identity, there had been no lessening of love for the family with whom she had spent the greater part of her life. If anything, the revelation of the true circumstances of her birth had only brought a keener realization that it was to Margarita and Juan Rodrigo's love that she owed her life. And Carlos, dear Carlos who was making steady improvements each day in health, could be no more truly her brother than . . .

Gritting her teeth against the torment her unfinished

thought evoked, Angelica stumbled, only to feel Peter's arm steady her as he looked toward a group of trees nearby and urged her in their direction. Reaching the destination they sought, Peter took her reins from her hand and tossed them with his over a nearby branch. His eyes soft with understanding, he raised his hand to cup her cheek.

"I dinna mean to upset ye, Angelica. The thought was on my mind . . ."

"You needn't worry. Papa Jon sent one of the men to post my letter the day after . . ." She had been about to state the day after Gareth left the Circle D, but chose instead, ". . . after you arrived."

Aware of her hesitation, Peter shook his head. "I have the feelin' that ye dinna think of that day with happy thoughts. But I must confess that although I was the bearer of news which shook ye, I am glad to be here now."

Peter's hand had slipped into her hair at her temple and Angelica frowned. His feelings for her were too obvious and she had no desire to encourage them. No, her heart and mind were too raw . . .

"Dinna frown, lass." His voice softer still, Peter smiled into her face. "It is nae my intention to make ye uncomfortable. I've been with ye here for over a month, and Jon has asked me to stay till I can get the project safely on its way. He does nae expect that the hostilities with Mexico will threaten the Circle D."

Angelica nodded and averted her eyes. She had regretted Jon's invitation to the earnest Scot, reading a more devious reasoning into his action. But she was being unfair, overly suspicious . . .

Startling her with his perceptiveness, Peter continued quietly. "Aye, lass, I suspect ye're right. Yer father hopes to provide ye with a way to get yer mind off the past with me presence. And I tell ye now, I be grateful for the opportunity . . ."

"Peter, I . . ."

"Nay, lass, dinna say more." Raising his hand to her shoulder, Peter held her fast. His eyes moved over her disturbed expression as his other hand stroked the gleaming surface of her hair. "I count myself lucky to be able to be near ye . . . to touch ye like this. I dinna expect to have ye jump into me arms. I did nae know the truth of the situation between ye and Gareth when I made up my mind to come here in Brock's place. I but knew I needed to see ye again, to make certain ye were well and happy before I cou' get on with me life. I dinna like to see yer pain . . . to see ye suffer, Angelica. I wou' do all in me power to spare ye yer pain if it was within me power. But I canna change things to the way ye wou' best prefer. That way is out of me hands . . . out of all our hands. So I be willin' to wait, lass . . . until ye're ready to love someone again. And I'm hopin' that someone will be me . . ."

"Peter, I cannot promise. I don't want to use you . . . "

"If usin' me will let me closer to ye, Angelica, I dinna mind bein' used. I wou' be happy for the chance . . . to have ye even look at me that way. I've nae had the chance to make ye love me, but I'll nae let this one slip by." His voice dropping to a husky whisper, Peter repeated softly, "Nay, I'll nae let this chance slip by . . ."

Lowering his head unexpectedly, Peter brushed her lips with his. Her spontaneous frown was met with a small mischievous smile.

"Ye wou' nae begrudge a thirsty man a drop of water, or a hungry man a crumb of bread, wou' ye?"

Her frown fading, Angelica managed to return his smile.

"No, I suppose a drop of water or a crumb of bread is easily spared . . ."

"Aye, lass. Ye have a generous heart."

The momentary flash of a stronger emotion in Peter's eyes caused her a brief doubt before Peter slid his arm around her waist and urged her back toward the waiting horses.

"And I think it be time to return. Jon will be askin' if I tried to steal ye off." Swinging her up into the saddle, Peter paused, his long-fingered hands covering hers as she looked down into his face. "And I wou' have to answer him, 'Nae yet, mon . . . nae yet . . .'"

Within minutes they were galloping back toward the

Circle D. Her eyes darting to the man riding beside her, Angelica swallowed hard. She had lived a full lifetime in her seventeen years, so why did it still come as a surprise to her that life was not fair . . . not fair at all?

Gareth's eyes swept the darkness surrounding Goliad. His gaze returning to the men at his side, he felt their tension. Planters, most of them, from the neighborhood of Matagorda and the banks of the Caney, joined by volunteers such as he, who had answered Colonel George Collingwsorth's call for aid. The marauding Mexicans at Victoria could no longer be countenanced, and Colonel Collingsworth was determined to capture Goliad.

The company of anxious Texans had arrived below the town at midnight, and the major body of the men now awaited the return of the scouts who had been sent to reconnoiter Goliad. Gareth smiled. While separated from the remainder of the men, some of his fellow volunteers had come across Colonel Milam hiding in a thicket. Having escaped from the Mexican prison at Monterey, he had made his way alone through the country, riding night and day to reach Texas. He had already volunteered to assist in the enterprise, and the morale of the men was heightened by his presence. It would not be long now before . . .

The shadowed darkness was parting to reveal their scouts, and Gareth released a relieved breath. Watching as the men moved to Colonel Collingsworth's side, Gareth joined the men who gathered to hear the scout's eager report.

"Everything's quiet, Captain. There's one guard on duty outside Captain Sandoval's quarters, and the rest of the garrison appears to be asleep. If we move now, we'll meet very little resistance. The town is all but ours, Captain . . ."

His eyes moving to the men surrounding him, Colonel Collingsworth directed them a meaningful glance. "Made to order for us boys. Nothing can stop us now . . ."

Within minutes the silent column was moving swiftly in the darkness, Gareth surging forward in the first wave of the attacking force which surrounded the quarters of Lieu-

tenant Sandoval. A rifle shot cracked in the night, only to
be answered by another charge as the sentinel fell to the
ground. His gun ready, Gareth followed the first lunge of
men into the garrison. The surprised Mexican soldiers were
disoriented, moving in an inept pattern which was only too
easy to overcome.

Finding it unnecessary to fire a single shot, Gareth
ushered the stumbling soldiers into the yard, his eyes
snapping to his rear where other soldiers followed under the
guns of his fellow Texans. Within minutes the compound
was secured. Taking a deep breath of satisfaction, Gareth
watched as Lieutenant Sandoval was ushered into the yard,
Colonel Collingsworth to his immediate rear. With a few
more words, surrender had officially been accepted and
their mission had been accomplished. Resistance had been
slight and casualties low. Goliad was theirs.

Pen in hand, Gareth sat at the much abused table, his
eyes on the empty sheet of paper before him. The flush of
victory had passed, and the sounds of celebration coming
from the street below his hotel room held little attraction.
He raised his hand and raked it unconsciously through his
heavy dark hair, his eyes glued to the blank sheet which
mocked him. He was only too aware that it was time he
wrote home. He had been gone over a month, had left the
Circle D the day after Peter Macfadden's arrival, stating
only his intention to join the volunteers. He had not
communicated with home since.

He had not meant to keep his father in ignorance, but
damn . . . what could he say? Could he tell his father that
he had plunged himself wholeheartedly into the revolutionary movement in the hope of freeing himself of the torment
that was with him day and night? Could he relate that the
success of his ploy had been temporary at best, that he
knew little relief even in victory?

Gareth gave a low laugh. How may months before had
his whole life revolved around the struggle in which he was
now so deeply emeshed? Freedom for Texas . . . independence . . . it had filled his thoughts, given impetus to his

life. In a Texas free of Mexico's stifling influence, he had seen the Circle D growing, expanding, its vast bounty encompassing those around him and providing a good life for generations to come. He had been annoyed to be taken from the growing struggle for independence by his father's infatuation for the land and hopes for improving it. His journey to Real del Monte was to have been his last concession to his father's obsession, and then he was to have considered himself free to join an active fight for total liberty.

He had not anticipated Angelica. Angelica. Jeanette . . . No, he would never think of her other than as Angelica. She was his angel . . . his love . . . the driving force of his life, which had been taken from him with the first glinting reflection of a small gold ring. Even now he was incredulous at the thought . . . unable to accept it in the dark reaches of his mind. It couldn't be true. He would have known . . . would have felt . . .

And now, a month after the shock of confirmation, his mind still balked at acceptance. He had employed all manner of distraction in an effort to drive Angelica from his mind, but none had provided him relief. God, he wanted her . . . he wanted her still. He need not even close his eyes to see her face before him, the memory of her scent, the smooth texture of her skin under his palms, the warmth of her sweet and tight against him returning so vividly as to start his heart pounding. He gave another low laugh. Were he free to write to Angelica . . . tell her his feelings, he would have no difficulty filling this page before him.

The words flowed so easily from his heart.

"I miss you, darlin'. Nothin' keeps you from my mind for very long. I miss lookin' at you, touchin' you. I miss your smile . . . the sound of your voice. I miss the challenge and the joy of you, darlin', and I miss lovin' you. I miss holdin' you in my arms . . . wakin' with you beside me. I feel empty . . . lost without you. Nothin' can make me believe what I feel for you is wrong, Angelica. Deep in my heart I know there's another explanation for that gold ring. But you believe it, darlin', everythin' that gold ring seems to mean. I saw it on your face and I have no defense against your belief. I've tried to put the way I feel aside, but I've come to accept that my love for you will never change.

"I ache to be with you, and a deep regret will give me no peace. I held back the words. I didn't want to rush you. I wanted your feelin's for me to grow gradually, unimpeded by pressure of any sort. I thought we had so much time . . ."

Emotion a tight knot in his throat, Gareth felt the warm heat under his weary lids growing, and he shook his head. His last thought tore at his waning self-control. "I waited too long, darlin', and now I can never tell you I love you . . ."

Allowing his pen to slip from his fingers, Gareth dug the heels of his palms into his eyes in an effort to dispel the burning heat there. The trembling which had beset his frame was changing into deep shudders which shook his broad frame, finally manifesting themselves in the low, hoarse sounds which escaped his choked throat.

Exerting the last of his restraint, Gareth took a deep breath and dropped his hands from his face. With a trembling hand he picked up the pen and moved his gaze again to the blank sheet in front of him. No, he couldn't write to Angelica, but he would not put off writing a letter home again. He would write to his father . . . tell him of the progress of the war. He would tell him that he was well . . . how he might be reached should there be such a need. He would not tell him that he could not come home . . .

. . . and our forays against Gonzales and Goliad have seen tremendous success. Goliad itself netted us two cannon and hundreds of muskets to aid our cause. Our army is now five hundred strong and we are to set out within a few days to throw General Cos out of Texas. Our banner is a white cloth decorated with black paint. At the top is a lone star and then a cannon barrel. Underneath is painted, Come And Take It.

We have no doubt our efforts against Cos will know

success now that Steve Austin has agreed to lead us. I was extremely happy to see him again, although he does not look well, and I am honored that he has asked me to serve at his side.

Communication will eventually reach me through the address I set below, should there be need. My regards to all those on the Circle D and my hopes are that you are seeing success with the project you have initiated.

Most cordially,
Gareth.

His voice trailing off as his eyes left the letter in front of him, Jon looked up into Angelica's pale face. He noted with a particularly painful twinge that Peter had stepped close behind her as he read Gareth's letter, silently lending her his support.

"Is . . . is that all Gareth had to say?"

"Yes, that's all, Angelica."

In the time since Gareth had left they had settled into an accepted manner of addressing each other with which Jon was finally comfortable. Jeanette, his daughter, was ill at ease with the name she had not borne for so long, and had requested that he call her Angelica. He had agreed, grateful for the fact that she continued to address him as "Papa Jon." The term brought back warm memories and he hoped they did the same for her.

But Jon suspected Angelica did not indulge herself in memory . . . not willingly. In the time since Gareth had left he had become accustomed to the haunted look in her great silver eyes, the mood changes which indicated she was having a difficult time eluding her past and putting her priority on the present. The future . . . he knew she did not allow herself to think in those terms. Time . . . they all needed time . . .

But Angelica's face was still, the sudden flush that covered her previously pale cheeks indicative of her vacillating emotions. Peter's arm moved around her waist and she looked up into his concerned expression. The young Scot loved her. He had seen that from the first, and had hoped Peter's presence would help her to . . .

But Angelica's face had turned back to his. It was obvious her hold on her emotions was tenuous.

"Gareth . . . he does not state when he will be coming home?"

Shaking his head, Jon offered softly, "No, he doesn't, Angelica. It looks as if he'll be involved at San Antonio for a while. It won't be an easy city to overcome. Cos is well entrenched."

"Gareth won't come home . . . not while I'm here."

Angelica's statement was flat, emotionless.

"Angelica, he's involved with the army of volunteers. He won't be able to return for at least . . ."

"He won't return at all, not while I'm still in this house. He doesn't want to see me, or even think of me, and I can't blame him." Taking a few quick steps to his side, Angelica rested her hand on Jonathan Dawson's arm. Her voice was suddenly firm with determination. "I'm going back to Real del Monte, Papa Jon."

"No." Shaking his head in refutation of her statement, Jon Dawson covered her small hand with his own. "No, that isn't the answer, darlin'."

"Yes, it is. I'll go back to my family there and Gareth will be free to return to the Circle D. This is his home, not mine. He has worked alongside you to build it . . . to protect it. I have no right to displace him, and I will not . . ."

"You aren't displacin' him, darlin'. This is just a temporary time of adjustment. When Gareth is finished at San Antonio, he'll come back and . . ."

"He won't come back. I know . . ." Her voice breaking, Angelica bit back the sob which had risen to her throat. Turning unexpectedly toward Peter, she said quietly, "You'll take me back, won't you, Peter? You will be traveling to Real del Monte soon. I won't be a burden. I am accustomed to the rigors of an extended journey. I am easily adaptable."

"Ye wou' never be a burden to me, Angelica. Ye needna

482

be concerned that I wou' find yer company anythin' but a pleasure."

"It's settled then."

Turning back to Jon, Angelica was startled at the angry flush that had transfused his face, was unprepared for the fury of his words as he stated harshly, "No, it isn't settled! You're not leavin'! You're disturbed because of Gareth's letter, and I can understand your feelin's. I feel much the same myself. But runnin' away will accomplish nothin'!"

"It will allow Gareth to return!"

"No! I will not sacrifice one of my children for another!"

Jon's harsh declaration snapped Angelica into silence, holding her unmoving as his arms moved to draw her into a comforting embrace.

"Angelica, just give it a little more time." He was rubbing his hand in small, soothing circles on her back, the familiarity of the lulling stroke succeeding in drawing hot tears to her eyes. His voice was low. "You said you had agreed with Gareth to stay a year . . ."

"Yes, but circumstances have changed."

"Yes, they have changed, darlin'. Now there's even more reason for you to stay."

Angelica's response was muffled against the surface of his chest. "No, there is even more reason for me to leave."

Sliding his hands up to her shoulders, Jon gently extricated Angelica from his embrace, holding her just far enough away from him that he might look into her tear-filled eyes.

"Angelica, darlin', wait a little longer. Just until the year you promised Gareth is over. It won't be too long."

"It will be a lifetime."

"All right . . . then wait until after your birthday . . . in February. I wasn't going to tell you yet, but I received a letter from Tante Minette. You remember her, don't you?"

"Tante Minette?" Her mind slipping back into the past, to the nanny who had been her mother's and her only family, she shook her head incredulously. "Mama's Tante Minette?"

"Yes, darlin'. She's still livin' in New Orleans. I've been

doin' all I can to help her since your mama and you disappeared. I suppose it was the only link I still had with you both, and I wasn't able to sever it. Besides, if she hadn't been recuperating from the fever, she'd have been on that wagon train with your mama and you. She was already packed to follow when she got the letter sayin' you and your mama were gone. When you came back, I wrote to Tante Minette and she said she was comin' out here for your eighteenth birthday. It was supposed to be a surprise. You don't want to disappoint her, do you, darlin'?"

"Papa Jon . . ."

"Or disappoint me . . . ?"

Unable to withstand the hope in Jon Dawson's eyes, Angelica released a slow, weary breath.

"All right. I'll stay until then. I . . . I've never celebrated my birthday. February twenty-fifth. I never knew . . ."

Drawing her words to an abrupt halt, Angelica turned away and started toward the staircase to her room. Reality was hard, unrelenting. Yes, she knew who she was now. She knew the true date of her birth, the meaning of her haunted dreams. She now had not one family that loved her, but two. She was no longer in a position of subservience, but was the accepted daughter of the household, with all its privileges. She had even gained the respect of the Circle D hired hands once the gold ring had established her identity without doubt, although she knew they wished Gareth were here instead of her. But in gaining all of this, she had sacrificed Gareth.

The price had been too high . . .

General Martin Perfecto de Cos, commandant general of the eastern internal provinces and brother-in-law of el presidente, glared at the man standing opposite him in his headquarters. Cos's short, broad frame was stiff with anger, his swarthy complexion flushed. But the well-uniformed young aristocrat was unintimidated by his rising fury.

"You dare to instruct me in my duties, Esteban? That very uniform you wear is the result of a political appoint-

ment, not earned in battle! I do not need your instructions
. . . your incitements!' "

"I have not desire to instruct you, Martin. Instead, I
only wished to remind you of the danger inherent in this
situation. The Texans come fresh from victories . . . at
Concepcion, Gonzales, and Goliad. Their army is reported
to number five hundred strong . . ."

"And I have more than enough men to withstand their
attack! My preparations have been more than adequate."

"You are certain of that?"

"I am more than certain! You are not as observant as
you would have Antonio believe, Esteban, or you would not
have felt the need to voice your concerns. Besides the
barricades which have been erected in the streets, I have
stationed sharpshooters in the houses, even installed a
small cannon on the church tower that commands the area.
I have even taken the precaution to move my own headquarters here." His eyes moving pointedly to the stone walls
of the old mission, he continued haughtily, "where I might
command the action of battle from a place of safety. I am
far enough removed in this position across the river from
town, and these walls will withstand even the most stringent assault, should it come to that. In any case, I do not
need to give you an accounting of my preparations. I do so
only to demonstrate how foolish are your concerns."

Taking a firm hold on his temper, Esteban stifled his
response. He was doing no good irritating Martin in this
way. The relationship between them had begun to deteriorate at the first word of the force marching in their
direction. The next step would be a total collapse of
amenities, and Esteban had no desire to find himself and
his private guards ostracized from the remainder of the
contingent at San Antonio, at least not until he was ready.
Preparing to make the sacrifice of an apology, Esteban
allowed a practiced, conciliatory smile to move across his
well-shaped lips.

"Martin, *lo siento*. I beg you to forgive my needless
concerns. San Antonio de Bejar . . . retaining possession of
this city is crucial to our cause. I would not want to

disappoint Antonio with its fall."

"San Antonio de Bejar is *my* concern, Esteban, not yours. I admit to considerable annoyance that I should be forced to remind you of that fact!"

"The defeat of the upstart Texans is a concern of us all, Martin. But I do beg your indulgence, for my own personal involvement here tends to color my thinking and my emotions."

"Personal involvement?" Despite himself, General Cos could not suppress the satisfaction that lit his dark eyes. "Do you speak of a romantic involvement, Esteban? If that is so, it would account for your surprising lack of endeavors in that direction since you have arrived in San Antonio. I confess, I had begun to attribute your tension to your surprising celibacy. I had almost reached the point where I was considering offering you the use of the woman I have employed since arrival in San Antonio. She does not attain the standards of the *putas* available in the capital, but she is clean and willing, and not totally unattractive . . ."

Doing his best to conceal his distaste, Esteban broadened his smile. Well, at least he had hit on the right note to dispel Cos's indignation. Affairs of the heart were common to all men, and not beneath this particular man's interest. He had just to stir the right sentiment in the fool's mind.

"*Sí*, Martin, you are extremely astute. There is a woman . . . a very beautiful woman, and the Texan cause stands between her and myself. It causes me no little grief, and I admit to a great anxiety to see this insurrection settled and our control once again firmly established so that I might dispense with the impediment between us."

"And that is why you have requested administrative duties in this area when the conflict is over . . . ?"

His expression reflecting his surprise at Cos's knowledge of his request, Esteban was about to attempt a denial when the smiling general laughed aloud.

"No, do not bother with a denial. Antonio confided his surprise in your interest in such menial duties. But it is written in your face, Esteban. So, the untouchable has been touched . . . the conqueror of women's hearts conquered!

486

Ah, Esteban, you do realize that you have allowed a legend to die . . ."

No longer able to disguise his annoyance, Esteban responded haughtily, "A legend, Martin?"

"*Si*, a legend! Second only to Antonio, your amorous escapades were the talk of the capital. I confess you stirred no little jealousy with your considerable success . . ."

"I am so happy to know I provided the capital scene with such a measure of entertainment."

"And you were also well entertained, were you not, Esteban? In any case, it appears that has all come to an end. So, you have found a woman who means more to you than all the others . . ."

"I suppose that is true . . ."

"And she has managed to elude you. Ah, for shame, Esteban! How did you allow that to happen?"

"Martin, I find I am becoming bored with this conversation."

"Yes, I suppose you find little enjoyment in discussing an unaccustomed defeat in an affair of the heart. But now that I realize the true cause of your agitation, I admit to an inclination to be more tolerant of your unnecessary concern here, even a tendency to dismiss your irritating agitations."

His handsome face all but twitching, Esteban nodded sharply. "You are too kind, Martin."

"Yes, I am." His dark eyes putting more meaning to his short statement than the words would indicate, General Cos pulled his sturdy frame to its full, meager height. "In any case, you may relieve your worries in the knowledge that everything is under control. When and if an attack comes here, we will be well prepared, and will emerge victorious."

"Your reassurance allows me no measure of alleviation, Martin." His words conveying a sarcasm he could not quite control, Esteban inclined his head politely. "Now, if you will excuse me, I will return to my quarters."

"Certainly, Esteban. And you may feel free to discuss your concerns with me at any time . . ."

"Thank you, General."

"You are most welcome, Colonel."

Turning abruptly on his heel, Esteban made a quick exit from the temporary quarters. Stupid fool that he was, Cos was underestimating the Texans! It was a mistake he himself had made once, and he did not intend to make it again! No . . . he would not be caught in a situation from which there would possibly be no escape. When the attack came, he would retire to a place of safety with his personal guards. He had not been sent here as a soldier, but as an observer and an adviser to el presidente. He would function in that capacity, and that capacity alone. He would not be among the possible ranks of the vanquished. He would see to it that he was in a position to advise Antonio of his warnings should San Antonio fall, and that fool inside would stand alone in the face of defeat.

Yes, Cos was a fool . . . even insofar as the place he had taken for his headquarters. Glancing to the hard stone walls surrounding him as he pulled open the massive carved doors, Esteban walked out into the yard. Glancing back, he surveyed the structure with contempt.

A former mission . . . used occasionally as barracks, it had nothing to recommend it other than the fact that it had stood the assault of years and had once sheltered a Spanish colonial company. As a matter of fact, it was still referred to by a portion of that company's name. What was it they called this place, the Alamo?

Shrugging his impressive shoulders in disgust, Esteban walked haughtily toward town. Whatever . . . he cared little.

Her pleasant wrinkled face imparting a dignity unaffected by age, Mademoiselle Minette Beauchamps steadied herself against the bump and roll of the stagecoach in which she had been riding since early morning. Her hold was firm on the frame of the open window through which she surveyed the sprawling countryside, her posture erect despite the long uncomfortable hours since she had first boarded the jolting conveyance. Slim in her youth, she had become thinner still as advancing years had taken their toll. White hair streaked with gray was twisted in a neat bun at the back of her neck, the dark dress and hat which covered her delicate frame lending an appearance of deceiving fragility which was immediately negated at first contact with the small, keen dark eyes with which she viewed the world. Her acute gaze fervently consumed the landscape flashing past as the stagecoach traveled into the afternoon sun. So this was Texas . . .

Her sharp mind reverting to a point in the past, Minette remembered her dear Celeste's voice, as clear and sweet as the chimes of a bell as she had called to her from the next room many years before.

"Minette . . . Minette! It is a letter from Jonathan! He is asking Jeanette and me to come to him . . . in Texas!"

There had been a short lapse of sound before Celeste had appeared in the doorway to her room, her face sparkling with happiness. "He wants me to come to him immediately . . . immediately! He says he will not bow to appearances and wait any longer. His wife has been buried and his son informed of his decision to ask me to come. He says we have been separated long enough . . . that we will be married as soon as I arrive!"

"Bon . . . bon, ma petite."

A momentary shadow had fallen across her darling's lovely face.

"But you are not yet well, Minette. You have not yet regained your strength. I . . . I will write to Jonathan and tell him we must wait . . ."

Her own response had been instantaneous. "No . . . no, you will not do that. Monsieur Jonathan is right. You have both waited long enough."

"But what of you, Minette? I cannot leave you . . ."

"And since when have I been your concern? It is I who have always taken care of you and *ma poupée*, Jeanette, have I not? It will be no hardship to take care of myself once you are firmly on your way to Texas."

"But . . . I cannot leave you here."

"It will only be temporary. I will be well within a few weeks, perhaps a month. My strength will be returned. This fever . . . it was never a match for me, despite my age."

Celeste's lovely face had openly reflected her love. "You are not of an 'age.' You are ageless, Minette, and . . . I am very glad that you are."

"Then you agree that I am able to take care of myself while you are gone, when in truth, my care will only necessitate rest."

"I . . . I suppose so . . ."

"Then you will arrange transportation for Jeanette and yourself immediately as Monsieur Jonathan requests. You will travel to Texas and marry the man you love. Jeanette will have a true papa at last, and I will follow within a month's time and join you there."

"But you will not be present at the time of our marriage, Minette. You will not hear us speak our vows . . ."

"In truth, will it matter, *ma chérie*? I will be with you the rest of your life, and I will see love reflected in both your and Monsieur Jonathan's eyes as true testimony of the words you spoke. I will need no more."

But Celeste had hesitated still, her great luminous eyes uncertain. And she had urged, "Promise me you will go, Celeste. I do not wish to bear the burden of standing in the way of your happiness."

Hesitating only a moment longer, Celeste had nodded, turning to stretch out her hand to the beautiful child who had appeared in the doorway.

"Come, Jeanette. I have some very exciting news I must tell you. We are going home . . . home to your papa at last."

The child had come to sit on the side of her bed, great gray eyes so like her mother's moving between their faces as she had whispered in breathless incredulity, "*C'est vrai, Mama?*"

"*Oui, c'est vrai, ma petite.* We are going home . . . at last."

How many times had she regretted the words she had spoken that day? She had lost her beautiful Celeste and her little *poupée* Jeanette. Life had gone on, but she had suffered the void of the loss. She suffered it still.

But she would see Jeanette again, and seeing the child of

her dear Celeste grown, her mission would be accomplished and she would return to New Orleans a happy woman again.

A small frown tightened the lines on Minette's pale brow. Her gaze became pensive and the passing landscape faded from her vision. In her heart she knew the necessity of her visit. From the moment the letter had arrived from Monsieur Jonathan she had determined that she must make the journey. Despite her eagerness to see her Jeanette grown, it was a reluctant journey. But all choice had been taken from her memory of Celeste's trusting gaze, and her final words in parting.

"You will do that for me, *ma chéri* Minette?"

And her own fervent reply.

"*Oui, ma petite, je vous le promets.* I promise."

Chapter XV

The scene was of utter chaos. From his covert vantage point on a rise of land a safe distance away, his safety in trust of his personal guards, Esteban Arricalde watched the progress of the Texans' assault against San Antonio de Bejar. The town, besieged for over a month by Texas volunteers, had fought valiantly, but its cause was lost.

Before his eyes desertion began to manifest itself within the ranks. Cries of "Treachery! Treachery!" sounded over the din, the impression that deserters had gone over to the enemy compounding the confusion which abounded. At the Alamo itself half-starved women and children flocked by hundreds in indescribable panic. In the belief that the soldiers withdrawn from San Antonio had been utterly routed, soldiers and citizen hustled each other in one common crowd in an effort to escape.

In the midst of the furor General Cos stood in a vain attempt to allay the commotion. His voice unheard in the melee, he was pushed and shoved in the encroaching darkness, a small, ineffective figure in the midst of the ensuing madness. A humiliating end to an heroic effort!

Esteban took a deep, angry breath. This disaster had not gone unforeseen by him. His gaze darting to the two men behind him whose eyes searched the immediate area for any sign of threat, Esteban grunted low in his throat. Martin had called him a fool, but the validity of his assessment was being shamefully proved before his eyes at this very moment.

Martin had refused to listen to him from the beginning. Had reinforcements been requested, a strengthening of the fortress by additional troops or a signal devised with which they would have been able to summon help if needed, there would have been a different end to the devastating blow of the soon-to-be-surrendered San Antonio de Bejar. But he had been true to his determination not to fall in defeat with the stubborn General Cos. In the dark of the previous night he had summoned his guard. Civilian clothes . . . the same poor Texan garments which had disguised him once before, had hidden his rank as he had escaped from the besieged compound with his similarly clothed men. Even now, as he stood viewing the humiliating scene progressing within the fortress from a safe distance, his guards stood with their hands on their guns, ready to defend him.

Yes, he would leave this mortifying scene and would report back to the capital . . . to el presidente himself. If he knew anything at all, he knew that el Presidente Antonio Lopez de Santa Anna would not allow this affront to be unavenged. And unlike his poor generals, he would lead his men to victory over these rag-tag Texans. Ah, yes, and when he did, he, Esteban Arricalde, would be beside him, his confidant, his adviser, his friend. Could any man ask for more?

Yes, perhaps he could, and he had no doubt that Antonio's gratitude would be such after his faithful service that he would be able to name his own reward. He had been very patient in working toward this end but the particular reward he would receive had been a driving incentive. It was a reward which would warm him through the long nights and fill his days with challenge. It was a reward from which he would demand the ultimate and which would afford him more pleasure than he had ever known. Yes, it was now only a matter of time.

Turning his back on the humiliation of San Antonio de Bejar, Esteban grunted in low command. "Vamos, Ricardo . . . Ramon. I do not care to watch any more of this disgrace. The next time we look at San Antonio de Bejar we will be at el presidente's side, and when we are done, our flag will be flying freely above it once again. But for now we leave it behind us with contempt."

Taking the few steps to his horse, Esteban was mounted within minutes. Spurring his stallion forward, Esteban heard the clatter of his guard's animals as they closed in behind him. Yes, it was now only a matter of time.

Angelica's hands were trembling as she fastened the last hairpin into her upswept coiffure. Satisfied at last that heavy, gleaming mass was secure, she glanced up into the mirror to assess her appearance. The sight that met her eyes was startling. Suddenly it was no longer a mystery how her father had recognized her the moment he had seen her. Her gown of blue velvet, a birthday gift from him, duplicated a picture that was now vivid in her memory.

Her eyes moving to the slight image behind her, Angelica held the gaze of the small black eyes which met hers, acutely aware that they were filled with tears.

You are lovely, *ma chérie*, the image of your mother."

Her throat tightening, Angelica turned to embrace Tante Minette's fragile form. Her arrival at the Circle D the day before had brought with it the return of memories so poignant that Angelica had been unable to control her emotion. She and Tante Minette had talked long into the night, and she was thankful for the gift of love the aging woman made so freely to her.

But Tante Minette disengaged herself from Angelica's arms with a soft sound of protest.

"No, you must not spoil your beautiful gown. Now, let me look at you one last time before we go downstairs."

Standing back, Tante Minette surveyed her more closely, her smile becoming distant, and Angelica was aware that the ageless woman was seeing the subtle differences between her mother and herself which were not apparent at first glance. True, her hair was the same shade of midnight black as her mother's . . . her skin the same creamy tone in color. Her eyes . . . yes . . . she remembered her mother's eyes were the same clear gray, her features small and fine. How many times in her former life had she despaired of that fine detail which had marked her with no true claim to the Rodrigo name?

But even as she had been refused acceptance as the child of Margarita and Juan's union, in her heart she was not

494

truly the daughter Papa Jon would have her to be. For part of that heart remained in Real del Monte with the family who had raised her and given her their love. And the greater portion of her heart had been given in another hopeless love. It was that separation from the child she had been to the woman she now was which was reflected in the sober depths of her eyes, the unmistakable firmness of her small, well-shaped chin, the determined set to delicate shoulders which had borne heavy burdens with spirit and courage . . . which bore them still. No, she was not the Jeanette DuBois she might have been, and neither was she Celeste.

But it was apparent Tante Minette approved of the woman she saw, and was content.

"There are no improvements that can be made on perfection, *ma chérie*." Glancing to the clock on the table, Tante Minette continued quietly. "It is almost time to go downstairs to your birthday celebration, so I must go to my own room for a few minutes. There are some things I must do. I will join you downstairs shortly."

Leaning forward, Tante Minette pressed a light kiss on her cheek. "*Ma petite poupée* . . . if Celeste could only see you now . . ."

Her eyes perilously close to overflowing, Tante Minette turned quickly and within minutes had moved across the room and was closing Angelica's bedroom door behind her. Her own eyes warm with the heat of tears, Angelica took a deep breath in an attempt to overcome the emotion the old woman had stirred inside her.

Her eyes moving back to the mirror, Angelica allowed her eyes to travel over the lush fabric of the gown Papa Jon had given her, knowing the true significance of the blue velvet in his eyes. To Papa Jon it was the realization of a dream . . . his Celeste with him again through his daughter. She had wanted to give him that before leaving . . . to let him know that a part of her mother would remain alive for him.

But the blue velvet had come to have a much deeper significance for her. Gareth . . . his love had changed the beauty of the blue velvet to a meaning which was now almost effective in destroying her tenuous composure as the smooth fabric caressed her skin. Gareth . . . he had said he would be her blue velvet, and in truth, she still wished it could be so. The passage of time since Gareth had gone had done little to alleviate her torn emotions, and she was more certain than ever that her only alternative was to leave the Circle D.

Papa Jon had finally accepted her decision, even though he insisted that her absence would be temporary. She supposed the fact that Gareth had not returned for the Christmas holidays, deciding instead to stay in the newly conquered San Antonio, had brought her words into true perspective. No, Gareth would not return while she remained at the Circle D. The letter received from Gareth only two days before had served to make Gareth's intentions to remain estranged from them only too clear.

Angelica closed her eyes against the pain the missive had induced. It was with her still. Gareth was once again with his friend, Bill Travis, who had been promoted to lieutenant-colonel, and who had been in charge of recruiting men for a new cavalry unit stipulated in the war plans of the state. Gareth had written that it was his intention to remain with Travis in his new assignment at the Alamo where they had yet to decide whether to defend or destroy the scarred fortress in the event of an attack.

Angelica winced at the thought. Because of her, because he could not come home, Gareth was exposing himself to constant danger. Papa Jon had denied it was so, claiming that Gareth had always been involved in the Texan bid for liberty. But the fact remained that even when the opportunity had presented itself, Gareth had not come home.

But he would come home now. It had been tentatively settled that Peter and she would be returning to Real del Monte at the end of the week. Tante Minette's decision to stay until that time was delaying their departure, but Angelica could not bear to leave before the dear woman was safely on her way back to New Orleans. How deeply she regretted the fact that she could not ask her to stay, but it was impossible for her, truly displaced herself, to make arrangements for Tante Minette.

If only she could . . .

A sharp knock on the door breaking into her thoughts, Angelica turned in its direction. Her bid to enter was answered by the immediate opening of the door and the appearance of Peter's tall, lanky frame. She had taken two steps in his direction when the expression on his face stopped her in her tracks.

After the space of a short silence, Peter offered simply, "Angelica, ye take away me breath. I have never seen anyone more beautiful."

"Peter, you are quite beautiful yourself."

Sincere in her compliment, Angelica allowed her eyes to move appreciately over Peter's handsome form. "So this is the reason you went into town so secretively earlier this week." Indicating the new dark suit and the manner in which it fit his lean proportions to perfection, she continued with a smile. "You look quite handsome."

Surprised by the flush that colored Peter's fair complexion, Angelica watched as he closed the door behind him and advanced to a point directly in front of her. Reaching out, Peter took her arm gently, drawing her closer as he lowered his head to brush her lips with his.

"You're kind, lass, but seein' you tonight only serves to remind me how very sharply I fall short in that respect. My looks are common, Angelica, but me heart is uncommonly filled with love for ye . . . filled to overflowin'."

Deeply touched by Peter's earnest declaration, Angelica was at a loss for words. She had become accustomed to Peter's patient attentions in the past months. This was not the first time he had declared his love for her, but she detected something different in his manner this night and she frowned.

"I dinna desire to raise a frown to yer brow, Angelica, but this time I'm not aboot to allow it to put a premature end to my words." Surprising her with the determination in his grip, Peter drew her into the circle of his arms. His clear, ardent face close to hers, his breath fanning the skin of her cheek, Peter began slowly.

"It is my thought that I must speak my mind this night. Ye've long known the way I feel about ye, lass. I have loved ye from the first moment my eyes touched on yer beautiful face. But my own backwardness allowed ye to slip away from me before I cou' declare how I felt. I dinna expect to allow that to happen again."

Pausing, Peter lowered his head, his mouth finding hers again. His kiss was thorough and gentle. His mouth was soft consolation for the gnawing ache deep inside which would allow her no peace, and she remained unresisting under his kiss. But the gradual escalation of Peter's heart-beat against her breast as his kiss became more urgent stirred pangs of guilt. No, she would not allow herself to lead this good man on. She felt nothing for him except a strong affection and the comfort of friendship. To allow him to think anything else was unfair, even cruel. She was attempting to withdraw herself from Peter's arms when he drew his mouth from hers. His smile reflected a sad understanding.

"Ye need nae panic, lass. I'm well aware ye dinna share me feelin's. But in truth, ye do have a warm affection for me, do ye nae?"

"Peter, you have proved to be my good friend. Were it not so, I would not have asked you to allow me to accompany you back to Real del Monte."

"Aye . . . yer friend . . ."

Seeing the flicker of frustration in Peter's eyes, Angelica shook her head. "But . . . but if you have changed your mind . . . if I would make you uncomfortable in any way . . ."

"Angelica, I've nae changed my mind. In truth, I have thought of nawt else but havin' you to myself for the duration of the journey back to the mines. Aye . . . My thoughts are so strong that I felt I must make myself more plain to ye this night. I've kept my emotions keenly in check these last months, lass, but it has nae been an easy matter. I love ye, and I want ye badly. In truth, I can think of nae else when I am near ye."

"Peter, I . . ."

"Let me finish, lass." Raising his hand to stroke her cheek, Peter continued softly. "It will be a long journey, and in all truth, I'm nae sure I will be up to withstandin' the temptations which will be involved." His gaze imploring her understanding, Peter shook his head at her silence. His pale-eyed gaze held her fast. "Do ye nae realize how much I want ye, Angelica? Ye have been the sole woman on my mind since I touched down on the foreign soil of Mexico, and the past months have done nawt but raise the fervor of my feelin's. We'll be alone for a great part of the journey. Many of the nights ye will be sleepin' beside me, within reach of my touch, with no one around to say yea or nae . . ."

"No one but me, Peter . . ."

"Aye, I've nae lost track of that fact. But it is my feelin' that once away from this place, ye will find a truer feeling for me, and it wou' be my hope that ye wou' allow that feelin' to take its natural course . . ."

Angelica's heart had begun a nervous pounding, the last words of Peter's statement effective in setting it to racing as she sought the true meaning of his words.

"What . . . what is it you're asking me, Peter? Are you asking me to allow you to make love to me?" Tears springing to her eyes, Angelica balked at the thought. There were no arms she wanted to hold her but Gareth's . . . no man she wanted to love her but him. He was lost to her forever, but she could accept no other man in his place, not even this good man who loved her . . .

She continued tentatively. "Because if that is what you're asking, I . . . I cannot say yes. Peter, please try to understand. My heart does battle with my mind. As much as I would wish it to be so, I am not free to love anyone . . ."

"I am only askin' that ye try to turn yer heart loose when we are alone . . . that ye nae turn from me. I give me word nae to force ye . . ."

"Peter . . ."

"And I'm askin' ye to be my wife . . . to marry me before

499

we leave so that ye willna feel guilt in comin' to me."

The heavy thudding of Peter's heart was mingling with her own, his ardent tone echoing in her ear, and Angelica closed her eyes against their mutual torment. Hot tears squeezed past her closed lids, and Angelica felt Peter's stiffening the moment before he pulled her close against him once again. This time his embrace was hard, unyielding.

"I canna allow yer tears to soften me, lass. I canna weaken now for to do so wou' be to take ye with me with less than the truth between us. I need ye to tell me that ye will try to make yerself love me. At least try . . ."

Peter's strong arms were trembling even in their strength and Angelica felt a deep sob shake her. What perverse sense forced her to perpetuate such useless emotional torment . . . to deny Peter her love, to allow her own hopeless love for Gareth to linger on?

Peter's lips were warm against her cheek, following the path of her tears. His mouth covered hers and she remained passive under its persuasion, allowing his kiss to deepen searchingly. His hands were moving warmly on her back, straining her closer . . . closer still.

Suddenly tearing his lips from hers, Peter gritted tightly, his emotions obviously in tenuous control, "Answer me, lass. Ye know this place can never be a home to ye now, as much as Jon loves ye. But we can make a home together in Real del Monte . . . near yer family there. I'll love ye and take care of ye. And I will see to Carlos. Ye need nae give thought to the worry that he'll fall short of the funds needed to get him well. Had ye come to me before leavin' Real del Monte I wou' gladly have helped ye, and I'd nae turn my back on him now."

Peter's eyes assessed her obvious bemusement. He groaned low in his throat as he drew her close again in a more restrained embrace. "Tell me ye trust me enough to consent to be my wife, lass. I will nae let ye doon. I will love ye and honor ye always. I will hold ye in my heart . . ."

An unexpected knock on the door to Angelica's room interrupted Peter's hoarse whisper.

Swallowing against the tight lump which had formed in her throat, Angelica responded softly, "Yes, who is it?"

Tante Minette's soft reply caused Peter to release her reluctantly, his eyes reflecting his obvious frustration as Angelica bid her to enter. Her small dark eyes moving assessingly between them, Tante Minette acknowledged Peter's presence politely. Her voice bearing no hint of apology, she stated quietly, "I did not think I heard you leave your room, and I thought to accompany you downstairs. Monsieur Jonathan awaits us, *ma petite*. He has looked forward to this celebration tonight, as have I. It will not do to keep him waiting."

Nodding her consent, Angelica took a step in the direction of the doorway. Tante Minette's hand gripping her arm in firm restraint, she turned to Peter unexpectedly.

"Monsieur Macfadden, if you will excuse us, Angelica need attend to some details of her toilette before leaving. You will please tell Monsieur Jonathan that we will be with him soon . . ."

"Of course."

Taking his dismissal with limited grace, Peter walked stiffly toward the door, and within minutes the sound of his step moved down the hallway. Turning back to Angelica, Tante Minette instructed quietly, "Now, bathe your face, *ma petite*, and erase all sign of your tears. Tonight we celebrate your coming of age and your freedom from the past. That is a joyous occasion with no place for distress."

Waiting the short minutes while Angelica refreshed herself, Tante Minette turned Angelica's chin gently in her direction.

"Now smile for me, ma petite. It is a great occasion, and I thank the Lord that he has spared us both that we might celebrate it together. Shall we not show him our appreciation? Smile, *ma petite poupée* . . . smile!"

Her heart lifting at the whispered encouragement, Angelica looked into Tante Min's bright, lined face. The smile that curved her lips bore no trace of its former uncertainty.

"*Oui*, Tante Minette. You are right. Papa Jon awaits us. Shall we go?"

Nodding, Tante Minette accepted her hand. Turning, the two slender figures walked quickly toward the door and within a few moments were walking down the staircase toward the brightly lit dining room and those who awaited them.

Conversation moved briskly around the crowded table. Nodding to Tante Minette's softly spoken comments, Angelica was intensely aware that her father's eyes had scarcely moved from her person since she had come into the room. Brilliant blue and glazed with a suspicious brightness, they had followed her entrance proudly as she had approached him. The arms that had closed around her in a warm embrace as she paused to kiss his cheek had trembled, and her determination to avoid tears had been almost shattered.

But the party had gone well. Bowing to her desire to celebrate modestly the occasion of her coming of age, Jonathan had invited no strangers to join their group. Instead the participants in the affair included merely the hired hands, Peter, Tante Minette, Papa Jon and herself. But that was enough . . . more than enough.

Angelica had been surprisingly touched by the trouble the hired hands had taken to show their appreciation for the event. Dressed in their Sunday best, clean shaven, their hair slicked back in uncommon neatness, they had obviously arrived promptly and were waiting as she entered the room. Their appreciative comments on her appearance had been more than generous, and Angelica had responded with considerable warmth, grateful that the hostility that had accompanied Gareth's departure from the ranch had finally been put to rest.

Maria and Sophie, once again in sole control of the kitchen, had prepared a feast which had included several incredibly delicious roasts from a steer freshly slaughtered in her honor, potatoes and vegetables in steaming mounds, and mountains of biscuits from her own recipe. Crowning the spectacular meal was a great fruited cake, elaborately iced and served to her with great ceremony. Doing the honors of cutting and serving the impressive confection, Angelica was unable to keep her mind from the path her mind had taken since the festivities had started.

The good wishes she had received this night had been many and sincere. There had been no doubting the warmth they had carried, but the smile on her face was becoming more stiff and forced with each moment that passed. Gareth . . . how long since she had seen his face . . . felt his touch. His absence in this room grew more painful by the moment. She would not be able to sustain this bright facade much longer.

But deep signs of satisfaction were sounding around the table as the men leaned back comfortably in their chairs. Taking the opportunity in the sudden lapse of conversation, Jonathan drew himself to his feet. Walking quickly toward her, he leaned down to press a light kiss on Angelica's cheek before reaching into his pocket to withdraw a small, crudely wrapped package.

"It just isn't a proper party without presents, Angelica, and I'm figuring it's the proper time to open mine."

Angelica protested with a small frown.

"But you have already given me this lovely gown. I did not expect more."

Jonathan's eyes misted over unexpectedly, stirring similar response within her as he replied quietly, "The gown was truly a gift for me. Seein' you wear it has fulfilled a dream . . ." His voice breaking off, Jon took a deep breath and continued with a new depth of tone, indicating the small package she still held in her hand. "This is a gift for you."

Averting her face, unable to say more, Angelica unwrapped the package. Her fingers trembling, she opened the small hinged box to see a single strand of pearls with dainty matching earbobs.

"Your mama said she received her pearls on her eighteenth birthday. She intended to pass them to you on this occasion, but . . ." Swallowing hard, Jon continued with a forced smile. "Well, her pearls are gone with her, but I wanted to give you these in their stead, darlin'. Celeste would have approved."

Not realizing she had risen to her feet, Angelica circled Jonathan's chest spontaneously with her arms and rested her cheek on its reassuring strength. Managing to restrain her tears, she finally drew back to whisper hoarsely, "I will treasure them always, Papa Jon."

The remainder of the gifts had been presented: a gold locket from Peter, and a fine shawl presented shyly by Brett on behalf of Maria, Sophie and the men. Angelica had expressed her appreciation with heartfelt gratitude when Tante Minette raised herself slowly to her feet.

Gaining the attention of all as she approached Angelica in her stately manner, Tante Minette took Angelica's hand solemnly.

"My gift to you is too personal to be presented at this table, *ma chérie*. If I might beg your indulgence . . ." Turning toward the many gazes locked on her sober face, Tante Minette continued quietly. "Monsieur Jon . . . Monsieur Macfadden, I think it would be best if you are both present when it is given, since you are both intimately concerned here."

Taking Angelica's hand, Tante Minette waited until she had risen to her feet before turning back to those remaining. "If you will please excuse us."

Exchanging brief looks with her father and Peter, Angelica allowed herself to be led by Tante Minette's firm hand out of the dining room toward the study. Her heart was pounding, a strange premonition heightening her senses.

Turning as the door to the study closed behind them, Angelica was aware of Jon's hand on her arm. She had not realized she was trembling visibly until Jon urged her to a chair.

But Tante Minette would allow no distraction to her purpose. Reaching into the small embroidered bag she carried on her arm, she withdrew an envelope.

"*Ma petite* Jeanette . . ." Hesitating, Tante Minette reached out a tentative hand. "I beg your indulgence in referring to you by the name with which you were christened. It means much to me at this moment."

At Angelica's tight nod, Tante Minette continued quietly. "Monsieur Jonathan and you both know that I should have made that fateful journey with your mama and yourself to this place many years ago. And indeed, I would have had I not been recuperating from the fever. For many years I was tormented by the caprice of fate which saw fit to spare me while taking my two beautiful loves in terrible and premature deaths. It was when I received the letter from Monsieur Jonathan, saying that you were alive and back with him, that I knew the true reason I had been spared. It is for that reason that I am here tonight.

"*Ma petite*, your mama did not leave New Orleans to come to this place with true peace of mind. In the short period before departure from our home there, she suffered many nights of tortured dreams, which in fact proved to be a strange premonition of the events which actually occurred. But her love for Monsieur Jonathan was too strong to allow 'such foolishness' to put yet another impediment in the way of their being together at last. Her only concession to that warning was this letter."

Pausing, her lined face filled with emotion, Tante Minette took a deep breath. "*Ma très belle* Celeste put this letter into my hand before leaving. She extracted a promise that should she not survive to be present on your eighteenth birthday, that I put it in your hand as she had put it in mine. Your mother loved you very deeply, *ma chérie*. I give this letter to you now with her love . . . and with mine . . ."

Her hands trembling so wildly that she was barely able to grasp the missive Tante Minette had placed in her hand, Angelica closed her eyes and held it tightly in an attempt to draw herself under control. The touch of a warm hand on her arm turned her to Jonathan's disturbed expression, and suddenly realizing that he suffered as much as she, Angelica delayed no longer. Carefully ripping open the seal, she drew out the neatly transcribed sheets.

"*Ma chérie*," Tante Minette's soft voice interrupted her concentration, turning her toward her deeply affected face as she continued, "despite the difficulty it may entail, I ask that you read the letter aloud. Monsieur Jonathan is intimately concerned with its contents, and he has waited a long time to hear from his dear Celeste again."

Nodding, momentarily unable to respond, Angelica unfolded the letter which still bore a light, remembered scent. Realizing by the mist which had glazed over her father's eyes that the scent had struck a similar chord in his memory as well, Angelica turned her attention to the sight of her mother's written hand. Her voice a husky whisper in the silence of the room, Angelica began to read:

Ma bien-aimée, Jeanette,

It is my fervent hope that you do not have cause to read this letter, for in order for you to do so, it will mean that I am not with you on this day of your eighteenth birthday. *Ma chérie*, I wish to tell you first that this day, eighteen years ago, was the happiest of my life despite the circumstances of your birth. You are a grown woman—you know that I was not married to your father when you were born, but it is my most honest declaration to you now that that fact in no way inhibited my joy in seeing your beautiful face for the first time. Please always remember that I love you and that I have loved you from the moment you were born. It is for that reason that I write to you now so you might understand the true circumstances of your birth. But to do so, I find I must start from the beginning. I implore your patience, *ma chérie*.

You have never met your grandparents, Jeanette, and I do not expect you ever will, so I think you will be surprised to learn that they were wealthy people, high-born in the society of New Orleans. I, being their only daughter and considered fair of face and totally pleasing to the eye, was spoiled outrageously from birth. There was nothing I wanted which was denied me and no place within reason where I could not go. My loyal Minette, dearer to me than my own mother, was the only sobering influence in my life, and I fought the few restrictions she imposed as my nanny, my tutor, and my friend with all the zeal of my rebellious spirit. But Minette was no match for my permissive parents' desire to please me.

I was seventeen years of age when I fell wildly in love. Prior to that time I had been exposed to a limited society of high-born Creoles such as myself. I was no match for the worldliness of Jacques LeClaire when I met him. He was a beautiful man, Jeanette. His hair was black as the midnight sky, his eyes dark and piercing. His broad, manly physique far outshone that of any of the boys whom I had known. I threw myself wholeheartedly into this first romance, certain that he felt for me the same which I felt for him.

After I had known Jacques for only a month, he proposed marriage to me, and I was enraptured. But my joy was doomed to an early death. My parents were shocked! Jacques was without family . . . without prospects . . . an adventurer who was taking advantage of my youth! They would not allow me to see him again and I was shattered. But Jacques did not give up. Swearing his love for me, he convinced me to meet with him. His ardor was profound, and deeply in its throes, I allowed him to make intimate love to me.

Once I had taken that first step outside the restrictions of society, I was more determined than ever to marry Jacques. In a stringent campaign, I pleaded, demanded, ranted, and carried on, but my parents would not relent. They would not allow me to see Jacques again, and determined not to allow them to get in the way of our love, I consented when Jacques suggested that we run away together.

Stealing out in the middle of the night, I joined Jacques and we escaped to a place just outside the city where Jacques said we would not be found. I was deeply in love, but disturbed that we had not gone straight to a priest to be married. Jacques explained that he would write a letter to my parents, telling him we were together. He stated that the fact that we were living together without benefit of wedlock would be an added pressure on them to give their consent. He declared that we would soon be back at my home with my parent's blessing on our marriage, and that we would shortly thereafter be the central figures in the wedding of the year.

But Jacques's plans did not take into account my father's fury on learning of my rebellion. Letter after letter failed to obtain a response, and Jacques became desperate. In a final attempt to speak to them, Jacques went into the city to my home without my knowledge. He returned in a state of extreme agitation. His cheek marked with the cruel cut of a riding crop, he vented his full fury on me. He stated that my parents had disowned me, that they had no desire to ever see me return. He said that they had turned me over into his care without so much as a penny with which to support me. I was shocked, but I begged Jacques to calm himself, stating that our love would see us through this unexpected setback.

It was then that Jacques told me he had never loved me . . . that I was vain and stupid with little to offer a man besides my physical beauty. He said he had long ago become bored with that, and the only thing which had truly held him with me had been the prospect of a generous settlement from my parents upon our marriage. He said that since that prospect was gone, he wanted no part of me.

Jacques left me that night . . . abandoned me in the country while he took what was left of my jewelry. I was shattered, but managed to find my way back to the city the following day. I returned to my home, only to discover that my parents refused to see me. Turned away from their door, I made my way to a public house and took a room. I was in shock and frightened. Managing to sell a ring which I had salvaged from Jacques's greed, I supported myself for a few days before returning ashamed and repentant to my parents' home once again. But I was informed at the door that Monsieur and Madame DuBois had no daughter.

After a week of seclusion in my rented room, my money was running out. Near to despair, I dressed myself in my best garments, taking especial care with my toilette, and made my way to the bank. I was aware that my grandmother DuBois had left me a sizable sum which could help me to support myself until I was able to decide what course to take. I approached the bank with carefully concealed trepidation, only to find that the sum I needed was held in trust for me until I turned eighteen years of age.

That final blow too much for my weakened defenses, I was only able to make it out of the door of that establishment before bursting into tears. It was then, in my state of utter desperation, that I met Jonathan Dawson. Kind, generous, and concerned, he took me back to my rooms and remained until I had gained control of myself once again. Telling him only as much of my story as I dared, I managed to stir his sympathy enough that he paid the rent on my room and arranged for my first hearty meal in days. He told me that he was in New Orleans to speak to the impresarios who were attempting to bring Americans into the virgin land of Texas.

Jonathan Dawson returned to my rooms many times that week to assure himself of my safety. During one of those visits he explained that he was from an area not far from New Orleans, that he was married . . . had been so for many years, and that he had a son. He did not need to explain that his marriage was not a happy one, for his eyes had clouded over at the mention of his married state, only coming to life at the mention of the boy, who he stated was named Gareth after his own father.

It was during this week of reprieve from my uncertainty in the face of Jonathan's platonic consolation that my worst fear was confirmed. I was pregnant. Bitter and desperate, I was in a state of total collapse when Jonathan again called at my room. Not knowing the full reason for my collapse, Jonathan did his best to console me, to alleviate my despair. His arms were warm and comforting. I was in the circle of their concern when I looked up into his face, truly seeing him for the first time. I was lost and frightened, and at that moment knew nothing but the desire to be held and loved, to know safety and peace if for only a short time. In the end it was I who seduced Jonathan, giving myself to him with all the fervor of my aching heart.

It was the next day when I awoke in his arms that I realized what I had done . . . and a devious plan formed in my mind. Jonathan Dawson was an honest man. In my newfound wisdom I had no doubt about that, and in my newfound bitterness, I realized this was the best opportunity I would have to find a way out of my dilemma. Jonathan Dawson had already indicated his intention to stay in New Orleans until plans could be completed for his intended move to the Texas grants. I needed only keep him with me for that time, and my future would be secure.

As it turned out, it was not a difficult proposition to keep Jonathan with me, and it was not long before I realized his feelings for me far transcended simple lust. The only situation I had not anticipated was the growth of my feelings for him. At the end of the month when it came time for Jonathan to leave, I found I could not bring myself to go through with my plan to declare him the father of my child.

Jonathan left New Orleans but not before he had settled a sum on me that was sufficient to see me through the next month. I was grateful and wished him a tearful good-bye. But I was not prepared for the desolation I suffered when he was gone. It was then that I realized in all the time I had spent with Jacques, I had not found even a portion of the happiness I had found in my short month with Jonathan.

My funds had all but run out when Jonathan returned. Ecstatic with happiness on seeing him again, I realized the true depth of my feelings, and from that day on my love for him has never deviated. It was only through accident that Jonathan found out about my pregnancy. There was no doubt in his mind from the moment of my confirmation that the child I carried was his, and in my love for him, I could not declare the child to be that of Jacques LeClaire. I have asked God to forgive me many times for that deceit, but, in truth, the happiness in my dear Jonathan's eyes when he saw you for the first time, Jeanette, was worth the weight of my sin.

There is not much more I need to tell you, Jeanette. Your Papa Jon was with me as often as he was able. He returned to New Orleans at least once a month during my pregnancy and the love between us grew. It was through my dear Jon that Minette was able to locate me at last. She came to stay with me, and is the only person who knew the true circumstances of your conception, other than myself. My family found out about your birth, and though unwilling to see me or acknowledge me, settled an allotment on me which allowed me to raise you comfortably without any undue pressure on Jonathan.

Because of his desire to stay near us, Jonathan did not make his move to the Texas grants for many years, until he was forced, by a reversal in his own financial position, to take the step. We have seen him less often this past year, but he has not forgotten us. Now, at the first opportunity he has sent for us to be with him. I long for the day when I will repeat my vows to him . . . the same vows I have voiced silently over the years of our association.

Jonathan, when you read this letter I ask you to forgive me my deceit. It was done in love, *mon cheri*, with all the love in my heart. But I have not borne it lightly. I can only tell you that I am grateful to Jacques LeClaire for having taken me from the life which I would have known had he not practiced his wiles on me. For without his poorly intentioned interference, I would never have come to know you—would never have known the depth of your love—would never have known what true love could be. I thank you for your love. It has given true purpose to my life and has made me complete. *Je t'aime*, Jonathan. *Je t'aime.*

Of you, *ma chérie* Jeanette, I ask forgiveness, too, for concealing the true circumstances of your birth for so long. But Jonathan Dawson was and is your father more truly than the man whose seed conceived you, the man who was killed shortly after your birth in a gambling incident. Remember, it was Jonathan Dawson who smiled with pride when you were introduced to the world, his arms who held and rocked you in love, his voice who sang you to sleep in the hoarse monotone which was so lulling, his bright eyes who watched you grow with such enduring love. And it is he who loves you still, wherever you both may be.

To Minette, more truly my mother than the woman who bore me, thank you for your love and for giving me peace at last.

If there is a forgiving God, I am smiling down on all of you right now—my true mother, my beautiful daughter, and my love, Jonathan, truer husband to me than I could ever have known, than I ever deserved.

Je t'aime. Your own, Celeste.

Silence met the cessation of Angelica's soft whisper. Not realizing tears were running down her face, Angelica carefully placed the letter on the desk beside her and raised her eyes to the man who stood at her side. A low gasp escaping her lips when she saw Jonathan Dawson's face also wet with tears, she moved immediately to her feet, and without hesitation, stepped into his anxious embrace.

Jon's voice was low, broken.

"Angelica . . . Darlin', how many times must I lose

512

you . . . ?"

Suppressing a sob at the sorrow in Jon's tone, Angelica drew away to look up into his broken expression. The joy beginning to dawn on her face held him motionless for her breathless reply.

"Do you not see, Papa Jon? You have not truly lost me. I am your daughter now as much as I have ever been . . . but you have regained your son. Gareth . . . Gareth can now come home! And we both will be waiting for him, Papa Jon! I will be . . ."

Her words drawing to a sudden halt, Angelica stiffened before turning around in a jerking movement toward the lanky figure who still leaned against the far wall. Peter . . . She had forgotten . . .

Her eyes meeting Peter's pale-eyed gaze, Angelica gasped at the anguish displayed so openly there. Looking back to her father for a short moment and seeing the understanding she sought, she turned and walked to Peter's side. Her arms moving around his chest to embrace him, she felt his despair, and she emitted a soft sob. In each joy there was sorrow. Tonight she would spend in consolation, but tomorrow .. tomorrow ..

Spurring her horse into a faster pace, Angelica stared into the distance unseeingly. Her responsive mare, seeming to sense her impatience, leaned heavily into her stride. The brisk March air whipped free the curling tendrils at Angelica's hairline, temporarily freeing with them the weight of anxiety which had begun to color her days.

It had been weeks since Tante Minette had delivered Celeste DuBois's letter into her hand. Angelica had written immediately to Gareth, explaining the contents of her mother's touching missive, telling him she needed him, wanted him to come home. But there had been no response. Tante Min had bid a touching farewell to the Circle D only the week before, and Angelica's tension had increased.

Papa Jon . . . Angelica's thoughts stopped on the name. She would never think of Jonathan Dawson in any other way, and she had been assured by the conflicting emotions she had seen in his eyes when her mother's letter had been read, that he felt the same as she. But she had sensed his growing tension as well, the same tension which had seemed stronger after the last meeting of the Safety Committee only a week before.

The sound of hoofbeats to her rear cut unconsciously into Angelica's thoughts. She did not have to look back to know their source. Reining her horse automatically to a slower place, she finally glanced over her shoulder and shot Peter a smile. But there was no smile in return as he drew up alongside.

"Ye canna escape from yer tensions in a quick, headlong rush, lass."

Shaking her head, willing away the warmth that filled her eyes, Angelica responded hoarsely, "How is it that you're so understanding, Peter?"

"It is nae difficult to understand someone you love."

Angelica had no response, and Peter finally smiled.

"Did I leave ye wordless, lass? I dinna mean to frustrate ye with my words or my presence. It's just that I canna make myself leave this place until everything is finished once and for all in my mind."

Her eyes holding his for a few seconds more, Angelica nodded. She had been selfishly thinking only of her own torment in waiting to hear from Gareth. But Peter suffered too, and she had been callously insensitive to his pain of late.

Knowing true regret, Angelica offered simply, "What could be keeping Gareth away, Peter? It has been weeks since I wrote to him. Do you suppose . . ." Halting her words, Angelica shook her head in frustration. "Oh, I am sorry, Peter. I know you know no more about the delay in Gareth's response than Papa Jon and I, but . . ."

"Jon wrote a letter to Gareth as well ye, did he nae? I dinna believe they could both have gone astray. It is far more logical to believe that Gareth has moved on from San Antonio . . . possibly to a point where he can nae be reached. He was committed to traveling with Bill Travis, was he nae? And Bill Travis is workin' in the service of the governor, is that nae also the truth?''

"Yes, that is what the Safety Committee reports. But it is near the end of March, Peter . . ."

"Aye, I know how long it has been. And I nae have a doot that Gareth wou' be here did he know the truth of that letter from yer mother . . ."

Allowing herself to face the fear she sustained deep inside for the first time, Angelica averted her eyes momentarily, only to lift them slowly to Peter's once again.

"You . . . you do not think he has found someone else . . . another woman, and he hesitates to write or return knowing I am here . . .?"

His expression showing the first spark of the turmoil which reigned inside him, Peter shook his head. "I cou' nae be so lucky as to have that happen. You ask the truth and I give it to ye squarely. I have nae always admired Gareth Dawson. In Real del Monte I despised his treatment of ye, his flauntin' of the intimacy between ye. I considered him then and still think of him now as a mon who has managed to demand more love and loyalty than he truly deserves. But nae, in all that time and hard feelin's that existed between us, I dinna ever consider Gareth Dawson a fool. There was no doot of his feelin's fer ye, lass, before he left. And because he is nae a fool, I have no doot he will return here as soon as he receives yer letter.''

"Then . . . then why do you stay, Peter? I . . ."

"I stay for the simple reason that I can nae make myself leave until I have seen this through. And since Jon is wantin' to start up with the project again . . ."

"Peter, I am sorry." Raising her hand to brush absent-mindedly at a flying wisp of hair, Angelica grumbled as she turned her head toward the distance, "I should not have allowed Papa Jon to dissuade me. I could have been in San Antonio by now . . ."

"Aye, in the midst of the turmoil that surrounds it. And if Gareth was nae there? His letters have nae been regular. Ye know only that he travels with the mon Travis. Wou' ye follow him from place to place . . .?"

"It is what I should have done."

515

"Nae. Jon was right. Better that Gareth come here than have ye chasin' . . ."

But Peter did not finish his sentence. Instead, he strained his eyes into the distance, toward the figure racing toward the Circle D. Catching the line of his gaze, Angelica felt her pulse quicken. Could that racing figure be Gareth? No, it would be too much to ask, too much to believe, that he was home at last.

Not sparing time for another thought, Angelica wheeled her horse back in the direction of the house. The rider did not see them. If she judged her position correctly, they would both reach the house at about the same time . . .

Angelica was flying along the trail, her body bent low over her mare's glistening neck, but she had no thought for the glory of the ride. Instead her mind was intent on her objective, the racing figure that even now was drawing closer to the Circle D.

She was breathless, her heart pounding in her ears as she reined up sharply in front of the house and jumped down from the saddle. She had tossed her mare's reins over the hitching post and was running toward Jon where he stood in front of the barn. She was not aware of Peter's heavy tread behind her, his eyes concentrating on the rider that was nearing.

Her step drawing to an abrupt halt, Angelica felt disappointment choke her throat. No, it was not Gareth. The rider was smaller, lighter-haired. It was Dennis Fairclough on another run for the Committee of Safety. The boy's enthusiasm for his assignment was unfailing, but somehow Angelica could not rise above her disappointment. Almost tempted to turn back to the house, Angelica forced herself to continue, to come to stand by Jon's side as Dennis reined up sharply.

But the boy was excited beyond the norm, his face flushed to a heated color. His obvious emotional involvement in his message caused a new fluttering in her stomach. Her fists clenching at her sides, Angelica watched as the boy swallowed and then swallowed again. When he spoke his voice was unsteady.

"It . . . it's San Antonio, sir. It's fallen! On March sixth . . . The last defense was made at the Alamo. Over one hundred and eighty of our men, sir, they're all dead! It was Santa Anna! He had five thousand troops. He sounded the Deguello at the outset . . . no quarter. He burned all the bodies, sir, in a funeral pyre . . . Crockett, Bowie, Travis . . ."

The boy continued speaking, but Angelica heard no more. Her shocked mind had seemed to jar to a stop at the words that kept echoing again and again inside her brain. All dead . . . all of them at the Alamo . . .

Her eyes shooting to Jon's white face, Angelica saw the anguish reflected there. Gareth had been with Travis. His last letter had stated his commitment to remain at Travis's side . . . No! It couldn't be true!

Taking a shaky step forward, Angelica rasped harshly, "You're sure . . . no one got away . . ."

"Ma'am, they're all dead. Them that wasn't dead when the Mexicans stormed over the wall was put immediately to the sword. Nobody got away. The only people who was spared was Almaron Dickinson's wife, their little daughter, and two nigger slaves."

The boy's sobbing voice was beginning to escape her, but Angelica pressed her quest. The ground was moving beneath her feet but she stared firmly into his tear-filled eyes.

"You said Travis . . ."

"They took him off the cannon where he fell with a shot through his forehead and they threw him on the fire . . ."

The world rocked sharply. Angelica opened her mouth in spontaneous protest, but no sound emerged. The words were caught in her mind, going around and around in a dizzying circle. Oh, God, no! Gareth . . . dead! Oh, God, he's dead . . .

There was a lapse of sound as the world came to a shuddering halt, holding Angelica frozen as the words ran over themselves inside her brain. Gareth appeared before her and she reached out to touch him, but there was no substance to the vision . . . nothing but the empty air, the empty sky, the empty earth and the deep, empty blackness

517

which welcomed her.

It was a week later and Angelica still walked as if in a sleep. In the time since Dennis Fairclough's frantic account of San Antonio's fall, it had been confirmed. Gareth's name had been on the rolls at San Antonio. The great funeral pyre built at Santa Anna's direction, in which the bodies of the heroes of the Alamo had been burned, had eliminated the possibility of positive identification of his remains. He was gone . . . Gareth was gone.

Time seemed to stand still, refusing to allow her pain alleviation. The pall that hung over the Circle D was deadening, the anger and frustration of Gareth's as well as the other loyal patriots' deaths stirring a rage that could not be quelled. Each day more men flocked to Sam Houston's call, and it was said that his army was growing to unbelievable proportions. There was now complete unity of purpose among Texans . . . cries for revenge . . . to remember the Alamo . . .

But Angelica was disconsolate. None of it would bring Gareth back. She would never know his arms around her again, hear his husky voice in her ear, know the wonder of his kiss or the soul-shaking tenderness of his love.

Unable to stand the torture of her own thoughts a moment longer, Angelica drew herself to her feet and took a last glance around her room. The brilliance of the afternoon sun shone brightly through her window, and she felt its siren call. Yes, she needed to feel the sun on her head, fresh air blowing against her face. She needed to clear her mind so she might be able to think again. She turned and started rapidly toward the door.

She would go out for a ride. She would give her mare her head . . . allow her all the leeway she desired, and would ride until she could ride no more. Then she would stop and think, away from the Circle D, free of the sorrow that filled the air, the troubled gazes that followed her. Yes, she needed her escape.

Moving rapidly, her mind set on her course, Angelica hesitated only long enough to snatch up her hat before walking silently down the front staircase. It was fortunate for her intentions that Peter had gone to town earlier on business of his own. Papa Jon had ridden out with the boys after their noon meal, allowing her an even greater opportunity for the solitude she desired. Sounds of activity from the kitchen confirmed the fact that Marie and Sophie were involved in their usual chores, and satisfied that no objections would be expressed against her solitary ride, Angelica walked quickly out the front door. She wanted no one near . . . no one but the one man whom she would never see again.

Her step quick and sure, Angelica went directly to the barn, and within moments she had saddled her mare and was leading it outside. Mounting easily, Angelica spurred her forward, knowing a deep satisfaction in her sense of escape. Yes, this was what she had needed . . . had needed badly . . .

She had been riding for an endless time. Running her mare hard at first, she had later slowed her to a cooling walk before resuming a rapid pace once again. She had no destination in mind, no actual idea of the ground she had covered. Her only thought had been to escape from the torment which filled her mind with pain. Perhaps . . . perhaps in exhaustion there would be freedom . . .

That thought giving her hope, she spurred her horse onward into the endless horizon.

The sun was well past the midpoint in the sky. Suddenly conscious of her mare's labored breathing, Angelica was filled with remorse. Her eyes moving to a group of trees in the distance, Angelica turned her tired mare in its direction. A cooling walk there and a long drink would refresh them both. Yes, it was time for a rest.

Relieved when the cover of trees had been reached, Angelica dismounted quickly and stretched her cramped muscles. Her mare's soft whinny brought a small smile to her lips.

"All right, girl, I know you're thirsty now that you've cooled off a bit. We'll get to that water right away."

Leading her anxious animal toward the small stream that

glittered in the rays of the golden sun, Angelica watched absentmindedly as her mare dipped her head toward the swirling ripples. The quiet of the grove was balm to Angelica's troubled heart. Yes, she would rest here for a while before returning.

Securing her reins to the saddle, knowing her mare would not wander far from the sparkling stream and the green grass that abounded around her, Angelica lowered herself to the ground and leaned back against the gnarled tree trunk behind her. Thankful for the numbness which had seemed to pervade her mind, she allowed her eyes to drop closed. Oh, God, she needed peace. She needed it so desperately.

She was drifting in a world colored by the brilliant glow of the sun against her closed lids. Golden dreams invaded her mind . . . treasured thoughts which gave her bitter-sweet pain. Gareth's face, sober, his dark eyes unyielding, looked steadily into hers. But his lips were parting to whisper to her and she waited silently for his remembered words . . .

"The way you feel in my arms, darlin' . . . the beauty we have when we come together . . . it's sweeter, more heady than wine, and it's ours . . . ours alone."

Oh, Gareth . . . When had she begun to love him? It had come so gradually, starting on that first day in the heat of Gareth's desire for her and the response she had felt deep inside. It had grown in the midst of the conflict between them, but it had been brought to full, magnificent bloom by Gareth's soul-shaking tenderness. Echoes of loving phrases, memories of searing passion assaulted her mind, and she felt the full depth of the love Gareth had given her so freely. It was lost . . . lost to her forever, and she would never. . .

Her mare's sharp whinny stirred her from her drifting sleep, and Angelica opened her eyes. Two unexpected male figures standing above her, silhouetted in darkness against the glow of the sun, startled her into abrupt wakefulness. Snapping to a sitting position, she had raised her hand to shield her eyes against the glare, straining to see the faces held in shadow, when one of the men reached down to offer her his hand.

"*Buenos tardes*, Señorita Rodrigo. Please, you will raise yourself to your feet. There is a matter we must discuss."

The coarse voice, heavily accented with Spanish, was unfamiliar. Straining to clear her mind of the fogginess of sleep, Angelica refused the proffered hand, and drew herself up quickly to her feet. Apprehension stiffened her spine as she squinted into the faces of the two unknown men. They were Mexican, short, with the tightly muscles physiques and erect postures of working soldiers. Their florid complexions were darkened by days in the sun, their dark mustaches heavy over unsmiling mouths. They were distinctly foreigners to this part of Texas where hostility ran so high against them at this particular point in time, and obviously were not casual transients as they had used her name . . . the name she had borne in a time which now seemed long ago.

Refusing to allow a hint of the trepidation which shook her, Angelica replied coolly to the man's opening remark.

"Who are you? What business do you have with me?"

Clearly unintimidated, the first fellow flicked an assessing glance over her face.

"Señorita, it matters little who my compatriot and I are. What matters is this letter I carry to you." His lips parting in a small smile which revealed uneven, tobacco-stained teeth, he continued in a carefully cultivated air of polite resolve as he drew a letter from a small pouch at his side and presented it to her with a mocking flourish. "For you *señorita*. We have traveled far in our effort to bring this to you and had all but despaired of a way to put it personally into your hands without being seen when you rode out so unexpectedly this afternoon."

Her brow furrowing into a frown at the appearance of the official-looking document, Angelica made no attempt to take it from his hand. Her hesitation stimulated a sharp comment from the second man who demanded harshly, "Señorita, we have no time to waste. It is to your advantage to read this missive quickly."

Her frown deepening, Angelica hesitated only a moment more before taking the letter and breaking the seal. The sheets were covered with a flowery, elaborate hand. Her eyes flicking to the bottom of the second sheet, Angelica experienced a flash of apprehension. Esteban Arricalde! Straining to suppress the sudden trembling the signature evoked, Angelica swallowed tightly and began to read.

Querida Angelica,

I can only think that you are greatly surprised to have this letter put into your hand. It is my thought that you never expected to hear from me again, but as you can see, I have not forgotten you. There is a matter long unresolved between us, an omission which I expect to correct at last.

First, I must give you my deepest thanks for the letter you sent so opportunely to San Antonio. Of course, it was not addressed to me, but you must understand that a missive of any sort to an addressee by the name of Gareth Dawson would be sure to gain my attention. It was a lovely letter, *querida*, and I confess to considerable jealousy that it was addressed to an individual unworthy of your so eloquently expressed feelings. But it is my thought that you will soon adequately salve my jealousy . . . that you will apply yourself with great diligence to the soothing of my wounded feelings.

No, do not allow your anger to overcome your good sense, my beautiful *puta*. And you must allow me a brief lapse into my old manner of addressing you now that you find yourself to be a respected daughter of a beautiful New Orleans Creole of good blood. But you are still a bastard, are you not, *querida*, a woman with no father's name to add to her own? Yes, your letter was very informative, and it is now easy for me to understand the reason for your extraordinary beauty, your indominable spirit, and your fire. It is that fire that I intend to bank, *querida*, to keep to a steady flame which will only flare to a blazing glory

522

under my persuasive, intimate touch.

You are pensive . . . angry at my words . . . feel
that they are a useless exercise in vanity. No, *querida*,
you are wrong. For you see, I hold the key to your
adherence to the plan I have devised so brilliantly.
Your letter clarifies the strength of my advantage only
too clearly. The key I hold is simple. You see, Gareth
Dawson is my prisoner.

Si, querida, your love . . . the man whom you
implored to return to you at the Circle D, was not
killed at our great victory of the Alamo. The truth of
that matter is that prior to the battle, your dear
Gareth, seemingly putting little value on his life,
volunteered to attempt to work his way through our
lines to deliver a call for aid for his friend, Lieutenant
Colonel Travis. He was wounded and removed to our
headquarters for interrogation. El President General
Santa Anna finally became disgusted with his uncooperative attitude and turned him over to me. Gareth
Dawson is my prisoner still, *querida*, and I now put it
to you bluntly. His life is in your hands.

I must tell you that I did not choose to allow
Gareth to read your letter. No, I do not have it in my
heart to alleviate the anguish I am sure he experiences, believing that you are related so closely by
blood as to make your continued alliance a sin in the
eyes of the world.

So, if you value your lover's life, you will follow the
instructions of my two very trusted lieutenants. Their
instructions are to deliver you to me with the utmost
haste, for you see, should there be an unnecessary
delay in their return, I have determined to execute
Señor Dawson.

It is my advice that you tell no one where and with
whom you are departing, for each word you speak
puts a heavier weight on the slender thread by which
Señor Dawson's life hangs.

Ramon y Ricardo await your decision, *querida*
Angelica. I advise you to decide quickly whether you

intend to return with them, for each moment you hesitate takes your lover closer to death.

Querida Anglica, I feel I must emphasize most clearly that Gareth Dawson is my prisoner. His disposition is in my hands. It is my thought that you will be able to persuade me to be generous with his life. You have it in your power to do so. The choice is yours.

Adios, querida. Hasta la vista. Your obedient servant, Colonel Esteban Arricalde.

Her shocked mind still reeling at the message the letter conveyed, Angelica slid her eyes back across the carefully drawn words. Finding the ones she sought, she read the sentence again and again.

"The key I hold is simple. You see, Gareth Dawson is my prisoner."

Gareth alive . . . Gareth, alive!

Hope soaring to life in her breast, Angelica raised her eyes to the two men before her. Holding the spokesman's eyes firmly with her own, she questioned breathlessly, "Is it true? Gareth Dawson . . . you have seen him? He is alive and well?"

"He is wounded, señorita, but he was making a satisfactory recovery when we left on this assignment. Colonel Arricalde wanted me to reassure you that the prisoner's treatment would be sure to improve as soon as you arrive at our destination."

Biting back the response that rose to her lips, Angelica replied quietly, "And where is that destination, Lieutenant?"

"Señorita, I am not so much a fool as to divulge that information to you so you might attempt escape to gain help to rescue Senor Dawson. I have been instructed to answer only the questions to which I have already responded. Now, what is your decision?"

Bending down to scoop her hat from the ground beside her feet, Angelica raised her eyes once again to the soldier's intense scrutiny.

"How soon may we leave, Lieutenant?"

In answer, the man turned to signal his compatriot, and her mare was drawn to her side. Within a few moments the efficient soldier had assisted her into her saddle and was mounted beside her.

Turning back, he responded in a low voice, "I offer you a final word of warning, Señorita Rodrigo. Your cooperation in this endeavor is of the utmost importance. We have been instructed to return within a stipulated length of time or the prisoner will be executed. We have already lost two days in an attempt to define a way to reach you covertly. If we are to arrive at our destination before it is too late, you must employ your considerable skill as a horsewoman and not attempt to hold us back. Señor Dawson's life is in your hands. *Comprende, señorita?*"

Swallowing tightly, Angelica choked a brief response. *"Sí. Comprendo."*

Assuming the position indicated between the two men, Angelica spurred her horse forward. There had been no choice to her decision. Gareth, alive . . . Almost afraid to accept the hope offered in those two words, Angelica fought the heavy thudding of her heart, the joy that had soared into life within her. She could not afford to indulge herself in those emotions now. Gareth's future depended on the speed of their journey to an unknown destination. She could afford to think no more.

Chapter XVI

Esteban raised himself to his feet. He walked around the modest desk in the room he had assumed as his office and approached the crystal decanter on the sideboard. He stood for a few silent moments, his eyes moving over the sparkling amber liquid magnified within the prisms of the well-cut piece, but his mind was far from its mellow color. He took a moment to adjust the perfect cut of his uniform. He had had it made especially for this occasion, aware that the deep blue of its color did much to enhance the rich tone of his skin, that the masterful tailoring made the most of his well-maintained physique, that he had never looked more handsome. Yes, he had prepared well for this moment.

Reaching out, Esteban removed the crystal knob from the top of the decanter and carefully poured himself a glass of the rare brandy. Tonight was a special night, indeed. In an effort to restrain the anticipation he felt building inside him, he took a deep breath. Slowly raising his glass to his lips, he took a modest swallow and allowed the smooth liquor to slip slowly down his throat. Yes, brandy was made to be sipped slowly . . . savored . . . enjoyed from the first moment to the last. That was the manner in which he was going to enjoy Angelica. He had spent countless nights in ardent contemplation of this evening, and his plans were deeply defined. He had already put them into play . . . and that play would soon be evolving.

A low laugh sounding in his throat, Esteban raised his glass again to his lips, this time taking a deeper swallow. The result was a warmth that surged to the surface of his skin almost at the same moment the fluid heat reached inside to warm him. Angelica had always had that effect on him . . . the sudden flush of desire, the heat which all but consumed him the moment he touched her pale skin . . . the overwhelming need to steep himself deeply in the joys she offered . . . the joys which had never been truly his to indulge.

But that time would soon be over. Angelica . . . she had arrived with his lieutenants only a short hour before, and according to his instructions had been shown to her room. He had no desire to see her as she would appear after days and nights on the trail in a frantic ride to arrive in time to save her lover. No, he had no desire to see her with the anguish of concern hot in her eyes.

Instead, he had sent women in with a hot bath, a light meal, and had then instructed that she be dressed in the attire he had ordered for this occasion. When Angelica appeared before him this evening she would come as his concubine, eager to please him. He would allow her a short glimpse of her lover . . . so that she might be inclined to exert her best effort in his behalf, and then he would escort her to his room where he would proceed to take her slowly, with great enjoyment.

He had arranged for this house, on the outskirts of the conquered town, and had seen to it that it was carefully surrounded by Antonio's guards. Antonio's joy in the success of his endeavors at the Alamo was such, his prospects for a quick victory over these upstart Texans so brilliant, that his magnanimity in allowing Gareth Dawson to keep his life temporarily was unrestrained.

A small frown slipped across Esteban's brow. For a short time it had indeed looked as if Gareth Dawson was going to cheat him from his vengeance. The Texan's shoulder wound, unattended for several days, had become infected and it was due only to vigilance on the part of the local surgeon and himself that Gareth was now alive to play his part in this episode of revenge. Now it would be up to Angelica to convince him if Gareth should keep his life.

His eyes darting to the clock on the mantel, Esteban restrained his impatience. Just fifteen minutes more and Angelica would be walking through his door. He would welcome her warmly . . . very warmly indeed . . . and the first act would begin.

Her hands trembling, her stomach churning at the aroma rising from the untouched food which had been sent in to her room, Angelica attempted to adjust the daring décolletage of the gown which had just been slipped over her head. Uncertain whether she was indeed moving in a frightening dream or a farce of reality, she had arrived at this sprawling home an hour before. Exhausted from extended days and nights of travel, she had been shown to a room which had been carefully prepared for her. Her demands to see Colonel Arricalde had come to naught as she had been informed the colonel would see her within the hour, after she had had time to prepare herself.

She had been bathed and cosseted, a special meal sent in to her, and she had begun to realize that Esteban was taking great pleasure in this torment he had devised. Mentally consenting to allow him his sadistic enjoyment if it advanced her own cause as well, Angelica allowed herself to be prepared like the whore he had intended her to feel. The nimble hands of the women presently fussing over her had arranged her hair into a gleaming mass of dark curls atop her head, applied a delicate scent to her throat and shoulders, and now, after assuming the incredibly delicate undergarments provided, she was being dressed in a beautiful gown of gold-colored silk.

Realizing the last button had been fastened, Angelica

turned to the wide eyes of the young woman who had provided the service. The envy in the dark eyes looking into hers could not be denied, and Angelica was hard pressed not to make bitter comment. But her position was too tenuous. She could not be certain how much of her words would eventually reach Esteban's ears and she would not risk Gareth's life for so brief a satisfaction.

Closing her eyes for a few minutes' escape, Angelica attempted to control her rioting emotions. She would allow herself to be led to Esteban in the manner of a practiced whore if it gave him a perverse satisfaction to view her as such, but she would demand to see Gareth . . . immediately. Her anxiety was now such that she . . .

A sudden knock on the door interrupted her thoughts. Angelica jerked in its direction at the same moment the door was pushed open and a face, remarkably similar to those of the two men who had escorted her to this place, appeared in the opening.

"Colonel Arricalde awaits you, Señorita Rodrigo."

Her heart leaping in her breast, Angelica gave a sharp nod and stepped immediately forward. She would never be any more ready to face Esteban Arricalde than she was now.

Her small hands balling into anxious fists, Angelica walked quickly to the door and fell in place behind the two guards waiting there. Her heart pounding, she assumed their moderate pace.

Gareth paced the small, windowless room which had been his prison for the past two weeks. He had become sorely sick of the stark gray walls and the colorless floor. The hard cot on which he had lain, the first week in a delirium that had left his memory of that time sporadic at best, and the second week in silent recuperation, had become too strong a reminder of his helplessness.

But he was not as totally helpless as he pretended. Slipping off the sling in which he rested his arm, Gareth adjusted the thick cotton padding wadded against his wound. It was awkward and bulky, insisted upon by the cautious doctor, but it served to perpetuate the idea that his wound was still draining, and he had no desire to negate that impression. He raised his elbow in a slow, deliberate move calculated to flex his stiff shoulder. Yes, it was growing stronger every day. And for that bit of comfort he had to thank the silent Dr. Escobar. He had much more to thank the slender Mexican for, also. It was only due to the doctor's influence that the amount of food he had been served as he had slowly regained his health had increased, that he had been given a clean shirt to replace the ripped and bloodstained one he had worn since he had been captured, and that he had been given the small comfort each day of a pitcher of water and a cloth with which to bathe. But most of all he need thank him for not divulging the full extent of his recuperation.

The sling had become an excellent ploy and he had played it to the hilt on his visits from the gloating Esteban Arricalde. Pompous, vain, and far more deadly than he appeared, Esteban had visited him frequently, and had taken great pains to relate the complete annihilation of the Texan contingent at the Alamo. His spirits sinking at the reminder of the great loss, Gareth closed his eyes in heartsick despair. Bill Travis, Davey Crockett, Jim Bowie, Jim Bonham . . . countless other good men heartlessly butchered. The Deguello . . . how proudly Esteban had related the manner in which Santa Anna's troops had responded to the bugle's call of "no quarter." "No quarter" . . . and here was he, formerly a part of that brave force, being carefully, oh so carefully, nursed back to health.

Raising his hand, Gareth ran his fingers through his shaggy dark hair in an anxious gesture, his hand slipping down across the dark growth of beard which covered his formerly clean-shaven cheeks. Why? What was it Esteban had in mind? His desire to wipe the gloating expression from Esteban's aristocratic face during his visit that morning had been almost too difficult to withstand. But he was not prepared to demonstrate the full extent of his recuperation yet.

Raising his injured shoulder again, Gareth carefully

rotated his elbow another revolution. Yes, he would wait until Esteban played out his hand. He had no intention . . .

But the sound of conversation outside his door broke into Gareth's thoughts, drawing a frown to his face. What was it the guard had said: ". . . and she goes to him now . . .?" There was more furtive whispering and then a quick denial, "Oh, no, Ramon says she is very beautiful . . . and very determined. He says she kept up with both of them, asking no special considerations. He says he would not like to be Colonel Arricalde should he turn his back on her."

There was another low murmur and the laughing reply, "Well, then he shall have to sleep facing her!"

Gareth sneered his contempt. Doubtless Esteban was causing talk with his entertainment of his latest whore. Whoever she was, the woman was a fool. It would be best if she obtained her money now, before he was done with her, or she would find herself used and tossed out on the street like so much excess baggage.

Suddenly a face ever present in the shadows of his mind invaded his thoughts. Attempting to avoid the familiar torment, he closed his eyes, only to invite a clearer picture of great gray eyes which seared him even in memory. He took a slow, anguished breath. It had been Esteban's intention to use Angelica in that way . . . But she was safe from him now . . . safe at the Circle D. His father would keep her there, free from harm. He had that much to be thankful for . . .

The mumbled voice outside the door was retreating. It spoke again from a distance, to be answered by his guard's unmistakable reply.

"You need not worry, Pablo, our prisoner is secure."

Clenching his teeth in frustration at the truth of the guard's statement, Gareth deliberately enlarged the circles he made with his injured arm. Yes, his imprisonment was secure . . . for now, but Esteban would reveal his hand soon, and when he did . . .

His dark eyes trained on the doorway, Esteban responded to the sharp knock with a bid to enter. Secure in his position, having awaited the opportunity approaching for endless months, he was still unprepared for the moment when the door opened and Angelica stood before him. Suppressing a gasp with sheer force of will, he allowed his eyes to devour Angelica's breathtaking presence.

Majestic . . . more beautiful than any woman he had ever known, Angelica stood stiffly in the doorway. Animosity had turned her great gray eyes to silver ice and his heart jumped a beat at the cutting edge of their glare. The magnificent planes of her face were composed, allowing no sign of the anxiety he knew filled her mind. He signaled to his men to leave them, and her lushly trimmed lids lowered to regard him cautiously. She stood just inside the doorway in silence, awaiting his next move. Esteban allowed her the discomfort he knew she experienced as he indulged his hungry gaze a few moments longer. She was a goddess, finally come to her own, a vision in silver and gold, far more beautiful than he had imagined in his wildest dreams.

Slowly walking forward, Esteban came to stand directly in front of her. Looking down, his eyes holding her stare, he reached for her hand and raised it slowly to his lips. But the first contact of his mouth against her smooth flesh was almost his undoing. A small laugh escaped his lips as he forced himself to step back. He cupped her elbow with his hand and urged her farther into the room.

Angelica was rigid under his touch, and feeling some measure of satisfaction in the fact that she was not as coolly composed as she would have him think, Esteban turned to face her once again.

"Do you not have some words of greeting for me, Angelica? Many months and many miles have been passed since we last saw each other. Speaking for myself, I find I am very pleased to have you with me tonight."

Angelica made an obvious effort to maintain her control. Her voice was like shards of glass cutting into the passion smoldering inside him.

"Do not be deceived by the picture you see before you, Don Esteban. I have allowed myself to be bathed and dressed in this *puta's* garment you would have me wear. My

532

body has been scented, my hair dressed like a woman of the society to which you have acclimated yourself, but I am not one of your capital whores who is impressed by the sheen of fabric or the cut of rich garments. And neither am I a servant in your family's hacienda, a woman to be treated like the *puta* you believed me to be. I came here tonight for one purpose only. I wish to see Ga—"

"But you see, it matters little to me what it is that you desire Angelica. It matters solely what I desire, and I desire you!"

Anger surging to the surface, Esteban had interrupted her without hesitation. Having made his stiff declaration, he cupped Angelica's face with his palms, his fingers biting cruelly into the soft flesh of her cheeks.

"That should come as no surprise to you, my beautiful little bitch, and that is what you truly are. You have not changed, except to have become more beautiful, and I admit to satisfaction in that. I have spent too many nights in contemplation of the ways in which I would capture the fire that burns within you, bask in its heat, indulge myself in its color without being consumed. I would not wish to be cheated of that challenge."

Her face beginning to twitch with the fierce emotion she suppressed so stringently, Angelica retorted hotly, "I care for none of this that you speak. Gareth . . . I want to see Gareth! You claim he is your prisoner, but I have only your word and the word of your lackeys that it is indeed so. I do not intend to play your games . . . to do anything until I know that he is alive and well."

A new flame coming alive in his eyes at her words, Esteban slipped his hands to Angelica's neck, his fingers curling around the smooth column in a grip that was just short of constricting. His eyes were trained on her perfect lips and he experienced a fleeting satisfaction at the slight tremor he saw there.

"And if I tell you I would have you prove your good faith before I show him to you . . . ?"

"I want to see him now . . ."

"Oh, no, not yet . . . not yet . . ."

Esteban's hands tightened on her throat, restricting just enough of her breathing to cause Angelica to gasp. His reaction was quick, spontaneous, as his mouth swooped down to cover hers, taking advantage of her parted lips to deepen his kiss. His one hand slipped to the back of her neck to hold her firmly in his control as the other crushed her tight against the hard length of his body. Her struggles had no chance against the power of his voracious kiss, the strength of the arms which confined her, the cruelty of the pain he inflicted so carelessly. But Angelica fought his touch in writhing desperation. She had all but succeeded in tearing her mouth from his when he bit down fiercely on her lower lip, extracting a spontaneous cry of pain.

Thoroughly enjoying her helplessness, Esteban released her slowly, allowing her to draw back just enough that he might survey her pale face. His eyes lingered on her reddened lower lip, and he gave a harsh laugh.

"You see, Angelica, it will not do to oppose me too stringently. I am not your Gareth Dawson, to be easily manipulated. Before I allow you to see your precious Gareth, to content yourself that he is improving in health, I would have you understand a few, very important points. But first, you are pale, *querida*. Come, take some brandy with me. It is a special year, aged and saved for this day and the celebration which I am to conduct this night."

"I don't want . . ."

Angelica's tense response was interrupted by Esteban's dark glance.

"You have not been listening, Angelica. I have already told you that it makes very little difference to me what you want. I want you to share some brandy with me. It will soothe your nerves . . ."

Angelica forced herself to remain silent as Esteban took the few steps to the sideboard and returned within a few minutes with two filled glasses. She accepted the glass he gave her, and held it stiffly.

"I wish to propose a toast, Angelica." A frown flickering across his brow at Angelica's lightly disguised resistance, he continued with a touch of anger. "Smile, Angelica. It would be well if you showed your appreciation of my interest. Much hinges on my good will . . ."

Her smile little more than a grimace, Angelica watched satisfaction move across Esteban's smoothly handsome features.

"That is better. You will learn to obey me . . . and to please me . . . and I will show you how very well I will please you. But first, we must raise our glasses in a toast." His gaze sharpening, Esteban continued slowly, "To this night, and all it will mean . . ."

Her chin lifting in spontaneous protest, Angelica refused to raise the glass to her lips even as Esteban drank deeply. Aware that anger was growing in his eyes, Angelica stiffened, preparing herself as Esteban lowered his glass at last.

"Am I to assume your refusal to drink to my toast means that you expect to remain hostile to my attentions, Angelica? That is indeed unfortunate. Gareth was doing so well. I had expected to allow you to see him within a few minutes, but . . . well, I can see no point in tormenting you with his recuperation. I was, after all, the only thing which stood between him and the fate of all the other members of the Alamo garrison, and since I will no longer have an interest in him . . ."

Angelica regarded Esteban through half-lidded eyes, despising the quiver in her voice as she spoke.

"You know I will do all in my power to have you spare Gareth's life. But first I must know that he is indeed alive. That is all I ask of you . . . to allow me to see that Gareth is truly alive and well."

Lowering his glass to the desk beside him, Esteban closed the distance between them, his expression adamant. "You forget, Angelica, I am in the position to set the conditions here. You will see Gareth in good time, but you have not impressed me with your desire to please me. And I do, most sincerely, wish to be convinced."

His quickened breathing divulging the true extent of his agitation, Esteban instructed hoarsely, "Kiss me, Angelica. Show me how much it means to you to win my favor. Show me now, before I lose my patience and instruct my men to go directly to Gareth's room and . . ."

"No!" The horror of his unfinished statement reflected on her beautiful face, Angelica shook her head in adamant refutation of his threat. "No, Esteban, please . . ."

"Then put your arms around my neck . . ." His face flushing with color as Angelica lowered her glass to the desk beside them and slowly followed his command, Esteban drew her flush against him. His breath was hot on her lips.

"Now, kiss me, Angelica, kiss me the way you kiss your Gareth. Show me all that I have missed and all that I may expect to gain if I spare his life." His voice dropping a notch lower, Esteban grated harshly, ". . . and show me it will be well worth the effort I will expend in keeping him alive . . ."

Her body shuddering its revulsion, her senses screaming in revolt, Angelica slowly lifted her gaze. Exerting the full force of her will, she closed her lips against Esteban's waiting mouth.

Desire exploding inside him at the first touch of her lips, Esteban crushed Angelica in his arms, his mouth devouring hers, his arms seeking to destroy the last remaining trace of resistance from her body with the power of his mindless passion. His mouth cruelly demanding, he forced apart her lips, capturing her tongue to suck it hungrily in his voracious desire, drawing it into his mouth, gasping at the sensations that ensued. Lost in the ecstasy of his enforced embrace, Esteban tore his mouth from hers at last to trail a line of rough, bruising kisses down her cheek, to the column of the throat his hands had encircled so cruelly only minutes before. Sucking deeply of her flesh, he caused her to cry out in protest, his enjoyment seeming to grow at each soft expression of her pain.

His mouth was searing the white skin of her shoulders, following the plunge of the daring décolletage when he suddenly became impatient with its restrictions. Pushing the dress roughly from her shoulders, he bared Angelica's breasts, his eyes darting back to her face for a breathless moment before his head dipped to cover the peak of one small, rounded breast and then the other. Seeming only content when he caused her pain, he bit down hard on the tender peaks again and again as she struggled to break free.

Suddenly realizing her cries granted him a perverse satisfaction, Angelica clenched her teeth tightly closed, refusing to allow him the reward he sought.

Lifting his mouth from the bruised mounds, Esteban dragged his heated gaze back to her pale face.

"Yes, you are correct, Angelica. If I cannot have you come to me with desire, I will have you come to me in fear . . . even hatred. Better either of those two heated emotions than the cold resistance you were determined to offer me."

Backing her up tight against the desk, Esteban trapped her there with the weight of his body, his full arousal tight against her. Staring hotly into her eyes, he watched revulsion move across her face as he took her breasts in his hands and kneaded them roughly.

"Yes . . . that is it, Angelica . . . allow yourself to hate me. Let the emotion surge through your body . . . allow it to shake you . . . control your response. Do you feel it making you shudder, recoil against my touch?" Lowering his head, Esteban took the full, rounded curve of her breast in his mouth again, sucking it deeply, his teeth finally bearing down in cruel torment.

When still Angelica refused him the satisfaction of crying out, he tore his mouth from the tortured flesh and raised his flushed face to hers once again.

"*Puta* . . . bitch! You would refuse me even the meager satisfaction of your cries. Must I take you here, in this room, force you to submit to me in pain before you will give me even that honest emotion? Answer me bitch! Answer me!"

Her lips trembling so hard that she could barely form the words, Angelica stammered roughly, "Gareth . . . I must see Gareth first . . . see if he is . . ."

Esteban's hand rose in a swift, unexpected movement to descend with a blow that snapped her face sharply to the side. Enraged at her continued silence, he struck her again and again, halting abruptly as Angelica's face lost its color and she began to sag weakly in his arms. Supporting her roughly, Esteban cupped Angelica's head with his hand. Taking up the filled glass she had placed on the desk only minutes before, he forced the amber liquid down her throat. The color began to return to her face and he forced her to drink until the glass was emptied.

The light of sensibility returned to Angelica's eyes and she slowly began to stiffen in his arms.

"So, you have only to take a moment to regain your senses and you again attempt to oppose me!"

Angelica's response was soft, shaken. "I . . . I want only to know that Gareth is alive. Then I will do whatever . . ."

"All right!"

His handsome face contorted with rage, Esteban took a few moments to rein his emotions under control. Stepping back, leaving her to support herself shakily against the desk, he allowed his eyes to move over her still face, the curve of her shoulders, her naked breasts.

"Cover yourself!"

Turning his back, Esteban walked to the sideboard and refilled his glass. Lifting it to his lips, he emptied it before returning it to the sideboard. His back still turned, he took a deep breath and pulled himself stiffly erect. Reaching out, he again filled his glass, this time taking only a small sip before turning back slowly in Angelica's direction.

Angelica returned his stare through eyes cold and still as ice. Her dress flawlessly readjusted, her shoulders were erect, her chin unyielding. The only trace of their violent conflict of a few minutes before were the bright marks of color on her smooth cheeks, the reddened trail of abused skin on her neck and shoulders, and the faint bruises on the tender flesh exposed in her décolletage.

Reluctant admiration surging to life within him, Esteban lifted his glass in her direction.

"Ah, yes, Angelica, you will prove a worthy opponent. You whet my anticipation. You make me more certain than ever that you will be well worth the effort I have expended to assure that you will be mine."

His eyes moving to the doorway, Esteban raised his voice in summons.

"Pablo!"

The door snapped open, the soldier who had brought Angelica to the office responding sharply, "*Si, mi colonel!*"

"Bring Señor Dawson to me now."

Turning back to Angelica as the soldier closed the door behind him, Esteban experienced a flush of jealousy at the new trembling that had beset her frame.

"You may see your lover, Angelica, and satisfy yourself that he is well. And tonight . . . then you may attempt to convince me, with all the powers of persuasion at your command, that he should remain that way . . ."

Her body quaking, Angelica fought to retain her tenuous grip on reality. Esteban's vicious attack on her body had been unexpected. Somehow she did not believe it had been part of Esteban's plan. No, he had been far too shaken by the encounter, and she was beginning to see that he had planned a far more subtle vengeance with which to soothe his damaged ego.

But she cared little for the disruption of Esteban's plans. She had one thought in mind. Gareth . . . Her heart beginning a steady pounding, she frowned at her unceasing fears.

Why had Esteban hesitated to allow her to see Gareth? In what condition would they bring him to her? Had he suffered deeply? Did he suffer still? Was he . . .

"Do not disturb yourself, Angelica. Your dear Gareth will soon be here." His expression beginning to show signs of a new agitation, Esteban walked slowly to her side. He had refilled her glass and held it out to her. She glanced toward the decanter. It was near to empty and she realized that Esteban had imbibed liberally. He was obviously more shaken by their encounter than she had realized.

"No, you need not worry that I will drink myself into oblivion, *querida*. I have too much to look forward to this night. Instead, I would suggest that you fortify yourself for the interview to come with a bit more of this excellent stimulant." His eyes taking on a steely glint, Esteban warned quietly, "I will expect you to act in a well-restrained manner. You are under my protection now, as is your

539

Gareth Dawson, and should you wish to have it remain in effect, I will expect complete deference to my instructions. Do you understand, Angelica?''

Taking a deep breath, Angelica returned Esteban's gaze unblinkingly. "Yes, I understand."

Pausing, Esteban added in unmistakable emphasis, "If you understand completely, you will realize that any effort you make to speak to Gareth out of turn will only result in his pain." At Angelica's stiffening, Esteban added, "You see, it was never my intention to hurt you. My plans for you include far more pleasure than pain. No, I would much prefer to vent my vengence on the man who took you so arrogantly from me and sent me off on my horse to die. Should you decide to show unwise enthusiasm at your lover's entrance, your disobedience will only allow me an opportunity to obtain the satisfaction so far denied me because of his weakened condition. *Comprendes*, Angelica?''

Taking a short, shaking breath, Angelica nodded. *"Si, comprendo."*

Angelica had accepted the glass Esteban offered her, and was making a pretense of sipping the brandy when Esteban stepped closer to her side. His voice was low with a new and startling emotion.

"I would have you see Gareth Dawson, and satisfy yourself as to his health. Then I would have you dismiss him from your thoughts, and eventually expel him completely from your heart. You see, I have decided, Angelica, that I am going to make you love me."

Her spontaneous gasp at his unexpected remark brought a smile to Esteban's lips.

"Is that so difficult a premise to consider? It is not for me. You have dominated my mind, my thoughts, my action for more time than I care to account. You have more spirit, more fire, and are more beautiful than any woman I have ever known. The blood of the lower classes does not run in your veins as I once believed, and although the circumstances of your birth are less than favorable, I would no longer feel that I would compromise my breeding to align myself with you."

"Esteban, what you feel for me . . . the emotion you demonstrated so vividly only minutes ago, does not transcend simple lust."

Choosing to ignore her words, Esteban raised his hand to stroke her cheek.

"Two bright spots of color mark your cheeks, *querida*. They compensate for your paleness, but your skin is bruised here and here . . ." Running his finger down the curve of her neck and across her shoulder, he hesitated before trailing it along the daring plunge of her neckline. Suppressing the desire to slap away his touch, Angelica clenched her teeth tightly shut.

"I confess to remorse at the sight of those marks, but tonight I will bathe your bruised flesh with my kisses and soothe away all memory of the pain. You will stay with me and I will convince you that . . ."

A brief knock on the door interrupted Esteban's impassioned speech, and Angelica turned sharply in its direction. Her heart pounding, anticipation flushed her face with the color absent before. Hardly realizing Esteban had slipped his arm around her waist and that he held her firmly against his side, Angelica awaited Esteban's bid to enter.

His back curved to accommodate the pull of the sling in which he rested his arm, Gareth had allowed the two guards who had entered his room unexpectedly to drag him roughly to the door. He had walked silently between them up the narrow hallway, making certain to lean heavily to the side of his wounded shoulder in order to exaggerate his disability. But he did not need to feign pain. Their rough treatment had indeed stirred the aching throb which still returned intermittently.

This unexpected audience with his holiness, Esteban Arricalde, was difficult to understand. Had he correctly understood the whispers behind the closed door to his room only a short half hour before, Esteban should be in the midst of entertaining his whore. But he had come to the conclusion during the pain-filled nights recently passed, that Esteban Arricalde was capable of anything in the hope of perpetuating his vain perception of his own worth. He would not put it past Esteban to . . .

But the men were jerking him to a halt before a room he had visited once before. Esteban's office. Perhaps he would finally find out why it was that Esteban had sought to extend his life, when he knew, in truth, Esteban would like nothing better than to see him join the ranks of his fallen comrades.

A harsh knock and the two guards exchanged a meaningful glance as Esteban's voice sounded from within.

"*Entra.*"

Preceded by the first guard, Gareth was unable to see past his uniformed figure until the man stepped unexpectedly aside. His breath catching in a sharp gasp, Gareth looked wordlessly into Angelica's still face.

Spontaneous, mindless joy had moved him a step in her direction when he was jerked back roughly to his former position by the guard at his side. His low gasp of pain as his injured shoulder screamed its protest of the rough handling, drew a soft protest from Angelica's white lips.

"Gareth . . ."

"Silence, Angelica." Esteban's voice was warm with enjoyment of the moment. "Do you not see Gareth is in pain? We must give him a few minutes to compose himself before we add to his stress."

The stabbing pain in his shoulder fading to a dull ache, Gareth was suddenly aware of the arm Esteban curved possessively around Angelica's waist, the manner in which his hand stroked the side of her breast. His gaze snapped to Angelica's anguished eyes and he felt a different, more searing distress.

"Angelica, what are you doing here? Why did Pa . . ."

But Esteban would not allow her response. Instead, he pulled Angelica closer to his side, his brief glance toward her averted head loving.

"Your father has no idea where Angelica is right now, Gareth. You see, Angelica ran away without telling him so she might join me here. We have much unfinished business to settle, and she is most eager to please." Turning his eyes

542

back to Angelica, Esteban waited until she raised her face to his gaze.

"Yes, see, Gareth, how accommodating she has become. I have but to indicate my desire and she responds. Is that not so, Angelica? Come, speak. Tell Gareth how very much you wish to please me."

Angelica's eyes snapped back to Gareth. Her gaze pleaded his understanding.

"Gareth . . ."

"Tell him, Angelica . . ."

"Yes I . . . I want to please Esteban . . ."

Turning back to Esteban, Angelica addressed him softly.

"I . . . I would like to speak to Gareth, Esteban, for just a few moments."

Choosing not to respond, Esteban addressed Gareth insidiously, "Your sister would like to speak to you, Gareth. Oh, yes, I am aware of the surprising turn of events at your homestead. A dreadful situation . . . shocking. It is no wonder you left your home to join that pathetic group at the Alamo. But as it turns out, your sudden attention to your patriotic duty had put me in a position to bring Angelica back into my life again. And you may rest assured I will not allow her to slip from my fingers again. Oh, no, Gareth. I would not be so much a fool . . .

"She is beautiful, is she not, Gareth? She is dressed as she always should have been dressed, and when she returns to Mexico City with me, she will be the toast of society. We will be inseparable . . . day and night . . ."

Inwardly raging at his helplessness, Gareth looked to the men at his sides. Their eyes were fixed on him, awaiting his move.

"No, do not try it, Gareth. You are no match for my men in your present condition. I would prefer to keep you alive, but if you make that condition uncomfortable, well . . ."

"Gareth, please. I'm fine. You needn't worry. I just wanted to make sure you were . . ."

"Angelica, I don't remember giving you permission to speak to Gareth . . ."

"Esteban . . ." Biting her lips, Angelica continued

543

tightly, "Just a few more words . . ."

"What is it you would like to tell him, Angelica? Oh, did you want to explain to him as you did in your letter that he is not truly your brother?"

The spontaneous jolt of shock that shook Gareth at his offhand remark caused a low laugh to escape Esteban's well-shaped lips. Turning to Gareth, Esteban continued smoothly, "Oh, yes, it is true, Gareth! You see, Angelica found out through a very surprising set of circumstances that she is not truly Jonathan Dawson's daughter, but the daughter of a clever fortune hunter whose plans were foiled by Celeste DuBois's uncooperative parents. So you see, you need never have left the Circle D! Had you remained until the letter from her mother had been delivered . . ." Esteban's voice trailed to a halt, his enjoyment obviously increasing at Gareth's incredulity as he continued. "But you did not, did you, Gareth? Your torment was undoubtedly too severe. That is unfortunate, but I must thank you for your impetuousness . . ."

Uncertain whether Esteban's remarks were truth or merely a cruel joke, Gareth suppressed the hope growing inside him as he questioned cautiously, "Angelica, is it true?"

The tears that sprang to her great eyes and her short nod sent a flush of elation moving through Gareth's veins. He took another step forward, only to be jerked backward by the rough hands of his guards, his gasp of pain drawing Angelica toward him in a spontaneous step. But Esteban would permit her no farther. His eyes lifting to her anguish, Gareth heard her low appeal.

"Gareth, please don't! Yes, it's true. My father's name was Jacques LeClaire. You and I are not related by blood. We . . ."

"Touching . . . very touching, but I find I am tiring of your dramatic displays. Pablo, Jorge, you may remove Señor Dawson from the room now."

"Esteban, no please! Just a few minutes more! I need . . ."

"You need, Angelica?" His jealous anger reflected in the

544

sudden flush of his face and in the cruel tightening of his arm around her waist, Esteban gritted harshly from between clenched teeth, "Your needs are simple. You need convince me that I should not turn Gareth Dawson over to the firing squad right now! He lives on borrowed time and I warn you, each endearing word, each loving glance you bestow on this worthless, uncultured Texan shortens his life!"

"Esteban, no, I just wanted . . ."

"Take him away!"

"Esteban . . ."

But the guards had gripped Gareth roughly in an attempt to remove him bodily from the room. Startled by the unexpected strength of his resistance; they struggled momentarily, jerking Esteban's attention in their direction even as he restrained Angelica's attempt to move to Gareth's side.

"Fools! Idiots! You cannot even manage a wounded man? Get him out of here now! I . . ."

But Esteban's violent tirade was interrupted by an unexpected commotion in the hallway outside the door. All eyes jerked in its direction even as the door burst open to admit a rushing thrust of men into the room. Abandoning their attempt to subdue Gareth, his guards scrambled to draw their guns, only to be halted by the menacing command of Jonathan Dawson's low voice and the drawn guns of the men behind him.

"Don't be damned fools! Step back!"

Motionless until the guards slowly followed Jonathan's command, Angelica was about to move toward Gareth when Esteban's arm snaked around her throat from behind, jerking her back against him as an efficient shield. A cold, hard object was jammed against her ribs, and she strained to look down in his choking hold. Her heart jumped at the sight of a small pistol pressed tightly against the gold silk of her gown.

Esteban's voice grated harshly in her ear.

"*Sí*, Angelica. If you move other than to obey my command, you will not live to see yourself triumph as you imagine . . ."

"Angelica!"

Gareth's voice rang out over the confusion of men and shifting positions, freezing the scene into a dramatic tableau with Angelica and Esteban at its center.

Esteban's voice was the first to cut the uneasy silence.

"Yes . . . Angelica . . . And do not hesitate to believe that I will pull this trigger if even the slightest move is made against me. Now, all of you . . ." His eyes on the men who still stood in the doorway, guns drawn, Esteban ordered tightly, "Drop your guns to the floor carefully."

Her eyes jerking to the doorway, Angelica fought to catch her breath in Esteban's choking hold. Papa Jon . . . Peter . . . Brett . . . Charlie. They were following Esteban's command. Their guns hit the floor with a resounding thud and Angelica was filled with despair. His hold tightening, Esteban caused her to emit a low gasp.

"Yes, that it right, Angelica. Show them how sincere I am in my threats, so they will not attempt any foolish heroics. Pablo, Jorge, pick up the guns."

His eyes on his men, Esteban watched as they moved quickly to his command. Angelica felt the pressure of the pistol removed from her side as Esteban relaxed momentarily and in the next moment she saw it flick forward as Gareth made a quick lunge in their direction.

The pistol barked and Gareth clutched at his chest and toppled to the floor. A choked shriek sounding in her throat, Angelica attempted to break free of Esteban's hold, only to gasp for breath as it tightened mercilessly.

Esteban's voice hissed in sharp command as he waved his pistol toward the men frozen in the doorway.

"All right . . . move into the corner . . . that is correct." His eyes darting to Gareth's unmoving form in contempt he backed toward it, pulling Angelica with him as he attempted to force the Texans into the corner while his men picked up their guns.

Barely retaining consciousness under Esteban's constricting grip on her throat, Angelica could see nothing but the sight of Gareth's falling body flashing again and again

546

in front of her mind.

Gareth . . . Gareth. Oh, God, no . . .

But there was a scrambling sound from behind and Angelica felt the sudden vibration as Esteban's body shuddered under an unanticipated blow. Freed unexpectedly from his choking hold on her throat, Angelica turned swiftly to see Esteban and Gareth locked in a violent struggle. The room suddenly burst into action as the men in the corner abruptly attacked the startled guards.

Still struggling to regain her breath, Angelica was unable to take her eyes from the savage conflict rapidly drawing to a halt as Gareth, his body pinning Esteban to the floor, delivered a smashing blow to his face. Esteban's head fell to the side in unconsciousness, and breathing heavily, Gareth drew himself to his feet. Within moments Angelica was in his arms.

Crushing her in a fierce embrace, Gareth rained kisses on her hair, her cheek, his mouth finally seeking and finding her waiting mouth. Abandoning herself to the wonder of his kiss, Angelica emitted a soft protest as Gareth withdrew his mouth from hers at last.

"Angelica . . ." His voice a ragged whisper, Gareth looked into the clear, glowing depths of her eyes. "I thought . . . I was beginning to believe I would never hold you like this again."

Hardly aware that Jonathan and the remainder of the men, their guns restored to them, were again in command of the situation, Angelica responded in sudden realization, "But he shot you! Gareth, are you all right?" Drawing back, Angelica blanched at the small bullet hole which had burned through his shirt. She shook her head disbelievingly.

Reaching inside his shirt, his fingers fumbling as he winced in momentary pain, Gareth pulled out his hand and produced a small bullet. The corners of his mouth turning up in a small smile, he said softly, "You didn't think a little thing like this was goin' to stop me from tellin' you I love you, did you, darlin'?"

Shaking her head, too incredulous to speak, Angelica

watched Gareth's smile widen.

"Dr. Escobar was sympathetic to the Texan cause, darlin'. He insisted on my keepin' on a heavy dressin' of wadded cotton. I think it was his way of protectin' me a little while longer from the fate he expected would overcome me when I was adjudged well. He did me an even greater favor than he thought, darlin'. The impact of the bullet stunned me, but I don't think it did much more than irritate the wound I already had."

Her hand moving to lovingly stroke his injured shoulder, her eyes intent on his mouth, Angelica whispered in soft inquiry, "Are you in pain, Gareth?"

Gareth's response was a low, hungry whisper. "Oh, yes, darlin'. I ache so bad with wantin' you . . ."

"Gareth . . ."

Turning at the sound of his father's voice, Gareth faced his concerned expression.

"We can't afford to waste any time in gettin' away from here. We've been lucky so far, but this house is too close to the main body of the Mexican forces . . ."

Gareth frowned as he glanced down at Esteban's unconscious form being carefully bound by Brett's hand. He shot a short glance to the two similarly bound guards.

"What about them?"

"We'll gag them and leave them. We have to get as far away from here as we can by daylight. Are you well enough to ride?"

"I'll make it."

"Then let's go."

Allowing the others to precede them out the door, Gareth hung back, pulling Angelica into his arms as the others began to make a cautious sweep of the hallway. His eyes suddenly anxious, he whispered into her upturned face. "I just wanted to be sure before we leave . . . I want to make certain you heard what I said, darlin'. I've cursed myself a thousand times because I never said the words . . . never told you . . . I love you, darlin'. Nothin' is any good without you. Nothin' will ever be good for me again if you're not with me. That was a damned fool agreement we

548

made when you agreed to come to Texas with me. Before we ever reached the Circle D, I knew I'd never be satisfied with just a year with you. But I thought we had so much time. I wanted to teach you to love me . . . the way I loved you. I wanted to be everythin' to you . . . your lover, your protector, your confidant, your friend. I wanted you to need me, to depend on me, to love me. I wanted us to wrap ourselves in each other so tight that we'd never be separated. I wanted to be your blue velvet for you, darlin', all the consolation . . . all the love you'd ever need for the rest of your life.

"But I lost the chance to say all those things to you, and I thought I'd never have the chance again. So I'm sayin' them now. I love you, Angelica. I love you more than I love my own life, and I've found out that my life's not worth much to me without you bein' a part of it. Angelica darlin', I love you. I want to speak my vows to you . . . the same vows I've repeated to you in my mind every time I've held you in my arms. I want you to be my wife, darlin' . . ."

Gareth's words drifted away into silence. His gaze intent on her face, he waited as Angelica's eyes held his.

Indulging herself for a few breathless moments in the sober black velvet of his eyes, Angelica reached up to stroke his bearded cheek. Her voice was husky with the myriad emotions assailing her.

"I love you too, Gareth. I'll be your wife. I'll be your wife, your lover. You're the only blue velvet I'll ever want or need . . ."

"Gareth! Angelica!"

Appearing in the doorway unexpectedly, Jon hesitated only a fraction of a moment at the sight of Gareth and Angelica in each other's arms before exclaiming gruffly, "You two don't have time for than now. Come on, the horses are ready. We have to get movin'."

Slipping his arm around her waist, Gareth gave his father a quick nod. His voice was deep, filled with happiness as he urged Angelica to follow his father's retreating form.

"Pa's right, darlin'. Once we get out of here we'll have time . . . all the time in the world . . ."

Heeding his entreaty, Angelica stepped out into the hallway and started running down the narrow passage toward the rear door. She was aware of Gareth's step close beside her. The sound bore its own sweet consolation. She gloried in the knowledge that it would be with her, always.

Epilogue

Angelica pulled back the curtain and looked out the window of her room. The bright morning light was beaming down on a brilliant summer landscape of level, sunswept land that moved uninterrupted to low, rolling hills in the infinite distance. Angelica paused to lift her unbound hair from her neck, remaining momentarily motionless as a cool breeze entered the window to bathe the damp surface with cool relief. The buzz of insects had begun early, forcasting another day of high temperatures. It had been a wickedly hot summer, the air heavy and moist, but it had been the most beautiful summer of Angelica's life.

Experiencing a joy so sweet that it brought hot tears to her eyes, she watched the slender, dark-haired boy as he gingerly rode the sleek chestnut mare around the corral. Turning unexpectedly toward her window, he caught her eye and waved proudly in her direction. She waved back, her heart filled to bursting at the health shining from Carlos's smiling face.

She had never thought her life could be so full, her mind at peace. Thankfully, her whole world was at peace. The conflict between Mexico and Texas had been resolved months earlier. Forty-six days after the Alamo had fallen, Sam Houston had led an army of Texans to defeat Santa Anna's forces at San Jacinto in a battle that had annihilated Santa Anna's forces in less than an hour. Santa Anna had been captured, and was still in the process of talking his way out of his defeat.

Gareth had been with Houston at the last battle, and she had waited in anguish for his return. They had been married immediately afterward in a Texas that was now a full-fledged republic.

Their wedding had been surrounded by a circle of love. Jon, insisting on giving her away, had walked her down the makeshift aisle in their small living room, his face beaming. Tante Minette had been present to witness the exchange of their vows, claiming her sweet Celeste was doubtless smiling down with true happiness in the face of their union. The hired hands, no longer split in their loyalty between Gareth and Angelica, had celebrated with true abandon. The affair had drawn every neighbor within a radius of one hundred miles, and the celebration had gone long into the night.

Conspicuously absent from the affair had been Peter Macfadden. The project he had overseen had been near enough to completion to proceed without him, and he had left a week before the wedding. His good wishes to Angelica and Gareth had been sincere but brief, and Angelica had wept in Gareth's arms as Peter's horse had disappeared into the distance on the long road back to Real del Monte.

After considerable coaxing by mail, Mama and Papa Rodrigo had consented to visit with Carlos. They were presently staying at the Circle D, and her joy in holding Carlos in her arms again had been overwhelming.

With her Mexican parents had come word of Esteban Arricalde. Seemingly invincible, he was back in Mexico City, purportedly deeply involved in affairs of state. His parents had been overheard to say that Esteban had found his true vocation in life in serving his country, and they were very proud. It had been Gareth and Angelica's opinion that Esteban would never serve anyone but himself. Nevertheless, in a way which seemed to cheat true justice, it appeared he would always land on his feet. But their happiness had been too complete to chafe at the consolation Esteban's good parents received from the harmless self-deception they employed to console themselves.

Her eyes following Carlos's progress as he urged his mare to a faster pace, Angelica again lifted her hair from her neck to expose it to the refreshing morning breeze. Unexpectedly she felt Gareth's long, hard length behind her as he slipped his arms around her waist. Leaning forward, he pressed light, fleeting kisses against the white column of her throat and cupped her breasts in a familiar, loving gesture. His mouth pressed against her ear, his sweet breath sent little shivers down her spine with his whisper.

"So, Carlos is up early this morning. He can't seem to get enough of riding that mare . . ."

"Carlos has never owned anything as beautiful as her before. It was a generous and thoughtful gift, Gareth, and I thank you for it."

"Was it really so generous of me, Angelica?" Turning her toward him, Gareth allowed his eyes to move over the exceptional beauty of his wife's face. "I owe Carlos everything I have. Had it not been for your love for him, you would never have come to me. I might have left Real del Monte without ever knowing the beauty we have together. I might be now, as I was then, existing on a plane of loveless duty, searching for something to make my life complete. Had I not found you, it would have been a fruitless search. But instead . . ."

His hands moving from her shoulders, Gareth slipped them to her widening waist and the small bulge that rose below it.

"Instead I have you . . . the child you carry inside you . . . more love than I ever expected . . . more love than I could ever hope to be worthy of . . ."

Angelica's brows raising in slow, considered retort, she replied thoughtfully, "I suppose that is true, Gareth. You are a very difficult man to live with. You are, after all, very opinionated, domineering, unyielding, determined, set in your ways . . ."

His mouth quirking in suppressed amusement at her response, Gareth replied slowly, "And you, Angelica, you are . . ."

"Oh, I am intelligent . . . generous . . . loving . . .

patient . . . and modest to a fault."

At Gareth's growing smile, Angelica nodded.

"Oh, yes, I am, Gareth!" Continuing with an air of true innocence, her great gray eyes widening generously, Angelica continued. "And I am determined to smooth your rough edges . . ."

Raising her mouth Angelica brushed his lips with hers, fully aware that the first contact would stir Gareth's hunger for more. Drawing herself back as Gareth leaned full into the kiss, she paused to whisper against his mouth.

"Come, Gareth. It is early. Lie beside me for a while before we go downstairs. We can discuss the best method in which we might work together to achieve that ultimate goal."

Sweeping Angelica unexpectedly into his arms, Gareth held her high against his chest as he walked slowly to their rumpled bed. His smile broadening, Gareth lowered her gently to the surface and leaned over her, looking deep into the crystal depths of her eyes.

"You may find the job more difficult than you thought, darlin'. We may have to spend a long time workin' this out between us."

Reaching up, Angelica drew Gareth's weight full against her, a soft sigh escaping her lips as their warm flesh met.

"We can devote as much time as you think we will need, darling." Her mouth moving ardently against his chin, Angelica mumbled, "I am thoroughly devoted to that goal . . ."

Gareth did not bother to respond. He was too busy . . . just loving her.

A note to the Reader

Dear Readers:

A visit to the Alamo in San Antonio is a truly emotional experience. The names of its gallant defenders line the walls of the great stone fortress, bringing the story of those fateful thirteen days in 1836 vividly to life. Colonel William Barret Travis's last written call for aid in the face of the certain death that awaited him and his men is so touching in its selfless heroism that one could not help but become affected.

It was a visit to this inspiring national shrine that brought the first seeds of Love's Defiant Mistress to life in my mind. In it I have attempted to put you in touch with the stress of the times and the thinking that forced the citizens of the Mexican state of Texas to seek their independence from the tyranny of Santa Anna's rule. I have set my two fictional protagonists in this setting and woven their lives through the myriad events which contributed to the Texas War for Independence. I hope you have enjoyed the result.

I truly enjoy sharing the romance of American history with you in this way. Your letters have been marvelous. Your thoughts and the insight they have provided have been invaluable to me in so many ways. It is always my pleasure to hear from you and to respond to your letters personally.

Regards,

Elaine Barbieri
P. O. Box 536
W. Milford, NJ 07480

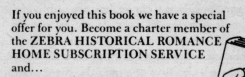

Each month you'll receive 4 brand new Zebra Historical Romance novels as soon as they are published. Look them over *Free* for 10 days. If you're not delighted simply return them and owe nothing. But if you enjoy them as much as we think you will, you'll pay *only* $3.50 each and save 45¢ over the cover price. (You save a total of $1.80 each month.) *There is no shipping and handling charge or other hidden charges.*

———— *Fill Out the Coupon* ————

Start your subscription now and start saving. Fill out the coupon and mail it *today*. You'll get your **FREE** book along with your first month's books to preview.

Mail to: Zebra Home Subscription Service, Inc.

120 Brighton Road
P.O. Box 5214
Clifton, New Jersey 07015-5214

YES. Send me my *FREE* Zebra Historical Romance novel along with my 4 new Zebra Historical Romances to preview. You will bill me only $3.50 each; a total of $14.00 (a $15.80 value—I save $1.80) with *no* shipping or handling charge. I understand that I may look these over FREE for 10 days and return them if I'm not satisfied and owe nothing. Otherwise send me 4 new novels to preview each month as soon as they are published at the same low price. I can always return a shipment and I can cancel this subscription at any time. There is no minimum number of books to purchase. In any event the *FREE* book is mine to keep regardless.

_____
NAME

_____
ADDRESS   APT. NO.

_____
CITY   STATE   ZIP

_____
SIGNATURE   (if under 18, parent or guardian must sign)

        Terms and prices are subject to change.   *1839*